W9-DDY-749

A GIRL OF THE

LIMBERLOST

LADDIE

A TRUE BLUE STORY

**GENE
STRATTON
PORTER**

Printing History
Doubleday edition/1909
Tyndale House edition/1991
First combined hardcover edition for
Christian Herald Family Bookshelf: 1992
Library of Congress Catalog Card Number 90-71542
ISBN 0-8423-1015-0

96   95   94   93   92   91
5   4   3   2

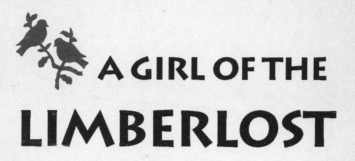

A GIRL OF THE
LIMBERLOST

**GENE
STRATTON
PORTER**

Printing History
Doubleday edition/1909
Tyndale House edition/1991
Library of Congress Catalog Card Number 90-71542
ISBN 0-8423-1015-0

96 95 94 93 92 91
5   4   3   2

To
all girls of the Limberlost
in general
and one
Jeanette Helen Porter
in particular

CONTENTS

CHAPTER

1

Wherein Elnora Goes to High School, and Learns Many Lessons Not Found in Her Books

"Elnora Comstock, have you lost your senses?" demanded the angry voice of Katharine Comstock as she glared at her daughter.

"Why, mother?" faltered the girl.

"Don't you 'why mother' me!" cried Mrs. Comstock. "You know very well what I mean. You've given me no peace until you've had your way about this going to school business; I've fixed you good enough, and you're ready to start. But no child of mine walks the streets of Onabasha looking like a play-actress woman. You wet your hair and comb it down modest and decent and then be off, or you'll have no time to find where you belong."

Elnora gave one despairing glance at the white face, framed in a most becoming riot of reddish-brown hair, which she saw in the little kitchen mirror. Then she untied the narrow black ribbon, wet the comb and plastered the waving curls close to her head, bound them fast, pinned on the skimpy black hat and started for the back door.

"You've gone so plum daffy you are forgetting your dinner," jeered her mother.

"I don't want anything to eat," replied Elnora without stopping.

"You'll take your dinner or you'll not go one step. Are you crazy? Walk nearly three miles and no food from six in the morning until six at night. A pretty figure you'd cut if you had your way about things! And after I've gone and bought you this nice new pail and filled it especial for the first day!"

Elnora came back with a face still whiter and picked up the lunch. "Thank you, mother! Good-bye!" she said. Mrs. Comstock did not reply. She watched the girl down the long walk to the gate and out of sight on the road in the bright sunshine of the first Monday of September.

"I bet a dollar she gets enough of it by night!" Mrs. Comstock said positively.

Elnora walked by instinct for her eyes were blinded with tears. She left the road where it turned south at the corner of the Limberlost, climbed a snake fence and entered a path worn by her own feet. Dodging under willow and scrub oak branches she at last came to the faint outline of an old trail made in the days when the precious timber of the swamp was guarded by armed men. This path she followed until she reached a thick clump of bushes. From the débris in the end of a hollow log she took a key that unlocked the padlock of a large weatherbeaten old box, inside of which lay several books, a butterfly apparatus, and an old cracked mirror. The walls were lined thickly with gaudy butterflies, dragonflies, and moths. She set up the mirror and once more pulling the ribbon from her hair, she shook the bright mass over her shoulders, tossing it dry in the sunshine. Then she straightened it, bound it loosely, and replaced her hat. She tugged vainly at the low brown calico collar and gazed despairingly at the generous length of the narrow skirt. She lifted it as she would have liked it to be cut if possible. That disclosed the heavy leather high shoes, at sight of which she looked positively ill, and hastily dropped the skirt. She opened the pail, took out the lunch, wrapped it in the napkin, and placed it in a small pasteboard box. Locking the case again she hid the key and hurried down the trail.

She followed it around the north end of the swamp and then struck into a footpath crossing a farm in the direction of the spires of the city to the northeast. Again she climbed a fence and was on the open road. For an instant she leaned against the fence staring before her, then turned and looked back. Behind her lay the land on which she had been born to drudgery and a mother who made no pretence of loving her; before her lay the city through whose schools she hoped to find means of escape and the way to reach the things for which she cared. When she thought of how she looked she leaned more heavily against the fence and groaned; when she thought of turning back and wearing such clothing in ignorance all the days of her life, she set her teeth firmly and went hastily toward Onabasha.

At the bridge crossing a deep culvert at the suburbs she glanced around, and then kneeling she thrust the lunch box between the foundation and the flooring. This left her empty-handed as she approached the great stone high school building. She entered bravely and inquired her way to the office of the superintendent. There she learned that she should have come the week before and arranged for her classes. There were many things incident to the opening of school, and one man unable to cope with all of them.

"Where have you been attending school?" he asked, as he advised the teacher of the cooking department not to telephone for groceries until she saw how many she would have in her classes; wrote an order for chemicals for the students of science; and advised the leader of the orchestra to try to get a professional to take the place of the bass violist, reported suddenly ill.

"I finished last spring at Brushwood school, district number nine," said Elnora. "I have been studying all summer. I am quite sure I can do the first year work, if I have a few days to get started."

"Of course, of course," assented the superintendent. "Almost invariably country pupils do good work. You may enter first year, and if you don't fit, we will find it out speedily. Your teachers will tell you the list of books you must have, and if you will come with me I will show you the way to the auditorium. It is now time for opening exercises. Take any seat you find vacant." He was gone.

Elnora stood before the entrance and stared into the largest room she ever had seen. The floor sloped down to a yawning stage on which a band of musicians, grouped around a grand piano, were tuning their instruments. She had two fleeting impressions. That it was all a mistake; this was no school, but a grand display of enormous ribbon bows; and the second, that she was sinking, and had forgotten how to walk. Then a burst from the orchestra nerved her while a bevy of daintily clad, sweet-smelling things that might have been birds, or flowers, or possibly gaily dressed, happy young girls, pushed her forward. She found herself plodding across the back of the auditorium, praying for guidance, to an empty seat.

As the girls passed her, vacancies seemed to open to meet them. Their friends were moving over, beckoning and whispering invitations. Everyone else was seated, but no one paid any attention to the white-faced girl stumbling half-blindly down the aisle next the farthest wall. So she went on to the very end facing the stage. No one moved, and she could not summon courage to crowd past others to several empty seats she saw. At the end of the aisle she paused in desperation, as she stared back at the whole forest of faces most of which were now turned upon her.

In one burning flash came the full realization of her scanty dress, her pitiful little hat and ribbon, her big, heavy shoes, her ignorance of where to go or what to do; and from a sickening wave which crept over her, she felt she was going to become very ill. Then out of the mass, she saw a pair of big, brown boy eyes, three seats from her, and there was a message in them. Without moving his body he reached forward and with a pencil touched the back of the seat before him. Instantly Elnora took another step which brought her to a row of vacant front seats.

She heard the giggle behind her, the knowledge that she wore the only hat in the room, burned her; every matter of moment, and some of none at all, cut and stung. She had no books. Where should she go when this was over? What would she give to be on the trail going home! She was shaking with a nervous chill when the music ceased, and the superintendent arose and, coming down to the front of the flower-decked platform, opened a Bible and began to read. Elnora did not know what he was reading, and she felt that she did not care. Wildly she was racking her brain to decide whether she should sit still when the rest left the room or follow, and ask some one where the Freshmen went first.

In the midst of the struggle one clean-cut sentence fell on her ear. "Hide me under the shadow of Thy wings."

Elnora began to pray frantically. "Hide me, O God, hide me, under the shadow of Thy wings."

Again and again she implored that prayer, and before she

realized what was coming, everyone had risen and the room was emptying rapidly. Elnora hurried after the nearest girl and in the press at the door touched her sleeve timidly.

"Will you please tell me where the Freshmen go?" she asked huskily.

The girl gave her one surprised glance, and drew away.

"Same place as the fresh women," she answered, and those nearest her laughed.

Elnora stopped praying suddenly and the colour swept into her face. "I'll wager you are the first person I meet when I find it," she said and stopped short. "Not that! Oh, I must not do that!" she thought in dismay. "Make an enemy the first thing I do. Oh, not that!"

She followed with her eyes as the young people separated in the hall, some climbing stairs, some disappearing down side halls, some entering doors nearby. She saw the girl overtake the brown-eyed boy and speak to him, and he glanced back at Elnora and now there was a scowl on his face. Then she stood alone in the hall.

Presently a door opened and a young woman came out and entered another room. Elnora waited until she returned, and hurried to her. "Would you tell me where the Freshmen are?" she panted.

"Straight down the hall, three doors to your left," was the answer, as the girl passed.

"One minute please, oh, please," begged Elnora. "Do I knock or just open the door?"

"Go in and take a seat," replied the teacher.

"What if there aren't any seats?" gasped Elnora.

"Class rooms are never half-filled, there will be plenty," was the answer.

Elnora removed her hat. There was no place to put it, so she carried it in her hand. She looked infinitely better without it. After several efforts she at last opened the door and stepping inside faced a smaller and more concentrated battery of eyes.

"The superintendent sent me. He thinks I belong here," she said to the professor in charge of the class, but she never before heard the voice with which she spoke. As she stood waiting, the girl of the hall passed on her way to the blackboard, and suppressed laughter told Elnora that her thrust had been repeated.

"Be seated," said the professor, and then because he saw Elnora was desperately embarrassed he proceeded to loan her a book and to ask her if she had studied algebra. She said she had a little, but not the same book they were using. He asked her if she felt that she could do the work they were beginning, and she said she did.

That was how it happened, that three minutes after entering the room she was compelled to take her place beside the girl who had gone last to the board, and whose flushed face and angry eyes avoided meeting Elnora's. Being compelled to concentrate on her proposition she forgot herself. When the professor asked that all pupils sign their work she firmly wrote "Elnora Comstock" under her demonstration. Then she took her seat and waited with white lips and trembling limbs, as one after another the professor called the names on the board, while their owners arose and explained their propositions, or flunked if they had not found a correct solution. She was so eager to catch their forms of expression and prepare herself for her recitation, that she never took her eyes from the work on the board, until clearly and distinctly, "Elnora Cornstock," called the professor.

The dazed girl stared at the board. One tiny curl added to the top of the first curve of the m in her name, had transformed it from a good old English patronymic that any girl might bear proudly, to Cornstock. Elnora stared speechless. When and how did it happen? She could feel the wave of smothered laughter in the air around her. A rush of anger turned her face scarlet and her soul sick. A hot answer was on her lips. The voice of the professor addressed her straightly.

"This proposition seems to be beautifully demonstrated, Miss Cornstalk," he said. "Surely, you can tell us how you did it."

That word of praise saved her. She could do good work. They might wear their pretty clothes, have their friends and make life a greater misery than it ever before had been for her, but not one of them should do better work or be more womanly. That lay with her. She was tall, straight, and handsome as she arose.

"Of course, I can explain my work," she said in natural tones.

"What I can't explain is how I happened to be so stupid as to make a mistake in writing my own name. I must have been a little nervous. Please, excuse me."

She went to the board, swept off the signature with one stroke, then without a tremor she rewrote it clearly. "My name is Comstock," she said distinctly. She returned to her seat and following the formula used by the others made her first high school recitation.

The face of Professor Henley was a study. As Elnora took her seat he looked at her steadily. "It puzzles me," he said deliberately, "how you can write as beautiful a demonstration, and explain it as clearly as ever has been done in any of my classes, and still be so disturbed as to make a mistake in your own name. Are you very sure you did that yourself, Miss Comstock?"

"It is impossible that anyone else should have done it," answered Elnora steadily.

"I am very glad you think so," said the professor. "Being Freshmen, all of you are strangers to me. I should hate to begin the year with you feeling there was one among you small enough to do a trick like that. The next proposition, please."

When the hour was gone the class filed back to the study room and Elnora followed in desperation, because she did not know where else to go. She could not study as she had no books, and when the class again left the room to go to another professor for the next recitation, she went also. At least they could put her out if she did not belong there. Noon came at last, and she kept with the others until they dispersed on the sidewalk. She was so abnormally self conscious she fancied all the hundreds of that laughing throng saw and jested at her. When she passed the brown-eyed boy walking with the girl of her encounter she knew, for she heard him say, "Did you really let that gawky piece of calico get ahead of you?" The answer was indistinct.

Elnora hurried from the city. She intended to get her lunch, eat it in the shade of the first tree, and then decide whether she would go back or go home. She knelt on the bridge and reached for her box, but it was so very light that she was prepared for the fact that it was empty before opening it. There was just one thing for which to be thankful. The boy or tramp who had seen her hide it, had left the napkin. She would not have to face her mother and account for its loss. She put it in her pocket, and threw the box into the ditch. Then she sat on the bridge and tried to think, but her brain was confused.

"Perhaps the worst is over," she said at last. "I will go back. What would mother say to me if I came home now?"

So she returned to the high school, followed some other pupils to the coat room, hung her hat, and found her way to the study where she had been in the morning. Twice that afternoon, with aching head and empty stomach, she faced strange professors, in different branches. Once she escaped notice, the second time the worst happened. She was asked a question she could not answer.

"Have you not decided on your course, and secured your books?" inquired the professor.

"I have decided on my course," replied Elnora, "I do not know who to ask for my books."

"Ask?" the professor was bewildered.

"I understood the books were furnished," faltered Elnora.

"Only to those bringing an order from the township trustee," replied the professor.

"No! Oh, no!" cried Elnora. "I will get them to-morrow," and gripped her desk for support for she knew that was not true. Four books, ranging perhaps at a dollar and a half apiece; would her mother get them? Of course she would not—could not.

Did not Elnora know the story by heart. There was enough land, but no one to do clearing and farm. Tax on all those acres, recently the new gravel road tax added, the expense of living and only the work of two women to meet all of it. She was insane to think she could come to the city to school. Her mother had been right. The girl decided that if only she lived to get home, she would stay there and lead any sort of life to avoid more of this torture. Bad as what she wished to escape had been, it was nothing like this. She never could live down the movement that went through the class when she inadvertently revealed the fact that she had expected her books to be furnished. Her mother would not get them; that settled the question.

But the end of misery is never in a hurry to come, for before the day was over the superintendent entered the room and explained that pupils from the country were charged a tuition of twenty dollars a year. That really was the end. Previously Elnora had canvassed a dozen wild plans for securing the money for books, ranging all the way from offering to wash the superintendent's dishes to breaking into the bank. This additional expense made the thing so wildly impossible, there was nothing to do but hold up her head until she was out of sight.

Down the long corridor alone among hundreds, down the long street alone among thousands, out into the country she came at last. Across the fence and field, along the old trail once trodden by a boy's bitter agony, now stumbled a white-faced girl, sick at heart. She sat on a log and began to sob in spite of her efforts at self-control. At first it was physical breakdown, later, thought came crowding.

Oh, the shame, the mortification! Why had she not known of the tuition? How did she happen to think that in the city books were furnished? Perhaps it was because she had read they were in several states. But why did she not know? Why did not her mother go with her? Other mothers—but when had her mother ever been or done anything at all like other mothers? Because she never had been it was useless to blame her now. Elnora felt she should have gone to town the week before, called on some one and learned all these things herself. She should have remembered how her clothing would look, before she wore it in public places. Now she knew, and her dreams were over. She must go home to feed chickens, calves, and pigs, wear calico and coarse shoes, and pass a library with averted head all her life. She sobbed again.

"For pity's sake, honey, what's the matter?" asked the voice of the nearest neighbour, Wesley Sinton, as he seated himself by Elnora. "There, there," he continued, smearing tears all over her face in an effort to dry them. "Was it so bad as that, now? Maggie has been just about wild over you all day. She's got nervouser every minute. She said we were foolish to let you go. She said your clothes were not right, you ought not to carry that tin pail, and that they would laugh at you. By gum, I see they did!"

"Oh, Uncle Wesley," sobbed the girl, "why didn't she tell me?"

"Well, you see, Elnora, she didn't like to. You got such a way of holding up your head, and going through with things. She thought someway that you'd make it, till you got started, and then she begun to see a hundred things we should have done. I reckon you hadn't reached that building before she remembered that your skirt should have been pleated instead of gathered, your shoes been low, and lighter for hot September weather, and a new hat. Were your things right, Elnora?"

The girl broke into hysterical laughter. "Right!" she cried. "Right! Uncle Wesley, you should have seen me among them! I was a picture! They'll never forget me. No, they won't get the chance, for they'll see the same things to-morrow!"

"Now, that is what I call spunk, Elnora! Downright grit," said Wesley Sinton. "Don't you let them laugh you out. You've helped Margaret and me for years at harvest and busy times, what you've earned must amount to quite a sum. You can get yourself a good many clothes with it."

"Don't mention clothes, Uncle Wesley," sobbed Elnora. "I don't care now how I look. If I don't go back all of them will know it's because I am so poor I can't buy my books."

"Oh, I don't know as you are so dratted poor," said Sinton meditatively. "There are three hundred acres of good land, with fine timber as ever grew on it."

"It takes all we can earn to pay the tax, and mother wouldn't cut a tree for her life."

"Well, then, maybe, I'll be compelled to cut one for her," suggested Sinton. "Anyway, stop tearing yourself to pieces and tell me. If it isn't clothes, what is it?"

"It's books and tuition. Over twenty dollars in all."

"Humph! First time I ever knew you to be stumped by twenty dollars, Elnora," said Sinton, patting her hand.

"It's the first time you ever knew me to want money," answered Elnora. "This is different from anything that ever happened to me. Oh, how can I get it, Uncle Wesley?"

"Drive to town with me in the morning and I'll draw it from the bank for you. I owe you every cent of it."

"You know you don't owe me a penny, and I wouldn't touch one from you, unless I really could earn it. For anything that's past I owe you and Aunt Margaret for all the home life and love I've ever known. I know how you work, and I'll not take your money."

"Just a loan, Elnora, just a loan for a little while until you can earn it. You can be proud with all the rest of the world, but there's no secrets between us, is there, Elnora?"

"No," said Elnora, "there are none. You and Aunt Margaret have given me all the love there has been in my life. That is the one reason above all others why you shall not give me charity. Hand me money because you find me crying for it! This isn't the first time this old trail has known tears and heartache. All of us know that story. Freckles stuck to what he undertook and won out. I stick, too. When Duncan moved away he gave me all Freckles left in the swamp, and as I have inherited his property maybe his luck will come with it. I won't touch your money, but I'll win some way. First, I'm going home and try mother. It's just possible I could find second-hand books, and perhaps all the tuition need not be paid at once. Maybe they would accept it quarterly. But, oh, Uncle Wesley, you and Aunt Margaret keep on loving me! I'm so lonely, and no one else cares!"

Wesley Sinton's jaws met with a click. He swallowed hard on bitter words and changed the thing he would have said three times before it became articulate.

"Elnora," he said at last, "if it hadn't been for one thing I'd have tried to take legal steps to make you ours when you were three years old. Maggie said then it wasn't any use, but I've always held on. You see, I was the first man there, honey, and there are things you see, that you can't ever make anybody else understand. She loved him Elnora, just made an idol of him. There was that oozy green hole, with the thick scum broke, and two or three big bubbles slowly rising that were the breath of his body. There she was in spasms of agony, and beside her the great heavy log she'd tried to throw him. I can't ever forgive her for turning against you, and spoiling your childhood as she has, but I couldn't forgive anybody else for abusing her. Maggie has got no mercy on her, but Maggie didn't see what I did, and I've never tried to make it very clear to her. It's been a little too plain for me ever since. Whenever I look at your mother's face, I see what she saw, so I hold my tongue and say, in my heart, 'Give her a mite more time.' Some day it will come. She does love you, Elnora. Everybody does, honey. It's just that she's feeling so much, she can't express herself. You be a patient girl and wait a little longer. After all, she's your mother, and you're all she's got, but a memory, and it might do her good to let her know that she was fooled in that."

"It would kill her!" cried the girl swiftly. "Uncle Wesley, it would kill her! What do you mean?"

"Nothing," said Wesley Sinton soothingly. "Nothing, honey. That was just one of them fool things a man says, when he is trying his best to be wise. You see, she loved him mightily, and they'd been married only a year, and what she was loving was what she thought he was. She hadn't really got acquainted with the man yet. If it had been even one more year, she could have borne it, and you'd have got justice. Having been a teacher she was better educated and smarter than the rest of us, and so she was more sensitive like. She can't understand she was loving a dream. So I say it might do her good if somebody that knew, could tell her, but I swear to gracious, I never could. I've heard her out at the edge of that quagmire calling in them wild spells of hers off and on for the last sixteen years, and imploring the swamp to give him back to her, and I've got out of bed when I was pretty tired, and come down to see she didn't go in herself, or harm you. What she feels is too deep for me. I've got to respectin' her grief, and I can't get over it. Go home and tell your ma, honey, and ask her nice and kind to help you. If she won't, then you got to swallow that little lump of pride in your neck, and come to Aunt Maggie, like you been a-coming all of your life."

"I'll ask mother, but I can't take your money, Uncle Wesley, indeed I can't. I'll wait a year, and earn some, and enter next year."

"There's one thing you don't consider, Elnora," said the man earnestly. "And that's what you are to Maggie. She's a little like your ma. She hasn't given up to it, and she's struggling on brave, but when we buried our second little girl the light went out of Maggie's eyes, and it's not come back. The only time I ever see a hint of it is when she thinks she's done something that makes you happy, Elnora. Now, you go easy about refusing her anything she wants to do for you. There's times in this world when it's our bounden duty to forget ourselves, and think what will help other people. Young woman, you owe me and Maggie all the comfort we can get out of you. There's the two of our own we can't ever do anything for. Don't you get the idea into your head that a fool thing you call pride, is going to cut us out of all the pleasure we have in life beside ourselves."

"Uncle Wesley, you are a dear," said Elnora. "Just a dear! If I can't possibly get that money any way else on earth, I'll come and borrow it of you, and then I'll pay it back if I dig ferns from the swamp and sell them from door to door in the city. I'll even plant them, so that they will be sure to come up in the spring. I have been sort of panic stricken all day and couldn't think. I can gather nuts and sell them. Freckles sold moths and butterflies, and I've a lot collected. Of course, I am going back to-morrow! I can find a way to get the books. Don't you worry about me. I am all right!"

"Now, what do you think of that?" inquired Wesley Sinton of the swamp in general. "Here's our Elnora come back to stay. Head high and right as a trivet! You've named three ways in three minutes that you could earn ten dollars, which I figure would be enough to start you. Let's go to supper and stop worrying!"

Elnora unlocked the case, took out the pail, put the napkin in it, pulled the ribbon from her hair, binding it down tight again and followed out to the road. From afar she could see her mother in the doorway. She blinked her eyes, and tried to smile as she answered Wesley Sinton, and indeed she did feel better. She knew now what she had to expect, where to go, and what to do. Get the books she must; when she got them, she would show those city girls and boys how to prepare and recite lessons, how to walk with a brave heart; and they could show her how to wear pretty clothes and have good times.

As she neared the door her mother reached for the pail. "I forgot to tell you to bring home your scraps for the chickens," she said.

Elnora entered. "There weren't any scraps, and I'm hungry again as I ever was in my life."

"I thought likely you would be," said Mrs. Comstock, "and so I got supper ready. We can eat first, and do the work afterward. What kept you so? I expected you an hour ago."

Elnora looked into her mother's face and smiled. It was a queer sort of a little smile, and would have reached the depths with any normal mother.

"I see you've been bawling," said Mrs. Comstock. "I thought you'd get your fill in a hurry. That's why I wouldn't go to any expense. If we keep out of the poorhouse we have to cut the corners close. It's likely this Brushwood road tax will eat up all we've saved in years. Where the land tax is to come from I don't know. It gets bigger every year. If they are going to dredge the swamp ditch again they'll just have to take the land to pay for it. I can't, that's all! We'll get up early in the morning and gather and hull the beans for winter, and put in the rest of the day hoeing the turnips."

Elnora again smiled that pitiful smile.

"Do you think I didn't know that I was funny and would be laughed at?" she asked.

"Funny?" cried Mrs. Comstock hotly.

"Yes, funny! A regular caricature," answered Elnora. "No one else wore calico, not even one other. No one else wore high heavy shoes, not even one. No one else had such a funny little old hat; my hair was not right, my ribbon invisible compared with the others, I did not know where to go, or what to do, and I had no books. What a spectacle I made for them!" Elnora laughed nervously at her own picture. "But there's always two sides! The professor said in the algebra class that he never had a better solution and explanation than mine of the proposition he gave me, which scored one for me in spite of my clothes."

"Well, I wouldn't brag on myself!"

"That was poor taste," admitted Elnora. "But, you see, it is a case of whistling to keep up my courage. I honestly could see that I would have looked just as well as the rest of them if I had been dressed as they were. We can't afford that, so I have to find something else to brace me. It was pretty bad, mother!"

"Well, I'm glad you got enough of it!"

"Oh, but I haven't!" hurried in Elnora. "I just got a start. The hardest is over. To-morrow they won't be surprised. They will know what to expect. I am sorry to hear about the dredge. Is it really going through?"

"Yes. I got my notification to-day. The tax will be something enormous. I don't know as I can spare you, even if you are willing to be a laughing-stock for the town."

With every bite Elnora's courage rose, for she was a healthy young thing.

"You've heard about doing evil that good might come from it," she said. "Well, mother mine, it's a little like that with me. I'm willing to bear the hard part to pay for what I'll learn. Already I have selected the ward building in which I shall teach in about four years. I am going to ask for a room with a south exposure so that the flowers and moths I bring in from the swamp to show the children will do well."

"You little idiot!" said Mrs. Comstock. "How are you going to pay your expenses?"

"Now, that is just what I was going to ask you!" said Elnora. "You see, I have had two startling pieces of news to-day. I did not know I would need any money. I thought the city furnished the books, and there is an out-of-town tuition, also. I need ten dollars in the morning. Will you please let me have it?"

"Ten dollars!" cried Mrs. Comstock. "Ten dollars! Why don't you say a hundred and be done with it! I could get one as easy as the other. I told you! I told you I couldn't raise a cent. Every year expenses grow bigger and bigger. I told you not to ask for money!"

"I never meant to," replied Elnora. "I thought clothes were all I needed and I could bear them. I never knew about buying books and tuition."

"Well, I did!" said Mrs. Comstock. "I knew what you would run into! But you are so bull-dog stubborn, and so set in your way, I thought I would just let you try the world a little and see how you liked it!"

Elnora pushed back her chair and looked at her mother.

"Do you mean to say," she demanded, "that you knew, when you let me go into a city classroom and reveal the fact before all of them that I expected to have my books handed out to me; do you mean to say that you knew I had to pay for them?"

Mrs. Comstock evaded the direct question.

"Anybody but an idiot mooning over a book or wasting time prowling the woods would have known you had to pay. Everybody has to pay for everything. Life is made up of pay, pay, pay! It's always and forever pay! If you don't pay one way you do another!

Of course, I knew you had to pay. Of course, I knew you would come home blubbering! But you don't get a penny! I haven't one cent, and can't get one! Have your way if you are determined, but I think you will find the road pretty rocky!"

"Swampy, you mean, mother," corrected Elnora. She arose white and trembling. "Perhaps some day God will teach me how to understand you. He knows I do not now. You can't possibly realize just what you let me go through to-day, or how you let me go, but I'll tell you this. You understand enough that if you had the money, and would offer it to me, I wouldn't touch it now. And I'll tell you this much more. I'll get it myself. I'll raise it, and do it some honest way. I am going back to-morrow, the next day, and the next. You need not come out, I'll do the night work, and hoe the turnips."

It was ten o'clock when the chickens, pigs, and cattle were fed, the turnips hoed, and a heap of bean vines was stacked by the back door.

2

Wherein Wesley and Margaret Go Shopping, and Elnora's Wardrobe Is Replenished

Wesley Sinton walked down the road a half-mile and turned in at the lane leading to his home. His heart was hot and filled with indignation. He had told Elnora he did not blame her mother, but he did. His wife met him at the door.

"Did you see anything of Elnora, Wesley?" she questioned.

"Most too much, Maggie," he answered. "What do you say to going to town? There's a few things has to be got right away!"

"Where did you see her, Wesley?"

"Along the old Limberlost trail, my girl, torn to pieces sobbing. Her courage always has been fine, but the thing she met to-day was too much for her. We ought to have known better than to let her go that way. It wasn't only clothes; there were books, and entrance fees for out-of-town people, that she didn't know about; while there must have been jeers, whispers, and laughing. Maggie, I feel as if I'd been a traitor to those girls of ours. I ought to have gone in and seen about this school business. I'm no man to let a fatherless girl run into such trouble. Don't cry, Maggie. Get me some supper, and I'll hitch up and see what we can do now."

"What can we do, Wesley?"

"I don't just know. But we've got to do something. Kate Comstock will be a handful, while Elnora will be two, but between us we must see that the girl is not too hard pressed about money, and that she is dressed so she is not ridiculous. She's saved us the wages of a woman many a day, can't you make her some decent dresses, Maggie?"

"Well, I'm not just what you call expert, but I could beat Kate Comstock all to pieces. I know that skirts should be pleated to the band instead of gathered, and full enough to sit in, and short enough to walk in. I could try. There's patterns for sale. Let's go right away, Wesley."

"Well, set me a bite of supper, while I hitch up."

Margaret Sinton started for the cupboard when she remembered that Wesley had worked all day and was hungry as usual, so she built a fire, made coffee, and fried ham and eggs. She set out pie and cake and had enough for a hungry man by the time the carriage was at the door, but she had no appetite. She dressed while Wesley ate, put away the food while he dressed, and then they drove toward the city through the beautiful September evening, and as they went they planned for Elnora. The only trouble was, not whether they were generous enough to get what she needed, but whether she would accept what they got, and what her mother would say.

They went to a large dry goods store and when a clerk asked what they wanted to see neither of them knew, so they stepped to one side and held a whispered consultation.

"What had we better get, Wesley?"

"Dresses," said Wesley promptly.

"But how many dresses, and what kind?"

"Blest if I know!" exclaimed Wesley. "I thought you would manage that. I know about some things I'm going to get."

At that instant several school girls came into the store and approached them.

"There!" exclaimed Wesley breathlessly. "There, Maggie! Like them! That's what she needs! Buy like they have!"

Margaret stared. What did they wear? They were rapidly passing, they seemed to have so much, and she could not decide so quickly. Before she knew it she was among them.

"I beg your pardon, but won't you wait one minute?" she asked.

The girls stopped with wondering faces.

"It's your clothes," explained Mrs. Sinton. "You look just beautiful to me. You look exactly as I should have wanted to see my girls. They both died of diphtheria when they were little, but they had yellow hair, dark eyes and pink cheeks, and everybody thought they were lovely. If they had lived, they'd been near your age now, and I'd want them to look like you."

There was nothing but sympathy in every girl face before Margaret Sinton.

"Why, thank you!" said one of them. "We are very sorry for you."

"Of course, you are," said Margaret. "Everybody always has been. And because I can't ever have the joy of a mother in thinking for my girls and buying pretty things for them, there is nothing left for me, but to do what I can for some one who has no mother to care for her. I know a girl, who would be just as pretty as any of you, if she had the clothes, but her mother does not think about her, so I got to mother her some myself."

"She must be a lucky girl," said another.

"Oh, she loves me," said Margaret, "and I love her. I want her to look just like you do. Please tell me about your clothes. Are these the dresses and hats you wear to school? What kind of goods are they, and where do you buy them?"

The girls began to laugh and cluster around Margaret. Wesley Sinton strode down the store with his head high in pride of her, but his heart was sore over the memory of two little faces under Brushwood sod. He inquired his way to the shoe department.

"Why, every one of us have on gingham or linen dresses," they said, "and they are our school clothes."

For a few moments there was a babel of laughing voices explaining to the delighted Margaret that school dresses should be bright and pretty, but simple and plain, and until cold weather they should wash.

"I'll tell you," said Ellen Brownlee, "my father owns this store, I know all the clerks. I'll take you to Miss Hartley. You tell her just how much you want to spend, and what you want to buy, and she will know how to get the most for your money. I've heard papa say she was the best clerk in the store for people who didn't know precisely what they wanted."

"That's the very thing," agreed Margaret. "But before you go, tell me about your hair. Elnora's hair is bright and wavy, but yours is silky as hackled flax. How do you do it?"

"Elnora?" asked four girls in concert.

"Yes, Elnora is the name of the girl I want these things for."

"Did she come to the high school to-day?" questioned one of them.

"Was she in your classes?" demanded Margaret without reply.

Four girls stood silent and thought fast. Had there been a strange girl among them, and had she been overlooked and passed by with indifference, because she was so very shabby? If she had appeared as much better than they, as she had looked worse, would her reception have been the same?

"There was a strange girl from the country in the Freshman class to-day," said Ellen Brownlee, "and her name was Elnora."

"That was the girl," said Margaret.

"Are her people so very poor?" questioned Ellen.

"No, not poor at all, come to think of it," answered Margaret. "It's a peculiar case. Mrs. Comstock had a great trouble and she let it change her whole life and make a different woman of her. She used to be lovely, now she is forever saving and scared to death for fear they will go to the poor-house; but there is a big farm, covered with lots of good timber. The taxes are high for women who can't manage to clear and work the land. There ought to be enough to keep two of them in good shape all their lives, if they only knew how to do it. But no one ever told Kate Comstock anything, and never will, for she won't listen. All she does is droop all day, and walk the edge of the swamp half the night, and neglect Elnora. If you girls would make life just a little easier for her, it would be the finest thing you ever did."

All of them promised they would.

"Now tell me about your hair," persisted Margaret Sinton.

So they took her to a toilet counter, and she bought the proper hair soap, also a nail file, and cold cream, for use after windy days. Then they left her with the experienced clerk, and when at last Wesley found her she was loaded with bundles and the glint of other days was in her beautiful eyes. Wesley carried some packages also.

"Did you get any stockings?" he whispered.

"No, I didn't," she said. "I was so interested in dresses and hair ribbons and a—a hat—" she hesitated and glanced at Wesley. "Of course, a hat!" prompted Wesley. "That I forgot all about those horrible shoes. She's got to have decent shoes, Wesley."

"Sure!" said Wesley. "She's got decent shoes. But the man said some brown stockings ought to go with them. Take a peep, will you!"

Wesley opened a box and displayed a pair of thick soled, beautifully shaped brown walking shoes of low cut. Margaret cried out with pleasure.

"But, do you suppose they are the right size, Wesley? What did you get?"

"I just said for a girl of sixteen with a slender foot."

"Well, that's about as near as I could come. If they don't fit when she tries them, we will drive straight in and change them. Come on, now, let's get home."

All the way they discussed how they should give Elnora their purchases and what Mrs. Comstock would say.

"I am afraid she will be awful mad," said Margaret Sinton tremulously.

"She'll just rip!" replied Wesley graphically. "But if she wants to leave the raising of her girl to the neighbours, she needn't get fractious if they take some pride in doing a good job. From now on I calculate Elnora shall go to school; and she shall have all the clothes and books she needs, if I go around on the back of Kate Comstock's land and cut a tree, or drive off a calf to pay for them. Why I know one tree she owns that would put Elnora in heaven for a year. Just think of it, Margaret! It's not fair. One-third of what is there belongs to Elnora by law, and if Kate Comstock raises a row I'll tell her so, and see that the girl gets it. You go to see Kate in the morning, and I'll go with you. Tell her you want Elnora's pattern, that you are going to make her a dress, for helping us. And sort of hint at a few more things. If Kate balks, I'll take a hand and settle her. I'll go to law for Elnora's share of that land and sell enough to educate her."

"Why, Wesley Sinton, you're perfectly wild."

"I'm not! Did you ever stop to think that such cases are so

frequent there have been laws made to provide for them? I can bring it up in court and force Kate to educate Elnora, and board and clothe her till she's of age, and then she can take her share."

"Wesley, Kate would go crazy!"

"She's crazy now. The idea of any mother living with as sweet a girl as Elnora, and letting her suffer till I find her crying like a funeral. It makes me fighting mad. All uncalled for. Not a grain of sense in it. I've offered and offered to oversee clearing her land and working her fields. Let her sell a good tree, or a few acres. Something is going to be done, right now. Elnora's been fairly happy up to this, but to spoil the school life she's planned, is to ruin all her life. I won't have it! If Elnora won't take these things, so help me, I'll tell her what she is worth, and loan her the money and she can pay me back when she comes of age. I am going to have it out with Kate Comstock in the morning. Here we are! You open up what you got while I put away the horses, and then I'll show you."

When Wesley came from the barn Margaret had four pieces of crisp gingham, a pale blue, a pink, a gray with green stripes and a rich brown and blue plaid. On each of them lay a yard and a half of wide ribbon to match. There were handkerchiefs and a brown leather belt. In her hands she held a wide-brimmed tan straw hat, having a high crown banded with velvet strips each of which fastened with a tiny gold buckle.

"It looks kind of bare now," she explained. "It had three quills on it here."

"Did you have them taken off?" asked Wesley dubiously.

"Yes, I did. The price was two and a half for the hat, and those things were a dollar and a half apiece. I couldn't pay that."

"It does seem considerable," admitted Wesley, "but will it look right without them?"

"No, it won't!" said Margaret. "It's going to have quills on it. Do you remember those beautiful peacock wing feathers that Phoebe Simms gave me? Three of them go on just where those came off, and nobody will ever know the difference. They match the hat to a moral, and they are just a little longer and richer than the ones that I had taken off. I was wondering whether I better sew them on to-night while I remember how they set, or wait till morning."

"Don't risk it!" exclaimed Wesley anxiously. "Don't you risk it! Sew them on right now!"

"Open your bundles, while I get the thread," said Margaret.

Wesley set out the shoes. Margaret took them up and pinched the leather and stroked them.

"My, but they are pretty!" she cried.

Wesley picked up one and slowly turned it in his big hands. He glanced at his foot and back to the shoe.

"It's a little bit of a thing, Margaret," he said softly. "Like as not I'll have to take it back. It don't look as if it could fit."

"It don't look like it dared do anything else," said Margaret. "That's a happy little shoe to get the chance to carry as fine a girl as Elnora to high school. Now, what's in the other box?"

Wesley looked at Margaret doubtfully.

"Why," he said, "you know there's going to be rainy days, and those things she has now ain't fit for anything but to drive up the cows—"

"Wesley, did you get high shoes, too?"

"Well, she ought to have them! The man said he would make them cheaper if I took both pairs at once."

Margaret laughed aloud. "Those will do her past Christmas," she exulted. "What else did you get?"

"Well, sir," said Wesley, "I saw something to-day. You told me about Kate getting that tin pail for Elnora to carry to high school and you said you told her it was a shame. I guess Elnora was ashamed all right, for to-night she stopped at the old case Duncan gave her, and took out that pail, where it had been all day, and put a napkin inside it. Coming home she confessed she was half starved because she hid her dinner under a culvert, and a tramp took it. She hadn't had a bite to eat the whole day. But she never complained at all, she was tickled to death that she hadn't lost the napkin. So I just inquired around till I found this, and I think it's about the ticket. Decent looking and handy as you please. See here, now!"

Wesley opened the package and laid a brown leather lunch box on the table. "Might be a couple of books, or drawing tools or most anything that's neat and genteel. You see, it opens this way."

It did open, and inside was a space for sandwiches, a little porcelain box for cold meat or fried chicken, another for salad, a glass with a lid which screwed on, held by a ring in a corner, for custard or jelly, a flask for tea or milk, a beautiful little knife, fork, and spoon fastened in holders, and a place for a napkin.

Margaret was almost crying over it.

"How I'd love to fill it!" she exclaimed.

"Do it the first time, just to show Kate Comstock what love is!" said Wesley. "Get up early in the morning and make one of those dresses to-morrow. Can't you make a plain gingham dress in a day? I'll pick a chicken, and you fry it and fix a little custard for the cup, and do it up brown. Go on, Maggie, you do it!"

"I never can," said Margaret. "I am slow as the itch about sewing, and these are not going to be plain dresses when it comes to making them. There are going to be edgings of plain green, pink, and brown to the bias strips, and tucks and pleats about the hips, fancy belts and collars, and all of it takes time."

"Then Kate Comstock's got to help," said Wesley. "Can the two of you make one, and get that lunch to-morrow?"

"Easy, but she'll never do it!"

"You see if she don't!" said Wesley. "You get up and cut it out, and soon as Elnora is gone I'll go after Kate myself. She'll take what I'll say better alone. But she'll come, and she'll help make the dress. These other things are our Christmas gifts to Elnora. She'll no doubt need them more now than she will then, and we can give them just as well. That's yours, and this is mine, or whichever way you choose."

Wesley untied a good brown umbrella and shook out the folds of a long, brown raincoat. Margaret dropped the hat, arose and took the coat. She tried it on, felt it, cooed over it and matched it with the umbrella.

"Did it look anything like rain to-night?" she inquired so anxiously that Wesley laughed.

"And this last bundle?" she said, dropping back in her chair, the coat still over her shoulders.

"I couldn't buy this much stuff for any other woman and nothing for my own," said Wesley. "It's Christmas for you, too, Margaret!" He shook out fold after fold of soft gray satiny goods that would look lovely against Margaret's pink cheeks and whitening hair.

"Oh, you old darling!" she exclaimed, and fled sobbing into his arms.

But she soon dried her eyes, raked together the coals in the cooking stove and boiled one of the dress patterns in salt water for a half-hour. Wesley held the lamp while she hung the goods on the line to dry. Then she set the irons on the stove so they would get hot the first thing in the morning.

3

Wherein Elnora Visits the Bird Woman, and Opens a Bank Account

At four o'clock next morning Elnora was shelling beans. At six she fed the chickens and pigs, swept two of the rooms of the cabin, built a fire, and put on the kettle for breakfast. Then she climbed the narrow stairs to the attic she had occupied since a very small child, and dressed in the hated shoes and brown calico, plastered down her crisp curls, ate what breakfast she could, and pinning on her hat started for town.

"There is no sense in your going for an hour yet," said her mother.

"I must try to discover some way to earn those books," replied Elnora. "I am perfectly positive I shall not find them lying along the road wrapped in tissue paper, and tagged with my name."

She went toward the city as on yesterday. Her perplexity as to where tuition and books were to come from was worse but she did not feel quite so badly. She never again would have to face all of it for the first time. She had been through it once, and was yet living. There had been times yesterday when she had prayed to be hidden, or to drop dead, and neither had happened. "I guess the best way to get an answer to prayer is to work for it," muttered Elnora grimly.

Again she took the trail to the swamp, rearranged her hair and left the tin pail. This time she folded a couple of sandwiches in the napkin, and tied them in a neat light paper parcel which she carried in her hand. Then she hurried along the road to Onabasha and found a bookstore. There she asked the prices of the list of books that she needed, and learned that six dollars would not quite supply them. She anxiously inquired for second-hand books, but was told that the only way to secure them was from the last year's Freshmen. Just then Elnora felt that she positively could not approach any of those she supposed to be Sophomores and ask to buy their old books. The only balm the girl could see for the humiliation of yesterday was to appear that day with a set of new books.

"Do you wish these?" asked the clerk hurriedly, for the store was rapidly filling with school children wanting anything from a dictionary to a pen.

"Yes," gasped Elnora, "Oh, yes! But I cannot pay for them just now. Please let me take them, and I will pay for them on Friday, or return them as perfect as they are. Please trust me for them a few days."

The clerk looked at her doubtfully and took her name.

"I'll ask the proprietor," he said. When he came back Elnora knew the answer before he spoke.

"I'm sorry," he said, "but Mr. Hann doesn't recognize your name. You are not a customer of ours, and he feels that he can't take the risk. You'll have to bring the money."

Elnora clumped out of the store, the thump of her heavy shoes beating as a hammer on her brain. She tried two other houses with the same result, and then in sick despair came into the street. What could she do? She was too frightened to think. Should she stay from school that day and canvass the homes appearing to belong to the wealthy, and try to sell beds of wild ferns, as she had suggested to Wesley Sinton? What would she dare ask for bringing in and planting a clump of ferns? How could she carry them? Would people buy them? She slowly moved past the hotel and then glanced around to see if there was a clock anywhere, for she felt sure the young people passing constantly were on their way to school.

There it stood in a bank window in big black letters staring straight at her:

Wanted: Caterpillars. Cocoons. Chrysalides. Pupae cases. Butterflies. Moths. Indian relics of all kinds. Highest scale of prices paid in cash.

Elnora caught the wicket at the cashier's desk with both hands to brace herself against disappointment.

"Who is it wants to buy cocoons, butterflies, and moths?" she panted.

"The Bird Woman," answered the cashier. "Have you some for sale?"

"I have some, I do not know if they are what she would want."

"Well, you had better see her," said the cashier. "Do you know where she lives?"

"Yes," said Elnora. "Would you tell me the time?"

"Twenty-one after eight," was the answer.

She had nine minutes to reach the auditorium or be late. Should she go to school, or to the Bird Woman? Several girls passed her walking swiftly and she remembered their faces. They were hurrying to school. Elnora caught the infection. She would see the Bird Woman at noon. Algebra came first, and that professor was kind. Perhaps she could slip to the superintendent and ask him for a book for the next lesson, and at noon—"Oh, dear Lord make it come true," prayed Elnora, at noon maybe she could sell some of those wonderful shining-winged things she had been collecting all her life around the outskirts of the Limberlost.

As she went down the long hall she noticed the professor of mathematics standing in the door of his recitation room. When she came up to him he smiled and spoke to her.

"I have been watching for you," he said, and Elnora stopped bewildered.

"For me?" she questioned.

"Yes," said Professor Henley. "Step inside."

Elnora followed him into the room and he swung the door behind them.

"At teachers' meeting last evening, one of the professors mentioned that a pupil had betrayed in class that she had expected her books to be furnished by the city. I thought possibly it was you. Was it?"

"Yes," breathed Elnora.

"That being the case," said Professor Henley, "it just occurred to me as you had expected that, you might require a little time to secure them, and you are too fine a mathematician to fall behind for want of supplies. So I telephoned one of our Sophomores to bring her last year's books this morning. I am sorry to say they are somewhat abused, but the text is all here. You can have them for two dollars, and pay when you get ready. Would you care to take them?"

Elnora sat suddenly, because she could not stand another instant. She reached both hands for the books, and said never a word. The professor was silent also.

At last Elnora arose, hugging those books to her heart as a mother grasps a lost baby.

"One thing more," said the professor. "You can pay your tuition quarterly. You need not bother about the first instalment this month. Any time in October will do."

It seemed as if Elnora's gasp of relief must have reached the soles of her brogans.

"Did any one ever tell you how beautiful you are!" she cried.

As the professor was lank, tow-haired and so near-sighted that he peered at his pupils through spectacles, no one ever had.

"No," said Professor Henley, "I've waited some time for that; for which reason I shall appreciate it all the more. Come, now, or we shall be late for opening exercises."

So Elnora entered the auditorium a second time. Her face was like the brightest dawn that ever broke over the Limberlost. No matter about the lumbering shoes and skimpy dress just now. No matter about anything, she had the books. She could take them home. In her garret she could commit them to memory, if need be. She could show that clothes were not all. If the Bird Woman did not want any of the many different kinds of specimens she had collected, she was quite sure now she could sell ferns, nuts, and a great many things. Then, too, someone moved over this morning, and several girls smiled and bowed. Elnora forgot everything save her books, and that she was where she could use them intelligently—everything except one little thing away back in her head. Her mother had known about the books and the tuition, and had not told her when she agreed to her coming.

At noon Elnora took her little parcel of lunch and started to the home of the Bird Woman. She must know about the specimens first and then she would go out to the suburbs somewhere and eat a few bites. She dropped the heavy iron knocker on the door of the big red log cabin, and her heart thumped at the resounding stroke.

"Is the Bird Woman at home?" she asked of the maid.

"She is at lunch," was the answer.

"Please ask her if she will see a girl from the Limberlost about some moths?" inquired Elnora.

"I never need ask, if it's moths," laughed the girl. "Orders are to bring anyone with specimens right in. Come this way."

Elnora followed down the hall and entered a long room with high panelled wainscoting, old English fireplace with an overmantel and closets of peculiar china filling the corners. At a bare table of oak, yellow as gold, sat a woman Elnora often had watched and followed covertly around the Limberlost. The Bird Woman was holding out a hand of welcome.

"I heard!" she laughed. "A little pasteboard box, or just the bare word 'specimen,' passes you at my door. If it is moths I hope you have hundreds. I've been very busy all summer and unable to collect, and I need so many. Sit down and lunch with me, while we talk it over. From the Limberlost, did you say?"

"I live near the swamp," replied Elnora. "Since it's so cleared I dare go around the edge in daytime, though we are still afraid at night."

"What have you collected?" asked the Bird Woman, as she helped Elnora to sandwiches unlike any she ever before had tasted, salad that seemed to be made of many familiar things, but you were only sure of celery and apples, and a cup of hot chocolate that would have delighted any hungry schoolgirl.

Elnora said "Thank you," and set the things before her, but her eyes were on the Bird Woman's face.

"I am afraid I am bothering you for nothing, and imposing on you," she said. "That 'collected' frightens me. I've only gathered. I always loved everything outdoors, and so I made friends and playmates of them. When I learned that the moths die so soon, I saved them especially, because there seemed no wickedness in it."

"I have thought the same thing," said the Bird Woman encouragingly. Then because the girl could not eat until she learned about the moths, the Bird Woman asked Elnora if she knew what kinds she had.

"Not all of them," answered Elnora. "Before Mr. Duncan moved away he often saw me near the edge of the swamp, and he showed me the box he had fixed for Freckles, and gave me the key. There were some books and things, so from that time on I studied and tried to take moths right, but I am afraid they are not what you want."

"Are they the big ones that fly mostly June nights?" asked the Bird Woman.

"Yes," said Elnora. "Great gray ones with reddish markings, pale blue-green, yellow with lavender, and red and yellow."

"What do you mean by 'red and yellow?'" asked the Bird Woman so quickly that the girl almost jumped.

"Not exactly red," explained Elnora, with tremulous voice. "A reddish, yellowish brown, with canary-coloured spots and gray lines on their wings."

"How many of them?" It was the same quick question.

"Well, I had over two hundred eggs," said Elnora, "but some of them didn't hatch, and some of the caterpillars died, but there must be at least a hundred perfect ones."

"Perfect! How, perfect?" cried the Bird Woman.

"I mean whole wings, no down gone, and all their legs and antennae," faltered Elnora.

"Young woman, that's the rarest moth in America," said the Bird Woman solemnly. "If you have a hundred of them, they are worth a hundred dollars according to my list. I can use all that are whole."

"What if they are not pinned right," quavered Elnora.

"If they are perfect, that does not make the slightest difference. I know how to soften them so that I can put them into any shape I choose. Where are they? When may I see them?"

"They are in Freckles's old case in the Limberlost," said Elnora. "I couldn't carry many for fear of breaking them, but I could bring a few after school."

"You come here at four," said the Bird Woman, "and we will drive out with some specimen boxes, and a price list, and see what you have to sell. Are they your very own? Are you free to part with them?"

"They are mine," said Elnora. "No one but God knows I have them. Mr. Duncan gave me the books and the box. He told Freckles about me, and Freckles told him to give me all he left. He said for me to stick to the swamp and be brave, and my hour would come, and it has! I know most of them are all right, and oh, I do need the money!"

"Could you tell me?" asked the Bird Woman softly.

"You see the swamp and all the fields around it are so full," explained Elnora. "Every day I felt smaller and smaller, and I wanted to know more and more, and pretty soon I got desperate, just as Freckles did. But I am better off than he was, for I have his books, and I have a mother; even if she don't care for me as other girls' mothers do for them, it's better than no one."

The Bird Woman's glance fell, for the girl was not conscious of how much she was revealing. Her eyes were fixed on a black pitcher filled with goldenrod in the centre of the table and she was saying what she thought.

"As long as I could go to the Brushwood school I was happy, but I couldn't go further just when things got the most interesting, so I was bound I'd come to high school and mother wouldn't consent. You see there's plenty of land, but father was drowned when I was a baby, and mother and I can't make money as men do. The taxes get bigger every year, and she said it was too expensive. I wouldn't give her any rest, until at last she got me this dress, and these shoes and I came. It was awful!"

Elnora stopped short and stared into the Bird Woman's face.

"Do you live in that beautiful cabin at the northwest end of the swamp?" asked the Bird Woman.

"Yes," said Elnora.

"I remember the place and a story about it now. You entered the high school yesterday?"

"Yes."

"It was pretty bad?"

"Pretty bad!" echoed Elnora.

The Bird Woman laughed.

"You can't tell me anything about that," she said. "I once entered a city school straight from the country. My dress was brown calico, and my shoes were quite heavy."

The tears began to roll down Elnora's cheeks.

"Did they—?" she faltered.

"They did!" said the Bird Woman. "All of it. I am quite sure they did not miss one least little thing."

Then she wiped away some tears that began rolling down her cheeks, and laughed at the same time.

"Where are they now?" asked Elnora suddenly.

"Well, they are pretty widely scattered, but none of them have attained heights out of range. Some of the rich are poor, and some of the poor are rich. Some of the brightest died insane, and some of the dullest worked out high positions, some of the very worst to bear have gone out, and I frequently hear from others. Now I am here, able to remember it, and mingle laughter with what used to be all tears; for every day I have my beautiful work, and almost every day God sends some one like you to help me. What is your name, my girl?"

"Elnora Comstock," answered Elnora. "Yesterday on the board it changed to Cornstock, and for a minute I thought I'd die, but I can laugh over that already."

The Bird Woman arose and kissed her. "Finish your lunch," she said, "and I will get my price lists, and take down a memorandum of what you think you have, so I will know how many boxes to prepare. And remember this. What you are lies with you. If you are lazy, and accept your lot, you may live in it. If you are willing to work, you can write your name anywhere you choose, among the only ones who live past the grave in this world, the people who write books that help, make exquisite music, carve statues, paint pictures, and work for others. Never mind the calico dress, and the coarse shoes. Dig into the books, and before long you will hear yesterday's tormentors boasting that they were once classmates of yours. 'I could a tale unfold'—!"

She laughingly left the room and Elnora sat thinking, until she remembered how hungry she was, so she ate the food, drank the hot chocolate and began the process of getting a grip on herself.

Then the Bird Woman came back and showed Elnora a long printed slip giving a list of graduated prices for moths, butterflies and dragon flies.

"Oh, do you want them!" exulted Elnora. "I have a few and I can get more by the thousand, with every color in the world on their wings."

"Yes," said the Bird Woman, "I will buy them, also the big moth caterpillars that are creeping everywhere now, and the cocoons that they will spin just about this time. I have a sneaking impression that the mystery, wonder, and the urge of their pure beauty, are going to force me to picture and paint our moths and put them into a book for all the world to see and know. We Limberlost people must not be selfish with the wonders God has given to us. We must share with those poor cooped-up city people the best we can. To send them a beautiful book, that is the way, is it not, little new friend of mine?"

"Yes, oh yes!" cried Elnora. "And please God they find a way to earn the money to buy the books, as I have those I need so badly."

"I will pay good prices for all the moths you can find," said the Bird Woman, "because you see I exchange them with foreign collectors. I want a complete series of the moths of America to trade with a German scientist, another with a man in India, and another in Brazil. Others I can exchange with home collectors for those of California and Canada, so you see I can use all you can raise, or find. The banker will buy stone axes, arrow points, and Indian pipes. There was a teacher from the city grade schools here to-day for specimens. There is a fund to supply the ward buildings. I'll help you get in touch with that. They want leaves of different trees, flowers, grasses, moths, insects, birds' nests and anything about birds."

Elnora's eyes were blazing. "Had I best go back to school or open a bank account and begin being a millionaire? Uncle Wesley and I have a bushel of arrow points gathered, a stack of axes, pipes, skin-dressing tools, tubes and mortars. I don't know how I ever will wait three hours."

"You must go, or you will be late," said the Bird Woman. "I will be ready at four."

After school closed Elnora, seated by the Bird Woman, drove

to Freckles's old room in the Limberlost. One at a time the beautiful big moths were taken from the interior of the old black case. Not a fourth of them could be moved that night and it was almost dark when the last box was closed, the list figured, and into Elnora's trembling fingers were paid fifty-nine dollars and sixteen cents. Elnora clasped the money closely.

"Oh you beautiful stuff!" she cried. "You are going to buy the books, pay the tuition, and take me to high school."

Then because she was a woman, she sat on a log and looked at her shoes. Long after the Bird Woman drove away Elnora remained. She had her problem, and it was a big one. If she told her mother, would she take the money to pay the taxes? If she did not tell her, how could she account for the books, and things for which she would spend it? At last she counted out what she needed for the next day, placed the rest in the farthest corner of the case, and locked the door. She then filled the front of her skirt from a heap of arrow points beneath the case and started home.

4

Wherein the Sintons Are Disappointed, and Mrs. Comstock Learns That She Can Laugh

With the first streak of red above the Limberlost Margaret Sinton was busy with the gingham and the intricate paper pattern she had purchased. Wesley cooked the breakfast and worked until he thought Elnora would be gone, then he started to bring her mother.

"Now you be mighty careful," cautioned Margaret. "I don't know how she will take it."

"I don't either," said Wesley philosophically, "but she's got to take it some way. That dress has to be finished by school time in the morning."

Wesley had not slept well that night. He had been so busy framing diplomatic speeches to make to Mrs. Comstock that sleep had little chance with him. Every step nearer to her he approached his position seemed less enviable. By the time he reached the front gate and started down the walk between the rows of asters and lady slippers he was perspiring, and every plausible and convincing speech had fled his brain. Mrs. Comstock helped him. She met him at the door.

"Good morning," she said. "Did Margaret send you for something?"

"Yes," said Wesley. "She sent me for you. She's got a job that's too big for her, and she wants you to help."

"Of course I will," said Mrs. Comstock. It was no one's affair how lonely the previous day had been, or how the endless hours of the present would drag. "What is she doing in such a rush?"

Now was his chance.

"She's making a dress for Elnora," answered Wesley. He saw Mrs. Comstock's form straighten, and her face harden, so he continued hastily. "You see Elnora has been helping us at harvest time, butchering, and with unexpected visitors for years. We've made out that she's saved us a considerable sum, and as she wouldn't ever touch any pay for anything, we just went to town and got a few clothes we thought would fix her up a little for the high school. We want to get a dress done to-day mighty bad, but Margaret is slow about sewing, and she never can finish alone, so I came for you."

"And it's such a simple little matter, so dead easy; and all so between old friends like, that you can't look above your boots while you explain it," sneered Mrs. Comstock. "Wesley Sinton, what put the idea into your head that Elnora would take things bought with money, when she wouldn't take the money?"

Then Sinton's eyes came up straightly.

"Finding her on the trail last night sobbing as hard as I ever saw any one at a funeral. She wasn't complaining at all, but she's come to me all her life with her little hurts, and she couldn't hide how she'd been laughed at, twitted, and run face to face against the fact that there was books and tuition, unexpected, and nothing will ever make me believe you didn't know that, Kate Comstock."

"If any doubts are troubling you on that subject, sure I knew it! She was so anxious to try the world, I thought I'd just let her take a few knocks and see how she liked it."

"As if she'd ever taken anything but knocks all her life!" cried Wesley Sinton. "Kate Comstock, you are a heartless, selfish woman. You've never showed Elnora any real love in her life. If ever she finds out that thing you'll lose her, and it will serve you right."

"She knows it now," said Mrs. Comstock icily, "and she'll be home to-night just as usual."

"Well, you are a brave woman if you dared put a girl of Elnora's make through what she suffered yesterday, and will suffer again to-day, and let her know you did it on purpose. I admire your nerve. But I've watched this since Elnora was born, and I got enough. Things have come to a pass where they go better for her, or I interfere."

"As if you'd ever done anything but interfere all her life! Think I haven't watched you? Think I, with my heart raw in my breast, and too numb to resent it openly, haven't seen you and Mag Sinton trying to turn Elnora against me day after day? When did you ever tell her what her father meant to me? When did you ever try to make her see the wreck of my life, and what I've suffered? No indeed! Always it's been poor little abused Elnora, and cakes, kissing, extra clothes, and encouraging her to run to you with a pitiful mouth every time I tried to make a woman of her."

"Kate Comstock, that's unjust," cried Sinton. "Only last night I tried to show her the picture I saw the day she was born. I begged her to come to you and tell you pleasant what she needed, and ask you for what I happen to know you can well afford to give her."

"I can't!" cried Mrs. Comstock. "You know I can't!"

"Then get so you can!" said Wesley Sinton. "Any day you say the word you can sell six thousand worth of rare timber off this place easy. I'll see to clearing and working the fields cheap as dirt, for Elnora's sake. I'll buy you more cattle to fatten. All you've got to do is sign a lease, to pull thousands from the ground in oil, as the rest of us are doing all around you."

"Cut down Robert's trees!" shrieked Mrs. Comstock. "Tear up his land! Cover everything with horrid, greasy oil! I'll die first!"

"You mean you'll let Elnora go like a beggar, and hurt and mortify her past bearing. I've got to the place where I tell you plain what I am going to do. Maggie and I went to town last night, and we got what things Elnora needs most urgent to make her look a little like the rest of the high school girls. Now here it is in plain English. You can help get these things ready, and let us give them to her as we want—"

"She won't touch them!" cried Mrs. Comstock.

"Then you can pay us, and she can take them as her right—"

"I won't!"

"Then I will tell Elnora just what you are worth, what you can afford, and how much of this she owns. I'll loan her the money to buy books and decent clothes, and when she is of age she can sell her share and pay me."

Mrs. Comstock gripped a chair-back and opened her lips, but no words came.

"And," Sinton continued, "if she is so much like you that she won't do that, I'll go to the county seat and lay complaint against you as her guardian before the judge. I'll swear to what you are worth, and how you are raising her, and have you discharged, or have the judge appoint some man who will see that she is comfortable, educated and decent looking!"

"You—you wouldn't!" gasped Mrs. Comstock.

"I won't need to, Kate!" said Sinton, his heart softening the instant the hard words were said. "You won't show it, but you do love Elnora! You can't help it! You must see how she needs things; come help us fix them, and be friends. Maggie and I couldn't live without her, and you couldn't either. You've got to love such a fine girl as she is; let it show a little!"

"You can hardly expect me to love her," said Mrs. Comstock coldly. "But for her a man would stand back of me now, who would beat the breath out of your sneaking body for the cowardly thing with which you threaten me. After all I've suffered you'd drag me to court and compel me to tear up Robert's property. If I ever go they carry me. If they touch one tree, or put down one greasy old oil well, it will be over all I can shoot, before they begin. Now, see how quick you can clear out of here!"

"You won't come and help Maggie with the dress?"

For answer Mrs. Comstock looked about swiftly for some object on which to lay her hands. Knowing her temper, Wesley Sinton left with all the haste consistent with dignity. But he did not go home. He crossed a field, and in an hour brought another neighbour who was skilful with her needle. With sinking heart Margaret saw them coming.

"Kate is too busy to help to-day, she can't sew before to-morrow," said Wesley cheerfully as they entered.

That quieted Margaret's apprehension a little, though she had some doubts. Wesley prepared the lunch, and by four o'clock the pretty dress was finished as far as it possibly could be until it was fitted on Elnora. If that did not entail too much work, it could be completed in two hours.

Then the neighbour left and Margaret packed their purchases into the big market basket. Wesley took the hat, umbrella, and raincoat, and they went down to Mrs. Comstock's. As they reached the step, Margaret spoke pleasantly to Mrs. Comstock, who sat reading just inside the door, but she did not answer and deliberately turned a leaf without looking up.

Wesley Sinton opened the door and went in followed by Margaret.

"Kate," he said, "you needn't take out your mad over our little racket on Maggie. I ain't told her a word I said to you, or you said to me. She's not so very strong, and she's sewed since four o'clock this morning to get this dress ready for to-morrow. It's done and we came down to try it on Elnora."

"Is that the truth, Mag Sinton?" demanded Mrs. Comstock.

"You heard Wesley say so," proudly affirmed Mrs. Sinton.

"I want to make you a proposition," said Wesley. "Wait till Elnora comes. Then we'll show her the things and see what she says."

"How would it do to see what she says without bribing her," sneered Mrs. Comstock.

"If she can stand what she did yesterday, and will to-day, she can bear 'most anything," said Wesley. "Put away the clothes if you want to, till we tell her."

"Well, you don't take this waist I'm working on," said Margaret, "for I have to baste in the sleeves and set the collar. Put the rest out of sight if you like."

Mrs. Comstock picked up the basket and bundles, placed them inside her room and closed the door.

Margaret threaded her needle and began to sew. Mrs. Comstock returned to her book, while Wesley fidgeted and raged inwardly. He could see that Margaret was nervous and almost in tears, but the lines in Mrs. Comstock's impassive face were set and cold. So they sat and the clock ticked off the time—one hour, two, dusk, and no Elnora. Margaret long since had taken the last stitch she could. Occasionally she and Wesley exchanged a few words. Mrs. Comstock regularly turned a leaf, and once arose and moved nearer a window. Just when Margaret and Wesley were discussing whether he had not best go to town to meet Elnora, they heard her coming up the walk. Wesley dropped his tilted chair and squared himself. Margaret gripped her sewing, and turned pleading eyes to the door. Mrs. Comstock closed her book and grimly smiled.

"Mother, please open the door," called Elnora.

Mrs. Comstock arose, and swung open the screen. Elnora stepped in beside her, bent half double, the whole front of her dress gathered into a sort of bag filled with a heavy load, and one arm stacked high with books. In the dim light she did not see the Sintons.

"Please hand me the empty bucket in the kitchen, mother," she said. "I just had to bring these arrow points home, but I'm scared for fear I've soiled my dress and will have to wash it. I'm to clean them, and take them to the banker in the morning, and oh, mother, I've sold enough stuff to pay for my books, my tuition, and maybe a dress and some lighter shoes besides. Oh, mother I'm so happy! Take the books and bring the bucket!"

Then she saw Margaret and Wesley. "Oh, glory!" she exulted. "I was just wondering how I'd ever wait to tell you, and here you are! It's too perfectly splendid to be true!"

"Tell us, Elnora," said Sinton.

"Well, sir," said Elnora, doubling down on the floor and spreading out her skirt, "set the bucket here, mother. These points are brittle and have to be put in one at a time. If they are chipped I can't sell them. Well, sir! I've had a time! You know I just had to have books. I tried three stores, and they wouldn't trust me, not even three days, I didn't know what in this world I could do quickly enough. Just when I was about frantic I saw a sign in a bank window asking for caterpillars, cocoons, butterflies, arrow points, and everything. I went in, and it was this Bird Woman wants the insects, and the banker wants the stones. I had to go to school then, but, if you'll believe it"—Elnora beamed on all of them in turn as she talked and slipped the arrow points from her dress to the pail—"if you'll believe it—but you won't, hardly, until you look at the books—there was the mathematics teacher, waiting at his door, and he had a set of books for me that he had telephoned a Sophomore to bring."

"How did he happen to do that, Elnora?" interrupted Sinton.

Elnora blushed.

"It was a fool mistake I made yesterday in thinking books were just handed out to you. There was a teachers' meeting last night and the history teacher told about that. Professor Henley thought it was me. You know I told you what he said about my algebra, mother. Ain't I glad I studied out some of it myself this summer! So he just telephoned and a girl brought the books. Because they are marked and abused some I get the whole outfit for two dollars. I can erase most of the marks, paste down the covers, and fix them so they look better. But I must hurry to the joy part. I didn't stop to eat, at noon, I just ran to the Bird Woman's, and I had lunch with her. It was salad, hot chocolate, and lovely things, and she wants to buy most every old scrap I ever gathered. She wants dragon flies, moths, butterflies, and he—the banker, I mean—wants everything Indian. This very night she came to the swamp with me and took away enough stuff to pay for the books and tuition, and to-morrow she is going to buy some more."

Elnora laid the last arrow point in the pail and arose, shaking leaves and bits of baked earth from her dress. She reached into her pocket and produced her money and waved it before their wondering eyes.

"And that's the joy part!" she exulted. "Put it up in the clock till morning, mother. That pays for the books and tuition and—" Elnora hesitated, for she saw the nervous grasp with which her mother's fingers closed on the bills. Then she went on, but more slowly and thinking before she spoke.

"What I get to-morrow pays for more books and tuition, and maybe a few, just a few, things to wear. These shoes are so dreadfully heavy and hot, and they make such a noise on the floor. There isn't another calico dress in the whole building, not among hundreds of us. Why, what is that! Aunt Margaret, what are you hiding in your lap?"

She snatched the waist and shook it out, and her face was beaming. "Have you taken to waists all fancy and buttoned in the back? I bet you this is mine!"

"I bet you so, too," said Margaret Sinton. "You undress right away and try it on, and if it fits, it will be done for morning. There are some low shoes, too!"

Elnora began to dance. "Oh, you dear people!" she cried. "I can pay for them to-morrow night! Isn't it too splendid! I was just thinking on the way home that I certainly would be compelled to have cooler shoes until later, and I was wondering what I'd do when the fall rains begin."

"I meant to get you some heavy dress skirts and a coat then," said Mrs. Comstock.

"I know you said so!" cried Elnora. "But you needn't now! I can get every single stitch I need myself. Next summer I can gather up a lot more stuff, and all winter on the way to school. I am sure I can sell ferns, I know I can nuts, and the Bird Woman says the grade rooms want leaves, grasses, birds' nests, and cocoons. Oh, isn't this world lovely? I'll be helping with the tax, next, mother!"

Elnora waved the waist and started for the bedroom. When she opened the door she gave a little cry.

"What have you people been doing?" she demanded. "I never saw so many interesting bundles in all my life. I'm 'skeered' to death for fear I can't pay for all of them, and will have to give up something."

"Wouldn't you take them, if you could not pay for them, Elnora?" asked her mother instantly.

"Why, not unless you did," answered Elnora. "People have no right to wear things they can't afford, have they?"

"But from such old friends as Maggie and Wesley!" Mrs. Comstock's voice was oily with triumph.

"From them least of all," cried Elnora stoutly. "From a stranger sooner than from them, to whom I owe so much more than I ever can pay them now."

"Well, you don't have to," said Mrs. Comstock. "Maggie just selected these things, because she is more in touch with the world, and has got such good taste. You can pay as long as your money holds out, and if there's more necessary, maybe I can sell the butcher a calf, or if there's things too costly for us, of course, they can take them back. Anything that ain't used can be returned. They were only brought here on trial. Put on the waist now, and then you can look over the rest and see if they are suitable, and what you want."

Elnora stepped into the adjoining room and closed the door.

Mrs. Comstock picked up the bucket and started for the well with it. At the bedroom she paused.

"Elnora, were you going to wash these arrow points?"

"Yes. The Bird Woman says they sell better if they are clean, so it can be seen that there are no defects in them."

"Of course," said Mrs. Comstock. "Some of them seem quite baked. Shall I put them to soak? Do you want to take them in the morning?"

"Yes, I do," answered Elnora. "If you would just fill the pail with water."

Mrs. Comstock left the room. Wesley Sinton sat with his back to the window in the west end of the cabin which overlooked the well. A suppressed sound behind him caused him to turn quickly. Then he arose and leaned over Margaret.

"She's out there laughing like a blamed monkey!" he whispered indignantly.

"Well, she can't help it!" exclaimed Margaret.

"I'm going home!" said Wesley.

"Oh, no, you are not!" retorted Margaret. "You are missing the point. The point is not how you look, or feel. It is to get these things in Elnora's possession past dispute. You go now, and to-morrow Elnora will wear calico, and Kate Comstock will return these goods. Right here I stay until everything we bought is Elnora's."

"What are you going to do?" asked Wesley.

"You'll have to watch me," said Margaret. "I don't know yet, myself."

Then she arose and peered from the window. At the well curb stood Katharine Comstock. The strain of the day was finding reaction. Her chin was in the air, she was heaving, shaking and strangling to suppress any sound. The word that slipped between Margaret Sinton's lips shocked Wesley until he dropped on his chair, and recalled her to her senses. She was fairly composed as she turned to Elnora, and began the fitting. When she had pinched, pulled, and patted she called, "Come see if you think this fits, Kate."

Mrs. Comstock had gone around to the back door and answered from the kitchen. "You know more about it than I do. Go ahead! I'm getting supper. Don't forget to allow for what it will shrink in washing!"

"I set the colours and washed the goods last night; it can be made to fit right now," answered Margaret past the pins between her teeth.

When she could find nothing more to alter she told Elnora to see how quickly she could heat a pail of water. After she had done that the girl began opening packages.

The hat came first.

"Mother!" cried Elnora. "Mother, of course, you have seen this, but you haven't seen it on me. I must try it on."

"Don't you dare put that on your head until your hair is washed and properly combed," said Margaret.

"Oh!" cried Elnora. "Is that water to wash my hair? I thought it was to set the color in another dress."

"Well, you thought wrong," said Margaret simply. "Your hair is going to be washed and brushed until it shines like copper. While it dries you can eat your supper, and this dress will be finished. Then you can put on your new ribbon, and your hat. You can try your shoes now, and if they don't fit, you and Wesley can drive to town and change them. That little round bundle on the top of the basket is your stockings."

Margaret sat down and began sewing swiftly, and a little later opened the machine, and ran several long seams.

Elnora was back in a few minutes holding up her skirts and stepping daintily in the beautiful new shoes.

"Don't soil them, honey, else you're sure they fit," cautioned Wesley.

"They seem just a trifle large, maybe," said Elnora dubiously, and Wesley got down to feel. He and Margaret thought them a fit, and then Elnora appealed to her mother. Mrs. Comstock appeared wiping her hands on her apron. She examined the shoes critically.

"They seem to fit," she said, "but they are away too fine to walk country roads."

"I think so, too," said Elnora instantly. "We had better take these back and get a cheaper pair."

"Oh, let them go for this time," said Mrs. Comstock. "They are so pretty, I hate to part with them. You can get cheaper ones after this."

Wesley and Margaret scarcely breathed for a long time.

Then Wesley went to do the feeding. Elnora set the table. When the water was hot, Margaret pinned a big towel around Elnora's shoulders and washed and dried the lovely hair according to the instructions she had been given the previous night. As the hair began to dry it billowed out in a sparkling sheen that caught the light and gleamed and flashed.

"Now, the idea is to let it stand naturally, just as the curl will make it. Don't you do any of that nasty, untidy snarling, Elnora," cautioned Margaret. "Wash it this way every two weeks while you are in school, shake it out, and dry it. Then part it in the middle and turn a front quarter on each side from your face. You tie the back at your neck with a string—so, and the ribbon goes in a big, loose bow. I'll show you." One after another Margaret Sinton tied the ribbons, creasing each of them so they could not be returned, as she explained that she was trying to see which was most becoming. Then she produced the raincoat which carried Elnora into transports.

Mrs. Comstock objected. "That won't be warm enough for cold weather, and you can't afford it and a coat, too."

"I'll tell you what I thought," said Elnora. "I was planning on the way home. These coats are fine because they keep you dry. I thought I would get one, and a warm sweater to wear under it cold days. Then you always would be dry, and warm, too. The sweater only costs three dollars, so I could get it and the raincoat both for half the price of a heavy cloth coat."

"You are right about that," said Mrs. Comstock. "You can change more with the weather, too. Keep the raincoat, Elnora."

"Wear it until you try the hat," said Margaret. "It will have to do until the dress is finished."

Elnora picked up the hat dubiously. "Mother, may I wear my hair as it is now?" she asked.

"Let me take a good look," said Katharine Comstock.

Heaven only knows what she saw. To Wesley and to Margaret the bright young face of Elnora, with its pink tints, its heavy dark brows, its bright blue-gray eyes, and its frame of curling reddish brown hair was the sweetest sight on earth, and at that instant Elnora was radiant.

"So long as it's your own hair, and combed back as plain as it will go, I don't suppose it cuts much ice whether it's tied a little tighter or looser," conceded Mrs. Comstock. "If you stop right there, you may let it go at that."

Elnora set the hat on her head. It was just a wide tan straw with three exquisite peacock quills at one side. Margaret Sinton cried out, Wesley slapped his knee and sighed like a blast, and Mrs. Comstock stood speechless for a second.

"I wish you had asked the price before you put that on," she said impatiently. "We never can afford it."

"It's not so much as you think," said Margaret. "Don't you see what I did? I had them take off the quills, and I put on some of those Phoebe Simms gave me from her peacocks. The hat will only cost you a dollar and a half."

She avoided Wesley's eyes, and looked straight at Mrs. Comstock. Elnora removed the hat to examine it.

"Why, they are those reddish tan quills of yours!" she cried. "Mother, look how beautifully they are set on! I think they are fine. I'd much rather have them than those from the store."

"So would I," said Mrs. Comstock. "If Margaret wants to spare them, that will make you a beautiful hat; dirt cheap, too! You must go past Mrs. Simms and show her. She would be pleased to see them."

Elnora sank into a chair because she couldn't stand any longer and contemplated her toe. "Landy, ain't I a queen?" she murmured. "What else have I got?"

"Just a belt, some handkerchiefs, and a pair of top shoes for rainy days and colder weather," said Margaret, handing over parcels.

"About those high shoes, that was my idea," said Wesley. "Soon as it rains, low shoes won't do, and by taking two pairs at once I could get them some cheaper. The low ones are two and the high ones two fifty, together three seventy-five. Ain't that cheap?"

"That's a real bargain," said Mrs. Comstock, "if they are good shoes, and they look it."

"This," said Wesley, producing the last package, "is your Christmas present from your Aunt Maggie. I got mine, too, but it's at the house. I'll bring it up in the morning."

He handed Margaret the umbrella, and she passed it over to Elnora who opened it and sat laughing under its shelter. Then she kissed both of them. She got a pencil and a slip of paper and set down the prices they gave her of everything they had brought except the umbrella, added the sum, and said laughingly, "Will you please wait till to-morrow for the money? I will have it then, sure."

"Elnora," said Wesley Sinton. "Wouldn't you—"

"Elnora, hustle here a minute!" called Mrs. Comstock from the kitchen. "I need you!"

"One second, mother," answered Elnora, throwing off the coat and hat, and closing the umbrella as she ran. There were several errands to do in a hurry, and then supper. Elnora chattered incessantly, Wesley and Margaret talked all they could, while Mrs. Comstock said a word now and then, which was all she ever did. But Wesley Sinton was watching her, and time and again he saw a peculiar little twist around her mouth. He knew that for the first time in sixteen years she really was laughing over something. She had all she could do to preserve her usually sober face. Wesley knew what she was thinking.

After supper the dress was finished, the plans for the next one discussed, and then the Sintons went home. Elnora gathered her treasures.

As she started for the stairs she stopped. "May I kiss you good-night, mother?" she asked lightly.

"Never mind any slobbering," said Mrs. Comstock. "I should think you'd lived with me long enough to know that I don't care for it."

"Well, I'd love to show you in some way how happy I am, and how I thank you."

"I wonder what for?" said Mrs. Comstock. "Mag Sinton picked that stuff and brought it here and you pay for it."

"Yes, but you seemed willing for me to have it, and you said you would help me if I couldn't pay all," insisted Elnora.

"Maybe I did," said Mrs. Comstock. "Maybe I did. I meant to

get you some heavy dress skirts about Thanksgiving, and I still can get them. Go to bed, and for any sake don't begin mooning before a mirror, and make a dunce of yourself."

Mrs. Comstock picked up several papers and blew out the kitchen light. She stood in the middle of the sitting-room floor for a time and then went into her room and closed the door. Sitting on the edge of the bed she thought for a few minutes and then suddenly buried her face in the pillow and again heaved with laughter.

Down the road plodded Margaret and Wesley Sinton. Neither of them had words to utter their united thought.

"Done!" hissed Wesley at last. "Done brown! Did you ever feel like a bloomin', confounded donkey? How did the woman do it?"

"She didn't do it!" gulped Margaret through her tears. "She didn't do anything. She just trusted to Elnora's great big soul to bring her out right, and really she was right, and so it had to bring her. She's a darling, Wesley! But she's got a time before her. Did you see Kate Comstock grab that money? Before six months she'll be out combing the Limberlost for bugs and arrow points to help pay the tax. I know her."

"Well, I don't!" exclaimed Sinton, "She's too many for me. But there is a laugh left in her yet! I didn't s'pose there was. Bet you a dollar, if we could see her this minute, she'd be chuckling over the way we got left."

Both of them stopped in the road and looked back.

"There's Elnora's light in her room," said Margaret. "The poor child will feel those clothes, and pore over her books till morning, but she'll look decent to go to school, anyway. Nothing is too big a price to pay for that."

"Yes, if Kate lets her wear them. Ten to one, she makes her finish the week with that old stuff!"

"No, she won't," said Margaret. "She don't dare. Kate made some concessions, all right; big ones for her—if she did get her way in the main. She bent some, and if Elnora proves that she can walk out barehanded in the morning and come back with that much money in her pocket, an armful of books, and buy a turnout like that, she proves that she is of some consideration, and Kate's smart enough. She'll think twice before she'll do that. Elnora won't wear a calico dress to high school again. You watch and see if she does. She may have got the best clothes she'll get for a time, for the least money, but she won't know it until she tries to buy goods herself at the same rates. Wesley, what about those prices? Didn't they shrink considerable?"

"You began it," said Wesley. "Those prices were all right. We didn't say what the goods cost us, we said what they would cost her. Surely, she's mistaken about being able to pay all that. Can she pick up stuff of that value around the Limberlost? Didn't the Bird Woman see her trouble, and just give her the money?"

"I don't think so," said Margaret. "Seems to me I've heard of her paying, or offering to pay them that would take the money, for bugs and butterflies, and I've known people who sold that banker Indian stuff. Once I heard that his pipe collection beat that of the Government at the Philadelphia Centennial. Those things have come to have a value."

"Well, there's about a bushel of that kind of valuables piled up in the woodshed, that belongs to Elnora. At least, I picked them up because she said she wanted them. Ain't it queer that she'd take to stones, bugs, and butterflies, and save them. Now they are going to bring her the very thing she wants the worst. Lord, but this is a funny world when you get to studying! Looks like things didn't all come by accident. Looks as if there was a plan back of it, and somebody driving that knows the road, and how to handle the lines. Anyhow, Elnora's in the wagon, and when I get out in the night and the dark closes around me, and I see the stars, I don't feel so cheap. Maggie, how the nation did Kate Comstock do that?"

"You will keep on harping, Wesley. I told you she didn't do it. Elnora did it! She walked in and took things right out of our hands. All Kate had to do was to enjoy having it go her way, and she was cute enough to put in a few questions that sort of guided Elnora. But I don't know, Wesley. This thing makes me think, too. S'pose we'd got Elnora when she was a baby, and we'd heaped on her all the love we can't on our own, and we'd coddled, petted, and shielded her, would she have made the woman that living alone, learning to think for herself, and taking all the knocks Kate Comstock could give, have made of her?"

"You bet your life!" cried Wesley, warmly. "Loving anybody don't hurt them. We wouldn't have done anything but love her. You can't hurt a child loving it. She'd have learned to work, be sensible, study, and grown into a woman with us, without suffering like a poor homeless dog."

"But you don't get the point, Wesley. She would have grown into a fine woman with us; just seems as if Elnora was born to be fine, but as we would have raised her, would her heart ever have known the world as it does now? Where's the anguish, Wesley, that child can't comprehend? Seeing what she's seen of her mother hasn't hardened her. She can understand any mother's sorrow. Living life from the rough side has only broadened her. Where's the girl or boy burning with shame, or struggling to find a way, that will cross Elnora's path and not get a lift from her? She's had the knocks, but there'll never be any of the thing you call 'false pride' in her. I guess we better keep out. Maybe Kate Comstock knows what she's doing. Sure as you live, Elnora has grown bigger on knocks than she would on love."

"I don't s'pose there ever was a very fine point to anything but I missed it," said Wesley, "because I am blunt, rough, and have no book learning to speak of. Since you put it into words I see what you mean, but it's dinged hard on Elnora, just the same. And I don't keep out. I keep watching closer than ever. I got my slap in the face, but if I don't miss my guess, Kate Comstock learned her lesson, same as I did. She learned that I was in earnest, that I would haul her to court if she didn't loosen up a bit, and she'll loosen. You see if she don't. It may come hard, and the hinges creak, but she'll fix Elnora decent after this, if Elnora don't prove that she can fix herself. As for me, I found out that what I was doing was as much for myself as for Elnora. I wanted her to take those things from us, and love us for giving them. It didn't work, and but for you, I'd messed the whole thing and stuck like a pig crossing a bridge. But you helped me out; Elnora's got the clothes, and by morning, maybe I won't grudge Kate the only laugh she's had in sixteen years. You been showing me the way quite a spell now, ain't you, Maggie?"

Then they went out of the night, and lay down together with Margaret's hand just touching Wesley's sleeve.

Up in the attic Elnora lighted two candles, set them on her little table, stacked the books, and put away the precious clothes. How lovingly she hung the hat and umbrella, folded the raincoat, and spread the new dress over a chair. She fingered the ribbons, and tried to smooth the creases from them. She put away the hose neatly folded, touched the handkerchiefs, and tried the belt. Then she slipped into her little white nightdress, shook down her hair that it might become thoroughly dry, set a chair before the table, and reverently opened one of the books. A stiff draught swept the attic, for it stretched the length of the cabin, and had a window in each end. Elnora arose and going to the east window closed it. She stood for a minute looking at the stars, the sky, and the dark outline of the straggling trees of the rapidly dismantling Limberlost. In the region of her case a tiny point of light flashed and disappeared. Elnora straightened and wondered. Was it wise to leave her precious money there? The light flashed once more, wavered a few seconds, and died out. The girl waited. She did not see it again, and so she went back to her books.

In the Limberlost the hulking figure of a man slouched down the trail.

"The Bird Woman was at Freckles's room this evening," he muttered. "Wonder what for?"

He left the trail, entered the enclosure still distinctly outlined and approached the case. The first point of light flashed from the tiny electric lamp on his vest. He took a duplicate key from his pocket, felt for the padlock and opened it. The door swung wide. The light flashed the second time. Swiftly his glance swept the interior.

"'Bout a fourth of her moths gone. Elnora must have been with the Bird Woman and given them to her." Then he stood tense. His keen eyes discovered the roll of bills hastily thrust back in the bottom of the case. He snatched them up, shut off the light, relocked the case by touch, and swiftly went down the trail. Every few seconds he paused and listened intently. Just as he reached the road, the low hoot of a screech owl, waveringly prolonged, fell on his ears, and he stopped. An instant later a second figure approached him.

"Is it you, Pete?" came the whispered question.

"Yes," said the first man.

"I was coming down to take a peep, when I saw your flash," he said. "I heard the Bird Woman had been at the case to-day. Anything doing?"

"Not a thing," said Pete. "She just took away about a fourth of the moths. Probably had the Comstock girl getting them for her. Heard they were together. Likely she'll get the rest to-morrow. Ain't picking gettin' bare these days?"

"Well, I should say so," said the second man, turning back in disgust. "Coming home, now?"

"No, I am going down this way," answered Pete, for his eyes caught the gleam from the window of the Comstock cabin, and he had a desire to learn why Elnora's attic was lighted at that hour.

He slouched down the road, occasionally feeling the size of the roll he had not taken time to count. He chuckled frequently.

"Feels fat enough to pay," he whispered. "Bill, I beat you just about seven minutes."

The attic was too long, the light too near the other end, and the cabin stood much too far back from the road. He could see nothing although he climbed the fence and walked back opposite the window. He knew Mrs. Comstock was probably awake, and that she sometimes went to the swamp behind her home at night. At times a cry went up from that locality that paralyzed anyone near, or sent them fleeing as if for life. He did not care to cross behind the cabin. He returned to the road, passed, and again climbed the fence. Opposite the west window he could see Elnora. She sat before a small table reading from a book between two candles. Her hair fell in a bright sheen around her, and with one hand she lightly shook, and tossed it as she studied. The man stood out in the night and watched.

For a long time a leaf turned occasionally and the hair-drying went on. The man drew nearer. The picture grew more beautiful as he approached. He could not see as well as he desired, for the screen was of white mosquito netting, and it angered him. He cautiously crept closer. The elevation shut off his view. Then he remembered the great willow tree shading the well and branching across the window at the west end of the cabin. From childhood Elnora had stepped from the sill to a limb and slid down the slanting trunk of the tree. He reached it and noiselessly swung himself up. Three steps out on the big limb the man shuddered. He was within a few feet of the girl.

He could see the throb of her breast under its thin covering and smell the fragrance of the tossing hair. He could see the narrow bed with its pieced calico cover, the whitewashed walls with gay lithographs, and every crevice stuck full of twigs with dangling cocoons. There were pegs for the few clothes, the old chest, the little table, the two chairs, the uneven floor covered with rag rugs, and braided corn husk. But nothing was worth a glance save the perfect face and form within reach by one spring through the rotten mosquito bar. He gripped the limb above that on which he stood, licked his lips, and breathed through his throat to be sure he was making no sound. Elnora closed the book and laid it aside. She picked up a towel, and turning the gathered ends of her hair rubbed them across it, and dropping the towel on her lap, tossed the hair again. Then she sat in deep thought. By and by words began to come softly. Near as he was the man could not hear at first. He bent closer and listened intently.

"—ever could be so happy," murmured the soft voice. "The dress is so pretty, such shoes, the coat and everything. I won't have to be ashamed again, not ever again, for the Limberlost is full of precious moths, and I always can collect them. The Bird Woman will buy more to-morrow, and the next day, and the next. When they are all gone, I can spend every minute gathering cocoons, and hunting other things I can sell. Oh, thank God, for my precious, precious money. Why, I didn't pray in vain after all! I thought when I asked the Lord to hide me, there in that big hall, that He wasn't doing it, because I wasn't covered from sight that instant. But I'm hidden now, I feel that." Elnora lifted her eyes to the beams above her. "I don't know much about praying properly," she muttered, "but I do thank you, Lord, for hiding me in your own time and way."

Her face was so bright that it shone with a white radiance. Two big tears welled from her eyes, and rolled down her smiling cheeks. "Oh, I do feel that you have hidden me," she breathed. Then she blew out the lights, and the little wooden bed creaked under her weight.

Pete Corson dropped from the limb and found his way to the road. He stood still a long time, then started back to the Limberlost. A tiny point of light flashed in the region of the case. He stopped with an oath.

"Another hound trying to steal from a girl," he exclaimed. "But it's likely he thinks if he gets anything it will be from a woman who can afford it, as I did."

He went on, but beside the fences, and very cautiously.

"Swamp seems to be alive to-night," he muttered. "That's three of us out."

He entered a deep place at the northwest corner, sat on the ground and taking a pencil from his pocket, he tore a leaf from a little notebook, and laboriously wrote a few lines by the light he carried. Then he went back to the region of the case and waited. Before his eyes swept the vision of the slender white creature with tossing hair. He smiled, and worshipped it, until a distant rooster faintly announced dawn.

Then he unlocked the case again, and replaced the money, laid the note upon it, and went back to concealment, where he remained until Elnora came down the trail in the morning, looking very lovely in her new dress and hat.

5

Wherein Elnora Receives a Warning, and Billy Appears on the Scene

It would be difficult to describe just how happy Elnora was that morning as she hurried through her work, bathed and put on the neat, dainty gingham dress, and the tan shoes. She had a struggle with her hair. It crinkled, billowed, and shone, and she could not avoid seeing the becoming frame it made around her face. But in deference to her mother's feelings the girl set her teeth, and bound her hair close to her head with a shoe-string. "Not to be changed at the case," she told herself.

That her mother was watching she was unaware. Just as she picked up the beautiful brown ribbon Mrs. Comstock spoke.

"You had better let me tie that. You can't reach behind yourself and do it right."

Elnora gave a little gasp. Her mother never before had proposed to do anything for the girl that by any possibility she could do herself. Her heart quaked at the thought of how her mother would arrange that bow, but Elnora dared not refuse. The offer was too precious. It might never be made again.

"Oh, thank you!" said the girl, and sitting down she held out the ribbon.

Her mother stood back and looked at her critically.

"You haven't got that like Mag Sinton had it last night," she announced. "You little idiot! You've tried to plaster it down to suit

---

me, and you missed it. I liked it away better as Mag fixed it, after I saw it. You didn't look so peeled."

"Oh, mother, mother!" laughed Elnora, with a half sob in her voice.

"Hold still, will you?" cried Mrs. Comstock. "You'll be late, and I haven't packed your dinner yet."

She untied the string and shook out the hair. It rose with electricity and clung to her fingers and hands. Mrs. Comstock jumped back as if bitten. She knew that touch. Her face grew white, and her eyes angry.

"Tie it yourself," she said shortly, "and then I'll put on the ribbon. But roll it back loose like Mag did. It looked so pretty that way."

Almost fainting Elnora stood before the glass, divided off the front parts of her hair, and rolled them as Mrs. Sinton had done; tied it at the nape of her neck, then sat while her mother arranged the ribbon.

"If I pull it down till it comes tight in these creases where she had it, it will be just right won't it?" queried Mrs. Comstock, and the amazed Elnora stammered "Yes."

When she looked in the glass the bow was perfectly tied, and how the gold tone of the brown did match the lustre of the shining hair! "That's awful pretty," commented Mrs. Comstock's soul, but her stiff lips had said all that could be forced from them for once. Just then Wesley Sinton came to the door.

"Good morning," he cried heartily. "Elnora, you look a picture! My, but you're sweet! If any of them city boys get sassy you tell your Uncle Wesley, and he'll horsewhip them. Here's your Christmas present from me." He handed Elnora the leather lunch box, with her name carved across the strap in artistic lettering.

"Oh, Uncle Wesley!" and that was all Elnora could say.

"Your Aunt Maggie filled it for me for a starter," he said. "Now, if you are ready, I'm going to drive past your way and you can ride almost to Onabasha with me, and save the new shoes that much."

Elnora was staring at the box. "Oh, I hope it isn't impolite to open it before you," she said. "I just feel as if I must see inside."

"Don't you stand on no formality with the neighbors," laughed Sinton. "Look at your box if you want to!"

Elnora slipped the strap and turned back the lid.

This disclosed the knife, fork, napkin, and spoon, the milk flask, and the interior packed with dainty sandwiches wrapped in tissue paper, and the little compartments for meat, salad, and the custard cup.

"Oh, mother!" cried Elnora. "Oh, mother, isn't it fine? What made you think of it, Uncle Wesley? How will I ever thank you? No one will have a finer lunch box than I. Oh, I do thank you! That's the nicest gift I ever had. How I love Christmas in September!"

"It's a mighty handy thing," assented Mrs. Comstock, taking in every detail with sharp eyes. "I guess you are glad now you went and helped Mag and Wesley when you could, Elnora?"

"Deedy, yes," laughed Elnora, "and I'm going again first time they have a big day if I stay out of school to do it."

"You'll do no such thing!" said the delighted Sinton. "Come now, if you're going!"

"If I ride, can you spare me time to run into the swamp to my box just a minute?" asked Elnora.

The light she had seen the previous night troubled her.

"Sure," said Wesley largely. He was having such a good time nothing could hurry him. So they drove away and left a white-faced woman watching them from the door, her heart just a little sorer than usual.

"I'd give a pretty to hear what he'll say to her!" she said bitterly. "Always sticking in, always doing things I can't ever afford. Where on earth did he get that thing and what did it cost?"

Then she entered the cabin and began the day's work, but mingled with the brooding bitterness of her soul was the vision of a sweet young face, glad with a gladness never before seen on it, and over and over she repeated, "I wonder what he'll say to her!"

What he said was that she looked as fresh and sweet as a posy, and to be careful not to step in the mud or scratch her shoe when she went to the case.

Elnora found her key and opened the door. Not where she had placed it, but conspicuously in front lay her little heap of bills, and a crude scrawl of writing beside it. Elnora picked up the note in astonishment.

dere elnory,

the lord amighty is hiding you all right done you ever dout it this money of yourn was took for some time las nite but it is returned with intres for god sake done ever come to the swamp at nite or late evnin or mornin or far in any time sompin worse an you know could git you

a frend.

Elnora began to tremble. She hastily glanced about. The damp earth before the case had been trodden by large, roughly shod feet. She caught up the money and the note, thrust them into her guimpe, locked the case, and ran for the road.

She was so breathless and her face so white Sinton noticed it.

"What in the world's the matter, Elnora?" he asked as he helped her into the carriage.

"I am half afraid!" she panted.

"Tut, tut, child!" said Wesley Sinton. "Nothing in the world to be afraid of. What happened?"

"Uncle Wesley," said Elnora, "I had more money than I brought home last night, and I put it in my case. Someone has been there. The ground is all trampled, and they left this note."

"And took your money, I'll wager," said Sinton angrily.

"No," answered Elnora. "Read the note and, oh, Uncle Wesley, tell me what it means!"

Sinton's face was a study. "I don't know what it means," he said. "Only one thing is clear. It means some beast who doesn't really want to harm you, has got his eye on you, and he is telling you plain as he can, not to give him a chance. You got to keep along the roads, in the open, and not let the biggest moth that ever flew toll you out of hearing of us, or your mother. It means that, plain and distinct."

"Just when I can sell them! Just when everything is so lovely on account of them! I can't! I can't stay away from the swamp. The Limberlost is going to buy the books, the clothes, pay the tuition, and even start a college fund. I just can't!"

"You've got to," said Sinton. "This is plain enough. You go far in the swamp at your own risk, even in daytime."

"Uncle Wesley," said the girl in a whisper, "last night before I went to bed, I was so happy I tried to pray, and I thanked God for hiding me 'under the shadow of His wing.' But how in the world could anyone know it?"

Wesley Sinton's heart gave one great leap in his breast. His face was whiter than the girl's now.

"Was you praying out loud, honey?" he almost whispered.

"I might have said words," answered Elnora. "I know I do sometimes. I've never had anyone to talk to, and I've played with and talked to myself all my life. You've caught me at it often, but it always makes mother angry when she does. She says it's silly. I forget and do it, when I'm alone. But, Uncle Wesley, if I said anything last night, you know it was the merest whisper, because I'd have been so afraid of waking mother. Don't you see? I sat up late, and did two lessons."

Sinton was steadying himself. "I'll stop and examine the case as I come back," he said. "Maybe I can find some clue. That other—that was just accidental. It's a common expression. All the preachers use it. If I was going to pray, that would be the very first thing I'd say."

The colour came back to Elnora's face.

"Did you tell your mother about this money, Elnora?" he asked.

"No, I didn't," said Elnora. "It's dreadful not to, but I was afraid. You see they are clearing the swamp so fast. Every year it grows harder to find things, and Indian stuff gets scarcer. I want to graduate, and that's four years unless I can double on the course. That means twenty dollars tuition each year, and new books, and clothes. There won't ever be so much at one time again, that I know. I just got to hang to my money. I was afraid to tell her, for fear she would want it for taxes, and she really must sell a tree or some cattle for that, mustn't she, Uncle Wesley?"

"On your life, she must!" said Wesley. "You put your little wad in the bank all safe, and never mention it to a living soul. It don't seem right, but your case is peculiar. Every word you say is a true word. Each year you will get less from the swamp, and things everywhere will be scarcer. If you ever get a few dollars ahead, that can start your college fund. You know you are going to college, Elnora!"

"Of course I am," said Elnora. "I settled that as soon as I knew what a college was. I will put all my money in the bank, except what I owe you. I'll pay that now."

"If your arrows are heavy," said Wesley, "I'll drive on to Onabasha with you."

"But they are not. Half of them were nicked, and this little box held all the good ones. It's so surprising how many are spoiled when you wash them."

"What does he pay?"

"Ten cents for any common perfect one, fifty for revolvers, a dollar for obsidian, and whatever is right for enormous big ones."

"Well, that sounds fair," said Sinton. "It's more than I would want to give for the things. You can come down Saturday and wash up the stuff at our house, and I'll take it in when we go marketing in the afternoon."

Elnora jumped from the carriage. She soon found that with her books, her lunch box, and the points she had a heavy load. She was almost to the bridge crossing the culvert when she heard the distressed screams of a child. Across an orchard of the suburbs came a small boy, after him a big dog, urged by a man in the background. Elnora's heart was with the small flying figure in any event whatever. She dropped her load on the bridge, and with practised hand caught up a stone and flung it at the dog. The beast curled double with a howl. The boy reached the fence, and Elnora was there to help him over. As he touched the top she swung him to the ground, but he clung to her, clasping her tightly, sobbing and shivering with fear. Elnora carried him to the bridge, and sat with him in her arms. For a time his replies to her questions were indistinct, but at last he became quieter and she could understand.

He was a mite of a boy, nothing but skin-covered bones, his burned, freckled face in a mortar of tears and dust, his clothing unspeakably dirty, one great toe in a festering mass from a broken nail, and sores all over the visible portions of the small body.

"You won't let the mean old thing make his dog get me!" he wailed.

"Indeed no," said Elnora, hugging him closely.

"You wouldn't set a dog on a boy for just taking a few old apples when you fed 'em to pigs with a shovel every day, would you?"

"No, I would not," said Elnora hotly.

"You'd give a boy all the apples he wanted, if he hadn't any breakfast, and was so hungry he was all twisty inside, wouldn't you?"

"Yes, I would," said Elnora.

"If you had anything to eat you would give me something right now, wouldn't you?"

"Yes," said Elnora. "There's nothing but just stones in the package. But my dinner is in that case. I'll gladly divide."

She opened the box. The famished child gave a little cry and reached both hands. Elnora caught them back.

"Did you have any supper?"

"No."

"Any dinner yesterday?"

"An apple and some grapes I stole."

"Whose boy are you?"

"Old Tom Billings's."

"Why don't your father get you something to eat?"

"He does most days, but he's drunk now."

"Hush, you must not!" said Elnora. "He's your father!"

"He's spent all the money to get drunk, too," said the boy, "and Jimmy and Belle are both crying for breakfast. I'd a got out all right with an apple for myself, but I tried to get some for them, and the dog got too close. Say, you can just throw, can't you?"

"Yes," admitted Elnora. She poured half the milk into the cup. "Drink this," she said, holding it to him.

The boy gulped the milk and swore joyously, gripping the cup with shaking fingers.

"Hush!" cried Elnora. "That's dreadful!"

"What's dreadful?"

"To say such awful words."

"Huh! pa says worser 'an that every breath he draws."

Elnora stared into the quaint little face, and saw that the child was older than she had thought. He might have been forty by his hard, unchildish expression.

"Do you want to be like your father?"

"No, I want to be like you. Couldn't a angel be prettier 'an you. Can I have more milk?"

Elnora emptied the flask. The boy drained the cup. He drew a breath of satisfaction as he gazed into her face.

"You wouldn't go off and leave your little boy, would you?" he asked.

"Did someone go away and leave you?" questioned Elnora in return.

"Yes, my mother went off and left me, and left Jimmy and Belle, too," said the boy. "You wouldn't leave your little boy, would you?"

"No."

The boy looked eagerly at the box. Elnora lifted a sandwich and uncovered the fried chicken. The boy gasped with delight.

"Say, I could eat the stuff in the glass, and the other box and carry the bread and the chicken to Jimmy and Belle," he offered.

Elnora silently uncovered the custard with preserved cherries on top and handed it and the spoon to the child. Never did food disappear faster. The salad went next, and a sandwich and half a chicken breast followed.

"I better leave the rest for Jimmy and Belle," he said, "they're 'ist fightin' hungry."

Elnora gave him the remainder of the carefully prepared lunch. The boy clutched it and ran with a sidewise hop like a wild thing.

Elnora covered the dishes and cup, polished the spoon, replaced it, and closed the beautiful case. She caught her breath in a tremulous laugh.

"If Aunt Margaret knew that, she'd never forgive me," she said. "It seems as if secrecy is literally forced upon me, and I hate it. What will I do for lunch? I'll have to go sell my arrows and keep enough money for a restaurant sandwich."

So she walked hurriedly into town, sold her points at a good price, deposited her funds, and went away with a neat little bank book and the note from the Limberlost carefully folded inside. Elnora passed down the great hall that morning, and no one paid the slightest attention to her. The truth was she looked so like everyone else that she was perfectly inconspicuous. But in the coat room there were members of her class. Surely no one intended it, but the whisper was too loud.

"Look at the girl from the Limberlost in the clothes that woman gave her!"

Elnora turned on them. "I beg your pardon," she said unsteadily, "I couldn't help hearing that! No one gave me these clothes. I paid for them myself."

Some one muttered, "Pardon me," but incredulous faces greeted her.

Elnora felt driven. "Aunt Margaret selected them, and she meant to give them to me," she explained, "but I wouldn't take them. I paid for them myself." There was a dead silence.

"Don't you believe me?" panted Elnora.

"Really, it is none of our affair," said another girl. "Come on, let's go."

Elnora stepped before the girl who had spoken. "You have made this your affair," she said, "because you told a thing which was not true. No one gave me what I am wearing. I paid for my clothes myself with money I earned selling moths to the Bird Woman. I just came from the bank where I deposited what I did not use. Here is my credit." Elnora drew out and offered the little red book. "Surely you will believe that," she said.

"Why, of course," said the girl who first had spoken. "We met such a lovely woman in Brownlee's store, and she said she wanted our help to buy some things for a girl, and that's how we came to know."

"Dear Aunt Margaret," said Elnora, "it was like her to ask you. Isn't she splendid?"

"She is indeed," chorused the girls. Elnora set down her lunch box and books, unpinned her hat, hanging it beside the others, and taking up the books she reached to set the box in its place and dropped it. With a little cry she snatched at it and caught the strap on top. That pulled from the fastening, the cover unrolled, the box fell away as far as it could, two porcelain lids rattled on the floor, and the one sandwich rolled like a cartwheel across the room. Elnora lifted a ghastly face. For once no one laughed. She stood an instant staring.

"It seems to be my luck to be crucified at every point of the compass," she said at last. "First two days you thought I was a pauper, now you will think I'm a fraud. All of you will believe I bought an expensive box, and then was too poor to put anything but a restaurant sandwich in it. You must stop till I prove to you that I'm not."

Elnora gathered up the lids, and kicked the sandwich into a corner.

"I had milk in that bottle, see! And custard in the cup. There was salad in the little box, fried chicken in the large one, and nut sandwiches in the tray. You can see the crumbs of all of them. A man set a dog on a child who was so starved he was stealing apples. I talked with him, and I thought I could bear hunger better, he was such a little boy, so I gave him my lunch, and got the sandwich at the restaurant."

Elnora held out the box. The girls were laughing by that time. "You goose," said one, "why didn't you give him the money, and save your lunch?"

"He was such a little fellow, and he really was hungry," said Elnora. "I often go without anything to eat at noon in the fields and woods, and never think of it."

She closed the box and set it beside the lunches of other country pupils. While her back was turned, into the room came the girl of her encounter on the first day, walked to the rack, and with an exclamation of approval took down Elnora's hat.

"Just the thing I have been wanting!" she said. "I never saw such beautiful quills in all my life. They match my new broadcloth to perfection. I've got to have that kind of quills for my hat. I never saw the like! Whose is it, and where did it come from?"

No one said a word, for Elnora's question, the reply, and her answer, had gone the rounds of the high school. Everyone knew that the Limberlost girl had come out ahead and Sadie Reed had not felt amiable, when the little flourish had been added to Elnora's name in the algebra class. Elnora's swift glance was pathetic, but no one helped her. Sadie Reed glanced from the hat to the faces around her and wondered.

"Why, this is the Freshman section, whose hat is it?" she asked again, this time impatiently.

"That's the tassel of the cornstock," said Elnora with a forced laugh.

The response was genuine. Everyone shouted. Sadie Reed blushed, but she laughed also.

"Well, it's beautiful," she said, "especially the quills. They are exactly what I want. I know I don't deserve any kindness from you, but I do wish you would tell me at whose store you got those quills." "Gladly!" said Elnora. "You can't get quills like those at a store. They are from a living bird. Phoebe Simms gathers them in her orchard as her peacocks shed them. They are wing quills from the males."

Then there was a perfect silence. How was Elnora to know that not a girl there would have told that?

"I haven't a doubt but I can get you some," she offered. "She gave Aunt Margaret a great bunch, and those are part of them. I am quite sure she has more, and would spare some."

Sadie Reed laughed shortly. "You needn't trouble," she said, "I was fooled. I thought they were expensive quills. I wanted them for a twenty-dollar velvet toque to match my new suit. If they are picked off the ground, really, I couldn't use them."

"Only in spots!" said Elnora. "They don't just cover the earth. Phoebe Simm's peacocks are the only ones within miles of Onabasha, and they moult but once a year. If your hat only cost twenty dollars, it's hardly good enough for those quills. You see, the Almighty made and coloured those Himself; and He puts the same kind on Phoebe Simm's peacocks, that He put on the head of the family in the forests of Ceylon, away back in the beginning. Any old manufactured quill from New York or Chicago will do for your little twenty-dollar hat. You ought to have something infinitely better than that to be worthy of quills that are made by the Creator."

How those girls did laugh! One of them walked by Elnora to the auditorium, sat with her during exercises, and tried to talk whenever she dared, to keep Elnora from seeing the curious and admiring looks bent upon her. For the brown-eyed boy whistled, and there was pantomime of all sorts going on behind Elnora's back that day. Happy with her books, no one knew how much she saw, and from her absorption in her studies it was evident she cared too little to notice. It soon developed that to be inconspicuous and to work was all Elnora craved.

After school she went again to the home of the Bird Woman, and together they visited the swamp and took away more specimens. This time Elnora asked the Bird Woman to keep the money until noon of the next day, when she would call for it and have it added to her bank account. She slowly walked home, for the visit to the swamp had brought back full force the experience of the morning. Again and again she examined the crude little note, for she did not know what it meant, yet it bred vague fear. The only thing on earth of which Elnora knew herself afraid was her mother; when with wild eyes and ears deaf to childish pleading, she sometimes lost control of herself in the night and visited the pool where her husband had sunk before her, calling his name in unearthly tones and begging of the swamp to give back its dead.

6

Wherein Mrs. Comstock Indulges in "Frills," and Billy Reappears

It was Wesley Sinton who really wrestled with the problem as he drove about his business. He did not have to ask himself what it meant; he knew. The old Corson gang was still holding together. Elder members who had escaped the law had been joined by a younger brother of Jack's, and they met in the thickest of the few remaining fast places of the swamp to drink, gamble, and loaf. Then, suddenly, there would be a robbery in some country house where a farmer that day had sold his wheat or corn and not paid a visit to the bank; or in some neighbouring village.

The home of Mrs. Comstock and Elnora adjoined the swamp. Sinton's land lay next, and not another residence or man easy to reach in case of trouble. Whoever wrote that note had some human kindness in his breast, but the fact stood revealed that he feared his strength if Elnora was delivered into his hands. Where had he been the previous night when he heard that prayer? Was that the first time he had been in such proximity? Sinton drove fast, for he wished to reach the swamp before Elnora and the Bird Woman would go there for more moths.

At almost four he came to the case, and dropping on his knees studied the ground, every sense alert. He found two or three little heel prints. Those were made by Elnora or the Bird Woman. What Sinton wanted to learn was whether all the rest were the footprints of one man. It was easily seen, they were not. There were deep, even tracks made by fairly new shoes, and others where a well-worn heel cut deeper on the inside of the print than at the outer edge. Undoubtedly some of Corson's old gang were watching the case, and the visits of the women to it. There was no danger that anyone would attack the Bird Woman. She never went to the swamp at night, and on her trips in the daytime, every one knew that she carried a revolver, understood how to use it, and pursued her work in a fearless manner.

Elnora, prowling around the swamp and lured into the interior by the flight of moths and butterflies; Elnora, without father, money, or friends save himself, to defend her—Elnora was a different proposition. For the thing to happen just when the Limberlost was bringing light, hope, and the very desire of her heart to the girl, it was too bad.

Sinton was afraid for her, yet he did not want to add the burden of fear to Katharine Comstock's trouble, or to disturb the joy of Elnora in her work. He stopped at the cabin and slowly went up the walk. Mrs. Comstock was sitting on the front step with some sewing. The work looked to Sinton as if she might be engaged in putting a tuck in a petticoat. He thought of how Margaret had shortened Elnora's dress to the accepted length for girls of her age, and made a mental note of Mrs. Comstock's occupation.

Mrs. Comstock dropped her work on her lap, laid her hands on it and looked into his face with a sneer.

"You didn't let any grass grow under your feet," she said.

Sinton saw her white, drawn face and comprehended.

"I went to pay a debt and see about this opening of the ditch, Kate."

"You said you were going to prosecute me."

"Good gracious, Kate!" cried Sinton. "Is that what you have been thinking all day? I told you before I left yesterday that I would not need do that. And I won't! We can't afford to quarrel over Elnora. She's all we've got. Now that she has proved that if you don't do just what I think you ought by way of clothes and schooling, she can take care of herself, I put that out of my head. What I came to see you about is a kind of scare I've had to-day. I want to ask you if you ever see anything about the swamp that makes you think the old Corson gang is still alive?"

"Can't say that I do," said Mrs. Comstock. "There's kind of dancing lights there sometimes, but I supposed it was just people passing along the road with lanterns. Folks hereabout are none too fond of the swamp. I hate it like death. I've never stayed here a night in my life without Robert's revolver, clean and loaded, under my pillow, and the shotgun, same condition, by the bed. I can't say that I'm afraid here at home. I'm not. I can take care of myself. But none of the swamp for me!"

"Well, I'm glad you are not afraid, Kate, because I got to tell you something. Elnora stopped at the case this morning, and somebody had been into it in the night."

"Broke the lock?"

"No. Used a duplicate key. To-day I heard there was a man here last night. I want to nose around a little."

Sinton went to the east end of the cabin and looked up at the window. There was no way anyone could have reached it without a ladder, for the logs were hewed and mortar filled the cracks even. Then he went to the west end, the willow faced him as he turned the corner. He examined the trunk carefully. There was no mistake about small particles of black swamp muck adhering to the sides of the tree. He reached the low branches and climbed the willow. There was earth on the large limb crossing Elnora's window. He stood on it, holding the branch as had been done the night before, and looked into the room. He could see very little, but he knew that if it had been dark outside and sufficiently light for Elnora to study inside he could have seen vividly. He brought his face close to the netting, and he could see the bed with its head to the east, at its foot the table with the candles and the chair before it, and then he knew where the man had been who had heard Elnora's prayer.

Mrs. Comstock had followed around the corner and stood watching him. "Do you think some slinking hulk was up there peekin' in at Elnora?" she demanded indignantly.

"There is muck on the trunk, and plenty on the limb," said Sinton. "Hadn't you better get a saw and let me take this branch off?"

"No, I hadn't," said Mrs. Comstock. "First place, Elnora's

climbed from that window on that limb all her life, and it's hers. Second place, no one gets ahead of me after I've had warning. Any crow that perches on that roost again, will get its feathers somewhat scattered. Look along the fence, there, and see if you can find where he came in."

The place was easy to find as was a trail leading for some distance west of the cabin.

"You just go home, and don't fret yourself," said Mrs. Comstock. "I'll take care of this. If you should hear the dinner bell at any time in the night you come down. But I wouldn't say anything to Elnora. She best keep her mind on her studies, if she's going to school."

When the work was finished that night Elnora took her books and went to her room to prepare some lessons, but every few minutes she looked toward the swamp to see if there were lights near the case. Mrs. Comstock raked together the coals in the cooking stove, got out the lunch box, and sitting down she studied it grimly. At last she arose.

"Wonder how it would do to show Mag Sinton a frill or two," she murmured.

She went to her room, knelt by a big black-walnut chest and hunted through its contents until she found an old-fashioned cook book. She tended the fire as she read and presently was in action. She first sawed an end from a fragrant, juicy, sugar-cured ham and put it to cook. Then she set a couple of eggs boiling, and after long hesitation began creaming butter and sugar in a crock. An hour later the odour of the ham, mingled with some of the richest spices of "happy Araby," in a combination that could mean nothing save spice cake, crept up to Elnora so strongly that she lifted her head and sniffed amazedly. She would have given all her precious money to go down and throw her arms around her mother's neck, but she did not dare move, even to open the door for a better smell.

Mrs. Comstock was up early, and without a word handed Elnora the case as she left the next morning.

"Thank you, mother," said Elnora, and went on her way.

She walked down the road looking straight ahead until she came to the corner, where she usually entered the swamp. She paused, glanced that way and smiled. Then she turned and looked back. There was no one coming in any direction. She kept to the road until well around the corner, then she stopped and sat on a grassy spot, laid her books beside her and opened the lunch box. Last night's odours had in a measure prepared her for what she would see, but not quite. She scarcely could believe her senses. Half the bread compartment was filled with dainty sandwiches of bread and butter sprinkled with the yolk of egg and the rest with three large slices of the most fragrant spice cake imaginable. The meat dish contained shaved cold ham, of which she knew the quality, the salad was tomatoes and celery, and the cup held preserved pear, clear as amber. There was milk in the bottle, two tissue-wrapped cucumber pickles in the folding drinking-cup, and a fresh napkin in the ring. No lunch was ever daintier or more palatable; of that Elnora was perfectly sure. And her mother had prepared it for her!

She glanced around her and then to her old refuge, the sky. "She does love me!" cried the happy girl. "Sure as you're born she loves me; she just hasn't found it out yet!"

She touched the papers daintily, and smiled at the box as if it were a living thing. As she began closing it a breath of air swept by, lifting the covering of the cake. It was like an invitation, and breakfast was several hours away. Elnora picked up a piece and ate it. That cake tasted even better than it looked. Then she tried a sandwich. How did her mother come to think of making them that way. They never had any at home. She slipped out the fork, sampled the salad, and one-quarter of pear. Then she closed the box and started down the road nibbling one of the pickles and trying to decide exactly how happy she was, but just then she could find no standard high enough for a measure.

She was to go to the Bird Woman's after school for the last load from the case. Saturday she would take the arrow points and specimens to the bank. That would exhaust her present supplies and give her enough money ahead to pay for books, tuition, and clothes for at least two years. She would work early and late gathering nuts. In October she would sell all the ferns she could find. She must collect specimens of all tree leaves before they fell, gather nests and cocoons later, and keep her eyes wide open for anything the grades could use. She would see the superintendent that night about selling specimens to the ward buildings. She must be ahead of anyone else if she wanted to furnish these things. So she approached the bridge.

That it was occupied could be seen from a distance. As she came up she found the small boy of yesterday awaiting her with a confident smile.

"We brought you something!" he announced without greeting. "This is Jimmy and Belle—and we brought you a present."

He offered a parcel wrapped in brown paper.

"Why, how lovely of you!" said Elnora. "I supposed you had forgotten me when you ran away so fast yesterday."

"Naw, I didn't forget you," said the boy. "I wouldn't forget you, not ever! Why, I was 'ist a-hurrying to take them things to Jimmy and Belle. My, they was glad!"

Elnora glanced at the children. They sat on the edge of the bridge, obviously clad in a garment each, very dirty and unkept, a little boy and a girl of about seven and nine. Elnora's heart began to ache.

"Say," said the boy. "Ain't you going to look what we have gave you?"

"I thought it wasn't polite to look before people," answered Elnora. "Of course, I will, if you would like to have me."

Elnora opened the package. She had been presented with a quarter of a stale loaf of baker's bread, and a big piece of ancient bologna.

"But don't you want this yourselves?" she asked in surprise.

"Gosh, no! I mean 'ist plain no," said the boy. "We always have it. We got stacks this morning. Pa's come out of it now, and he's so sorry he got more 'an ever we can eat. Have you had any before?"

"No," said Elnora, "I never did!"

The boy's eyes brightened and the girl moved restlessly.

"We thought maybe you hadn't," said the boy. "First you ever have, you like it real well; but when you don't have anything else for a long time, years an' years, you git so tired."

He hitched at the string which held his trousers and eyed Elnora speculatively.

"I don't s'pose you'd trade what you got in that box for 'ist old bread and bologna now, would you? Mebby you'd like it! And I know, I 'ist know, what you got would taste like heaven to Jimmy and Belle. They never had nothing like that! Not even Belle, and she's most ten! No, sir-ee, they never tasted things like you got!"

It was in Elnora's heart to be thankful that she had got even a taste in time, as she knelt on the bridge, opened the box and divided her lunch into three equal parts, the smaller boy getting most of the milk. Then she told them it was school time and she must go.

"Why don't you put your bread and bologna in the nice box?" asked the boy.

"Of course," said Elnora. "I didn't think."

When the box was arranged to the children's satisfaction all of them accompanied Elnora to the corner where she turned toward the high school. Elnora and Billy led the way, Jimmy and Belle followed.

"Billy," said Elnora, "I would like you much better if you were cleaner. Surely, you have water! Can't you children get some soap and wash yourselves? Gentlemen are never dirty. You want to be a gentleman, don't you?"

"Is being clean all you have to do to be a gentleman?"

"No," said Elnora. "You must not say bad words, and you must be kind and polite to your sister."

"Must Belle be kind and polite to me, else she ain't a lady?"

"Yes."

"Then Belle's no lady!" said Billy succinctly.

Elnora could say nothing more just then, and she bade them good-bye and started them home.

"The poor little souls!" she mused. "I think the Almighty put them in my way to show me real trouble. I won't be likely to spend much time pitying myself while I can see them." She glanced at the lunch box. "What on earth do I carry this for? I never had anything that was so strictly ornamental! One sure thing! I can't take this stuff to the high school. You never seem to know just what is going to happen to you while you are there."

As if to provide a way out of her difficulty a big dog arose from a lawn, and came toward the gate wagging his tail. "If those children ate the stuff, it can't possibly kill him!" thought Elnora, so she offered the bologna. The dog accepted it graciously, and being a pedigreed beast he trotted around to a side porch and laid the bologna before his mistress. The woman snatched it, screaming, "Come, quick! Someone is trying to poison Pedro!" Her daughter came running from the house. "Go see who is on the street. Hurry!" cried the excited mother.

Ellen Brownlee ran and looked. Elnora was a half block away, and no one nearer. Ellen called loudly, and Elnora stopped. Ellen came running toward her.

"Did you see anyone give our dog something?" she cried as she approached.

Elnora saw no escape.

"I gave it a piece of bologna myself," she said. "It was fit to eat. It wouldn't hurt the dog."

Ellen stood and looked at her. "Of course, I didn't know it was your dog," explained Elnora. "I just had something I wanted to throw to some dog, and that one looked big enough to manage it."

Ellen had arrived at her conclusions. "Pass over that lunch box," she demanded.

"I will not!" said Elnora.

"Then I will have you arrested for trying to poison our dog," laughed the girl as she took the box. "One chunk of stale bread, one half mile of antique bologna contributed for dog feed; the remains of cake, salad and preserves in an otherwise empty lunch box. One ham sandwich yesterday. I think it's lovely you have the box. Who got your lunch?"

"Same," confessed Elnora, "but there were three of them today."

"Wait, until I run back and tell mother about the dog, and get my books."

Elnora waited, and that morning she walked down the hall and into the auditorium beside one of the very nicest girls in Onabasha, and it was the fourth day. But the surprise came at noon when Ellen insisted upon Elnora lunching at the Brownlee home, and convulsed her parents and family, and overwhelmed Elnora by a greatly magnified, but moderately accurate history of her lunch box.

"Gee! but it's a box, daddy!" cried the laughing girl. "It's carved leather and fastens with a strap that's got her name on it. Inside are trays for things all complete, and it bears evidence of having enclosed delicious food, but Elnora never gets any. She's carried it two days now, and both times it has been empty before she reached school. Isn't that killing?"

"It is, Ellen, in more ways than one. No girl is going to eat breakfast at six o'clock, walk three miles, and do good work with no lunch. You can't tell me anything about that box. I sold it last Monday night to Wesley Sinton, one of my good country customers. He told me it was a present for a girl who was worthy of it, and I see he was right."

"He's so good to me," said Elnora. "Sometimes I look at him and wonder if a neighbour can be so kind to one, what a real father would be like. I envy a girl with a father unspeakably."

"You have cause," said Ellen Brownlee. "A father is the very nicest thing in the whole round world, except a mother, who is just as nice." The girl, starting to pay tribute to her father, saw that she must include her mother, and said the thing before she remembered what Mrs. Sinton had told the girls in the store. She stopped in dismay. Elnora's face paled a trifle, but she smiled bravely.

"Then I'm fortunate in having a mother," she said.

Mr. Brownlee lingered at the table after the girls had excused themselves and returned to school.

"There's a girl Ellen can't see too much of, in my opinion," he said. "She is every inch a lady, and not a foolish notion or action about her. I can't understand just what combination of circumstances produced her in this day."

"It has been an unusual case of repression, for one thing. She waits on her elders and thinks before she speaks," said Mrs Brownlee.

"She's mighty pretty. She looks so sound and wholesome, and she's neatly dressed."

"Ellen says she was a fright the first two days. Long brown calico dress almost touching the floor, and big, lumbering shoes. Those Sinton people bought her clothes. Ellen was in the store, and the woman stopped her crowd and asked them about their dresses. She said the girl was not poor, but her mother was selfish and didn't care for her. But Elnora showed a bankbook the next day, and declared that she paid for the things herself, so the Sinton people must just have selected them. There's something peculiar about it, but nothing wrong I am sure. I'll encourage Ellen to ask her again."

"Well, I should say so, especially if she is going to keep on giving away her lunch."

"She lunched with the Bird Woman one day this week."

"She did!"

"Yes, she lives out by the Limberlost. You know the Bird Woman works there a great deal, and probably knows her that way. I think the girl gathers specimens for her. Ellen says she knows more than the teachers about any nature question that comes up, and she is going to lead all of them in mathematics, and make them work in any branch."

When Elnora entered the coat room after having had luncheon with Ellen Brownlee there was such a difference in the atmosphere that she could feel it.

"I am almost sorry I have these clothes," she said to Ellen.

"In the name of sense, why?" cried the astonished girl.

"Everyone is so nice to me in them, it just sets me to wondering if in time I could have made them be equally friendly in the others."

Ellen looked at her introspectively.

"Well, sir, I believe you could," she announced at last. "But it would have taken time and heartache, and your mind would have been less free to work on your studies. No one is happy without friends, and I just simply can't study when I am unhappy."

That night the Bird Woman made the last trip to the swamp. Every specimen she possibly could use had been purchased at a fair price, and three additions had been made to the bank-book, carrying the total a little past two hundred dollars. There remained the Indian relics to sell on Saturday, and Elnora had secured the order to furnish material for nature work for the grades. Life suddenly grew very full. There was the most excitingly interesting work for every hour, and that work was to pay high-school expenses and start the college fund. There was just one little rift in her joy. All of it would have been so much better if she could have told her mother, and given the money into her keeping. But the struggle to get a start had been so terrible, Elnora was afraid to take the risk.

When she reached home, she only told her mother that the last of the things had been sold that evening.

"I think," said Mrs. Comstock, "that we will get Wesley to move that box over here back of the garden for you. There you are apt to get tolled farther into the swamp than you intend to go, and you might mire or something. There ought to be just the same things in our woods, and along our swampy places, as there are in the Limberlost. Can't you hunt your stuff here?"

"I can try," said Elnora. "I don't know what I can find until I do. Our woods are undisturbed, and there is a possibility they might be even better hunting than the swamp. But I wouldn't have Freckles's case moved for the world. He might come back some day, and not like it. I've tried to keep his room the best I could, and taking out the box would make a great hole in one side of it. Store boxes don't cost much. I will have Uncle Wesley buy me one, and set it up wherever hunting looks the best, early in the spring. I would feel safer at home."

"Shall we do the work or have supper first?"

"Let's do the work," said Elnora. "I can't say that I'm hungry now. Don't seem as if I ever could be hungry again with such a lunch. I am quite sure no one carried more delicious things to eat than I."

Mrs. Comstock was pleased. "I put in a pretty good hunk of cake," she said. "Did you divide it with anyone?"

"Why, yes, I did," admitted Elnora.

"Who?"

Things were getting uncomfortable. "I ate the biggest piece myself," said Elnora, "and gave the rest to a couple of boys named Jimmy and Billy and a girl named Belle. They said it was very best cake they ever tasted in all their lives."

Mrs. Comstock sat straight. "I used to be a master hand at spice cake," she boasted. "But I'm a little out of practice. I must get to work again. With the very weeds growing higher than our heads, we should get plenty of good stuff to eat off this land, if we can't afford anything else but taxes."

Elnora laughed and hurried up stairs to change her dress.

Margaret Sinton came that night bringing a beautiful blue one in its stead, and carried away the other to launder.

"Do you mean to say those dresses are to be washed every two days?" questioned Mrs. Comstock.

"They have to be, to look fresh," replied Margaret. "We want our girl sweet as a rose."

"Well, of all things!" cried Mrs. Comstock. "Every two days! Any girl who can't keep a dress clean longer than that is a dirty girl. You'll wear the goods out and fade the colours with so much washing."

"We'll have a clean girl, anyway."

"Well, if you like the job you can have it," said Mrs. Comstock. "I don't mind the washing, but I'm so inconvenient with an iron."

Elnora sat late that night working hard over her lessons. The next morning she put on her blue dress and ribbon and in those she was a picture. Mrs. Comstock caught her breath with a queer stirring around her heart, and looked twice to be sure of what she saw. As Elnora gathered her books her mother silently gave her the lunch box.

"Feels heavy," said Elnora gaily. "And smelly! Like as not I'll be called upon to divide again."

"Then you divide!" said Mrs. Comstock. "Eating is the one thing we don't have to economize on, Elnora. Spite of all I can do food goes to waste in this soil every day. If you can give some of those city children a taste of the real thing, why, don't be selfish."

Elnora went down the road thinking of the city children with whom she probably would divide. Of course, the bridge would be occupied again. So she stopped and opened the box. Undoubtedly Mrs. Comstock was showing Margaret Sinton the "frills." The cake was still fresh, and there were four slices. The sandwiches had to be tasted twice before Elnora discovered that beechnuts had been used in a peanut recipe, and they were a great improvement. There were preserved strawberries in the cup, potato salad with mint and cucumber in the dish, and a beautifully browned squab from the stable loft.

"I don't want to be selfish," murmured Elnora, "but it just seems as if I can't give away this lunch. If mother did not put love into it, she's substituted something that's likely to fool me."

She almost felt her steps lagging as she approached the bridge. A very hungry dog had been added to the trio of children. Elnora loved all dogs, and, as usual, this one came to her in friendliness. The children said "Good morning!" with alacrity, and another paper parcel lay conspicuous.

"How are you this morning?" inquired Elnora.

"All right!" cried the three, while the dog sniffed ravenously at the lunch box, and beat a perfect tattoo with his tail.

"How did you like the bologna?" questioned Billy eagerly.

"One of the girls took me to lunch at her home yesterday," answered Elnora.

Dawn broke beautifully over Billy's streaked face. He caught the package and thrust it toward Elnora.

"Then maybe you'd like to try the bologna to-day!"

The dog leaped in glad apprehension of something, and Belle scrambled to her feet and took a step forward. The look of famished greed in her eyes was more than Elnora could bear. It was not that she cared for the food so much. Good things to eat had been in abundance all her life. She wanted with this lunch to try to absorb what she felt must be an expression of some sort from her mother, and if it was not a manifestation of love, she did not know what to think it. But it was her mother who had said "be generous." She knelt on the bridge. "Keep back the dog!" she warned the elder boy.

She opened the box and divided the milk between Billy and the girl. She gave each a piece of cake leaving one and a sandwich. Billy pressed forward eagerly, bitter disappointment on his face, and the elder boy forgot his charge.

"Aw, I thought they'd be meat!" lamented Billy.

Elnora gave way.

"There is!" she said gladly. "There is a little pigeon bird. I want just a teeny piece of the breast, for a sort of keepsake, just one bite, and you can have the rest among you."

Elnora drew the knife from its holder and cut off the wishbone. Then she held the bird toward the girl.

"You can divide it," she said. The dog made a bound and seizing the squab sprang from the bridge and ran for life. The girl and boy hurried after him. With awful eyes Billy stared and swore tempestuously. Elnora caught him and clapped her hand over the little mouth. A delivery wagon came tearing down the street, the horse running full speed, passed the fleeing dog with the girl and boy in pursuit, and stopped at the bridge. High school girls began to roll from all sides of it.

"A rescue! A rescue!" they shouted.

It was Ellen Brownlee and her crowd, and every girl of them carried a big parcel. They took in the scene as they approached. The fleeing dog with something in its mouth, the half-naked girl and boy chasing it told the story. Those girls screamed with laughter as they watched the pursuit.

"Thank goodness, I saved the wishbone!" said Elnora. "As usual, I can prove that there was a bird." She turned toward the box. Billy had improved the time. He had the last piece of cake in one hand, and the last bite of salad disappeared in one great gulp. Then the girls shouted again.

"Let's have a sample ourselves," suggested one. She caught up the box and handed out the remaining sandwich. Another girl divided it into bites each little over an inch square, and then she lifted the cup lid and deposited a preserved strawberry on each bite. "One, two, three, altogether now!" she cried.

Billy let out a roar. "You old mean things!" he screamed.

In an instant he was down in the road and handfuls of dust began to fly among them. The girls scattered before him.

"Billy!" cried Elnora. "Billy! I'll never give you another bite as long as I live, if you throw dust on anyone!"

Then Billy dropped the dust, bored both fists into his eyes, and fled sobbing into Elnora's new blue skirt. She stooped to meet him and consolation began. Those girls laughed on. They screamed and shouted until the little bridge shook.

"To-morrow might as well be a clear day," said Ellen, passing around and feeding the remaining berries to the girls as they could compose themselves enough to take them. "Billy, I admire your taste more than your temper."

Elnora looked up. "The little soul is nothing but skin and bones," she said. "I never was really hungry myself; were any of you?"

"Well, I should say so," cried a plump, rosy girl. "I'm famished right now. Let's have breakfast immediate!"

"We got to refill this box first!" said Ellen Brownlee. "Who's got the butter?" A girl advanced with a wooden tray.

"Put it in the preserve cup, a little strawberry flavour won't hurt it. Next!" called Ellen.

A loaf of bread was produced and Ellen cut off a piece which filled the sandwich box.

"Next!" A bottle of olives was unwrapped. The grocer's boy who was waiting opened that, and Ellen filled the salad dish.

"Next!"

A bag of macaroons was produced and the cake compartment filled.

"Next!"

"I don't suppose this will make quite as good dog feed as a bird," laughed a girl holding open a bag of sliced ham while Ellen filled the meat dish.

"Next!"

A box of candy was handed her and she stuffed every corner of the lunch box with chocolates and nougat. Then it was closed and formally presented to Elnora. The girls each helped themselves to candy and olives, and gave Billy the remainder of the food. Billy took one bite of ham, and approved. Belle and Jimmy had given up chasing the dog and, angry and ashamed, stood waiting a half block away.

"Come back!" screamed Billy. "You great big dunces, come back! They's a new kind of meat, and cake and candy."

The boy delayed, but the girl joined Billy. Ellen wiped her fingers, stepped to the cement abutment and began reciting "Horatio at the Bridge!" substituting Elnora wherever the hero appeared in the lines.

Elnora gathered up the sacks, and gave them to Belle telling her to take the food home, cut and spread the bread, set things on the table, and eat nicely.

Then Elnora was hustled into the wagon with the girls, and driven on the run to the high school. They sang a song beginning—

Elnora please give me a sandwich.
I'm ashamed to ask for cake

as they went. Elnora did not know it, but that was her initiation. She belonged to "the crowd." She only knew that she was happy, and vaguely wondered what her mother and Aunt Margaret would have said about the proceedings.

CHAPTER
7

Wherein Mrs. Comstock Manipulates Margaret, and Billy Acquires a Residence

Saturday morning Elnora helped her mother with the work. When she had finished Mrs. Comstock told her to go to Sinton's and wash her Indian relics, so that she would be ready to accompany Wesley to town in the afternoon. Elnora hurried down the road and was soon at the cistern with a tub busily washing arrow points, stone axes, tubes, pipes, and skin-cleaning implements. There were not so many points as she had supposed, and some she had thought the finest were chipped and broken; still there was quite a large box of perfect pieces to carry to the city.

Then Elnora hurried home, dressed and was waiting when the carriage reached the gate. She stopped at the bank with the box, and Sinton went to do his marketing and a little shopping for his wife.

At the dry goods store Mr. Brownlee called to him, "Hello, Sinton! How do you like the fate of your lunch box?" Then he began to laugh.

"I always hate to see a man laughing alone," said Sinton. "It looks so selfish! Tell me the fun, and let me help you."

Brownlee wiped his eyes.

"I supposed you knew, but I see she hasn't told."

Then the three days' history of the lunch box was repeated with particulars which included the dog.

"Now laugh!" concluded Brownlee.

"Blest if I see anything funny!" replied Sinton. "And if you had bought that box and furnished one of those lunches yourself, you wouldn't either. I call such a work a shame! I'll have it stopped."

"Some one must see to that, all right. They are little leeches. Their father earns enough to support them, but they have no mother, and they run wild. I suppose they are crazy for cooked food. But it is funny, and when you think it over you will see it, if you don't now."

"About where would a body find that father?" inquired Sinton grimly. Mr. Brownlee told him and he started, locating the house with little difficulty. House was the proper word, for of home there was no sign. Just a small empty house with three unkept little children racing through and around it. The girl and the elder boy hung back, but dirty little Billy greeted Sinton with, "What you want here?"

"I want to see your father," said Sinton.

"Well, he's asleep," said Billy.

"Where?" asked Sinton.

"In the house," answered Billy, "and you can't wake him."

"Well, I'll try," said Wesley.

Billy led the way. "There he is!" he said. "He is drunk again."

On a dirty mattress in a corner lay a sleeping man who appeared to be strong and well.

Billy was right. You could not awake him. He had gone the limit, and a little beyond. He was now facing eternity.

Sinton went out and closed the door.

"Your father is sick and needs help," he said. "You stay here, and I will send a man to see him."

"If you just let him 'lone, he'll sleep it off," volunteered Billy. "He's that way all the time, but he wakes up and gets us something to eat after awhile. Only waitin' twists you up inside pretty bad."

The boy wore no air of complaint. He was merely stating facts.

Wesley Sinton looked hard at Billy. "Are you twisted up inside now?" he asked.

Billy laid a grimy hand on the region of his stomach and the filthy little waist sank close to the backbone. "Bet yer life, boss," he said cheerfully.

"How long have you been twisted?" asked Sinton.

Billy appealed to the others. "When was it we had the stuff on the bridge?"

"Yesterday morning," said the girl.

"Is that all gone?" asked Sinton.

"She went and told us to take it home," said Billy ruefully, "and 'cause she said to, we took it. Pa had come back, he was drinking some more, and he ate a lot of it—'most the whole thing, and it made him sick as a dog, and he went and wasted all of it. Then he got drunk some more, and now he's asleep again. We didn't get hardly none."

"You children sit on the steps until the man comes," said Sinton. "I'll send you some things to eat with him. What's your name, sonny?"

"Billy," said the boy.

"Well, Billy, I guess you better come with me. I'll take care of him," Sinton promised the others. He reached a hand to Billy.

"I ain't no baby, I'm a boy!" said Billy, as he shuffled along beside Sinton, taking a kick at every movable object without regard to his battered toes.

Once they passed a great Dane dog lolling after its master, and Billy ascended Sinton as if he was a tree, and clung to him with trembling hot hands.

"I ain't afraid of that dog," scoffed Billy, as he was again placed on the walk, "but onc't he took me for a rat or somepin' and his teeth cut into my back. If I'd a done right, I'd a took the law on him."

Sinton looked down into the indignant little face. The child was bright enough, he had a good head, but, oh, such a body!

"I 'bout got enough of dogs," said Billy. "I used to like 'em, but I'm getting pretty tired. You ought to seen the lickin' Jimmy and Belle and me give our dog when we caught him, for taking the little bird she gave us. We waited till he was asleep 'nen laid a board on him and all of us jumped on it to onc't. You could a heard him yell a mile. Belle said mebbe we could squeeze the bird out of him. But, squeeze nothing! He was holler as us, and that bird was lost long 'fore it got to his stummick. It was 'ist a little one, anyway. Belle said it wouldn't 'a' made a bite apiece for three of us nohow, and the dog got one good swaller. We didn't get much of the meat, either. Pa took most of that. Seems like pas and dogs gets everything."

Billy laughed ruefully. Involuntarily Wesley Sinton reached his hand. They were coming into the business part of Onabasha and the streets were crowded. Billy understood it to mean that he might lose his companion and took a grip. The little hot hand clinging tight to his, the sore feet recklessly scouring the walk, the hungry child panting for breath as he tried to keep even, the brave soul jesting in the face of hard luck, caught Sinton in a tender, empty spot.

"Say, son," he said. "How would you like to be washed clean, and have all the supper your skin could hold, and sleep in a good bed?"

"Aw, gee!" said Billy. "I ain't dead yet! Them things is in heaven! Poor folks can't have them. Pa said so."

"Well, you can have them if you want to go with me and get them," promised Sinton.

"Honest?"

"Yes, honest."

"Crost yer heart?"

"Yes," said Sinton.

"Kin I take some to Jimmy and Belle?"

"If you'll come with me and be my boy, I'll see that they have plenty."

"What will pa say?"

"Your pa is in that kind of sleep now where he won't wake up, Billy," said Sinton. "I am pretty sure the law will give you to me, if you want to come."

"When people don't ever wake up they're dead," announced Billy. "Is my pa dead?"

"Yes, he is," answered Sinton.

"And you'll take care of Jimmy and Belle, too?"

"I can't adopt all three of you," said Sinton. "I'll take you, and see that they are well provided for. Will you come?"

"Yep, I'll come," said Billy. "Let's eat, first thing we do."

"All right," agreed Sinton. "Come into this restaurant." He lifted Billy to the lunch counter and ordered the clerk to give him as many glasses of milk as he wanted, and a biscuit. "I think there's going to be fried chicken when we get home, Billy," he said, "so you just take the edge off now, and fill up later."

While Billy lunched Sinton called up the different departments and notified the proper authorities ending with the Women's Relief Association. He sent a basket of food to Belle and Jimmy, bought Billy a pair a trousers, and a shirt, and went to bring Elnora.

"Why, Uncle Wesley!" cried the girl. "Where did you find Billy?"

"I've adopted him for the time being, if not longer," replied Sinton.

"Where did you get him?" queried the astonished Elnora.

"Well, young woman," said Sinton, "Mr. Brownlee told me the history of your lunch box. It didn't seem so funny to me as it does to the rest of them; so I went to look up the father of Billy's family, and make him take care of them, or allow the law to do it for him. It will have to be the law."

"He's deader than anything!" broke in Billy. "He can't ever take all the meat any more."

"Billy!" gasped Elnora.

"Never you mind!" said Sinton. "A child don't say such things about a father who loved and raised him right. When it happens, the father alone is to blame. You won't hear Billy talk like that about me when I cross over."

"You don't mean you are going to take him to keep!"

"I'll soon need help," said Sinton. "Billy will come in just about right ten years from now, and if I raise him I'll have him the way I want him."

"But Aunt Margaret don't like boys," objected Elnora.

"Well, she likes me, and I used to be a boy. Anyway, as I remember she has had her way about everything at our house ever since we were married. I am going to please myself about Billy. Hasn't she always done just as she chose so far as you know? Honest, Elnora!"

"Honest!" replied Elnora. "You are beautiful to all of us, Uncle Wesley; but Aunt Margaret won't like Billy. She won't want him in her home."

"In our home," corrected Sinton.

"What makes you want him?" marvelled Elnora.

"God only knows," said Sinton. "Billy ain't so beautiful, and he ain't so smart, I guess it's because he's so human. My heart goes out to him."

"So did mine," said Elnora. "I love him. I'd rather see him eat my lunch than have it myself any time."

"What makes you like him?" asked Sinton.

"Why, I don't know," pondered Elnora. "He's so little he needs so much, he's got such splendid grit, and he's perfectly unselfish with his brother and sister. But we must wash him before Aunt Margaret sees him. I wonder if mother—?"

"You needn't bother. I'm going to take him home the way he is," said Sinton. "I want Maggie to see the worst of it."

"I'm afraid—" began Elnora.

"So am I," said Sinton, "but I won't give him up. He's taken a sort of grip on my heart. I've always been crazy for a boy. Don't let him hear us."

"Don't let him get killed!" cried Elnora. During their talk Billy had wandered to the edge of the walk and barely escaped the wheels of a passing automobile in an effort to catch a stray kitten that seemed in danger.

Sinton drew Billy back to the walk, and held his hand closely. "Are you ready, Elnora?"

"Yes; you were gone a long time," she said.

Sinton glanced at a package she carried. "Have to have another book?" he asked.

"No, I got this for mother. I've had such splendid luck selling my specimens, I didn't feel right about keeping all the money for myself, so I saved enough from the Indian relics to get a few things I wanted. I would have liked to have gotten her a dress, but I didn't dare, so I compromised on a book."

"What did you select, Elnora?" asked Sinton wonderingly.

"Well," said she, "I have noticed mother always seemed interested in anything Mark Twain wrote in the newspapers, and I thought it would cheer her up a little, so I just got his 'Innocents Abroad.' I haven't read it myself, but I've seen mention made of it all my life, and the critics say it's genuine fun."

"Good!" cried Sinton. "Good! You've made a splendid choice. It will take her mind off herself a lot. But she will scold you."

"Of course," assented Elnora. "But possibly she will read it, and feel better. I'm going to serve her a trick. I am going to hide it until Monday, and set it on her little shelf of books the last thing before I go away. She must have all of them by heart. When she sees a new one she can't help being glad, for she loves to read, and if she has all day to get interested, maybe she'll like it so she won't scold so much."

"We are both in for it, but I guess we are prepared. I don't know what Margaret will say, but I'm going to take Billy home and see. Maybe he can win with her, as he did with us."

Elnora had her doubts, but she did not say anything more.

When they started home Billy sat on the front seat. He drove with the hitching strap tied to the railing of the dashboard, flourished the whip, and yelled with delight. At first Sinton laughed with him, but by the time he left Elnora with several packages at her gate, he was looking serious enough.

Margaret was at the door as they drove up the lane. Sinton left Billy in the carriage, hitched the horses and went to explain to her. He had not reached her before she cried, "Look, Wesley, that child! You'll have a runaway!"

Wesley looked and ran. Billy was standing in the carriage slashing the mettlesome horses with the whip.

"See me make 'em go!" he shouted as the whip fell a second time.

He did make them go. They took the hitching post and a few fence palings, which scraped the paint from a wheel. Sinton missed the lines at the first effort, but the dragging post impeded the horses, and he soon caught them. He led them to the barn, and ordered Billy to remain in the carriage while he unhitched. Then leading Billy and carrying his packages he entered the yard.

"You run play a few minutes, Billy," he said. "I want to talk to the nice lady."

The nice lady was looking rather stupefied as Sinton approached her.

"Where in the name of sense did you get that awful child?" she demanded.

"He is a young gentleman who has been stopping Elnora and eating her lunch every day, part of the time with the assistance of his brother and sister, while our girl went hungry. Brownlee told me about it at the store. It's happened three days running. The first time she did without anything, the second time Brownlee's girl took her to lunch, and the third a crowd of high school girls bought a lot of stuff and met them at the bridge. The youngsters seemed to think they could rob her every day, so I went to see their father about having it stopped."

"Well, I should think so!" cried Margaret.

"There were three of them, Margaret," said Sinton, "that little fellow—"

"Hyena, you mean," interpolated Margaret.

"'Hyena'," corrected Sinton gravely, "and another boy and a girl, all equally dirty and hungry. The man was dead. They thought he was in a drunken sleep, but he was stone dead. I brought the little boy with me, and sent the officers and other help to the house. He's half starved. I want to wash him, and put clean clothes on him, and give him some supper."

"Have you got anything to put on him?"

"Yes."

"Where did you get it?"

"Bought it. It ain't much. All I got didn't cost a dollar."

"A dollar is a good deal when you work and save for it the way we do."

"Well, I don't know a better place to put it. Have you got any hot water? I'll use this tub at the cistern. Please give me some soap and towels."

Instead Margaret pushed by him with a shriek. Billy had played by producing a cord from his pocket, and having tied the tails of Margaret's white kittens together, he had climbed on a box and hung them across the clothes line. Wild with fright the kittens were clawing each other to death, and the air was white with fur. The string had twisted and the frightened creatures could not recognize friends. Margaret stepped back with bleeding hands. Sinton cut the cord with his knife and the poor little cats raced under the house bleeding and disfigured. Margaret white with wrath faced Sinton.

"If you don't hitch up and take that animal back to town," she said, "I will."

Billy threw himself on the grass and began to scream.

"You said I could have fried chicken for supper," he wailed. "You said she was a nice lady!"

Sinton lifted him and something in his manner of handling the child infuriated Margaret. His touch was so gentle. She reached for Billy and gripped his shirt collar in the back. Sinton's hand closed over hers.

"Gently, girl!" he said. "This little body is covered with sores."

"Sores!" she ejaculated. "Sores? What kind of sores?"

"Oh, they might be from bruises made by fists or boot toes, or they might be bad blood, from wrong eating, or they might be pure filth. Will you hand me some towels?"

"No, I won't!" said Margaret.

"Well, give me some rags, then."

Margaret compromised on pieces of old tablecloth.

Sinton led Billy to the cistern, pumped cold water into the tub, poured in a kettle of hot, and beginning at the head scoured him. The boy shut his little teeth, and said never a word though he twisted occasionally when the soap struck a raw spot. Margaret watched the process from the window in amazed, and ever-increasing anger. Where did Wesley learn it? How could his big hands be so gentle? Sinton came to the door.

"Have you got any peroxide?" he asked.

"A little," she answered stiffly.

"Well, I need about a pint, but I'll begin on what you have."

Margaret handed him the bottle. Wesley took a cup, weakened the drug and said to Billy. "Man, these sores on you must be healed. Then you must eat the kind of food that's fit for little men. I am going to put some medicine on you, and it is going to sting like fire. If it just runs off, I won't use any more. If it boils, there is poison in these places, and they must be tied up, dosed everyday, and you must be washed, and kept mighty clean. Now, hold still, because I am going to put it on."

"I think the one on my leg is the worst," said the undaunted Billy, holding out a raw place. Sinton poured on the drug. Billy's body twisted and writhed, but he did not run.

"Gee, look at it boil!" he cried. "I guess they's poison. You'll have to do it to all of them."

Sinton's teeth were set, as he watched the boy's face. He poured the drug, strong enough to do effective work, on a dozen places over that little body and bandaged all he could. Billy's lips quivered at times, and his chin jumped, but he did not shed a tear or utter a sound other than to take a deep interest in the boiling. As Sinton put the small shirt on the boy, and fastened the trousers, he was ready to reset the hitching post and mend the fence without a word.

"Now am I clean?" asked Billy.

"Yes, you are clean outside," said Sinton. "There is some dirty blood in your body, and some bad words in your mouth, that we have to get out, but that takes time. If we put right things to eat into your stomach that will do away with the sores, and if you know that I don't like bad words you won't say them any oftener than you can help, will you Billy?"

Billy leaned against Sinton in apparent indifference.

"I want to see me!" he demanded.

Sinton led the boy into the house, and lifted him to a mirror.

"My, I'm purty good-looking, ain't I?" bragged Billy. Then as Sinton stooped to set him on the floor Billy's lips passed close to the big man's ear and hastily whispered a vehement "No!" as he ran for the door.

"How long until supper, Margaret?" asked Sinton as he followed.

"You are going to keep him for supper?" she asked.

"Sure!" said Sinton. "That's what I brought him for. It's likely he never had a good square meal of decent food in his life. He's starved to the bone."

Margaret arose deliberately, removed the white cloth from the supper table and substituted an old red one she used to wrap the bread. She put away the pretty dishes they commonly used and set the table with old plates for pies and kitchen utensils. But she fried the chicken, and was generous with milk and honey, snowy bread, gravy, potatoes, and fruit.

Sinton repainted the scratched wheel. He mended the fence, with Billy holding the nails and handing the pickets. Then he filled the old hole, dug a new one and set the hitching post.

Billy hopped on one foot at his task of holding the post steady as the earth was packed around it. There was not the shadow of a trouble on his little freckled face. Sinton threw in stones and pounded the earth solid around the post. The sound of a gulping sob attracted him to Billy. The tears were rolling down his cheeks. "If I'd a knowed you'd have to get down in a hole, and work so hard I wouldn't 'a' hit the horses," he said.

"Never you mind, Billy," said Sinton. "You will know next time, so you can think over it, and make up your mind whether you really want to before you strike."

Sinton went to the barn to put away the tools. He thought Billy at his heels, but the boy lagged on the way. A big snowy turkey gobbler resented the small intruder in his especial preserves, and with spread tail and dragging wings came at him threateningly. If that turkey gobbler had known the sort of things with which Billy was accustomed to holding his own, he never would have issued that challenge. Billy accepted instantly. He danced around with stiff arms at his sides and imitated the gobbler. Then came his opportunity, and he jumped on the big turkey's back. Wesley heard Margaret's scream in time to see the flying leap and admire its dexterity. The turkey tucked its tail and scampered. Billy slid from its back and as he fell he clutched wildly, caught the folded tail, and instinctively hung on for life. The turkey gave one scream and relaxed its muscles. Then it fled in disfigured defeat to the haystack. Billy scrambled to his feet holding the tail, and his eyes were bulging.

"Why, the blasted old thing came off!" he said to Sinton, holding out the tail in amazed wonder.

Sinton, caught suddenly, forgot everything and roared. Seeing which, Billy thought a turkey tail of no account and flung that one high above him shouting in wild childish laughter, as the feathers scattered and fell.

Margaret, watching, burst into tears. Wesley had gone mad. For the first time in her married life she wanted to tell her mother. When Wesley had waited until he was so hungry he could wait no longer he invaded the kitchen to find a cooked supper baking on the back of the stove, while Margaret with red eyes nursed a pair of demoralized white kittens.

"Is supper ready?" he asked.

"It has been for an hour," answered Margaret.

"Why didn't you call us?"

That "us" had too much comradeship in it. It irritated Margaret.

"I supposed it would take you even longer than that to fix things decent again. As for my turkey, and my poor little kittens, they don't matter."

"I am mighty sorry about them, Margaret, you know that. Billy is very bright, and he will soon learn—"

"Soon learn!" cried Margaret. "Wesley Sinton, you don't mean to say that you think of keeping that creature here for some time?"

"No, I think of keeping a decent, well-behaved little boy."

Margaret set the supper on the table. Seeing the old red cloth Wesley stared in amazement. Then he understood. Billy capered around in delight.

"Ain't that pretty?" he exulted. "I wish Jimmy and Belle could see. We, why we 'ist eat out of our hands or off a old dry goods box, and when we fix up a lot, we have newspaper. We ain't ever had a nice red cloth like this."

Wesley looked straight at Margaret, so intently that she turned away, her face flushing. He stacked the dictionary and the geography of the world on a chair, and lifted Billy beside him. He heaped a plate generously, cut the food, put a fork into Billy's little fist, and made him eat slowly and properly. Billy did his best. Occasionally greed overcame him, and he used his left hand to pop a bite into his mouth with his fingers. These lapses Wesley patiently overlooked, and went on with his general instructions. Luckily Billy did not spill anything on his clothing or the cloth. After supper Wesley took him to the barn until he finished the night work. Then he went and sat by Margaret on the front porch. Billy appropriated the hammock, and swung by pulling a rope tied around a tree. The very energy with which he went at the work of swinging himself appealed to Wesley.

"Mercy, but he's an active little body," he said. "There isn't a lazy bone in him. See how he works to pay for his fun."

"There goes his foot through it!" cried Margaret. "Wesley, he shall not ruin my hammock."

"Of course he shan't!" said Wesley. "Wait, Billy, let me show you."

Thereupon he explained to Billy that ladies wearing beautiful white dresses sat in hammocks, so little boys must not put their dusty feet in them. They must just sit in them, and let their feet hang down. Billy immediately sat, and allowed his feet to swing.

"Margaret," said Sinton after a long silence on the porch, "isn't it true that if Billy had been a half-starved sore cat, dog, or animal of any sort, that you would have pitied, and helped care for it, and been glad to see me get any pleasure out of it I could?"

"Yes," said Margaret coldly.

"But because I brought a child with an immortal soul, there is no welcome."

"That isn't a child, it's an animal."

"You just said you would have welcomed an animal."

"Not a wild one. I meant a tame beast."

"Billy is not a beast!" said Wesley hotly. "He is a very dear little boy. Margaret, you've always done the church-going and Bible reading for this family. How do you reconcile that 'Suffer little children to come unto Me' with the way you are treating Billy?"

Margaret arose. "I haven't treated that child. I have only let him alone. I can barely hold myself. He needs the hide tanned about off him!"

"If you'd cared to look at his body, you'd know that you couldn't find a place to strike without cutting into a raw spot," said Sinton. "Besides, Billy has not done a thing for which a child should be punished. He is only full of life, no training, and with a boy's love of mischief. He did abuse your kittens, but an hour before I saw him risk his life to save one from being run over. He minds what you tell him, and doesn't do anything he is told not to. He thinks of his brother and sister right away when anything pleases him. He took that stinging medicine with the grit of a bulldog. He is just a bully little chap, and I love him."

"Oh, good heavens!" cried Margaret, going into the house as she spoke.

Sinton sat still. At last Billy tired of the swing, came to him and leaned his slight body against the big knee.

"Am I going to sleep here?" he asked.

"Sure you are!" said Sinton.

Billy swung his feet as he laid across Wesley's knee.

"Come on," said Sinton, "I must clean you up for bed."

"You have to be just awful clean here," announced Billy. "I like to be clean, you feel so good, after the hurt is over."

Sinton registered that remark, and worked with especial tenderness as he redressed the ailing places and washed the dust from Billy's feet and hands.

"Where can he sleep?" he asked Margaret.

"I'm sure I don't know," she answered.

"Oh, I can sleep 'ist any place," said Billy. "On the floor or anywhere. Home, I sleep on pa's coat on a storebox, and Jimmy and Belle they sleep on the storebox, too. I sleep between them, so's I don't roll off and crack my head. Ain't you got a storebox and a old coat?"

Sinton arose and opened a folding lounge. Then he brought an armload of clean horse blankets from a closet.

"These don't look like the nice white bed a little boy should have, Billy," he said, "but we'll make them do. This will beat a storebox all hollow."

Billy took a long leap for the lounge. When he found it bounced, he proceeded to bounce, until he was tired. By that time the blankets had to be refolded. Wesley had Billy take one end and help, while both of them seemed to enjoy the job. Then Billy lay down and curled up in his clothes like a little dog. But sleep would not come. Finally he sat up. He stared around restlessly. Then he arose, went to Sinton, and leaned against his knee. Sinton picked up the boy and folded his arms around him. Billy sighed in rapturous content.

"That bed feels so lost like," he said. "Jimmy always jabbed me on one side, and Belle on the other, and so I knew I was there."

Sinton laughed the best he could.

"Do you know where they are?" asked Billy.

"They are with kind people who gave them a fine supper, a clean bed, and will always take good care of them."

"I wisht I was"—Billy hesitated and looked earnestly at Sinton. "I mean, I wish they was here."

"You are about all I can manage, Billy," said Sinton.

Billy sat up. "Can't she manage anything?" he asked, waving toward Margaret.

"Indeed, yes," said Sinton. "She has managed me for twenty years."

"My, but she made you nice!" said Billy. "I just love you. I wisht she'd take Jimmy and Belle and make them nice as you."

"She isn't strong enough to do that, Billy. They will grow into a good boy and girl where they are."

Billy slid from Sinton's arms and walked toward Margaret until he reached the middle of the room. Then he stopped, and at last sat on the floor. Finally he lay down and closed his eyes. "This feels more like my bed; if only Jimmy and Belle was here to crowd up a little, so it wasn't so alone like."

"Won't I do, Billy?" asked Sinton in a husky voice.

Billy moved restlessly. "Seems like—seems like—towards night as if a body got kind o' lonesome for a woman person—like her."

Billy indicated Margaret and then closed his eyes so tight his small face wrinkled.

Soon he was up again. "'Wisht I had Snap," he said. "Oh, I 'ist wisht I had Snap!"

"I thought you laid a board on Snap and jumped on it," said Sinton.

"We did!" cried Billy—"oh, you ought to heard him squeal!" Billy laughed loudly then his face clouded. "But I want Snap to lay beside me so bad now—that if he was here I'd give him a piece of my chicken, 'fore I ate any. Do you like dogs?"

"Yes, I do," said Sinton.

Billy was up instantly. "Would you like Snap?"

"I am sure I would," said Sinton.

"Would she?" Billy indicated Margaret. And then he answered his own question. "But of course, she wouldn't, cos she likes cats, and dogs chases cats. Oh, dear, I thought for a minute maybe Snap could come here." Billy lay down and closed his eyes resolutely.

Suddenly they flew open. "Does it hurt to be dead?" he demanded.

"Nothing hurts you after you are dead, Billy," said Sinton.

"Yes, but I mean does it hurt getting to be dead?"

"Sometimes it does. It did not hurt your father, Billy. It came softly while he was asleep."

"It 'ist came softly?"

"Yes."

"I kind o' wisht he wasn't dead!" said Billy. "'Course I like to stay with you, and the fried chicken, and the nice soft bed, and—and everything, and I like to be clean, but he took us to the show, and he got us gum, and he never hurt us when he wasn't drunk."

Billy drew a deep breath, and tightly closed his eyes. But very soon they opened. Then he sat up. He looked at Sinton pitifully, and then he glanced at Margaret. "You don't like boys, do you?" he questioned.

"I like good boys," said Margaret.

Billy was at her knee instantly. "Well, say, I'm a good boy!" he announced joyously.

"I do not think boys who hurt helpless kittens and pull out turkeys' tails are good boys."

"Yes, but I didn't hurt the kittens," explained Billy. "They got mad 'bout 'ist a little fun and scratched each other. I didn't s'pose they'd act like that. And I didn't pull the turkey's tail. I 'ist held on to the first thing I grabbed, and the turkey pulled. Honest, it was the turkey pulled." He turned to Sinton. "You tell her! Didn't the turkey pull? I didn't know its tail was loose, did I?"

"I don't think you did, Billy," said Sinton.

Billy stared into Margaret's cold face. "Sometimes at night, Belle sits on the floor, and I lay my head in her lap. I could pull up a chair and lay my head in your lap. Like this, I mean." Billy pulled up a chair, climbed on it and laid his head on Margaret's lap. Then he shut his eyes again. Margaret could have looked little more repulsed if he had been a snake.

Billy was soon up.

"My, but your lap is hard," he said. "And you are a good deal fatter 'an Belle, too!" He slid from the chair and came back to the middle of the room.

"Oh, but I wisht he wasn't dead!" he cried. The flood broke and Billy screamed in desperation.

Out of the night a soft, warm young figure flashed through the door and with a swoop caught him in her arms. She dropped into a chair, nestled him closely, and drooped her fragrant brown head over his little bullet-eyed red one, and rocked softly as she crooned over him—

Billy, boy, where have you been?
Oh, I have been to seek a wife,
She's the joy of my life,
But then she's a young thing and she can't leave her mammy!

Billy gripped her with a death grip. Elnora wiped his eyes, kissed his face, swayed and sang.

"Why aren't you asleep?" she asked at last.

"I don't know," said Billy. "I tried. I tried awful hard 'cos I thought he wanted me to, but it 'ist wouldn't come. Please tell her I tried." He appealed to Margaret.

"He did try to go to sleep," admitted Margaret.

"Maybe he can't sleep in his clothes," suggested Elnora. "Haven't you an old dressing sacque? I could roll the sleeves."

Margaret got an old sacque, and Elnora put it on Billy. Then she brought a basin of water and bathed his face and head. She gathered him up and began to rock again.

"Have you got a pa?" asked Billy.

"No," said Elnora.

"Is he dead like mine?"

"Yes."

"Did it hurt him to die?"

"I don't know."

Billy was wide awake again. "It didn't hurt my pa," he boasted; "he 'ist died while he was asleep. He didn't even know it was coming."

"I am glad of that," said Elnora, pressing the little head against her breast again.

Billy escaped her hand and sat up. "I guess I won't go to sleep," he said. "It might 'come softly' and get me."

"It won't get you, Billy," said Elnora, rocking and singing between sentences. "It don't get little boys. It just takes big people who are sick."

"Was my pa sick?"

"Yes," said Elnora. "He had a dreadful sickness inside him that burned, and made him drink things. That was why he would forget his little boys and girl. If he had been well, he would have gotten you good things to eat, clean clothes, and had the most fun with you."

Billy leaned against her and closed his eyes and Elnora rocked hopefully.

"If I was dead would you cry?" he was up again.

"Yes, I would," said Elnora gripping him closer until Billy almost squealed with the embrace.

"Do you love me tight as that?" he questioned blissfully.

"Yes, bushels and bushels," said Elnora. "Better than any little boy in the whole world."

Billy looked at Margaret. "She don't!" he said. "She'd be glad if it would get me 'softly,' right now. She don't want me here 't all."

Elnora smothered his face against her breast and rocked.

"You love me, don't you?"

"I will, if you will go to sleep."

"Every single day you will give me your dinner for the bologna, won't you," said Billy.

"Yes, I will," replied Elnora. "But you will have as good a lunch as I do after this. You will have milk, eggs, chicken, all kinds of good things, little pies, and cakes, maybe."

Billy shook his head. "I am going back home soon as it is light," he said, "she don't want me. She thinks I'm a bad boy. She's going to whip me—if he lets her. She said so. I heard her. Oh, I wish he hadn't died! I want to go home." Billy shrieked again.

Mrs. Comstock had started to walk slowly and meet Elnora. The girl had been so late that her mother reached the Sinton gate and came up the path until the picture inside became visible. Elnora had told her about Sinton taking Billy home. Mrs. Comstock had some curiosity to see how Margaret bore the unexpected addition to her family. Billy's voice raised with excitement, was plainly audible. She could see Elnora holding him, and hear his excited wail. Sinton's face was drawn and haggard, and Margaret's set and defiant. A very imp of perversity entered the breast of Mrs. Comstock and danced there.

"Hoity, toity!" she said as she suddenly appeared in the door.

"Blest if I ever heard a man making sounds like that before!"

Billy ceased suddenly. Mrs. Comstock was tall, angular, and her hair was prematurely white, for she was only thirty-six, though she looked fifty. But there was an expression on her usually cold face that was attractive just then, and Billy was in search of attractions.

"Have I stayed too late, mother?" asked Elnora anxiously. "I truly intended to come straight back, but I thought I could get Billy to sleep first. Everything is strange, and he's so nervous."

"Is that your ma?" demanded Billy.

"Yes."

"Does she love you?"

"Of course!"

"My mother didn't love me," said Billy. "She went away and left me, and never came back. She don't care what happens to me. You wouldn't go away and leave your little girl, would you?" questioned Billy of Mrs. Comstock.

"No," said Katharine Comstock, "and I wouldn't leave a little boy, either."

Billy was half off Elnora's knees.

"Do you like boys?" he questioned.

"If there is anything I love it is a boy," said Mrs. Comstock assuringly. Billy was on the floor.

"Do you like dogs?"

"Yes. Almost as well as boys. I am going to buy a dog just as soon as I can find a good one."

Billy swept toward her with a whoop.

"Do you want a boy?" he shouted.

Katharine Comstock stretched out her arms, and gathered him in.

"Of course, I want a boy!" she rejoiced.

"Maybe you'd like to have me?" offered Billy.

"Sure I would," triumphed Mrs. Comstock. "Anyone would like to have you. You are just a real boy, Billy,"

"Will you take Snap?"

"I'd like to have Snap almost as well as you."

"Mother!" breathed Elnora imploringly. "Don't! Oh, don't! He thinks you mean it!"

"And so I do mean it," said Mrs. Comstock. "I'll take him in a jiffy. I throw away enough to feed a little tyke like him every day. His chatter would be great company while you are gone. Blood soon can be purified with right food and baths, and as for Snap, I meant to get a bulldog, but possibly Snap will serve just as well. All I ask of a dog is to bark at the right time. I'll do the rest. Would you like to come and be my boy, Billy?"

Billy leaned against Mrs. Comstock, reached his arms around her neck and gripped her with all his puny might. "You can whip me all you want to," he said. "I won't make a sound."

Mrs. Comstock held him closely and her hard face was softening, of that there could not be a doubt.

"Now, why would anyone whip a nice little boy like you?" she asked wonderingly.

"She"—Billy from his refuge waved toward Margaret—"she was going to whip me 'cause her cats fought, when I tied their tails together and hung them over the line to dry. How did I know her old cats would fight?"

Mrs. Comstock began to laugh suddenly, and try as she would she could not stop as soon as she desired. Billy studied her.

"Have you got turkeys?" he demanded.

"Yes, flocks of them," said Mrs. Comstock, vainly struggling to suppress her mirth, and settle her face in its accustomed lines.

"Are their tails fast?" demanded Billy.

"Why, I think so," marvelled Mrs. Comstock.

"Hers ain't!" said Billy with the wave toward Margaret that was becoming familiar. "Her turkey pulled, and its tail comed right off. She's going to whip me if he lets her. I didn't know the turkey would pull. I didn't know its tail would come off. I won't ever touch one again, will I?"

"Of course, you won't," said Mrs. Comstock. "And what's more, I don't care if you do! I'd rather have a fine little man like you than all the turkeys in the country. Let them lose their old tails if they want to, and let the cats fight. Cats and turkeys don't compare with boys, who are going to be fine big men some of these days."

Then Billy and Mrs. Comstock hugged each other rapturously, and their audience stared in silent amazement.

"You like boys!" exulted Billy, and his head dropped against Mrs. Comstock in unspeakable content.

"Yes, and if I don't have to carry you the whole way home, we must start right now," said Mrs. Comstock. "You are going to be asleep before you know it."

Billy opened his eyes and braced himself. "I can walk," he said proudly.

"All right, we must start. Come, Elnora! Good night, folks!" Mrs. Comstock set Billy on the floor, and arose gripping his hand. "You take the other side, Elnora, and we will help him as much as we can," she said.

Elnora stared piteously at Margaret, then at Wesley, and arose in white-faced bewilderment.

"Billy, are you going to leave without even saying good-bye to me?" asked Sinton, with a great gulp in his throat.

Billy held tight to Mrs. Comstock and Elnora.

"Good-bye!" he said casually. "I'll come and see you some time."

Wesley Sinton gave a smothered sob, and strode from the room.

Mrs. Comstock started for the door, dragging at Billy as Elnora pulled back, but Mrs. Sinton was before them, her eyes flashing.

"Kate Comstock, you think you are mighty smart, don't you?" she cried.

"I ain't in the lunatic asylum, where you belong, anyway," said Mrs. Comstock. "I am smart enough to tell a dandy boy when I see him, and I'm good and glad to get him. I'll love to have him!"

"Well, you won't have him!" exclaimed Margaret Sinton. "That boy is Wesley's! He got him, and brought him here. You can't come in and take him like that! Let go of him!"

"Not much, I won't!" cried Mrs. Comstock. "Leave the poor sick little soul here for you to beat, because he didn't know just how to handle things! Of course, he'll make mistakes. He's got to have a lot of teaching, but not the kind he'll get from you! Clear out of my way!"

"You let go of our boy," ordered Margaret.

"Why? Do you want to whip him, before he can go to sleep?" jeered Mrs. Comstock.

"No, I don't!" said Margaret. "He's Wesley's, and nobody shall touch him. Wesley!"

Wesley Sinton appeared behind Margaret in the doorway, and she turned to him. "Make Kate Comstock let go of our boy!" she demanded.

"Billy, she wants you now," said Wesley Sinton. "She won't whip you, and she won't let anyone else. You can have stacks of good things to eat, ride in the carriage, and have a great time. Won't you stay with us?"

Billy drew away from Mrs. Comstock and Elnora.

He faced Margaret, his eyes shrewd with unchildish wisdom. Necessity had taught him to strike the hot iron, to drive the hard bargain.

"Can I have Snap to live here always?" he demanded.

"Yes, you can have all the dogs you want," said Margaret Sinton.

"Can I sleep close enough so's I can touch you?"

"Yes, you can move your lounge up so that you can hold my hand," said Margaret.

"Do you love me now?" questioned Billy.

"I'll try to love you if you are a good boy," said Margaret.

"Then I guess I'll stay," said Billy walking over to her.

Out in the night Elnora and her mother went down the road in the moonlight, and every few rods Mrs. Comstock laughed aloud.

"Mother, I don't understand you," sobbed Elnora.

"Well, maybe when you have gone to high school longer you will," said Mrs. Comstock. "Anyway, you saw me bring Mag Sinton to her senses, didn't you?"

"Yes, I did," answered Elnora, "but I thought you were in earnest. So did Billy, and Uncle Wesley, and Aunt Margaret."

"Well, wasn't I?" inquired Mrs. Comstock.

"But you just said you brought Aunt Margaret to!"

"Well, didn't I?"

"I don't understand you."

"That's the reason I am recommending more schooling!"

Elnora took her candle and went to bed. Mrs. Comstock was feeling too good to sleep. Twice of late she really had enjoyed herself for the first in sixteen years, and a sort of greediness for more of the same feeling crept into her blood like intoxication. As she sat brooding alone she knew the truth. She would have loved to take Billy. She would not have minded his mischief, his chatter, or his dog. He would have meant a sort of salvation from herself that she greatly needed, she was even sincere about the dog. She meant to tell Sinton to buy her one at the very first opportunity. Her last thought was of Billy. She chuckled softly, for she was not saintly, and now she knew what she could do that would fill her soul with grim satisfaction.

8

Wherein the Limberlost Tempts Elnora, and Billy Buries His Father

Immediately after dinner on Sunday Wesley Sinton stopped at the Comstock gate to ask if Elnora wanted to go to town with them. Billy sat beside him and he did not look as if he were on his way to a funeral. Elnora said she had to study and could not go, but she suggested that her mother take her place. Mrs. Comstock put on her hat and went at once, which surprised Elnora. She did not know that her mother was anxious for an opportunity to speak with Sinton alone. Elnora knew why she was repeatedly cautioned not to leave their land, if she went specimen hunting, to remain along the roads, or at least not to enter the swamp.

She studied two hours and was several lessons ahead of her classes. There was no use to go further. She would take a walk and see if she could gather any caterpillars or find any freshly spun cocoons. She searched the bushes and low trees behind the garden and all about the edge of the woods on their land, and having little success, at last came out to the road. Almost the first thorn bush she examined yielded a Polyphemus cocoon. Elnora lifted her head with the instinct of a hunter on the chase, and began work. She reached the swamp before she knew it, carrying five fine cocoons of different species as her reward. She pushed back her hair and gazed around longingly. A few rods inside she thought she saw cocoons on a bush, to which she went, and found several. Sense of caution was rapidly vanishing, she was in a fair way to forget everything and plunge into the swamp when she thought she heard footsteps coming down the trail. She went back, and came out almost facing Pete Corson.

That ended her difficulty. She had known him since childhood. When she sat on the front bench of the Brushwood schoolhouse, Pete had been one of the big boys at the back of the room. He had been rough and wild, but she never had been afraid of him, and often he had given her pretty things from the swamp.

"What luck!" she cried. "I promised mother I would not go inside the swamp alone, and will you look at the cocoons I've found! There are more just screaming for me to come get them, because the leaves will fall with the first frost, and then the jays and crows will begin to tear them open. I haven't much time, since I'm going to school. You will go with me, Pete! Please say yes! Just a little way!"

"What are those things?" asked the man, his keen black eyes fast upon her.

"They are the cases these big caterpillars spin for winter, and in the spring they come out great night moths, and I can sell them. Oh, Pete, I can sell them for enough to take me through high school and dress me so like the rest that I don't look different, and if I have very good luck I can save some for college. Pete, please go with me?"

"Why don't you go like you always have?"

"Well, the truth is, I had a little scare," said Elnora. "I never did mean to go alone; sometimes I sort of wandered inside farther than I intended, chasing things. You know Duncan gave me Freckles's books, and I have been gathering moths like he did. Lately I found I could sell them. If I can make a complete collection, I can get three hundred dollars for it. Three such collections would take me almost through college, and I've four years in the high school yet. That's a long time. I might get them."

"Can every kind there is be found here?"

"No, not all of them, but when I get more than I need of one kind, I can trade them with collectors farther north and west, so I can complete sets. It's the only way I see to earn the money. Look what I have already. Big gray Cecropias come from this kind;

brown Polyphemus from that, and green Lunas from these. You aren't working on Sunday. Go with me just an hour, Pete!"

The man looked at her narrowly. She was young, wholesome, and beautiful. She was innocent, intensely in earnest, and she needed the money, he knew that.

"You didn't tell me what scared you," he said.

"Oh, I thought I did! Why, you know, I had Freckles's box packed full of moths and specimens, and one evening I sold some to the Bird Woman. Next morning I found a note telling me it wasn't safe to go inside the swamp. That sort of scared me. I think I'll go alone, rather than miss the chance, but I'd be so happy if you would take care of me. Then I could go anywhere I chose, because if I mired you could pull me out. You will take care of me, Pete?"

That was the finishing stroke.

"Yes, I'll take care of you," promised Pete Corson.

"Goody!" said Elnora. "Let's start quick! And Pete, you look at these closely, and when you are hunting or going along the road, if one dangles under your nose, you cut off the little twig and save it for me, will you?"

"Yes, I'll save you all I see," promised Pete. He pushed back his hat and followed Elnora. She plunged fearlessly through bushes, over underbrush, and across dead logs. One minute she was crying wildly, that here was a big one, the next she was reaching for a limb above her head or on her knees overturning dead leaves under a hickory or oak tree, or pushing aside black muck with her bare hands as she searched for buried pupae cases. For the first hour Pete bent back bushes and followed, carrying what Elnora discovered. Then he found one.

"Is this the kind of thing you are looking for?" he asked, bashfully, as he presented a wild cherry twig.

"Oh, Pete, that's a Promethea! I didn't even hope to find one."

"What's the bird like?" asked Pete.

"Almost black wings," said Elnora, "with clay-coloured edges, and the most wonderful wine-coloured flush over the under side if it's a male, and stronger wine above and below if it's a female. Oh, aren't I happy!"

"How would it do to make what you have into a bunch that we could leave here, and come back for them?"

"That would be all right."

Relieved of his load Pete began work. First, he narrowly examined the cocoons Elnora had found. He questioned her as to what other kinds would be like. He began to use the eyes of a trained woodman and hunter in her behalf. He saw several so easily, and moved through the forest so softly, that Elnora forgot the moths in watching him. Presently she was carrying the specimens, and he was making the trips of investigation to see which was a cocoon and which a curled leaf, or he was down on his knees digging around stumps. As he worked he kept asking questions. What kind of logs were best to look beside, what trees were pupae cases most likely to be under; on what bushes did caterpillars spin most frequently? Time passed, as it always does when one's occupation is absorbing.

When the Sintons had taken Mrs. Comstock home, they stopped to see if Elnora was safe. She was not at home, and they had not seen her along the way. Mrs. Comstock called about the edge of her woods and received no reply. Then Sinton turned and drove back to the Limberlost. He left Margaret and Mrs. Comstock holding the team and entertaining Billy, and entered the swamp.

Elnora and Pete had left a wide trail behind them. Before Sinton had thought of calling, he heard voices and approached with some caution. Soon he saw Elnora, her flushed face beaming as she bent with an armload of twigs and branches and talked to a kneeling man.

"Now go cautiously!" she was saying. "I am just sure we will find an Imperialis here. It's their very kind of a place. There! What did I tell you! Isn't that splendid? Oh, I am so glad you came with me!"

Sinton stood and stared in speechless astonishment, for the man had risen, brushed the dirt from his hands, and held out to Elnora a small shining dark pupa case. As his face swung into view Sinton almost cried out, for he was the one man of all others Wesley knew with whom he most feared for Elnora's safety. She had him on his knees digging pupae cases for her from the loose swamp loam.

"Elnora!" called Sinton. "Elnora!"

"Oh, Uncle Wesley!" cried the girl. "See what luck we've had! I know we have a dozen and a half cocoons and we have three pupae cases. It's much harder to get the cases because you have to dig for them, and you can't see where to look. But Pete is fine at it! He's found three, and he says he will keep watch along the roads, and through the woods as he hunts. Isn't that splendid of him? Uncle Wesley, there is a college over there on the western edge of the swamp. Look closely, and you can see the great dome up among the clouds."

"I should say you have had luck," said Sinton, striving to make his voice natural. "But I thought you were not coming to the swamp?"

"Well, I wasn't," said Elnora, "but I couldn't find many anywhere else, honest, I couldn't, and just as soon as I came to the edge I began to see them here. I kept my promise. I didn't come in alone. Pete came with me. He's so strong, he isn't afraid of anything, and he's perfectly splendid to locate cocoons! He's found half of these. Come on, Pete, it's getting dark now, and we must go."

They started for the trail, Pete carrying the cocoons. He left them at the case, while Elnora and Sinton went on to the carriage together.

"Elnora Comstock, what does this mean?" demanded her mother.

"It's all right, one of the neighbours was with her, and she got several dollars' worth of stuff," interposed Sinton.

"You oughter seen my pa," shouted Billy. "He was 'ist all whited out, and he laid as still as anything. They put him away deep in the ground."

"Billy!" breathed Margaret in a prolonged groan.

"Jimmy and Belle are going to be together in a nice place. They are coming to see me, and Snap is right down here by the wheel. Here, Snap! My, but he'll be tickled to get something to eat! He's 'most twisted as me. They get new clothes, and all they want to eat, too, but they'll miss me. They couldn't have got along without me. I took care of them. I had a lot of things give to me 'cause I was the littlest, and I always divided with them. But they won't need me now."

When she left the carriage Mrs. Comstock gravely shook hands with Billy. "Remember," she said to him, "I love boys, and I love dogs. Whenever you don't have a good time up there, take your dog and come right down and be my little boy. We will just have loads of fun. You should hear the whistles I can make. If you aren't treated right you come straight to me."

Billy wagged his head sagely. "You 'ist bet I will!" he said.

"Mother, how could you?" asked Elnora as they walked up the path.

"How could I, missy? You better ask how couldn't I? I just couldn't! Not for enough to pay my road tax! Not for enough to pay the road tax, and the dredge tax, too!"

"Aunt Margaret always has been lovely to me, and I don't think it's fair to worry her."

"I choose to be lovely to Billy, and let her sweat out her own worries just as she has me, these sixteen years. There is nothing in all this world so good for people as getting a dose of their own medicine. The difference is that I am honest. I just say in plain English, 'if they don't treat you right, come to me.' They have only said it in actions and inferences. I want to teach Mag Sinton how her own doses taste, but she begins to sputter before I fairly get the spoon to her lips. Just you wait!"

"When I think what I owe her—" began Elnora.

"Well, thank goodness, I don't owe her anything, and so I'm perfectly free to do what I choose. Come on, and help me get supper. I'm hungry as Billy!"

Margaret Sinton rocked slowly back and forth in her chair. On her breast lay Billy's red head, one hand clutched her dress front with spasmodic grip, even after he was unconscious.

"You mustn't begin that, Margaret," said Sinton. "He's too heavy. And it's bad for him. He's better off to lie down and go to sleep alone."

"He's very light, Wesley. He jumps and quivers so. He has to be stronger than he is now, before he will sleep soundly."

9

Wherein Elnora Discovers a Violin, and Billy Disciplines Margaret

Elnora missed the little figure at the bridge the next morning. She slowly walked up the street and turned in at the wide entrance to the school grounds. She scarcely could comprehend that only a week ago she had gone there friendless, alone, and so sick at heart that she was physically ill. To-day she had decent clothing, books, friends, and her mind was at ease to work on her studies.

As she approached home that night the girl paused in amazement. Her mother had company, and she was laughing. Elnora entered the kitchen softly and peeped into the sitting room. Mrs. Comstock sat in her chair holding a book and every few seconds a soft chuckle broke into a real laugh. Mark Twain was doing his work; while Mrs. Comstock was not lacking in a sense of humour. Elnora entered the room before her mother saw her. Mrs. Comstock looked up with flushed face.

"Where did you get this?" she demanded.

"I bought it," said Elnora.

"Bought it! With all the taxes due!"

"I paid for it out of my Indian money, mother," said Elnora. "I couldn't bear to spend so much on myself and nothing at all on you. I was afraid to buy the dress I should have liked to, and I thought the book would be company, while I was gone. I haven't read it, but I do hope it's good."

"Good! It's the biggest piece of foolishness I have read in all my life. I've laughed all day, ever since I found it. I had a notion to go out and read some of it to the cows and see if they wouldn't laugh."

"If it made you laugh, it's a wise book," said Elnora.

"Wise!" cried Mrs. Comstock. "You can stake your life it's a wise book. It takes the smartest man there is to do this kind of fooling," and she began laughing again.

Elnora, highly satisfied with her purchase, went to her room and put on her working clothes. Thereafter she made a point of getting a book that she thought would interest her mother, from the library every week, and leaving it on the sitting-room table. Every night she carried home at least two school books and studied until she had mastered the points of each lesson. She did her share of the work faithfully, and every available minute she was in the fields searching for cocoons, for the moths promised to become her best source of income.

She gathered large baskets of nests, flowers, mosses, insects, and all sorts of natural history specimens and sold them to the grade teachers. At first she tried to tell these instructors what to teach their pupils about the specimens; but recognizing how much more she knew than they, one after another begged her to study at home, and use her spare hours in school to exhibit and explain nature subjects to their pupils. Elnora loved the work, and she needed the money, for every few days some matter of expense arose that she had not expected.

From the first week she had been received and invited with the crowd of girls in her class, and it was their custom in passing through the business part of the city to stop at the confectioners' and take turns in treating to expensive candies, ice cream sodas, hot chocolate, or whatever they fancied. When first Elnora was asked she accepted without understanding. The second time she went because she seldom had tasted these things, and they were so delicious she could not resist. After that she went because she knew all about it, and had decided to go.

She had spent a half-hour on the log by the trail in deep thought and had arrived at her conclusions. She worked harder than usual for the next week, but she seemed to thrive on work. It was October and the red leaves were falling when her first time came to treat. As the crowd flocked down the broad walk that night Elnora called "Girls, it's my treat to-night! Come on!"

She led the way through the city to the grocery they patronized when they had a small spread, and entering came out with a basket, which she carried to the bridge on her home road. There she arranged the girls in two rows on the cement abutments and opening her basket she gravely offered each girl an exquisite little basket of bark, lined with red leaves, in one end of which nestled a juicy big red apple and in the other a spicy doughnut not an hour from Margaret Sinton's frying basket.

Another time she offered big balls of popped corn stuck together with maple sugar, and liberally sprinkled with beechnut kernels. Again it was hickory nut kernels glazed with sugar, another time maple candy, and once a basket of warm pumpkin pies. She never made any apology, or offered any excuse. She simply gave what she could afford, and the change was as welcome to those city girls, accustomed to sodas and French candy as were these same things to Elnora surfeited on pop-corn and pie. In her room was a little slip containing a record of the number of weeks in the school year, the times it would be her turn to treat and the dates on which such occasions would fall, with a number of suggestions by each. Once the girls almost fought over a basket lined with yellow leaves, and filled with fat, very ripe red haws. In late October there was a riot over one which was lined with red leaves and contained big fragrant pawpaws frost-bitten to a perfect degree. Then hazel nuts were ripe, and once they served. One day Elnora at her wits' end, explained to her mother that the girls had given her things and she wanted to treat them. Mrs. Comstock, with characteristic stubbornness, had said she would leave a basket at the grocery for her, but firmly declined to say what would be in it. All day Elnora struggled to keep her mind on her books. For hours she wavered in tense uncertainty. What would her mother do? Should she take the girls to the confectioner's that night or risk the basket? Mrs. Comstock could make delicious things to eat, but would she?

As they left the building Elnora made a final rapid mental calculation. She could not see her way clear to a decent treat for ten people for less than two dollars, and if the basket was nice, then the money would be wasted. She decided to risk it. As they went to the bridge the girls were betting on what the treat would be, and crowding near Elnora like spoiled small children. Elnora set down the basket.

"Girls," she said, "I don't know what this is myself, so all of us are going to be surprised. Here goes!"

She lifted the cover and perfumes from the land of spices rolled up. In one end of the basket lay ten enormous sugar cakes the tops of which had been liberally dotted with circles cut from stick candy. The candy had melted in baking and made small transparent wells of waxy sweetness and in the centre of each cake was a fat turtle made from a raisin with cloves for head and feet. The remainder of the basket was filled with big spiced pears that could be held by their stems while they were eaten. The girls shrieked and attacked the cookies, and of all the treats Elnora offered perhaps none was quite so long remembered as that.

When Elnora took her basket, placed her books in it, and started home, all the girls went with her as far as the fence where she crossed the field to the swamp. When they parted they kissed her good-bye. Elnora was a happy girl as she hurried home to thank her mother. She was happy over her books that night, and happy all the way to school the next morning.

When the music swelled from the orchestra her heart almost broke with throbbing joy. For music always had affected her strangely, and since she had been comfortable enough in her surroundings to notice things, she had listened to every note to find what it was that literally hurt her heart, and at last she knew. It was the talking of the violins. They were human voices, and they spoke a language Elnora understood. It seemed to her that she must climb up on the stage, take the instruments from the fingers of the players and make them speak what was in her heart. She fairly prayed to get hold of one, if only for a second.

That night she said to her mother, "I am perfectly crazy for a violin. I am sure I could play one, sure as I live. Did anyone—" Elnora never completed that sentence.

"Hush!" thundered Mrs. Comstock. "Be quiet! Never mention those things before me again—never as long as you live! I loathe them! They are a snare of the very devil himself! They were made to lure men and women from their homes and their honour. If ever I see you with one in your fingers I will smash it in pieces."

Naturally Elnora hushed, but she thought of nothing else after she had done justice to her lessons. At last there came a day when for some reason the leader of the orchestra left his violin on the grand piano. That morning Elnora made her first mistake in algebra. At noon, as soon as the great building was empty, she slipped into the auditorium, found the side door which led to the stage, and going through the musicians' entrance she took the violin. She carried it back into the little side room where the orchestra assembled, closed all the doors, opened the case and lifted out the instrument.

She laid it on her breast, dropped her chin on it and drew the bow softly across the strings. One after another she tested the open notes. They reminded her of things. Gradually her stroke ceased to tremble and she drew the bow firmly. Then her fingers began to fall and softly, slowly she searched up and down those strings for sounds she knew. Standing in the middle of the floor, she tried over and over. It seemed scarcely a minute before the hall was filled with the sound of hurrying feet, and she was forced to put away the violin and go to her classes. Of food she never thought until she noticed how heavy her lunch box was on the way home, so she sat on the log by the swamp and remedied that. The next day she prayed that the violin would be left again, but her petition was not answered.

That night when she returned from the school she made an excuse to go down to see Billy. He was engaged in hulling walnuts by driving them through holes in a board. His hands were protected by a pair of Margaret's old gloves, but he had speckled his face generously. He looked well, and greeted Elnora hilariously.

"Me an' the squirrels are laying up our winter stores," he shouted. "'Cos the cold is coming, an' the snow an' if we have any nuts we have to fix 'em now. But I'm ahead, 'cos Uncle Wesley made me this board, and I can hull a big pile while the old squirrel does only 'ist one with his teeth."

Elnora picked him up and kissed him. "Billy, are you happy?" she asked.

"Yes, and so's Snap," answered Billy. "You ought to see him

make the dirt fly when he gets after a chipmunk. I bet you he could dig up pa, if anybody wanted him to."

"Billy!" gasped Margaret as she came out to them.

"Well, me and Snap don't want him up, and I bet you Jimmy and Belle don't either. I ain't been twisty inside once since I been here, and I don't want to go away, and Snap don't either. He told me so."

"Billy! That is not true. Dogs can't talk," cautioned Margaret.

"Then what makes you open the door when he asks you to?" demanded Billy.

"Scratching and whining isn't talking."

"Anyway, it's the best Snap can talk, and you get up and do things he wants done. Chipmunks can talk too. You ought to hear them dang things holler when Snap gets them!"

"Billy! When you want a cooky for supper and I don't give it to you it is because you said a wrong word."

"Well, for—" Billy clapped his hand over his mouth and stained his face in swipes. "Well, for—anything! Did I go an' forget again! The cookies will get all hard, won't they? I bet you ten dollars I don't say that any more."

He espied Wesley and ran to show him a walnut too big to go through the holes, and Elnora and Margaret went into the house.

They talked of many things for a time and then Elnora said suddenly, "Aunt Margaret, I like music."

"I've noticed that in you all your life," answered Margaret.

"If dogs can't talk, I can make a violin talk," announced Elnora, and then in amazement watched the face of Margaret Sinton grow pale.

"A violin!" she wavered. "Where did you get a violin?"

"They fairly seemed to speak to me in the orchestra. One day the conductor left his in the auditorium, and I took it, and, Aunt Margaret, I can make it do the wind in the swamp, the birds, and the animals. I can make any sound I ever heard on it. If I had a chance to practise a little, I could make it do the orchestra music, too. I don't know how I know, but I do."

"Did—did you ever mention it to your mother?" faltered Margaret.

"Yes, and she seems prejudiced against them. But, oh, Aunt Margaret, I never felt so about anything, not even going to school.

I just feel as if I'd die if I didn't have one. I could keep it at school, and practise at noon a whole hour. Soon they'd ask me to play in the orchestra. I could keep it in the case and practise in the woods in summer. You'd let me play here over Sunday. Oh, Aunt Margaret, what does one cost? Would it be wicked for me to take of my money and buy a very cheap one? I could play on the least expensive one made."

"Oh, no you couldn't! A cheap machine makes cheap music. You got to have a fine fiddle to make it sing. But there's no sense in your buying one. There isn't a decent reason on earth why you shouldn't have your fa—"

"My father's!" cried Elnora. She caught Margaret Sinton by the arm. "My father had a violin! He played it. That's why I can! Where is it! Is it in our house? Is it in mother's room?"

"Elnora!" panted Margaret. "Your mother will kill me! She always hated it."

"Mother dearly loves music," said Elnora.

"Not when it took the man she loved away from her to make it!"

"Where is my father's violin?"

"Elnora!"

"I've never seen a picture of my father. I've never heard his name mentioned. I've never had a scrap that belonged to him. Was he my father, or am I a charity child like Billy, and so she hates me?"

"She's got good pictures of him. Seems she just can't bear to hear him talked about. Of course, he was your father. They lived right there when you were born. She don't dislike you, she just tries to make herself think she does. There's no sense in the world in you not having his violin. I've a great notion—"

"Has she got it?"

"No. I've never heard her mention it. It was not at home when he—when he died."

"Do you know where it is?"

"Yes. I'm the only person on earth who does, except the one who has it."

"Who is that?"

"I can't tell you, but I will see if they have it yet, and get it if I can. But, if your mother finds it out she will never forgive me."

"I can't help it," said Elnora. "I want that violin. I want it now."

"I'll go to-morrow, and get it if it has not been destroyed."

"Destroyed! Oh, Aunt Margaret! Would anyone dare?"

"I hardly think so. It was a good instrument. He played it like a master."

"Tell me!" breathed Elnora.

"His hair was red and curled more than yours, and his eyes were blue. He was tall, slim, and the very imp of mischief. He joked and teased all day until he picked up that violin. Then his head bent over it, and his eyes got big and earnest. He seemed to listen as if he first heard the notes, and then copied them. Sometimes he drew the bow tremblely, like he wasn't sure it was right, and he might have to try again. He could almost drive you crazy when he wanted to, and no man that ever lived could make you dance as he could. He made it all up as he went. He seemed to listen for his dancing music, too. It appeared to come to him; he'd begin to play and you had to keep time or die. You couldn't be still; he loved to sweep a crowd around with that bow of his. I think it was the thing you call inspiration. I can see him now, his handsome head bent, his cheeks red, his eyes snapping, and that bow going across the strings, and driving us like sheep. He always kept his body swinging, and he loved to play. He often slighted his work shamefully, and sometimes her a little; that is why she hated it—Elnora, what are you making me do?"

The tears were rolling down Elnora's cheeks. "Oh, Aunt Margaret," she sobbed. "Why haven't you told me about him sooner? I feel as if you had given my father to me living, so that I could touch him. I can see him, too! Why didn't you ever tell me before? Go on! Go on!"

"I can't, Elnora! I'm scared to death! I never meant to say anything. If I hadn't promised her not to talk of him to you she wouldn't have let you come here. She made me swear it."

"But why? Why? Was he a shame? Was he disgraced?"

"Maybe it was that unjust feeling that took possession of her when she couldn't help him from the swamp. She had to blame some one, or go crazy, so she took it out on you. At times, those first ten years, if I had talked to you, and you had repeated anything to her, she might have struck you too hard. She was not master of herself. You must be patient with her, Elnora. God only knows what she has gone through, but I think she is a little better lately."

"So do I," said Elnora. "She seems more interested in my clothes, and she fixes me such delicious lunches that the girls bring fine candies and cake and beg to trade. I gave half my lunch for a box of candy one day, brought it home to her, and told her. Since, she has wanted me to carry a market basket and treat the crowd every day, she was so pleased. Life has been too monotonous for her. I think she enjoys even the little change made by my going and coming. She sits up half the night to read the library books I bring, but she is so stubborn she won't even admit that she touches them. Tell me more about my father."

"Wait until I see if I can get the violin."

So Elnora went home in suspense, and that night she added to her prayers, "Dear Lord, be merciful to my father, and, oh, do help Aunt Margaret to get his violin."

Wesley and Billy came in to supper tired and hungry. Billy ate heartily, but his eyes often rested on a plate of tempting cookies, and when Wesley offered them to the boy he reached for one. Margaret was compelled to explain that cookies were forbidden that night.

"What!" said Wesley. "Wrong words been coming again. Oh, Billy, I do wish you could remember! I can't sit and eat cookies before a little boy who has none. I'll have to put mine back, too."

Billy's face was a puzzle. It twisted in despair.

"Aw, go on!" he said gruffly, but his chin was jumping, for Wesley was his idol.

"Can't do it," said Wesley. "It would choke me."

Billy turned to Margaret. "You make him," he appealed.

"He can't, Billy," said Margaret. "I know how he feels. You see, I can't myself."

Then Billy slid from his chair, ran to the couch, buried his face in the pillow and cried heart-brokenly. Wesley hurried to the barn, and Margaret to the kitchen. When the dishes were almost washed Billy slipped from the back door.

Wesley piling hay into the mangers heard a sound behind him and inquired, "That you, Billy?"

"Yes," answered Billy, "and it's all so dark you can't see me now, isn't it?"

"Well, mighty near," answered Wesley.

"Then you stoop down and open your mouth."

Sinton had shared bites of apple and nuts for weeks, for Billy had not learned how to eat anything without dividing with Jimmy and Belle. Since he was separated from them, he shared with Wesley and Margaret. So he bent over the small figure and received an instalment of cooky that almost choked him.

"Now you can eat it!" shouted Billy in delight. "It's all dark! I can't see what you're doing 't all!"

Wesley picked up the small figure and set the boy on the back of a horse to bring his face level so that they could talk as men. He never towered from his height above Billy, but always lifted the little soul when important matters were to be discussed.

"Now what a dandy scheme," he commented. "Did you and Aunt Margaret fix it up?"

"No. She ain't had hers yet. But I got one for her. 'Ist as soon as you eat yours, I am going to take hers, and feed her first time I find her in the dark."

"But, Billy, where did you get the cookies? You know Aunt Margaret said you were not to have any."

"I 'ist took them," said Billy, "I didn't take them for me. I 'ist took them for you and her."

Wesley swallowed hard and thought fast. In the warm darkness of the barn the horses crunched their corn, a rat gnawed at a corner of the granary, and among the rafters the white pigeon cooed a soft sleepy note to his dusky mate.

"Did—did—I steal?" wavered Billy through the darkness.

Wesley's big hands closed until he almost hurt the boy.

"No!" he said vehemently. "That is too big a word. You just made a mistake. You were trying to be a fine little man, but you went at it the wrong way. You only made a mistake. All of us do that, Billy. The world grows that way. When we make mistakes we can see them; that teaches us to be more careful the next time, and so we learn."

"How wouldn't it be a mistake?"

"If you had told Aunt Margaret what you wanted to do, and

asked her for the cookies she would have given them to you."

"But I was 'fraid she wouldn't, and you 'ist had to have it."

"Not if it was wrong for me to have it, Billy. I don't want it that much."

"Must I take it back?"

"You think hard, and decide yourself," suggested Wesley.

"Lift me down," said Billy, after a silence. "I got to put this in the jar, and tell her."

Wesley set the boy on the floor, but as he did so he paused one second and strained him close to his breast.

Margaret sat in her chair sewing, Billy slipped in and crept up beside her. The little face was lined with tragedy.

"Why, Billy, whatever is the matter?" she cried as she dropped her sewing and held out her arms. Billy stood back. He gripped his little fists tight and squared his shoulders. "I got to be shut up in the closet," he said.

"Oh, Billy! What an unlucky day! What have you done now?"

"I stold!" gulped Billy. "He said it was 'ist a mistake, but it was worser 'an that. I took something you told me I wasn't to have."

"Stole!" Margaret was in despair. "What, Billy?"

"Cookies!" answered Billy in equal trouble.

"Billy!" wailed Margaret. "How could you?"

"It was for him and you," sobbed Billy. "He said he couldn't eat it 'fore me, but out in the barn it's all dark and I couldn't see. I thought maybe he could there. Then we might put out the light and you could have yours. He said I only made it worse, 'cos I mustn't take things, and I know I mustn't, so I got to go in the closet."

Margaret gazed at him helplessly.

"Will you hold me tight a little bit first? He did."

Margaret opened her arms and Billy rushed in and clung to her a few seconds, with all the force of his being, then he slipped to the floor and marched to the closet. Margaret opened the door. Billy gave one glance at the light, clinched his fists and walking inside climbed on a box. Margaret shut her eyes and closed the door.

Then she sat and listened. Was the air pure enough? Possibly he might smother. She had read something once. Was it very dark? What if there should be a mouse in the closet and it should run across his foot and frighten him into spasms. Somewhere she had heard—Margaret leaned forward with tense face and listened. Something dreadful might happen. She could bear it no longer. She arose hurriedly and opened the door. Billy was drawn up on the box in a little heap, and he lifted a disapproving face to her.

"Shut that door!" he said. "I ain't been in here near long enough yet!"

10

Wherein Elnora Has More Financial Troubles, and Mrs. Comstock Again Hears the Song of the Limberlost

The next night Elnora hurried to Sinton's. She threw open the back door and searched Margaret's face with anxious eyes.

"You got it!" panted Elnora. "You got it! I can see by your face that you did. Oh, give it to me!"

"Yes, I got it, honey, I got it all right, but don't be so fast. You can't have it before Saturday. It had been kept in such a damp place it needed glueing, it had to have strings, and a key was gone. I knew how much you wanted it, so I sent Wesley right to town with it. They said they could fix it good as new, but it should be varnished, and that it would take several days for the glue to set. You can have it Saturday."

"You found it where you thought it was? You know it's his?"

"Yes, it was just where I thought, and it's the same violin I've seen him play hundreds of times. It's all right, only laying so long it needs fixing."

"Oh, Aunt Margaret! Can I ever wait?"

"It does seem a long time, but how could I help it? You couldn't do anything with it as it was. You see, it had been hidden away in a garret, and it needed cleaning and drying to make it fit to play again. You can have it Saturday sure."

"Saturday morning?"

"He just said Saturday. But Elnora, you've got to promise me that you will leave it here, or in town, and not let your mother get a hint of it. I don't know what she'd do."

"Uncle Wesley can bring it here until Monday. Then I will take it to school so that I can practise at noon. Oh, I don't know how to thank you. And there's more than the violin for which to be thankful. You've given me my father. Last night I saw him plain as life."

"Elnora you were dreaming! You couldn't have seen him."

"I know I was dreaming, but I saw him. I saw him so closely that a tiny white scar at the corner of his eyebrow showed. I was just reaching out to touch him when he disappeared."

"Who told you there was a scar on his forehead?"

"No one ever did in all my life. I saw it last night just as he went down. And, oh, Aunt Margaret! I saw what she did, and I heard his cries! No matter what she does, I don't believe I ever can be angry with her again. Her heart is broken, and she can't help it. Oh, it was terrible, but I am glad I saw it. Now, I will always understand."

"I don't know what to make of that," said Margaret. "I don't believe in such stuff at all, but you couldn't make it up, for you didn't know."

"I only know that I played the violin last night, as he played it, and while I played he came through the woods from the direction of Carney's. It was summer and all the flowers were in bloom. He wore gray trousers and a blue shirt, his head was bare, and his face was beautiful. I could almost touch him when he sank."

Margaret Sinton stood perplexed. "Well, I don't know what to think of that!" she ejaculated. "I was next to the last person who saw him before he was drowned. It was late on a June afternoon, and he was dressed as you describe. He was bareheaded because he had found a quail's nest before the bird began to brood, and he gathered the eggs in his hat and left it in a fence corner to get on his way home; they found it afterward."

"Was he coming from Carney's?"

"He was on that side of the quagmire. Why he ever skirted it so close as to get caught is a mystery you will have to dream out. I never could understand it."

"Was he doing something he didn't want my mother to know?"

"Why?"

"Because if he was, he might have cut close the swamp so he couldn't be seen from the garden. You know, the whole path straight to the pool where he sank can be seen from our back door. It's firm on our side. The danger is on the north and east. If he didn't want mother to know he might have tried to pass on either of those sides and gone too close. Was he in a hurry?"

"Yes, he was," said Margaret. "He had been away longer than he expected, and he almost ran when he started home."

"And he'd left his violin somewhere that you knew, and you went and got it. I'll wager he was going to play, and didn't want mother to find it out!"

"It wouldn't make any difference to you if you knew every little thing, so quit thinking about it, and just be glad you are to have what he loved best of anything."

"That's true, and I must hurry home, or I'll have to be cutting too close the swamp myself. I am dreadfully late."

Elnora sprang up and ran down the road, but when she was near the cabin she climbed the fence, crossed the open woods pasture diagonally and entered at the back garden gate. As she often came that way when she had been looking for cocoons her mother asked no questions.

Elnora lived by the minute until Saturday, when, contrary to his usual custom, Sinton went to town in the forenoon, taking her along to buy some groceries. Sinton drove straight to the music store, and asked for the violin he had left to be mended.

In its new coat of varnish, with new keys and strings, it looked greatly like any other violin to Sinton, but to Elnora it was the most beautiful instrument ever made, and a priceless treasure. She held it in her arms, touched the strings softly and then she drew the bow across them in whispering measure. She had no time to think what a remarkably good bow it was for sixteen years' disuse. The tan leather case might have impressed her as being in fine condition also, had she been in a state to question anything. She did remember to ask for the bill and she was gravely presented with a slip calling for four strings, one key, and a coat of varnish, total, one dollar fifty. It seemed to Elnora she never could put the precious instrument in the case and start home. Wesley left her in the music store where the proprietor showed her all he could about tuning, and gave her several beginners' sheets of notes and scales. She carried the violin in her arms as far as the crossroads at the corner of their land, then reluctantly put it under the carriage seat.

As soon as her work was done she ran down to Sintons' and began to play, and on Monday the violin went to school with her. She made arrangements with the superintendent to leave it in his office and scarcely took time for her food at noon, she was so eager to practise. Often one of the girls asked her to stay in town all night for some lecture or entertainment. She could take the violin with her, practise, and secure help. Her skill was so great that the leader of the orchestra offered to give her lessons if she would play to pay for them, so her progress was rapid in technical work. But from the first day the instrument became hers, with perfect faith that she could play as her father did, she spent half her practice time in imitating the sounds of all outdoors and improvising the songs her happy heart sang in those days.

So the first year went, and the second and third were a repetition; but the fourth was different, for that was the close of the course, ending with graduation and all its attendant ceremonies and expenses. To Elnora these appeared mountain high. She had hoarded every cent, thinking twice before she parted with a penny, but teaching natural history in the grades had taken time from her studies in school which must be made up outside. She was a conscientious student, ranking first in most of her classes, and standing high in all branches. Her interest in her violin had grown with the years. She went to school early and practised a half-hour in the little room off the stage, while the orchestra gathered. She put in a full hour at noon, and remained another half hour at night. She carried the violin to Sinton's on Saturday and practised all the time she could there, while Margaret watched the road to see that Mrs. Comstock was not coming. She had become so skilful that it was a delight to hear her play the music of any composer, but when she played her own, that was joy inexpressible, for then the wind blew, the water rippled, the Limberlost sang her songs of sunshine, shadow, black storm, and white night.

Since her dream Elnora had regarded her mother with peculiar tenderness. The girl realized, in a measure, what had happened. She avoided anything that possibly could stir bitter memories or draw deeper a line on the hard, white face. This cost many sacrifices, much work, and sometimes delayed progress, but the horror of that awful dream remained with Elnora. She worked her way cheerfully, doing all she could to interest her mother in things that happened in school, in the city, and by carrying books that were interesting from the public libraries.

Three years had changed Elnora from the girl of sixteen to the very verge of womanhood. She had grown tall, round, and her face had the loveliness of perfect complexion, beautiful eyes and hair and an added touch from within that might have been called comprehension. It was a compound of self-reliance, hard knocks, heart hunger, unceasing work, and generosity. There was no form of suffering with which the girl could not sympathize, no work she was afraid to attempt, no subject she had investigated she did not understand. These things combined to produce a breadth and depth of character altogether unusual. She was so absorbed in her classes and her music that she had not been able to gather specimens as usual. When she realized this and hunted assiduously, she soon found that changing natural conditions had affected such work. Men all around were clearing available land. The trees fell wherever corn would grow. The swamp was broken by several gravel roads, dotted in places around the edge with little frame houses, and the machinery of oil wells; one especially low place around the region of Freckles's room was nearly all that remained of the original. Wherever the trees fell the moisture dried, the creeks ceased to flow, the river ran low, and at times the bed was dry. With unbroken sweep the winds of the west came, gathering force with every mile and howled and raved; threatening to tear the shingles from the roof, blowing the surface from the soil in clouds of fine dust and rapidly changing everything. From coming in with two or three dozen rare moths in a day, in three years' time Elnora had grown to be delighted with finding two or three. Big pursy caterpillars could not be picked from their favourite bushes, when there were no bushes. Dragon flies would not hover over dry places, and butterflies became scarce in proportion to the flowers, while no land yields over three crops of Indian relics.

All the time the expense of books, clothing and incidentals had continued. Elnora added to her bank account whenever she could, and drew out when she was compelled, but she omitted the important feature of calling for a balance. So, one early spring morning in the last quarter of the fourth year, she almost fainted when she learned that all her funds were gone. Commencement with its extra expense was coming, she had no money, and very few cocoons to open in June, which would be too late. She had one collection for the Bird Woman complete to a pair of Imperialis moths, and that was her only asset. On the day she added these big yellow Emperors she would get a check for three hundred dollars, but she would not get it until these specimens were secured. She remembered that she never had found an Emperor before June.

Moreover, that sum was for her first year in college. Then she would be of age, and she meant to sell enough of her share of her father's land to finish. She knew her mother would oppose her bitterly in that, for Mrs. Comstock had clung to every acre and tree that belonged to her husband. Her land was almost complete forest where her neighbours owned cleared farms, dotted with wells that every hour sucked oil from beneath her holdings, but she was too absorbed in the grief she nursed to know or care. The Brushwood road and the redredging of the great Limberlost ditch had been more than she could pay from her income, and she had trembled before the wicket as she asked the banker if she had funds to pay it, and wondered why he laughed as he assured her she had. For Mrs. Comstock had spent no time on compounding interest, and never added the sums she had been depositing through nearly twenty years. Now she thought her funds were almost gone, and every day she worried over expenses. She could see no reason in going through the forms of graduation when pupils had all in their heads that was required to graduate. Elnora knew she had to have her diploma in order to enter the college she wanted to attend, but she did not dare utter the word, until high school was finished, for, instead of softening as she hoped her mother had begun to do, she seemed to remain very much the same.

When the girl reached the swamp she sat on a log and thought bitterly over the absolute expense she was compelled to meet.

Every member of her particular set was having an expensive photograph taken to exchange with the others. Elnora loved these girls and boys, and to say she could not have their pictures to keep was more than she could bear. Each one would give to all the others a handsome graduation present. She knew they would prepare gifts for her whether she could make a present in return or not. Then it was the custom for each graduating class to give a great entertainment and use the funds to present the school with a statue for the entrance hall. Elnora had been cast for and was practising a part in that performance. She was expected to furnish her dress and personal necessities. She had been told that she must have a green dress, and where was it to come from?

Every girl of the class would have three beautiful new frocks for Commencement; one for the baccalaureate sermon, another, which could be plainer, for graduation exercises, and a handsome one for the banquet and ball. Elnora faced the past three years and wondered how she could have spent so much money and not kept account of it. She did not realize where it had gone. She did not know what she could do now. She thought over the photographs, and at last settled that question to her satisfaction. She studied longer over the gifts, ten handsome ones there must be, and at last decided she could arrange for them. The green dress came first. The lights would be dim in the scene, and the setting deep woods. She could manage that. She simply could not have three dresses. She would have to get a very simple one for the sermon and do the best she could for graduation. Whatever she got for that must be made with a guimpe that could be taken out to make it a little more festive for the ball. But where could she get even two pretty dresses?

The only hope she could see was to break into the collection of the man from India, sell some moths, and try to replace them in June. But in her soul she knew that never would do. No June ever brought just the things she hoped it would. If she spent the college money she knew she could not replace it. If she did not, the only way was to try for a room in the grades and teach a year. Her work there had been so appreciated that Elnora felt with the recommendation she knew she could get from the superintendent and teachers she could secure a position. She was sure she could pass the examinations easily. She had once gone on Saturday, taken them and secured a licence for a year before she left the Brushwood school.

She wanted to start to college when the other girls were going. If she could make the first year alone, she could manage the rest. But make that first year herself, she must. Instead of selling any of her collection, she must hunt as she never before had hunted and find a yellow Emperor. She had to have it, that was all. Also, she had to have those dresses. She thought of Sinton and dismissed it. She thought of the Bird Woman, and knew she could not tell her. She thought of every way in which she ever had hoped to earn money and realized that with the play, committee meetings, practising, and final examinations she scarcely had time to live, much less to do more than the work required for her pictures and gifts. Again Elnora was in trouble, and this time it seemed the worst of all.

It was dark when she arose and went home.

"Mother," she said, "I have a piece of news that is decidedly not cheerful."

"Then keep it to yourself!" said Mrs. Comstock. "I think I have enough to bear without a great girl like you piling trouble on me."

"My money is all gone!" said Elnora.

"Well, did you think it would last forever? It's been a marvel to me that it's held out as well as it has, the way you've dressed and gone."

"I don't think I've spent any that I was not compelled to," said Elnora. "I've dressed on just as little as I possibly could to keep going. I am heartsick. I thought I had over fifty dollars to put me through Commencement, but they tell me it's all gone."

"Fifty dollars! To put you through Commencement! Well, what on earth are you proposing to do?"

"The same as the rest of them, in the very cheapest way possible."

"And what might that be?"

Elnora omitted the photographs, the gifts and the play. She told only of the sermon, graduation exercises, and the ball.

"Well, I wouldn't trouble myself over that," sniffed Mrs. Comstock. "If you want to go to a sermon, put on the dress you always use for meeting. If you need white for the exercises wear the new dress you got last spring. As for the ball, the best thing for you to do is to stay a mile away from such folly. In my opinion you'd best bring home your books, and quit right now. You can't be fixed like the rest of them, don't be so foolish as to run into it. Just stay here and let these last few days go. You can't learn enough more to be of any account."

"But, mother," gasped Elnora. "You don't understand!"

"Oh, yes, I do!" said Mrs. Comstock. "I understand perfectly. So long as the money lasted, you held up your head, and went sailing without even explaining how you got it from the stuff you gathered. Goodness knows I couldn't see. But now it's gone, you come whining to me. What have I got? Have you forgot that the ditch and the road completely strapped me? I haven't any money. There's nothing for you to do but get out of it."

"I can't!" said Elnora desperately. "I've gone on too long. It would make a break in everything. They wouldn't let me have my diploma!"

"What's the difference? You've got the stuff in your head. I wouldn't give a rap for a scrap of paper. That don't mean anything!"

"But I've worked four years for it, and I can't enter—I ought to have it to help me get a school, when I want to teach. If I don't have my grades to show, people will think I quit because I couldn't pass my examinations. I must have my diploma!"

"Then get it!" said Mrs. Comstock.

"The only way is to graduate with the rest."

"Well, graduate if you are bound to!"

"But I can't, unless I have things enough like the others, that I don't look as I did that first day."

"Well, please remember I didn't get you into this, and I can't get you out. You are set on having your own way. Go on, and have it, and see how you like it!"

Elnora went upstairs and did not come down again that night, which her mother called pouting.

"I've thought all night," said the girl at breakfast, "and I can't see any way but to borrow the money of Uncle Wesley and pay it back from some that the Bird Woman will owe me, when I get one more specimen. But that means that I can't go to—that I will have to teach this winter, if I can get a city grade or a country school."

"Just you dare go dinging after Wesley Sinton for money," cried Mrs. Comstock. "You won't do any such a thing!"

"I can't see any other way. I've got to have the money!"

"Quit, I tell you!"

"I can't quit!—I've gone too far!"

"Well, then, let me get your clothes, and you can pay me back."

"But you said you had no money!"

"Maybe I can borrow some at the bank. Then you can return it when the Bird Woman pays you."

"All right," said Elnora. "I don't have to have expensive things. Just some kind of a pretty cheap white dress for the sermon, and a white one a little better than I had last summer, for Commencement and the ball. I can use the white gloves and shoes I got myself for last year, and you can get my dress made at the same place you did that one. They have my measurements, and do perfect work. Don't get expensive things. It will be warm so I can go bareheaded."

Then she started to school, but was so tired and discouraged she scarcely could walk. Four years' plans going in one day! For she felt that if she did not get started to college that fall she never would. Instead of feeling relieved at her mother's offer, she was almost too ill to go on. For the thousandth time she groaned, "Oh, why didn't I keep account of my money?"

After that the days went so swiftly she scarcely had time to think, but several trips her mother made to town, and the assurance that everything was all right, satisfied Elnora. She worked very hard to pass good final examinations and perfect herself for the play. For two days she had remained in town with the Bird Woman in order to spend more time practising and at her work.

Often Margaret had asked about her dresses for graduation, and Elnora had replied that they were with a woman in the city who had made her a white dress for last year's Commencement when she was a junior usher, and they would be all right. So Margaret, Wesley, and Billy concerned themselves over what they would get her for a present. Margaret suggested a beautiful dress. Sinton said that would look to every one as if she needed dresses. The thing was to get a handsome gift like all the rest would have. Billy wanted to present her a five-dollar gold piece to buy music for her violin. He was positive Elnora would like that best of anything.

It was toward the close of the term when they drove to town one evening to try to settle this important question. They knew Mrs. Comstock had been alone several days, so they asked her to accompany them. She had been more lonely than she would admit, filled with unusual unrest besides, and so she was glad to go. But before they had driven a mile Billy had told that they were going to buy Elnora a graduation present, and Mrs. Comstock devoutly wished that she had remained at home. She was prepared when Billy asked, "Aunt Kate, what are you going to give Elnora when she graduates?"

"Plenty to eat, a good bed to sleep in, and do all the work while she trollops," answered Mrs. Comstock dryly.

Billy reflected. "I guess all of them have got that," he said. "I mean a present you buy at the store, like Christmas?"

"It is only rich folks that buy presents at stores," replied Mrs. Comstock. "I can't afford it."

"Well, we ain't rich," he said, "but we are going to buy Elnora something as fine as the rest of them have if we sell a corner of the farm. Uncle Wesley said so."

"A fool and his land is soon parted," said Mrs. Comstock tersely. Wesley and Billy laughed, but Margaret did not enjoy the remark.

While they were searching the stores for something on which all of them could decide, and Margaret was holding Billy to keep him from saying anything before Mrs. Comstock about the music on which he was determined, Mr. Brownlee met Wesley and stopped to shake hands.

"I see your boy came out finely," he said.

"I don't allow any boy anywhere to be finer than Billy," said Sinton.

"I guess you don't allow any girl to surpass Elnora," said Mr. Brownlee. "She comes home with Ellen often, and my wife and I love her. Ellen says she is great in her part to-night. Best thing in the whole play! Of course, you are in to see it! If you haven't reserved seats, you'd best start pretty soon, for the high school auditorium only seats a thousand. It's always jammed at these home-talent plays. All of us want to see how our children perform."

"Why, yes, of course," said the bewildered Sinton. Then he hurried to Margaret. "Say," he said, "there is going to be a play at the high school to-night; and Elnora is in it. Why hasn't she told us?"

"I don't know," said Margaret, "but I'm going."

"So am I," said Billy.

"Me, too!" said Wesley, "unless you think for some reason she don't want us. Looks like she would have told us if she had. I'm going to ask her mother."

"Yes, that's what she's been staying in town for," said Mrs. Comstock. "It's some sort of a swindle to raise money for her class to buy some silly thing to stick up in the school house hall to remember them by. I don't know whether it's now or next week, but there's something of the kind to be done."

"Well, it's to-night," said Wesley, "and we are going. It's my treat, and we've got to hurry or we won't get in. There's reserved seats, and we have none, so it's the gallery for us, but I don't care so I get to take one good peep at Elnora."

"S'pose she plays?" whispered Margaret in his ear.

"Aw, tush! She couldn't!" said Wesley.

"Well, she's been doing it three years in the orchestra, and working like a slave at it."

"Oh, well that's different. She's in the play to-night. Brownlee told me so. Come on, quick! We'll drive and hitch closest place we can find to the building."

Margaret went in the excitement of the moment, but she was troubled.

When they reached the building Wesley tied the team to a railing and Billy sprang out to help Margaret. Mrs. Comstock sat still.

"Come on, Kate," said Wesley, reaching his hand.

"I'm not going anywhere," said Mrs. Comstock, settling comfortably back against the cushions.

All of them begged and pleaded, but it was no use. Not an inch would Mrs. Comstock budge. The night was warm and the carriage comfortable, the horses were securely hitched. She did not care to see what idiotic thing a pack of school children were doing, she would wait until the Sintons returned. Wesley told her it might be two hours, and she said she did not care if it was four, so they left her.

"Did you ever see such—?"

"Cookies!" cried Billy.

"Such blamed stubbornness in all your life?" demanded Sinton. "Won't come to see as fine a girl as Elnora in a stage performance. Why, I wouldn't miss it for fifty dollars!"

"I think it's a blessing she didn't," said Margaret placidly. "I begged unusually hard so she wouldn't. I'm scared of my life for fear Elnora will play."

They found seats near the door where they could see fairly well. Billy stood at the back of the hall and had a good view. By and by, a great volume of sound welled from the orchestra, but Elnora was not playing.

"Told you so!" said Sinton. "Got a notion to go out and see if Kate won't come now. She can take my seat, and I'll stand with Billy."

"You sit still!" said Margaret emphatically. "This is not over yet."

So Wesley remained in his seat. The play opened and went on very much like all high school plays have gone for the past fifty years. But Elnora did not appear in any of the scenes.

Out in the warm summer night a sour, grim woman nursed an aching heart and tried to justify herself. The effort irritated her intensely. She felt that she could not afford the things that were being done. The old fear of losing the land that she and Robert Comstock had purchased and began to clear, was strong upon her. She was thinking of him, how she needed him, when the orchestra music poured from the open windows near her. She leaned back, closed her eyes and tried to make her mind a blank, to shut out even the music, when the leading violin began a solo. Mrs. Comstock bore it as long as she could, and then slipped from the carriage and fled down the street.

She did not know how far she went or how long she stayed, but everything was still, save an occasional raised voice when she wandered back. She stood looking at the building. Slowly she entered the wide gates and followed up the walk. Elnora had been coming here for almost four years. When Mrs. Comstock reached the door she looked inside. The wide hall was lighted with electricity, and the statuary and the decorations of the walls did not seem like pieces of foolishness. The marble looked pure, white, and the big pictures most interesting. She walked the length of the hall and slowly read the titles of the statues and the names of the pupils who had donated them. She speculated on where the piece Elnora's class would buy could be placed to advantage.

Then she wondered if they were having a large enough audience to buy marble. She liked it better than the bronze, but it looked as if it cost more. How white the broad stairway was! Elnora had been climbing those stairs for years and never told her they were marble. Of course, she thought they were wood. Probably the upper hall was even grander than this. She went over to the fountain, took a drink, climbed to the first landing and looked about her, and then without thought to the second. There she came opposite the wide open doors and the entrance to the auditorium packed with people and a crowd standing outside. When they noticed a tall woman with white face and hair and black dress, one by one they stepped a little aside, so that Mrs. Comstock could see the stage. It was covered with curtains, and no one was doing anything. Just as she turned to go a sound so faint that everyone leaned forward and listened, drifted down the auditorium. It was difficult to tell just what it was; after one instant half the audience looked toward the windows, for it seemed only a breath of wind rustling freshly opened leaves, just a hint of stirring air.

Then the curtains were swept aside swiftly. The stage had been transformed into a lovely little corner of creation, where trees and flowers grew and moss carpeted the earth. A soft wind blew and it was the gray of dawn. Suddenly a robin began to sing, then a song sparrow joined him, and then several orioles began talking at once. The light grew stronger, the dew drops trembled, flower perfume began to creep out to the audience; the air moved the branches gently and a rooster crowed. Then all the scene was shaken with a babel of bird notes in which you could hear a cardinal whistling, and a blue finch piping. Back somewhere among the high branches a dove cooed and then a horse neighed shrilly. That set a blackbird crying, "T' check," and a whole flock answered it. The crows began to caw and a lamb bleated. Then the grosbeaks, chats, and vireos had something to say, the sun rose higher, the light grew stronger and the breeze rustled the tree-tops loudly; a cow bawled and the whole barnyard answered. The guineas were clucking, the turkey gobbler strutting, the hens calling, the chickens cheeping, the light streamed down straight overhead and the bees began to hum. The air stirred strongly, and off in an unseen field a reaper clacked and rattled through ripening wheat while the driver whistled. An uneasy mare whickered to her colt, the colt answered, and the light began to decline. Miles away a rooster crowed for twilight, and dusk was coming down. Then a catbird and a brown thrush sang against a grosbeak and a hermit thrush. The air was tremulous with heavenly notes, the lights went out in the hall, dusk swept across the stage, a cricket sang and a katydid answered, and a wood pewee wrung the heart with its lonesome cry. Then a night hawk screamed, a whip-poor-will complained, a belated killdeer swept the sky, and the night wind sang a louder song. A little screech owl tuned up in the distance, a barn owl replied, and a great horned owl drowned both their voices. The moon shone and the scene was warm with mellow light. The bird voices died and soft exquisite melody began to swell and roll. In the centre of the stage, piece by piece the grasses, mosses and leaves dropped from an embankment, the foliage softly blew away, while plainer and plainer came the outlines of a lovely girl figure draped in soft clinging green. In her shower of bright hair a few green leaves and white blossoms clung, and they fell over her robe down to her feet. Her white throat and arms were bare, she leaned forward a little and swayed with the melody, her eyes fast on the clouds above her, her lips parted, a pink tinge of exercise in her cheeks as she drew her bow. She played as only a peculiar chain of circumstances puts it in the power of a very few to play. All nature had grown still, the violin sobbed, sang, danced and quavered on alone, no voice in particular, just the soul of the melody of all nature combined in one great outpouring.

At the doorway, a white-faced woman bore it as long as she could and then fell senseless. The men nearest carried her down the hall to the fountain, revived her, and then placed her in the carriage to which she directed them. The girl played on and never knew. When she finished, the uproar of applause sounded a block down the street, but the half-senseless woman scarcely realized what it meant. Then the girl came to the front of the stage, bowed, and lifting the violin she played her conception of an invitation to dance. Every living soul within sound of her notes strained their nerves to sit still and let only their hearts dance with her. When that began the woman ran toward the country. She never stopped until the carriage overtook her half-way to her cabin. She only said she had grown tired of sitting, and walked on ahead. That night she asked Billy to remain with her and sleep on Elnora's bed. Then she pitched headlong upon her own, and suffered agony of soul such as she never before had known. The swamp had sent back the soul of her loved dead and put it into the body of the daughter she resented, and it was almost more than she could bear and live.

CHAPTER
11

Wherein Elnora Graduates, and Freckles and the Angel Send Gifts

That was Friday night. Elnora came home Saturday morning and went to work. Mrs. Comstock asked no questions, and the girl only told her that the audience had been large enough to more than pay for the piece of statuary the class had selected for the hall. Then she inquired about her dresses and was told they would be ready for her. She had been invited to go to the Bird Woman's to prepare for both the sermon and Commencement exercises. Since there was so much practising to do, it had been arranged that she should remain there from the night of the sermon until after she was graduated. If Mrs. Comstock decided to attend she was to drive in with the Sintons. When Elnora begged her to come she said she thought not. She cared nothing about such silliness.

It was almost time for Wesley to come to take Elnora to the city when, fresh from her bath, with shining, crisply washed hair, and dressed to her outer garment, she stood with expectant face before her mother and cried, "Now my dress, mother!"

Mrs. Comstock was pale as she replied, "It's on my bed. Help yourself."

Elnora opened the door and stepped into her mother's room with never a misgiving. Since the night Margaret and Wesley had brought her clothing, when she first started to school, her mother had selected all of her dresses, with Mrs. Sinton's help made most of them, and Elnora had paid the bills. The white dress of the previous spring was her first made at a dressmaker's. She had worn that as junior usher at Commencement. But her mother had selected the goods, had it made, and it had fitted perfectly and had been suitable in every way. So with her heart at rest on that point, Elnora hurried to the bed to find only her last summer's white dress, freshly washed and ironed. For an instant she stared at it, then she picked up the garment, looked at the bed beneath it, and then her gaze slowly swept the room.

It was a very unfamiliar room. Perhaps this was the third time she had been in it since she was a very small child. Her eyes ranged over the beautiful walnut dresser, the tall bureau, the big chest, inside which she never had seen, and the row of masculine attire hanging above it. Somewhere a dainty lawn or mull dress simply must be hanging. But it was not. Elnora dropped on the chest because she felt too weak to stand. In less than two hours she must be in the church, at Onabasha. She could not wear a last year's washed dress. She had nothing else. She leaned against the wall and her father's overcoat brushed her face. She caught the folds and clung to it with all her might.

"Oh, father! Father!" she moaned. "I need you! I don't believe you would have done this!"

She clung to the coat in dry-eyed agony and tried to think what she could do. At last she opened the door.

"I can't find my dress," she said.

"Well, as it's the only one there I shouldn't think it would be much trouble."

"You mean for me to wear an old washed dress tonight?"

"It's a good dress. There isn't a hole in it! There's no reason on earth why you shouldn't wear it."

"Except that I will not," said Elnora. "Didn't you get me any dress for Commencement, either?"

"If you soil that to-night, I've plenty of time to wash it again."

Sinton's voice called from the gate.

"In a minute," answered Elnora.

She ran upstairs and in an incredibly short time came down wearing one of her gingham school dresses. With a cold, hard face she passed her mother and went into the night. A half hour later Margaret and Billy stopped for Mrs. Comstock with the carriage. She had determined fully that she would not go before they called. With the sound of their voices a sort of horror of being left seized her, so she put on her hat, locked the door and went out to them.

"How did Elnora look?" inquired Margaret anxiously.

"Like she always does," answered Mrs. Comstock curtly.

"I do hope her dresses are as pretty as the rest," said Margaret. "None of them will have prettier faces or nicer ways."

"They just don't have one-half as pretty faces or one-tenth as nice ways," boasted Billy, who was wrestling with fractions.

"Oh, you two make me tired!" scoffed Mrs. Comstock.

Wesley was waiting before the big church to take care of the team. As they stood watching the people enter the building, Mrs. Comstock felt herself growing ill, without knowing why. When they went inside among the lights, saw the flower-decked stage, and the masses of finely dressed people, she grew no better. She could hear Margaret and Billy softly commenting on what was being done.

"That first chair in the very front row is Elnora's," exulted Billy, "'cos she's got the highest grades, and so she gets to lead the procession to the platform."

"The first chair!" "Lead the procession!" Mrs. Comstock was dumfounded. The notes of the pipe organ began to fill the building in a slow rolling march. Would Elnora lead the procession in a gingham dress? Or would she be absent and her chair vacant on this great occasion? For now, Mrs. Comstock could see that it was a great occasion. Everyone would remember how Elnora had played a few nights before, and they would miss her and pity her. Pity? Because she had no one to care for her. Because she was worse off than if she had no mother. For the first time in her life, Mrs. Comstock began to study herself as she would appear to others. Every time a junior girl came fluttering down the aisle, leading someone to a seat, and Mrs. Comstock saw a beautiful white dress pass, a wave of positive illness swept over her. What had she done? What would become of Elnora?

As Elnora rode to the city, she answered Wesley's questions in monosyllables so that he thought she was nervous or rehearsing her speech and did not care to talk. Several times the girl tried to tell him and realized that if she said the first word it would bring a torrent of tears. The Bird Woman opened the screen and stared unbelievingly.

"Why, I thought you would be ready; you are so late!" she said. "If you have waited to dress here, we will have to hurry."

"I have nothing to put on," said Elnora.

In bewilderment the Bird Woman drew her inside.

"Did—did—" she faltered, "did you think you would wear that?"

"No. I thought I would telephone Ellen that there had been an accident and I could not come. I don't know yet how to explain. I'm too sick to think. Oh, do you suppose I can get something made by Tuesday, so that I can graduate?"

"Yes; and you'll get something on you to-night, so that you can lead your class, as you have done for four years. Go to my room and take off that gingham, quickly. Anna, drop everything, and come help me."

The Bird Woman ran to the telephone and called Ellen Brownlee.

"Elnora has had an accident. She will be a little late," she said. "You have got to make them wait. Have them play an extra musical number before the march."

Then she turned to the maid. "Tell Benson to have the carriage at the gate, just as soon as he can get it there. Then come to my room. Bring the thread box from the sewing room, that roll of wide white ribbon on the cutting table, and gather all the white pins from every dresser in the house. But first come with me a minute."

"I want that trunk with the Swamp Angel's stuff in it, from the cedar closet," she panted as they reached the top of the stairs.

They hurried down the hall together and dragged the big trunk to the Bird Woman's room. She opened it and began tossing out white stuff.

"How lucky that she left these things!" she cried. "Here are white shoes, gloves, stockings, fans, everything!"

"I am all ready but a dress," said Elnora.

The Bird Woman began opening closets and pulling out drawers and boxes.

"I think I can make it this way," she said.

She snatched up a creamy lace yoke with long sleeves that recently had been made for her and held it out. Elnora slipped into it, and the Bird Woman began smoothing out wrinkles and sewing in pins. It fitted very well with a little lapping in the back. Next, from among the Angel's clothing she caught up a white silk waist with low neck and elbow sleeves, and Elnora put it on. It was large enough, but distressingly short in the waist, for the Angel had worn it at a party when she was sixteen. The Bird Woman loosened the sleeves and pushed them to a puff on the shoulders, catching them in places with pins. She began on the wide draping of the yoke, fastening it front, back and at each shoulder. She pulled down the waist and pinned it. Next came a soft white silk dress skirt of her own. By pinning her waist band quite four inches above Elnora's, the Bird Woman could secure a perfect Empire sweep, with the clinging silk. Then she began with the wide white ribbon that was to trim a new frock for herself, bound it three times around the high waist effect she had managed, tied the ends in a knot and let them fall to the floor in a beautiful sash.

"I want four white roses, each with two or three leaves," she cried.

Anna ran for them, while the Bird Woman added pins.

"Elnora," she said, "forgive me, but tell me truly. Is your mother so extremely poor as to make this necessary?"

"No," answered Elnora. "Next year I am heir to my share of over three hundred acres of land covered with almost as valuable timber as was in the Limberlost. We adjoin it. There could be dozens of oil wells drilled that would yield to us the thousands our neighbours are draining from under us, and the bare land is worth over one hundred dollars an acre for farming. She is not poor, she is—I don't know what she is. A great trouble soured and warped her. It made her peculiar. She does not in the least understand, but it is because she don't care to, instead of ignorance. She does not—"

Elnora stopped.

"She is—is different," finished the girl.

Anna came with the roses. The Bird Woman set one on the front of the draped yoke, one on each shoulder and the last among the bright masses of brown hair. Then she turned the girl facing the tall mirror.

"Oh!" panted Elnora. "Is that me? You are a genius! Why, I will look as well as any of them."

"Well, thank goodness for that!" cried the Bird Woman. "If it wouldn't do, I should have been ill. You are lovely; altogether lovely! Ordinarily I shouldn't say that; but when I think of how you are carpentered, I'm adoring the result."

The organ began rolling out the march as they came in sight. Elnora took her place at the head of the procession, while everyone wondered. Secretly they had hoped that she would be dressed well enough, that she would not appear poor and neglected. What this radiant young creature, gowned in the most recent style, her smooth skin flushed with excitement, and a rose-set coronet of red gold on her head, had to do with the girl they knew was difficult to decide. The signal was given and Elnora began the slow march across the vestry and down the aisle. The music welled softly, and Margaret began to sob without knowing why.

Mrs. Comstock gripped her hands together and shut her eyes. It seemed an eternity to the suffering woman before Margaret caught her arm and whispered, "Oh, Kate! For any sake look at her! Here! The aisle across!"

Mrs. Comstock opened her eyes and directing them where she was told, gazed intently, and slid down in her seat on the verge of collapse. She was saved by Margaret's tense grip and her command, "Here! Idiot! Stop that!"

In the blaze of light Elnora climbed the steps to the palm-embowered platform, crossed it and took her place. Sixty young men and women, each of them dressed the best possible, followed her. There were manly, fine looking men in that class which Elnora led. There were girls of beauty and grace, but not one of them was handsomer or clothed in better taste than she.

Billy thought the time never would come when Elnora would see him, but at last she caught his eye, then Margaret and Wesley got faint signs of recognition in turn, but there was no softening of the girl's face and no hint of a smile when she saw her mother.

Heartsick, Katharine Comstock gripped her seat and tried to

prove to herself that she was justified in what she had done, but she could not. She tried to blame Elnora for not saying that she was to lead a procession and sit on a platform in the sight of hundreds of people; but that was impossible for she realized that she would have scoffed and not understood if she had been told. Her heart pained until she suffered acute agony with every breath.

When at last the exercises were over she climbed into the carriage and rode home without a word. She did not hear what Margaret and Billy were saying. She scarcely heard Sinton, who drove behind, when he told her that Elnora would not be home until Wednesday. Early the next morning Mrs. Comstock was on her way to Onabasha. She was waiting when the Brownlee store opened. She examined ready-made white dresses, but they had only one of the right size, and it was marked forty dollars. Mrs. Comstock did not hesitate over the price, but whether the dress would be suitable. She would have to ask Elnora. She inquired her way to the home of the Bird Woman and knocked.

"Is Elnora Comstock here?" she asked the maid.

"Yes, but she is still in bed. I was told to let her sleep as long as she would."

"Maybe, I could sit here and wait," said Mrs. Comstock. "I want to see about getting her a dress for tomorrow. I am her mother."

"Then you don't need wait or worry," said the girl cheerfully. "There are two women up in the sewing-room at work on a dress for her right now. It will be done in time, and it will be a beauty."

Mrs. Comstock turned and trudged back to the Limberlost. The bitterness in her soul became a physical actuality, and water would not wash the taste of wormwood from her lips. She was too late! She was not needed. Another woman was mothering her girl. Another woman would prepare a beautiful dress such as Elnora had worn last night. The girl's love and gratitude would go to her. Mrs. Comstock tried the old process of blaming someone else, but she felt no better. She nursed her grief as closely as ever in the long days of the girl's absence. She brooded over Elnora's possession of the forbidden violin and her ability to play it until the performance could not have been told from her father's. She tried every refuge her mind could conjure, to quiet her heart and remove the fear that the girl never would come home again, but it persisted. Mrs. Comstock could neither eat nor sleep. She wandered about the cabin and garden. She kept far from the pool where Robert Comstock had sunk from sight for she felt that it would entomb her also if Elnora did not come home Wednesday morning. The mother told herself that she would wait, but the waiting was bitter as anything she ever had known.

When Elnora awoke Monday another dress was in the hands of a seamstress and was soon fitted. It had belonged to the Angel, and was a soft white thing that with a little alteration would serve admirably for Commencement and the ball. All that day Elnora worked, helping prepare the auditorium for the exercises, rehearsing the march and the speech she was to make in behalf of the class. The next day was even more busy. But her mind was at rest, for the dress was a soft delicate lace, easy to change, and the marks of alteration impossible to detect.

The Bird Woman had telephoned to Grand Rapids, explained the situation and asked the Angel if she might use it. The reply had been to give the girl all the things the chest contained. When the Bird Woman told Elnora, tears filled her eyes.

"I will write at once and thank her," she said. "With all her beautiful things she does not need them, and I do. They will serve for me often, and be much finer than anything I could afford. It is lovely of her to give me the dress and of you to have it altered for me, as I never could."

The Bird Woman laughed. "I feel quite religious to-day," she said. "You know the first and greatest rock of my salvation is 'Do unto others.' I'm only doing to you what there was no one to do to me when I was a girl very like you. Anna tells me your mother was here early this morning and that she came to see about getting you a dress."

"She is too late!" said Elnora coldly. "She had over a month to prepare my dresses, and I was to pay for them, so there is no excuse."

"Nevertheless, she is your mother," said the Bird Woman, softly. "I think almost any kind of a mother must be better than none at all, and you say she has had great trouble."

"She loved my father and he died," said Elnora. "The same

thing, in quite as tragic a manner, has happened to thousands of other women, and they have gone on with calm faces and found happiness in life by loving others. There was something else I am afraid I never shall forget; this I know I shall not, but talking does not help. I must deliver my presents and photographs to the crowd. I have a picture and I made a present for you, too, if you would care for them."

"I shall love anything you give me," said the Bird Woman. "I know you well enough to know that whatever you do will be beautiful."

Elnora felt good over that, and as she tried on her dress for the last fitting she was really happy. She looked lovely in the dainty gown, it would serve finely for the ball and many other like occasions, and it was her very own.

The Bird Woman's driver took Elnora in the carriage and she called on all the girls with whom she was especially intimate, and left her picture and the package containing her gift to them. By the time she returned, parcels for her were arriving. Friends seemed to spring from everywhere. Almost everyone she knew had some gift for her, while because they so loved her the members of her crowd had made her beautiful presents. There were books, vases, silver pieces, handkerchiefs, fans, boxes of flowers and candy. One big package settled the trouble at Sintons', for it contained a dainty dress from Margaret, a five-dollar gold piece, conspicuously labeled, "I earned this myself," from Billy, with which to buy music; and a gorgeous cut glass perfume bottle, it would have cost five dollars to fill with even a moderate-priced scent, from Wesley.

In an expressed crate was a fine curly-maple dressing table, sent by Freckles. The drawers were filled with wonderful toilet articles from the Angel. The Bird Woman added an embroidered linen cover and a small silver vase for a few flowers and no girl of the class had finer gifts. Elnora laid her head on the table sobbing happily, and the Bird Woman was almost crying herself. Professor Henley sent an elegantly printed and illustrated butterfly book, the grade rooms in which Elnora had taught gave her a set of volumes covering every phase of life afield, in the woods, and water. Elnora had no time to read so she just carried one of these books around with her hugging it as she went. After she had gone to dress a queer looking package was brought by a small boy who hopped on one foot as he handed it in and said, "Tell Elnora that is from her ma."

"Who are you?" asked the Bird Woman, as she took the bundle.

"I'm Billy!" announced the boy. "I gave her the five dollars. I earned it myself dropping corn, sticking onions, and pulling weeds. My, but you got to drop, and stick, and pull a lot before it's five dollars' worth."

"Would you like to come in and see Elnora's gifts?"

"Yes, ma'm!" said Billy trying to stand quietly.

He followed into the room and gazed around.

"Gee-mentley!" he gasped. "Does Elnora get all this?"

"Yes."

"I bet you a thousand dollars I be first in my class when I graduate. Say, have the others got a lot more than Elnora?"

"I think not."

"Well, Uncle Wesley said to find out if I could, and if she didn't have as much as the rest, he'd buy till she did, if it took a hundred dollars. Say, you ought to know him! He's just scrumptious! There ain't anybody anywhere finer 'an he is. My, he's grand!"

"I'm quite sure of it!" said the Bird Woman. "I've often heard Elnora say so."

Billy strutted around the table admiringly.

"I bet you nobody can beat this!" he boasted. Then he stopped, thinking deeply. "I don't know, though," he began reflectively. "Some of them are awful rich; they got big families to give them things and wagon loads of friends, and I haven't seen what they got. Now, maybe Elnora is getting left, after all!"

He lifted an anxious little freckled face to the Bird Woman. She cleared her throat.

"Don't worry, Billy," she said. "I will watch and if I find Elnora is 'getting left' I'll buy her some more things myself. But I'm sure she is not. She has more beautiful gifts now than she will know what to do with, and others will come. Tell your Uncle Wesley his girl is bountifully remembered, very happy, and she sends her dearest love to all of you. Now you must go, so I can help her dress. You will be there to-night to see her, of course?"

"Yes, sir-ee! She got me a seat, third row from the front, middle section, so I can see, and she's going to wink at me, after she gets her speech off her mind. She kissed me, too! She's a perfect lady, Elnora is. I'm going to marry her when I get big enough."

"Why isn't that splendid!" laughed the Bird Woman as she hurried upstairs.

"Dear!" she called. "Here is another gift for you."

Elnora was half disrobed as she took the package and, sitting on a couch, opened it. The Bird Woman bent over her and tested the fabric with her fingers.

"Why, bless my soul!" she cried. "Hand woven, hand embroidered linen, fine as silk. It's priceless! I haven't seen such things in years. My mother had garments like those when I was a child, but my sisters had them cut up for collars, belts, and fancy waists while I was small. Look at the exquisite work!"

"Where could it have come from?" cried Elnora.

She shook out a petticoat, with a hand-wrought ruffle a foot deep, then an old-fashioned chemise the neck and sleeve work of which was elaborate and perfectly wrought. On the breast was pinned a note that she hastily opened.

"I was married in these," it read, "and I had intended to be buried in them, but perhaps it would be more sensible for you to graduate and get married in them yourself, if you would like. Your mother."

"From my mother!" Wide-eyed, Elnora looked at the Bird Woman. "I never in my life saw the like. Mother does things I think I never can forgive, and when I feel hardest, she turns around and does something that makes me think she just must love me a little bit, after all. Any of the girls would give almost anything to graduate in hand-embroidered linen like that. Money can't buy such things. And they came just when I was thinking she didn't care what became of me. Do you suppose she can be insane?"

"Yes," said the Bird Woman. "Stark, staring mad! Wildly insane, if she does not love you and care what becomes of you."

Elnora rose and held the petticoat to her. "Will you look at it?" she cried. "Only imagine her not getting my dress ready, and then turning around and sending me such a petticoat as this! Ellen would pay a hundred dollars for it and never blink. I suppose mother has had it all my life, and I never saw it before."

"Go, take your bath and put on those things," said the Bird Woman. "Forget everything and be happy. She is not insane! She is embittered. She did not understand how things would be. When she saw, she came at once to get you a dress. This is her way of saying she is sorry she did not get the other. You notice she has not spent any money, so perhaps she is quite honest in saying she has none."

"Oh, she is honest!" said Elnora. "She wouldn't care enough to tell an untruth. She'd say just how things were, no matter what happened."

Soon Elnora was ready for her dress. She never had looked so well as when she again headed the procession across the flower and palm decked stage of the high school auditorium. As she sat there she could have reached over and dropped a rose she carried into the seat she had occupied that September morning four years previously when she entered the high school. She spoke the few words she had to say in behalf of the class beautifully, had the tiny wink ready for Billy, and the smile and nod of recognition for Wesley and Margaret. When at last she looked into the eyes of a white-faced woman next them, she slipped a hand to her side and raised her skirt the fraction of an inch, just enough to let the embroidered edge of a petticoat show a trifle. When she saw the look of relief which flooded her mother's face, Elnora knew that forgiveness was in her heart, and that she would go home in the morning.

It was late afternoon before she arrived, and a dray followed with a load of packages. Mrs. Comstock was overwhelmed. She sat half dazed and made Elnora show her each costly and beautiful or simple and useful gift, tell her carefully what it was and from where it came. She studied the faces of Elnora's particular friends intently. The gifts from them had to be selected and set in a group. Several times she started to speak and then stopped. At last, between her dry lips, came a harsh whisper.

"Elnora, what did you give back for these things?"

"I'll show you," said Elnora cheerfully. "I got the same thing for the Bird Woman, Aunt Margaret and you, if you care for it. But I have to run upstairs to get it."

When she returned she handed her mother an oblong frame, hand carved, enclosing Elnora's picture, taken by a schoolmate's camera. She wore her storm-coat and carried a dripping umbrella. From under it looked her bright face; her books and lunchbox were on her arm, and across the bottom of the frame was carved, "Your Country Classmate."

Then she offered another frame.

"I am strong on frames," she said. "They seemed to be the best I could do without money. I located the maple and the black walnut myself, in a little corner that had been overlooked between the river and the ditch. They didn't seem to belong to anyone so I just took them. Uncle Wesley said it was all right, and he cut and hauled them for me. I gave the mill half of each tree for sawing and curing the remainder. Then I gave the wood-carver half of that for making my frames. A photographer gave me a lot of spoiled plates, and I boiled off the emulsion, and took the specimens I framed from my stuff. The man said the white frames were worth three and a half, and the black ones five. I exchanged those little framed pictures for the photographs of the others. For presents, I gave each one of my crowd one like this, only a different moth. The Bird Woman gave me the birch bark. She got it up north last summer."

Elnora handed her mother a handsome black-walnut frame a foot and half wide by two long. It finished a small shallow glass-covered box of birch bark, to the bottom of which clung a big night moth with delicate pale green wings and long exquisite trailers. A more beautiful thing would have been difficult to imagine.

"So you see I did not have to be ashamed of my gifts," said Elnora. "I made them myself and raised and mounted the moths."

"Moth, you call it," said Mrs. Comstock. "I've seen a few of the things before."

"They are thick around us every June night, or at least they used to be," said Elnora. "I've sold hundreds of them, with butterflies, dragon flies, and other specimens. Now, I must put away these and get to work, for it is almost June and there are a few more I want dreadfully. When I get them I will be paid some money for which I have worked a long time."

She was afraid to say college just then. She thought it would be better to wait a few days and see if an opportunity would not come when it would work in more naturally. Besides, unless she could secure the yellow Emperor she needed to complete her collection, she could not talk college until she was of age, for she would have no money.

CHAPTER
12

Wherein Margaret Sinton Reveals a Secret, and Mrs. Comstock Possesses the Limberlost

"Elnora, bring me the towel, quick!" cried Mrs. Comstock.

"In a minute, mother," mumbled Elnora.

She was standing before the kitchen mirror, tying the back part of her hair, while the front turned over her face.

"Hurry! There's a varmint of some kind!"

Elnora ran into the sitting room and thrust the heavy kitchen towel into her mother's hand. Mrs. Comstock swung open the screen door and struck at some object. Elnora tossed the hair from her face so that she could see past her mother. The girl screamed wildly.

"Don't! Mother, don't!"

Mrs. Comstock struck again. Elnora caught her arm.

"It's the one I want! It's worth a lot of money! Don't! Oh, you shall not!"

"Shan't, missy?" blazed Mrs. Comstock. "When did you get to bossing me?"

The hand that held the screen swept a half-circle and stopped at Elnora's cheek. She staggered with the blow, and across her face, paled with excitement, a red mark rose rapidly. The screen slammed shut, throwing the creature on the floor before them. Instantly Mrs. Comstock's foot crushed it. Elnora stepped back. Excepting the red mark, her face was very white.

"That was the last moth I needed," she said, "to complete a collection worth three hundred dollars. You've ruined it before my eyes!"

"Moth!" cried Mrs. Comstock. "You say that because you are mad. Moths have big wings. I know a moth!"

"I've kept things from you," said Elnora, "because I didn't dare confide in you. You had no sympathy with me. But you know I never told you untruths in all my life."

"It's no moth!" reiterated Mrs. Comstock.

"It is!" cried Elnora. "It's just out of a case in the ground. Its wings take two or three hours to expand and harden."

"If I had known it was a moth—" Mrs. Comstock wavered.

"You did know! I told you! I begged you to stop! It meant just three hundred dollars to me."

"Bah! Three hundred fiddlesticks!" sneered Mrs. Comstock.

"They are what have paid for books, tuition, and clothes for the last four years. They are what I could have started on to college. You've crushed the last one I needed before my face. You never have made any pretence of loving me. At last I'll be equally frank with you. I hate you! You are a selfish, wicked woman! I hate you!"

Elnora turned, went through the kitchen and out the back door. She followed the garden path to the gate and walked toward the swamp a short distance when reaction overtook her. She dropped on the ground and leaned against a big log. When a little child, desperate as now, she had tried to die by holding her breath. She had thought in that way to make her mother sorry, but she had learned that life was a thing thrust upon her and death would not come at her wish.

She was so crushed over the loss of that moth, which she had childishly named the yellow Emperor, that she scarcely remembered the blow. She had thought no luck in all the world would be so rare as to complete her collection, and she just had been forced to see a splendid Imperialis crushed to a mass before her. There was a possibility that she could find another, but now she was facing the certainty that the one she might have had and with which she undoubtedly could have attracted others, was ruined—by her mother. How long she sat there Elnora did not know or care. She simply suffered in dumb, abject misery, an occasional dry sob shaking her. Aunt Margaret was right. Elnora felt that morning that her mother never would be any different. The girl had reached the place where she realized that she could bear it no longer.

As Elnora left the room, Mrs. Comstock took one step after her. "You little huzzy!" she gasped.

But Elnora was gone. Her mother stood staring.

"She never did lie to me," she muttered. "I guess it was a moth. And the only one she needed to get three hundred dollars, she said. I wish I hadn't been so fast! I never saw anything like it. I thought it was some deadly, stinging, biting thing. A body does have to be mighty careful here. But likely I've spilt the milk now. Pshaw! She can find another! There's no use to be foolish. Maybe moths are like snakes, where there's one, there's two."

Mrs. Comstock took the broom and swept the moth out of the door. Then she got down on her knees and carefully examined the steps, logs and the earth of the flower beds at each side. She found the place where the creature had emerged from the ground, and the hard, dark brown case which had enclosed it, still wet inside. Then she knew Elnora had been right. It was a moth. Its wings had been damp and not expanded. Mrs. Comstock never before had seen one in that state, and she did not know how they originated. She had thought all of them came from cases spun on trees or against walls or boards. She only had seen enough to know that there were such things, just as a flash of white told her that an ermine was on her premises, or a sharp "buzzzzz" warned her of a rattler.

So it was from creatures like that Elnora had gotten her school money. In one sickening sweep there rushed into the heart of the woman a full realization of the width of the gulf which separated her from her child. Lately many things had pointed toward it, none more plainly than when Elnora, like a reincarnation of her father, had stood fearlessly before a large city audience and played with even greater skill than he, on what Mrs. Comstock felt very certain, was his violin. But that little crawling creature of earth, crushed by her before its splendid yellow and lavender wings could spread and carry it into the mystery of night, had brought a realizing sense.

"We are nearer strangers with each other than we are with any of the neighbours," she muttered.

So one of the Almighty's most delicate and beautiful creations was sacrificed without fulfilling the law, yet none of its species ever served so glorious a cause, for at last Mrs. Comstock's inner vision had cleared. She went through the cabin mechanically. Every few minutes she glanced toward the back walk to see if Elnora was coming. She knew arrangements had been made with Margaret to go to the city some time that day, so she grew more nervous and uneasy every moment. She was haunted by the fear that the blow might discolour Elnora's cheek, and that she would tell Margaret. She went down the back walk, looking intently in all directions, left the garden and took the swamp path. Her step was noiseless on the soft, black earth, and soon she came near enough to see Elnora. Mrs. Comstock stood looking at the girl in troubled uncertainty. Not knowing what to say, at last she turned and went back to the cabin.

Noon came and she prepared dinner, calling, as she always did, when Elnora was in the garden, but she got no response, and the girl did not come. A little after one o'clock Margaret stopped at the gate.

"Elnora has changed her mind. She is not going," called Mrs. Comstock.

She felt that she hated Margaret as she hitched her horse and came up the walk instead of driving on.

"You must be mistaken," said Margaret. "I was going on purpose for her. She asked me to take her. I had no errand. Where is she?"

"I will call her," said Mrs. Comstock.

She followed the path again, and this time found Elnora sitting on the log. Her face was swollen and discoloured, and her eyes red with crying. She paid no attention to her mother.

"Mag Sinton is here," said Mrs. Comstock harshly. "I told her you had changed your mind, but she said you asked her to go with you, and she had nothing to go for herself."

Elnora arose, recklessly took a short cut through the deep swamp grasses and so reached the path ahead of her mother. Mrs. Comstock followed as far as the garden, but she could not enter the cabin. She busied herself among the vegetables, barely looking up when the back door screen slammed noisily. Margaret Sinton approached colourless, and with such flaming eyes that Mrs. Comstock shrank back.

"What's the matter with Elnora's face?" demanded Margaret.

Mrs. Comstock made no reply.

"You struck her, did you?"

"I thought you wasn't blind!"

"I have been, for twenty long years now, Kate Comstock," said Margaret Sinton, "but my eyes are open at last. What I see is that I've done you no good and Elnora a big wrong. I had an idea that it would kill you to know, but I guess you are tough enough to stand anything. Kill or cure, you get it now!"

"What are you frothing about?" coolly asked Mrs. Comstock.

"You!" cried Margaret. "You! The woman who don't pretend to love her only child. Who lets her grow to a woman, as you have let Elnora, and can't be satisfied with every sort of neglect, but must add abuse yet; and all for a fool idea about a man who wasn't worth his salt!"

Mrs. Comstock picked up a hoe.

"Go right on!" she said. "Empty yourself. It's the last thing you'll ever do!"

"Then I'll make a tidy job of it," said Margaret. "You'll not touch me. You'll stand there and hear the truth at last, and because I dare face you and tell it, you will know in your soul it is truth. When Robert Comstock shaved that quagmire out there so close he went in, he wanted to keep you from seeing where he was coming from. He'd been to see Elvira Carney. They had plans to go to a dance that night—"

"Close your lips!" said Mrs. Comstock in a voice of deadly quiet.

"You know I wouldn't dare open them if I was not telling you the truth. I can prove what I say. I was coming from Reeds. It was hot in the woods and I stopped at Carney's as I passed for a drink. Elvira's bedridden old mother heard me, and she was so crazy for some one to talk with, I stepped in a minute. I saw Robert come down the path. Elvira saw him, too, and she ran out of the house to head him off. It looked funny, and I just deliberately moved where I could see and hear. He brought her his violin, and told her to get ready and meet him in the woods with it that night, and they would go to a dance. She took it and hid it in the little loft to the well-house and promised she'd go."

"Are you done?" demanded Mrs. Comstock.

"No. I am going to tell you the whole story. You don't spare Elnora anything. I shan't spare you. I hadn't been here that day, but I can tell you just how he was dressed, which way he went and every word they said, though they thought I was busy with her mother and wouldn't notice them. Put down your hoe, Kate. I went to Elvira, told her what I knew and made her give me Comstock's violin for Elnora over three years ago. She's been playing it ever since. I won't see her slighted and abused another day on account of a man who would have broken your heart if he had lived. Six months more would have showed you what everybody else knew. He was one of those men who couldn't trust himself, and so no woman was safe with him. Now, will you drop grieving over him, and do Elnora justice?"

Mrs. Comstock gripped the hoe tighter and turning she went down the walk, and started across the woods to the home of Elvira Carney. With averted head she passed the pool, steadily pursuing her way. Elvira Carney, hanging towels across the back fence, saw her coming and went toward the gate to meet her. Twenty years she had dreaded that visit. Since Margaret Sinton had compelled her to produce the violin she had hidden so long, because she was afraid to destroy it, she had come more near expectation than dread. The wages of sin are the hardest debts on earth to pay, and they are always collected at inconvenient times and unexpected places. Mrs. Comstock's face and hair were so white, that her dark eyes seemed burned into their setting. Silently she stared at the woman before her a long time.

"I might have saved myself the trouble of coming," she said at last, "I see you are guilty as sin!"

"What has Mag Sinton been telling you?" panted the miserable woman, gripping the fence.

"The truth!" answered Mrs. Comstock succinctly. "Guilt is in every line of your face, in your eyes, all over your wretched body. If I'd taken a good look at you any time in all these past years, no doubt I could have seen it just as plain as I can now. No woman or man can do what you've done, and not get a mark set on them for everyone to read."

"Mercy!" gasped weak little Elvira Carney. "Have mercy!"

"Mercy?" scoffed Mrs. Comstock. "Mercy! That's a nice word from you! How much mercy did you have on me? Where's the mercy that sent Comstock to the slime of the bottomless quagmire, and left me to see it, and then struggle on in agony all these years? How about the mercy of letting me allow my baby to be neglected all the days of her life? Mercy! Do you really dare use the word to me?"

"If you knew what I've suffered!"

"Suffered?" jeered Mrs. Comstock. "That's interesting. And pray, what have you suffered?"

"All the neighbours have suspected and been down on me. I ain't had a friend. I've always felt guilty of his death! I've seen him go down a thousand times, plain as ever you did. Many's the night I've stood on the other bank of that pool and listened to you, and I tried to throw myself in to keep from hearing you, but I didn't dare. I knew God would send me to burn forever, but I'd better done it; for now, He has set the burning on my body, and every hour it is slowly eating the life out of me. The doctor says it's a cancer—"

Mrs. Comstock exhaled a long breath. Her grip on the hoe relaxed and her stature lifted to towering height.

"I didn't know, or care, when I came here, just what I did," she said. "But my way is beginning to clear. If the guilt of your soul has come to a head, in a cancer on your body, it looks as if the Almighty didn't need any of my help in meting out His punishments. I really couldn't fix up anything to come anywhere near that. If you are going to burn until your life goes out with that sort of fire, you don't owe me anything!"

"Oh, Katharine Comstock!" groaned Elvira Carney, clinging to the fence for support.

"Looks as if the Bible is right when it says, 'The wages of sin is death,' don't it?" asked Mrs. Comstock. "Instead of doing a woman's work in life, you chose the smile of invitation, and the dress of unearned cloth. Now you tell me you are marked to burn to death with the unquenchable fire. And him! It was shorter with him, but let me tell you he got his share! He left me with an untruth on his lips, for he told me he was going to take his violin to Onabasha for a new key, when he carried it to you. Every vow of love and constancy he ever made me was a lie, after he touched your lips, so when he tried the wrong side of the quagmire, to hide from me the direction in which he was coming, it reached out for him, and it got him. It didn't hurry, either! It just sucked him down, slow and deliberate."

"Mercy!" groaned Elvira Carney. "Mercy!"

"I don't know the word," said Mrs. Comstock. "You took all that out of me long ago. The last twenty years haven't been of the sort that taught mercy. I've never had any on myself and none on my child. Why, in the name of justice, should I have mercy on you, or on him? You were both older than me, both strong, sane people, you deliberately chose your course when you lured him, and he, when he was unfaithful to me. When a Loose Man and a Light Woman face the death the Almighty ordained for them, why should they shout at me for mercy? What did I have to do with it?"

Elvira Carney sobbed in panting gasps.

"You've got tears, have you?" marvelled Mrs. Comstock. "Mine all dried long ago. I've none left to shed over my wasted life, my disfigured face and hair, my years of struggle with a man's work, my wreck of land among the tilled fields of my neighbours, or the final knowledge that the man I so gladly would have died to save, wasn't worth the sacrifice of a rattlesnake. If anything yet could wring a tear from me, it would be the thought of the awful injustice I always have done my girl. If I'd lay hand on you for anything, it would be for that."

"Kill me if you want to," sobbed Elvira Carney. "I know that I deserve it, and I don't care."

"You are getting your killing fast enough to suit me," said Mrs. Comstock. "I wouldn't touch you, any more than I would him, if I could. Once is all any man or woman deceives me about the holiest things in life. I wouldn't touch you any more than I would the black plague. I am going back to my girl."

Mrs. Comstock turned and started swiftly through the woods, but she had gone only a few rods when she stopped, and leaning on the hoe, she stood thinking deeply. Then she turned back. Elvira still clung to the fence, sobbing bitterly.

"I don't know," said Mrs. Comstock, "but I left a wrong impression with you. I don't want you to think that I believe the Almighty set a cancer to burning you as a punishment for your sins. I don't! I think a lot more of the Almighty. With a whole sky-full of worlds on His hands to manage, I'm not believing that He has time to look down on ours, and pick you out of all the millions of we sinners, and set a special kind of torture to eating you. It wouldn't be a gentlemanly thing to do, and, first of all, the Almighty is bound to be a gentleman. I think likely a bruise and bad blood is what caused your trouble. Anyway, I've got to tell you that the cleanest housekeeper I ever knew, and one of the noblest Christian women, was slowly eaten up by a cancer. She got hers from the careless work of a poor doctor. The Almighty is to forgive sin and heal disease, not to invent and spread it."

She had gone only a few steps when she again turned back.

"If you will gather a lot of red clover bloom, make a tea strong as lye of it, and drink quarts, I think likely it will help you, if you are not too far gone. Anyway, it will cool your blood and make the burning easier to bear."

Then she swiftly walked home. Enter the lonely cabin she could not, neither could she sit outside and think. She attacked a bed of beets and hoed until the perspiration ran from her face and body, then she began on the potatoes. When she was too tired to take another stroke she bathed and put on dry clothing. In securing her dress she noticed her husband's carefully preserved clothing lining one wall. She gathered it in a great armload and carried it out to the swamp. Piece by piece she pitched into the green maw of the quagmire all those articles she had dusted carefully and fought moths from for years, and stood watching as it slowly sucked them down. She went back to her room and gathered every scrap that had in any way belonged to Robert Comstock, excepting his gun and revolver, and threw it into the swamp. Then for the first time she set her door wide open.

She was too weary now to do more, but an urging unrest drove her. She wanted Elnora. It seemed to her she never could wait until the girl came and delivered her judgment. At last in an effort to get nearer to her, Mrs. Comstock climbed the stairs and stood looking around Elnora's room. It was very unfamiliar. The pictures were strange to her. Commencement had filled it with packages and bundles. The walls were covered with cocoons; moths and dragon flies were pinned about. Under the bed she could see a half-dozen large white boxes. She did not know what they contained. She pulled out one and lifted the lid. The bottom was covered with a sheet of thin cork, and on long pins sticking in it were dozens of great, velvet-winged moths. Each one was labelled, always there were two of a kind, in many cases four, showing under and upper wings of both male and female. They were of every colour and shape.

Mrs. Comstock caught her breath sharply. When and where had Elnora gotten all of them? They were the most exquisite sight the woman ever had seen, so she opened all the boxes to feast on their beautiful contents. As she did so there came more fully a sense of the distance between her and her child. She could not understand how Elnora had gone to school, and performed all this work secretly. When it was finished, up to the very last moth, she, the mother who should have been the first confidant and helper, had been the one to bring disappointment. Small wonder Elnora had come to hate her.

Mrs. Comstock carefully closed and replaced the boxes, and again stood looking around the room. This time her eyes rested on some books she did not remember having seen before, so she picked up one and found that it was a moth book. She glanced over the first pages and was soon eagerly reading. When the text reached the classification of species, she laid it down, took up another and read its introductory chapters. Then she found some papers and studied them. By that time her brain was in a confused jumble of ideas about capturing moths with differing baits and bright lights.

She went downstairs thinking deeply. Being unable to sit still and having nothing else to do she glanced at the clock and began preparing supper. The work dragged. A chicken was snatched up and dressed hurriedly. A spice cake sprang into being in short order. Strawberries that had been intended for preserves went into shortcake. Delicious odours crept from the cabin. She put many extra touches on the table and then commenced watching the road. Everything was ready, but Elnora did not come. Then began the anxious process of trying to keep cooked food warm and not spoil it. The birds went to bed and dusk came. Mrs. Comstock gave up the fire and set the supper on the table. Then she went out and sat on the front door step watching night creep all around her. She started eagerly as the gate creaked, but it was only Wesley Sinton coming down the walk.

"Katharine, Margaret and Elnora passed where I was working this afternoon, and Margaret got out of the carriage and called me to the fence. She told me what she had done. I've come to say to you that I am sorry. She has heard me threaten to do it a good many times, but I never would have got it done. I'd give a good deal if I could undo it, but I can't, so I've come to tell you how sorry I am."

"You've got something to be sorry for," said Mrs. Comstock, "but likely we ain't thinking of the same thing. It hurts me less to know the truth, than to live in ignorance. If Mag had the sense of a pewee, she'd told me long ago. That's what hurts me, to think that both of you knew Robert was not worth an hour of honest grief, yet you'd let me mourn him all these years and neglect Elnora while I did it. If I have anything to forgive you, that is what it is."

Sinton took off his hat and sat on a bench.

"Katharine," he said solemnly, "nobody ever knows how to take you."

"Would it be asking too much to take me for having a few grains of plain common sense?" she inquired. "You've known all this time that Comstock got what he deserved, when he undertook to sneak in an unused way across a swamp, with which he was none too familiar. Now I should have thought that you'd figure that knowing the same thing would be the best method to cure me of pining for him, and slighting my child."

"Heaven only knows we have thought of that, and talked of it often, but we were both too big cowards. We didn't dare tell you."

"So you have gone on year after year, watching me show indifference to Elnora, and yet a little horse-sense would have pointed out to you that she was my salvation. Why, look at it! Not married quite a year. All his vows of love and fidelity made to me before the Almighty forgotten in a few months, and a dance and a Light Woman so alluring he had to lie and sneak for them. What kind of a prospect is that for a life? I know men and women. An honourable man is an honourable man, and a liar is a liar; both are born and not made. One cannot change to the other any more than that some old leopard can change its spots. After a man tells a woman the first untruth of that sort, the others come piling thick, fast, and mountain high. The desolation they bring in their wake overshadows anything I have suffered completely. If he had lived six months more I should have known him for what he was born to be. It was in the blood of him. His father and grandfather before him were fiddling, dancing people; but I was certain of him. I thought we could leave Ohio and come out here alone, and I could so love him and interest him in his work, that he would be a man. Of all the fool, fruitless jobs, making anything of a creature that begins by deceiving her, is the foolest a sane woman ever undertook. I am more than sorry you and Margaret didn't see your way clear to tell me long ago. I'd have found it out in a few more months if he had lived, and I wouldn't have borne it a day. The man who breaks his vows to me once, don't get the second chance. I give truth and honour. I have a right to ask it in return. I am glad I understand at last. Now, if Elnora will forgive me, we will take a new start and see what we can make out of what is left of life. If she won't, then it will be my time to learn what suffering really means."

"But she will," said Sinton. "She must! She can't help it when things are explained. Don't you worry over her."

"I notice she isn't hurrying any about coming home. Do you know where she is or what she is doing?"

"I do not. But likely she will be along soon. I must go help Billy with the night work. Good-bye, Katharine. Thank the Lord you have come to yourself at last!"

They shook hands and Sinton went down the road while Mrs. Comstock entered the cabin. She went to the supper table, but she could not swallow food. She stood in the back door watching the sky for moths, but they did not seem to be very numerous. Her spirits sank and she breathed unevenly. Then she heard the front screen. She reached the middle door as Elnora touched the foot of the stairs.

"Hurry, and get ready, Elnora," she said. "Your supper is almost spoiled now."

Elnora closed the stair door behind her, and for the first time in her life, threw the heavy lever which barred out anyone from downstairs. Mrs. Comstock heard the thud, and knew what it meant. She reeled slightly and caught the doorpost for support. For a few minutes she clung there, then sank to the nearest chair. After a long time she arose and stumbling half blindly, she put the food in the cupboard and covered the table. She took the lamp in one hand, the butter in the other, and started for the spring house. Something brushed close by her face, and she looked just in time to see a winged creature rise above the cabin and sail away.

"That was a night bird," she muttered. As she stooped to set the butter in the water, came another thought. "Perhaps it was a moth!" Mrs. Comstock dropped the butter and hurried out with the lamp; she held it high above her head and waited until her arms ached. Small insects of night gathered, and at last a little dusty miller, but nothing came of any size.

"I got to go where they are, if I get them," muttered Mrs. Comstock.

She hurried into the cabin, set the lamp on the table, and stood thinking deeply. She went to the barn for the pair of stout high boots she used in feeding stock in deep snow. Throwing the boots by the back door she climbed to the loft over the spring house, and hunted an old lard oil lantern and one of first manufacture for oil. Both these she cleaned and filled. She listened until everything upstairs had been still for over a half-hour. By that time it was after eleven o'clock. Then she took the good lantern from the kitchen, the two old ones, a handful of matches, a ball of twine, and went from the cabin, softly closing the door.

Sitting on the back steps, she put on the boots, and then stood gazing into the sweet June night, first in the direction of the woods on her land, then toward the Limberlost. Its outline looked so dark and forbidding she shuddered and went down the garden, taking the path toward the woods, but as she neared the pool her knees wavered and her courage fled. The knowledge that in her soul she was now glad Robert Comstock was at the bottom of it made a coward of her, who fearlessly had mourned him there, nights untold. She could not go on. She skirted the back of the garden, crossed a field, and came out on the road. Soon she reached the Limberlost. She hunted until she found the old trail, then followed it stumbling over logs and through clinging vines and grasses. The heavy boots clumped on her feet, overhanging branches whipped her face and pulled her hair. But her eyes were on the sky as she went straining into the night, hoping to find signs of a living creature on wing.

By and by she began to see the wavering flight of something she thought near the right size. She had no idea where she was, but she stopped, lighted a lantern and hung it as high as she could reach. A little distance away she placed the second and then the third. The objects came nearer and sick with disappointment she saw that they were bats. Crouching in the damp swamp grasses, without a thought of snakes or venomous insects, she waited, her eyes roving from lantern to lantern. Once she thought a creature of high flight dropped near the lard oil light, so she arose breathlessly waiting, but either it passed or it was an illusion. She glanced at the old lantern, then at the new, and was on her feet in an instant creeping close. Something large as a small bird was fluttering around. Mrs. Comstock began to perspire, while her hand shook wildly. Closer she crept and just as she reached for it, something similar swept by and both flew away together.

Mrs. Comstock set her teeth and stood shivering. For a long time the locusts rasped, the whip-poor-wills cried and a steady hum of night life throbbed in her ears. Away in the sky she saw something coming when it was no larger than a falling leaf. Straight on toward the light it came. Without in the least realizing what she was doing, Mrs. Comstock began to pray aloud.

"This way, O Lord! Make it come this way! Please! You know how I need it! O Lord, send it lower!"

The moth hesitated at the first light, then slowly, easily it came toward the second, as if following a path of air. It touched a leaf near the lantern and settled. As Mrs. Comstock reached for it a thin yellow spray wet her hand and the surrounding leaves. When its wings raised above its back, her fingers came together. She held the moth to the light. It was nearer brown than yellow, and she remembered having seen some like it in the boxes that afternoon. It was not the one needed to complete the collection, but Elnora might want it, so Mrs. Comstock held on. Just there the Almighty was kind, or nature was sufficient, as you look at it, for following the law of its being when disturbed, the moth again threw the spray by which some suppose it attracts its kind, and liberally sprinkled Mrs. Comstock's dress front and arms. From that instant, she became the best moth bait ever invented. Every Polyphemus in range hastened to her, and other fluttering creatures of night followed. The influx came her way. She snatched wildly here and there until she had one in each hand and no place to put them. She could see more coming, and her aching heart, swollen with the strain of long excitement, hurt pitifully. She prayed in broken exclamations that did not always sound reverent, but never was human soul in more deadly earnest.

Moths were coming. She had one in each hand. They were not yellow, and she did not know what to do. She glanced around to try to discover some way to keep what she had, and her throbbing heart stopped and every muscle stiffened. There was the dim outline of a crouching figure not two yards away, and a pair of eyes their owner thought hidden, caught the light in a cold stream. Her first impulse was to scream and fly for life. Before her lips could open a big moth alighted on her breast while she felt another walking over her hair. All sense of caution deserted her. She did not care to live if she could not replace the yellow moth she had killed. She set her eyes on those among the leaves.

"Here, you!" she cried hoarsely. "I need you! Get yourself out here, and help me. These critters are going to get away from me, and I've got to have them. Hustle!"

Pete Corson parted the bushes and stepped into the light.

"Oh, it's you!" said Mrs. Comstock. "I might have known! But you gave me a start. Here, hold these until I make some sort of bag for them. Go easy! If you break them I don't guarantee what will happen to you!"

"Pretty fierce, ain't you!" laughed Pete, but he advanced and held out his hands. "For Elnora, I s'pose?"

"Yes," said Mrs. Comstock. "In a mad fit, I trampled one this morning, and by the luck of the old boy himself it was the last moth she needed to complete a collection. I got to get another one or die."

"Then I guess it's your funeral," said Pete. "There ain't a chance in a dozen the right one will come. What colour was it?"

"Yellow, and big as a bird."

"The Emperor, likely," said Pete. "You dig for that kind, and they are not numerous, so's 'at you can smash 'em for fun."

"Well, I can try to get one, anyway," said Mrs. Comstock. "I forgot all about bringing anything to put them in. You take a pinch on their wings until I make a poke."

Mrs. Comstock removed her apron, tearing off the strings. She unfastened and stepped from the skirt of her calico dress. With one apron string she tied shut the band and placket. She pulled a wire pin from her hair, stuck it through the other string, and using it as a bodkin ran it around the hem of her skirt. Her fingers flew, and shortly she had a large bag. She put several branches inside to which the moths could cling, closed the mouth partially and held it toward Pete.

"Put your hand well down and let the things go!" she ordered. "But be careful, man! Don't run into the twigs! Easy! That's one. Now the other. Is the one on my head gone? There was one on my dress, but I guess it flew. Here comes a kind of a gray-looking one."

Pete slipped several more moths into the bag.

"Now, that's five, Mrs. Comstock," he said. "I'm sorry, but you'll have to make that do. You must get out of here lively. Your lights will be taken for hurry calls, and inside the next hour a couple of men will ride here like fury. They won't be nice Sunday school men, and they won't hold bags and catch moths for you. You must go quick!"

Mrs. Comstock laid down the bag and pulled one of the lanterns lower.

"I won't budge a step," she said. "This land don't belong to you. You have no right to order me off it. Here I stay until I get a yellow Emperor, and no little petering thieves of this neighbourhood can scare me away."

"You don't understand," said Pete. "I'm willing to help Elnora, and I'd take care of you, if I could, but there will be too many for me, and they will be mad at being called out for nothing."

"Well, who's calling them out?" demanded Mrs. Comstock. "I'm catching moths. If a lot of good-for-nothings get fooled into losing some sleep, why, let them, they can't hurt me, or stop my work."

"They can, and they'll do both."

"Well, I'll see them do it!" said Mrs. Comstock. "I've got Robert's revolver in my dress, and I can shoot as straight as any man, if I'm mad enough. Anyone that interferes with me to-night will find me mad aplenty. There goes another!"

She stepped into the light and waited until a big brown moth settled on her and was easily taken. Then in light, airy flight came a delicate pale green thing, and Mrs. Comstock started in pursuit. But the scent was not right. The moth fluttered high, then dropped lower, still lower, and sailed away. With outstretched hands Mrs. Comstock pursued it. She hurried one way and another, then ran over an object which tripped her and she fell. She regained her feet in an instant, but she had lost sight of the moth. With livid face she turned on the crouching man.

"You nasty, sneaking son of Satan!" she cried. "Why are you hiding there? You made me lose the one I wanted most of any I've had a chance at yet. Get out of here! Go this minute, or I'll fill your worthless carcass so full of holes you'll do to sift cornmeal. Go, I say! I'm using the Limberlost to-night, and I won't be stopped by the devil himself! Cut like fury, and tell the rest of them they can just go home. Pete is going to help me, and he is all of you I need. Now go!"

The man turned and went. Pete leaned against a tree, held his mouth shut and shook inwardly. Mrs. Comstock came back panting.

"The old scoundrel made me lose that!" she said. "If anyone else comes snooping around here I'll just blow them up to start with. I haven't time to talk. Suppose that had been yellow! I'd have killed that man, sure! The Limberlost isn't safe to-night, and the sooner those whelps find it out, the better it will be for them."

Pete stopped laughing to look at her. He saw that she was speaking the truth. She was quite past reason, sense, or fear. The soft night air stirred the wet hair around her temples, the flickering lanterns made her face a ghastly green. She would stop at nothing, that was evident. Pete suddenly began catching moths with exemplary industry. In putting one into the bag, another escaped.

"We must not try that again," said Mrs. Comstock. "Now, what will we do?"

"We are close to the old case," said Pete. "I think I can get into it. Maybe we could slip the rest in there."

"That's a fine idea!" said Mrs. Comstock. "They'll have so much room there they won't be likely to hurt themselves, and the books say they don't fly in daytime unless they are disturbed, so they will settle when it's light, and I can come with Elnora to get them."

They captured two more, and then Pete carried them to the case.

"Here comes a big one!" he cried as he returned.

Mrs. Comstock looked up and stepped out with a prayer on her lips. She could not tell the colour at that distance, but the moth appeared different from the others. On it came, dropping lower and darting from light to light. As it swept near her, "O Heavenly Father!" exulted Mrs. Comstock, "it's yellow! Careful, Pete! Your hat, maybe!"

Pete made a long sweep. The moth wavered above the hat and sailed away. Mrs. Comstock leaned against a tree and covered her face with her shaking hands.

"That is my punishment!" she cried. "Oh, Lord, if you will give a moth like that into my possession, I'll always be a better woman!"

The Emperor again came in sight. Pete stood tense and ready. Mrs. Comstock stepped into the light and watched the moth's course. Then a second appeared in pursuit of the first. The larger one wavered into the radius of light once more. The perspiration rolled down the man's tense face. He half lifted the hat.

"Pray, woman! Pray now!" he panted.

"I guess I best get over by that lard oil light and go to work," breathed Mrs. Comstock. "The Lord knows this is all in prayer, but it's no time for words just now. Ready, Pete! You are going to get a chance first!"

Pete made another long, steady sweep, but the moth darted beneath the hat. In its flight it came straight toward Mrs. Comstock. She snatched off the remnant of apron she had tucked into her petticoat band and held the calico before her. The moth struck full against it and clung to the goods. Pete crept up stealthily. The second moth followed the first, and the spray showered the apron.

"Wait!" gasped Mrs. Comstock. "I think they have settled. The books say they won't leave now."

The big pale yellow creature clung firmly, lowering and raising its wings. The other came nearer. Mrs. Comstock held the cloth with rigid hands, while Pete could hear her breathing in short gusts.

"Shall I try now?" he implored.

"Wait!" whispered the woman. "Something seems to say wait!"

The night breeze stiffened and gently waved the apron. Locusts rasped, mosquitoes hummed and frogs sang uninterruptedly. A musky odour slowly filled the air.

"Now shall I?" questioned Pete.

"No. Leave them alone. They are safe now. They are mine. They are my salvation. God and the Limberlost gave them to me! They won't move for hours. The books all say so. O Heavenly Father, I am thankful to You, and you, too, Pete Corson! You are a good man to help me. Now, I can go home and face my girl."

Instead, Mrs. Comstock dropped suddenly. She spread the apron across her knees. The moths were undisturbed. Then her tired white head dropped, the tears she had thought forever dried gushed forth, and she sobbed for pure joy.

"Oh, I wouldn't do that now, you know!" comforted Pete. "Think of getting two! That's more than you ever could have expected. A body would think you would cry, if you hadn't got any. Come on, now. It's almost morning. Let me help you home."

Pete took the bag and the two old lanterns. Mrs. Comstock carried her moths and the best lantern and went ahead to light the way.

Elnora had sat by her window far into the night. At last she undressed and went to bed, but sleep would not come. She had gone to the city to talk with members of the School Board about a room in the grades. There was a possibility that she might secure the moth, and so be able to start to college that fall, but if she did not, then she wanted the school. She had been given some encouragement, but she was so unhappy that nothing mattered. She could not see the way open to anything in life, while she remained with her mother, save a long series of disappointments. Yet Margaret Sinton had advised her to go home and try once more. Margaret had seemed so sure there would be a change for the better, that Elnora had consented, although she had no hope herself. So strong is the bond of blood, she could not make up her mind to seek a home elsewhere, even after the day which had passed. Unable to sleep she arose at last, and the room being warm, she sat on the floor by the window. The lights in the swamp caught her eye. She was very uneasy, for quite a hundred of her best moths were in the case. However, there was no money, and no one ever had touched a book or any of her apparatus. Watching the lights set her thinking, and before she realized it, she was in a panic or fear.

She hurried down the stairway softly calling her mother. There was no answer. She lightly stepped across the sitting room and looked in at the open door. There was no one, and the bed had not been used. Her first thought was that her mother had gone to the pool; and the Limberlost was alive with signals. Pity and fear mingled in the heart of the girl. She opened the kitchen door crossed the garden and ran back to the swamp. As she neared it she listened, but she could hear only the usual voices of night.

"Mother!" she called softly. Then louder, "Mother!"

There was not a sound. Chilled with fright she hurried back to the cabin. She did not know what to do. She understood what the lights in the Limberlost meant. Where was her mother? She was afraid to enter, while she was growing very cold and still more fearful about remaining outside. At last she went to her mother's room, picked up the gun, carried it into the kitchen, and crowding in a little corner behind the stove, she waited in trembling anxiety. The time was dreadfully long before she heard her mother's voice. Then she decided that someone had been ill and sent for her, so she took courage, and stepping swiftly across the kitchen she unbarred the door and drew back out of sight by the table.

Mrs. Comstock entered dragging her heavy feet. Her dress skirt was gone, her petticoat wet and drabbled, and the waist of her dress was almost torn from her body. Her hair hung in damp strings; her eyes were red with crying. In one hand she held the lantern, and in the other stiffly extended before her, on a wad of calico reposed a magnificent pair of yellow Emperors. Elnora stared, her lips parted.

"Shall I put these others in the kitchen?" inquired a man's voice.

The girl shrank back to the shadows.

"Yes, anywhere inside the door," replied Mrs. Comstock as she moved a few steps to make way for him. Pete's head appeared. He set down the moths and was gone.

"Thank you, Pete, more than ever woman thanked you before!" said Mrs. Comstock.

She placed the lantern on the table and barred the door. As she turned Elnora came into view. Mrs. Comstock leaned toward her, and held out the moths. In a voice vibrant with tones never before heard she said: "Elnora, my girl, mother's found you another moth!"

Wherein Mother Love Is Bestowed on Elnora, and She Finds an Assistant in Moth Hunting

Elnora awoke at dawn and lay gazing around the unfamiliar room. She noticed that every vestige of masculine attire and belongings were gone, and knew, without any explanation, what that meant. For some reason every tangible evidence of her father was banished, and she was at last to be allowed to take his place. She turned to look at her mother. Mrs. Comstock's face was white and haggard, but on it rested an expression of profound peace Elnora never before had seen. As she studied the features on the pillow beside her, the heart of the girl throbbed in tenderness. She realized as fully as any one else could what her mother had suffered. Thoughts of the night brought shuddering fear. She softly slipped from the bed, went to her room, dressed and entered the kitchen to attend the Emperors and prepare breakfast. The pair had been left clinging to the piece of calico. The calico was there and a few pieces of beautiful wing. A mouse had eaten the moths!

"Well, of all the horrible luck!" gasped Elnora.

With the first thought of her mother, she caught up the remnants of the moths, burying them in the ashes of the stove. She took the bag to her room, hurriedly releasing its contents, but there was not another yellow one. Her mother had said some had been confined in the case in the Limberlost. There was still a hope that an Emperor might be among them. She peeped at her mother, who still slept soundly.

Elnora took a large piece of mosquito netting, and ran to the swamp. Throwing it over the top of the case, she unlocked the door. She reeled, faint with distress. The living moths that had been confined there in their fluttering to escape to night and the mates they sought not only had wrecked the other specimens of the case, but torn themselves to ribbons on the pins. A third of the rarest moths of the collection for the man of India were antennaeless, legless, wingless, and often headless. Elnora sobbed, aloud.

At last she closed the door, dropped the netting, and sank on a log, staring before her with unseeing eyes, trying to think.

"This is overwhelming," she said at last. "It is making a fatalist of me. I am beginning to think things happen as they are ordained from the beginning, this plainly indicating that there is to be no college, at least, this year, for me. My life is all mountain-top or canyon. I wish someone would lead me into a few days of 'green pastures.' Last night I went to sleep on mother's arm, the moths all secured, love and college, certainties. This morning I wake to find all my hopes wrecked. I simply don't dare let mother know that instead of helping me, she has ruined my collection. Everything is gone!—unless the love lasts. That actually seemed true. I believe I will go see."

The love remained. Indeed, in the overflow of the long hardened, pent-up heart, the girl was almost suffocated with tempestuous caresses and generous offerings. Before the day was over, Elnora realized that she never had known her mother at all. The woman who now busily went through the cabin, her eyes bright, eager, alert, constantly planning, was a stranger. Her very face was different, while it did not seem possible that during one night the acid of twenty years could disappear from a voice and leave it sweet and pleasant.

For the next few days Elnora worked at mounting the moths her mother had taken. She had to go to the Bird Woman and tell about the disaster, but Mrs. Comstock was allowed to think that Elnora delivered the moths when she made the trip. If she had told her what actually happened, the chances were that Mrs.

Comstock again would have taken possession of the Limberlost, hunting there until she replaced all the moths that had been destroyed. But Elnora knew from experience what it meant to collect such a list in pairs. Valiant as she was in any good cause, this time she was compelled to admit that she was defeated. It would require hard work for at least two summers to replace the lost moths. When she left the Bird Woman she went to the president of the Onabasha schools and asked him to do all in his power to secure her a room in one of the ward buildings.

The next morning the last moth was mounted, and the house work finished. Elnora said to her mother, "If you don't mind, I believe I will go into the woods pasture beside Sleepy Snake creek and see if I can catch some dragon flies or moths."

"Wait until I get a knife and a pail and I will go along," answered Mrs. Comstock. "The dandelions are plenty tender for greens among the deep grasses, and I might just happen to see something myself. My eyes are pretty sharp."

"I wish you could realize how young you are," said Elnora. "I know women in Onabasha who are ten years older than you, yet they look twenty years younger. So could you, if you would dress your hair becomingly, and wear appropriate clothes."

"I think my hair puts me in the old woman class permanently," said Mrs. Comstock, but there was no bitterness in her voice.

"Well, it don't!" cried Elnora. "There is a woman of twenty-eight who has hair as white as yours from sick headaches, but her face is young and beautiful. If your face would grow a little fuller and those lines would go away, you'd be lovely!"

"You little pig!" laughed Mrs. Comstock. "Anyone would think you would be satisfied with having a splinter new mother, without setting up a kick on her looks, first thing. Greedy!"

"That is a good word," said Elnora. "I admit the charge. I am greedy over every wasted year. I want you young, lovely, prettily dressed and enjoying life like the other girls' mothers."

Mrs. Comstock laughed softly as she pushed back her sunbonnet so that shrubs and bushes along the way could be scanned closely. Elnora walked ahead with a case over her shoulder, a net in her hand. Her head was bare, the rolling collar of her lavendar gingham dress was cut in a V at the throat, the sleeves only reached the elbows. Every few steps she paused and examined the shrubbery carefully, while Mrs. Comstock was watching until her eyes ached, but there were no dandelions in the pail she carried.

Early June was rioting in fresh grasses, bright flowers, bird songs, and gay-winged creatures of air. Down the footpath the two went through the perfect morning, the love of God and all nature in their hearts. At last they reached the creek, following it toward the bridge. Here Mrs. Comstock found a large bed of tender dandelions and stopped to fill her pail. Then she sat on the bank, picking over the greens, while she listened to the creek softly singing its June song.

Elnora remained within calling distance, and was having good success. At last she crossed the creek, following it up to a bridge. There she began a careful examination of the under sides of the sleepers and flooring for cocoons. Mrs. Comstock could see her and the creek for several rods above. The mother sat beating the long green leaves across her hand, carefully picking out the white buds, because Elnora liked them, when a splash up the creek attracted her attention.

Around the bend came a man. He was bareheaded, dressed in a white sweater, and waders which reached his waist. He kept on the bank, only entering the water when necessary. He had a queer basket strapped on his hip, and with a small rod he sent a long line spinning before him down the creek, deftly manipulating with it a little floating object. He was nearer Elnora than her mother, but Mrs. Comstock thought possibly by hurrying she could remain unseen and yet warn the girl that a stranger was coming. Thrusting the greens into the pail she ran down the creek bank. As she neared the bridge, she caught a sapling and leaned over the water to call Elnora. With her lips parted to speak, she hesitated a second to watch a sort of insect that flashed past on the water, when a splash from the man attracted the girl.

She was under the bridge, one knee planted in the embankment and a foot braced to support her. Her hair was tousled by wind and bushes, her face flushed, and she lifted her arms above her head, working to loosen a cocoon she had found. The call Mrs. Comstock had intended to utter never found voice, for as

Elnora looked down at the sound, "Possibly I could get that for you," suggested the man.

Mrs. Comstock drew back. He was a young man with a wonderfully attractive face, although it was too white for robust health, broad shoulders, and slender upright frame.

"Oh, I do hope you can!" answered Elnora. "It's quite a find! It's one of those lovely pale red cocoons described in the books. I suspect it comes from having been in a dark place and screened from the weather."

"Is that so?" cried the man. "Wait a minute. I've never seen one. I suppose it's a Cecropia, from the location."

"Of course," said Elnora. "It's so cool here the moth hasn't emerged. The cocoon is a big, baggy one, and it is as red as fox tail."

"What luck!" he cried. "Are you making a collection?"

He reeled in his line, laid his rod across a bush and climbed the embankment to Elnora's side, produced a knife and began the work of whittling a deep groove around the cocoon.

"Yes. I paid my way through the high school in Onabasha with them. Now I am starting a collection which means college."

"Onabasha!" said the man. "That is where I am visiting." He paused to rest, for the bridge flooring was hard lumber, and the task he had set himself not easy. "Possibly you know my people— Dr. Ammon's? The doctor is my uncle. My home is in Chicago. I've been having typhoid fever, something fierce. In the hospital six weeks. Didn't gain strength right, so Uncle Doc sent for me. I am to live out of doors all summer, and exercise until I get in condition again. Do you know my uncle?"

"Yes. He is Aunt Margaret's doctor, and he would be ours, only we are never ill."

"Well, you look it!" said the man, appraising Elnora at a glance.

"Strangers always mention it," sighed Elnora. "I wonder how it would feel to be a pale languid lady and ride in a carriage."

"Ask me!" laughed the man. "It feels like the—dickens! I'm so proud of my feet. It's quite a trick to stand on them now. I have to keep out of the water all I can and stop to baby every half-mile. But with interesting outdoor work I'll be myself in a week."

"Do you call that work?" Elnora indicated the creek.

"I do, indeed! Nearly three miles, banks too soft to brag on and never a strike. Wouldn't you call that hard labour?"

"Yes," laughed Elnora. "Work at which you might kill yourself and never get a fish. Did anyone tell you there were trout in Sleepy Snake Creek?"

"Uncle said I could try."

"Oh, you can," said Elnora. "You can try no end, but you'll never get a trout. This is too far south and too warm for them. If you sit on the bank and use worms you might get some perch or catfish."

"But that isn't exercise."

"Well, if you only want exercise, go right on fishing. You can get a creel full of invisible results every night."

"I object," said the man emphatically. He stopped work again and studied Elnora. Even the watching mother could not blame him. Against the embankment, in the shade of the bridge Elnora's bright head, and her lavender dress made a picture worthy of much contemplation.

"I object!" repeated the man. "When I work I want to see results. I'd rather exercise sawing wood, making one pile grow little and the other big, than to cast all day and catch nothing because there is not a fish to take. Work for work's sake don't appeal to me. I work for results."

He dug the groove around the cocoon with skilled hand.

"Now there is some fun in this!" he said. "It's going to be a fair job to cut it out, but when it comes, it is not only beautiful, but worth a price; it will help you on your way. I think I'll put up that rod and hunt moths. That would be something like! Don't you want help?"

Elnora parried the question.

"Have you ever hunted moths, Mr. Ammon?"

"Enough to know the ropes in taking them, and to distinguish the commonest ones. I go wild on Catocalæ. There's too many of them, all too much alike for Philip, but I know all these fellows. One flew into my room when I was about ten years old, and we thought it a miracle. None of us ever had seen one so we took it over to the museum to Dr. Dorsey. He said they were common enough, but we didn't see them because they flew at night. He showed me the museum collection, and I was so interested I took mine back home and started to hunt them. Every year after that we went to our cottage a month earlier, so I could find them, and all my family helped. I stuck to it until I went to college. Then, keeping the little moths out of the big ones was too much for the mater, so father advised that I donate mine to the museum. He bought a fine case for them with my name on it, which constitutes my sole contribution to science. I know enough to help you all right."

"Aren't you going north this year?"

"All depends on how this fever leaves me. Uncle says the nights are too cold and the days too hot there for me. He thinks I had better stay in an even temperature until I am strong again. I am going to stick pretty close to him until I know I am. I wouldn't admit it to anyone at home, but I was almost gone. I don't believe anything can eat up nerve much faster than the burning of a slow fever. No, thanks, I have enough. I stay with Uncle Doc, so if I feel it coming again he can do something quickly."

"I don't blame you," said Elnora. "I never have been sick, but it must be dreadful. I am afraid you are tiring yourself over that. Let me take the knife awhile."

"Oh, it isn't so bad as that! I wouldn't be wading creeks if it were. I just need a few more days to get steady on my feet again. I'll have this cut out in a minute."

"It is kind of you to get it," said Elnora. "I should have had to peel it, which would spoil the cocoon, for a specimen and ruin the moth."

"You haven't said yet whether I may help you while I am here." Elnora hesitated.

"You better say 'yes,'" he persisted. "It would be a real kindness. It would keep me out doors all day and give an incentive to work. I'm good at it. I'll show you if I am not in a week or so. I can 'sugar,' manipulate lights, and mirrors, and all the expert methods. I'll wager moths are thick in the old swamp over there."

"They are," said Elnora. "Most I have I took there. A few nights ago my mother caught a good many, but we don't dare go alone."

"All the more reason why you need me. Where do you live? I can't get an answer from you, I'll just go tell your mother who I am and ask her if I may help you. I warn you, young lady, I have a very effective way with mothers. They almost never turn me down."

"Then it's probable you will have a new experience when you meet mine," said Elnora. "She never was known to do what anyone expected she surely would."

The cocoon came loose. Philip Ammon stepped down the embankment turning to offer his hand to Elnora. She ran down as she would have done alone, and taking the cocoon turned it end for end to learn if the imago it contained was alive. Then Ammon took back the cocoon to smooth the edges. Mrs. Comstock gave them one long look as they stood there, and returned to her dandelions. She began the cleaning process all over again. While she worked she paused occasionally, listening intently. Presently they came down the creek, the man carrying the cocoon as if it were a jewel, while Elnora made her way along the bank, taking a lesson in casting. Her face was flushed with excitement, her eyes shining, the bushes taking liberties with her hair. For a picture of perfect loveliness she scarcely could have been surpassed, and the eyes of Philip Ammon seemed to be in working order.

"Moth-er!" called Elnora.

There was an undulent, caressing sweetness in the girl's voice, as she sung out the call in perfect confidence that it would bring a loving answer, that struck deep in Mrs. Comstock's heart. She never had heard that word so pronounced before and a lump rose in her throat.

"Here!" she answered.

She went on examining the dandelion leaves.

"Mother, this is Mr. Philip Ammon, of Chicago," said Elnora. "He has been ill and he is staying with Dr. Ammon in Onabasha. He came fishing down the creek and cut this cocoon from under the bridge for me. He feels that it would be better to hunt moths than to fish, until he gets well. What do you think about it?"

Philip Ammon extended his hand.

"I am glad to know you," he said.

"You may take the hand-shaking for granted," replied Mrs. Comstock. "Dandelions have a way of making the fingers sticky, and I like to know a man before I take his hand, anyway. That introduction seems mighty comprehensive on your part, but it still leaves me unclassified. My name is Comstock."

Philip bowed.

"I am sorry to hear you have been sick," said Mrs. Comstock. "But if people will live where they have such vile water as they do in Chicago, I don't see what else they are to expect."

Ammon studied her intently.

"I am sure I didn't have a fever on purpose," he said.

"You do seem a little wobbly on your legs," she observed. "Maybe you had better sit and rest while I finish these greens. It's late for the genuine article, but in the shade, among long grass they are still tender."

"May I have a leaf?" asked Ammon reaching for one as he sat on the bank, looking from the little creek at his feet, away through the dim cool spaces of the June forest on the opposite side. He drew a deep breath. "Glory, but this is good after almost two months inside hospital walls!"

He stretched on the grass and lay gazing up at the leaves, occasionally asking the interpretation of a bird note or the origin of an unfamiliar forest voice. Elnora began helping with the dandelions.

"Another, please," said the young man, holding out his hand.

"Do you suppose this is the kind of grass Nebuchadnezzar ate?" she asked, giving the leaf.

"He knew a good thing if it is."

"Oh, you should taste dandelions boiled with bacon and accompanied by mother's especial brand of cornbread."

"Don't! My appetite is twice my size now. While it is—how far is it to Onabasha, shortest cut?"

"Three miles."

The man lay in perfect content, nibbling leaves.

"This surely is a treat," he said. "No wonder you find good hunting here. There seems to be foliage for almost every kind of caterpillar. But I suppose you have to exchange for northern species and Pacific Coast kinds?"

"Yes. And everyone wants Regalis in trade. I never saw the like. They consider a Cecropia or a Polyphemus an insult, and a Luna is barely acceptable."

"What authorities have you?"

Elnora began to name text-books which started a discussion. Mrs. Comstock listened. She cleaned dandelions with greater deliberation than they ever before were examined. In reality she was taking stock of the young man's long, well-proportioned frame, his strong hands, his smooth, fine-textured skin, his thick shock of dark hair, and making mental notes of his simple manly speech and the fact that he evidently did know a great deal about moths. It pleased her to think that if he had been a neighbour boy who had lain beside her every day of his life while she worked, he could have been no more at home. She liked the things he said, but she was proud that Elnora had a ready answer which always seemed appropriate.

At last Mrs. Comstock finished the greens.

"You are three miles from the city and less than a mile from where we live," she said. "If you will tell me what you dare eat, I suspect you had best go home with us and rest until the cool of the day before you start back. Probably some one that you can ride in with will be passing before evening."

"That is mighty kind of you," said Philip. "I think I will. It don't matter so much what I eat, the point is that I must be moderate. I am hungry all the time."

"Then we will go," said Mrs. Comstock, "and we will not allow you to make yourself sick with us."

Philip Ammon was on his feet. Picking up the pail of greens and his fishing rod he stood waiting. Elnora led the way. Mrs. Comstock motioned Philip to follow and she walked in the rear. The girl carried the cocoon and the box of moths she had taken, searching every step for more. The young man frequently set down his load to join in the pursuit of a dragon fly or moth, while Mrs. Comstock watched the proceedings with sharp eyes. Every time Philip picked up the pail of greens she struggled to suppress a smile.

Elnora proceeded slowly chattering about everything along the trail. Philip was interested in all the objects she pointed out, noticing several things which escaped her. He carried the greens just as casually when they took a short cut down the roadway as along the trail. When Elnora turned toward the gate of her home Philip Ammon stopped, took a long look at the big hewed log cabin, the vines which clambered over it, the flower garden ablaze with beds of bright bloom interspersed with strawberries and tomatoes, the trees of the forest rising north and west like a green wall and exclaimed, "How beautiful!"

Mrs. Comstock was pleased. "If you think that," she said, "perhaps you will understand, how in all this present-day rush to be modern, I have preferred to remain as I began. My husband and I took up this land, and enough trees to build the cabin, stable, and out buildings are about all we ever cut. Of course, if he had lived, I suppose we should have kept with our neighbours. I hear considerable about the value of the land, the trees which are on it, and the oil which is supposed to be under it, but, as yet I haven't brought myself to change anything. So we stand for one of the few remaining homes of first settlers in this region. Come in. You are very welcome to what we have."

Mrs. Comstock stepped forward and took the lead. She had a bowl of soft water and a pair of boots to offer for the heavy waders, for outer comfort, a glass of cold buttermilk and a bench on which to rest, in the circular arbour until dinner was ready. Philip Ammon splashed in the water. He followed to the stable and exchanged boots there. He was ravenous for the buttermilk, and when he stretched on the bench in the arbour the flickering patches of sunlight so tantalized his tired eyes, while the bees made such splendid music, he was soon sound asleep.

When Elnora and her mother came out with a table they stood a short time looking at him. It is probable Mrs. Comstock voiced a united thought when she said, "What a refined, decent looking young man! How proud his mother must be of him! We must be careful what we let him eat."

Then they returned to the kitchen where Mrs. Comstock proceeded to be careful. She broiled ham of her own sugar-curing, creamed potatoes, served asparagus on toast, and made a delicious strawberry shortcake. As she cooked dandelions with bacon, she feared to serve them to him, so she made an excuse that it took too long to prepare them, blanched some, and made a salad. When everything was ready she touched Ammon's sleeve.

"Best have something to eat, lad, before you get too hungry," she said.

"Please, hurry!" he begged laughingly as he held a plate toward her to be filled. "I thought I had enough self-restraint to start out alone, but I see I was mistaken. If you would allow me, just now, I am afraid I should start a fever again. I never did smell food so good as this. It's mighty kind of you to take me in. I hope I will be man enough in a few days to do something worth while in return."

Spots of sunshine fell on the white cloth and blue china, the bees and an occasional stray butterfly came searching for food. A rose-breasted grosbeak, released from a three hours' siege of brooding, while his independent mate took her bath and recreation, mounted the top branch of a maple in the west woods from which he serenaded the dinner party with a joyful chorus in celebration of his freedom. Ammon's eyes strayed to the beautiful cabin, to the mixture of flowers and vegetables stretching down to the road, and to the singing bird with his red-splotched breast of white and he said, "I can't realize now that I ever lay in ice packs in a hospital. How I wish all the sick folks could come here to grow strong!"

The grosbeak sang on, a big Turnus butterfly sailed through the arbour and poised over the table. Elnora held up a lump of sugar and the butterly, clinging to her fingers, tasted daintily. With eager eyes and parted lips, the girl held steadily. When at last it wavered away, "That made a picture!" said Ammon. "Ask me some other time how I lost my illusions concerning butterflies. I always thought of them in connection with sunshine, flower pollen, and fruit nectar, until one sad day."

"I know!" laughed Elnora. "I've seen that, too, but it didn't destroy any illusion for me. I think just as much of the butterflies as ever."

Then they talked of flowers, moths, dragon flies, Indian relics, and all the natural wonders the swamp afforded, straying from those subjects to books and school work. When they cleared the table Ammon assisted, carrying several tray loads to the kitchen. He and Elnora mounted specimens while Mrs. Comstock washed the dishes. Then she came out with a ruffle she was embroidering.

"I wonder if I did not see a picture of you in Onabasha, last night," Ammon said to Elnora. "Aunt Anna took me to call on Miss Brownlee. She was showing me her crowd—of course, it was you!

But it didn't half do you justice, although it looked the nearest human of any of them. Miss Brownlee is very fond of you. She said the finest things."

Then they talked of Commencement, and at last Ammon said he must go or his friends would become anxious about him.

Mrs. Comstock brought him a blue bowl of creamy milk and a plate of bread. She stopped a passing team and secured a ride to the city for him, as his exercise of the morning had been a little too violent, and he was forced to admit he was tired.

"May I come to-morrow afternoon and chase moths awhile?" he asked Mrs. Comstock as he arose. "We will 'sugar' a tree and put a light by it, if I can get stuff to make the preparation. Possibly we can take some that way. I always enjoy moth hunting, I'd like to help Miss Elnora, and it would be a charity to me. I've got to remain outdoors some place, and I'm quite sure I'd get well faster here than anywhere else. Please say I may come."

"I have no objections, if Elnora really would like help," said Mrs. Comstock.

In her heart she wished he would not. She wanted her newly found treasure all to herself, for a time, at least. But Elnora's were eager, shining eyes. She thought it would be splendid to have help, and great fun to try book methods for taking moths, so it was arranged. As Ammon rode away, Mrs. Comstock's eyes followed him. "What a nice young man!" she said.

"IIe seems fine," agreed Elnora.

"He comes of a good family, too. I've often heard of his father. He is a great lawyer."

"I am glad he likes it here. I need help. Possibly—"

"Possibly what?"

"We can get a great many moths."

"What did he mean about the butterflies?"

"That he always had connected them with sunshine, flowers, and fruits, and thought of them as the most exquisite of creations; then one day he found some clustering thickly over carrion."

"Come to think of it, I have seen butterflies—"

"So had he," laughed Elnora, "and that is what he meant."

CHAPTER
14

*Wherein a New Position Is
Tendered Elnora,
and Philip Ammon
Is Shown Limberlost Violets*

The next morning Mrs. Comstock called to Elnora, "The mail carrier stopped at our box."

Elnora ran down the walk and came back carrying an official looking letter. She tore it open and read:

My Dear Miss Comstock:

At the weekly meeting of the Onabasha School Board last night, it was decided to add the position of Lecturer on Natural History to our corps of city teachers. It will be the duty of this person to spend two hours a week in each of the grade schools exhibiting and explaining specimens of the most prominent objects in nature; animals, birds, insects, flowers, vines, shrubs, bushes, and trees. These specimens and lectures should be appropriate to the seasons and the comprehension of the grades. This position was unanimously voted to you. I think you will find the work delightful and much easier than the routine grind of the other teachers. It is my advice that you accept and begin to prepare yourself at once. Your salary will be $750 a year, and you will be allowed $200 for expenses in procuring specimens and books. Let us know at once if you want the position, as it is going to be difficult to fill satisfactorily if you do not.

Very truly yours,

David Thompson, President, Onabasha Schools.

"I hardly understand," marvelled Mrs. Comstock.

"It is a new position. They never have had anything like it before. I suspect it arose from the help I've been giving the grade teachers in their nature work. They are trying to teach the children something, and half the instructors don't know a blue jay from a kingfisher, a beech leaf from an elm, or a wasp from a hornet."

"Well, do you?" anxiously inquired Mrs. Comstock.

"Indeed, I do!" laughed Elnora, "and several other things beside. When Freckles bequeathed me the swamp, he gave me a bigger inheritance than he knew. While you have thought I was wandering aimlessly, I have been following a definite plan, studying hard, and storing up the stuff that will earn these seven hundred and fifty dollars. Mother, dear, I am going to accept this, of course. The work will be a delight. I'd love it most of anything in teaching. You must help me. We must find nests, eggs, leaves, queer formations in plants and rare flowers. I must have flower boxes made for each of the rooms and filled with wild things. I should begin to gather specimens this very day."

Elnora was on her feet. Her face was flushed and her eyes bright.

"Oh, what great work that will be!" she cried. "You must go with me so you can see the little faces when I tell them how the goldfinch builds its nest, and how the bees make honey."

So Elnora and her mother went into the woods behind the cabin to study nature.

"I think," said Elnora, "the idea is to begin with fall things in the fall, keeping to the seasons throughout the year."

"What are fall things?" inquired Mrs. Comstock.

"Oh, fringed gentians, asters, ironwort, every fall flower, leaves from every tree and vine, what makes them change colour, abandoned bird nests, winter quarters of caterpillars and insects, what becomes of the butterflies and grasshoppers—just myriads of stuff. I never can use the half there will be to show. I shall have to be very wise to select the things it will be most beneficial for the children to learn."

"Can I really help you?" Mrs. Comstock's strong face was pathetic.

"Indeed, yes!" cried Elnora. "I never can get through it alone. There will be an immense amount of work connected with securing and preparing specimens."

Mrs. Comstock lifted her head proudly and began doing business at once. Her sharp eyes ranged from earth to heaven. She investigated everything, asking innumerable questions. By noon she was as eager and interested as Elnora. The morning was filled with happiness for both of them. Near noon Mrs. Comstock took the specimens they had collected, and went to prepare dinner, while Elnora followed the woods down to Sintons' to show her letter.

She had to explain what became of her moths, and why college would have to be abandoned for that year, but Margaret and Wesley vowed not to tell. Wesley waved the letter excitedly, explaining it to Margaret as if it was a personal possession. Margaret was deeply impressed, while Billy volunteered first aid in gathering material.

"Now, anything you want in the ground, Snap can dig it out," he said. "Uncle Wesley and I found a hole three times as big as Snap, that he dug at the roots of a tree."

"We will train him to hunt pupae cases," said Elnora.

"Are you going to the woods this afternoon?" asked Billy.

"Yes," answered Elnora. "Dr. Ammon's nephew from Chicago is visiting in Onabasha. He is going to show me how men put some sort of compound on a tree, hang a light by it, and take moths that way. It will be interesting to watch and learn."

"May I come?" asked Billy.

"Of course, you may come!" answered Elnora.

"Is this nephew of Dr. Ammon a young man?" inquired Margaret.

"About twenty-six, I should think," said Elnora. "He said he had been out of college and at work in his father's law office three years."

"Does he seem nice?" asked Margaret, and Wesley smiled.

"Finest kind of a person," said Elnora. "He can teach me so much. It is very interesting to hear him talk. He knows considerable about moths that will be a help to me. He had a fever and he has to stay outdoors until he grows strong again."

"Billy, I guess you better help me this afternoon," said Margaret. "Maybe Elnora had rather not bother with you."

"There's no reason on earth why Billy should not come!" cried Elnora, and Wesley smiled again.

"I must hurry home and get my dinner or I won't be ready," she added.

Hastening down the road with glowing face she entered the cabin.

"I thought you never would come," said Mrs. Comstock. "If you don't hurry Mr. Ammon will be here before you get dressed."

"I forgot about him until just now," said Elnora. "I am not going to dress. He's not coming to visit. We are only going to the woods for more specimens. I can't wear anything that requires care. The limbs take the most dreadful liberties with hair and clothing."

Mrs. Comstock opened her lips, looked at Elnora and closed them. In her heart she was pleased that the girl was so interested in her work that she had forgotten Philip Ammon's coming. But it did seem to her that such a pleasant young man should have been greeted by a girl in a fresh dress. "If she isn't disposed to primp at the coming of a man, heaven forbid that I should be the one to start her," thought Mrs. Comstock. So she did the primping in honour of the occasion. It consisted of a fresh gingham dress and hair coiled a little more loosely than usual.

Ammon came whistling down the walk between the cinnamon pinks, pansies, and strawberries. He carried several packages, while his face flushed with more colour than on the previous day.

"Only see what has happened to me!" cried Elnora, offering her letter.

"I'll wager I know!" answered Ammon. "Isn't it great! Everyone in Onabasha is talking about it. At last there is something new under the sun. All of them are pleased. They think you'll make a big success. This will give an incentive to work. In a few days more I'll be myself again, and we'll overturn the fields and woods around here."

He went on to congratulate Mrs. Comstock.

"Aren't you proud of her, though?" he asked. "You should hear what folks are saying! They say she created the necessity for the position, and everyone seems to feel that it is a necessity. Now, if she succeeds, and she will, all of the other city schools will have such departments, and first thing you know she will have made the whole world just a little better. Let me rest a few seconds; my feet are acting up again. Then we will cook the compound and put it to cool."

He laughed as he sat breathing shortly.

"It doesn't seem possible that a fellow could lose his strength like this. My knees are actually trembling, but I'll be all right in a minute. Uncle Doc said I could come. I told him how you took care of me, and he said I would be safe here."

Then he began unwrapping packages and explaining to Mrs. Comstock how to cook the compound to attract the moths. He followed her into the kitchen, kindled the fire, and stirred the preparation as he talked. While the mixture cooled, he and Elnora walked through the vegetable garden behind the cabin and strayed from there into the woods.

"What about college?" he asked. "Miss Brownlee said you were going."

"I had hoped to," replied Elnora, "but I had a streak of dreadful luck, so I'll have to wait until next year. If you won't speak of it I'll tell you."

Ammon promised, and Elnora recited the history of the yellow Emperor. She was so interested in doing the Emperor justice she did not notice how many personalities went into the story. A few pertinent questions told Ammon the rest. He looked at the girl in wonder. In face and form she was as lovely as any one of her age and type he ever had seen. Her school work far surpassed that of most girls of her age he knew. She differed in other ways. This vast store of learning she had gathered from field and forest was a wealth of attraction no other girl possessed. Her frank, matter-of-fact manner was an inheritance from her mother, but there was something more. Once, as they talked he thought "sympathy" was the word to describe it and again "comprehension." She seemed to possess a large sense of brotherhood for all human and animate creatures. She spoke to him as if she had known him all her life. She talked to the grosbeak in exactly the same manner, as she laid strawberries and potato bugs on the fence for his family. She did not swerve an inch from her way when a snake slid by her, while the squirrels came down from the trees and took corn from her fingers. She might as well have been a boy, so lacking was she in any touch of feminine coquetry toward him. He studied her wonderingly.

As they went along the path they reached a large slime-covered pool surrounded by decaying stumps and logs thickly covered with water hyacinths and blue flags. Ammon stopped.

"Is that the place?" he asked.

Elnora assented.

"The doctor told you?"

"Yes. It was tragic. Is that pool really bottomless?"

"So far as we ever have been able to discover."

Ammon stood looking at the water, while the long, sweet grasses, thickly sprinkled with blue flag bloom, over which wild bees clambered, swayed around his feet. Then he turned to the girl. She had worked hard. The same lavender dress she had worn the previous day clung to her in limp condition. But she was as evenly coloured and of as fine grain as a wild rose petal, her hair was really brown, but never was such hair touched with a redder glory, while her heavy arching brows added a look of strength to her big gray-blue eyes.

"And you were born here?"

He had not intended to voice that thought.

"Yes," she said looking into his eyes. "Just in time to prevent my mother from saving the life of my father. She came near never forgiving me."

"Ah, cruel!" cried Ammon.

"I find a great deal in life that is cruel, from our standpoints," said Elnora. "It takes the large wisdom of the Unfathomable, the philosophy of the Almighty, to bear some of it. But there is always right somewhere, and at last it seems to come."

"Will it come to you?" asked Ammon, who found himself suffering intensely.

"It has come," said the girl serenely. "It came a week ago. It came in fullest measure when my mother ceased to regret that I had been born. Now, work that I love has come—that should constitute happiness. A little farther along is my violet bed. I want you to see it."

As Philip Ammon followed he definitely settled upon the name of the unusual feature of Elnora's face. It should be called "experience." She had known hard experiences early in life. Suffering had been her familiar more than joy. He watched her with intense earnestness, his heart deeply moved. She led him into a swampy half-open space in the woods, stopped and stepped aside. Ammon uttered a cry of surprised delight.

A few decaying logs were scattered around, the grass grew in tufts long and fine. Blue flags waved, clusters of cowslips nodded gold heads, but the whole earth was purple with a thick blanket of violets nodding from stems a foot in length. Elnora knelt and slipping her fingers through the leaves and grasses to the roots, gathered a few violets and gave them to Philip.

"Can your city greenhouses surpass them?" she asked.

Ammon sat on a log to examine the blooms.

"They are superb!" he said. "I never saw such length of stem or such rank leaves, while the flowers are the deepest blue, the truest violet I ever saw growing wild. They are coloured exactly like the eyes of the girl I am going to marry."

Elnora handed him several others to add to those he held.

"She must have wonderful eyes," she commented.

"No other blue eyes are quite so beautiful," he said. "In fact, she is altogether lovely."

"It is customary for a man to think the girl he is going to marry lovely. I wonder if I should find her so."

"You would," said Ammon. "No one ever fails to. She is tall as you, very slender, but perfectly rounded; you know about her eyes; her hair is black and wavy—while her complexion is clear and flushed with red."

Elnora knelt among the flowers as she looked at him.

"Why, she must be the most beautiful girl in the whole world!" she cried.

Ammon laughed.

"No, indeed!" he said. "She is not a particle better looking in her way than you are in yours. She is a type of dark beauty, but you are just as perfect. She is unusual in her combination of black hair and violet eyes, although everyone thinks them black at a little distance. You are quite as unusual with your fair face, black brows and brown hair; indeed, I know many people who would prefer your bright head to her dark one. It's all a question of taste—and being engaged to the girl," he added.

"That would be likely to prejudice one," laughed Elnora.

"Edith has a birthday soon; if these last will you let me have a box of them to send her?"

"I will help gather and pack them for you, so they will carry nicely. Does she hunt moths with you?"

Back went Philip Ammon's head in a gale of laughter.

"No!" he cried. "She says they are 'creepy.' She would scream herself into a spasm if she were compelled to touch those young caterpillars I saw you handling yesterday."

"Why would she?" marvelled Elnora. "Haven't you told her that they are perfectly clean, helpless, and harmless as so much animate velvet?"

"No, I have not told her. She wouldn't care enough about caterpillars to listen."

"In what is she interested?"

"What interests Edith Carr? Let me think! First, I believe she takes pride in being just a little handsomer and better dressed than any girl of her set. She is interested in having a beautiful home, fine appointments about her, in being petted, praised, and the acknowledged leader of society. She likes to find new things which amuse her, and to always and in all circumstances have her own way about everything."

"Good gracious!" cried Elnora, staring at him. "But what does she do? How does she spend her time?"

"'Spend her time!'" repeated Ammon. "Well, she would call that a joke. Her days are never long enough. There is endless shopping, to find the pretty things; regular visits to the dressmakers, calls, parties, theatres, entertainments. She is always rushed. I never get to see half as much of her as I would like."

"But I mean work," persisted Elnora. "In what is she interested that is useful to the world?"

"Me!" cried Ammon promptly.

"I can understand that," laughed Elnora. "What I can't understand is how you can be in—" She stopped short in confusion, but she saw that he had finished the sentence as she had intended. "I beg your pardon!" she cried. "I didn't mean to say that. But I cannot understand these people I hear about who live only for their own amusement. Perhaps it is very great; I'll never have a chance to know. To me, it seems the only pleasure in this world worth having is the joy we get out of living for those we love, and those we can help. I hope you are not angry with me."

Ammon sat silently looking far away, with deep thought in his eyes.

"You are angry," faltered Elnora.

His look came back to her as she knelt before him among the flowers and he gazed at her steadily.

"No doubt I should be," he said, "but the fact is I am not. I cannot understand a life purely for personal pleasure myself. But she is only a girl, and this is her playtime. When she is a woman in her own home, then she will be different, will she not?"

Elnora never resembled her mother so closely as when she answered that question.

"I would have to be well acquainted with her to know, but I should hope so. To make a real home for a tired business man is a very different kind of work from that required to be a leader of society. It demands different talent and education. Of course, she means to change, or she would not have promised to make a home for you. I suspect our dope is cool now, let's go try for some butterflies."

As they went back along the path together Elnora talked of many things but Ammon answered absently. Evidently he was thinking of something else. But the moth bait recalled him and he was ready for work as they made their way back to the woods. He wanted to try the Limberlost, but Elnora was firm about keeping on home ground. She did not tell him that lights hung in the swamp would be a signal to call up a band of men whose presence she dreaded. So they set out, Ammon carrying the dope, Elnora the net, Billy and Mrs. Comstock following with cyanide boxes and lanterns.

First they tried for butterflies and captured several fine ones with little trouble. They also called swarms of ants, beetles, bees, and flies. When it grew dusk, Mrs. Comstock and Ammon went to prepare supper. Elnora and Billy remained until the butterflies went to bed. Then they lighted the lanterns, repainted the trees and followed the home trail.

"Do you 'spect you'll get just a lot of moths?" asked Billy, as he walked beside Elnora.

"I am sure I hardly know," said the girl. "This is a new way for me. Perhaps they will come to the lights, but few moths eat; and I have some doubt about those which the lights attract settling on the right trees. Maybe the smell of that dope will draw them. Between us, Billy, I think I like the old way best. If I can find a hidden moth, slip up and catch it unawares, or take it in full flight, it's my captive, and I can keep it until it dies naturally. But this way you seem to get it under false pretences, it has no chance, and it will probably ruin its wings struggling for freedom before morning."

"Well, any moth ought to be proud to be taken anyway, by you," said Billy. "Just look what you do! You can make everybody love them. People even quit hating caterpillars when they see you handle them and hear you tell all about them. You just must have some to show people how they are. It's not like killing things to see if you can, or because you want to eat them, the way most men kill birds. I think it is right for you to take enough for collections, to show city people, and to illustrate the Bird Woman's books. You go on and take them! The moths don't care. They're glad to have you. They like it!"

"Billy, I see your future," said Elnora. "We will educate you and send you up to Mr. Ammon to make a great lawyer. You'd beat the world as a special pleader. You actually make me feel that I am doing the moths a kindness to take them."

"And so you are!" cried Billy. "Why, just from what you have taught them, Uncle Wesley and Aunt Margaret never think of killing a caterpillar until they look whether it's the beautiful June moth kind, or the horrid tent ones. That's what you can do. You just go ahead!"

"Billy, you are a jewel!" cried Elnora, throwing her arm across his shoulders as they came down the path.

"My, I was scared!" said Billy with a deep breath.

"Scared?" questioned Elnora.

"Yes, sir-ee! Aunt Margaret scared me. May I ask you a question?"

"Of course, you may!"

"Is that man going to be your beau?"

"Billy! No! What made you think such a thing?"

"Aunt Margaret said likely he would fall in love with you, and you wouldn't want me around any more. Oh, but I was scared! It isn't so, is it?"

"Indeed, no!"

"I am your beau, ain't I?"

"Surely you are!" said Elnora, tightening her arm.

"I do hope Aunt Kate has ginger cookies," said Billy with a little skip of delight.

CHAPTER
15

Wherein Mrs. Comstock Faces the Almighty, and Philip Ammon Writes a Letter

Mrs. Comstock and Elnora were finishing breakfast the next morning when they heard a cheery whistle down the road. Elnora with surprised eyes looked at her mother.

"Could that be Mr. Ammon?" she questioned.

"I did not expect him so soon," commented Mrs. Comstock.

It was just sunrise, but the musician was Philip Ammon. He looked stronger than yesterday.

"I hope I am not too early," he said. "I am consumed with anxiety to learn if we have made a catch. If we have, we should beat the birds to it. I promised Uncle Doc to put on my waders and keep dry for a few days yet, when I go to the woods. Let's hurry! I am afraid of crows. There might be a rare moth."

The sun was topping the Limberlost when they started. As they neared the place Ammon stopped.

"Now we must use great caution," he said. "The lights and the odours always attract numbers that don't settle on the baited trees. Every bush, shrub, and limb may hide a specimen we want."

So they approached with much care.

"There is something, anyway!" cried Ammon, who was leading the way.

"There are moths! I can see them!" exulted Elnora.

"Those you see are fast enough. It's the ones for which you

must search that will get away. The grasses are dripping, and I have boots, so you look along the path while I take the outside," suggested Ammon.

Mrs. Comstock wanted to hunt moths, but she was timid about making a wrong movement, so she wisely sat on a log and watched Ammon and Elnora to learn how they proceeded. Back in the deep woods a hermit thrush was singing his chant to the rising sun. Orioles were sowing the pure, sweet air with notes of gold, poured out while on wing. The robins were only chirping now, for their morning songs had awakened all the other birds an hour ago. Scolding red-wings tilted on half the bushes. Excepting late species of haws, tree bloom was almost gone, but wild flowers made the path border and all the wood floor a riot of colour. Elnora, born among such scenes, worked eagerly, but to the city man, shortly from a hospital, they seemed too good to miss. He frequently stooped to examine a flower face, paused to listen intently to the thrush or lifted his head to see the gold flash which accompanied the oriole's trailing notes. So Elnora uttered the first cry, as she softly lifted branches and peered among the grasses.

"My find!" she called. "Bring the box, mother!"

Ammon came hurrying also. When they reached her she stood on the path holding a pair of moths. Her eyes were wide with excitement, her cheeks pink, her red lips parted, and on the hand she held out to them clung a pair of delicate blue-green moths, with white bodies, and touches of lavender and straw colour. All about her lay flower-brocaded grasses, behind the deep green background of the forest, while the sun slowly sifted gold from heaven to burnish her hair. Mrs. Comstock heard a sharp breath behind her.

"Oh, what a picture!" exulted Ammon at her shoulder. "She is absolutely and altogether lovely! I'd give a small fortune for that faithfully set on canvas!"

He picked the box from Mrs. Comstock's fingers and slowly advanced with it. Elnora held down her hand and transferred the moths. Ammon closed the box carefully, but the watching mother saw that his eyes were following the girl's face. He was not making the slightest attempt to conceal what he felt.

"I wonder if a woman ever did anything lovelier than to find a pair of Luna moths on a forest path, early on a perfect June morning," he said to Mrs. Comstock, as he returned the box.

She glanced at Elnora. The girl had gone back to work, and was intently searching the bushes.

"Look here, young man," said Mrs. Comstock. "You seem to find that girl of mine about right."

"I could suggest no improvement," said Ammon. "I never saw a more attractive girl anywhere. She seems absolutely perfect to me."

"Then suppose you don't start any scheme calculated to spoil her!" suggested Mrs. Comstock dryly. "I don't think you can, or that any man could, but I'm not taking any risks. You asked to come here to help in this work. We are both glad to have you, if you confine yourself to work; but it's the least you can do to leave us as you find us."

"I beg your pardon!" said Ammon. "I intended no offence. I admire her as I admire any perfect creation."

"And nothing in all this world spoils the average girl so quickly and so surely," said Mrs. Comstock. She raised her voice. "Elnora, fasten up that tag of hair over your left ear. These bushes muss you so you remind me of a sheep poking its nose through a hedge fence."

Mrs. Comstock started down the path toward her log again, and as she reached it she called sharply, "Elnora, come here! I believe I have found something myself."

The "something" was a Citheronia Regalis which had just emerged from its case on the soft earth by the log. It climbed up the wood, its stout legs dragging a big pursy body, while it wildly flapped tiny wings the size of a man's thumb-nail. Elnora gave one look and a cry which brought Ammon.

"That's the rarest moth in America!" he announced. "Mrs. Comstock, you've gone up head. You can put that in a box with a screen cover to-night, and attract a half-dozen, possibly."

"Is it rare, Elnora?" inquired Mrs. Comstock as if no one else knew.

"It surely is," answered Elnora. "If we can find it a mate to-night, it will lay from two hundred and fifty to three hundred eggs to-morrow. With any luck at all I can raise two hundred caterpillars from them. I did once before. And they are worth a dollar apiece."

"Was the one I killed like that?" gasped Mrs. Comstock.

"No. That was a different moth, but its life processes were the same as this. The Bird Woman calls this the King of the Poets."

"Why does she?"

"Because it is named for Citheron who was a poet, and regalis refers to king. You mustn't touch it or you may stunt wing development. You watch and don't let that moth out of sight, or anything come near it. When the wings are expanded and hardened we will put it in a box."

"I am afraid it will race itself to death," objected Mrs. Comstock.

"That's a part of the game," said Ammon. "It is starting circulation now. When the right moment comes, it will stop and develop its wings. If you watch closely you can see them expand."

Presently the moth found a rough projection of bark and clung with its feet, back down, its wings hanging. The body was an unusual orange red, the tiny wings were gray, striped with the red and splotched here and there with markings of canary yellow. Mrs. Comstock watched breathlessly. Presently she slipped off the log and knelt to get a better view.

"Are its wings growing?" called Elnora.

"They are getting larger and the markings coming stronger every minute."

"Let's watch, too," said Elnora to Ammon.

They came and looked over Mrs. Comstock's shoulder. Lower drooped the gray wings, wider they spread, brighter grew the markings as if laid off in geometrical patterns. They could hear Mrs. Comstock's tense breath and see her absorbed expression.

"Young people," she said solemnly, "if your studying science and the elements has ever led you to feel that things just happen, kind of evolve by chance, as it were, this sight will be good for you. Maybe earth and air accumulate, but it takes the wisdom of the Almighty God to devise the wing of a moth. If there ever was a miracle, this whole process is one. Now, as I understand it, this creature is going to keep on spreading those wings, until they grow to size and harden to strength sufficient to bear its body. Then it flies away, mates with its kind, lays its eggs on the leaves of a certain tree, and the eggs hatch tiny caterpillars which eat just that kind of leaves, and the worms grow and grow, and take on different forms and colours until at last they are big caterpillars six inches long, with large horns. Then they burrow into the earth, build a house around themselves from material which is inside them, and lie through rain and freezing cold for months. A year from egg laying they come out like this, and begin the process all over again. They don't eat, they don't see distinctly, they live but a few days and fly only at night; then they drop off easy, but the process goes on."

A shivering movement went over the moth. The wings drooped and spread wider. Mrs. Comstock fell into soft awed tones.

"There never was a moment in my life," she said, "when I felt so in the Presence, as I do now. I feel as if the Almighty was so real, and so near, that I could reach out and touch Him, as I could this wonderful work of His, if I dared. I feel like saying to Him, 'To the extent of my brain power I realize Your presence, and all it is in me to comprehend of Your power. Help me to learn, even this late, the lessons of Your wonderful creations. Help me to unshackle and expand my soul to the fullest realization of *Your* wonders. Almighty God, make me bigger, make me broader!'"

The moth climbed to the end of the projection, up it a little way, then suddenly reversed its wings, turning the hidden sides out and dropping them along its abdomen, like a great fly. The outside of the wings, thus exposed, was far richer colour, more exquisite texture than the under, and they slowly half lifted and drooped again. Mrs. Comstock turned her face to Ammon.

"Am I an old fool, or do you feel it, too?" she half whispered.

"You are wiser than you ever have been before," answered Ammon. "I feel it, too."

"I also," breathed Elnora.

The moth spread its wings, shivered them tremulously, opening and closing them rapidly. Ammon handed the box to Elnora. She shook her head.

"I can't take that one," she said. "Let her go."

"But, Elnora," protested Mrs. Comstock, "I don't want to let her go. She's mine. She's the first one I ever found this way. Can't you put her in a big box, and let her live without hurting her? I can't bear to let her go. I want to learn all about her."

"Then watch while we get these on the trees," said Elnora. "We will take her home until night and then decide what to do. She won't fly for a long time yet."

Mrs. Comstock settled on the ground, an elbow on her knee, her chin in her palm, gazing at the moth. Elnora and Ammon went to the baited trees, placing several large moths and a number of smaller ones in the cyanide jar, and searching the bushes beyond where they found several paired specimens of differing families. When they returned Elnora showed her mother how to hold her hand before the moth so that it would climb upon her fingers. Then they started back to the cabin, Elnora and Ammon leading the way; Mrs. Comstock followed slowly, stepping with great care lest she stumble and jar the moth. Her face wore a look of comprehension, in her eyes was an exalted light. On she came to the blue-bordered pool lying beside her path.

A turtle scrambled from a log and splashed into the water, while a red-wing shouted, "O-ka-lee!" to her. Mrs. Comstock paused and looked intently at the slime-covered quagmire, framed in a flower riot and homed over by sweet-voiced birds. Then she gazed at the thing of incomparable beauty clinging to her fingers and said softly: "If you had known about wonders like these in the days of your youth, Robert Comstock, could you ever have done what you did?"

Elnora missed her mother, and turning to look for her, saw her standing beside the pool. Would the old fascination return? A panic of fear seized the girl. She went back swiftly.

"Are you afraid she is going?" Elnora asked. "If you are, cup your other hand over her for shelter. Carrying her through this air and in the hot sunshine will dry her wings and make them ready for flight very quickly. You can't trust her in such air and light as you can in the cool dark woods."

As she talked she took hold of her mother's sleeve, anxiously smiling a pitiful little smile that Mrs. Comstock understood. Ammon set his load at the back door, returning to hold open the garden gate for Elnora and Mrs. Comstock. He reached it just in time to see them standing together beside the pool. The mother bent swiftly and kissed the girl on the lips. Ammon wheeled and was busily hunting moths on the raspberry bushes when they reached the gate. And so excellent are the rewards of attending your own business, that he found a splendid Promethea on a lilac in a corner, a moth of such rare wine-coloured, velvety shades that it almost sent Mrs. Comstock to her knees again. But this one was fully developed, able to fly, and had to be taken into the cabin hurriedly. Mrs. Comstock stood in the middle of the room holding up her Regalis.

"Now what must I do?" she asked.

Elnora glanced at Philip Ammon. Their eyes met and both of them smiled; he with amusement at the tall, spare figure, with dark eyes and white crown, asking the childish question so confidingly; and Elnora with exultant pride. The girl was beginning to appreciate the greatness of her mother.

"How would you like to sit and see her finish development? I'll get dinner," proposed the girl.

After they had dined, Ammon and Elnora carried the dishes to the kitchen, brought out boxes, sheets of cork, pins, ink, paper for slips and everything necessary for mounting and classifying the moths they had taken. When the housework was finished Mrs.Comstock brought her ruffle and sat near, watching and listening. She remembered all they said that she understood, and when uncertain she asked questions. Occasionally she laid down her work to straighten some flower which needed attention or to go to the garden for a bug for the grosbeak. In one of these absences Elnora said to Ammon, "These replace quite a number of the moths I lost for the man of India. With a week of such luck I could almost begin to talk college again."

"There is no reason why you should not have the week and the luck," said Ammon. "I have taken moths until the middle of August, though I suspect one is more apt to find late ones in the north where it is colder than here. The next week is hay-time, but we can count on a few double-brooders and strays, and by working the exchange method for all its worth, I think we can complete the collection again."

"You almost make me hope," said Elnora, "but I must not allow myself. I don't truly think I can replace all I lost, not even with your help. If I could, I can't see my way clear to leave mother this winter. I have found her so recently, and she is so precious, I can't risk losing her again. I am going to take the nature position in the Onabasha schools, and I shall be most happy doing the work. Only, these are a temptation."

"I wish you might go to college this fall with the other girls," said Ammon. "I feel that if you don't you never will. Isn't there some way?"

"I can't see it if there is, and I really don't want to leave mother."

"Well, mother is mighty glad to hear it," said Mrs. Comstock, entering the arbour.

Ammon noticed that her face was pale, her lips quivering, her voice cold.

"I was just saying to your daughter that she should go to college this winter," he explained, "but she says she don't want to leave you."

"If she wants to go, I wish she could," said Mrs. Comstock, a look of relief spreading over her face.

"Oh, all girls want to go to college," said Ammon. "It's the only proper place to learn bridge and embroidery; not to mention midnight lunches of mixed pickles and fruit cake, and all the delights of the sororities."

"I have thought a great deal about going to college," said Elnora, "but I never thought of any of those things."

"That is because your education in fudge and bridge has been sadly neglected," said Ammon. "You should hear my sister Polly! This was her last year! Lunches and sororities were all I heard her mention, until Tom Levering came on deck; now he is the leading subject. I can't see from her daily conversation, that she knows half as much really worth knowing as you do, but she can beat you miles on fun."

"Oh, we had some good times in the high school," said Elnora. "Life hasn't been all work and study. Is Edith Carr a college girl?"

"No. She is the very selectest kind of a private boarding school girl."

"Who is she?" asked Mrs. Comstock.

Ammon opened his lips.

"She is a girl in Chicago, that Mr. Ammon knows very well,"

said Elnora. "She is beautiful and rich, and a friend of his sister's. Or, didn't you say that?"

"I don't remember, but she is," said Ammon. "This moth needs an alcohol bath to take off the dope."

"Won't the down come, too?" asked Elnora anxiously.

"No. You watch and you will see it come out, as Polly would say, 'a perfectly good' moth."

"Is your sister younger than you?" inquired Elnora.

"Yes," said Ammon, "but she is three years older than you. She is the dearest sister in all the world. I'd love to see her now."

"Why don't you send for her," suggested Elnora. "Perhaps she'd like to help us catch moths."

"Yes, I think Polly in a Virot hat, Picot embroidered frock and three-inch heels would take more moths than anyone that ever struck the Limberlost," laughed Ammon.

"Well, you get lots of them, and you are her brother."

"Yes, but that is different. Father was raised in Onabasha, and he loved the country. He trained me his way and mother took charge of Polly. I don't just understand it. Mother is a great home body herself, but she did succeed in making Polly strictly ornamental."

"Does Tom Levering need a 'strictly ornamental' girl?"

"You are too matter of fact! Too 'strictly' material! He needs a darling girl who will love him plenty, and Polly is that."

"Well, then, does the Limberlost need a 'strictly ornamental' girl?"

"No!" cried Ammon. "You are ornament enough for the Limberlost. I have changed my mind. I don't want Polly here. She would not enjoy catching moths, or anything we do."

"She might," persisted Elnora. "You are her brother, and surely you care for these things."

"The argument does not hold," said Ammon. "Polly and I do not like the same things when we are at home, but we are very fond of each other. The member of my family who would go crazy about this is my father. I wish he could come, if only for a week. I'd send for him, but he is tied up in preparing some papers for a great corporation case this summer. He likes the country. It was his vote that brought me here."

Ammon leaned back in the arbour, watching the grosbeak as it hunted food between a tomato vine and a day lily. Elnora set him to making labels, and when he finished them he asked permission to write a letter. He took no pains to conceal his page, and from where she sat opposite him, Elnora could not look his way without reading, "My dearest Edith." He wrote busily for a time and then sat staring out across the garden.

"Have you run out of material so quickly?" asked Elnora.

"That's about it," said Ammon. "I have said that I am getting well as rapidly as possible, that the air is fine, the folks at Uncle Doc's all well, and entirely too good to me; that I am spending most of my time in the country helping catch moths for a collection, which is splendid exercise; now I can't think of another thing that will be interesting."

There was a burst of exquisite notes in the maple.

"Put in the grosbeak," suggested Elnora. "Tell her you are so friendly with him you feed him potato bugs."

Ammon dropped the pen to the sheet, bent forward, then hesitated.

"Blest if I do!" he cried. "She'd think a grosbeak was a depraved person with a large nose. She'd never dream that it was a black-robed lover, with a breast of snow and a crimson heart. She don't care for hungry babies and potato bugs. I shall write that to father. He will find it exquisite."

Elnora deftly picked up a moth, pinned it and placed its wings. She straightened the antennae, drew each leg into position and set it in perfectly lifelike manner. As she lifted her work to see if she had it right, she glanced at Ammon. He was still frowning and hesitating over the paper.

"I dare you to let me dictate a couple of paragraphs," she said.

"Done!" cried Ammon. "Go slowly enough that I can write it."

Elnora laughed softly.

"I am writing this," she began, "in an old grape arbour in the country, near a log cabin where I had my dinner. From where I sit I can see directly into the home of the next-door neighbour on the west. His name is R. B. Grosbeak. From all I have seen of him, he is a gentleman of the old school; the oldest school there is, no doubt. He always wears a black suit and cap and a white vest, decorated with one large red heart, which I think must be the emblem of some ancient order. I have been here a number of times, and I never have seen him wear anything else, or his wife appear in other than a brown dress with touches of white.

"It has appeared to me at times that she was a shade neglectful of her home duties, but he does not seem to see it that way. He cheerfully stays about the sitting room, while she is away having a good time, and sings as he cares for the four small children. I must tell you about his music. I am sure he never saw inside a conservatory. I think he merely picked up what he knows by ear and without vocal training, but there is a tenderness in his tones, a depth of pure melody, that I never have heard surpassed. It may be that I think more of his music than that of some other good vocalists hereabout, because I see more of him and appreciate his devotion to his home life.

"I just had an encounter with him at the west fence, and induced him to carry a small gift to his children. When I see the perfect harmony in which he lives, and the depth of content he and the brown lady find in life, I am almost persuaded to—now this is going to be poetry," said Elnora. "Move your pen over here and begin with a quote and a cap."

Ammon's face had been an interesting study as he took down her sentences. Now he gravely set the pen where she indicated, and Elnora dictated—

"Buy a nice little home in the country,
And settle down there for life."

"That's the truth!" cried Ammon. "It's as big a temptation as I ever had. Go on!"

"That's all," said Elnora. "You can finish. The moths are done. I am going hunting for whatever I can find for the grades."

"Wait a minute," begged Ammon. "I am going, too."

"No. You stay with mother and finish your letter."

"It is done. I couldn't add anything to that."

"All right! Sign your name and come on. But I forgot to tell you all the bargain. Maybe you won't send the letter when you hear that. The rest is that you show me the reply to my part of it."

"Oh, that's easy! I wouldn't have the slightest objection to showing you the whole letter."

He signed his name, folded the sheets and slipped them into his pocket.

"Where are we going and what do we take?"

"Will you go, mother?" asked Elnora.

"I have a little work that should be done," said Mrs. Comstock. "Could you spare me? Where do you want to go?"

"We will go down to Aunt Margaret's and see her a few minutes and get Billy. We will be back in time for supper."

Mrs. Comstock smiled as she watched them down the road. What a splendid looking pair of young creatures they were! How finely proportioned, how full of vitality! Then her face grew troubled as she saw them in earnest conversation. Just as she was wishing she had not trusted her precious girl with so much of a stranger, she saw Elnora stoop to lift a branch and peer under. The mother grew content. Elnora was thinking only of her work. She was to be trusted utterly.

16

Wherein the Limberlost Sings for Ammon, and the Talking Trees Tell Great Secrets

A few days later Ammon handed Elnora a sheet of paper and she read: "In your condition I should think the moth hunting and life at the cabin would be very good for you, but for any sake keep away from that Grosbeak person, and don't come home with your head full of granger ideas. No doubt he has a remarkable voice, but I can't bear untrained singers, and don't you get the idea that a June song is perennial. You are not hearing the music he will make when the four babies get the scarlet fever and the measles, and the gadding wife leaves him at home to care for them then. Poor soul, I pity her! How she exists where rampant cows bellow at you, frogs croak, mosquitoes consume you, the butter goes to oil in summer and bricks in winter, while the pump freezes every day, and there is no earthly amusement, and no society! Poor things! Can't you influence him to move? No wonder she gads when she has a chance! I should die. If you are thinking of settling in the country, think also of a woman who is satisfied with white and brown to accompany you! Brown! Of all deadly colours! I should go mad in brown."

Elnora laughed as she read. Her face was dimpling as she handed back the sheet. "Who's ahead?" she asked.

"Who do you think?" he parried.

"She is," said Elnora. "Are you going to tell her in your next that

R. B. Grosbeak is a bird, and that he probably will spend the winter in a wild plum thicket in Tennessee?"

"No," said Ammon. "I shall tell her that I understand her ideas of life perfectly, and, of course, I never shall ask her to deal with oily butter and frozen pumps—"

"—and measley babies," interpolated Elnora.

"Exactly!" said Ammon. "Just the same I find so much to counterbalance those things, that I should not object to bearing them myself, in view of the recompense. Where do we go and what do we do to-day?"

"We will have to wander along the roads and around the edge of the Limberlost to-day," said Elnora. "Mother is making strawberry preserves, and she can't come until she finishes. Suppose we go down to the swamp and I'll show you what is left of the flower-room that Terrence O'More, the big lumber man of Great Rapids, made when he was a homeless boy here. Of course, you have heard the story?"

"Yes, and I've met the O'Mores who are frequently in Chicago society. They have friends there. I think them one ideal couple."

"That sounds like they might be the only one, or close to it," said Elnora, "and, indeed, they are not. I know dozens. Aunt Margaret and Uncle Wesley are another, the Brownlees another, and my mathematics professor and his wife. The world is full of happy people, but no one ever hears of them. You have to fight and make a scandal to get into the papers. No one knows about all the happy people. I am happy myself, and just look how perfectly inconspicuous I am."

"You only need go where you will be seen," began Ammon, when he remembered and finished. "What do we take to-day?"

"Ourselves," said Elnora. "I have a vagabond streak in my blood and it's in evidence. I am going to show you where real flowers grow, real birds sing, and if I feel quite right about it, perhaps I shall raise a note or two myself."

"Oh, do you sing?" asked Ammon politely.

"At times," answered Elnora. "'As do the birds, because I must,' but don't be scared. The mood does not possess me often. Perhaps I shan't raise a note when we get there."

They went down the road to the swamp, climbed the snake

fence, followed the path to the old trail and then turned south along it. Elnora indicated to Ammon the trail with remnants of sagging barbed wire.

"It was ten years ago," she said. "I was just a little school girl, but I wandered widely even then, and no one cared. I saw him often. He had been in a city institution all his life, when he took the job of keeping timber thieves out of this swamp, before many trees had been cut. It was strong man's work, and he was a frail boy, but he grew hardier as he lived out of doors. This trail we are on is the path his feet first wore, in those days when he was insane with fear and eaten up with loneliness, but he stuck to his work and won out. I used to come down to the road and creep in among the bushes as far as I dared, to watch him pass. He walked mostly, sometimes he rode a wheel.

"Some days his face was dreadfully sad, some days it was so determined a little child could see the force in it, and once it was radiant. That day the Swamp Angel was with him. I can't tell you what she was like. I never saw any one who resembled her. He stopped near here to show her a bird's nest. Then they went on to a sort of flower-room he had made, and he sang for her. By the time he left, I had gotten bold enough to come out on the trail, and I met the big Scotchman Freckles lived with. He saw me catching moths and butterflies, so he took me to the flower-room and gave me everything there. I don't dare come alone often, and so I can't keep it up as he did, but you can see something of how it was."

Elnora led the way and Ammon followed. The outlines of the room were not distinct, because many of the trees were gone, but Elnora showed how it had been as nearly as she could.

"The swamp is almost ruined now," she said. "The maples, walnuts, and cherries are all gone. The talking trees are the only things left worth while."

"The 'talking trees'! I don't understand," commented Ammon.

"No wonder!" laughed Elnora. "They are my discovery. You know all trees whisper and talk during the summer, but there are two that have so much to say they keep on the whole winter, when the others are silent. The beeches and oaks so love to talk, they cling to their dead, dry leaves. In the winter the winds are stiffest and blow most, so these trees whisper, chatter, sob, laugh, and at times roar until the sound is deafening. They never cease until new leaves come out in the spring to push off the old ones. I love to stand beneath them with my ear to the great trunks, interpreting what they say to fit my moods. The beeches branch low, and their leaves are small so they only know common earthly things; but the oaks run straight above almost all other trees before they branch, their arms are mighty, their leaves large. They meet the winds that travel around the globe, and from them learn the big things."

Ammon studied the girl face. "What do the beeches tell you, Elnora?" he asked gently.

"To be patient, to be unselfish, to do unto others as I would have them do to me."

"And the oaks?"

"They say 'be true,' 'live a clean life,' 'send your soul up here and let the winds of the world teach it what honour achieves.'"

"Wonderful secrets, those!" marvelled Ammon. "Are they telling them now? Could I hear?"

"No. They are only gossiping now. This is playtime. They tell the big secrets to a white world, when the music inspires them."

"The music?"

"All other trees are harps in the winter. Their trunks are the frames, their branches the strings, the winds the musicians. When the air is cold and clear, the world very white, and the harp music swelling, then the talking trees tell the strengthening, uplifting things."

"You wonderful girl!" cried Ammon. "What a woman you will be!"

"If I am a woman at all worth while, it will be because I have had such wonderful opportunities," said Elnora. "Not every girl is driven to the forest to learn what God has to say there. Here are the remains of Freckles's room. The time the Angel came here he sang to her, and I listened. I never heard music like that. No wonder she loved him. Everyone who knew him did, and they do yet. Try that log, it makes a fairly good seat. This old store box was his treasure house, just as it's now mine. I will show you my dearest possession. I do not dare take it home because mother can't overcome her dislike for it. It was my father's, and in some ways I am like him. This is the strongest."

Elnora lifted the violin and began to play. She wore a school dress of green gingham, with the sleeves rolled to the elbows. She seemed a part of the setting all around her. Her head shone like a small dark sun, and her face never had seemed so rose-flushed and fair. From the instant she drew the bow, her lips parted and her eyes fastened on something far away in the swamp, and never did she give more of that impression of feeling for her notes and repeating something audible only to her. Ammon was too near to get the best effect. He arose and stepped back several yards, leaning against a large tree, looking and listening with all his soul.

As he changed positions he saw that Mrs. Comstock had followed them, and was standing on the trail, where she could not have helped hearing everything Elnora had said. So to Ammon before her and the mother watching on the trail, Elnora played the Song of the Limberlost. It seemed as if the swamp hushed all its other voices and spoke only through her dancing bow. The mother out on the trail had heard it all, once before from the girl, many times from her father. To the man it was a revelation. He stood so stunned he forgot Mrs. Comstock. He tried to realize what a great city audience would say to that music, from such a player, with a like background, and he could not imagine.

He was wondering what he dared say, how much he might express, when the last note fell and the girl laid the violin in the case, closed the door, locked it and hid the key in the rotting wood at the end of a log. Then she came to him. Ammon stood looking at her curiously.

"I wonder," he said, "what people would say to that?"

"I did it in public once," said Elnora. "I think they liked it, fairly well. I had a note yesterday offering me the leadership of the high school orchestra in Onabasha. I can take it as well as not. None of my talks to the grades come the first thing in the morning. I can play a few minutes in the orchestra and reach the rooms in plenty of time. It will be more work that I love, and like finding the money. I would gladly play for nothing, just to be able to express myself."

"With some people it makes a regular battlefield of the human heart—this struggle for self-expression," said Ammon. "You are going to do beautiful work in the world, and do it well. When I realize that your violin belonged to your father, that he played it before you were born, and it no doubt affected your mother strongly, and then couple with that the years you have roamed these fields and swamps finding in nature all you had to lavish your great heart upon, I can see how you evolved. I understand what you mean by self-expression. I know something of what you have to express. The world never so wanted your message as it does now. It is hungry for the things you know. I can see easily how your position came to you. What you have to give is taught in no college, and I am not sure but you would spoil yourself if you tried to run your mind through a set groove with hundreds of others. I never thought I should say such a thing to anyone, but I do say to you, and I honestly believe it; give up the college idea. Your mind does not need that sort of development, it is far past it. Stick close to your work in the woods. You are getting so infinitely greater on it, than the best college student I ever knew, that there is no comparison. When you have money to spend, take that violin and go to one of the world's great masters and let the Limberlost sing to him; if he thinks he can improve it, very well. I have my doubts."

"Do you really mean that you would give up all idea of going to college, if you were me?"

"I really mean it," said Ammon. "If I now held the money to send you in my hands, and could give it to you in some way you would accept I would tear it up and throw it away first. I do not know why it is the lot of the world always to want something different from what life gives them. If you only could realize it, my girl, you are in college, and have been always. You are in the school of experience, and it has taught you to think, and given you a heart. God knows I envy the man who wins it! You have been in the college of the Limberlost all your life, and I never met a graduate from any other institution who could begin to compare with you in sanity, clarity, and interesting knowledge. I wouldn't even advise you to read too many books on your lines. You get your stuff first hand, and you know that you are right. What you should do is to begin early to practise self-expression. Don't wait too long to tell us about the woods as you know them."

"Follow the course of the Bird Woman, you mean?" asked Elnora.

"In your own way; with your own light. She won't live forever.

You are younger, and you will be ready to begin where she ends. The swamp has given you all you need so far, now you give it to the world in payment. College be confounded! Go to work and show people what there is in you!"

Not until then did he remember that Mrs. Comstock was somewhere very near.

"Should we go out to the trail and see if your mother is coming?" he asked.

"Here she is now," said Elnora. "Gracious, it's a mercy I got that violin put away in time! I didn't expect her so soon," whispered the girl as she turned and went toward her mother. Mrs. Comstock's face was a study as she looked at Elnora.

"I forgot that you were making sun-preserves and they didn't require much cooking," she said. "We should have waited for you."

"Not at all!" answered Mrs. Comstock. "Have you found anything yet?"

"Nothing that I can show you," said Elnora. "I am not sure but I have found an idea that will revolutionize the whole course of my work, thought, and ambitions."

"'Ambitions!' My, what a hefty word!" laughed Mrs. Comstock. "Now, who would suspect a little red-haired country girl of harbouring such a deadly germ in her body? Can you tell mother about it?"

"Not if you talk to me that way, I can't," said Elnora.

"Well, I guess we better let ambition lie. I've always heard it was safest asleep. If you ever get a bona fide attack, it will be time to attend it. Let's hunt specimens. It is June. Philip and I are in the grades. You have an hour to put an idea into our heads that will stick for a lifetime, and grow for good. That's the way I look at your job. Now, what are you going to give us? We don't want any old silly stuff that has been hashed over and over, we want a big new idea to plant in our hearts. Come on, Miss Teacher, what is the boiled-down, double-distilled essence of June? Give it to us strong. We are large enough to furnish it developing ground. Hurry up! Time is short and we are waiting. What is the miracle of June? What one thing epitomizes the whole month, and makes it just a little different from any other?"

"The birth of these big night moths," said Elnora promptly.

Ammon clapped his hands. The tears started to Mrs. Comstock's eyes. She took Elnora in her arms, and kissed her forehead.

"You'll do!" she said. "June is June, not because it has bloom, bird, fruit, or flower, exclusive to it alone. It's half May and half July in all of them. But as I figure it, it's just June, when it comes to these great, velvet-winged night moths which sweep its moonlit skies, consummating their scheme of creation, and dropping like a bloomed-out flower. Give them moths for June. Then make that the basis of your year's work. Find the distinctive feature of each month, the one thing which marks it a time apart, and hit them squarely between the eyes with it. Even the babies of the lowest grades can comprehend moths when they see a few emerge, and learn their history, as it can be lived before them. You should show your specimens in pairs, then their eggs, the growing caterpillars, and then the cocoons. You want to dig out the red heart of every month in the year, and hold it pulsing before them.

"I can't name all of them off-hand, but I think of one more right now. February belongs to our winter birds. It is then the great horned owl of the swamp courts his mate, the big hawks pair, and even the crows begin to take notice. These are truly our birds. Like the poor we have them always with us. You should hear the musicians of this swamp in February, Philip, on a mellow night. Oh, but they are in earnest! For twenty-one years I've listened by night to the great owls, all the smaller sizes, the foxes, coons, and every resident left in these woods, and by day to the hawks, yellow-hammers, sap-suckers, titmice, crows, and all our winter birds. Only just now it's come to me that the distinctive feature of February is not linen bleaching, nor sugar making; it's the love month of our very own birds. Give them hawks and owls for February, Elnora."

The girl looked at Ammon with flashing eyes. "How's that?" she said. "Don't you think I will make it, with such help? You should hear the concert she is talking about! It is simply indescribable when the ground is covered with snow, and the moonlight white."

"It's about the best music we have," said Mrs. Comstock. "I just wonder if you couldn't copy that alone and make a strong, original piece out of it for your violin, Elnora?"

There was one tense breath, then— "I could try," said Elnora simply.

Ammon rushed to the rescue. "We must go to work," he said, and began examining a walnut branch for Luna moth eggs. Elnora joined him while Mrs. Comstock drew her embroidery from her pocket and sat on a log. She said she was tired, they could come for her when they were ready to go. She could hear their voices all around her until she called them at supper time. When they came to her she stood waiting on the trail, the sewing in one hand, the violin in the other. Elnora became very white, but took the trail without a word. Ammon, unable to see a woman carry a heavier load than he, reached for the instrument. Mrs. Comstock shook her head. She carried the violin home, took it into her room and closed the door. Elnora turned to Ammon.

"If she destroys that, I will die!" cried the girl.

"She won't!" said Ammon. "You misunderstand her. She wouldn't have said what she did about the owls, if she had meant to. She is your mother. No one loves you as she does. Trust her! Myself—I think she's simply great!"

Mrs. Comstock returned with serene face, and all of them helped with supper. When it was over Ammon and Elnora sorted and classified the afternoon's specimens, and made a trip to the woods to paint and light several trees for moths. When they came back Mrs. Comstock sat in the arbour, and they joined her. The moonlight was so intense, print could have been read by it. The damp night air held odours near to earth, making flower and tree perfume strong. A thousand insects were serenading, and in the maple the grosbeak occasionally said a reassuring word to his wife, while she answered that all was well. A whip-poor-will wailed in the swamp and back by the blue-bordered pool a chat complained disconsolately. Mrs. Comstock went into the cabin, but she returned almost instantly, laying the violin and bow across Elnora's lap. "I wish you would give us a little music," she said.

CHAPTER
17

Wherein Mrs. Comstock Dances in the Moonlight, and Elnora Makes a Confession

Billy was swinging in the hammock, at peace with himself and all the world, when he thought he heard something. He sat bolt upright, his eyes staring. Once he opened his lips, then thought again and closed them. The sound persisted. Billy vaulted the fence, and ran down the road with his queer sidewise hop. When he neared the Comstock cabin, he left the warm dust of the highway and stepped softly at slower pace over the rank grasses by the roadside. He had heard aright. The violin was in the grape arbour, singing like mad, singing a perfect jumble of everything, poured out in an exultant tumult. The strings were voicing the joy of a happy girl heart.

Billy climbed the fence enclosing the west woods and crept down toward the arbour. He was not a spy and not a sneak. He merely wanted to satisfy his childheart as to whether Mrs. Comstock was at home, and Elnora at last playing her loved violin with her mother's consent. One peep sufficed. Mrs. Comstock sat in the moonlight, her head leaning against the arbour; on her face was a look of perfect peace and contentment. As he stared at her the bow hesitated a second and Mrs. Comstock spoke.

"That's all very melodious and sweet," she said, "but I do wish you could play Money Musk and some of the tunes I danced as a girl."

Elnora had been avoiding carefully every note that might be reminiscent of her father. At the words she laughed softly and struck into "Turkey in the Straw." An instant later Mrs. Comstock was dancing like mad in the moonlight. Ammon sprang to her side, caught her in his arms, while to Elnora's laughter and the violin's impetus they danced until they dropped panting on the arbour bench.

Billy scarcely knew when he got back on the road. His light feet barely touched the soft way, so swiftly he flew. He vaulted the fence and burst into the house.

"Aunt Margaret! Uncle Wesley!" he screamed. "Listen! Listen! She's playing it! Elnora's playing her violin at home! And Aunt Kate is dancing like anything before the arbour! I saw her in the moonlight! I ran down! Oh, Aunt Margaret!"

Billy fled to his haven and sobbed on Margaret's breast.

"Why, Billy!" she chided. "Don't cry, you little dunce! That's what we've all prayed for these many years; but you must be mistaken about Kate. I can't believe it."

Billy lifted his head. "Well, you just have to!" he said. "When I say I saw anything, Uncle Wesley knows I did. The city man was dancing with her. They danced together and Elnora laughed. But it didn't look funny to me; I was scared."

"Who was it said 'wonders would never cease'?" asked Wesley. "You mark my word, once you get Kate Comstock started, you can't stop her. There's a wagon load of penned-up force in her. Dancing in the moonlight! Well, I'll be hanged!"

Billy was at his side instantly. "Well, whoever does it will have to hang me, too," he cried.

Sinton threw his arm around Billy and drew him close. "Tell us all about it, son," he said. Billy told. "And when Elnora just stopped a breath, 'Can't you play some of the old things I knew when I was a girl?' said her ma. Then Elnora began to do a thing that made you want to whirl round and round, and quicker 'an scat there was her ma a-whirling. The city man, he ups and grabs her and whirls, too, and back in the woods I was going just like they did. Elnora begins to laugh, and I ran to tell you, 'cos I knew you'd like to know. Now, all the world is right, ain't it?" ended Billy as he leaned against Sinton in supreme satisfaction.

"You just bet it is!" said Wesley.

Billy looked steadily at Margaret. "Is it, Aunt Margaret?"

Margaret Sinton smiled at him bravely.

An hour later when Billy was ready to climb the stairs to his room, he went to Margaret to say good night. He leaned against her an instant, and brought his lips close to her ear. "Wish I could get your little girls back for you!" he whispered and dashed for the stairs.

Down at the Comstock cabin the violin played on until Elnora was so tired she scarcely could lift the bow. Then Ammon went home. The women walked to the gate with him, and stood watching him from sight.

"That's what I call one decent young man!" said Mrs. Comstock. "To see him fit in with us, you'd think he'd been raised in a cabin; but it's likely he's always had the very cream o' the pot."

"Yes, I think so," laughed Elnora, "but it hasn't hurt him. I've never seen anything I could criticize. He's teaching me so much, unconsciously. You know he graduated from Harvard, and has several degrees in law. He's coming in the morning, and we are going to put in a big day on Catocalae."

"Which is ——?"

"Those gray moths with wings that fold back like big flies, and they appear as if they had been carved from old wood. Then, when they fly, the lower wings flash out and they are red and black, or gold and black, or pink and black, or dozens of bright, beautiful colours combined with black. No one has ever classified all of them and written their complete history, unless the Bird Woman is doing it now. She wants everything she can get about them."

"I remember," said Mrs. Comstock. "They are mighty pretty things. I've started up slews of them from the vines covering the logs, all my life. I must be cautious and catch them after this, but they seem powerful spry. I might get hold of something rare." She thought intently and added, "And wouldn't know it if I did. It would just be my luck. I've had the rarest thing on earth in reach this many a day and only had the wit to cinch it just as it was going. I'll bet I don't let anything else escape me."

Next morning Ammon came early, and he and Elnora went at once to the fields and woods. Mrs. Comstock had come to believe so implicitly in him that she now stayed at home to complete the work before she joined them, and when she did she often sat sewing, leaving them wandering hours at a time. It was noon before she finished, and then she packed a basket of lunch. She found Elnora and Philip near the violet patch, which was still in its prime. They all lunched together in the shade of a wild crab thicket, with flowers spread at their feet, and the gold orioles streaking the air with flashes of light and trailing ecstasy behind them, while the red-wings, as always, asked the most impertinent questions. Then Mrs. Comstock carried the basket back to the cabin, and Ammon and Elnora sat on a log, resting a few minutes. They had unexpected luck, and both were eager to continue the search.

"Do you remember your promise about these violets?" asked Ammon. "To-morrow is Edith's birthday, and if I'd put them special delivery on the morning train, she'd get them in the late afternoon. They ought to keep well that long. She leaves for the North next day."

"Of course, you can have them," said Elnora. "We will quit long enough before supper to gather a great bunch. They can be packed so they will carry all right. They should be perfectly fresh, especially if we gather them this evening and let them drink all night."

Then they went back to hunt Catocalae. It was a long and a happy search. It led them into new, unexplored nooks of the woods, by a red-poll nest, and where goldfinches prospected for thistledown for the cradles they would line a little later. It led them into real forest, where deep, dark pools lay, where the hermit thrush and the wood robin extracted the essence from all other bird melody, and poured it out in their pure belltone notes. It seemed as if every old gray tree-trunk, slab of loose bark, and prostrate log yielded the flashing gray treasures; while of all others they seemed to take alarm most easily, and be most difficult to capture.

Ammon came to Elnora at dusk, daintily holding one by the body, its dark wings showing and its long slender legs trying to clasp his fingers and creep from his hold.

"Oh, for mercy's sake!" cried Elnora, and stared at him.

"I half believe it!" exulted Ammon.

"Did you ever see one?"

"Only in collections, and mighty seldom there."

Elnora studied the black wings intently. "I surely believe that's Sappho," she marvelled. "The Bird Woman will be overjoyed."

"We must get the cyanide jar quickly," said Ammon. "I wouldn't lose her for a hundred dollars. Such a chase as she led me!"

Elnora got the jar and began gathering up paraphernalia.

"When you make a find like that," she said, "it's the right time to quit and feel glorious all the rest of that day. I tell you I'm proud! We will go now. We have barely time to carry out our plans before supper. Won't mother be pleased to see that we have a rare one?"

"I'd like to see anyone more pleased than I am!" said Philip Ammon. "I feel as if I'd earned my supper to-night. Let's go."

He took the greater part of the load and stepped aside for Elnora to precede him. She went down the path, broken by the grazing cattle, toward the cabin and nearest the violet patch she stopped, laid down her net, and the things she carried. Ammon passed her and hurried straight toward the back gate.

"Aren't you going to ——?" began Elnora.

"I'm going to get this moth home in a hurry," he said. "This cyanide has lost its strength, and it's not working well. We need some fresh in the jar."

He had forgotten the violets! Elnora stood looking after him, a curious expression on her face. One second so—then she picked up the net and followed. At the blue-bordered pool she paused and half turned back, then she closed her lips firmly and went on. It was nine o'clock when Ammon said good-bye, and started to town. His gay whistle floated to them from the farthest corner of the Limberlost. Elnora complained of being tired, so she went to her room and to bed. But sleep would not come. Thought was racing in her brain and the longer she lay the wider awake she grew. At last she softly slipped from bed, lighted her lamp and began opening boxes. Then she went to work. Two hours later a beautiful birch bark basket, strongly and artistically made stood on her table. She set a tiny alarm clock at three, returned to bed and fell asleep instantly with a smile on her lips.

She was on the floor with the first tinkle of the alarm, and hastily dressing, she picked up the basket and a box to fit it, crept down the stairs, and out to the violet patch. She was unafraid as it was so near morning, and lining the basket with damp mosses she swiftly began picking with practised hands, the youngest of the flowers. It was so dark she scarcely could tell which were freshest at times, but day soon came creeping over the Limberlost and peeped down at her. The robins awoke all their neighbours, and a babel of bird notes filled the air. The dew was dripping, and the first strong rays of light fell on a world in which Elnora worshipped. When the basket was filled to overflowing, she set it in the stout pasteboard box, packed it solid with mosses, tied it firmly and slipped under the cord a note she had written the previous night.

Then she took a short cut across the woods and walked swiftly to Onabasha. It was after six o'clock, but all of the city she wished to avoid were asleep. She had no trouble in finding a small boy out, and she stood at a distance waiting while he rang Dr. Ammon's bell and delivered the package for Philip to a maid, with the note which was to be given him at once.

On the way home through the woods passing some baited trees she collected the captive moths. She entered the kitchen with them so naturally that Mrs. Comstock made no comment. After breakfast Elnora went to her room, cleared away all trace of the night's work and was out in the arbour mounting moths when Ammon came down the road. "I am tired sitting," she said to her mother. "I think I will walk a few rods and meet him."

"Who's a trump?" called Ammon from afar.

"Well, not you!" retorted Elnora. "Confess that you forgot!"

"Completely!" said Ammon. "But luckily it would not have been fatal. I wrote Polly last week to send Edith something appropriate and handsome to-day, with my card. But that touch from the woods will be mighty effective. Thank you more than I can say. Aunt Anna and I unpacked it to see the basket, and it was a beauty. She says you are always doing things like that."

"Well, I hope not!" laughed Elnora. "If you'd seen me sneaking out before dawn, not to waken mother and coming in with moths to make her think I'd been to the trees, you'd know it was a most especial occasion."

Then Ammon understood two things. Elnora's mother did not know of the early morning trip to the city, and the girl had come to meet him to tell him so.

"You were a brick to do it!" he whispered as he closed the gate behind them. "I'll never forget you for it. Thank you ever so much. You are too kind to me."

"I did not do that for you," said Elnora tersely. "I did it mostly to preserve my own self-respect. I saw you were forgetting. If I did it for anything besides that, I did it for her."

"Just look what I've brought!" said Ammon, entering the arbour and greeting Mrs. Comstock. "Borrowed it of the Bird Woman. And it isn't hers. A rare edition of Catocalae with coloured plates. I told her the best I could, and she said to try for Sappho here. I suspect the Bird Woman will be out presently. She was all excitement."

Then they bent over the book together and with the mounted moth before them determined her family. The Bird Woman did come later, and carried the moth away to put into a book and Elnora and Ammon were freshly filled with enthusiasm.

So these days were the beginning of the weeks that followed. Six of them flying on Time's wings, each filled to the brim with interest. After June, the moth hunts grew less frequent; the fields and woods were scoured for material for Elnora's grade work. The most absorbing occupation they found was in carrying out Mrs. Comstock's suggestion to learn the vital thing for which each month was distinctive, and make that the key to the nature work. They wrote out a list of the months, opposite each the things all of them could suggest which seemed to pertain to that month alone, and then tried to sift until they found something typical. Mrs. Comstock was a great help. Her mother had been Dutch and had brought from Holland numerous quaint sayings and superstitions easily traceable to Pliny's Natural History; and in Mrs. Comstock's early years in Ohio she had heard much Indian talk among her elders, so she knew the signs of each season, and sometimes they helped. Always her practical thought and sterling common-sense were useful. When they were afield until exhausted they came back to the cabin for food, to prepare specimens and classify them, and to talk over the day. Sometimes

Ammon brought books and read while Elnora and her mother worked, and every night Mrs. Comstock asked for the violin. Her perfect hunger for music was sufficient evidence of how she had suffered without it. So the days crept by, golden, filled with useful work and pure pleasure.

The grosbeak had led the family in the maple abroad and a second brood, in a wild grape vine clambering over the well, was almost ready for flight. The dust lay thick on the country roads, the days grew warmer; summer was just poising to slip into fall, and Ammon stayed on, coming each day as if he had belonged there always and expected to remain forever.

One warm August afternoon Mrs. Comstock looked up from the ruffle on which she was engaged to see a blue-coated messenger enter the gate.

"Is Philip Ammon here?" asked the boy.

"He is," said Mrs. Comstock.

"I have a message for him."

"He is in the woods back of the cabin. I will ring the bell, and he will come. Do you know if it is important?"

"Urgent," said the boy; "I rode hard."

Mrs. Comstock stepped to the back door and clanged the dinner bell sharply, paused a second, and rang again. In a short time Ammon and Elnora came down the path on the run.

"Are you ill, mother?" cried Elnora.

Mrs. Comstock indicated the boy. "There is an important message for Philip," she said.

Ammon muttered an excuse and tore open the telegram. His colour faded slightly. "I have to take the first train," he said. "My father is ill and I am needed."

He handed the sheet to Elnora. "I have about two hours, as I remember the trains north, but my things are all over Uncle Doc's house, so I must go at once."

"Certainly," said Elnora giving back the message. "Is there anything I can do to help? Mother, get Philip a glass of buttermilk to start on. I will gather what you have here."

"Never mind. There is nothing of importance. I don't want to be hampered. I'll send for it if I miss anything I need."

Ammon drank the milk, said good-bye to Mrs. Comstock,

repeatedly thanked her for all her kindness, and turned to Elnora. "Will you walk to the edge of the Limberlost with me?" he asked. Elnora assented. Mrs. Comstock followed to the gate, urged him to come again soon, and repeated her good-bye. Then she went back to the arbour to await Elnora's return. As she watched down the road she smiled softly.

"I had an idea he would speak to me first," she thought, "but this may change things some. He hasn't time. Elnora will come back a happy girl, and she has good reason. He is a model young man. Her lot will be mighty different from mine."

She picked up her embroidery and began setting dainty, precise little stitches, possible only to certain women.

On the road Elnora spoke first. "I do hope it is nothing serious," she said. "Is he usually strong?"

"Quite strong," said Philip. "I am not at all alarmed but I am very much ashamed. I have been well enough for the last month to have gone home and helped him with some critical cases that were keeping him at work in this heat. I was enjoying myself so I wouldn't offer to go, and he would not ask me to come, so long as he could help it. I have allowed him to overtax himself until he is down, and mother and Polly are north at our cottage. He's never been sick before, and it's probable I am to blame that he is now."

"He intended you to stay this long when you came," urged Elnora.

"Yes, but it's hot in Chicago. I should have remembered him. He is always thinking of me. Possibly he has needed me for days. I am ashamed to go to him in splendid condition and admit that I was having such a fine time I forgot to come home."

"You have had a fine time, then?" asked Elnora.

They had reached the fence. Ammon vaulted over to take a short cut across the fields. He turned and looked at her.

"The best, the sweetest, and most wholesome time any man ever had in this world," he said. "Elnora, if I talked hours I couldn't make you understand what a girl I think you are. I never in all my life hated anything as I hate leaving you. It seems to me that I have not strength to do it."

"If you have gotten anything worth while from me," said Elnora, "that should be it. Just to have strength to go to your duty, and to go quickly."

Ammon caught the hand she held out to him in both his. "Elnora, these days we have had together, have they been sweet to you?"

"Beautiful days!" said Elnora. "Each like a perfect dream to be thought over and over all my life. Oh, they have been the only really happy days I've ever known; these days rich with mother's love, and doing useful work with your help. Good-bye! You must hurry!"

Ammon gazed at her. He tried to drop her hand, and only clutched it closer. Suddenly he drew her toward him. "Elnora," he whispered, "will you kiss me good-bye?"

Elnora drew back and stared at him with wide eyes. "I'd strike you sooner!" she said. "Have I ever said or done anything in your presence that made you feel free to ask that, Philip Ammon?"

"No!" panted Ammon. "No! I think so much of you, I just wanted to touch your lips once before I left you. You know Elnora—"

"Don't distress yourself," said Elnora calmly. "I am broad enough to judge you sanely. I know what you mean. It would be no harm to you. It would not matter to me, but here we will think of someone else. Edith Carr would not want your lips to-morrow if she knew they had touched mine to-day. I was wise to say 'Go quickly!'"

Ammon still clung to her. "Will you write me?" he begged.

"No," said Elnora. "There is nothing to say, save good-bye. We can do that now."

Ammon held on. "Promise that you will write me only one letter," he urged. "I want just one message from you to lock in my desk, and keep always. Promise you will write once, Elnora."

Elnora looked straight into his eyes, and smiled serenely. "If the talking trees tell me this winter, the secret of how a man may grow perfect, I will write you what it is, Philip. In all the time I have known you, I never have liked you so little. Good-bye."

She drew away her hand and swiftly turned back to the road. Philip Ammon, wordless, started toward Onabasha on a run.

Elnora crossed the road, climbed the fence and sought the

shelter of their own woods. She took a diagonal course and followed it until she came to the path leading past the violet patch. She went down this hurriedly. Her hands were clenched at her sides, her eyes dry and bright, her cheeks red-flushed, and her breath coming fast. When she reached the patch she turned into it and stood looking around her.

The mosses were dry, the flowers gone, weeds a foot high covered it. She turned away and went on down the path until she was almost in sight of the cabin.

Mrs. Comstock smiled and waited in the arbour until it dawned on her that Elnora was a long time coming, so she went to the gate. The road stretched away toward the Limberlost empty and lonely. Then she knew that Elnora had gone into their own woods and would come in the back way. She could not understand why the girl did not hurry to her with what she would have to tell. She went out and wandered around the garden. Then she stepped into the path and started back along the way leading to the woods, past the pool now framed in a thick setting of yellow lilies. Then she saw, and stopped, gasping for breath. Her hands flew up and her lined face grew ghastly. She stared at the sky and then at the prostrate girl figure. Over and over she tried to speak, but only a dry breath came. She turned and fled back to the garden.

In the familiar enclosure she gazed around her like a caged animal seeking escape. The sun beat down on her bare head mercilessly, and mechanically she moved over to the shade of a half-grown hickory tree that voluntarily had sprouted by the milk house. At her feet lay an axe with which she made kindlings for fires. She stooped and picked it up. That prone figure sobbing in the grass caught her with a renewed spasm. She shut her eyes as if to close it out. That made hearing so acute she felt certain she heard Elnora moaning by the path. The eyes flew open. They fell squarely on a few spindling tomato plants set too near the tree and stunted by its shade. Mrs. Comstock whirled on the hickory and swung the axe. Her hair shook down, her clothing became disarranged, in the heat the perspiration streamed, but stroke fell on stroke until the tree crashed over, grazing a corner of the milk house and smashing the garden fence on the east.

At the sound Elnora sprang to her feet and came running down the garden walk. "Mother!" she cried. "Mother! What in the world are you doing?"

Mrs. Comstock wiped her ghastly face on her apron. "I've laid out to cut that tree for years," she said. "It shades the beets in the morning, and the tomatoes in the afternoon!"

Elnora uttered one wild little cry and fled into her mother's arms. "Oh, mother!" she sobbed. "Will you ever forgive me?"

Mrs. Comstock's arms swept together in a tight grip around Elnora.

"There isn't a thing on God's footstool from a to izzard I won't forgive you, my precious girl!" she said. "Tell mother what it is!"

Elnora lifted her wet face. "He told me," she panted, "just as soon as he decently could—that second day he told me. Almost all his life he's been engaged to a girl at home. He never cared anything about me. He was just interested in the moths and growing strong."

Mrs. Comstock's arms tightened. With a shaking hand she stroked the bright hair.

"Tell me, honey," she said. "Is he to blame for a single one of these tears?"

"Not one!" sobbed Elnora. "Oh, mother, I won't forgive you if you don't believe that. Not one! He never said, or looked, or did anything all the world might not have known. He likes me very much as a friend. He hated to go dreadfully!"

"Elnora!" the mother's head bent until the white hair mingled with the brown. "Elnora, why didn't you tell me at first?"

Elnora caught her breath in a sharp snatch. "I know I should!" she sobbed. "I will bear any punishment for not, but I didn't feel as if I possibly could. I was afraid."

"Afraid of what?" the shaking hand was on the hair again.

"Afraid you wouldn't let him come!" panted Elnora. "And, oh, mother, I wanted him so!"

CHAPTER
18

Wherein Mrs. Comstock Experiments with Rejuvenation, and Elnora Teaches Natural History

For the next week Mrs. Comstock and Elnora worked so hard there was no time to talk, and they were compelled to sleep from physical exhaustion. Neither of them made any pretense of eating, for they could not swallow without a great effort, so they drank milk and worked. Elnora went on setting bait for Catacolae and Sphinginae, which, unlike the big moths of June, live several months. She took all the dragon flies and butterflies she could, and when she went over the list for the man of India, she found, to her amazement, that with Ammon's help she once more had it complete save a pair of Yellow Emperors.

This circumstance was so amazing she had a fleeting thought of writing Ammon and asking him to see if he could not secure her a pair. She did tell the Bird Woman, and from every source at her command she tried to complete the series with these moths, and could not find any for sale.

"I think the mills of the Gods are grinding this grist," said Elnora, "and we might as well wait patiently until they choose to send a Yellow Emperor."

Mrs. Comstock invented work. When she had nothing more to do, she hoed in the garden although the earth was hard and dry and there were no plants that really needed attention. Then came a notification that Elnora would be compelled to attend a week's session of the Teachers' Institute held at the county seat twenty miles north of Onabasha the following week. That gave them something of which to think and real work to do. Elnora was requested to bring her violin. As she was on the programme of one of the most important sessions for a talk on nature work in grade schools, she was driven to prepare her speech, and to select and practise some music. Her mother turned her attention to clothing.

They went to Onabasha together and purchased a simple and appropriate fall suit and hat, goods for a dainty little coloured frock, and a dress skirt and several fancy waists. Margaret Sinton came down and the sewing began. When everything was finished and packed, Elnora kissed her mother good-bye at the depot, and the train pulled out. Mrs. Comstock went into the waiting-room and dropped into a seat to rest. Her heart was so sore her whole right side felt tender. She was half starved for the food she had no appetite to take. She had worked in dogged determination until she was exhausted. For a time she simply sat and rested. Then she began to think. She was glad Elnora had gone where she would be compelled to fix her mind on other things for a few days. She remembered the girl had said she wanted to go.

School would begin the following week. She thought over what Elnora would have to do to accomplish her work successfully. She would be compelled to arise at six o'clock, walk three miles through varying weather, lead the high school orchestra, and then put in the rest of the day travelling from building to building over the city, teaching a specified length of time every week in each room. She must have her object lessons ready, and she must do a certain amount of practising with the orchestra. Then a cold lunch at noon, and a three-mile walk at night.

"Humph!" said Mrs. Comstock, "To get through that the girl would have to be made of cast-iron. I wonder how I can help her best?"

She plunged in deepest thought again.

"The less she sees of what she's been having all summer, the sooner she'll feel better about it," she muttered.

She arose, went to the bank and inquired for the cashier.

"I want to know just how I am fixed here," she said.

The cashier laughed. "Well, you haven't been in a hurry," he replied. "We have been ready for you any time these twenty years, but you didn't seem to pay much attention. Your account is rather flourishing. Interest, when it gets to compounding is quite a money breeder. Come back here to a table and I will show you your balances."

Mrs. Comstock sank into a chair and waited while the cashier read a jumble of figures to her. It meant that her deposits had exceeded her expenses from one to three hundred dollars a year, according to the cattle, sheep, hogs, poultry, butter, and eggs she had sold. The aggregate of these sums had been compounding interest throughout the years. Mrs. Comstock stared at the total with dazed and unbelieving eyes. Through her sick heart rushed the realization that if she merely had stood before that wicket and asked one question, she would have known that all those bitter years of skimping for Elnora and herself had been unnecessary. She arose and went back to the depot.

"I want to send a message," she said. She picked up the pencil and, with rash extravagance, wrote, "Found money at bank didn't know about. If you want to go to college, come on first train and get ready." She hesitated a second and then she said to herself grimly, "Yes, I'll pay for that, too," and recklessly added, "With love, Mother." Then she sat waiting for the answer. It came in less than an hour. "Going to teach this winter. With dearest love, Elnora."

Mrs. Comstock held the message a long time. When she arose she was ravenously hungry, but the pain in her heart was a little easier. She went to a restaurant and got some food, then to a dressmaker where she ordered four dresses; two very plain everyday ones, a serviceable dark gray cloth suit, and a soft light gray silk with touches of lavender and lace. She made a heavy list of purchases at Brownlees, and the remainder of the day she did business in her direct and spirited way. At night she was so tired she scarcely could walk home, but she built a fire and cooked and ate a hearty meal.

Later she went out by the west fence and gathered an armful of tansy which she boiled to a thick green tea. Then she stirred in oatmeal until it was a stiff paste. She spread a sheet over her bed and began tearing strips of old muslin. She bandaged each hand and arm with the mixture and plastered the soggy, evil-smelling stuff in a thick poultice over her face and neck. She was so tired she had to sleep, and when she awoke she was half skinned. She bathed her face and hands, did the work and went back to town, coming home at night to go through the same process.

By the third morning she was a raw even red, the fourth she had faded to a brilliant pink under the soothing influence of a cream recommended. That day came a letter from Elnora saying that she would remain where she was until Saturday morning, and then come to Ellen Brownlee's at Onabasha and stay for the Saturday's session of teachers to arrange their year's work. Sunday was Ellen's last day at home, and she wanted Elnora very much. She had to get together the orchestra and practise them Sunday; and could not come home until after school Monday night. That suited Mrs. Comstock, and she at once answered the letter saying so.

The next day Mrs. Comstock was a pale pink, and the following a delicate porcelain white. That day she went to a hairdresser and had the great rope of snowy hair which covered her scalp washed, dressed, and fastened with such pins and combs as were decided to be most becoming. She took samples of her dresses, went to a milliner, and bought a street hat to match her suit, and a gray satin with lavender orchids to wear with the silk dress. Her last investment was a loose coat of soft gray broadcloth with white lining, and touches of lavender on the embroidered collar, and gray gloves to match.

Then she went home, rested and worked by turns until Monday. When school closed on that evening, and Elnora, so tired she almost trembled, came down the long walk after a late session of teachers' meeting, a messenger boy stopped her.

"There's a lady wants to see you most important. I am to take you to the place," he said.

Elnora groaned. She could not imagine who wanted her, but there was nothing to do but go and find out, tired and anxious to see her mother as she was.

"This is the place," said the boy, and went his way whistling. Elnora was three blocks from the high school building on the same street. She was before a quaint old house, fresh with paint and covered with vines. There was a long wide lot, grass-covered, closely set with trees, and a barn and chicken park at the back that seemed to be occupied. Elnora stepped on the veranda which was furnished with straw rugs, bent-hickory chairs, hanging baskets, and a table with a work-box and magazines, and knocked at the screen door.

Inside she could see bare polished floors, walls freshly papered in low-toned harmonious colours, straw rugs and madras curtains. It seemed to be a restful, homelike place to which she had come, and a second later down an open stairway came a tall, dark-eyed woman with cheeks faintly pink and a crown of fluffy snow-white hair. She wore a lavender gingham dress with white collar and cuffs, and she called as she advanced, "That screen isn't latched! Open it and come see your brand-new mother, my girl."

Elnora stepped inside the door. "Mother!" she cried. "You my mother! I don't believe it."

"Well, you better!" said Mrs. Comstock, "because it's true! You said you wished I were like the other girls' mothers, and I've shot as close the mark as I could without any practice. I thought that walk would be too much for you this winter, so I just rented this house and moved in, to be near you, and help more in case I'm needed. I've only lived here a day, but I like it so well I've a mortal big notion to buy the place."

"But, mother!" protested Elnora, clinging to her wonderingly. "You are perfectly beautiful, and this house is a little paradise, but how will we ever pay for it? We can't afford it!"

"Humph! Have you forgotten I telegraphed you I'd found some money I didn't know about? All I've done is paid for, and plenty more to settle for all I propose to do."

Mrs. Comstock glanced around with supreme satisfaction.

"I may get homesick as a pup before spring," she said, "but if I do I can go back. If I don't, I'll sell some timber and put a few oil wells where they don't show much. I can have land enough cleared for a few fields and put a tenant on our farm, and we will buy this and settle here. It's for sale."

"You don't look it, but you've surely gone mad!" exclaimed Elnora.

"Just the reverse, my girl," said Mrs. Comstock. "I've gone sane. If you are going to undertake this work, you must be convenient to it. And your mother should be where she can see that you are properly dressed, fed, and cared for. This is our—let me think—reception room. How do you like it? This door leads to your workroom and study. I didn't do much there because I wasn't sure of my way. But I knew you would want a rug, curtains, table, shelves for books, and a case for your specimens, so I had a carpenter shelve and enclose that end of it. Looks pretty neat to me. The dining room and kitchen are back, one of the cows in the barn, and some chickens in the coop. I understand that none of the other girls' mothers milk a cow, so a neighbour boy will tend to ours for a third of the milk. There are three bedrooms, and a bath upstairs. Go take one, get in some fresh clothes, and come to supper. You can find your room because your things are in it."

Elnora kissed her mother over and over, and hurried upstairs. She identified her room by the dressing-case. There was a pretty rug, and curtains, white iron bed, plain and rocking chairs to match her case, a shirtwaist chest, and the big closet was filled with her old clothing and several new dresses. She found the bathroom, bathed, dressed in fresh linen and went down to a supper that was an evidence of Mrs. Comstock's highest art in cooking. Elnora was so hungry she ate her first real meal in two weeks. But the bites went down slowly because she forgot about them in watching her mother.

"How on earth did you do it?" she said at last. "I always thought you were naturally brown as a nut."

"Oh, that was just tan and sunburn!" explained Mrs. Comstock. "I always knew I was white underneath it. I hated to shade my face because I hadn't anything but a sunbonnet, and I couldn't stand for it to touch my ears, so I went bareheaded and took all the colour I accumulated. But when I began to think of moving you in to your work, I saw I must put up an appearance that wouldn't disgrace you, so I thought I'd best remove the crust. It took some time, and I hope I may die before I ever endure the feel and the smell of the stuff I used again, but it skinned me nicely. What you now see is my own with just a little dust of rice powder, for protection. I'm sort of tender yet."

"And your lovely, lovely hair?" breathed Elnora.

"Hair dresser did that!" said Mrs. Comstock. "It cost like smoke. But I watched her, and with a little help from you I can wash it alone next time, though it will be hard work. I let her monkey with it until she said she had found 'my style.' Then I tore it down and had her show me how to build it up again three times. I thought my arms would drop. When I paid the bill for her work, the time I'd taken, the pins, and combs she'd used, I nearly had heart failure, but I didn't turn a hair before her. I just smiled at her sweetly and said, 'How reasonable you are!' Come to think of it, she was! She might have charged me ten dollars for what she did just as well as nine seventy-five. I couldn't have helped myself. I had made no bargain to begin on."

Then Elnora leaned back in her chair and shouted, in a gust of hearty laughter, and a little of the ache ceased in her breast. There was no time to think, the remainder of that evening, she was so tired she had to sleep, and her mother did not awaken her until she barely had time to dress, breakfast and get to school. There was nothing in the new life to remind her of the old, while it seemed as if there never came a minute for retrospection, but her mother appeared on the scene with more work, or some entertaining thing to do.

Mrs. Comstock invited Elnora's friends to visit her, and proved herself a bright and interesting hostess. She digested a subject before she spoke; and when she advanced a view, her point was sure to be original and tersely expressed. Before three months people waited to hear what she had to say. She kept her appearance so in mind that she made a handsome and a distinguished figure.

Elnora never mentioned Philip Ammon, neither did Mrs. Comstock. Early in December came a note and a big box from him. It contained several books on nature subjects which would be a great help in school work, a number of conveniences Elnora could not afford, and a pair of glass-covered plaster casts, for each large moth she had. In these the upper and under wings of male and female showed. Ammon explained that she would break her specimens easily, carrying them about in boxes. He had seen these and thought they would be of use. Elnora was delighted with them, and at once began the tedious process of softening the mounted moths and fitting them to the casts moulded to receive them. Her time was so taken in school, she progressed slowly, so her mother undertook this work. After trying one or two very common ones she learned to handle the most delicate with ease. She took keen pride in relaxing the tense moths, fitting them to the cases, polishing the glass covers to the last degree and sealing them. The results were beautiful to behold.

Soon after Elnora wrote Ammon:

Dear Friend:

I am writing to thank you for the books, and the box of conveniences sent me for my work. I can use everything with fine results. Hope I am giving good satisfaction in my position. You will be interested to learn that when the summer's work was classified and pinned, I again had my complete collection for the man of India, save a Yellow Emperor. I have tried everywhere I know, so has the Bird Woman. We cannot find a pair for sale. Fate is against me, at least this season. I shall have to wait until next year and try again.

Thank you very much for helping me with my collection and for the books and things.

Sincerely yours,
Elnora Comstock.

Ammon was disappointed over that note and instead of keeping it he tore it into bits and dropped them into the waste basket.

That was precisely what Elnora hoped he would do. Christmas brought beautiful cards of greeting to Mrs. Comstock and Elnora, Easter others, and the year went rapidly toward spring. Elnora's work had been intensely absorbing, and she had gone into it with all her power. She had made it a wonderful success and won new friends. Mrs. Comstock had helped in every way she could, and she was very popular also.

Throughout the winter they had enjoyed the city thoroughly, and the change of life it afforded, but signs of spring did wonderful things to the hearts of the country-bred women. A restlessness began on bright February days, calmed during March storms and attacked full force in April. When neither could bear it any longer they were forced to discuss the matter and admit they were growing ill with pure homesickness. They decided to keep the city house during the summer, but to go back to the farm to live just as soon as school closed.

So Mrs. Comstock would prepare breakfast and lunch and then slip away to the farm to make up beds in her ploughed garden, plant seeds, trim and tend her flowers, and prepare the cabin for occupancy. Then she would go home and make the evening as cheerful as possible for Elnora; in these days she lived only for the girl.

Both of them were glad when the last of May came and the schools closed. They packed the books and clothing they wished to take into a wagon and walked across the fields to the old cabin. As they approached it, Mrs. Comstock said to Elnora, "You are sure you won't be lonely here?"

Elnora knew what she really meant.

"Quite sure," she said. "For a time last fall I was glad to be away, but that all wore out with the winter. Spring made me homesick as I could be. I can scarcely wait until we get back again."

So they began that summer just as they had begun all others— with work. But both of them took a new joy in everything, and the violin sang by the hour in the twilight.

CHAPTER 19

Wherein Philip Ammon Gives a Ball in Honour of Edith Carr, and Hart Henderson Appears on the Scene

Edith Carr stood in a vine-enclosed side veranda of the Lake Shore Club House waiting while Philip Ammon gave some important orders. In a few days she would sail for Paris to select a wonderful trousseau she had planned for her marriage in October. To-night Philip was giving a club dance in her honour, and three hundred of their friends were bidden to share their happiness. Philip had spent days in devising new and exquisite effects in decorations, entertainment, and supper. Weeks before the favoured guests had been notified. Days before they had received the invitations asking them to participate in this entertainment by Philip Ammon in honour of Miss Carr. They spoke of it as 'Phil's' dance for Edith!

As Edith Carr stood waiting, she smiled softly. She could hear the rumble of carriages and the panting of automobiles as in a steady stream they rolled to the front entrance. She could catch glimpses of floating draperies of gauze and lace, the flash of jewels, and the passing of exquisite colour. Everyone was newly arrayed in her honour in the loveliest clothing, and the most expensive jewels they could command. As she thought of it she lifted her head a trifle higher and her eyes flashed proudly.

She was robed in a French creation suggested and designed by Philip. He had said to her, "I know a competent judge who says the distinctive feature of June is her exquisite big night moths. I want you to be the very essence of June that night, as you will be the embodiment of love. Be a moth. The most beautiful of them is either the pale green Luna or the Yellow Imperialis. Be my moon lady, or my gold Empress."

He took her to the museum and showed her the moths. She instantly decided on the yellow. Secretly because she knew the shades would make her more startlingly beautiful than any other colour. To him she said, "A moon lady seems so far away and cold. I would be of earth and very near on that night. I choose the Empress."

So she matched the colours exactly, wrote out the idea and forwarded the order to Paquin. To-night when Philip Ammon came for her, he stood speechless for a minute and then silently kissed her hands.

For she stood tall, lithe, of grace inborn, her dark waving hair high piled and crossed by gold bands studded with amethyst and at one side an enamelled lavender orchid rimmed with diamonds, which flashed and sparkled. The soft yellow robe of lightest weight velvet fitted her form perfectly, while from each shoulder fell a great velvet wing lined with lavender, and flecked with embroidery of that colour in imitation of the moth. Around her throat was a wonderful necklace and on her arms were bracelets of gold set with amethyst and rimmed with diamonds. Philip had said that her gloves, fan, and slippers must be lavender, because the feet of the moth were that colour. These accessories had been made to order and embroidered with gold. It had been arranged that her mother, Philip's, and a few best friends should receive his guests. She was to appear when she led the grand march with Philip Ammon. Miss Carr was as positive that she would be the most beautiful, and most exquisitely gowned woman present as she was of life. In her heart she thought of herself as "Imperialis Regalis," as the Yellow Empress. In a few moments she would stun her world into feeling it as Philip Ammon had done, for she had taken pains that the history of her costume should be whispered to a few who would give it circulation. She lifted her head proudly and waited, for was not Philip planning something unusual and unsurpassed in her honour? Then she smiled.

But in all the fragmentary thoughts crossing her brain the one that never came was that of Philip Ammon as the Emperor. Philip the king of her heart, and at least her equal in all things. She was the Empress—yes, but Philip was a mere man, to devise entertainments, to provide luxuries, to humour whims, to kiss hands!

"Ah, my luck!" cried a voice behind her.

Edith Carr turned and smiled exquisitely.

"I thought you were on the ocean," she said.

"I only reached the dock," replied the man. "When I had a letter that recalled me by the first limited."

"Oh! Important business?"

"The only business of any importance in all the world to me. I'm triumphant that I came. Edith, you are the most superb woman in every respect that I have ever seen. One glimpse is worth the whole journey."

"You like my dress?" she moved toward him and turned, lifting her arms. "Do you know what it is intended to represent?"

"Yes, Polly Ammon told me. I knew when I heard about it how you would look, so I started a sleuth hunt, to get the first peep. Edith, I can become intoxicated just with looking at you to-night."

He half-closed his eyes and smilingly stared straight at her. He was taller than she, a lean man, with close-cropped light hair, steel gray eyes, a square chin and "man of the world" written all over him.

Edith Carr flushed. "I thought you realized when you went away that you were to stop that, Hart Henderson," she cried.

"I did, but this letter of which I tell you called me back to start it all over again."

She came a step closer. "Who wrote that letter, and what did it contain concerning me?" she demanded.

"One of your most intimate chums wrote it. It contained the hazard that possibly I had given up too soon. It said that in a fit of petulance you had broken your engagement with Ammon twice this winter, and he had come back because he knew you did not really mean it. I thought hard there on the dock when I read that, and my boat sailed without me. I argued that anything so weak as an engagement twice broken and patched up again was a mighty frail affair indeed, and likely to smash completely at any time, so

I came on the run. I said once I would not see you marry any other man. Because I could not bear it, I planned to go into exile of any sort to escape that. I have changed my mind. I have come back to haunt you until the ceremony is over. Then I go, not before. I was insane!"

The girl laughed merrily. "Not half so insane as you are now, Hart!" she cried gaily. "You know that Philip Ammon has been devoted to me all my life. Well, now I'll tell you something else, because this looks serious for you. I love him with all my heart. Not while he lives shall he know it, and I will laugh at him if you tell him, but the fact remains: I intend to marry him, but no doubt I shall tease him constantly. It's good for a man to be uncertain. If you could see Ammon's face at the quarterly return of his ring, you would understand the fun of it. You had better have taken your boat."

"Possibly," said Henderson calmly. "But you are the only woman in the world for me, and while you are free, as I now see my light, I stay by you. You know the old adage."

"But I'm not 'free'!" cried Edith Carr. "I'm just telling you I am not. This night is my public acknowledgment that Phil and I are promised, as our world has surmised since we were children. That promise is an actual fact, because of what I just have told you. My little fits of temper don't count with Phil. He's been raised on them. In fact, I often invent one in a perfect calm to see him perform. He is the most amusing spectacle. But, please, please, do understand that I love him, and always will, and that we will be married."

"Just the same, I'll wait and see it an accomplished fact," said Henderson. "And, Edith, because I love you, with the sort of love it is worth a woman's while to inspire, I want your happiness before my own. So I am going to say this to you, for I never dreamed you were capable of the feeling you have displayed for Phil. If you do love him, and have loved him always, a disappointment would cut you deeper than you know. Go careful from now on! Don't strain that patched engagement of yours any further. I've known Philip all my life. I've known him through boyhood, in college, and since. All men respect him. Where the rest of us confess our sins, he stands clean. You can go to his arms with nothing to forgive. Mark this thing! I have heard him say, 'Edith is my slogan,' and I have seen him march home strong in the strength of his love for you, in the face of temptations before which every other man of us fell. Before the gods! that ought to be worth something to a girl, if she really is the delicate, sensitive, refined thing she would have man believe. It would take a woman with the organism of an ostrich to endure some of the men here to-night, if she knew them as I do; but Phil is sound to the core. So this is what I would say to you. First, your instincts are right in loving him, why not let him feel it in the ways a woman knows? Second, don't break your engagement again. As men know the man, any of us would be afraid to the soul. He loves you, yes! He is long-suffering for you, yes! But men know he has a limit. When the limit is reached, he will stand fast, and all the powers can't move him. You don't seem to think it, but you can go too far!"

"Is that all?" laughed Edith Carr sarcastically.

"No, there is one thing more," said Henderson. "Here or here-after, now and so long as I breathe, I am your slave. You can do anything you choose and know that I will kneel before you again. So carry this in the depths of your heart; now or at any time, in any place or condition, merely lift your hand, and I will come. Any-thing you want of me, that thing will I do. I am going to wait; if you need me, it is not necessary to speak; only give me the faintest sign. All your life I will be somewhere near you waiting for it."

"Idjit! You rave!" laughed Edith Carr. "How you would frighten me! What a bugbear you would raise! Be sensible and go find what keeps Phil. I was waiting patiently, but my patience is going. I won't look nearly so well as I do now when it is gone."

At that instant Philip Ammon entered. He was in full evening dress and exceptionally handsome. "Everything is ready," he said; "they are waiting for us to lead the march. It is formed."

Edith Carr smiled entrancingly. "Do you think I am ready?"

Philip looked what he thought, and offered his arm. Edith Carr nodded carelessly to Henderson, and moved away. Servants parted the curtains and the Yellow Empress bowing right and left, swept the length of the ballroom and took her place at the head of the formed procession. The great open dancing pavilion was draped with yellow silk caught up with lilac flowers. Every corner was filled with bloom of those colours. The music was played by harpers dressed in yellow and violet, and the ball opened.

The midnight supper was served with the same colours and the last half of the programme was well under way. Never had girl been more complimented and petted in the same length of time than Edith Carr. Every minute she seemed to grow more worthy of praise. A partners' dance was called and the floor was filled with couples waiting for the music. Ammon stood whispering delightful things to Edith facing him. From out of the night, in at the wide front entrance to the pavilion there swept in slow wavering flight a great yellow moth and fluttered toward the centre cluster of glaring electric lights. Philip Ammon and Edith Carr saw it at the same instant.

"Why, isn't that—?" she began excitedly.

"It's a Yellow Emperor! This is fate!" cried Ammon. "The last one Elnora needs for her collection. I must have it! Excuse me!"

He ran toward the light. "Hats! Handkerchiefs! Fans! Anything!" he panted. "Everyone hold up something and stop that! It's a moth; I've got to catch it!"

"He wants it for Edith!" ran in a murmur around the hall. The girl's face flushed, while she bit her lip in vexation.

Instantly everyone began holding up something to keep the moth from flying back into the night. One fan held straight before it served, and the moth gently settled on it.

"Hold steady!" cried Ammon. "Don't move for your life!" he rushed toward the moth, made a quick sweep and held it up between his fingers. "All right!" he called. "Thanks, everyone! Excuse me a minute."

He ran to the office.

"An ounce of gasolene, quick!" he ordered. "A cigar box, a cork, and the glue bottle."

He poured some glue into the bottom of the box, set the cork in it firmly, dashed the gasoline over the moth repeatedly, pinned it to the cork, poured the remainder of the liquid over it, closed the box, and fastened it. Then he laid a bill on the counter.

"Pack that box with cork around it, in one twice its size, tie securely and express to this address at once."

He scribbled on a sheet of paper and shoved it over.

"On your honour, will you do that faithfully as I say?" he asked the clerk.

"Certainly," was the reply.

"Then keep the change," called Ammon as he ran back to the pavilion.

Edith Carr stood where he left her, thinking rapidly. She heard the murmur that went up when Philip started to capture the exquisite golden creature she was impersonating. She saw the flash of surprise that went over unrestrained faces when he ran from the room, without even showing it to her. "The last one Elnora needs," rang in her ears. He had told her that he helped collect moths the previous summer, but she had understood that the Bird Woman, with whose work Miss Carr was familiar, wanted them to put in a book.

He had spoken of a country girl he had met who played the violin wonderfully, and at times, he had showed a disposition to exalt her as a standard of womanhood. Miss Carr had ignored what he said, and talked of something else. But that girl's name had been Elnora. It was she who was collecting moths! No doubt she was the competent judge who was responsible for the yellow costume Philip had devised. Had Edith Carr been in her room, she would have torn off the dress at the thought.

Being in a circle of her best friends, which to her meant her keenest rivals and harshest critics, she grew rigid with anger. Her breath hurt her paining chest. No one thought to speak to the musicians and, seeing the floor filled, they began the waltz. Only half the guests could see what had happened, and at once the others formed and commenced to dance. Laughing couples came sweeping past her.

Edith Carr grew very white as she stood alone. Her lips turned pale, while her dark eyes flamed with anger. She stood perfectly still where Philip had left her, and the approaching men guided their partners around her, while the girls, looking back, could be seen making exclamations of surprise.

The idolized only daughter of the Carr family hoped that she would drop dead from mortification, but nothing happened. She was too perverse to step aside laughingly and say that she was waiting for Philip. Then came Tom Levering dancing with Polly

Ammon. Being in the scales with the Ammon family, Tom scented trouble from afar, so he whispered to Polly, "Edith is standing in the middle of the floor, and she's awful mad about something."

"That won't hurt her," laughed Polly. "It's an old pose of hers. She knows she looks superb when she is angry, so she keeps herself furious half the time on purpose."

"She looks like the mischief!" answered Tom. "Hadn't we better steer over and wait with her? She's the ugliest sight I ever saw!"

"Why Tom!" cried Polly. "Stop, quickly!"

They hurried to Edith.

"Come, dear," said Polly. "We are going to wait with you until Phil gets back. Let's go for a drink. I am so thirsty!"

"Yes, do!" begged Tom, offering his arm. "Let's get out of here until Phil comes."

There was an opportunity to laugh and walk away, but Edith Carr would not accept it. Anger only seemed to flame higher.

"My betrothed left me here," she said. "Here I shall remain until he returns for me, and then—he will be my betrothed no longer!"

Polly grasped Edith's arm.

"Oh, Edith!" she implored. "Don't make a scene here, and to-night. Edith, this has been the loveliest dance ever given at the club house. Everyone is saying so. Edith! Darling, do come! Phil will be back in a second. He can explain! It's only a breath since I saw him go out. I thought he had returned."

As Polly panted these disjointed ejaculations, Tom Levering began to grow angry on her account.

"He has been gone just long enough to show every one of his guests that he will leave me standing alone, like a neglected fool, for any passing whim of his. Explain! His explanation would sound well! Do you know for whom he caught that moth? It is being sent to a girl he flirted with all last summer. It has just occurred to me that the dress I am wearing is her suggestion. Let him try to explain!"

Speech unloosed the fountain. She stripped off her gloves to free her hands. At that instant the dancers parted to admit Philip. Instinctively they stopped as they approached and with wondering faces walled in Edith and Philip, Polly and Tom.

"Mighty good of you to wait!" cried Ammon, his face beaming with delight over his success in capturing the Yellow Emperor. "I thought when I heard the music you were going on."

"How did you think I was going on?" demanded Edith Carr in frigid tones.

"I thought you would step aside and wait a few seconds for me, or dance with Henderson. It was most important to have that moth. It just completes a valuable collection for a person who needs the money. Come!"

He held out his arms.

"I 'step aside' for no one!" stormed Edith Carr. "I await no other girl's pleasure! You may 'complete the collection' with that!"

She drew her engagement ring from her finger and reached to place it in one of Philip's outstretched hands. Ammon saw and drew back. Instantly Edith dropped the ring. As it fell, almost instinctively Philip caught it in air. With amazed face he looked closely at Edith Carr. Her distorted features were scarcely recognizable. He held the ring toward her.

"Edith, for the love of mercy, wait until I can explain," he begged. "Put on your ring and let me tell you how it is."

"I know perfectly 'how it is,'" she answered. "I never will wear that ring again."

"You won't even hear what I have to say? You won't take back your ring?" he cried.

"Never! Your conduct is infamous!"

"Come to think of it," said Ammon deliberately, "it is infamous to cut a girl, who has danced all her life, out of a few measures of a waltz. As for asking forgiveness for so black a sin as picking up a moth, and starting it to a friend who lives by collecting them, I don't see how I could! I have not been gone three minutes by the clock, Edith. Put on your ring and finish the dance like a dear girl."

He thrust the glittering ruby into her fingers and again held out his arms. She dropped the ring and it rolled some distance from them. Henderson followed its shining course, and caught it before it was lost.

"You really mean it?" demanded Ammon in a voice as cold as hers ever had been.

"You know I mean it!" cried Edith Carr.

"I accept your decision in the presence of these witnesses," said Philip Ammon.

"Where is my father?" he asked of those around them. The elder Ammon with a distressed face hurried to him. "Father, take my place," said Philip. "Excuse me to my guests. Ask all my friends to forgive me. I am going out for a time."

He turned and walked from the pavilion. As he went Hart Henderson rushed to Edith Carr and forced the ring into her fingers. "Edith, quick! Come, quick!" he implored. "There's just time to catch him. If you let him go that way, he never will return in this world. Remember what I told you."

"Great prophet! aren't you, Hart?" she sneered. "Who wants him to return? If that ring is thrust upon me again I shall fling it into the lake. Signal the musicians to begin, and take this dance with me."

Henderson put the ring into his pocket, and began the dance. He could feel the muscular spasms of the girl in his arms, her face was cold and hard, but her breath burned with the scorch of fever. She finished the dance and all others, taking Phil's numbers with Henderson, who had arrived too late to arrange a programme. She left with the others, merely inclining her head as she passed Ammon's father taking his place, and entered the big touring car for which Henderson had telephoned.

She sank limply into a seat and moaned softly.

"Shall I drive awhile in the night air?" asked Henderson.

She nodded. Henderson instructed the chauffeur.

She raised her head in a few seconds. "Hart, I'm going to pieces," she said. "Won't you put your arm around me a little while?"

Henderson gathered her into his arms and her head fell on his shoulder. "Closer!" she cried.

Henderson gripped her with the strength of a practised athlete, and held her until his arms were numb, but he did not know it. The tricks of fate are cruel enough, but there scarcely could have been a worse one than that. To care for a woman as he loved Edith Carr and have her given into his arms because she was so numb with misery over her trouble with another man that she did not know or care what she did. Dawn was streaking the east when he spoke to her.

"Edith, it is growing light."

"Take me home," she said.

Henderson helped her up the steps and rang the bell. When the door was opened he went inside and guided her to her room.

"Miss Carr is ill," he said to the footman. "Rouse her maid instantly, and have her prepare something hot as quickly as possible."

"Edith," he cried, "just a word. I have been thinking. It isn't too late yet. Take your ring and put it on. I will go find Phil at once and tell him you have, that you are expecting him, and he will come."

"Think what he said!" she cried. "He accepted my decision as final, 'in the presence of witnesses,' as if it were court. He can return it to me, if I ever wear it again."

"You think that now, but in a few days you will find that you feel very differently. Living a life of heartache is no joke, and no job for a woman. Put on your ring and send me to tell him to come."

"No."

"Edith, there was not a soul who saw that, but sympathized with Phil. It was ridiculous for you to get so angry over a thing which was never intended for the slightest offence, and by no logical reasoning could have been so considered."

"Do you think that?" she demanded.

"I do!" said Henderson. "If you had laughed and stepped aside an instant, or laughed and stayed where you were, Phil would have been back; or, if he needed punishment in your eyes, to have found me having one of his dances would have been enough. I was waiting. You could have called me with one look. But to publicly do and say what you did, my lady—I know Phil, and I know you went too far. Put on that ring, and send him word you are sorry, before it is too late."

"I will not! He shall come to me."

"Then God help you!" said Henderson, "for you are plunging into misery whose depth you do not dream. Edith, I beg of you—!"

She swayed where she stood. Her maid opened the door and caught her. Henderson went down the hall and out to his car.

CHAPTER
20

Wherein the Elder Ammon Offers Advice, and Edith Carr Experiences Regrets

Philip Ammon walked from among his friends a humiliated and a wounded man. Never before had Edith Carr appeared quite so beautiful. All evening she had treated him with unusual consideration. Never had he loved her so deeply. Then in a few seconds everything was different. Seeing the change in her face, and hearing her meaningless accusations, killed something in his heart. Warmth went out and a cold weight took its place. But even after that, he had offered the ring to her again, and asked her before others to reconsider. The answer had been further insult.

He walked straight ahead, paying no heed to where he went. He had traversed many miles when he became aware that his feet had chosen familiar streets. He was passing his home. Dawn was near, but the first floor was lighted. He staggered up the steps and was instantly admitted. The library door stood open, while his father sat with a book pretending to read. At Philip's entrance the father scarcely glanced up.

"Come on!" he called. "I have just told Banks to bring me a cup of coffee before I turn in. Have one with me!"

Philip sat by the table and leaned his head on his hands, but he drank a cup of steaming coffee and felt better.

"Father," he said, "father, may I talk with you a little while?"

"Of course," answered Mr. Ammon. "I am not at all tired. I

think I must have been waiting in the hope that you would come. I want no one's version of this but yours. Tell me the straight of the thing, Phil."

Philip told all he knew, while his father sat in deep thought.

"On my life I can't see any occasion for such a display of temper, Phil. It passed all bounds of reason and breeding. Can't you think of anything more?"

"I cannot!"

"Polly says everyone expected you to carry the moth you caught to Edith. Why didn't you?"

"She screams if a thing of that kind comes near her. She never has taken the slightest interest in them. I was in a big hurry. I didn't want to miss one minute of my dance with her. The moth was not so uncommon, but by a combination of bad luck it had become the rarest in America for a friend of mine, who is making a collection to pay college expenses. For an instant last June the series was completed; when a woman's uncontrolled temper ruined this specimen and the search for it began over. A few days later a pair was secured, and again the money was in sight for several hours. Then an accident wrecked one-fourth of the collection. I helped replace those last June, all but this Yellow Emperor which we could not secure, and we haven't been able to find, buy or trade for one since. So my friend was compelled to teach this past winter instead of going to college. When that moth came flying in there to-night, it seemed to me like fate. All I thought of was, that to secure it would complete the collection and get the money. So I caught the Emperor and started it to Elnora. I declare to you that I was not out of the pavilion over three minutes at a liberal estimate. If I only had thought to speak to the orchestra! I was sure I would be back before enough couples gathered and formed for the dance."

The eyes of the elder Ammon were very bright.

"The friend for whom you wanted the moth is a girl?" he asked indifferently, as he ran the book leaves through his fingers.

"The girl of whom I wrote you last summer, and told you about in the fall. I helped her all the time I was away."

"Did Edith know of her?"

"I tried many times to tell her, to interest her, but she was so indifferent that it was insulting. She would not hear me."

"We are neither one in any condition to sleep. Why don't you begin at the first and tell me about this girl? To think of other matters for a time may clear our vision for a sane solution of this. Who is she, just what is she doing, and what is she like? You know I was reared among those Limberlost people, I can understand readily. What is her name and where does she live?"

Philip gave a man's version of the previous summer, while his father played with the book industriously.

"You are very sure as to her refinement and education?" he asked.

"In almost two months' daily association, could a man be mistaken? She can far and away beat Polly, Edith, or any girl of our set on any common, high school, or supplementary branch, and you know high schools have French, German, and physics now. Besides, she is a graduate of two other institutions. All her life she has been in the school of Hard Knocks. She has the biggest, tenderest, most human heart I ever knew in a girl. She has known life in its most cruel phases, and instead of hardening her, it has set her trying to save other people suffering. Then this nature position of which I told you; she graduated in the School of the Woods, before she got that. The Bird Woman, whose work you know, helped her there. Elnora knows more interesting things in a minute than any other girl I ever met knew in an hour, provided you are a person who cares to understand plant and animal life."

The book leaves slid rapidly through his fingers as the father drawled, "What sort of looking girl is she?"

"Tall as Edith, a little heavier, pink, even complexion, wide open blue-gray eyes with heavy black brows, and lashes so long they touch her cheeks. She has a rope of waving, shining hair that makes a real crown on her head, and it appears almost red in the light. She is as handsome as any fair woman I ever saw, but she doesn't know it. Every time anyone pays her a compliment, her mother, who is a caution, discovers that, for some reason, the girl is a fright, so she has no appreciation of her looks."

"And you were in daily association two months with a girl like that! How about it, Phil?"

"If you mean, did I trifle with her, no!" cried Philip hotly. "I told her the second time I met her all about Edith. Almost every day I wrote to Edith in her presence. Elnora gathered violets and made a fancy basket to put them in for Edith's birthday. I started to err in too open admiration for Elnora, but her mother brought me up with a whirl I never forgot. Fifty times a day in the swamps and forests Elnora made a perfect picture, but I neither looked nor said anything. I never met any girl so downright noble in bearing and actions. I never hated anything as I hated leaving her, for we were dear friends, like two wholly congenial men. Her mother was almost always with us. She knew how much I admired Elnora, but so long as I concealed it from the girl, the mother did not care."

"Yet you left such a girl and came back whole-hearted to Edith Carr!"

"Surely! You know how it has been with me about Edith all my life."

"Yet the girl you picture is far her superior to an unprejudiced person, when thinking what a man would require in a wife to be happy."

"I never have thought what I would 'require' to be happy! I only thought whether I could make Edith happy. I have been an idiot! What I've borne you'll never know! To-night is only one of many outbursts like that, in varying and lesser degrees."

"Phil, I love you, when you say you have thought only of Edith! I happen to know that it is true. You are my only son, and I have had a right to watch you closely. I believe you utterly. Anyone who cares for you as I do, and has had my years of experience in this world over yours, knows that in some ways, tonight would be a blessed release, if you could take it; but you cannot! Go to bed now, and get some rest. To-morrow, go back to her and fix it up."

"You heard what I said when I left her! I said it because something in my heart died a minute before that, and I realized that it was my love for Edith Carr. Never again will I voluntarily face such a scene. If she can act like that at a ball, before hundreds, over a thing of which I thought nothing at all, she would go into actual physical fits and spasms, over some of the household crises I've seen the Mater meet with a smile. Sir, it is truth that I have thought only of her up to the present. Now, I will admit I am thinking about myself. Father, did you see her? Life is too short, and it can be too sweet, to throw away in a battle with an unrestrained woman. I am no fighter—where a girl is concerned, anyway. I respect and love her or I do nothing. Never again is either respect or love possible between me and Edith Carr. Whenever I think of her in the future, I will see her as she was to-night. But I can't face the crowd just yet. Could you spare me a few days?"

"It is only ten days until you were to go north for the summer, go now."

"I don't want to go north. I don't want to meet people I know. There, the story would precede me. I do not need pitying glances or rough condolences. I wonder if I could not hide at Uncle Ed's in Wisconsin for awhile?"

The book closed suddenly. The father leaned across the table and looked into the son's eyes.

"Phil, are you sure of what you just have said?"

"Quite sure!"

"Do you think you are in any condition to decide to-night?"

"Death cannot return to life, father. My love for Edith Carr is dead. I hope never to see her again."

"If I thought you could be certain so soon! But, come to think of it, you are very like me in many ways. I am with you in this. Public scenes and disgraces I would not endure. It would be over with me, were I in your position, that I know."

"It is done for all time," said Philip Ammon. "Let us not speak of it further."

"Then, Phil," the father leaned closer and looked at the son tenderly, "Phil, why don't you go to the Limberlost?"

"Father!"

"Why not? No one can comfort a hurt heart like a tender woman; and, Phil, have you ever stopped to think that you may have a duty in the Limberlost, if you are free? I don't know! I only suggest it. But, for a country schoolgirl, unaccustomed to men, two months with a man like you might well awaken feelings of which you do not think. Because you were safeguarded is no sign the girl was. She might care to see you. You can soon tell. With you, she comes next to Edith, and you have made it clear to me that you appreciate her in many ways above. So I repeat it, why not go to the Limberlost?"

A long time Philip Ammon sat in deep thought. At last he raised his head.

"Well, why not!" he said. "Years could make me no surer than I am now, and life is short. Please ask Banks to get me some coffee and toast, and I will bathe and dress so I can take the early train."

"Go to your bath. I will attend to your packing and everything. And Phil, if I were you, I would leave no addresses."

"Not an address!" said Ammon. "Not even Polly."

When the train pulled out, the elder Ammon went home to find Hart Henderson waiting.

"Where is Phil?" he demanded.

"He did not feel like facing his friends at present, and I am just back from driving him to the station. He said he might go to Siam, or Patagonia. He would leave no address."

Henderson almost staggered. "He's not gone? And left no address? You don't mean it! He'll never forgive her!"

"Never is a long time, Hart," said Mr. Ammon. "And it seems even longer to those of us who are well acquainted with Phil. Last night was not the last straw. It was the whole straw-stack. It crushed Phil so far as she is concerned. He will not see her again voluntarily, and he will not forget if he does. You can take it from him, and from me, we have accepted the lady's decision. Will you have a cup of coffee?"

Twice Henderson opened his lips to speak of Edith Carr's despair. Twice he looked into the stern, inflexible face of Mr. Ammon and could not betray her. He held out the ring.

"I have no instructions as to that," said the elder Ammon, drawing back. "Possibly Miss Carr would have it as a keepsake."

"I am sure not," said Henderson curtly.

"Then suppose you return it to Peacock. I will 'phone him. He will give you the price of it, and you might add it to the children's Fresh Air Fund. We would be obliged if you would do that. No one here cares to handle the object."

"As you choose," said Henderson. "Good morning!"

Then he went to his home, but he could not think of sleep. He ordered breakfast, but he could not eat. He paced the library for a time, but it was too small. Going out on the streets he walked until exhausted, then he called a hansom and was driven to his club. He had thought himself familiar with every depth of suffering; that night had taught him that what he felt for himself was not to be compared with the anguish which wrung his heart over the agony of Edith Carr. He tried to blame Philip Ammon, but being an honest man, Henderson knew that was unjust. The fault lay wholly with her, but that only made it harder for him, as he realized it would in time for her. As he sauntered into the room an attendant hurried to him.

"You are wanted most urgently at the 'phone, Mr. Henderson," he said. "You have had three calls from Main 5770."

Henderson shivered as he picked down the receiver and gave the call.

"Is that you, Hart?" came Edith's voice.

"Yes."

"Did you find Phil?"

"No."

"Did you try?"

"Yes. As soon as I left you I went straight there."

"Wasn't he home yet?"

"He has been home and gone again."

"Gone!"

The cry tore Henderson's heart.

"Shall I come and tell you, Edith?"

"No! Tell me now."

"When I got to the house Banks said Mr. Ammon and Phil were out in the motor, so I waited. Mr. Ammon came back soon. Edith, are you alone?"

"Yes. Go on!"

"Call your maid. I can't tell you until someone is with you."

"Tell me instantly!"

"Edith, he said he had been to the station. He said Phil had started to Siam or Patagonia, he didn't know which, and left no address. He said—"

Distinctly Henderson heard her fall. He set the buzzer ringing, and in a few seconds heard voices, so he knew she had been found. Then he crept into a private den and shook with a hard, nervous chill.

The next day Edith Carr started on her trip to Europe. Henderson felt certain she hoped to meet Philip there. He was sure she would be disappointed, though he had no idea where Ammon could have gone. But after much thought he decided he would see Edith soonest by remaining at home, so he spent the summer in Chicago.

21

Wherein Philip Ammon Returns to the Limberlost, and Elnora Studies the Situation

"We must be thinking about supper, mother," said Elnora, as she set the wings of a Cecropia with great care. "It seems as if I can't get enough to eat, or enough of being at home. I enjoyed that city house. I don't believe I could have gotten through my work if I had been compelled to walk back and forth. I thought at first I never wanted to come here again. Now, I feel as if I could not live anywhere else."

"Elnora," said Mrs. Comstock, "there's someone coming down the road."

"Coming here, do you think?"

"Yes, coming here, I suspect."

Elnora glanced quickly at her mother and then turned to the road as Philip Ammon reached the gate.

"Careful, mother!" the girl instantly warned. "If you change your treatment of him a hair's breadth, he will suspect. Come with me to meet him."

She dropped her work and sprang up.

"Well, of all the delightful surprises!" she cried.

She was a trifle thinner than during the previous summer. On her face there was a more mature, patient look, but the sun struck her bare head with the same ray of red gold. She wore one of the old blue gingham dresses, open at the throat and rolled to the elbows. Mrs. Comstock did not look at all the same woman, but Ammon saw only Elnora; heard only her greeting. He caught both hands where she offered but one.

"Elnora," he cried, "if you were engaged to me, and we were at a ball, among hundreds, where I offended you very much, and didn't even know I had done anything, and if I asked you before all of them to allow me to explain, to forgive me, to wait, would your face grow distorted and unfamiliar with anger? Would you drop my ring on the floor and insult me repeatedly? Oh, Elnora, would you?"

Elnora's big eyes seemed to leap, while her face grew very white. She wrenched away her hands.

"Hush, Phil! Hush!" she protested. "That fever has you again! You are dreadfully ill. You don't know what you are saying."

"I am sleepless and exhausted; I'm heartsick; but I am well as I ever was. Answer me, Elnora, would you?"

"Answer nothing!" cried Mrs. Comstock. If Wesley Sinton had been speaking to her just then he would have called her "Kate." "Answer nothing! Hang your coat there on your nail, Phil, and come split some kindling. Elnora, clean away that stuff, and set the table. Can't you see the boy is starved and tired? He's come home to rest and get a decent meal. Come on, Phil!"

Mrs. Comstock marched away, and Ammon hung his coat in its old place and followed. Out of sight and hearing she turned on him.

"Do you call yourself a man or a hound?" she flared.

"I beg your pardon—!" stammered Philip Ammon.

"I should think you would!" she ejaculated. "I'll admit you did the square thing and was a man last summer, though I'd liked it better if you'd faced up and told me you were promised; but to come back here babying, and take hold of Elnora like that, and talk that way because you have had a fuss with your girl, I don't tolerate. Split that kindling and I'll get your supper, and then you best go. I won't have you working on Elnora's big heart, because you have quarreled with some one else. You'll have it patched up in a week and be gone again, so you can go right away."

"Mrs. Comstock, I came here to ask Elnora to marry me."

"The more fool you, then!" cried Mrs. Comstock. "This time

yesterday you were engaged to another woman, no doubt. Now, for some little flare-up you come racing here to use Elnora as a tool to spite the other girl. A week of sane living, and you will be sorry and ready to go back to Chicago, or, if you really are man enough to be sure of yourself, she will come to claim you. She has her rights. An engagement of years is a serious matter, and not broken for a whim. If you don't go, she'll come. Then, when you patch up your affairs and go sailing away together, where does my girl come in?"

"I am a lawyer, Mrs. Comstock," said Ammon. "It appeals to me as beneath your ordinary sense of justice to decide a case without hearing the evidence. It is due me that you hear me first."

"Hear your side!" flashed Mrs. Comstock. "I'd a heap sight rather hear the girl!"

"I wish to my soul that you had heard and seen her last night, Mrs. Comstock," said Ammon. "Then, my way would be clear. I never even thought of coming here to-day. I'll admit I would have come in time, but not for many months. My father sent me."

"Your father sent you!" repeated Mrs. Comstock. "Why?"

"Father, mother, and Polly were present last night. They, and all my friends, saw me insulted and disgraced in the worst exhibition of uncontrolled temper any of us ever witnessed. All of them knew it was the end. Father liked what I had told him of Elnora, and he advised me to come here, so I came. If she does not want me, I can leave instantly, but, oh, I hoped she would understand!"

"You people are not splitting wood," called Elnora from the back door.

"Oh, yes, we are!" answered Mrs. Comstock. "You set out the things for biscuit, and lay the table." She turned again to Ammon. "I know considerable about your father," she said. "I have met your Uncle's family frequently this winter. I've heard your Aunt Anna say that she didn't at all like Miss Carr, and that she and all your family secretly hoped that something would happen to prevent your marrying her. That chimes right in with your saying that your father sent you here. I guess you better speak your piece."

Ammon gave his version of the previous night.

"Do you believe me?" he finished.

"Yes," said Mrs. Comstock.

"May I stay?"

"Oh, it looks all right for you, but what about her?"

"Nothing, so far as I am concerned. Her plans were all made to start to Europe to-day. I suspect she is on the way by this time. Elnora is very sensible, Mrs. Comstock. Hadn't you better let her decide this?"

"The final decision rests with her, of course," admitted Mrs. Comstock. "But look you one thing! She's all I have. As Solomon says, 'she is the one child, the only child of her mother.' I've suffered enough in this world that I fight against any suffering which threatens her. So far as I know you've always been a man, and you may stay. But if you bring tears and heartache to her, don't have the assurance to think I'll bear it tamely. I'll get right up and fight like a catamount, if things go wrong for Elnora!"

"I have no doubt but you will," replied Ammon, "and I don't blame you in the least if you do. I have the utmost devotion to offer Elnora, a good home, fair social position, and my family will love her dearly. Think it over. I know it is sudden, but my father advised it."

"Yes, I reckon he did!" said Mrs. Comstock dryly. "I guess instead of me being the catamount, you had the genuine article up in Chicago, masquerading in peacock feathers, and posing as a fine lady, until her time came to scratch. Human nature seems to be pretty much the same the world over. But I'd give a pretty to know that secret thing you say you don't, that set her to raving over your just catching a moth for Elnora. You might get that crock of strawberries in the spring house."

They prepared and ate supper. Afterward they sat in the arbour and talked, or Elnora played until time for Ammon to go.

"Will you walk to the gate with me?" he asked Elnora as he arose.

"Not to-night," she answered lightly. "Come early in the morning if you like, and we will go over to Sleepy Snake Creek and hunt moths and gather dandelions for dinner."

Ammon leaned toward her. "May I tell you tomorrow why I came?" he asked.

"I think not," replied Elnora. "The fact is, I don't care why you came. It is enough for me that we are your very good friends, and that in trouble, you have found us a refuge. I fancy we had better live a week or two before you say anything. There is a possibility what you have to say may change in that length of time."

"It will not change one iota!" cried Ammon.

"Then it will have the grace of that much age to give it some small touch of flavour," said the girl. "Come early in the morning."

She lifted the violin and began to play a dainty fairy dance.

"Well, bless my soul!" softly ejaculated the astounded Mrs. Comstock. "To think I was worrying for fear you couldn't take care of yourself!"

Elnora laughed as she played.

"Shall I tell you what he said?" inquired Mrs. Comstock.

"Nope! I don't want to hear it!" said Elnora. "He is only six hours from Chicago. I'll give her a week to find him and fix it up, if he stays that long. If she don't put in an appearance then, he can tell me what he wants to say, and I'll take my time to think it over. Time in plenty, too! There are three of us in this, and one has got to be left with a sore heart for life. If the decision rests with me I propose to be very sure that it is the one who deserves such hard luck. Let's go to bed."

The next morning Ammon came early, dressed in the outing clothing he had worn the previous summer, and aside from a slight paleness seemed very much the same as when he left. Elnora met him on the old footing, and for a week life went on exactly as it had the previous summer. Mrs. Comstock made mental notes and watched in silence. She could see that Elnora was on a strain, though she hoped Ammon would not. The girl grew restless as the week drew to a close. Once when the gate clicked she suddenly lost colour and moved nervously. Billy came down the walk.

Ammon leaned toward Mrs. Comstock and said, "I am expressly forbidden to speak to Elnora as I would like just now. Would you mind telling her for me that I had a letter from my father this morning saying that Miss Carr is on her way to Europe for the summer?"

"Elnora," said Mrs. Comstock promptly, "I have just heard that Carr woman is on her way to Europe, and I wish to my gracious stars she'd stay there!"

Philip Ammon shouted, but Elnora rose hastily and went to meet Billy. They came into the arbour together and after speaking to Mrs. Comstock and Ammon, Billy said, "Uncle Wesley and I found something funny, and we thought you'd like to see."

"I don't know what I should do without you and Uncle Wesley to help me," said Elnora. "What have you found now?"

"Something I couldn't bring. You have to come to it. I tried to get one and I killed it. They are a kind of insecty things, and they got a long tail that is three fine hairs. They stick those hairs right into the hard bark of trees, and if you pull, the hairs stay fast and it kills the bug."

"We will come at once," laughed Elnora. "I know what they are, and I can use some in my work."

"Billy, have you been crying?" inquired Mrs. Comstock.

Billy lifted a chastened face. "Yes, ma'am," he replied. "This has been the worst day."

"What's the matter with the day?"

"The day is all right," admitted Billy. "I mean every single thing has gone wrong with me."

"Now, that is too bad!" sympathized Mrs. Comstock. "Tell me about it."

"Began early this morning," said Billy. "All Snap's fault too."

"Now, what has poor Snap been doing?" demanded Mrs. Comstock, her eyes beginning to twinkle.

"Digging for woodchucks, just like he always does. He gets up at two o'clock to dig for them. He was coming in from the woods all tired and covered thick with dirt. I was going to the barn with the pail of water for Uncle Wesley to use in milking. I had to set down the pail to shut the gate so the chickens wouldn't get into the flower beds, and old Snap stuck his dirty nose into the water and began to lap it down. I knew Uncle Wesley wouldn't use that, so I had to go 'way back to the cistern for more, and it pumps awful hard. Made me mad, so I threw the water on Snap."

"Well, what of it?"

"Nothing, if he'd stood still. But it scared him awful, and when he's afraid he just goes a-humping for Aunt Margaret. When he got right up against her he stiffened out and gave a big shake. You oughter seen the nice blue dress she had put on to go to Onabasha!"

Mrs. Comstock and Ammon laughed, but Elnora put her arms around the boy. "Oh, Billy!" she cried. "That was too bad!"

"She got up early and ironed that dress to wear because it was cool. Then, when it was all dirty, she wouldn't go, and she wanted to real bad." Billy wiped his eyes. "That ain't all, either," he added.

"We'd like to know about it, Billy," suggested Mrs. Comstock, struggling with her face.

"'Cos she couldn't go to the city, she's most worked herself to death, to-day. She's done all the dirty, old hard jobs she could find. She's fixing her grape juice now."

"Sure!" cried Mrs. Comstock. "When a woman is disappointed she always works like a dog to gain sympathy!"

"Well, Uncle Wesley and I are sympathizing all we know how, without her working so. I've squeezed until I almost busted to get the juice out from the seeds and skins. That's the hard part. Now, she has to strain it through white flannel and seal it in bottles, and it's good for sick folks. Most wish I'd get sick myself, so I could have a glass. It's so good!"

Elnora glanced swiftly at her mother.

"I worked so hard," continued Billy, "that she said if I would throw the leavings in the woods, then I could come for you to see about the bugs. Do you want to go?"

"We will all go," said Mrs. Comstock. "I am mightily interested in those bugs myself."

From afar commotion could be seen at the Sinton home. Wesley and Margaret were running around wildly and peculiar sounds filled the air.

"What's the trouble?" asked Ammon, hurrying to Wesley.

"Cholera!" groaned Sinton. "My hogs are dying like flies."

Margaret was softly crying. "Wesley, can't I fix something hot? Can't we do anything? It means several hundred dollars and our winter meat."

"I never saw stock taken so suddenly and so hard," said Wesley. "I have 'phoned for the veterinary to come as soon as he can get here."

All of them hurried to the feeding pen into which the pigs seemed to be gathering from the woods. Among the common stock were big white beasts of pedigree which were Wesley's pride at county fairs. Several of these rolled on their backs, pawing the air feebly and emitting little squeaks. A huge Berkshire sat on his haunches, slowly shaking his head, the water dropping from his eyes, until he, too, rolled over with faint grunts. A pair crossing the yard on wavering legs collided, and attacked each other in anger, only to fall, so weak they scarcely could squeal. A fine snowy Plymouth Rock rooster after several attempts, flew to the fence, balanced with great effort, wildly flapped his wings and started to emit a guttural crow, but broke off and fell sprawling among the pigs, too helpless to stand.

"Did you ever see such a dreadful sight?" sobbed Margaret.

Billy climbed on the fence, took one long look and turned an astounded face to Wesley.

"Why them pigs is drunk!" he cried. "They act just like my pa!"

Wesley turned on Margaret.

"Where did you put the leavings from that grape juice?" he demanded.

"I sent Billy to throw it in the woods."

"Billy—" began Wesley.

"Threw it just where she told me to," cried Billy. "But some of the pigs came by there coming into the pen, and some were close in the fence corners."

"Did they eat it?" demanded Wesley.

"They just chanked into it," replied Billy graphically. "They pushed, and squealed, and fought over it. You couldn't blame 'em! It was the best stuff I ever tasted!"

Faint squealing, punctuated by feeble crows filled the long pause which ensued.

"Margaret," said Wesley, "run, 'phone that doctor he won't be needed. Billy, take Elnora and Mr. Ammon to see the bugs. Katherine, suppose you help me a little."

Wesley took the clothes basket from the back porch and started in the direction of the cellar. Margaret returned from the telephone.

"I just caught him," she said. "There's that much saved. Why, Wesley, what are you going to do?"

"You go sit on the front porch a little while," said Wesley. "You will feel better if you don't see this."

"Wesley," cried Margaret aghast. "Some of that wine is ten years old. There's days and days of hard work in it, and I couldn't say how much sugar. Dr. Ammon keeps people alive with it when nothing else will stay on their stomachs."

"Let 'em die, then!" said Wesley. "You heard the boy, didn't you?"

"It's a cold process. There's not a particle of fermentation about it!"

"Not a particle of fermentation! Great day, Margaret! Look at those pigs!"

Margaret took a long look. "Leave me a few bottles for mince-meat," she wavered.

"Not a smell for any cause on this earth! You heard the boy! He shan't say, when he grows to manhood that he learned to like it here!"

Wesley made a clean sweep, Mrs. Comstock cheerfully assisting. Then they all went to the woods to see and learn about the wonderful insects. The day ended with a big supper at Sintons', and then they went down to the Comstock cabin for a concert. Elnora played beautifully that night. When the Sintons left she kissed Billy with particular tenderness. She was so moved that she was kinder to Ammon than she had intended to be, and Elnora as an antidote to a disappointed lover, was a decided success in any mood.

However strong the attractions of Edith Carr had been, once the bond was finally broken, Philip Ammon could not help realizing that Elnora was the superior woman, and that he was fortunate to have escaped, just when he regarded his ties strongest. Every day, while working with Elnora, he saw more to admire. He grew very thankful that he was free to try to win her, and impatient to justify himself to her.

Elnora did not evince the slightest haste to hear what he had to say, but waited the week she had set, in spite of Philip's hourly manifest impatience. When she did consent to listen, Philip realized before he had talked five minutes, that she was putting herself in Edith Carr's place, and judging him from what the other girl's standpoint would be. That was so disconcerting, he did not plead his cause nearly so well as he had hoped, for when he ceased Elnora sat in silence.

"You are my judge," he said at last. "What is your verdict?"

"If I could hear her speak from her heart as I just have heard you, then I could decide," answered Elnora.

"She is on the ocean," said Philip. "She went because she knew she was wholly in the wrong. She had nothing to say, or she would have remained."

"That sounds plausible," reasoned Elnora, "but it is pretty hard to find a woman in an affair that involves her heart, with nothing at all to say. I fancy if I could meet her just now she would say several things. I should love to hear them. If I could talk with her three minutes, I could tell what answer to make you."

"Don't you believe me, Elnora?"

"Unquestioningly," answered Elnora. "But I would believe her also. If only I could meet her I soon would know."

"I don't see how that is to be accomplished," said Ammon, "but I am perfectly willing. There is no reason why you should not meet her, except that she probably would lose her temper and insult you."

"Not to any extent," said Elnora calmly. "I have a tongue of my own, while I am not without some small sense of personal values."

Ammon glanced into her face and began to laugh. Very different of facial formation and colouring, Elnora at times, closely resembled her mother. She joined in Ammon's laugh a little ruefully.

"The point is this," she said. "Someone is going to get hurt, most dreadfully. If the decision as to who it shall be rests with me, I must know it is the right one. Of course, no one ever hinted it to you, but you are a very attractive man, Philip. You are mighty good to look at, and you have a trained, refined mind, that makes you most interesting. For years Edith Carr has felt that you were hers. She has lived expecting to assume the closest relations of life with you. She has thought of you as hers, and you were hers. Now, how is she going to change? I have been thinking—thinking deep and long, Phil. If I were in her place, I simply could not give you up, unless you had made yourself unworthy of love. Undoubtedly, you never seemed so desirable to her as just now, when she is told she can't have you. What I think is that she will come to claim you yet."

"You overlook the fact that it is not in a woman's power to throw away a man and pick him up at leisure," said Ammon with some warmth. "She publicly and repeatedly cast me off. I accepted her decision as publicly as it was made. You have done all your thinking from a wrong viewpoint. You seem to have an idea that it lies with you to decide what I shall do, that if you say the word, I shall return to Edith. Get that thought out of your head! Now, and for all time to come, she is a matter of indifference to me. She killed all feeling in my heart for her so completely, that I do not even dread meeting her. I could see her coming down the walk now without the quickening of a heartbeat. I can meet her as casually as any woman I ever met, and liked least of all women.

"If I hated her, or was angry with her, I could not be sure the feeling would not die. As it is, she has deadened me into a creature of indifference. So you just revise your viewpoint a little, Elnora. Cease thinking it is for you to decide what I shall do, and that I will obey you. I make my own decisions in reference to any woman, save you. The question you are to decide is whether I may remain here, associating with you as I did last summer; but with the difference that it is understood that I am free; that it is my intention to care for you all I please, to make you return my feeling for you if I can. There is just one question for you to decide, and it is not triangular. It is between us. May I remain? May I love you? Will you give me the chance to prove what I think of you?"

"You speak very plainly," said Elnora.

"This is the time to speak plainly," said Philip Ammon. "There is no use in allowing you to go on threshing out a problem which does not exist. If you do not want me here, say so and I will go. Of course, I warn you before I start, that I will come back. I won't yield without the stiffest fight it is in me to make. I will have all you have to give any man if I can get it. But drop thinking it lies in your power to send me back to Edith Carr. If she were the last woman in the world, and I the last man, I'd jump off the planet before I would give her further opportunity to exercise her temper on me. Narrow this to us, Elnora. Will you take the place she vacated? Will you take the heart she threw away? I'd give my right hand and not flinch, if I could offer you my life, free from any contact with hers, but that is not possible. I can't undo things which are done. I can only profit by experience and build better in the future."

"I don't see how you can be sure of yourself," said Elnora. "I don't see how I could be sure of you. You loved her first, you never can care for me anything like that. Always I'd have to be afraid you were thinking of her and regretting."

"Folly!" cried Ammon. "Regretting what? That I was not married to a woman who was liable to rave at me any time or place, without my being conscious of having given offence? A man does relish that! I am likely to pine for more!"

"You'd be thinking she'd learned a lesson. You would think it wouldn't happen again."

"No, I wouldn't be 'thinking,'" said Ammon. "I'd be everlastingly sure! I wouldn't risk what I went through that night again, not to save my life! Just you and me, Elnora. Decide for us."

"I can't!" cried Elnora. "I am afraid!"

"Very well," said Ammon. "We will wait until you feel that you can. Wait until fear vanishes. Just decide now whether you would rather have me go for a few months, or remain with you. Which shall it be, Elnora?"

"You can never love me as you did her," wailed Elnora.

"I am happy to say I cannot," replied Ammon. "I've cut my matrimonial teeth. I'm cured of wanting to swell in society. I've gotten over being proud of a woman for her looks alone. I have no further use for lavishing myself on a beautiful, elegantly dressed creature, who thinks only of self. I have come to the surface. I have learned that I am just a common man. I admire beauty and beautiful clothing just as much as I ever did; but, first, I want an understanding, deep as the lowest recess of my soul, with the woman I marry. I want to work for you, to plan for you, to build you a home with every comfort, to give you all good things I can, to shield you from every evil. I want to interpose my body between yours and fire, flood, or famine. I want to give you everything; but I hate the idea of getting nothing at all on which I can depend in return. Edith Carr had only good looks to offer, and when anger overtook her, beauty went out like a snuffed candle.

"I want you to love me. I want some consideration. I even crave respect. I've kept myself clean. So far as I know how to be, I am honest and scrupulous. It wouldn't hurt me to feel that you took some interest in these things. Pretty fierce temptations strike a man, every few days, in this world. I can keep decent, for a woman who cares for decency, but when I do, I'd like to have the fact recognized, by just enough of a show of appreciation that I could see it. I am tired of this one-sided business. It has made me selfish. After this, I want to get a little in return for what I give. Elnora, you have love, tenderness, and honest appreciation of the finest in life. Take what I offer, and give what I ask."

"You do not ask much," said Elnora.

"As for not loving you as I did Edith," continued Ammon, "as I said before, I hope not! I have a newer and better idea of loving. The feeling I offer you was inspired by you. It is a Limberlost product. It is as much bigger, cleaner, and more wholesome than any feeling I ever had for Edith Carr, as you are bigger than she, when you stand before your classes and in calm dignity explain the marvels of the Almighty, while she stands on a ballroom floor, and gives way to uncontrolled temper. Ye gods, Elnora, if you could look into my soul, you would see it leap and rejoice over my escape! Perhaps it isn't decent, but it's human, and I'm only a common human being. I'm the gladdest thing alive that I'm free! I would turn somersaults and yell if I dared. What an escape! Just snatched out of it with a clean conscience, when I was most besotted. Stop straining after Edith Carr's viewpoint and take a look from mine. Put yourself in my place and try to study out how I feel.

"I am so happy I get religious over it. Fifty times a day I catch myself whispering, 'My soul is escaped!' As for you, take all the time you want. If you had rather be alone, I'll take the next train and stay away as long as I can bear it, but I'll come back. You can be most sure of that. Straight as your pigeons to their loft, I'll come back to you, Elnora. Shall I go?"

"Oh, what's the use to be extravagant?" murmured Elnora.

22

Wherein Philip Ammon Kneels to the Queen of Love, and Chicago Comes to the Limberlost

The month which followed was a reproduction of the previous June. There were long moth hunts, days of specimen gathering, wonderful hours with great books, big dinners all of them helped to prepare, and perfect nights filled with music. Everything was as it had been, with the difference that Philip was now an avowed suitor. He missed no opportunity to advance himself in Elnora's graces. At the end of the month he was no nearer any sort of understanding with her than he had been at the beginning. He revelled in the privilege of loving her, but he got no response. Elnora believed in his love, yet she hesitated to accept him, because she could not forget Edith Carr.

One afternoon early in July, Ammon came across the fields, through the Comstock woods, and entered the garden. He inquired for Elnora at the back door and was told that she was reading under the willow. He went around the west end of the cabin to her. She sat on a rustic bench they had made and placed beneath a drooping branch. Ammon had not seen her before in the dress she was wearing. It was clinging mull of pale green, trimmed with narrow ruffles and touched with knots of black velvet; a simple dress, but vastly becoming. Every tint of her bright hair, her luminous eyes, her red lips, and her rose-flushed face, neck, and arms grew a little more vivid with the delicate green setting.

Ammon stopped short. She was so near, so temptingly sweet, he lost control. He went to her with a half-smothered cry after that first long look, dropped on one knee beside her and reached an arm behind her to the bench back, so that he was very near. He caught her hands.

"Elnora!" he cried tensely, "end it now! Say this strain is over. I pledge you that you will be happy. You don't know! If you only would say the word, you would awake to new life and great joy! Won't you promise me now, Elnora?"

The girl sat staring into the west woods, while strong in her eyes was her father's look of seeing something invisible to others. Ammon's arm slipped from the bench around her. His fingers closed firmly over hers, his face came very near.

"Elnora," he pleaded, "you know me well enough. You have had time in plenty. End it now. Say you will be mine!"

He gathered her closer, pressing his face against hers, his breath on her cheek.

"Can't you quite promise yet, my girl of the Limberlost?"

Elnora shook her head. Instantly he released her.

"Forgive me," he begged. "I had no intention of thrusting myself upon you, but, Elnora, you are the veriest Queen of Love, this afternoon. From the tips of your toes to your shining crown, I worship you. All my life I will. I want no woman save you. You are so wonderful this afternoon, I couldn't help urging. Forgive me. Perhaps it was something that came this morning for you. I wrote Polly to send it. May we just try if it fits? Will you tell me if you like it?"

He drew a little white velvet box from his pocket and showed her a splendid emerald ring.

"It may not be right," he said. "The inside of a glove finger is not very accurate for a measure, but it was the best I could do. I wrote Polly to get it, because she and mother are home from the East this week, but next they will go on to our cottage in the north, and no one knows what is right quite so well as Polly."

He laid the ring in Elnora's hand.

"Dearest," he said, "don't slip that on your finger; put your arms around my neck and promise me, all at once and abruptly, or I'll keel over and die of sheer joy."

Elnora smiled.

"I won't! Not all those venturesome things at once; but, Phil, I'm ashamed to confess that ring simply fascinates me. It is the most beautiful one I ever saw, and do you know that I never owned a ring of any kind in my life? Would you think me unwomanly if I slip it on just a second, before I can say for sure. Phil, you know I care! I care very much! You know I will tell you the instant I feel right about it."

"Certainly you will," agreed Ammon promptly. "It is your right to take all the time you choose. I can't put that ring on you until it means a bond between us. I'll shut my eyes and you try it on, so we can see if it fits and looks well."

Philip turned his face toward the west woods and tightly closed his eyes. It was a boyish thing to do, and it caught the hesitating girl in the depths of her heart as the boy element in a man ever appeals to a motherly woman. Before she quite realized what she was doing, the ring slid on her finger. With both arms she caught Ammon and drew him to her breast, holding him closely. Her head drooped over his, her lips were on his hair. So an instant, then her arms dropped. Ammon lifted a convulsed, white face.

"Dear Lord!" he whispered. "You—you didn't mean that, Elnora! You— What made you do it?"

"You—you looked so boyish!" panted Elnora. "I didn't mean it! I—I forgot that you were older than Billy. Look—look at the ring!"

She thrust her hand before him to distract his attention.

"'The Queen can do no wrong,'" quoted Ammon between his set teeth. "But don't you do that again, Elnora, unless you do mean it. Kings are not so good as queens, and there is a limit with all men. As you say, we will look at your ring. It seems very lovely to me. Suppose you leave it on until time for me to go. Please do! I have heard of mute appeals; perhaps it will plead for me. I am wild for your lips this afternoon. I am going to take your hands."

He caught both of them and covered them with kisses. He lifted his face.

"Elnora," he said, "will you be my wife?"

"I must have a little more time," she whispered. "I must be absolutely certain, for when I say yes, and give myself to you, only death shall part us. I would not give you up. So I want just a little more time—but, I think I will."

"Thank you," said Ammon. "If at any time you feel that you have reached a decision, will you tell me? I don't feel as if I could lose a second waiting to stumble on that fact. Will you promise me to tell me instantly, or shall I keep asking you until the time comes?"

"You make it difficult," said Elnora. "But I will promise you that. Whenever the last doubt vanishes, I will let you know instantly—if I can."

"Would it be hard for you?" whispered Ammon.

"I—I don't know," faltered Elnora.

"It seems as if I can't be man enough to put this thought aside and give up this afternoon," said Ammon. "I am ashamed of myself, but I can't help it. I am going to ask God to make that last doubt vanish before I go this night. I am going to believe that ring will plead for me. I am going to hope that doubt will disappear suddenly. I will be watching. Every second I will be watching. If it happens and you can't speak, give me your hand. Just the least movement toward me, I will understand. Would it help you to talk it over with your mother? Shall I call her? Shall I—?"

Honk! Honk! Honk! Hart Henderson set the alarm of the big automobile going as it shot from behind the trees lining the Brushwood road. The picture of a vine-covered cabin, a great drooping tree, a green-clad girl, and a man bending over her very closely flashed into view. Edith Carr caught her breath with a snap. Polly Ammon gave Tom Levering a quick touch and wickedly winked at him.

Several days before, Edith had returned from Europe suddenly. She and Henderson had called at the Ammon residence saying that they were going to motor down to the Limberlost to see Philip a few hours, and urged that Polly and Tom accompany them. Mrs. Ammon knew that her husband would disapprove of the trip, but it was easy to see that Edith Carr had determined on going. So the mother thought it better to have Polly along to support Philip than to allow him to confront Edith unexpectedly and alone. Polly was full of spirit. She did not relish the thought of Edith as a sister. Always they had been in the same set, always

Edith, because of greater beauty and wealth, had patronized Polly. Although it had rankled, she had borne it sweetly. But two days before, her father had extracted a promise of secrecy, given her Philip's address and told her to send him the finest emerald ring she could select. Polly knew how that ring would be used. What she did not know was that the girl who accompanied her went back to the store afterward, made an excuse to the clerk that she had been sent to be absolutely sure that the address was right, and so secured it for Edith Carr.

Two days later Edith had induced Hart Henderson to take her to Onabasha. By the aid of maps they located the Comstock land and passed it, merely to see the place. Henderson hated that trip, and implored Edith not to take it, but she made no effort to conceal from him what she suffered, and it was more than he could endure. He pointed out that Philip had gone away without leaving an address, because he did not wish to see her, or any of them. But Edith was so sure of her power, she felt certain Philip needed only to see her to succumb to her beauty as he always had done, while now she was ready to plead for forgiveness. So they came down the Brushwood road, and Henderson had just said to Edith beside him, "This should be the Comstock land on our left."

A minute later the wood ended, while the sunlight, as always pitiless, etched with distinctness the scene at the west end of the cabin. Instinctively, to save Edith, Henderson set the whistle blowing. He had thought to go on to the city, but Polly Ammon stood, crying, "Phil! Phil!" Tom Levering was on his feet shouting and waving, while Edith in her most imperial manner ordered him to turn into the lane leading through the woods beside the cabin.

"Fix it some way that I get a minute alone with her," she commanded as he stopped the car.

"That is my sister Polly, her fiancé Tom Levering, a friend of mine named Henderson, and—" began Ammon.

"—and Edith Carr," volunteered Elnora.

"And Edith Carr," repeated Philip Ammon. "Elnora, be brave, for my sake. Their coming can make no difference in any way. I won't let them stay but a few minutes. Come with me!"

"Do I look scared?" inquired Elnora serenely. "This is why you haven't had your answer. I have been waiting just six weeks for that motor. You may bring them to me at the arbour."

Ammon glanced at her and broke into a laugh. She had not lost colour. Her self-possession was perfect. She deliberately turned and walked toward the grape arbour, while he sprang over the west fence and ran to the car.

Elnora standing in the arbour entrance made a perfect picture, framed in green leaves and tendrils. No matter how her heart ached, it was good to her, for it pumped steadily, and kept her cheeks and lips suffused with colour. She saw Philip reach the car and gather his sister into his arms. Past her he reached a hand to Levering, then to Edith Carr and Henderson. He lifted his sister to the ground, and assisted Edith to alight. Instantly, she stepped beside him, and Elnora's heart played its first trick.

She could see that Miss Carr was splendidly beautiful, while she moved with the hauteur and grace supposed to be the prerogatives of royalty. And she had instantly taken possession of Philip Ammon. But Ammon also had a brain which was working with rapidity. He knew Elnora was watching so he swung around to the others.

"Give her up, Tom!" he cried. "I didn't know I wanted to see the little nuisance so badly, but I do. How are father and mother? Polly, didn't the mater send me something?"

"She did!" said Polly Ammon, stopping on the path and lifting her chin as a little child, while she drew away her veil.

Philip caught her in his arms and stooped for his mother's kiss. "Be good to Elnora!" he whispered.

"Umhu!" assented Polly. And aloud—"Look at that ripping green and gold symphony! I never saw such a beauty! Thomas Asquith Levering, you come straight here and take my hand!"

Edith's move to compel Ammon to approach Elnora beside her had been easy to see; also its failure. Henderson stepped into Ammon's place as he turned to his sister. Instead of taking Polly's hand Levering ran to open the gate. Edith passed through first, but Polly darted in front of her on the run, with Phil holding her arm, and swept up to Elnora. Polly looked for the ring and saw it. That settled matters with her.

"You lovely, lovely, darling girl!" she cried, throwing her arms around Elnora and kissing her. With her lips near Elnora's ear, Polly whispered, "Sister! Dear, dear sister!"

Elnora drew back, staring at Polly in confused amazement. She was a beautiful girl, dressed in some wonderful way, her eyes were sparkling and dancing, and as she turned to make way for the others, she kept one of Elnora's hands in hers. Polly would have dropped very dead in that instant if Edith Carr could have killed with a look, for not until then did she realize that Polly would even many a slight, and that it had been a great mistake to bring her.

Edith bowed low, muttered something and touched Elnora's fingers. Tom Levering took his cue from Polly.

"I always follow a good example," he said, and before anyone could divine his intention he kissed Elnora as he gripped her hand and cried, "Mighty glad to meet you! Like to meet you a dozen times a day, you know!"

Elnora laughed and her heart pumped smoothly. They had accomplished their purpose. They had let her know they were there through compulsion, but on her side. In that instant only pity was in Elnora's breast for the flashing dark beauty, standing with smiling face while her heart must have been filled with exceeding bitterness. Elnora stepped back from the entrance.

"Come into the shade," she urged. "You must have found it warm on these country roads. Won't you lay aside your dust-coats and have a cool drink? Philip, would you ask mother to come, and bring that pitcher in the spring house?"

They entered the arbour exclaiming at the dim, green coolness. There was plenty of room and wide seats around the sides, a table in the centre, on which lay a piece of embroidery, magazines, books, the moth apparatus, and the cyanide jar containing several specimens. Polly rejoiced in the cooling shade, slipped off her duster, removed her hat, rumpled her pretty hair and seated herself to indulge in the delightful occupation of paying off old scores. Tom Levering followed her example. Edith took a seat, but refused to remove her hat and coat, while Henderson stood in the entrance.

"There goes something with wings! Should you have that?" cried Levering.

He seized a net from the table and raced across the garden

after a butterfly. He caught it and came back mightily pleased with himself. As the creature struggled in the net, Elnora noted a repulsed look on Edith Carr's face. Levering helped the situation beautifully.

"Now what have I got?" he demanded. "Is it just a common one that everyone knows and you don't keep, or is it the rarest bird off the perch?"

"You must have had practice, you took that so perfectly," said Elnora. "I am sorry, but it is quite common and not of a kind I keep. Suppose all of you see how beautiful it is and then it may go nectar hunting again."

She held the butterfly where all of them could see, showed its upper and under wing colours, answered Polly's questions as to what it ate, how long it lived, and how it died. Then she put it into Polly's hand saying, "Stand there in the light and loosen your hold slowly and easily."

Elnora caught a brush from the table and began softly stroking the creature's sides and wings. Delighted with the sensation the butterfly slowly opened and closed its wings, clinging to Polly's soft little fingers, while everyone cried out in surprise. Elnora laid aside the brush, and the butterfly sailed away.

"Why, you are a wizard! You charm them!" marvelled Levering.

"I learned that from the Bird Woman," said Elnora. "She takes soft brushes and coaxes butterflies and moths into the positions she wants for the illustrations of a book she is writing. I have helped her often. Most of the rare ones I get go to her."

"Then you don't keep all you take?" questioned Levering.

"Oh, dear, no!" cried Elnora. "Not a tenth! For myself, a pair of each kind to use in illustrating the lectures I give in the city schools in the winter, and one pair for each collection I make. One might just as well keep the big night moths of June, for they only live four or five days anyway. For the Bird Woman, I only save rare ones she has not yet secured. Sometimes I think it is cruel to take such creatures from freedom, even for an hour, but it is the only way to teach the masses of people how to distinguish the pests they should destroy, from the harmless ones of great beauty, and secure propagation privileges for them. Here comes mother with something cool to drink."

Mrs. Comstock came deliberately, talking to Ammon as she approached. Elnora gave her one searching look, but could discover only an extreme brightness of eye to denote any unusual feeling. She wore one of her lavender dresses, while her snowy hair was high piled. She had taken care of her complexion, and her face had grown fuller during the winter. She might have been anyone's mother with pride, and she was perfectly at ease.

Polly instantly went to her and held up her face to be kissed. Mrs. Comstock's eyes twinkled and she made the greeting hearty.

The drink was compounded of the juices of oranges and berries from the garden. It was cool enough to frost glasses and pitcher and delicious to dusty tired travellers. Soon the pitcher was empty, and Elnora picked it up and went to refill it. While she was gone Henderson asked Philip about some trouble he was having with his car. They went to the woods and began a minute examination to find a defect which did not exist. Polly and Levering were having an animated conversation with Mrs. Comstock. Henderson saw Edith arise, follow the garden path next the woods and stand waiting under the willow which Elnora would pass on her return. It was for that meeting he had made the trip. He got down on the ground, tore up the car, worked, asked for help, and kept Philip busy screwing bolts and applying the oil can. All the time Henderson kept an eye on Edith and Elnora under the willow. But he took pains to lay the work he asked Philip to do where that scene would be out of his sight. When Elnora came around the corner with the pitcher, she found herself facing Edith Carr.

"I want a minute with you," said Miss Carr.

"Very well," replied Elnora, walking on.

"Set the pitcher on the bench there," commanded Edith Carr, as if speaking to a servant.

"I prefer not to offer my guests a warm drink," said Elnora. "I'll come back if you really wish to speak with me."

"I came solely for that," said Edith Carr.

"It would be a pity to travel so far in this dust and heat for nothing. I'll only be gone a second."

Elnora set the pitcher before her mother. "Please serve this," she said. "Miss Carr wishes to speak with me."

"Well, don't you pay the least attention to anything she says," cried Polly. "Tom and I didn't come here because we wanted to. We just came to checkmate her. I hoped I'd get the opportunity to say a word to you, and now she has given it to me. I just want to tell you that she threw Phil over in perfectly horrid style. All of us detest her for it, as much as he does. She hasn't any right to lay the ghost of a claim to him, has she, Tom?"

"Nary a claim," said Tom Levering earnestly. "Why, even you, Polly, couldn't serve me as she did Phil, and ever get me back again. If I were you, Miss Comstock, I'd send my mother to talk with her and I'd stay here."

Tom had gauged Mrs. Comstock rightly. Polly put her arms around Elnora. "Let me go with you, dear," she begged.

"I promised I would speak with her alone," said Elnora, "and she has to be considered. But thank you, very much."

"How I shall love you!" exulted Polly, giving Elnora a parting hug.

The girl slowly and gravely walked back to the willow. She could not imagine just what was coming, but she was promising herself that she would be very patient and control her temper.

"Will you be seated?" she asked politely.

Edith Carr glanced at the bench, while a shudder shook her.

"No. I prefer to stand," she said. "Did Mr. Ammon give you the ring you are wearing, and do you consider yourself engaged to him?"

"By what right do you ask such personal questions as those?" inquired Elnora.

"By the right of a betrothed wife. I have been promised to Philip Ammon ever since I wore short skirts. All our lives we have expected to marry. An agreement of years cannot be broken in one insane moment. Always he has loved me devotedly. Give me ten minutes with him and he will be mine for all time."

"I seriously doubt that," said Elnora. "But I am perfectly willing that you should make the test. I will call him."

"Stop!" commanded Edith Carr. "I told you that it was you I came to see."

"I remember," said Elnora.

"Mr. Ammon is my betrothed," continued Edith Carr. "I expect to take him back to Chicago with me."

"You expect considerable," murmured Elnora. "I will raise no objection to your taking him, if you can—but, I tell you frankly, I don't think it possible."

"You are so sure of yourself as that," scoffed Edith Carr. "One hour in my presence will bring back the old spell, full force. We belong to each other. I will not give him up."

"Then it is untrue that you twice rejected his ring, repeatedly insulted him, and publicly renounced him?"

"That was through you!" cried Edith Carr. "Phil and I never had been so near and so happy as we were on that night. It was your clinging to him for things that caused him to desert me among his guests, while he tried to make me await your pleasure. I realize the spell of this place, for a summer season. I understand what you and your mother have done to inveigle him. I know that your hold on him is quite real. I can see just how you have worked to ensnare him!"

"Men would call that lying," said Elnora calmly. "The second time I met Philip Ammon he told me of his engagement to you, and I respected it. I did by you as I would want you to do by me. He was here parts of each day, almost daily last summer. The Almighty is my witness that never once, by word or look did I ever make the slightest attempt to interest him in my person or personality. He wrote you frequently in my presence. He forgot the violets for which he asked to send you. I gathered them and carried them to him. I sent him back to you in unswerving devotion, and the Almighty is also my witness that I *could* have changed his heart last summer, if I had tried. I wisely left that work for you. All my life I shall be glad that I lived and worked on the square. That he ever would come back to me free, by your act, I never dreamed. When he left me I did not hope or expect to see him again," Elnora's voice fell soft and low, "and, behold! You sent him—and free!"

"You exult in that!" cried Edith Carr. "Let me tell you he is not free! We have belonged for years. We always will. If you cling to him, and hold him to rash things he has said and done, because he thought me still angry and unforgiving with him, you will ruin all our lives. If he married you, before a month you would read heart-hunger for me, in his eyes. He could not love me as he has done, and give me up for a little scene like that!"

"There is a great poem," said Elnora, "one line of which reads, 'For each man kills the thing he loves.' Let me tell you that a woman can do that also. He did love you—that I concede. But you killed his love everlastingly, when you disgraced him in public. Killed it so completely he does not even feel resentment toward you. To-day, he would do you a favour, if he could; but love you, no! That is over!"

Edith Carr stood truly regal and filled with scorn. "You are mistaken! Nothing on earth could kill that!" she cried, and Elnora saw that the girl really believed what she said.

"You are very sure of yourself!" said Elnora.

"I have reason to be sure," answered Edith Carr. "We have lived and loved too long. I have had years with him to match against your days. He is mine! His work, his ambitions, his friends, his place in society are with me. You may have a summer charm for a sick man in the country; if he tried placing you in society, he soon would see you as others will. It takes birth to position, schooling, and endless practice to meet social demands gracefully. You would put him to shame in a week."

"I hardly think I should follow your example so far," said Elnora dryly. "I have a feeling for Philip that would prevent my hurting him purposely, either in public or private. As for managing a social career for him he never mentioned that he desired such a thing. What he asked of me was that I should be his wife. I understood that to mean that he desired me to keep him a clean house, serve him digestible food, mother his children, and give him loving sympathy and tenderness."

"Shameless!" cried Edith Carr.

"To which of us do you intend that adjective to apply?" inquired Elnora. "I never was less ashamed in all my life. Please remember I am in my own home, and your presence here is not on my invitation."

Miss Carr lifted her head and struggled with her veil. She was very pale and trembling violently, while Elnora stood serene, a faint smile on her lips.

"Such vulgarity!" panted Edith Carr. "How can a man like Ammon endure it?"

"Why don't you ask him?" inquired Elnora. "I can call him with one breath; but, if he judged us as we stand, I should not be the one to tremble at his decision. Miss Carr, you have been quite plain. You have told me in carefully selected words just what you think of me. You insult my birth, education, appearance, and home. I assure you I am legitimate. I will pass a test examination with you on any high school or supplementary branch, or French or German. I will take a physical examination beside you. I will face any social emergency you can mention with you. I am acquainted with a whole world in which Philip Ammon is keenly interested, that you scarcely know exists. I am not afraid to face any audience you can get together anywhere with my violin. I am not repulsive to look at, and I have a wholesome regard for the proprieties and civilities of life. Philip Ammon never asked anything more of me, why should you?"

"It is plain to see," cried Edith Carr, "that you took him when he was hurt and angry and kept his wound wide open. Oh, what have you not done against me?"

"I did not promise to marry him when an hour ago he asked me the last time, and offered me this ring, because there was so much feeling in my heart for you, that I knew I never could be happy, if I felt that in any way I had failed in doing justice to your interests. I did slip on this ring, which he had just brought, because I never owned one, and it is very beautiful, but I made him no promise, nor shall I make any, until I am quite, quite sure, that you fully realize he never would marry you if I sent him away this hour."

"You know perfectly that if your puny hold on him were broken, if he were back in his home, among his friends, and where he was meeting me, in one little week, he would be mine again, as he always has been. In your heart you don't believe what you say. You don't dare trust him in my presence. You are afraid to allow him out of your sight, because you realize what the results would be. Right or wrong, you have made up your mind to ruin him and me, and you are going to be selfish enough to do it. But—"

"That will do!" said Elnora. "Spare me the enumeration of how I will regret it. I shall regret nothing. I shall not act until I know there will be nothing to regret. I have decided on my course. You may return to your friends."

"What do you mean?" demanded Edith Carr.

"That is my affair," replied Elnora. "Only this! When your opportunity comes, seize it! Any time you are in Philip Ammon's presence, exert the charms of which you boast, and take him. I grant you are justified in doing it if you can. I want nothing more than I want to see you marry Philip, if he wants you. He is just across the fence under that automobile. Go spread your meshes and exert your wiles. I won't stir to stop you. Take him to Onabasha, and to Chicago with you. Use every art you possess. If the old charm can be revived I will be the first to wish both of you well. Now, I must return to my guests. Kindly excuse me."

Elnora turned and went back to the arbour. Edith Carr followed the fence and passed through the gate into the west woods where she asked Henderson if the car was ready. As she stood near him she whispered, "Take Phil back to Onabasha with us."

"I say, Ammon, can't you go to the city with us and help me find a shop where I can get this pinion fixed?" asked Henderson. "We want to lunch and start back by five. That will get us home by midnight. Why don't you bring your automobile here?"

"I am a working man," said Philip. "I have no time to be out motoring. I can't see anything the matter with your car, myself; but, of course, you don't want to break down in the night, on strange roads, with women on your hands. I'll see."

Philip went into the arbour, where Polly took possession of his lap, fingered his hair, and kissed his forehead and lips.

"When are you coming to the cottage, Phil?" she asked. "Come soon, and bring Miss Comstock for a visit. All of us would be so glad to have her."

Philip beamed on Polly. "I'll see about that," he said. "Sounds pretty good. Elnora, Henderson is in trouble with his automobile. He wants me to go to Onabasha with him to show him where the doctor lives and help him get fixed so he can start back this evening. It will take about two hours. May I go?"

"Of course, you must go," she said, laughing lightly. "You can't leave your sister. Why don't you go back to Chicago with them? There is plenty of room, and you could have a fine visit."

"I'll be back in just two hours," said Ammon. "While I am gone, you be thinking over what we were talking of when the folks came."

"Miss Comstock can go with us just as well as not," said Polly. "That back seat was made for three, and I can sit on your lap."

"Come on! Do come!" urged Ammon instantly, and Tom Levering joined him, but Henderson and Edith silently waited at the gate.

"No, thank you," laughed Elnora. "That would crowd you, and it's warm and dusty. We will say good-bye here."

She offered her hand to all of them, and when she came to Ammon she gave him one long steady look in the eyes, then shook hands with him also.

23

Wherein Elnora Reaches a Decision, and Freckles and the Angel Appear

"Well, she came, didn't she?" remarked Mrs. Comstock to Elnora as they watched the automobile speed down the road. As it turned the Limberlost corner, Ammon arose and waved to them.

"She hasn't got him yet, anyway," said Mrs. Comstock, taking heart. "What's that on your finger, and what did she say to you?"

Elnora explained about the ring as she drew it off.

"I have several letters to write, then I am going to change my dress and walk down toward Aunt Margaret's for a little exercise. I may meet some of them, and I don't want them to see this ring. You keep it until Philip comes," said Elnora. "As for what Miss Carr said to me, many things, two of importance. One, that I lacked every social requirement necessary for the happiness of Philip Ammon, and that if I married him I would see inside a month that he was ashamed of me—"

"Aw, shockins!" scorned Mrs. Comstock. "Go on!"

"The other was that she has been engaged to him for years, that he belongs to her, and she refuses to give him up. She said that if he were in her presence one hour, she would have him under a mysterious thing she calls 'her spell' again; if he were where she could see him for one week, everything would be made up. It is her opinion that he is suffering from wounded pride, and that the slightest concession on her part will bring him to his knees before her."

Mrs. Comstock giggled. "I do hope the boy isn't weak-kneed," she said. "I just happened to be passing the west window this afternoon—"

Elnora laughed. "Nothing save actual knowledge ever would have made me believe there was a girl in all this world so infatuated with herself. She speaks casually of her power over men, and boasts of 'bringing a man to his knees' as complacently as I would pick up a net and say, 'I am going to take a butterfly.' She actually and honestly believes that if Philip were with her a little while she could re-kindle his love for her and awaken in him every particle of the old devotion. Mother, the girl is honest! She is absolutely sincere! She so believes in herself and the strength of Phil's love for her, that all her life she will believe in and brood over that thought, unless she is taught differently. So long as she thinks that, she will nurse wrong ideas and pine over her blighted life. She must be taught that Phil is absolutely free, and yet he will not go to her."

"But how on earth are you proposing to teach her that?"

"The way will open."

"Lookey here, Elnora!" cried Mrs. Comstock. "That Carr girl is the handsomest dark woman I ever saw. She's got to the place where she won't stop at anything. Her coming here proves that. I don't believe there was a thing the matter with that automobile. I think that was a scheme she fixed up to get Phil where she could see him alone, as she worked to see you. If you are going deliberately to put Philip under her influence again, you've got to brace yourself for the possibility that she may win. A man is a weak mortal, where a lovely woman is concerned, and he never denied that he loved her once. You may make yourself downright miserable."

"But, mother, if she won, it wouldn't make me half so miserable as to marry Phil myself, and then read hunger for her in his eyes! Someone has got to suffer over this. If it proves to be me, I'll bear it, and you'll never hear a whisper of complaint from me. I know the real Philip Ammon better in our months of work in the fields, than she knows him in all her years of society engagements. So she shall have the hour she asked, many, many of them, enough to make her acknowledge that she is wrong. Now, I am going to write my letters and take my walk."

Elnora threw her arms around her mother and kissed her repeatedly. "Don't you worry about me," she said. "I will get along all right, and whatever happens, I always will be your girl and you my darling mother."

She left two sealed notes on her desk. Then she changed her dress, packed a small bundle which she dropped with her hat from the window by the willow, and softly went downstairs. Mrs. Comstock was in the garden. Elnora picked up the hat and bundle, hurried down the road a few rods, then climbed the fence and entered the woods. She took a diagonal course, and after a long walk reached a road two miles west and one south. There she straightened her clothing, put on her hat and a thin dark veil and waited the passing of the next trolley. She left it at the first town and took a train for Fort Wayne. She made that point just in time to climb on the evening train north, as it pulled from the station. It was after midnight when she left the car at Grand Rapids, and went into the depot to await the coming of day.

Tired out, she laid her head on her bundle and fell asleep on a seat in the women's waiting-room. Long after light she was awakened by the roar and rattle of trains. She washed, re-arranged her hair and clothing, and went into the general waiting-room to find her way to the street. She saw him as he entered the door. There was no mistaking the tall, lithe figure, the bright hair, the lean, brown-splotched face, the steady gray eyes. He was dressed for travelling, and carried a light overcoat and a bag. Straight to him Elnora went speeding.

"Oh, I was just starting to find you!" she cried.

"Thank you!" he said.

"You are going away?" she panted.

"Not if I am needed. I have a few minutes. Can you be telling me briefly?"

"I am the Limberlost girl to whom your wife gave the dress for Commencement last spring, and both of you sent lovely gifts. There is a reason, a very good reason, why I must be hidden for a time, and I came straight to you—as if I had a right."

"You have!" answered Freckles. "Any boy or girl who ever suffered one pang in the Limberlost, has a claim to the best drop of blood in my heart. You needn't be telling me anything more. The Angel is at our cottage on Mackinac. You shall tell her and play with the babies while you want shelter. This way!"

They breakfasted in a luxurious car, talked over the swamp, the work of the Bird Woman; Elnora told of her nature lectures in the schools, and soon they were great friends. In the evening they left the train at Mackinaw City and crossed the Straits by boat. Sheets of white moonlight flooded the water and paved a molten path across the breast of it straight to the face of the moon.

The island lay a dark spot on the silver surface, its tall trees sharply outlined on the summit, and a million lights blinked around the shore. The night guns boomed from the white fort and a dark sentinel paced the ramparts above the little city tucked down close to the water. A great tenor summering in the north came out on the upper deck of the big boat, and, baring his head, faced the moon and sang, "Oh, the moon shines bright on my old Kentucky home!" Elnora thought of the Limberlost, of Philip, and her mother, and almost choked with the sobs that would rise in her throat. On the dock a woman of exquisite beauty swept into the arms of Terrence O'More.

"Oh, Freckles!" she cried. "You've been gone a month!"

"Four days, Angel, just four days by the clock," remonstrated Freckles. "Where are the children?"

"Asleep! Thank goodness! I'm worn to a thread. I never saw such inventive, active children. I can't keep track of them!"

"I have brought you help," said Freckles. "Here is the Limberlost girl in whom the Bird Woman is interested. Miss Comstock needs a rest before beginning her school work for next year, so she came to us."

"You dear thing! How good of you!" cried the Angel. "We shall be so happy to have you!"

In her room that night, in a beautiful cottage furnished with every luxury, Elnora lifted a tired face to the Angel.

"Of course, you understand there is something back of this?" she said. "I must tell you."

"Yes," agreed the Angel. "Tell me! If you get it out of your system, you will stand a better chance of sleeping."

Elnora stood brushing the copper-bright masses of her hair as she talked. When she finished the Angel was almost hysterical. "You insane creature!" she cried. "How crazy of you to turn him over to her! I know both of them. I have met them often. She may be able to make good her boast. But it is perfectly splendid of you! And, after all, really it is the only way. I can see that. I think it is what I should have done myself, or tried to do. I don't know that I could have done it! When I think of walking off and leaving Freckles with a woman he once loved, to let her see if she can make him love her again, oh, it gives me a graveyard heart. No, I never could have done it! You are bigger than I ever was. I should have turned coward, sure."

"I am a coward," admitted Elnora. "I am soul-sick! I am afraid I shall lose my senses before this is over. I didn't want to come! I wanted to stay, to go straight into his arms, to bind myself with his ring, to love him with all my heart. It wasn't my fault that I came. There was something inside that just pushed me. She is beautiful—"

"I quite agree with you!"

"You can imagine how fascinating she can be. She used no arts on me. Her purpose was to cower me. She found she could not do that, but she did a thing which helped her more. She proved that she was honest, perfectly sincere in what she thought. She believes that if she merely beckons to Philip, he will go to her. So I am giving her the opportunity to learn from him what he will do. She never will believe it from anyone else. When she is satisfied, I shall be also."

"But child! Suppose she wins him back!"

"That is the supposition with which I shall eat and sleep for the next few weeks. Would one dare ask for a peep at the babies before going to bed?"

"Now, you are perfect!" announced the Angel. "I never should have liked you all I can if you had been content to go to sleep in this house without asking to see the babies. Come this way. We named the first boy for his father, of course, and the girl for Aunt Alice. The next boy is named for my father, and the baby for the Bird Woman. After this we are going to branch out."

Elnora began to laugh.

"Oh, I suspect there will be quite a number of them," said the Angel serenely. "I am told the more there are the less trouble they make. The big ones take care of the little ones. We want a large family. This is our start."

She entered a dark room and held aloft a candle. She went to the side of a small white iron bed in which lay a boy of eight and another of three. They were perfectly formed, rosy children, the elder a replica of his mother, the other very like. Then they came to a cradle where a baby girl of almost two slept soundly, and looked a picture.

"But just see here!" said the Angel. She threw the light on a sleeping girl of six. A mass of red curls swept the pillow. Line and feature the face was that of Freckles. Without asking, Elnora knew the colour and expression of the closed eyes. The Angel handed Elnora the candle, and stooping, straightened the child's body. She ran her fingers through the bright curls, and lightly touched the aristocratic little nose.

"The supply of freckles holds out in my family, you see!" she said. "Both of the girls will have them, and the second boy a few."

She stood an instant longer, then, bending, ran her hand caressingly down a rosy bare leg, while she kissed the babyish red mouth. There had been some reason for touching all of them; the kiss fell on the lips which were like Freckles's.

To Elnora she said a tender good night, whispering brave words of encouragement and making plans to fill the days to come. Then she went away. An hour later there was a light tap on the girl's door.

"Come!" she called as she lay staring into the dark.

The Angel felt her way to the bedside, sat down and took Elnora's hands.

"I just had to come back to you," she said. "I have been telling Freckles, and he is almost hurting himself with laughing. I didn't think it was funny, but he does. He thinks it's the funniest thing that ever happened. He says that to run away from Mr. Ammon, when you had made him no promise at all, when he wasn't sure of you, won't send him home to her; it will set him hunting you! He says if you had combined the wisdom of Solomon, Socrates, and all the rest of the wise men, you couldn't have chosen any course that would have sealed him to you so surely. He feels that now Ammon will perfectly hate her for coming down there and driving you away. And you went to give her the chance she wanted. Oh, Elnora! It is getting funny! I see it, too!"

The Angel rocked on the bedside. Elnora faced the dark in silence.

"Forgive me," gulped the Angel. "I didn't mean to laugh. I didn't think it was funny, until all at once it came to me. Oh, dear! Elnora, it *is* funny! I've got to laugh!"

"Maybe it is," admitted Elnora, "to others; but it isn't very funny to me. And it won't be to Philip, or to mother."

That was very true. Mrs. Comstock had been slightly prepared for stringent action of some kind, by what Elnora had said. The mother instantly had guessed where the girl would go, but nothing was said to Philip. That would have been to invalidate Elnora's test in the beginning, and Mrs. Comstock knew her child well enough to know that she never would marry Ammon, unless she felt it right that she should. The only way to know was to find out, and Elnora had gone to seek the information. There was nothing to do but wait until she came back, and her mother was not in the least uneasy but that the girl would return brave and self-reliant, as always.

Philip Ammon hurried back to the Limberlost, strong in the hope that now he might take Elnora into his arms and receive her promise to become his wife. His first shock of disappointment came when he found her gone. In talking with Mrs. Comstock he learned that Edith Carr had made an opportunity to speak with Elnora alone. He hastened down the road to meet her, coming back an agitated man. Then search revealed the notes. His read:

Dear Philip:

I find that I am never going to be able to answer your question of this afternoon fairly to all of us, when you are with me. So I am going away a few weeks to think over matters alone. I shall not tell you, or even mother, where I am going, but I shall be safe, well cared for, and happy. Please go back home and live among your friends, just as you always have done, and on or before the first of September, I will write you where I am, and what I have decided. Please do not blame Edith Carr for this, and do not avoid her. I hope you will call on her and be friends. I think she is very sorry, and covets your friendship at least. Until September, then, as ever,

Elnora.

Mrs. Comstock's note was much the same. Ammon was ill with disappointment. In the arbour he laid his head on the table, among the implements of Elnora's loved work, and gulped down dry sobs he could not restrain. Mrs. Comstock never had liked him so well. Her hand involuntarily crept toward his dark head, then she drew back. Elnora would not want her to do anything whatever to influence him.

"What am I going to do to convince Edith Carr that I do not love her, and Elnora that I am hers?" he demanded.

"I guess you have to figure that out yourself," said Mrs. Comstock. "I'd be glad to help you if I could, but it seems to be up to you."

Ammon sat a long time in silence. "Well, I have decided!" he said abruptly. "Are you perfectly sure Elnora had plenty of money and a safe place to go?"

"Absolutely!" answered Mrs. Comstock. "She has been taking care of herself ever since she was born, and she always has come out all right, so far; I'll stake all I'm worth on it, that she always will. I don't know where she is, but I'm not going to worry about her safety."

"I can't help worrying!" cried Philip. "I can think of fifty things that may happen to her when she thinks she is safe. This is distracting! First, I am going to run up to see my father. Then, I'll let you know what we have decided. Is there anything I can do for you?"

"Nothing!" said Mrs. Comstock.

But the desire to do something for him was so strong with her she scarcely could keep her lips closed or her hands quiet. She longed to tell him what Edith Carr had said, how it had affected Elnora, and to comfort him as she felt she could. But loyalty to the girl held her. If Elnora truly felt that she could not decide until

Edith Carr was convinced, then Edith Carr would have to yield or triumph. It rested with Philip. So Mrs. Comstock kept silent, while Philip took the night limited, a bitterly disappointed man.

By noon the next day he was in his father's offices. They had a long conference, but did not arrive at much until the elder Ammon suggested sending for Polly. Anything that might have happened could be explained after Polly had told of the private conference between Edith and Elnora.

"Talk about lovely woman!" cried Philip Ammon bitterly. "One would think that after such a dose as Edith gave me, she would be satisfied to let me go my way, but no! Not caring for me enough herself to save me from public disgrace, she must now pursue me to keep any other woman from loving me. I call that too much! I am going to see her, and I want you to go with me, father."

"Very well," said Mr. Ammon, "I will go."

When Edith Carr came into her reception room that afternoon, gowned for conquest, she expected only Philip, and him penitent. She came hurrying toward him, smiling, radiant, ready to use every allurement she possessed, and paused in dismay when she saw his cold face and his father.

"Why, Phil!" she cried. "When did you come home?"

"I am not at home," answered Philip. "I merely ran up to see my father on business, and to inquire of you what it was you said to Miss Comstock yesterday that caused her to disappear before I could get back to the Limberlost."

"Miss Comstock disappear! Impossible!" cried Edith Carr. "Where could she go?"

"I thought perhaps you could answer that, since it was through you that she went."

"Phil, I haven't the faintest idea where she is," said the girl gently.

"But you know perfectly why she went! Kindly tell me that."

"Let me see you alone, and I will."

"Here and now, or not at all."

"Phil!"

"What did you say to the girl I love?"

Then Edith Carr stretched out her arms.

"Phil, I am the girl you love!" she cried. "All your life you have loved me. Surely it cannot be all gone in a few weeks of misunderstanding. I was jealous of her! I did not want you to leave me an instant that night for any other girl living. That was the moth I was representing. Everyone knew it! I wanted you to bring it to me. When you did not, I knew instantly it had been for her that you worked last summer, she who suggested my dress, she who had power to take you from me, when I wanted you most. The thought drove me mad, and I said and did those insane things. Phil, I beg your pardon! I ask your forgiveness. Yesterday she said that you had told her of me at once. She vowed both of you had been true to me—and, Phil, I couldn't look into her eyes and not see that it was the truth. Oh, Phil, if you understood how I have suffered you would forgive me. Phil, I never knew how much I cared for you! I will do anything—anything!"

"Then tell me what you said to Elnora yesterday that drove her, alone and friendless, into the night, heaven knows where!"

"You have no thought for anyone save her?"

"Yes," said Ammon. "I have. Because I once loved you, and believed in you, my heart aches for you. I will gladly forgive anything you ask. I will do anything you want, save resume our old relations. That is impossible. It is hopeless and useless to ask it."

"You truly mean that!"

"Yes."

"Then find out from her what I said!"

"Come, father," said Philip rising.

"You were going to show Edith Miss Comstock's letter," suggested Mr. Ammon.

"I have not the slightest interest in Miss Comstock's letter," said Edith Carr.

"You are not even interested in the fact that she says you are not responsible for her going, and that I am to call on you and be friends with you?"

"That is interesting, indeed!" sneered Miss Carr.

She took the letter, read and returned it.

"She has done what she could for my cause, it seems," she said coldly. "How very generous of her! Do you propose calling out Pinkertons and instituting a general search?"

"No," replied Ammon. "I simply propose to go back to the Limberlost and live with her mother, until Elnora becomes convinced that I am not courting you, and never will be. Then, perhaps, she will come home to us. Good-bye. Good luck to you always!"

24

Wherein Edith Carr Wages a Battle, and Hart Henderson Stands Guard

Many people looked, a few followed, as Edith Carr slowly came down the main street of Mackinac, pausing here and there to note the glow of colour in one small booth after another, overflowing with gay curios. That street of packed white sand, winding with the curves of the shore, outlined with brilliant shops, and thronged with laughing, bare-headed people in outing costumes was a picturesque and fascinating sight. Thousands annually made long journeys and paid exorbitant prices to take part in that pageant.

As Edith Carr slowly progressed, she was the most distinguished figure of the old street. Her clinging black gown was sufficiently elaborate for a dinner dress. On her head was a large, wide, drooping-brimmed black hat, with immense floating black plumes, while on the brim, and among the laces on her breast, glowed velvety, deep red roses. Some way these made up for the lack of colour in her cheeks and lips, and while her eyes seemed unnaturally bright, to a close observer they looked weary. Despite the effort she made to move lightly she was very tired, and dragged her heavy feet with an effort.

She turned at the little street leading down to the dock, and went out to meet the big lake steamer ploughing up the Straits from Chicago. Past the landing place, on to the very end of the pier she went, then sat down, leaned against a dock support and closed her tired eyes. When the steamer came very near she languidly watched the people lining the railing. Instantly she marked one lean anxious face turned toward hers, and with a throb of pity she lifted a hand and waved to Hart Henderson. He was the first man off the boat, coming to her instantly. She spread her trailing skirts and motioned him to sit beside her. Silently they looked across the softly lapping water. At last she forced herself to speak to him.

"Did you have a successful trip?"

"I accomplished my purpose."

"You didn't lose any time getting back."

"I never do when I am coming to you."

"Do you want to go to the cottage for anything?"

"No."

"Then let us sit here and wait until the Petosky steamer comes in. I like to watch the boats. Sometimes I study the faces, if I am not too tired."

"Have you seen any new types to-day?"

She shook her head. "This has not been an easy day, Hart."

"And it's going to be worse," said Henderson bitterly. "There's no use putting it off. Edith, I saw someone to-day."

"You should have seen thousands," she said lightly.

"I did. But of them all, only one will be of interest to you."

"Man or woman?"

"Man."

"Where?"

"Lake Shore private hospital."

"An accident?"

"No. Nervous and physical breakdown."

"Phil said he was going back to the Limberlost."

"He went. He was there three weeks, but the strain broke him. He has an old letter in his hands that he has handled until it is ragged. He held it up to me and said, 'You can see for yourself that she says she will be well and happy, but we can't know until we see her again, and that may never be. She may have gone too near that place her father went down, some of that Limberlost gang may have found her in the forest, she may lie dead in some city morgue this instant, waiting for me to find her body."

"Hart! For pity sake stop!"

"I can't," cried Henderson desperately. "I am forced to tell you. They are fighting brain fever. He did go back to the swamp and he prowled it night and day. The days down there are hot now, and the nights wet with dew and cold. He paid no attention and forgot his food. A fever started and his uncle brought him home. They've never had a word from her, or found a trace of her. Mrs. Comstock thought she had gone to O'More's at Grand Rapids, so when Phil got sick he telegraphed there. They had been gone all summer, so her mother is as anxious as Phil."

"The O'Mores are here," said Edith. "I haven't seen any of them, because I haven't gone out much in the few days since we came, but this is their summer home."

"Edith, they say at the hospital that it will take careful nursing to save Phil. He is surrounded by stacks of maps and railroad guides. He is trying to frame up a plan to set the entire detective agency of the country to work. He says he will stay there just two days longer. The doctors say he will kill himself when he goes. He is a sick man, Edith. His hands are burning and shaky and his breath was hot against my face."

"Why are you telling me?" It was a cry of acute anguish.

"He thinks you know where she is."

"I do not! I haven't an idea! I never dreamed she would go away when she had him in her hand! I should not have done it!"

"He said it was something you said to her that made her go."

"That may be, but it don't prove that I know where she went."

Henderson looked across the water and suffered keenly. At last he turned to Edith and laid a firm, strong hand over hers.

"Edith," he said, "do you realize how serious this is?"

"I suppose I do."

"Do you want as fine a fellow as Phil driven any further? If he leaves that hospital now, and goes out to the exposure and anxiety of a search for her, there will be a tragedy that no after regrets can avert. Edith, what did you say to Miss Comstock that made her run away from Phil?"

The girl turned her face from him and sat still, but the man gripping her hands and waiting in agony could see that she was shaken by the jolting of the heart in her breast.

"Edith, what did you say?"

"What difference can it make?"

"It might furnish some clue to her action."

"It could not possibly."

"Phil thinks so. He has thought so until his brain is worn enough to give way. Tell me, Edith!"

"I told her Phil was mine! That if he were away from her an hour and back in my presence, he would be to me as he always had been."

"Edith, did you believe that?"

"I would have staked my life, my soul on it!"

"Do you believe it now?"

There was no answer. Henderson took her other hand and gripping both of them firmly he said softly, "Don't mind me, dear. I don't count! I'm just old Hart! You can tell me anything. Do you still believe that?"

The beautiful head barely moved in negation. Henderson gathered both her hands in one of his and stretched an arm across her shoulders to the post to support her. She dragged her hands from him and twisted them together.

"Oh, Hart!" she cried. "It isn't fair! There is a limit! I have suffered my share. Can't you see? Can't you understand?"

"Yes," he panted. "Yes, my girl! Tell me just this one thing yet, and I'll cheerfully kill anyone who annoys you further. Tell me, Edith!"

Then she lifted her great, dull, pain-filled eyes to his and cried, "No! I do not believe it now! I know it is not true! I killed his love for me. It is dead and gone forever. Nothing will revive it! Nothing in all this world. And that is not all. I did not know how to touch the depths of his nature. I never developed in him those things he was made to enjoy. He admired me. He was proud to be with me. He thought, and I thought, that he worshipped me; but I know now that he never did care for me as he cares for her. Never! I can see it! I planned to lead society, to make his home a place sought for my beauty and popularity. She plans to further his political ambitions, to make him comfortable physically, to stimulate his intellect, to bear him a brood of red-faced children. He likes her and her plans as he never did me and mine. Oh, my soul! Now, are you satisfied?"

She dropped back against his arm exhausted. Henderson held her and learned what suffering truly means. He fanned her with his hat, rubbed her cold hands and murmured broken, incoherent things. By and by great slow tears slipped from under her closed lids, but when she opened them her eyes were dull and hard.

"What a rag one is when the last secret of the soul is torn out and laid bare!" she cried.

Henderson thrust his handkerchief into her fingers and whispered, "Edith, the boat has been creeping up. It's very near. Maybe some of our crowd are on it. Hadn't we better get away from here before it lands?"

"If I can walk," she said. "Oh, I am so dead tired, Hart!"

"Yes, dear," said Henderson soothingly. "Just try to get past the landing before the boat anchors. If I only dared carry you!"

They struggled through the waiting masses, but directly opposite the landing there was a backward movement in the happy, laughing crowd, the gang-plank came down with a slam, and people began hurrying from the boat. Crowded against the fish house on the dock, Henderson could only advance a few steps at a time. He was straining every nerve to protect and assist Edith. He saw no one he recognized near them, so he slipped his arm across her back to help support her. He felt her stiffen against him and catch her breath. At the same instant, the clearest, sweetest male voice he ever had heard called, "Be careful there, little men!"

Henderson shot a swift glance toward the boat. Terrence O'More just had stepped from the gang-plank, escorting a little daughter, so like him, it was comical. There followed a picture not easy to describe. The Angel in the full flower of her beauty, richly dressed, a laugh on her cameo face, the setting sun glinting on her gold hair, escorted by her eldest son, who held her hand tightly and carefully watched her steps. Next came Elnora, dressed with equal richness, a trifle taller and slenderer, almost the same type of colouring, but with different eyes and hair, facial lines and expression. She was led by the second O'More boy who convulsed the crowd by crying, "Tareful, Elnora! Don't 'oo be 'teppin' in de water!"

People surged around them, purposely closing them in.

"What lovely women! Who are they? It's the O'Mores. The lightest one is his wife. Is that her sister? No, it is his! They say he has a title in England."

Whispers ran fast and audible. As the crowd pressed around the party an opening was left beside the fish sheds. Edith ran down the dock. Henderson sprang after her, catching her arm and assisting her to the street.

"Up the shore! This way!" she panted. "Everyone will go to dinner the first thing they do."

They left the street and started around the beach, but Edith was breathless from running, while the yielding sand made hard walking.

"Help me!" she cried clinging to Henderson. He put his arm around her, almost carrying her out of sight into a little cove walled by high rocks at the back, while there was a clean floor of white sand, and logs washed from the lake for seats. He found one of these with a back rest, and hurrying down to the water he soaked his handkerchief and carried it to her. She passed it across her lips, over her eyes, and then pressed the palms of her hands upon it. Henderson removed the heavy hat, fanned her with his, and wet the handkerchief again.

"Hart, what makes you?" she said wearily. "My mother doesn't care. She says this is good for me. Do you think this is good for me, Hart?"

"Edith, you know I would give my life if I could save you this," he said, and could not speak further.

She leaned against him, closed her eyes and lay silent so long the man fell into panic.

"Edith, you are not unconscious?" he whispered, touching her.

"No. Just resting. Please don't leave me."

He held her carefully, softly fanning her. She was suffering almost more than either of them could bear.

"I wish your boat was here," she said at last. "I want to sail fast with the wind in my face."

"There is no wind. I can get my motor around in a few minutes."

"Then get it."

"Lie on the sand. I can 'phone from the first booth. It won't take but a little while."

Edith lay on the white sand, and Henderson covered her face with her hat. Then he ran to the nearest booth and talked imperatively. Presently he was back bringing a hot drink that was stimulating. Shortly the motor ran close to the beach and stopped. Henderson's servant brought a row-boat ashore and took them to the launch. It was filled with cushions and wraps. Henderson made a couch and soon, warmly covered, Edith sped out over the water in search of peace.

Hour after hour the boat ran up and down the shore. The moon arose and the night air grew very chilly. Henderson put on an overcoat and piled more covers on Edith.

"You must take me home," she said at last. "The folks will be uneasy."

He was compelled to take her to the cottage with the battle still raging. He went back early the next morning, but already she had wandered out over the island. Instinctively Henderson felt that the shore would attract her. There was something in the tumult of rough little Huron's waves that called to him. It was there he found her, crouching so close the water the foam was dampening her skirts.

"May I stay?" he asked.

"I have been hoping you would come," she answered. "It's bad enough when you are here, but it is a little easier than bearing it alone."

"Thank God for that!" said Henderson sitting beside her. "Shall I talk to you?"

She shook her head. So they sat by the hour. At last she spoke.

"Of course, you know there is something I have got to do, Hart!"

"You have not!" cried Henderson violently. "That's all nonsense! Give me just one word of permission. That is all that is required of you."

"'Required'? You grant, then, that there is something 'required'?"

"One word. Nothing more."

"Did you ever know one word could be so big, so black, so desperately bitter? Oh, Hart!"

"No."

"But you know it now, Hart!"

"Yes."

"And still you say that it is 'required'?"

Henderson suffered unspeakably. He twisted and fumed impotently. At last he said. "If you had seen and heard him, Edith, you, too, would feel that it is 'required.' Remember—"

"No! No! No!" she cried. "Don't ask me to remember even the least of my pride and folly. Let me forget!"

She sat silent a long time.

"Will you go with me?" she whispered.

"Of course."

At last she arose.

"I might as well give up and get it over," she faltered.

That was the first time in her life that Edith Carr ever had proposed to give up anything she wanted.

"Help me, Hart!"

Henderson started around the beach assisting her all he could. Finally he stopped.

"Edith, there is no sense in this! You are too tired to go. You know you can trust me. You wait in any of these lovely places and send me. You will be safe, and I'll run. One word is all that is necessary."

"But I've got to say that word myself, Hart!"

"Then write it, and let me carry it. The message is not going to prove who went to the office and sent it."

"That is quite true," she said dropping wearily, but she made no movement to take the pen and paper he offered.

"Hart, you write it," she said at last.

Henderson turned away his face. He gripped the pen, while his breath sucked between his dry teeth.

"Certainly!" he said when he could speak. "Mackinac, August 27, 1908. Philip Ammon, Lake Shore Hospital, Chicago." He paused with suspended pen and glanced at Edith. Her white lips were working, but no sound came. "Miss Comstock is at Terrence O'More's on Mackinac Island," prompted Henderson.

Edith nodded.

"Signed, Henderson," continued the big man.

Edith shook her head.

"Say, 'She is well and happy,' and sign, Edith Carr!" she panted.

"Not on your life!" flashed Henderson.

"For the love of mercy, Hart, don't make this any harder! It is the least I can do, and it takes every ounce of strength in me to do it."

"Will you wait for me here?" he asked.

She nodded, and, pulling his hat lower over his eyes, Henderson ran around the shore. In less than an hour he was back. He helped her a little farther to where the Devil's Kitchen lay cut into the rocks; it furnished places to rest, and cool water. Before long his man came with the boat. From it they spread blankets on the sand for her, and made chafing-dish tea. She tried to refuse it, but the fragrance overcame her and she drank ravenously. Then Henderson cooked several dishes and spread an appetizing lunch. She was young, strong, and almost famished for food. She was forced to eat. That made her feel a world better. Then Henderson helped her into the boat and ran it through shady coves of the shore, where there were refreshing breezes. When she fell asleep the girl did not know, but the man did. Sadly in need of rest himself, he ran that boat for five hours through quiet bays, away from noisy parties, and where the shade was cool and deep. When she woke he took her home, and as they went she knew that she had been mistaken. She would not die. Her heart was not even broken. She had suffered horribly; she would suffer more; but eventually the pain must wear out. Into her head crept a few lines of an old opera—

Hearts do not break, they sting and ache,
For old love's sake, but do not die,
As witnesseth the living I.

That evening they were sailing down the Straits before a stiff breeze and Henderson was busy with the tiller when she said to him, "Hart, I want you to do something more for me."

"You have only to tell me," he said.

"Have I only to tell you Hart?" she asked softly.

"Haven't you learned that yet, Edith?"

"I want you to go away."

"Very well," he said quietly, but his face whitened visibly.

"You say that as if you had been expecting it."

"I have. I knew from the beginning that when this was over you would dislike me for having seen you suffer. I have grown my Gethsemane in a full realization of what was coming, but I could not leave you, Edith, so long as it seemed to me that I was serving you. Does it make any difference to you where I go?"

"I want you where you will be loved, and good care taken of you."

"Thank you!" said Henderson, smiling grimly. "Have you any idea where such a spot might be found?"

"It should be with your sister at Los Angeles. She always has seemed very fond of you."

"That is quite true," said Henderson, his eyes brightening a little. "I will go to her. When shall I start?"

"At once."

Henderson began to tack for the landing, but his hands shook until he scarcely could manage the boat. Edith Carr sat watching him indifferently, but her heart was throbbing painfully. "Why is there so much suffering in the world?" she kept whispering to herself. Inside her door Henderson took her by the shoulders almost roughly.

"For how long is this, Edith, and how are you going to say good-bye to me?"

She raised tired, pain-filled eyes to his.

"I don't know for how long it is," she said. "It seems now as if it had been a slow eternity. I wish to my soul that God would be merciful to me and make something 'snap' in my heart, as there did in Phil's, that would give me rest. I don't know for how long, but I'm perfectly shameless with you, Hart. If peace ever comes and I want you, I won't wait for you to find it out yourself, I'll cable, Marconigraph, anything. As for how I say good-bye; any way you please. I don't care in the least what happens to me."

Henderson studied her intently.

"In that case, we will shake hands," he said. "Good-bye, Edith. Don't forget that every hour I am thinking of you and hoping all good things will come to you soon."

CHAPTER

25

Wherein Philip Finds Elnora, and Edith Carr Offers a Yellow Emperor

"Oh, I need my own violin," cried Elnora. "This one may be a thousand times more expensive, and much older than mine; but it wasn't inspired and taught to sing by a man who knew how. It don't know 'beans,' as mother would say, about the Limberlost."

The guests in the O'More music room laughed appreciatively.

"Why don't you write your mother to come for a visit and bring yours?" suggested Freckles.

"I did that three days ago," acknowledged Elnora. "I am half expecting her on the noon boat. That is one reason why this violin gets worse every minute. There is nothing at all the matter with me."

"Splendid!" cried the Angel. "I've begged and begged her to do it. I know how anxious these mothers become. When did you send? What made you? Why didn't you tell me?"

"'When?' Three days ago. 'What made me?' You. 'Why didn't I tell you?' Because I can't be sure in the least that she will come. Mother is the most individual person. She never does what everyone expects she will. She may not come, and I didn't want you to be disappointed."

"How did I make you?" asked the Angel.

"Loving Alice. It made me realize that if you cared for your girl like that, with Mr. O'More and three other children, possibly my mother, with no one, might like to see me. I know good and plenty I want to see her, and you had told me to so often, I just sent for her. Oh, I do hope she comes! I want her to see this lovely place."

"I have been wondering what you thought of Mackinac," said Freckles.

"Oh, it is a perfect picture, all of it! I should like to hang it on the wall, so I could see it whenever I wanted to; but it isn't real, of course; it's nothing but a picture."

"These people won't agree with you," smiled Freckles.

"That isn't necessary," retorted Elnora. "They know this, and they love it; but you and I are acquainted with something different. The Limberlost is life. Here it is a carefully kept park. You motor, sail, and golf, all so secure and fine. But what I like is the excitement of choosing a path carefully, in the fear that the quagmire may reach out and suck me down; to go into the swamp naked-handed and wrest from it treasures that bring me books and clothing, and I like enough of a fight for things that I always remember how I got them. I even enjoy seeing a canny old vulture eyeing me as if it were saying, 'Ware the sting of the rattler, lest I pick your bones as I did old Limber's.' I like sufficient danger to put an edge on things. This is all so tame. I should have loved it when all the homes were cabins, and watchers for the stealthy Indian canoes patrolled the shores. You wait until mother comes, and if my violin isn't angry with me for leaving it, to-night we shall sing you the Song of the Limberlost. You shall hear the big gold bees over the red, yellow, and purple flowers, bird song, wind talk, and the whispers of Sleepy Snake Creek, as it goes past you. You will know!" Elnora turned to Freckles.

He nodded. "Who better?" he asked. "This is secure while the children are so small, but when they get larger, we are going farther north, into real forest, where they can learn self-reliance and develop backbone."

Elnora laid away the violin. "Come along, children," she said. "We must get at that backbone business at once. Let's race to the playhouse."

With the brood at her heels Elnora ran, and for an hour lively sounds stole from the remaining spot of forest on the Island, which lay beside the O'More cottage. Then Terry went to the playroom to bring Alice her doll. He came racing back, dragging it by one leg, and crying, "There's company! Someone has come that mamma and papa are just tearing down the house over. I saw through the window."

"It could not be my mother, yet," mused Elnora. "Her boat is not due until twelve. Terry, give Alice that doll—"

"It's a man-person, and I don't know him, but my father is shaking his hand right straight along, and my mother is running for a hot drink and a cushion. It's a kind of a sick person, but they are going to make him well right away, anyone can see that! This is the best place. I'll go tell him to come lie on the pine needles in the sun and watch the sails go by. That will fix him!"

"Watch sails go by," chanted Little Brother. "'At fix him! Elnora fix him, won't you?"

"I don't know about that," answered Elnora. "What sort of a looking person is he, Terry?"

"A beautiful white person; but my father is going to 'colour him up,' I heard him say so. He's just out of the hospital, and he is a bad person, 'cause he ran away from the doctors and made them awful angry. But father and mother are going to doctor him better. I didn't know they could make sick people well."

"'Ey do anyfing!" boasted Little Brother.

Before Elnora missed her, Alice, who had gone to investigate, came flying across the shadows and through the sunshine waving a paper. She thrust it into Elnora's hand.

"There is a man-person—a stranger-person!" she shouted. "But he knows you! He sent you that! You are to be the doctor! He said so! Oh, do hurry! I like him heaps!"

Elnora read Edith Carr's telegram to Philip Ammon and understood that he had been ill, that she had been located by Edith who had notified him. In so doing she had acknowledged defeat. At last Philip was free. Elnora looked up with a radiant face.

"I like him 'heaps' myself!" she cried. "Come on, children, we will go tell him so."

Terry and Alice ran, but Elnora had to suit her steps to Little Brother, who was her loyal esquire, and would have been heart-broken over desertion and insulted at being carried. He was rather dragged, but he was arriving, and the emergency was great, he could see that.

"She's coming!" shouted Alice.

"She's going to be the doctor!" cried Terry.

"She looked just like she'd seen angels when she read the letter," explained Alice.

"She likes you 'heaps'! She said so!" danced Terry. "Be waiting! Here she is!"

Elnora helped Little Brother up the steps, then deserted him and came at a rush. The stranger-person stood holding out trembling arms.

"Are you sure, at last, runaway?" asked Philip Ammon.

"Perfectly sure!" cried Elnora.

"Will you marry me now?"

"This instant! That is, any time after the noon boat comes in."

"Why such unnecessary delay?" demanded Ammon.

"It is almost September," explained Elnora. "I sent for mother three days ago. We must wait until she comes, and we either have to send for Uncle Wesley and Aunt Margaret, or go to them. I couldn't possibly be married properly without those dear people."

"We will send," decided Ammon. "The trip will be a treat for them. O'More, would you get off a message at once?"

Everyone met the noon boat. They went in the motor because Ammon was too weak to walk so far. As soon as people could be distinguished at all Elnora and Philip sighted an erect figure, with a head like a snowdrift. When the gang-plank fell the first person across it was a lean, red-haired boy of eleven, carrying a violin in one hand and an enormous bouquet of yellow marigolds and purple asters in the other. He was beaming with broad smiles until he saw Ammon. Then his expression changed.

"Aw, say!" he exclaimed reproachfully. "I bet you Aunt Margaret is right. He is going to be your beau!"

Elnora stooped to kiss Billy as she caught her mother.

"There, there!" cried Mrs. Comstock. "Don't knock my head-gear into my eye. I'm not sure I've got either hat or hair. The wind blew like bizzem coming up the river."

She shook out her skirts, straightened her hat, and came forward to meet Philip, who took her into his arms and kissed her repeatedly. Then he passed her along to Freckles and the Angel to whom her greetings were mingled with scolding and laughter over her windblown hair.

"No doubt I'm a precious spectacle!" she said to the Angel. "I saw your pa a little before I started, and he sent you a note. It's in my satchel. He said he was coming up next week. What a lot of people there are in this world! And what on earth are all of them laughing about? Did none of them ever hear of sickness, or sorrow, or death? Billy, don't you go to playing Indian or chasing woodchucks until you get out of those clothes. I promised Margaret I'd bring back that suit good as new."

Then the O'More children came crowding to meet Elnora's mother.

"Merry Christmas!" cried Mrs. Comstock, gathering them in. "Got everything right here but the tree, and there seems to be plenty of them a little higher up. If this wind would stiffen just enough more to blow away the people, so one could see this place, I believe it would be right decent looking."

"See here," whispered Elnora to Ammon. "You must fix this with Billy. I can't have his trip spoiled."

"Now, here is where I dust the rest of 'em!" complacently remarked Mrs. Comstock, as she climbed into the motor car for her first ride, in company with Ammon and Little Brother. "I have been the one to trudge the roads and hop out of the way of these things for quite a spell."

She sat very erect as the car rolled into the broad main avenue, where only stray couples were walking. Her eyes began to twinkle and gleam. Suddenly she leaned forward and touched the driver on the shoulder.

"Young man," she said, "just you toot that whistle suddenly and shave close enough a few of those people, so that I can see how I look when I leap for ragweed and snake fences."

The amazed chauffeur glanced questioningly at Ammon, who slightly nodded. A second later there was a quick "honk!" and a swerve at a corner. A man engrossed in conversation grabbed the woman to whom he was talking and dashed for the safety of a lawn. The woman tripped in her skirts, and as she fell the man caught and dragged her. Both of them turned red faces to the car and berated the driver. Mrs. Comstock laughed in unrestrained enjoyment. Then she touched the chauffeur again.

"That's enough," she said. "It seems a mite risky." A minute later she added to Ammon, "If only they had been carrying six pounds of butter and ten dozen eggs apiece, wouldn't that have been just perfect?"

Billy had wavered between Elnora and the motor, but his loyal little soul had been true to her, so the walk to the cottage began with him at her side. Long before they arrived the little O'Mores had crowded around and captured Billy, and he was giving them an expurgated version of Mrs. Comstock's tales of Big Foot and Adam Poe, boasting that Uncle Wesley had been in the camps of Me-shin-go-me-sia and knew Wa-ca-co-nah before he got religion and dressed like white men; while the mighty prowess of Snap as a woodchuck hunter was done full justice. When they reached the cottage Ammon took Billy aside, showed him the emerald ring and gravely asked his permission to marry Elnora. Billy struggled to be just, but it was going hard with him, when Alice, who kept close enough to hear, intervened.

"Why don't you let them get married?" she asked. "You are much too small for her. You wait for me!"

Billy studied her intently. At last he turned to Ammon. "Aw, well! Go on, then!" he said gruffly. "I'll marry Alice!"

Alice reached her hand. "If you got that settled let's put on our Indian clothes, get the boys, and go to the playhouse."

"I haven't got any Indian clothes," said Billy ruefully.

"Yes, you have," explained Alice. "Father got you some coming from the dock. You can put them on in the playhouse. The boys do."

Billy examined the playhouse with gleaming eyes. Never had he encountered such possibilities. He could see a hundred amusing things to try, and he could not decide which to do first. The most immediate attraction seemed to be a dead pine, held perpendicularly by its fellows, while its bark had decayed and fallen, leaving a bare, smooth trunk.

"If we just had some grease that would make the dandiest pole to play Fourth of July with!" he shouted.

The children remembered the Fourth. It had been great fun.

"Butter is grease. There is plenty in the 'frigerator," suggested Alice speeding away.

Billy caught the cold roll and began to rub it against the tree excitedly.

"How are you going to get it greased to the top?" inquired Terry.

Billy's face lengthened. "That's so!" he said. "The thing is to begin at the top and grease down. I'll show you!"

Billy put the butter in his handkerchief and took the corners between his teeth. He climbed the pole, greasing it as he slid down.

"Now, I got to try first," he said, "because I'm the biggest and so I have the best chance; only the one that goes first hasn't hardly any chance at all, because he has to wipe off the grease on himself, so the others can get up at last. See?"

"All right!" said Terry. "You go first and then I will, and then Alice. Phew! It's slick. He'll never get up."

Billy wrestled manfully, and when he was exhausted he boosted Terry, and then both of them helped Alice, to whom they awarded a prize of her own doll. As they rested Billy remembered.

"Do your folks keep cows?" he asked.

"No, we buy milk," said Terry.

"Gee! Then what about the butter? Maybe your ma needs it for dinner!"

"No, she don't!" cried Alice. "There's stacks of it! I can have all the butter I want."

"Well, I'm mighty glad of it!" said Billy. "I didn't just think. I'm afraid we've greased our clothes, too."

"That's no difference," said Terry. "We can play what we please in these things."

"Well, we ought to be all dirty, and bloody, and have feathers on us to be real Indians," said Billy.

Alice tried a handful of dirt on her sleeve and it streaked beautifully. Instantly all of them began smearing themselves.

"If we only had feathers," lamented Billy.

Terry disappeared and shortly returned from the garage with a feather duster. Billy fell on it with a shriek. Around each one's head he firmly tied a twisted handkerchief, and stuck inside it a row of stiffly upstanding feathers.

"Now, if we just only had some pokeberries to paint us red, we'd be real, for sure enough Indians, and we could go on the war path and fight all the other tribes and burn a lot of them at the stake."

Alice sidled up to him. "Would huckleberries do?" she asked softly.

"Yes!" shouted Terry, wild with excitement. "Anything that's a colour!"

Alice made another trip to the refrigerator. Billy crushed the berries in his hands and smeared and streaked all their faces liberally.

"Now are we ready?" asked Alice.

Billy collapsed. "I forgot the ponies! You got to ride ponies to go on the war path!"

"You ain't neither!" contradicted Terry. "It's the very latest style to go on the warpath in a motor. Everybody does! They go everywhere in them. They are much faster and better than any old ponies."

Billy gave one genuine whoop. "Can we take your motor?"

Terry hesitated.

"I suppose you are too little to run it?" said Billy.

"I am not!" flashed Terry. "I know how to start and stop it, and I drive lots for Stephens. It is hard to turn over the engine when you start."

"I'll turn it," volunteered Billy. "I'm strong as anything."

"Maybe it will start without. If Stephens has just been running it, sometimes it will. Come on, let's try."

Billy straightened up, lifted his chin and cried, "Houpe! Houpe! Houpe!"

The little O'Mores stared in amazement.

"Why don't you come on an whoop?" demanded Billy. "Don't you know how? You are great Indians! You got to whoop before you go on the warpath. You ought to kill a bat, too, and see if the wind is right. But maybe the engine won't run if we wait to do that. You can whoop, anyway. All together now!"

They did whoop, and after several efforts the cry satisfied Billy, so he led the way to the big motor, and took the front seat with Terry. Alice and Little Brother took the back.

"Will it go?" asked Billy, "or do we have to turn it?"

"It will go," said Terry as the machine gently slid out into the avenue and started under his guidance.

"This is no warpath!" scoffed Billy. "We got to go a lot faster than this, and we got to whoop. Alice, why don't you whoop?"

Alice arose, took hold of the seat in front and whooped.

"If I open the throttle, I can't squeeze the bulb to scare people out of our way," said Terry. "I can't steer and squeeze too."

"We'll whoop enough to get them out of the way. Go faster!" urged Billy.

Billy also stood, lifted his chin and whooped like the wildest little savage that ever came out of the West. Alice and Little Brother added their voices, and when he was not absorbed with the steering gear, Terry joined in.

"Faster!" shouted Billy.

Intoxicated with the speed and excitement, Terry threw the throttle wider and the big car leaped forward and shot down the avenue. In it four black, feather-bedecked children whooped in wild glee until suddenly Terry's war cry changed to a scream of panic.

"The lake is coming!"

"Stop!" cried Billy. "Stop! Why don't you stop?"

Paralyzed with fear Terry clung to the steering gear and the car sped onward.

"You little fool! Why don't you stop?" screamed Billy catching Terry's arm. "Tell me how to stop!"

A bicycle shot along beside them and Freckles standing on the pedals shouted, "Pull out the pin in that little circle at your feet!"

Billy fell on his knees and tugged and the pin yielded at last. Just as the wheels struck the white sand the bicycle sheered close, Freckles caught the lever and with one strong shove set the brake. The water flew as the car struck Huron, but luckily it was shallow and the beach smooth. Hub deep the big motor stood quivering as Freckles climbed in and backed it to dry sand.

Then he drew a deep breath and stared at his brood.

"Terrance, would you kindly be explaining?" he said at last.

Billy looked at the panting little figure of Terry.

"I guess I better," he said. "We were playing Indians on the warpath, and we hadn't any ponies, and Terry said it was all the style to go in automobiles now, so we—"

Freckles's head went back, and he did some whooping himself.

"I wonder if you realize how nearly you came to being four drowned children?" he said gravely, after a time.

"Oh, I think I could swim enough to get most of us out," said Billy. "Anyway, we need washing."

"You do indeed," said Freckles. "I will head this procession to the garage, and there we will remove the first coat." For the remainder of Billy's visit the nurse, chauffeur, and every servant of the O'More household had something of importance on their minds, and Billy's every step was shadowed.

"I have Billy's consent," said Philip to Elnora, "and all the other consent you have stipulated. Before you think of something more, give me your left hand, please."

Elnora gave it gladly, and the emerald slipped on her finger. Then they went together into the forest to tell each other all about it, and talk it over.

"Have you seen Edith?" asked Ammon.

"No," answered Elnora, "but she must be here, or she may have seen me when we went to Petosky a few days ago. Her people have a cottage over on the bluff, but the Angel never told me until to-day. I didn't want to make that trip, but the folks were so anxious to entertain me, and it was only a few days until I intended to let you know myself where I was."

"And I was going to wait just that long, and if I didn't hear then I was getting ready to turn over the country. I can scarcely realize yet that Edith sent me that telegram."

"No wonder! It's a difficult thing to believe. I can't express how I feel for her."

"Let us never again speak of it," said Ammon. "I came nearer feeling sorry for her last night than I have yet. I couldn't sleep on that boat coming over, and I couldn't put away the thought of what sending that message cost her. I never would have believed it possible that she would do it. But it is done. We will forget it."

"I scarcely think I shall," said Elnora. "It is the sort of thing I like to remember. How suffering must have changed her! I would give a great deal to bring her peace."

"Henderson came to see me at the hospital a few days ago. He's gone a pretty wild pace, but if he had been held from youth by the love of a good woman he might have lived differently. There are things about him one cannot help admiring."

"I think he loves her," said Elnora softly.

"He does! He always has! He never made any secret of it. He will cut in now and do his level best, but he told me that he thought she would send him away. He understands her thoroughly."

Edith Carr did not understand herself. She went to her room after her good-bye to Henderson, lay on her bed and tried to think why she was suffering as she was.

"It is all my selfishness, my unrestrained temper, my pride in my looks, my ambition to be first," she said. "That is what has caused this trouble."

Then she went deeper.

"How does it happen that I am so selfish, that I never controlled my temper, that I thought beauty and social position the vital things of life?" she muttered. "I think that goes a little past me. I think a mother who allows a child to grow up as I did, who educates it only for the frivolities of life, has a share in that child's ending. I think my mother has some responsibility in this," Edith Carr whispered to the night. "But she will recognize none. She would laugh at me if I tried to tell her what I have suffered and the bitter, bitter lesson I have learned. No one really cares, but Hart. I've sent him away, so there is no one! No one!"

Edith pressed her fingers across her burning eyes and lay still.

"He is gone!" she whispered at last. "He would go at once. He would not see me again. I should think he never would want to see me any more. But I will want to see him! My soul! I want him now! I want him every minute! He is all I have. And I've sent him away. Oh, these dreadful days to come, alone! I can't bear it. Hart! Hart!" she cried aloud. "I want you! No one cares but you. No one understands but you. Oh, I want you!"

She sprang from her bed and felt her way to her desk.

"Get me someone at the Henderson cottage," she said to Central, and waited shivering.

"They don't answer."

"They are there! You must get them. Turn on the buzzer."

After a time the sleepy voice of Mrs. Henderson answered.

"Has Hart gone?" panted Edith Carr.

"No! He came in late and began to talk about starting to California. He hasn't slept in weeks to amount to anything. I put him to bed. There is time enough to start to California when he wakens. Edith, what are you planning to do next with that boy of mine?"

"Will you tell him I want to see him before he goes?"

"Yes, but I won't wake him."

"I don't want you to. Just tell him in the morning."

"Very well."

"You will be sure?"

"Sure!"

Hart was not gone. Edith fell asleep. She arose at noon the next day, took a cold bath, ate her breakfast, dressed carefully, and leaving word that she had gone to the forest, she walked slowly across the leaves. It was cool and quiet there, so she sat where she could see him coming and waited. She was thinking hard and fast.

Henderson came swiftly down the path. A long sleep, food, and Edith's message had done him good. He had dressed in new light flannels that were becoming. Edith arose and went to meet him.

"Let us walk in the forest," she said.

They passed the old Catholic graveyard, and went back into the deepest wood of the Island. Back where all shadows were green, all voices of humanity ceased, and there was no sound save the whispering of the trees, a few bird notes and squirrel rustle. There Edith seated herself on a mossy old log, and Henderson studied her. He could detect a change. She was still pale and her eyes tired, but the dull, strained look was gone. He wanted to hope, but he did not dare. Any other man would have forced her to speak. The mighty tenderness in Henderson's heart shielded her in every way.

"What have you thought of that you wanted yet, Edith?" he asked lightly as he stretched himself at her feet.

"You!"

Henderson lay tense and very still.

"Well, I am here!"

"Thank Heaven for that!"

Henderson sat up suddenly, leaning toward her with questioning eyes. Not knowing what he dared say, afraid of the hope which found birth in his heart, he tried to shield her and at the same time to feel his way.

"I am more thankful than I can express that you feel so," he said. "I would be of use, of comfort, to you if I knew how, Edith."

"You are my only comfort," she said. "I tried to send you away. I thought I didn't want you. I thought I couldn't bear the sight of you, because of what you have seen me suffer. But I went to the root of this thing last night, Hart, and with self in mind, as usual, I found that I could not live without you."

Henderson began breathing lightly. He was afraid to speak or move.

"I faced the fact that all this is my own fault," continued Edith, "and came through my own selfishness. Then I went further back and realized that I am as I was reared. I don't want to blame my parents, but I was carefully trained into what I am. If Elnora Comstock had been like me, Phil would have come back to me. I can see how selfish I look to him, and how I appear to you, if you would admit it."

"Edith," said Henderson desperately, "there is no use to try to deceive you. You have known from the first that I found you wrong in this. But it's the first time in your life I ever thought you wrong about anything—and it's the only time I ever will. Understand, I think you the bravest, most beautiful woman on earth, the one most worth loving."

"I'm not to be considered in the same class with her."

"I don't grant that, but if I did, you must remember how I compare with Phil. He's my superior at every point. There's no use in discussing that. You wanted to see me, Edith. What did you want?"

"I didn't want you to go away."

"Not at all?"

"Not at all! Not ever! Not unless you take me with you, Hart."

She slightly extended one hand to him. Henderson took that hand, kissing it again and again.

"Anything you want, Edith," he said brokenly. "Just as you wish it. Do you want me to stay here, and go on as we have been?"

"Yes, only with a difference."

"Can you tell me, Edith?"

"First, I want you to know that you are the dearest thing on earth to me, right now. I would give up everything else, before I would you. I can't honestly say that I love you with the love you deserve. My heart is too sore. It's too soon to know. But I love you some way. You are necessary to me. You are my comfort, my shield. If you want me, as you know me to be, Hart, you can consider me yours. I give you my word of honour I will try to be as you would have me, just as soon as I can."

Henderson kissed her hand passionately. "Don't, Edith," he begged. "Don't say those things. I can't bear it. I understand. Everything will come right in time. Love like mine must bring a reward. You will love me some day. I can wait. I am the most patient fellow."

"But I must say it," cried Edith. "I—I think, Hart, that I have been on the wrong road to find happiness. I planned to finish life as I started it with Phil; and you can see how glad he was to change. He wanted the other sort of girl far more than he ever wanted me. And you, Hart, honest now—I'll know if you don't tell me the truth! Would you rather have a wife as I planned to live life with Phil, or would you rather have her as Elnora Comstock intends to live with him?"

"Edith!" cried the man, "Edith!"

"Of course, you can't say it in plain English," said the girl. "You are far too chivalrous for that. You needn't say anything. I am answered. If you could have your choice you wouldn't have a society wife, either. In your heart you'd like the smaller home of comfort, the furtherance of your ambitions, the palatable meals regularly served, and little children around you. I am sick of all we have grown up to, Hart. When your hour of trouble comes, there is no comfort for you. I am tired to death. You find out what you want to do, and be, that is a man's work in the world, and I will plan our home, with no thought save your comfort. I'll be the other kind of a girl, as fast as I can learn. I can't correct all my faults in one day, but I'll change as rapidly as I can."

"God knows, I will be different, too, Edith. You shall not be the only generous one. I will make all the rest of life worthy of you. I will change, too!"

"Don't you dare!" said Edith Carr, taking his head between her hands and holding it against her knees, while the tears slid down her cheeks. "Don't you dare change, you big-hearted, splendid lover! I am little and selfish. You are the very finest, just as you are!"

Henderson was not talking then, so they sat through a long silence. At last he heard Edith draw a quick breath, and lifting his head he looked where she pointed. Up a fern stalk climbed a curious looking object. They watched breathlessly. By lavender feet clung a big, pursy, lavender-splotched, yellow body. Yellow and lavender wings began to expand and take on colour. Every instant great beauty became more apparent. It was one of those double-brooded freaks, which do occur on rare occasions, or merely an Eacles Imperialis moth that in the cool damp northern forest had failed to emerge in June. Edith Carr drew back with a long, shivering breath. Henderson caught her hands and gripped them firmly. Steadily she looked the thought of her heart into his eyes.

"By all the powers, you shall not!" swore the man. "You have done enough. I will smash that thing!"

"Oh, no, you won't!" cried the girl, clinging to his hands. "I am not big enough yet, Hart, but before I leave this forest I shall have grown to breadth and strength to carry that to her. She needs two of each kind. Phil only got her one!"

"Edith I can't bear it! That's not demanded! Let me take it!"

"You may go with me. I know where the O'Mores' cottage is. I have been there often."

"I'll say you sent it!"

"You may watch me deliver it!"

"Phil may be there by now."

"I hope he is! I should like him to see me do one decent thing by which to remember me."

"I tell you that is not necessary!"

"'Not necessary!'" cried the girl, her great eyes shining. "Not necessary? Then what on earth is the thing doing here? I just have boasted that I would change, that I would be like her, that I would grow bigger and broader. As the words are spoken God gives me the opportunity to prove whether I am sincere. This is my test, Hart! Don't you see it? If I am big enough to carry that to her, you will believe that there is some good in me. You will not be loving me in vain. This is an especial Providence, man! Be my strength! Help me, as you always have done!"

Henderson arose and shook the leaves from his clothing. He drew Edith Carr to her feet and carefully picked the mosses from her skirts. He went down to the water and moistened his handkerchief to bathe her face.

"Now a dust of powder," he said when the tears were washed away.

From a tiny book Edith tore leaves that she passed over her face.

"All gone!" cried Henderson, critically eyeing her. "You look almost half as lovely as you really are!"

Edith Carr drew a wavering breath. She stretched one hand to him.

"Hold tight, Hart!" she said. "I know they handle these things, but I would quite as soon touch a snake."

Henderson clenched his teeth and held steadily. The moth had emerged too recently to be troublesome. It climbed on her fingers quietly and obligingly clung there without moving. So hand in hand they went down the dark forest path. But when they came to the avenue, the first person they met paused with an ejaculation of wonder. The next stopped also, and everyone following. They could make little progress on account of marvelling, interested people. A strange excitement took possession of Edith. She began to feel proud of the creature.

"Do you know," she said to Henderson, "this is growing easier every step. Its clinging is not disagreeable, as I thought it would be. I feel as if I were saving it, protecting it. I am proud that we are taking it to be put into a collection or a book. It seems like doing a thing worth while. Oh, Hart, I wish we could work together at something for which people would care as they seem to for this. Hear what they say! See them lift their little children to look at it!"

"Edith, if you don't stop," said Henderson, "I will take you in my arms and kiss the face half off you, here on the avenue. You are adorable!"

"Don't you dare!" laughed Edith Carr. The colour rushed to her cheeks and a new light leaped in her eyes.

"Oh, Hart!" she cried. "Let's work! Let's do something! That's the way she makes people love her so. There's the place, and, thank goodness, there is a crowd."

"You darling!" whispered Henderson as they passed up the walk. Her face was rose-flushed with excitement and her eyes shone.

"Hello, everyone!" she cried as she came on the wide veranda. "Only see what we found up in the forest! We thought you might like to have it for some of your collections."

She held out the moth as she walked straight to Elnora, who arose to meet her, crying, "How perfectly splendid! I don't even know how to begin to thank you."

Elnora took the moth. Edith shook hands with all of them and asked Philip if he were improving. She said a few polite words to Freckles and the Angel, declined to remain on account of an engagement, and went away, gracefully.

"Well, bully for her!" said Mrs. Comstock. "She's a little thoroughbred after all!"

"That was a mighty big thing for her to be doing," said Freckles in a hushed voice.

"If you knew her as well as I do," said Philip Ammon, "you would have a better conception of what that cost."

"It was a terror!" cried the Angel. "I never could have done it."

"'Never could have done it!'" echoed Freckles. "Why, Angel, dear, that is the one thing of all the world you would have done!"

"I have to take care of this," faltered Elnora, hurrying for the door to hide the tears which were rolling down her cheeks.

"I must help," said Ammon disappearing also. "Elnora," he called, catching up with her, "take me where I can cry, too. Wasn't she great?"

"Superb!" exclaimed Elnora. "I have no words. I feel so humbled!"

"So do I," said Ammon. "I think a great deed like that always makes one feel so. Now are you happy?"

"Unspeakably happy!" answered Elnora.   The End

LADDIE

A TRUE BLUE STORY

GENE
STRATTON
PORTER

Printing History
Doubleday edition/1913
Tyndale House edition/1991

Library of Congress Catalog Card Number 90-71543
ISBN 0-8423-2664-2
Copyright © 1913 by Doubleday, Page & Company
Cover artwork copyright © 1991 by Deborah L. Chabrian
All rights reserved
Printed in the United States of America

96   95   94   93   92   91
7   6   5   4   3   2

To Leander Elliot Stratton
"The Way To Be Happy Is To Be Good"

CONTENTS

CHARACTERS

Laddie, Who Loved and Asked No Questions.
The Princess, from the House of Mystery.
Leon, Our Angel Child.
Little Sister, Who Tells What Happened.
Mr. and Mrs. Stanton, Who Faced Life Shoulder to Shoulder.
Sally and Peter, Who Married Each Other.
Elizabeth, Shelley, May and Other Stanton Children.
Mr. and Mrs. Pryor, Father and Mother of the Princess.
Robert Paget, a Chicago Lawyer.
Mrs. Freshett, Who Offered Her Life for Her Friend.
Candace, the Cook.
Miss Amelia, the School Mistress.
Interested Relatives, Friends, and Neighbours.

CHAPTER

1

Little Sister

And could another child-world be my share,
I'd be a Little Sister there.

"Have I got a Little Sister anywhere in this house?" inquired Laddie at the door, in his most coaxing voice.

"Yes sir," I answered, dropping the trousers I was making for Hezekiah, my pet bluejay, and running as fast as I could. There was no telling what minute May might take it into her head that she was a little sister and reach him first. Maybe he wanted me to do something for him, and I loved to wait on Laddie.

"Ask mother if you may go with me a while."

"Mother doesn't care where I am, if I come when the supper bell rings."

"All right!" said Laddie.

He led the way around the house, sat on the front step and drew me near.

"Oh, is it going to be a secret?" I cried.

Secrets with Laddie were the greatest joy in life. He was so big and so handsome. He was so much nicer than any one else in our family, or among our friends, that to share his secrets, run his errands, and love him blindly was the greatest happiness.

Sometimes I disobeyed father and mother; I minded Laddie like his right hand.

"The biggest secret yet," he said gravely.

"Tell quick!" I begged, holding my ear to his lips.

"Not so fast!" said Laddie. "Not so fast! I have doubts about this. I don't know that I should send you. Possibly you can't find the way. You may be afraid. Above all, there is never to be a whisper. Not to any one! Do you understand?"

Nothing ever had sounded so grown up and important before. I drew back to study Laddie's face and found it full of trouble.

"What's the matter?" I asked.

"Something serious," said Laddie. "You see, I expected to have an hour or two for myself this afternoon, so I made an engagement to spend the time with a Fairy Princess in our Big Woods. Father and I broke the reaper taking it from the shed just now, and you know how he is about Fairies."

I did know how he was about Fairies. He hadn't a particle of patience with them. Neither had any one else in our family, except Laddie, and it was only lately that he would take the trouble even to lift a dock leaf, and see whether one was hiding beneath it. Now, he had found a Princess and was going to see her. That was something worth while. The Princess would be the Queen's daughter. My father's people were English, and I had heard enough talk to understand that. I was almost wild with excitement.

"Tell me the secret, hurry!" I cried.

Laddie gathered me close.

"It's just this," he said. "It took me a long time to coax the Princess into our Big Woods. I had to fix a throne for her to sit on; spread a Magic Carpet for her feet, and build a wall to screen her. Now, what is she going to think if I'm not there to welcome her when she comes? She promised to show me how to make sunshine on dark days."

"Tell father where you must go and he can have Leon help him."

"But it is a secret with the Princess, and it's *hers* as much as mine. If I tell, she may not like it, and then she won't make me her Prince and let me share her secrets and send me on her errands."

"Then you don't dare tell a breath," I said.

"Will you go in my place, and carry her a letter to explain why I'm not coming? Will you, Little Sister?"

"Of course!" I said stoutly, and then my heart turned right over; for I had never been in our Big Woods alone, and neither mother nor father wanted me to go. Passing Gypsies sometimes laid down the fence and went there to camp. Father thought all the wolves and wildcats were gone, he hadn't seen any in years, but every once in a while some one said they had, and he was not quite sure yet. And that wasn't the beginning of it. Paddy Ryan had come back from the war wrong in his head. He wore his old army overcoat summer and winter, slept on the ground, and ate whatever he could find. Once Laddie and Leon, hunting squirrels to make broth for mother on one of her bad days, saw him in our Big Woods and he was eating *snakes*. If I found Pat Ryan eating a snake, it would frighten me so I would stand still and let him eat me, if he wanted to, and perhaps he wasn't too crazy to see how plump I was. This was the worst trouble of my life. I seemed to see swarthy, dark faces; big, sleek cats dropping from limbs; and Paddy Ryan's matted gray hair, the flying rags of the old blue coat, and a snake in his hands. Laddie was slipping the letter into my apron pocket. My knees threatened to let me down.

"Must I lift the leaves and hunt for her, or will she come to me?" I wavered.

"That's the biggest secret of all," said Laddie. "Since the Princess consented to enter them, our woods are Enchanted, and there is no telling what wonderful things may happen any minute. One of them is this: Whenever the Princess comes there, she grows in size until she is as big as, say our Sally, and she fills all the place with glory, until you are so blinded you scarcely can see her face."

"What is she like, Laddie?" I questioned, so filled with awe and interest, that fear was forgotten.

"She is taller than Sally," said Laddie. "Her face is oval, and her cheeks are bright. Her eyes are big moonlit pools of darkness, and silken curls fall over her shoulders. One hair is strong enough for a lifeline that will draw a drowning man ashore, or strangle an unhappy one. But you will not see her. I'm purposely sending you early, so you can do what you are told and come back to me before she even reaches the woods."

"What am I to do, Laddie?"

"You must put one hand in your apron pocket and take the letter in it, and as long as you hold it tight, nothing in the world can hurt you. Go out our lane to the Big Woods, climb the gate and walk straight back the wagon road to the water. When you reach that, you must turn to your right and go toward Hoods' until you come to the pawpaw thicket. Go around that, look ahead, and you'll see the biggest beech tree you ever saw. You know a beech, don't you?"

"Of course I do," I said indignantly. "Father taught me beech with the other trees."

"Well then," said Laddie, "straight before you will be a purple beech, and under it is the throne of the Princess, the Magic Carpet, and the walls I made. Among the beech roots there is a stone hidden with moss. Roll the stone back and there will be a piece of bark. Lift that and lay the letter in the box you'll find, replace the stone, and scamper to me like flying. I'll be at the barn with father."

"Is that all?"

"Not quite," said Laddie. "It's possible that the Fairy Queen may have set the Princess spinning silk for the caterpillars to weave their little houses with this winter; and if she has, she may have left a letter there to tell me. If there is one, put it in your pocket, hold it close every step of the way, and you'll be safe coming home as you were going. But you mustn't let a soul see it; you must slip it into my pocket when I'm not looking, and when no one else can see. If you let any one see, then the Magic will be spoiled, and the Fairy won't come again."

I closed my lips and looked at Laddie.

"No one shall see," I promised.

"I knew you could be trusted," said Laddie, kissing and hugging me hard. "Now go! If anything gets after you that such a big girl as you really wouldn't be ashamed to be afraid of, climb on a fence and call. I'll be listening, and I'll come flying. Now I must hurry. Father will think it's going to take me the remainder of the day to find the bolts he wants."

We went down the front walk between the rows of hollyhocks and tasselled lady-slippers, out the gate, and followed the road. Laddie held one of my hands tight, and in the other I gripped the letter in my pocket. At the foot of the garden he turned to his left and went to the barn. I started toward the west lane leading to our Big Woods. So long as Laddie could see me, and the lane lay between open fields, I wasn't afraid. I was thinking so deeply about our woods being Enchanted and a tiny Fairy growing big as our Sally, because she was in them, that I stepped out bravely.

Every few days I followed the lane as far back as the Big Gate. This stood where four fields cornered, and opened into the road leading to the woods. Beyond it, I had walked on Sunday afternoons with father, while he taught me all the flowers, vines, and bushes he knew, only he didn't know some of the prettiest ones; I had to have books for them, and I was studying to learn enough that I could find out. Or I had ridden on the wagon with Laddie and Leon when they went to bring wood for the cookstove, outoven, and big fireplace. But to walk! To go all alone! Not that I didn't walk by myself over every other foot of the acres and acres of beautiful land my father owned; but plowed fields, grassy meadows, wood pasture, and the orchard were different. I played in them without a thought of fear.

The only things to be careful about were a little, shiny, slender snake, with a head as bright as mother's copper kettle, and a big thick one with patterns on its back like those in Laddie's geometry books, and a whole rattlebox on its tail; to not eat any berry or fruit I didn't know without first asking father; and to always be sure to measure how deep the water was before I waded in alone.

But our Big Woods! Leon said the wildcats would get me there. I sat in our catalpa and watched the Gypsies drive past every summer of my life. Mother hated them as hard as ever she could hate any one, because once they had stolen some fine shirts, with linen bosoms, that she had made by hand for father, and was bleaching on the grass. If Gypsies should be in our west woods to-day and steal me, she would hate them worse than ever; because my mother loved me now, even if she didn't want me when I was born.

But you could excuse her for that. She had already bathed,

spanked, sewed for, and reared eleven babies so big and strong not one of them ever even threatened to die. When you thought of that, you could see she wouldn't be likely to implore the Almighty to send her another, just to make her family even numbers. I never felt much hurt at her, but some of the others I never have forgiven and maybe I never will. As long as there had been eleven babies, they should have been so accustomed to children that they needn't all of them have objected to me, all except Laddie, of course. That was the reason I loved him so and tried to do every single thing he wanted me to, just the way he liked it done. That was why I was facing the only spot on our land where I was in the slightest afraid; because he asked me to. If he had told me to dance a jig on the ridgepole of our barn, I would have tried it.

So I clasped the note, set my teeth, and climbed over the gate. I walked fast and kept my eyes straight before me. If I looked on either side, sure as life I would see something I never had before, and be down digging up a strange flower, chasing a butterfly, or watching a bird. Besides, if I didn't look in the fence corners that I passed, maybe I wouldn't see anything to scare me. I was going along finely, and feeling better every minute as I went down the bank of an old creek that had gone dry, and started up the other side toward the sugar camp not far from the Big Woods. The bed was full of weeds and as I passed through, away! went Something among them.

Beside the camp shed there was corded wood, and the first thing I knew, I was on top of it. The next, my hand was on the note in my pocket. My heart jumped until I could see my apron move, and my throat went all stiff and dry. I gripped the note and waited. Maybe it was only a rabbit, but it might be a wolf, or a wildcat, or Paddy Ryan catching snakes. The weeds in that creek bed were high as a horse's back and I couldn't see. The things that make a noise when you can't see are always more scary than if you know what is doing it. I waited a long time, then stood up and looked toward the barn. The front door was open, and father and Laddie were working over the machine they had broken. I could see our church, the white stones in the graveyard around it, and the old schoolhouse across the road. Father believed God would take care of him. I was only a little girl and needed help much more than a big man; maybe God would take care of me. There was nothing wrong in carrying a letter to the Fairy Princess for Laddie. I thought perhaps it would help if I should kneel on the top of the woodpile and ask God to not let anything get me.

The more I thought about it, the less I felt like doing it, though, because really you have no business to ask God to take care of you, unless you *know* you are doing right. This was right, but in my heart I also knew that if Laddie had asked me, I would be shivering on top of that cordwood on a hot August day, when it was wrong. On the whole, I thought it would be more honest to-leave God out of it, and take the risk myself. That made me think of the Crusaders, and the little gold trinket in father's chest till. There were four shells on it and each one stood for a trip on foot or horseback to the Holy City when you had to fight almost every step of the way. Those shells meant that my father's people had gone four times, so he said; that, although it was away far back, still each of us had a tiny share of the blood of the Crusaders in our veins, and that it would make us brave and strong, and whenever we were afraid, if we would think of them, we never could do a cowardly thing or let any one else do one before us. He said any one with Crusader blood had to be brave as Richard the Lion-hearted. Thinking about that helped ever so much, so I gripped the note and turned to take one last look at the house before I made a dash for the gate that led into the Big Woods.

Home never looked so good. The house appeared as big, and white, and comfortable as my idea of Heaven. The garden this side of it, the orchard back, and the woods pasture beyond, surrounded it with pictures of perfect beauty. Even the open meadow across the road, with its fence almost a green wall of shrubs and trees father left for the birds, was beautiful. So was the yellow road running north down the Little Hill to the small creek that crossed our pasture and emptied into the big one in the meadow. Beyond our land lay the farm of Jacob Hood, and Mrs. Hood always teased me because Laddie had gone racing after her when I was born. She was in the middle of Monday's washing, and the bluing settled in the rinse water and stained her white clothes in streaks it took months to bleach out. I always liked Sarah Hood for coming and dressing me, though, because our Sally, who was big enough to have done it, was upstairs crying and wouldn't come down. I liked Laddie too, because he was the only one of our family who went to my mother and kissed her, said he was glad, and offered to help her. Maybe the reason he went was because he had an awful scare, but anyway he *went*, and that was enough for me.

You see it was this way: No one wanted me; as there had been eleven of us, every one felt that was enough. May was six years old and in school, and my mother thought there never would be any more babies. She was well as could be. She was growing ample and strong and making up for all she had missed while doing her best for the others. She had given away the cradle and divided the baby clothes among my big married sisters and brothers, and was having a fine time and enjoying herself the most she ever had in her life. The land was paid for long ago; the house she had planned, builded as she wanted it; she had a big team of matched grays and a carriage with side lamps and patent leather trimmings; and sometimes there was money in the bank. I do not know that there was very much, but any at all was a marvel, considering how many of us there were to feed, clothe, and send to college. Mother was forty-six and father was fifty; so they felt young enough yet to have a fine time and enjoy life, and just when things were going best, I announced that I was halfway over my journey to earth.

You can't blame my mother so much. She must have been tired of babies and disliked to go back and begin all over after resting six years. And you mustn't be too hard on my father if he was not just overjoyed. He felt sure the cook would leave, and she did. He knew Sally would object to a baby, when she wanted to begin having beaus, so he and mother talked it over and sent her away for a long visit to Ohio with father's people, and never told her. They intended to leave her there until I was over the colic, at least. They knew the big married brothers and sisters would object, and they did. They said it would be embarrassing for their children to be the nieces and nephews of an aunt or uncle younger than themselves. They said it so often and so emphatically that father was provoked and mother cried. Shelley didn't like it, because she was going to school in Groveville, where Lucy, one of our married sisters, lived, and she was afraid I would make so much work she would have to give up her books and friends and remain at home. There never was a baby born who was any less wanted than I was. I knew as much about it as any one else, because from the day I could understand, all of them, father, mother, Shelley, Sarah Hood, every one who knew, took turns telling me how badly I was not wanted, how much trouble I made, and how Laddie was the only one who loved me at first. Because of that I was on the cordwood trying to find courage to go farther. Over and over Laddie had told me himself. He had been to visit our big sister Elizabeth over Sunday and about eight o'clock Monday morning he came riding down the road, his head high, lungs and heart full, and on the top of the Little Hill he looked down the valley at his home, and saw the most dreadful thing. There was not a curl of smoke from the chimneys, not a tablecloth or pillowslip on the line, not a blind raised. Laddie said his heart went—just like mine did when the Something jumped in the creek bed, no doubt. Then he laid on the whip and rode.

He flung the rein over the hitching post, leaped the fence and reached the back door. The young green girl, who was all father could get when the cook left, was crying. So were Shelley and little May, although she said afterward she had a boil on her heel and there was no one to poultice it. Laddie leaned against the door casing, and it is easy enough to understand what he thought. He told me he had to try twice before he could speak, and then he could only ask: "What's the matter?"

Probably May never thought she would have the chance, but the others were so busy crying harder, now that they had an audience, that she was the first to tell him: "We have got a little sister."

"Great Day!" cried Laddie. "You made me think we had a funeral! Where is mother, and where is my Little Sister?"

He went bolting right into mother's room and kissed her like the gladdest boy alive; because he was only a boy then, and he told her how happy he was that she was safe, and then he *asked* for me. Mother told him father had wrapped me in an old shawl and laid me on the stair steps, and she was afraid I was smothering.

Laddie went and picked me up, and he said I was the only living creature in that house who was not shedding tears, and I didn't begin for about six months afterward. In fact, not until Shelley taught me by pinching me if she had to rock the cradle; then I would cry so hard mother would have to take me. He said he didn't believe I'd ever have learned by myself.

He took a pillow from the bed, fixed it in the rocking chair and laid me on it. When he found that father was hitching the horses to send Leon for Doctor Fenner, Laddie rode back after Sarah Hood and spoiled her washing. It may be that the interest he always took in me had its beginning in all of them scaring him with their weeping; even Sally, whom father had to telegraph to come home, was upstairs crying, and she was almost a woman. It may be that all the tears they shed over not wanting me so scared Laddie that he went farther in his welcome than he ever would have thought of going if he hadn't done it for joy when he learned his mother was safe. I don't care about the reason. It is enough for me that from the hour of my birth Laddie named me Little Sister, seldom called me anything else, and cared for me all he possibly could to rest mother. He took me to the fields with him in the morning and brought me back on the horse before him at noon. He could plow with me riding the horse, drive a reaper with me on his knees, and hoe corn while I slept on his coat in a fence corner. The winters he was away at college left me lonely, and when he came back for a vacation I was too happy for words. I could only hang around his neck and whisper in his ear how I loved him. Maybe it was wrong to love him most. I knew my mother cared for and wanted me now. And all my secrets were not with Laddie. I had one with father that I was never to tell so long as he lived, but it was about the one he loved best, next after mother. Perhaps I should never tell it, but I wouldn't be surprised if the family knew. I followed Laddie like a faithful dog, when I was not gripping his waving hair and riding in triumph on his shoulders. He never had to go so fast he couldn't take me on his back. He never was in too big a hurry to be kind. He always had patience to explain every shell, leaf, bird, and flower I asked about. I was just as much his, when pretty young girls were around, and the house full of company, as when we were alone. That was the reason I was shivering on the cordwood, gripping his letter and thinking of all these things in order to force myself to go farther.

I was excited about the Fairies too. I often had close chances of seeing them, but I always just missed. Now here was Laddie writing letters and expecting answers; our Big Woods Enchanted, a Magic Carpet and the Queen's daughter becoming our size so she could speak with him. No doubt the Queen had her grow big as Shelley, when she sent her on an errand to tell Laddie about how to make sunshine; because she was afraid if she went her real size he would accidentally step on her, he was so dreadfully big. Or maybe her voice was so fine he could not hear what she said. He had told me I was to hurry, and I had gone as fast as I could until Something jumped; since, I had been settled on that cordwood like Robinson Crusoe on his desert island. I had to get down and go on some time; I might as well start.

So I took one last look at the church, and the farm and the house. Oh, how safe home did seem! I gripped the letter, slid to the ground, and ran toward the big gate straight before me. I climbed it, clutched the note again, and ran blindly down the road through the forest toward the creek. I could hurry there. On either side of it I could not have run ten steps at a time. The big trees reached so high above me it seemed as if they would push through the floor of Heaven. Logs as large as the trees lay criss-crossed in heaps. You couldn't see far through the bushes. The ground was covered with brown leaves, mosses and lichens crept everywhere, ferns grew almost as tall as I was, a few birds chirped, and I could begin to hear the chuckle of the creek as it came toward me. I didn't stop to watch for Gypsies. I wouldn't have looked up for a farm bigger than ours for fear I might see something. I tried to shut my ears and run so fast I couldn't hear a sound, and so going, I soon came to the creek bank. There I turned to my right and went slower, watching for the pawpaw thicket. On leaving the road I thought I would have to crawl over logs and make my way; but there seemed to be kind of a path not very plain, but travelled enough to follow. It led straight to the thicket. We had hunted the big green and gold fruit there often enough that I felt more at home. There were no branches that would hold up a wildcat. At the edge I stopped to look for the beech. It was not nearly so far away as I had feared it would be. It could be reached in one breathless dash, but there seemed to be a green enclosure, so I walked around until I found an entrance. Once there I was so amazed I stood and stared. I was half indignant too.

Laddie hadn't done a thing but make an exact copy of my playhouse under the biggest maiden's-blush in our orchard. He used the immense beech for one corner, where I had the apple tree. His Magic Carpet was woolly-dog moss, and all the magic about it, was that on the damp woods floor, in the deep shade, the moss had taken root and was growing as if it always had been there. He had been able to cut and stick much larger willow sprouts for his walls than I could, and in the wet black mould they didn't look as if they ever had wilted. They were so fresh and green, no doubt they had taken root and were growing. Where I had a low bench under my tree, he had used a log; but he had hewed the top flat, and made a moss cover. In each corner he had set a fern as high as my head. On either side of the entrance he had planted a cluster of cardinal flower that was in full bloom, and around the walls in a few places thrifty bunches of Oswego tea and foxfire, that I would have walked miles to secure for my wild garden under the Bartlett pear tree. I stood gazing a second. It was so beautiful it took my breath away. There were the big trunk of the purple beech, the growing green walls high above my head, the broad flat beech branches roofing them, the floor like finest velvet, and here and there, flaming red, living flowers.

"If the Queen's daughter doesn't like this," I said softly, "she'll have to go to Heaven before she finds anything better, for there can't be another place on earth so pretty."

It was wonderful how the sound of my own voice gave me courage, even if it did seem a little strange. So I hurried to the beech, knelt and slipped the letter in the box, and put back the bark and stone. Laddie had said that nothing could hurt me while I had the letter, so my protection was gone as soon as it left my hands.

There was nothing but my feet to save me now. I thanked goodness I was a fine runner, and started for the pawpaw thicket without paying the least heed to the rules. I went fast as possible from the first jump. Once there, I paused only one minute to see whether the way to the stream was clear, and while standing tense and gazing, I heard something. For an instant it was every bit as bad as at the dry creek. Then I realized that this was a soft voice singing, and I forgot everything else in a glow of delight. The Princess was coming! There would be time for one peep at her before racing to Laddie. I turned and slipped through the thicket, never taking my eyes from the entrance. In a minute, there she came!

Never in all my life was I so surprised, and astonished, and bewildered. She was even larger than our Sally; her dress was pale green, like I thought a Fairy's should be; her eyes were deep and dark as Laddie had said, her hair hung from a part in the middle of her forehead over her shoulders, and if she had been in the sun, it would have gleamed like a blackbird's wing. She had a few tiny sprays of the first opening goldenrod in it. You wouldn't have thought she would, with her dark skin; but maybe she knew with her red lips and flushed cheeks it would be all right. She was just as Laddie said she would be; she was so much more beautiful than you would suppose any woman could be, I stood there dumbly staring. It is wonderful to count up the things you can think in an instant, if you must. I wouldn't have asked for any one more perfectly beautiful or more like Laddie had said the Princess would be; but she was no more the daughter of the Fairy Queen than I was. She was not any more of a Princess. If father ever would tell all about the little bauble he kept in the till of his big chest, maybe she was not as near! She was no one on earth but one of those new English people who had moved on the land that cornered with ours on the northwest. She had ridden over the roads, and been at our meeting house. There could be no mistake.

And neither father nor mother would want her on our place. They didn't like her or her family at all. Mother called them the neighbourhood mystery, and father spoke of them as the Infidels. If he had said devils it wouldn't have sounded any worse. It wouldn't have been so bad, in fact. No one wants to be a devil. That is just the result of having all your sins piled up in a heap at the end of life. You don't want or intend to be a devil. That comes to you if you are bad and you take your punishment. But of course, folks are only infidels because they want to be, so that makes it all the more disgraceful. They had dropped from nowhere, mother said, bought that splendid big farm, moved on and shut out every one. Before any one knew people were shut out, mother, dressed in her finest, with Laddie driving, went in the carriage, all shining, to make friends with them. This very girl opened the door and said that her mother was "indisposed," and could not see callers. "In-dis-posed!" That's a good word that fills your mouth, but our mother didn't like having it used to her. She said the "saucy chit" was insulting. Then the man came, and he said he was very sorry, but his wife would see no one. He did invite mother in, but she wouldn't go. She told us she could see past him into the house and there was such finery as she never in all her days had laid her eyes on. She said he was mannerly as could be, but he had the coldest, severest face she ever saw.

They had two men and a woman servant, and no one could coax a word from them, about why those people acted as they did. They said " 'orse," and " 'ouse," and "Hengland." They talked so funny you couldn't have understood them anyway. They never plowed or put in a crop. They made everything into a meadow and had more horses, cattle, and sheep than a country fair, and everything you ever knew with feathers, even peacocks. We could hear them scream whenever it was going to rain. Father said they sounded heathenish. I rather liked them. The man had stacks of money or they couldn't have lived the way they did. He came to our house twice on business: once to see about road laws, and again about tax rates. Father was mightily pleased at first, because Mr. Pryor seemed to have books, and to know everything, and father thought it would be fine to be neighbours. But the minute Mr. Pryor finished business he began to argue that every single thing father and mother believed was wrong. He said right out in plain English that God was a myth. Father told him pretty quickly that no man could say that in his house; so he left suddenly and had not been back since, and father didn't want him ever to come again.

Then their neighbours often saw the woman around the house and garden. She looked and acted quite as well as any one, so probably she was not half so sick as my mother, who had nursed three of us through typhoid fever, and then had it herself when she was all tired out. We did every single thing we knew, but she never could seem to grow strong enough again but that every little while she had to suffer dreadfully. She wouldn't let a soul know she had a pain until she dropped over and couldn't take another step, and father or Laddie carried her to bed. But she went everywhere, saw all her friends, and did more good from her bed than any other woman in our neighbourhood could on her feet. So we thought mighty little of those Pryor people.

Everyone said the girl was pretty. They had to. People would have known they were not honest or else jealous if they didn't. Then her clothes drove the other women crazy. Some of our neighbourhood came from far down east, like my mother. Our people back a little were from over the sea, and they knew how things should be, to be right. Many of the others were from Kentucky and Virginia, and they were well dressed, proud, handsome women; none better looking anywhere. They followed the fashions and spent much time and money on their clothes. When it was Quarterly Meeting or the Bishop dedicated the church or they went to town on court days, you should have seen them—until Pryors came. Then something new happened, and not a woman in our neighbourhood liked it. Pamela Pryor didn't follow the fashions. She set them. If every other woman made long tight sleeves to their wrists, she let hers flow to the elbow and filled them with silk lining, ruffled with lace. If they wore high neck bands, she had none, and used a flat lace collar. If they cut their waists straight around and gathered their skirts on six yards full, she ran hers down to a little point front and back, that made her look slenderer, and put only half as much goods in her skirt. Maybe Laddie rode as well as she could; he couldn't manage a horse any better, and aside from him there wasn't a man we knew who would have tried to ride some of the animals she did.

If she ever worked a stroke, no one knew it. All day long she sat in the parlour, the very best one, every day; or on benches under the trees with embroidery frames or books, some of them fearful, big, difficult looking ones, or rode over the country. She rode in sunshine and she rode in storm, until you would think she couldn't see her way through her tangled black hair. She rode through snow and in pouring rain, when she could have stayed out of it, if she had wanted to. She didn't seem to be afraid of anything on earth or in Heaven. Every one thought she was like her father and didn't believe there was any God; so when she came among us at church or any public gathering, as she sometimes did, people were in no hurry to be friendly, while she looked straight ahead and never spoke until she was spoken to, and then she was precise and cold, I tell you.

Men took off their hats, got out of the road when she came pounding along, and stared after her like "be-addled mummies," my mother said. But that was all she, or any one else, could say. The young fellows were wild about her, and if they tried to sidle up to her in the hope that they might lead her horse or get to hold her foot when she mounted, they always saw when they got sidled, that she wasn't there.

But she was here! I had seen her only a few times, but this was the Pryor girl, just as sure as I would have known if it had been Sally. What dazed me was that she answered in every particular the description Laddie had given me of the Queen's daughter. And worst of all, from the day she first came among us, moving so proud and cold, blabbing old Hannah Dover said she carried herself like a Princess—as if Hannah Dover knew *how* a Princess carried herself!—every living soul, my father even, had called her the Princess. At first it was because she was like they thought a Princess would be, but later they did it in meanness, to make fun. After they knew her name, they were used to calling her the Princess, so they kept it up, but some of them were proud of her in their hearts; because she could look, and do, and be what they would have given anything to, and knew they couldn't to save them.

I was never in such a fix in all my life. She looked more as Laddie had said the Princess would than you would have thought any woman could, but she was Pamela Pryor, nevertheless. Every one called her the Princess, but she couldn't make reality out of that. She just couldn't be the Fairy Queen's daughter; so the letter couldn't possibly be for her.

She had no business in our woods; you could see that they had plenty of their own. Most people had so much they spent their winters cutting them down to make fields. She went straight to the door of the willow room and walked in as if she belonged there.

What if she found the hollow and took Laddie's letter! Fast as I could slip over the leaves, I went back. She was on the moss carpet, on her knees, and the letter was in her fingers. It's a good thing to have your manners soundly thrashed into you. You've got to be scared stiff before you forget them. I wasn't so afraid of her as I would have been if I had known she *was* the Princess, and have Laddie's letter, she should not. What had the kind of a girl she was, from a home like hers, to teach any one from our house about making sunshine? I was at the willow wall by that time peering through, so I just parted it a little and said: "Please put back that letter where you got it. It isn't for you."

She knelt on the mosses, the letter in her hand, and her face, as she turned to me, was rather startled; but when she saw me she laughed, and said in the sweetest voice I ever heard: "Are you so very sure of that?"

"Well, I ought to be," I said. "I just put it there."

"Might I inquire for whom you put it there?"

"No ma'am! That's a secret."

You should have seen the light flame in her eyes, the red deepen on her cheeks, and the little curl of laughter that curved her lips.

"How interesting!" she cried. "I wonder now if you are not Little Sister."

I cannot tell you in what a soft, coaxing way she said it, but I didn't propose to be wheedled. Laddie never would trust me again if I bungled the most important errand on which he ever had sent me.

"I am to Laddie and our folks," I said. "You are a stranger."

All the dancing lights went from her face. She looked as if she were going to cry unless she hurried up and swallowed it down hard and fast.

"That is quite true," she said. "I am a stranger. Do you know that being a stranger is the loneliest, hardest thing that can happen to any one in all this world?"

"Then why don't you open your doors, invite your neighbours in, go to see them, and stop your father from saying such dreadful things?"

"They are not my doors," she said, "and could you keep your father from saying anything he chooses?"

I stood and blinked at her. Of course I wouldn't even dare try that.

"I'm so sorry," was all I could think to say.

I couldn't ask her to come to our house. I knew no one wanted her. But if I couldn't speak for the others, surely I might for myself. I let go the willows and went to the door. The Princess arose and sat on the seat Laddie had made for the Queen's daughter. It was an awful pity to tell her she shouldn't sit there, for I had my doubts if the real, true Princess would be half as lovely when she came—if she ever did. Some way the Princess, who was not a Princess, appeared so real, I couldn't keep from becoming confused and forgetting that she was only just Pamela Pryor. Already the lovely lights had gone from her face until it made me so sad I wanted to cry, and I was no easy cry-baby either. If I couldn't offer friendship for my family I would for myself.

"You may call me Little Sister, if you like," I said. "I won't be a stranger. After this, I'll speak to you, and you may say to yourself, she is my friend."

"Why how lovely!" cried the Princess, stretching out her arms.

You should have seen the dancing lights fly back to her eyes. Probably you won't believe this, but the first thing I knew I was beside her on the throne, her arm was around me, and it's the gospel truth that she hugged me tight. I just had sense enough to reach over and pick Laddie's letter from her fingers, and then I was on her side. I don't know what she did to me, but all at once I knew that she was dreadfully lonely; that she hated being a stranger; that she was sorry enough to cry because their house was one of mystery, and that she would open the door if she could.

"I like you," I said, reaching up to touch her curls.

I never had seen her that I did not want to. They were like I thought they would be. Father and Laddie and some of us had wavy hair, but hers was crisp—and it clung to your fingers, and wrapped around them and seemed to tug at your heart like it does when a baby grips you. I drew away my hand, and the hair stretched out until it was long as any of ours, and then curled up again, and you could see that no tins had stabbed into her head to make those curls. I began trying to single out one hair.

"What are you doing?" she asked, still holding me close.

"I want to know if only one hair is strong enough to draw a drowning man from the water or strangle an unhappy one," I said.

"Believe me, no!" cried the Princess. "It would take all I have, woven into a rope, to do that."

"Laddie knows curls that just one hair of them is strong enough," I boasted.

"I wonder now!" said the Princess. "I think he must have been making poetry or telling Fairy tales."

"He was telling the truth," I assured her. "Father doesn't believe in Fairies, and mother laughs, but Laddie and I know. Do you believe in Fairies?"

"Of course I do!" she said.

"Then you know that this *could* be an Enchanted Wood?"

"I have found it so," said the Princess.

"And *maybe* this is a Magic Carpet?"

"It surely is a Magic Carpet."

"And you *might* be the daughter of the Queen? Your eyes are 'moonlit pools of darkness.' If only your hair were stronger, and you knew about making sunshine!"

"Maybe it is stronger than I think. It never has been tested. Perhaps I do know about making sunshine. Possibly I am as true as the wood and the carpet."

I drew away and stared at her. The longer I looked the more uncertain I became. Maybe her mother was the Queen. Perhaps that was the mystery. It might be the reason she didn't want the people to see her. Maybe she was so busy making sunshine for the Princess to bring to Laddie that she had no time to sew carpet rags, and to go to quiltings, and funerals, and make visits. It was hard to know what to think.

"I wish you'd tell me plain out if you are the Queen's daughter,"

I said. "It's most important. You can't have this letter unless I *know*. It's the very first time Laddie ever trusted me with a letter, and I just can't give it to the wrong person."

"Then why don't you leave it where he told you?"

"But you have gone and found the place. You started to take it once; you would again, just as soon as I was gone."

"Look me straight in the eyes, Little Sister," said the Princess softly. "Am I like a person who would take anything that didn't belong to her?"

"No!" I said instantly.

"How do you think I happened to come to this place?"

"I don't know. Maybe our woods are prettier than yours."

"How do you think I knew where the letter was?"

I shook my head.

"If I show you some others exactly like the one you have there, then will you believe that is for me?"

"Yes," I answered.

I believed it anyway. It just *seemed* so, the better you knew her. The Princess slipped her hand among the folds of the trailing pale green skirt, and from a hidden pocket drew other letters exactly like the one I held. She opened one and ran her finger along the top line and I read, "To the Princess," and then she pointed to the ending and it was merely signed, "Laddie," but all the words written between were his writing. Slowly I handed her the letter.

"You don't want me to have it?" she asked.

"Yes," I said. "I want you to have it if Laddie wrote it for you—but mother and father won't, not at all."

"What makes you think so?" she asked gently.

"Why, don't you know what people say about you?" I asked her, instead of answering.

"Some of it, perhaps."

"Well?"

"'Well?'" repeated the Princess. "Do you think it is true?"

"Not that you're stuck up, and hateful and proud, not that you don't want to be neighbourly with other people, no, I don't think that. But your father said in our home that there was no God, and you wouldn't let my mother in when she put on her best dress and went in the carriage, and wanted to be friends. I have to believe that."

"Yes, you can't help believing that," said the Princess, sadly.

"Then can't you see why you'll be likely to show Laddie the way to find an awful lot of trouble, instead of sunshine?"

"I can see," said the Princess.

"Oh Princess, you won't do it, will you?" I cried.

"Don't you think such a big man as Laddie can take care of himself?" she asked, and the dancing lights that had begun to fade came sparkling back. "Over there," she pointed through our woods toward the southwest, "lives a man you know. What do his neighbours call him?"

"Stiff-necked Johnny," I answered promptly.

"And the man who lives next him?"

"Pinch-fist Williams."

Her finger veered to another neighbour's.

"The girls of that house?"

"Giggle-head Smithsons."

"What about the man who lives over there?"

"He beats his wife."

"And the house beyond?"

"Mother whispers about them. I don't know."

"And the woman on the hill?"

"She doesn't do anything but gossip and make every one trouble."

"Exactly!" said the Princess. "Yet most of these people come to your house, and your family goes to theirs, because they know all about them. Do you suppose people they know nothing about are so much worse than these others?"

"If your father will take it back about God, and your mother will let people in—my mother and father both wanted to be friends, you know."

The Princess slowly shook her head.

"That I can't possibly do," she said, "but maybe I could change their feelings toward me."

I watched her face. It would be better not to tell so much about her looks; but you couldn't see her without noticing how beautiful she was, and of course every one else saw too. Laddie must have seen how lovely she was, often and often, before he ever found courage to write all those letters, build the wall, and spread the Magic Carpet.

"Do it!" I cried. "Oh, I'd just love you to do it! I wish you would come to our house and be friends. Sally is pretty as you are, only a different way, and I know she'd like you, and so would Shelley. If Laddie writes you letters and comes here about sunshine, of course he'd be delighted if mother knew you; because she loves him best of any of us. She depends on him most as much as father."

"Then will you keep the secret until I have time to try—say until this time next year?"

"I'll keep it just as long as Laddie wants me to," I answered.

"Good!" said the Princess. "No wonder Laddie thinks you the finest Little Sister any one ever had."

"Does Laddie think that?" I asked.

"He does indeed!" said the Princess. "He has told me often."

"Then I'm not afraid to go home," I said. "And I'll bring his letter the next time he can't come."

"Were you scared this time?"

I told her about that Something in the dry bed, the wolves, wildcats, Paddy Ryan, and the Gypsies.

"You little goosie," said the Princess. "I am afraid that brother Leon of yours is the biggest rogue loose in this part of the country. Didn't it ever occur to you that people named Wolfe live over there, and they call that crowd next us 'wildcats,' because they just went on some land and took it, and began living there without any more permission than real wildcats ask to enter the woods? Do you suppose I would be here, and everywhere else I want to go, if there were any danger? Did anything really harm you coming?"

"You're harmed when you're scared until you can't breathe," I said. "Anyway, nothing could get me coming, because I held the letter tight in my hand, like Laddie said. If you'd write me one to take back, I'd be safe going home."

"I see," said the Princess. "But I have nothing to say, and I've no pencil, and no paper, unless I use the back of one of Laddie's letters, and that wouldn't be polite."

"You can make new fashions," I said, "but you don't know much about the woods, do you? I could fix fifty ways to send a message to Laddie."

"How would you?" asked the Princess.

Running to the pawpaw bushes I pulled some big tender leaves. Then I took the bark from the box and laid a leaf on it.

"Press with one of your rings," I said, "and print what you want to say. I write to the Fairies every day that way, only I use an old knife handle."

She tried. She spoiled two or three by bearing down so hard she cut the leaves. She didn't even know enough to write on the frosty side, until she was told. But pretty soon she got along so well she printed all over two big ones. Then I took a stick and punched little holes and stuck a piece of foxfire bloom through.

"What makes you do that?" she asked with greatest interest.

"That's the stamp," I explained.

"But it's my letter, and I didn't put it there."

"Has to be there or the Fairies won't like it," I said. "There's only one way to do it, and this is the way."

"Well then, let it go," said the Princess. "It does look pretty."

I put back the bark and replaced the stone, gathered up the scattered leaves, and put the two with writing on between fresh ones.

"Now I must run," I said, "or Laddie will think the Gypsies have got me sure."

"I'll go with you past the dry creek," she offered.

"You better not," I said. "I'd love to have you, but it would be best for you to change their opinion, before you let father and mother see you on their land."

"Perhaps it would," said the Princess. "Well, I'll wait here until you reach the fence and then you call and I'll know you are in the open and feel comfortable."

"I am most all over being afraid now," I told her. "Good-bye."

Just to show her, I walked to the creek, and then it was not so far, and wagon tracks, she could hear a call, and if I ran I might spoil the letter, so I kept on walking. I did stop and listen beside the cordwood, but there was not a sound, so I crossed the dry creek, climbed the gate and went down the lane. Almost to the road I began wondering what I could do with the letter, when looking ahead I saw Laddie coming.

"I was just starting to find you. You've been an age, child," he said.

I held up the letter.

"No one is looking," I said, "and this won't go in your pocket."

You should have seen his face.

"Where did you get it?" he asked.

I told him all about it. I told him everything—about the hair that maybe was stronger than she thought, and that she was going to change father's and mother's opinions, and that I put the red flower on, but she left it; and when I was done Laddie almost hugged the life out of me. I never did see him so happy. -

"If you be very, very careful never to breathe a whisper, I'll take you with me some day," he promised.

CHAPTER

2

Our Angel Boy

I had a brother once—a gracious boy,
Full of all gentleness, of calmest hope,
Of sweet and quiet joy,—there was the look
Of heaven upon his face.

It was supper time when we reached home, and Bobby was at the front gate to meet me. He always hunted me all over the place when the big bell in the yard rang at meal time, because if he crowed nicely when he was told, he was allowed to stand on the back of my chair and every little while I held up my plate and shared bites with him. I have seen many white bantams, but never another like Bobby. My big brothers bought him for me at a fair in Fort Wayne, and sent him in a box, alone on the cars. Father and I drove to Groveville to meet him. The minute father pried off the lid, Bobby hopped on the edge of the box and crowed—the biggest crow you ever heard from such a mite of a body; he wasn't in the least afraid of us and we were pleased about it. You scarcely could see his beady black eyes for his bushy topknot, his wing tips touched the ground, his tail had two beautiful plumy feathers much longer than the others, his feet were covered with feathers, and his knee tufts dragged. He was the sauciest, spunkiest little fellow, and white as muslin. We went to supper together, but no one asked where I had been, and because I was so bursting full of importance, I talked only to Bobby, in order to be safe.

After supper I finished Hezekiah's trousers, and May cut his coat for me. School would begin in September and our clothes were being made, so I used the scraps to dress him. His suit was done by the next forenoon, and father never laughed harder than when Hezekiah hopped down the walk to meet him dressed in pink trousers and coat. The coat had flowing sleeves like the Princess wore, so Hezekiah could fly and he seemed to like them. His suit was such a success I began a sunbonnet, and when that was tied on him, the folks almost had spasms. They said he wouldn't like being dressed; that he would fly away to punish me, but he did no such thing. He stayed around the house and was tame as ever. He and Bobby quarrelled all the time. He could come out best too, for he would fly down and give Bobby a good peck on the head with his strong, sharp beak, and then keep straight on wing into the cherry tree. Bobby had to reach his perching place in the Bartlett pear, by flying to the garden fence first, and then to a lower limb.

When I became tired sewing that afternoon, I went down the lane leading to our meadow, where Leon was killing thistles with a grubbing hoe. I thought he would be glad to see me, and he was. Every one had been busy in the house, so I went to the cellar the outside way and ate all I wanted from the cupboard. Then I spread two big slices of bread the best I could with my fingers, putting apple butter on one, and mashed potatoes on the other. If you never have tried it, you don't know how good cold mashed potatoes are on bread and butter halfway between dinner and supper. Leon leaned on the hoe and watched me coming. He was a hungry boy, and lonesome too, but he couldn't have been forced to say so.

"Laddie is at work in the barn," he said when he saw me.

"I'm going to play in the creek," I answered.

I always did love water. Crossing our meadow there was a little stream that had grassy banks, big trees, willows, bushes and vines for shade, a solid pebbly bed; it was all turns and bends so that the water hurried until it bubbled and sang as it went; in it lived tiny fish coloured brightly as flowers, beside it ran killdeer, plover and solemn blue herons almost as tall as I was came over from the river to fish; for a place to play on a hot August afternoon, it couldn't be beaten. The sheep had been put in the lower pasture; so the cross old Shropshire ram was gone and there was nothing to bother us.

"Come to the shade," I said to Leon, and when we were comfortably seated under a big maple weighted down with trailing grapevines, I offered the bread. Leon laid his hat aside, took a piece in each hand and began to eat as if he were starving. Laddie would have kissed me and said: "What a fine treat! Thank you, Little Sister."

Leon was different. He ate every crumb so greedily you had to know he was mighty glad to get it, but he wouldn't say so, not if he never got any more. When you knew him, you understood he wouldn't forget it, and he'd be almost certain to do something nice for you before the day was over to pay back. We sat there talking about everything we saw, and at last Leon said with a grin: "Shelley isn't getting much grape sap is she?"

"I didn't know she wanted grape sap."

"She read about it in a paper. It said to cut the vine of a wild grape, set a vessel under, catch the drippings and moisten your hair. This would make it glossy and fine, and grow faster."

"What on earth does Shelley want with more hair than she has?"

"Oh, she has heard it bragged on so much she thinks people would say more if she could improve it."

I looked and there was the vine, dry as could be, and a milk crock beneath it.

"Didn't the silly know she had to cut the vine in the spring when the sap was running?"

"Bear witness, O vine! that she did not," said Leon with a wave of his hand, "and speak, ye voiceless pottery, and testify that she expected to find you overflowing."

"Too bad that she's going to be disappointed."

"She isn't! She's going to find ample liquid to bathe her streaming tresses. Keep quiet and watch me."

He picked up the crock, carried it to the creek and dipped it full of water.

"That's too much," I objected. "She'll know she never got a crock full from a dry vine."

"She'll think the vine bled itself dry to accommodate her."

"She isn't that silly."

"Well, then, how silly is she?" asked Leon, spilling out half. "About so?"

"Not so bad as that. Less yet!"

"Anything to please the ladies," said Leon, pouring out more.

Then we sat and giggled a while.

"What are you going to do now?" asked Leon.

"Play in the creek," I answered.

"All right! I'll work near you."

He rolled his trousers above his knees and took the hoe, but he was in the water most of the time. We had to climb on the bank when we came to the deep curve, under the stump of the old oak that father cut because Pete Billings would climb it and yowl like a wildcat, on cold winter nights. Pete was wrong in his head like Paddy Ryan, only worse. As we passed we heard the faintest sounds, so we lay and looked, and there in the dark place under the roots, where the water was deepest, huddled some of the cunningest little downy wild ducks you ever saw. We looked at each other and never said a word. Leon chased them out with the hoe and they swam down stream faster than old ones. I stood in the shallow water behind them and kept them from going back to the deep place, while Leon worked to catch them. Every time he got one he brought it to me, and I made a bag of my apron front to put them in. The supper bell rang before we caught all of them. We were dripping wet with creek water and perspiration, but we had the ducks, every one of them, and proudly started home. I'll wager Leon was sorry he didn't wear aprons so he could carry them. He did keep the last one in his hands, and held its little fluffy body against his cheeks every few minutes.

"Couldn't anything be prettier than a young duck," he said.

"Except a little guinea."

"That's so!" said Leon. "They are most as pretty as quail. I guess all young things that have down are about as cunning as they can be. I don't believe I know which I like best, myself."

"Baby killdeers."

"I mean tame. Things we raise."

"I'll take guineas."

"I'll say white turkeys. They seem so innocent. Nothing of ours is pretty as these."

"But these are wild."

"So they are," said Leon. "Twelve of them. Won't mother be pleased?"

She was not in the least. She said we were a sight to behold; that she was ashamed to be the mother of two children as big as we were, who didn't know tame ducks from wild ones. She remembered instantly that Amanda Deam had set a speckled Dorking hen on Mallard duck eggs; where she got the eggs, and what she paid for them. She said the ducks had found the creek that flowed beside Deams' barnyard before it entered our land, and they had swum away from the hen, and both the hen and Amanda would be frantic. She put the ducks into a basket and said to take them back soon as ever we got our suppers, and we must hurry because we had to bathe and learn our texts for Sunday-school in the morning.

We went through the orchard, down the hill and across the meadow until we came to the creek. By that time we were tired of the basket. It was one father had woven himself of shaved and soaked hickory strips, and it was heavy. The sight of water suggested the proper place for ducks, anyway. We talked it over and decided that they would be much more comfortable swimming than in the basket, and it was more fun to wade than to walk, so we went above the deep place, I stood in the creek to keep them from going down, and Leon poured them on the water. Pigs couldn't have acted more contrary. Those ducks *liked* us. They wouldn't go to Deams'. They just fought to swim back to us. Anyway, we had the worst time you ever saw. Leon cut long switches to herd them with, and both of us waded and tried to drive them, but they would dart under embankments and roots, and dive and hide. We worked very hard and we were soaked.

Long before we reached Deams' I wished with all my might that we had carried them as mother told us, for we had lost three, and if we stopped to hunt them, more would hide. By the time we drove them under the floodgate crossing the creek between our land and Deams' four were gone. Leon left me on the gate with both switches to keep them from going back and he ran to call Mrs. Deam. She had red hair and a hot temper, and we were not very anxious to see her, but we had to do it. While Leon was gone I was thinking pretty fast and I knew exactly how things would happen. First time mother saw Mrs. Deam she would ask her if the ducks were all right, and she would tell that four were gone. Mother would ask how many she had, and she would say twelve, then mother would remember that she started us with twelve in the basket—Oh what's the use! Something had to be done. It had to be done quickly too, for I could hear Amanda Deam, her boy Sammy and Leon coming across the barnyard. I looked around in despair, but when things are the very worst, there is almost always some way out.

On the dry straw worked between and pushing against the panels of the floodgate, not three yards from me, I saw a monstrous big black water snake. I took one good look at it: no coppery head, no geometry patterns, no rattlebox, so I knew it wasn't poisonous and wouldn't bite until it was hurt, and if it did, all you had to do was to suck the place, and it wouldn't amount to more than a few little pricks as if pins had stuck you; but a big snake was a good excuse. I rolled from the floodgate among the ducks, and cried, "Snake!" with all my might. They scattered everywhere. The snake lazily uncoiled and slid across the straw so slowly that—thank goodness! Amanda Deam got a fair look at it. She immediately began to jump up and down and scream. Leon grabbed a stick and came running to the water. I cried so he had to help me out first.

"Don't let her count them!" I whispered.

Leon gave me one swift look and all the mischief in his baby blue eyes peeped out. He was the funniest boy you ever knew, anyway. Mostly he looked scowly and abused. He had a grievance against everybody and everything. He said none of us liked him, and we imposed on him. Father said that if he tanned Leon's jacket for anything, and set him down to think it over, he would pout a while, then he would look thoughtful, suddenly his face would light up and he would go away just sparkling; and you could depend upon it he would do the same thing over, or something worse, inside an hour. When he wanted to, he could smile the most winning smile you ever saw, and he could coax you into anything. Mother said she dreaded to have to borrow a dime from him, if a peddler caught her without change, because she knew she'd be kept paying it back for the next six months. Right now he was the busiest kind of boy.

"Where is it? Let me get a good lick at it! Don't scare the ducks!" he would cry, and chase them from one bank to the other, while Amanda danced and fought imaginary snakes. For a woman who had seen as many as she must have in her life, it was too funny. I don't think I could laugh harder, or Leon and Sammy. We enjoyed ourselves so much that at last she began to be angry. She quit dancing and commenced hunting ducks, for sure. She held her skirts high, poked along the banks, jumped the creek and didn't always get clear across. Her hair shook down, she lost a sidecomb, and she couldn't find half the ducks. That made her worse.

"You younguns pack right out of here," she said. "Me and Sammy can get them better ourselves, and if we don't find all of them, we'll know where they are."

"We haven't got any of your ducks," I said angrily, but Leon smiled his most angelic smile, and it seemed as if he were going to cry.

"Of course, if you want to accuse mother of stealing your ducks, you can," he said plaintively, "but I should think you'd be ashamed to do it, after all the trouble we took to catch them before they swam to the river, where you never would have found one of them. Come on, Little Sister, let's go home."

He started and I followed. As soon as we got around the bend we sat on the bank, hung our feet in the water, leaned against each other and laughed. We just laughed ourselves almost sick. When Amanda's face got fire red, and her hair came down, and she jumped and didn't go quite over, she looked a perfect fright.

"Will she ever find all of them?" I asked at last.

"Of course," said Leon. "She will comb the grass and strain the water until she gets every one."

"Hoo-hoo!"

I looked at Leon. He was watching so intently an old turkey

buzzard hanging in the air, he never heard the call that meant it was time for us to be home and cleaning up for Sunday. It was difficult to hurry, for after we had been soaped and scoured, we had to sit on the back steps and commit to memory verses from the Bible. At last we slid into the water and waded toward home. Two of the ducks we had lost swam before us all the way, so we knew they were alive, and all they needed was finding.

"If she hadn't accused mother of stealing her old ducks, I'd catch those and carry them back to her," said Leon. "But since she thinks we are so mean, I'll just let her and little Sammy find them."

Then we heard their voices as they came down the creek, so Leon reached me his hand and we scampered across the water and meadow, never stopping until we sat on the top rail of our back orchard fence. There we heard another call, but that was only two. We sat there, rested and looked at the green apples above our heads, wishing they were ripe, and talking about the ducks. We could see Mrs. Deam and Sammy coming down the creek, one on each side. We slid from the fence and ran into a queer hollow that was cut into the hill between the never-fail and the Baldwin apple trees. That hollow was overgrown with weeds, and full of trimmings from trees, stumps, everything that no one wanted any place else in the orchard. It was the only unkept spot on our land, and I always wondered why father didn't clean it out and make it look respectable. I said so to Leon as we crouched there watching down the hill where Mrs. Deam and Sammy hunted ducks with not such very grand success. They seemed to have so many they couldn't decide whether to go back or go on, so they must have found most of them.

"You know I've always had my suspicions about this place," said Leon. "There is somewhere on our land that people can be hidden for a long time. I can remember well enough before the war ever so long, and while it was going worst, we would find the wagon covered with more mud in the morning than had been on it at night; and the horses would be splashed and tired. Once I was awake in the night and heard voices. It made me want a drink, so I went downstairs for it, and ran right into the biggest, blackest man who ever grew. If father and mother hadn't been there I'd have been scared into fits. Next morning he was gone and there wasn't a whisper. Father said I'd had bad dreams. That night the horses made another mysterious trip. Now where did they keep the black man all that day?"

"What did they have a black man for?"

"They were helping him run away from slavery to be free in Canada. It was all right. I'd have done the same thing. They helped a lot. Father was a friend of the Governor. There were letters from him, and there was some good reason why father stayed at home, when he was crazy about the war. I think this farm was what they called an Underground Station. What I want to know is where the station was."

"Maybe it's here. Let's hunt," I said. "If the black men were here some time, they would have to be fed, and this is not far from the house."

So we took long sticks and began poking into the weeds. Then we moved the brush, and sure as you live, we found an old door with a big stone against it. I looked at Leon and he looked at me.

"Hoo-hoo!" came mother's voice, and that was the third call.

"Hum! Must be for us," said Leon. "We better go as soon as we get a little dryer."

He slid down the bank on one side, and I on the other, and we pushed at the stone. I thought we never would get it rolled away so we could open the door a crack, but when we did what we saw was most surprising. There was a little room, dreadfully small, but a room. There was straw scattered over the floor, very deep on one side, where an old blanket showed that it had been a bed. Across the end there was a shelf. On it was a candlestick, with a half-burned candle in it, a pie pan with some mouldy crumbs, crusts, bones in it, and a tin can. Leon picked up the can and looked in. I could see too.

It had been used for water or coffee, as the plate had for food, once, but now it was stuffed full of money. I saw Leon pull some out and then shove it back, and he came to the door white as could be, shut it behind him and began to push at the stone. When we got it in place we put the brush over it, and fixed everything like it had been. Then we looked at each other.

At last Leon said: "That's the time we got into something not intended for us, and if father finds it out, we are in for a good thrashing. Are you just a blubbering baby, or are you big enough to keep still?"

"I am old enough that I could have gone to school two years ago, and I won't tell!" I said stoutly.

"All right! Come on then," said Leon. "I don't know but mother has been calling us."

We started up the orchard path just as the fourth call came.

"Hoo-hoo!" answered Leon in a sick little voice to make it sound far away. Must have made mother think we were on Deams' hill. Then we went on side by side.

"Say Leon, you found the Station, didn't you?" I whispered.

"Don't talk about it!" snapped Leon.

I changed the subject.

"Whose money do you suppose that is?"

"Oh crackey! You can depend on a girl to see everything," groaned Leon. "Do you think you'll be able to stand the switching that job will bring you, without getting sick in bed?"

Now I never had been sick in bed, and from what I had seen of other people who were, I never wanted to be. The idea of being switched until it made me sick was too much for me. I shut my mouth tight and I never opened it about the Station place. Just as we reached the maiden's-blush apple tree came another call, and it sounded pretty cross, I can tell you. Leon reached his hand.

"Now, it's time to run," he said. "Let me do the talking."

We were out of breath when we reached the back door. There stood the tub on the kitchen floor, the boiler on the stove, soap, towels, and clean clothing on chairs. Leon had his turn at having his head and ears washed first because he could bathe himself while mother did my hair.

"Was Mrs. Deam glad to get her ducks back?" she asked as she fine-combed Leon.

"Aw, you never can tell whether she's glad about anything or not," growled Leon. "You'd have thought from the way she acted, that we'd been trying to steal her ducks. She said if she missed any she'd know where to find them."

"Well as I live!" cried mother. "Why, I wouldn't have believed that of Amanda Deam. You told her you thought they were wild, of course."

"I didn't have a chance to tell her anything. The minute the ducks struck the water they started right back down stream, and there was a big snake, and we had an awful time. We got wet nearly all over trying to head them back, and then we didn't get all of them. She and Sammy are in our meadow now trying to find the others."

"They are like little eels. You should have helped Amanda."

"Well, you called so cross we thought you would come after us, so we had to run."

"One never knows," sighed mother. "I thought you were loitering. Of course if I had known you were having trouble with the ducks! I think you had better go back and help them."

"Didn't I do enough to take them home? Can't Sammy Deam catch ducks as fast as I can?"

"I suppose so," said mother. "And I must get your bathing out of the way of supper. You use the tub while I do Little Sister's hair."

I almost hated Sunday, because of what had to be done to my hair on Saturday, to get ready for it. All week it hung in two long braids that were brushed and arranged each morning. But on Saturday it had to be combed with a fine comb, oiled and rolled around thin strips of tin until Sunday morning. Mother did everything thoroughly. She raked that fine comb over our scalps until she almost raised the blood. She hadn't time to fool with tangles, and we had so much hair she didn't know what to do with all of it, anyway. When she was busy talking she reached around too far and combed across our foreheads or raked the tip of an ear.

She made the oil she used herself. The colour was lovely. She fried out the fat from turkey gizzards, cut it with alcohol, and scented it with bergamot. It smelled beautifully, but when she wiped it into our eyes it smarted, and unless we kept our mouths tight shut we had to swallow some of it sometimes. Then she rolled the tins so tight they drew our necks up with the hair in little hills, and if we didn't sleep on our faces at night, the tins cut into us until we bled once in a while. But on Sunday morning we forgot all that, when we walked down the aisle with shining curls hanging below our waists. Mother was using the fine comb, when she looked up, and there stood Mrs. Freshett. We could see at a glance that she was out of breath, too. From the way she panted she might have been chasing ducks herself.

"Have I beat them?" she cried.

"Whom are you trying to beat?" asked mother as she told May to set a chair for Mrs. Freshett and bring her a drink.

"The grave-kiver men," she said. "I wanted to get to you first."

"Well, you have," said mother. "Rest a while and then tell me." But Mrs. Freshett was so excited she couldn't rest.

"I thought they were coming straight on down," she said, "but they must have turned off at the cross roads. I want to do what's right by my children here or there," panted Mrs. Freshett, "and these men seemed to think the contrivance they was sellin' perfectly grand, an' like to be an aid to the soul's salvation. Nice as it seemed, an' convincin' as they talked, I couldn't get the consent of my mind to order, until I knowed if you was goin' to kiver your dead with the contraption. None of the rest of the neighbours seem overly friendly to me, an' I've told Josiah many's the time, that I didn't care a rap if they wa'n't, so long as I had you. Says I, 'Josiah, to my way of thinkin', she is top crust in this neighbourhood, and I'm on the safe side apin' her ways clost as possible.'"

"I'll gladly help you all I can," said my mother.

"Thanky!" said Mrs. Freshett. "I knowed you would. Josiah he says to me, 'Don't you be apin' nobody.' 'Josiah,' says I, 'it takes a pretty smart woman in this world to realize what she doesn't know. Now I know what I know, well enough, but all I know is like to keep me an' my children in a log cabin an' on log cabin ways to the end of our time.' You ain't even got the remains of the cabin you started in for a cow shed. Says I, 'Josiah, Miss Stanton knows how to get out of a cabin an' into a grand big palace, fit fur a queen woman. She's a ridin' in a shinin' kerridge, 'stid of a spring wagon. She goes abroad dressed so's you men all stand starin' like cabbage heads. All hern go to church, an' Sunday-school, an' college, an' come out on the top of the heap. She does jest what I'd like to if I knowed how. An' she ain't come-uppety one morsel.' If I was to strike acrost fields to them stuck-up Pryors, I'd get the door slammed in my face if 'twas the missus, a sneer if 'twas the man, an' at best a nod cold as an iceberg if 'twas the girl. Them as wants to call her kind 'Princess,' and encourage her in being more stuck up 'an she was born to be, can, but to my mind a Princess is a person who thinks of some one besides herself once in a while."

"I don't find the Pryors easy to become acquainted with," said mother. "I have never met the woman; I know the man very slightly; he has been here on business once or twice, but the girl seems as if she would be nice, if one knew her. I rather like her looks myself."

"Well, I wouldn't have s'posed she was your kind," said Mrs. Freshett. "If she is, I won't open my head against her any more. Anyway, it was the grave-kivers I come about. The men are likely to get here soon, and I want your sentiments first."

"Just what is it, Mrs. Freshett?" asked mother, almost taking the top from my left ear with a sweep of the comb.

"It's two men sellin' a patent iron kiver for to protect the graves of your dead from the sun an' the rain."

"Who wants the graves of their dead protected from the sun and the rain?" demanded my mother sharply.

"I said to Josiah, 'I don't know how she'll feel about it, but I can't do more than ask.'"

"Do they carry a sample? What is it like?"

"Jest the len'th an' width of a grave. They got from baby to six-footer sizes. They are cast iron like the bottom of a cook stove on the under side, but atop they are polished so they shine somethin' beautiful. You can get them in a solid piece, or with a hole in the centre about the size of a milk crock to set flowers through. They come ten to the grave, an' they are mighty stylish lookin' things. I have been savin' all I could skimp from butter, an' eggs, an' garden sass, to get Samantha a organ; but says I to her, 'You are gettin' all I can do for you every day; there lays your poor brother 'at ain't had a finger lifted for him since he was took so sudden he was gone before I knowed he was goin'.' I never can get over Henry bein' took the way he was, so I says: 'If this would be a nice thing to have for Henry's grave, and the neighbours are goin' to have them for theirn, looks to me like some of the organ money will have to go, an' we'll make it up later.' I don't 'low for Henry to be slighted bekase he rid himself to death trying to make a president out of his pa's gin'ral."

"You never told me how you lost your son," said mother, feeling so badly she wiped one of my eyes full of oil.

"Law now, didn't I?" inquired Mrs. Freshett. "Well, mebby that is bekase I ain't had a chance to tell you much of anythin', your bein' always so busy like, an' me not wantin' to wear out my welcome. It was like this: All endurin' the war Henry an' me did the best we could without pa at home, but by the time it was over, Henry was most a man. Seemed as if when he got home, his pa was all tired out and glad to set down an' rest, but Henry was afire to be up an' goin'. His pa filled him so full o' Grant, it was runnin' out of his ears. Come the second run the Gin'ral made, peered like Henry set out to 'lect him all by hisself. He wore every horse on the place out, ridin' to rallies. Sometimes he was gone three days an' more at a stretch. He'd git one place an' hear of a rally on ten miles or so furder, an' blest if he didn't ride plum acrost the state 'fore he got through with one trip. He set out in July, and he rid right straight through to November, nigh onto every day of his life. He got white, an' thin, an' narvous, from loss of sleep an' lack of food, an' his pa got restless, said Henry was takin' the 'lection more serious 'an he ever took the war. Last few days before votin' was cold an' raw an' Henry rid constant. 'Lection day he couldn't vote, for he lacked a year of bein' o' age, an' he rid in with a hard chill, an' white as a ghost, an' he says, 'Ma,' says he, 'I've 'lected Grant, but I'm all tuckered out. Put me to bed an' kiver me warm.'

"I did so, but 'fore long I heard him mutterin', an' by the time his pa got home, took all my stren'th to hold Henry down. His pa went straight back for the doctor, an' he come by mornin'. He looked Henry over and he says: 'Lung fever. Bad!'"

I forgot the sting in my eyes watching Mrs. Freshett. She was the largest woman I knew, and strong as most men. Her hair was black and glisteny, her eyes black, her cheeks red, her skin a clear, even, dark tint. She was handsome, she was honest, and she was in earnest over everything. There was something about her, or her family, that had to be told in whispers, and some of the neighbours would have nothing to do with her. But mother said Mrs. Freshett was doing the very best she knew, and for the sake of that, and of her children, any one who wouldn't help her was not a Christian, and not to be a Christian was the very worst thing that could happen to you. I stared at her steadily. She talked straight along, so rapidly you scarcely could keep up with the words; you couldn't if you wanted to think about them any between. There was not a quiver in her voice, but from her eyes there rolled, steadily, the biggest, roundest tears I ever saw. They ran down her cheeks, formed a stream in the first groove of her double chin, overflowed it, and dripped drop, drop, a drop at a time, on the breast of her stiffly starched calico dress, and from there shot to her knees.

"'Twa'n't no time at all, 'til he was chokin' an burnin' red with fever, an' his pa and me, stout as we be, couldn't hold him down nor keep him kivered. He was speechifyin' to beat anythin' you ever heard. His pa said he was repeatin' what he'd heard said by every big stump speaker from Greeley to Logan. When he got so hoarse we couldn't tell what he said any more, he jest mouthed it, an' at last he dropped back and laid like he was pinned to the sheets, an' I thought he was restin', but 'twa'n't an hour 'til he was gone."

Suddenly Mrs. Freshett lifted her apron, covered her face and sobbed until her broad shoulders shook.

"Oh you poor soul!" said my mother. "I'm so sorry for you!"

Finally Mrs. Freshett wiped her eyes and stopped sobbing, though her voice was wavery.

"I never knowed he was a-goin' until he was gone," she said. "He was the only one of mine I ever lost, an' I thought it would jest lay me out. I couldn't 'a' stood it at all if I hadn't 'a' knowed he was saved. I well know my Henry went straight to Heaven if anybody ever did. Why Miss Stanton, he riz right up in bed at the last and clear and strong he jest yelled it: 'Hurrah fur Grant!'"

My mother's fingers tightened in my hair until I thought she would pull out a lot, and I could feel her knees stiffen against my sides. While I was twisting around to see her face, there was a yell from the kitchen. Leon just whooped. Mother sprang up and ran to the door.

"Leon!" she cried. Then there was a slam. "What in the world is the matter?" she asked.

"Stepped out of the tub right on the soap, and it threw me down," explained Leon.

"For mercy sake, be careful!" said my mother, and shut the door.

It wasn't a minute before the knob turned and it opened again a little.

I never saw mother's face look so queer, but at last she said softly: "You were thinking of the grave cover for him?"

"Yes, but I wanted to ask you before I bound myself. I heard you lost two when the scarlet fever was ragin' an' I'm goin' to do jest what you do. If you have kivers, I will. If you don't like them when you see how bright and shiny they are, I won't get any either."

"I can tell you without seeing them, Mrs. Freshett," said my mother, wrapping a strand of hair around the tin so tight I slipped up my fingers to feel whether my neck wasn't like a buckeye hull looks, and it was. "I don't want any cover for the graves of my dead but grass and flowers, and sky and clouds. I like the rain to fall on them, and the sun to shine, so that the grass and flowers will grow. If you are satisfied that the soul of Henry is safe in Heaven, that is all that is necessary. Laying a slab of iron on top of earth six feet above his body will make no difference to him. If he is singing with the angels, by all means save your money for the organ."

"I don't know about the singin'. He never sung none on earth, but I'd stake my last red cent he's still hollerin' fur Grant. I was kind o' took with the idea; the things was so shiny and scilloped at the edges, peered like it was payin' considerable respect to the dead to kiver them that-a-way."

"What good would it do?" asked mother. "The sun shining on the iron would make it so hot it would burn any flower you tried to plant in the opening; the water couldn't reach the roots, and all that fell on the slab would run off and make it that much wetter at the edges. The iron would soon rust and grow dreadfully ugly lying under winter snow. There is nothing at all in it, save a method to work on the feelings of the living, and get them to pay their money for something that wouldn't affect their dead a particle. I wouldn't think of such a thing."

" 'Twould be a poor idea for me," said Mrs. Freshett. "I said to the men that I wanted to honour Henry all I could, but with my bulk, I'd hev all I could do, come Jedgment Day, to bust my box, an' heave up the clods, without havin' to hist up a piece of iron an' klim from under it."

Mother stiffened and Leon slipped again. He could have more accidents than any boy I ever knew. But it was only a few minutes until he came to mother, clean and neat as a pin, and gave her a Bible to mark the verses he had to learn to recite at Sunday-school next day. Mother couldn't take the time when she had company, so she asked if he weren't big enough to pick out ten proper verses and learn them by himself, and he said of course he was. He took his Bible and he and May and I sat on the back steps and studied our verses. He and May were so big they had ten; but I had only two, and mine were not very long. I never saw such a boy as Leon. He giggled half the time he was studying. I haven't found anything so very funny in the Bible. Every few minutes he would whisper to himself: *"That's a good one!"*

He took the book and heard May do hers until she had them perfectly, then he went away alone, and sat on the back fence with his book and studied as I never before had seen him. Mrs. Freshett stayed so long mother had no time to hear him, but he told her he had them all learned so he could repeat them without a mistake.

Next morning mother was busy getting breakfast, the chickens fed, and dinner arranged before we dressed, so she had no time then. Father, Shelley, and I rode on the front seat, mother, May, and Sally on the back, while the boys started early and walked. We passed them on the bridge at the foot of the Big Hill, and father called to them to come along, as it would be time to begin when we got there.

When we reached the top of the hill, the road was lined with carriages, wagons, spring wagons, and saddle horses. Father found a place for our team and we went down the walk between the hitching rack and the cemetery fence. Mother opened the gate and knelt beside two small graves covered with grass, shaded by yellow rose bushes, and marked with little white stones. She laid some flowers on each and wiped the dust from the carved letters with her handkerchief. The little sisters who had scarlet fever and whooping cough lay there. Mother was still a minute and then she said softly: "'The Lord has given and the Lord has taken away. Blessed be the name of the Lord.'"

She was very pale when she came to us, but her eyes were bright and she smiled as she put her arms around as many of us as she could reach, and we went toward the church door.

"What a beautiful horse!" said Sally. "Look at that saddle and bridle! The Pryor girl is here."

"Why should she come?" asked Shelley.

"To show her fine clothes and queen it over us, of course."

"Children, children!" said mother. "'Judge not!' This is a house of worship. The Lord may be drawing her in His own way. It is for us to help Him by being kind and making her welcome, if she chooses to come among us."

At the church door we parted and sat with our teachers, but for the first time in my life, as I went down the aisle I was not thinking of my linen dress, my patent leather slippers, and my pretty curls. It suddenly seemed cheap to me to twist my hair when it was straight as a shingle, and cut my head on tin. If the Lord had wanted me to have curls, my hair would have been like Sally's. Seemed to me hers tried to see into what big soft curls it could roll. May said ours was so straight it bent back the other way. Anyway, I made up my mind to talk it over with father and always wear braids after that, if I could get him to coax mother to let me. Also, I made up my mind to another thing, but there was no chance just then.

Our church was quite new and it was beautiful. All the casings were oiled wood, and the walls had just a little yellow in the last skin coating used to make them smooth, so they were a creamy colour, and the blinds were yellow. The windows were wide open and the wind drifted through, while the birds sang as much as they ever do in August, among the trees and bushes of the cemetery. Every one had planted so many flowers of all kinds on the graves you could scent sweet odours. Often a big, black-striped, brown butterfly came sailing in through one of the windows, followed the draft across the room, and out of another. I was thinking something funny: it was about what the Princess had said of other people, and whether hers were worse. I looked at my father sitting in calm dignity in his Sunday suit and thought him quite as fine and handsome as mother did. Every Sabbath he wore the same suit, he sat in the same spot, he worshipped the Lord in his calm, earnest way. The ministers changed, but father was as much a part of the service as the Bible on the desk, or the communion table. I wondered if people said things about him, and if they did, what they were. I never had heard. Twisting in my seat, one by one I studied the faces on the men's side, and then the women. It was a mighty good-looking crowd. Some had finer clothes than others—that is always the way—but as a rule every one was clean, neat, and good to see. From some you scarcely could turn away. There was Widow Fall. She was French, from Virginia, and she talked like little tinkly notes of music. I just loved to hear her, and she walked like high-up royalty. Her dress was always black, with white bands at the neck and sleeves, black rustly silk, and her eyes and hair were like the dress. There was a little red on her cheeks and lips, and her face was always grave until she saw you directly before her, and then she smiled the sweetest smile.

Maybe Sarah Hood was not pretty, but there was something about her lean face and shining eyes that made you look twice before you were sure of it, and by that time you had got so used to her, you liked her better as she was, and wouldn't have changed her for anything. Mrs. Fritz had a pretty face, and dresses and manners, and so did Hannah Dover, only she talked too much. So I studied them and remembered what the Princess had said, and I wondered if she heard some one say that Peter Justice beat his wife, or if she showed it in her face and manner. She reminded me of a scared cowslip that had been cut and laid in the sun an hour. I don't know as that expresses it. Perhaps a flower couldn't look scared, but it could be wilted, and faded. I wondered if she ever had bright hair, laughing eyes, and red in her lips and cheeks. She must have been pretty if she had.

At last I reached my mother. There was nothing scared or faded about her, and she was dreadfully sick too, once in a while since she had the fever. She was a little bit of a woman, coloured like a wild rose petal, face and body—a piece of pink porcelain Dutch, father said. She had brown eyes, hair like silk, and she always had three best dresses. There was one of alpaca or woollen, of black, gray or brown, and two silks. Always there was a fine rustly black one with a bonnet and mantle to match, and then a softer, finer one of either gold brown, like her hair, or dainty gray, like a dove's wing. When these grew too old for fine use, she wore them to Sunday-school and had a fresh one for best. There was a new gray in her closet at home, so she put on the old brown to-day, and she was lovely in it. I shut my eyes and tried to think how she must have looked at twenty when father married her. He said her face then was like pink velvet, a rope of brown hair thick as his wrist reached her knees, and her eyes were big and shining. She weighed only ninety pounds, and he always put in that she was "plump as a partridge."

Usually the minister didn't come for church services until Sunday-school was half over, so the superintendent read a chapter, Daddy Debs prayed, and all of us stood up and sang: "Ring Out the Joy Bells." That was the prettiest song. Then the superintendent read the lesson over as impressively as he could. The secretary made his report, we sang another song, gathered the pennies, and each teacher took a class and talked over the lesson a few minutes. Then we repeated the verses we had committed to memory to our teachers; the member of each class who had learned the nicest texts, and knew them best, was selected to recite before the school. Beginning with the littlest people, we came to the big folks. Each one recited two texts until they reached the class above mine. We walked to the front, stood inside the altar, made a little bow, and the superintendent kept score. I could see that mother appeared worried when Leon's name was called for his class, for she hadn't heard him, and she was afraid he would forget.

Among the funny things about Leon was this: while you had to drive other boys of his age to recite, you almost had to hold him to keep him from it. Father said he was born for a politician or a preacher, if he would be good, and grow into the right kind of a man to do such responsible work.

He walked up the centre aisle, stood inside the railing, and made a smooth little bow. Then he turned to the secretary.

"I forgot several last Sabbath, so I have thirteen today," he said politely.

Of course no one expected anything like that. You never knew what might happen when Leon did anything. He must have been about sixteen. He was a slender lad, having almost sandy hair, like his English grandfather. He wore a white ruffled shirt with a broad collar, and cuffs turning back over his black jacket, and his trousers fitted his slight legs closely. The wind whipped his soft black tie a little and ruffled the light hair where it was longest and wavy above his forehead. Such a perfect picture of innocence you never saw. There was one part of him that couldn't be described any better than the way Mr. Rienzi told about his brother in his "Address to the Romans," in McGuffey's Sixth. "The look of heaven on his face" stayed most of the time; again, there was a dealish twinkle that sparkled and flashed while he was thinking up something mischievous to do. When he was fighting angry, and going to thrash Absalom Saunders or die trying, he was plain white and his eyes were like steel. Mother called him "Weiscope," half the time. I can only spell the way that sounds, but it means "white-head," and she always used that name when she loved him most. "The look of heaven" was strong on his face now.

"One," said the recording secretary.

"Jesus wept," answered Leon promptly.

There was not a sound in the church. You could almost hear the butterflies pass. Father looked down and laid his lower lip in folds with his fingers, like he did sometimes when it wouldn't behave to suit him of itself.

"Two," said the secretary after just a breath of pause.

Leon looked over the congregation easily and then fastened his eyes on Abram Saunders, the father of Absalom, and said reprovingly: "Give not sleep to thine eyes nor slumber to thine eyelids."

Abram straightened up suddenly and blinked in astonishment, and father held fast to his lip.

"Three," called the secretary hurriedly.

Leon shifted his gaze to Betsy Alton, whom every one knew hadn't spoken to her next door neighbour in five years.

"Hatred stirreth up strife," he told her softly, "but love covereth all sins."

Things were so quiet it seemed as if the air would snap.

"Four."

The mild blue eyes travelled back to the men's side and settled on Isaac Thomas, a man too lazy to plow and sow land his father had earned and left him. They were not so mild, and the voice was strongly touched with command: "Go to the ant, thou sluggard, consider her ways and be wise."

Still that silence.

"Five," said the secretary hurriedly, as if he wished it were over. Back came the eyes to the women's side and past all question looked straight at Hannah Dover.

"As a jewel of gold in a swine's snout, so is a fair woman without discretion."

"Six," said the secretary and looked appealingly at father, whose face was filled with dismay.

Again Leon's eyes crossed the aisle and he looked directly at the man whom everybody in the community called "Stiff-necked Johnny." I think he was rather proud of it, he worked so hard to keep them doing it.

"Lift not up your horn on high: speak not with a stiff neck," Leon commanded him.

Toward the door some one tittered.

"Seven," called the secretary hastily.

Leon glanced around the room.

"But how good and how pleasant it is for brethren to dwell together in unity," he announced in delighted tones as if he had found it out by himself, only that minute.

"Eight," called the secretary with something like a breath of relief.

Our angel boy never had looked so angelic, and he was beaming on the Princess.

"Thou art all fair, my love; there is no spot in thee," he told her.

Laddie would thrash him for that.

Instantly after, "Nine," he recited straight at Laddie, "I made a covenant with mine eyes; why then should I think upon a maid?"

More than one giggled that time.

"Ten!" came almost sharply.

Leon looked scared for the first time. He actually seemed to shiver. Maybe he realized at last that it was a pretty serious thing he was doing. When he spoke he said these words in the most surprised voice you ever heard: "I was almost in all evil in the midst of the congregation and assembly."

"Eleven."

Perhaps these words are in the Bible. They are not there to read the way Leon repeated them, for he put a short pause after the first name, and he glanced toward our father: "Jesus Christ, the *same,* yesterday, and to-day, and forever!"

Sure as you live my mother's shoulders shook.

"Twelve."

Suddenly Leon seemed to be forsaken. He surely shrank in size and appeared abused.

"When my father and my mother forsake me, then the Lord will take me up," he announced, and looked as happy over the ending as he had seemed forlorn at the beginning.

"Thirteen."

"The Lord is on my side; I will not fear; what can man do unto me?" inquired Leon of every one in the church. Then he soberly made his little bow and walked to his seat.

Father's voice broke that silence. "Let us kneel in prayer," he said.

He took a step forward, knelt, laid his hands on the altar, closed his eyes and turned his face upward.

"Our Heavenly Father, we come before Thee in a trying situation," he said. "Thy word of truth has been spoken to us by a thoughtless boy, whether in a spirit of helpfulness or of jest, Thou knowest. Since we are reasoning creatures, it little matters in what form Thy truth comes to us; the essential thing is that we soften our hearts for its entrance, and grow in grace by its application. Tears of compassion such as our dear Saviour wept are in our eyes this morning as we plead with Thee to help us to apply these words to the betterment of this community."

Then father began to pray. If the Lord had been standing six feet in front of him, and his life had depended on what he said, he could have prayed no harder. Goodness knows how fathers remember. He began at "Jesus wept" and told about this sinful world and why He wept over it; then one at a time he took those other twelve verses and hammered them down where they belonged much harder than

Leon ever could by merely looking at people. After that he prayed all around each one so fervently that those who had been hit the very worst cried aloud and said: "Amen!" You wouldn't think any one could do a thing like that; but I heard and saw my father do it.

When he arose the tears were running down his cheeks, and before him stood Leon. He was white as could be, but he spoke out loudly and clearly.

"Please forgive me, sir; I didn't intend to hurt your feelings. Please every one forgive me. I didn't mean to offend any one. It happened through hunting short verses. All the short ones seemed to be like that, and they made me think—"

He got no farther. Father must have been afraid of what he might say next. He threw his arms around Leon's shoulders, drew him to the seat, and with the tears still rolling, he laughed as happily as you ever heard, and he cried: "'Sweeping through the Gates!' All join in!"

You never heard such singing in your life. That was another wonderful thing. My father didn't know the notes. He couldn't sing; he said so himself. Neither could half the people there, yet all of them were singing at the tops of their voices, and I don't believe the angels in Heaven could make grander music. My father was leading:

"These, these are they, who in the conflict dire—"

You could tell Emanuel Ripley had been in the war from the way he roared:

"Boldly have stood amidst the hottest fire—"

The Widow Fall soared above all of them on the next line; her man was there, and maybe she was lonely and would have been glad to go to him:

"Jesus now says, 'Come up higher'—"

Then my little mother:

"Washed in the blood of the Lamb—"

Like thunder all of them rolled into the chorus:

"Sweeping through the gates to the New Jerusalem—"

You wouldn't have been left out of that company for anything in all this world, and nothing else ever could make you want to go so badly as to hear every one sing straight from the heart, a grand old song like that. It is no right way to have to sit and keep still, and pay other people money to sing about Heaven to you. No matter if you can't sing by note, if your heart and soul are full, until they are running over, so that you are forced to sing as those people did, whether you can or not, you are sure to be straight on the way to the Gates.

Before three lines were finished my father was keeping time like a choirmaster, his face all beaming with shining light; mother was rocking on her toes like a wood robin on a twig at twilight, and at the end of the chorus she cried, "Glory!" right out loud, and turned and started down the aisle, shaking hands with every one, singing as she went. When she reached Betsy Alton she held her hand and led her down the aisle straight toward Rachel Brown. When Rachel saw them coming she hurried to meet them, and they shook hands and were glad to make up as any two people you ever saw. It must have been perfectly dreadful to see a woman every day for five years, and not to give her a pie, when you felt sure yours were better than she could make, or loan her a new pattern, or tell her first who had a baby, or was married, or dead, or anything like that. It was no wonder they felt glad. Mother came on, and as she passed me the verses were all finished and every one began talking and moving. Johnny Dover forgot his neck and shook hands too, and father pronounced the benediction. He always had to when the minister wasn't there, because he was ordained himself, and you didn't dare pronounce the benediction unless you were.

Every one began talking again, and wondering if the minister wouldn't come soon, and some one went out to see. There was mother standing only a few feet from the Princess, and I remembered what I had wanted to do. I had seen it done often enough, but I never had tried it myself, yet I wanted it so badly, there was no time to think how scared I would be. I took mother's hand and led her a few steps farther and said: "Mother, this is my friend, Pamela Pryor."

I believe I did it fairly well. Mother must have been surprised, but she put out her hand.

"I didn't know Miss Pryor and you were acquainted," she said.

"It's only been a little while," I told her. "I met her when I was on some business with the Fairies. They know everything and they told me her father was busy"—I thought she wouldn't want me to tell that he was plain *cross*, where every one could hear, so I said "busy" for politeness—"and her mother not very strong, and that she was a good girl, and dreadfully lonesome. Can't you do something, mother?"

"Well I should think so!" said mother, for her heart was soft as rose leaves. Maybe you won't believe this, but it's quite true. My mother took the Princess' arm and led her to Sally and Shelley, and introduced her to all the girls. By the time the minister came and mother went back to her seat, she had forgotten all about the "indisposed" word she disliked, and as you live! she invited the Princess to go home with us to dinner. She stood tall and straight, her eyes very bright, and her cheeks a little redder than usual, as she shook hands and said a few pleasant words that were like from a book, they fitted and were so right. When mother asked her to dinner she said: "Thank you kindly. I should be glad to go, but my people expect me at home and they would be uneasy. Perhaps you would allow me to ride over some week day and become acquainted?"

Mother said she would be happy to have her, and Shelley said so too, but Sally was none too cordial. She had dark curls and pink cheeks herself, and every one had said she was the prettiest girl in the county before Shelley began to blossom out and show what she was going to be. Sally never minded that, but when the Princess came she was a little taller, and her hair was a trifle longer, and heavier, and blacker, and her eyes were a little larger and darker, and where Sally had pink skin and red lips, the Princess was dark as olive, and her lips and cheeks were like red velvet. Anyway, the Princess had said she would come over; mother and Shelley had been decent to her, and Sally hadn't been exactly insulting. It would be a little more than you could expect for her to be wild about the Princess. I believe she was pleased over having been invited to dinner, and as she was a stranger she couldn't know that mother had what we called the "invitation habit."

I have seen her ask from fifteen to twenty in one trip down the aisle on Sunday morning. She wanted them to come too; the more who came, the better she liked it. If the hitching-rack and barn-yard were full on Sunday she just beamed. If the sermon pleased her, she invited more. That morning she was feeling so good she asked seventeen; and as she only had dressed six chickens—third table, backs and ham, for me as usual; but when the prospects were as now, I always managed to coax a few gizzards from Candace; she didn't dare give me livers—they were counted. Almost every one in the church was the happiest that morning they had been in years. When the preacher came, he breathed it from the air, and it worked on him so he preached the best sermon he ever had, and never knew that Leon made him do it. Maybe after all it's a good thing to tell people about their meanness and give them a stirring up once in a while.

3

Mr. Pryor's Door

"Grief will be joy if on its edge
Fall soft that holiest ray,
Joy will be grief if no faint pledge
Be there of heavenly day."

"Have Sally and Peter said anything about getting married yet?" asked my big sister Lucy of mother. Lucy was home on a visit. She was bathing her baby and mother was sewing.

"Not a word!"

"Are they engaged?"

"Sally hasn't mentioned it."

"Well, can't you find out?"

"How could I?" asked mother.

"Why, watch them a little and see how they act when they are together. If he kisses her when he leaves, of course they are engaged."

"It would be best to wait until Sally tells me," laughed mother.

I heard this from the back steps. Neither mother nor Lucy knew I was there. When they began talking of other things I wandered around the house hunting something interesting to do; but as I was thinking more of what they had said than anything else, I found nothing. I went back to see if they would let me take the baby. Of course they wouldn't! Mother had it herself. She was rocking, and softly singing my Dutch song that I loved best; I can't spell it, but it sounds like this:

Trus, trus, trill;
Der power rid der fill,
Fill sphring aveck
Plodschlicter power in der dreck.

Once I asked mother to sing it in English, and she couldn't because it didn't rhyme that way and the words wouldn't fit the notes; it was just, "Trot, trot, trot, a boy rode a colt. The colt sprang aside, down went the boy in the dirt."

"Aw, don't sing my song to that little red, pug-nosed baldhead!" I said.

Really, it was a very nice baby; I only said that because I wanted to hold it, and mother wouldn't give it up. I tried to coax May to the dam snake hunting, but she couldn't go, so I had to amuse myself. I had a doll, but I never played with it except when I was dressed up on Sunday. Anyway, what's the use of a doll when there's a live baby in the house? I didn't care much for my playhouse since I had seen one so much finer that Laddie had made for the Princess. Of course I knew moss wouldn't take root in our orchard as it did in the woods, neither would willow cuttings, and there were red flowers nowhere else. Finally, I decided to go hunting. I went into the garden and gathered every ripe touch-me-not pod I could find, and all the portulaca. Then I stripped the tiger lilies of each little black ball at the bases of the leaves, and took all the four o'clock seed there was. Then I got my biggest alder popgun and started up the road toward Sarah Hood's.

I was going along singing a little verse; it wasn't Dutch either; the old baby could have that if it wanted it. Soon as I got from sight of the house I made a powder-horn of a curled leaf, loaded my gun with portulaca powder, rammed in a tiger lily bullet, laid the weapon across my shoulder, and stepped high and lightly as Laddie does when he's in the Big Woods hunting for squirrel. It must have been my own singing—I am rather good at hearing things, but I never noticed a sound that time, until a voice like a rusty saw said: "Good morning, Nimrod!"

I sprang from the soft dust and landed among the dog fennel of a fence corner, in a flying leap. Then I looked. It was the Princess' father, tall, and gray, and grim, riding a big black horse that seemed as if it had been curried with the fine comb and brushed with the grease rag.

"Good morning!" I said just as quickly as I could speak.

He stopped his horse.

"Am I correct in the surmise that you are on the chase with a popgun?" he asked politely.

"Yes sir," I answered, getting my breath the best I could.

It came easier after I noticed he didn't seem to be angry about anything.

"Where is your hunting ground, and what game are you after?" he asked gravely.

"You can see the great African jungle over there"—I pointed for him. "I am going to hunt for lions and tigers."

You always must answer politely any one who speaks to you; and you get soundly thrashed, at least at our house, if you don't be politest of all to an older person, especially with white hair. Father is extremely particular about white hair. It is a "crown of glory," when it is found in the way of the Lord. Mahlon Pryor had enough crown of glory for three men, but maybe his wasn't exactly glory, because he wasn't in the way of the Lord. He was in a way of his own. He must have had much confidence in himself. At our house we would rather trust in the Lord. I only told him about the lions and tigers because he asked me, and that was the way I played. But you should have heard him laugh. You wouldn't have supposed to look at his face that he could.

"Umph!" he said at last. "I am a little curious about your ammunition. Just how do you bring down your prey?"

"I use portulaca powder and tiger lily bullets on the tigers, and four o'clocks on the lions," I said.

You could have heard him a mile, dried up as he was.

"I used to wear a red coat and ride to the hounds fox hunting," he said. "It's great sport. Won't you take me with you to the jungle?"

I didn't want him in the least, but if any one older asks right out to go with you, what can you do? I am going to tell several things you won't believe, and this is one of them: He got off his horse, tied it to the fence, and climbed over after me. As we went down the cowpath beside the water, I was thankful for the height of the hill that would keep them from seeing at the house. He went on asking questions and of course I had to tell him. Most of what he wanted to know, his people should have taught him before he was ten years old, but father says they do things differently in England.

"There doesn't seem to be many trees in the jungle," he said.

"Well, there's one, and it's about the most important on our land," I told him. "Father wouldn't cut it down for a farm. You see that little dark bag nearly as big as your fist, swinging out there on that limb? Well, every spring one of these birds, yellow as orange peel, with velvet black wings, weaves a nest like that, and over on that big branch, high up, one just as bright red as the other is yellow, and the same black wings, builds a cradle for his babies. Father says a red and a yellow bird keeping house in the same tree is the biggest thing that ever happened in our family. They come every year and that is their tree. I believe father would shoot any one who drove them away."

"Your father is a gunner also?" he asked, and I thought he was laughing to himself.

"He's enough of a gunner to bring mother in a wagon from Pennsylvania all the way here, and he kept wolves, bears, Indians, and Gypsies from her, and shot things for food. Yes sir, my father can shoot if he wants to, better than any of our family except Laddie."

"And does Laddie shoot well?"

"Laddie does everything well," I answered proudly. "He won't try to do anything at all, until he practises so he can do it well."

"Score one for Laddie," he said in a queer voice.

"Are you in a hurry about the lions and tigers?" I asked.

"Not at all," he answered. "Pray follow any customary proceeding."

"Well, here I always stop and let Governor Oglesby go swimming," I said.

Mr. Mahlon Pryor sat on the bank of our Little Creek, took off his hat and shook back his hair as if the wind felt good on his forehead. I fished Dick Oglesby from the ammunition in my apron pocket, and held him toward the cross old man, and he wasn't cross at all. It's funny how you come to get such wrong ideas about people.

"My big married sister who lives in Westchester sent him to me last Christmas," I explained. "I have another doll, great big, with a Scotch plaid dress made from pieces of mine, but I only play with her on Sunday when I dare not do much else. I like Dick the best because he fits my apron pocket. Father wanted me to change his name and call him Oliver P. Morton, after a friend of his, but I told him this doll had to be called by the name he came with, and if he wanted me to have one named for his friend, to get it, and I'd play with it."

"What did he do?"

"He didn't want one named Morton that much."

Mr. Pryor took Dick Oglesby in his fingers and looked at his curly black hair and blue eyes, his chubby out-stretched arms, like a baby when it wants you to take it, and his plump little feet and the white shirt with red stripes all a piece of him as he was made, and said: "The honourable governor of our sister state seems a little weighty; I am at loss to understand how he swims."

"It's a new way," I said. "He just stands still and the water swims around him. It's very easy for him."

Then I carried Dick to the water, waded in and stood him against a stone. Something funny happened instantly. It always did. I never became tired trying it. I found it out one day when I got some apple butter on the governor giving him a bite of my bread, and put him in the wash bowl to soak. He was two and a half inches tall; but the minute you stood him in water he went down to about half that height and spread out to twice his size around. Then in the little red striped shirt and with his chubby hands and feet, he looked too funny. You should have heard Mr. Pryor.

"If you will lie on the bank and watch you'll have more to laugh at than that," I promised.

He lay down and never paid the least attention to his clothes. Pretty soon a little chub fish came swimming around to make friends with Governor Oglesby, and then a shiner and some more chub, and then one of those small ones about two inches long with a whole rainbow of bright stripes on its side. They nibbled at his hands and toes, and then went flashing away, and from under the stone came backing a big crayfish and seized the governor by the leg and started dragging him, so I had to jump in and stop it. I took a shot at the crayfish with the tiger ammunition and then loaded for lions.

We went on until the marsh became a thicket of cattails, bullrushes, willow bushes, and blue flags; then I found a path where the lions left the jungle, hid Mr. Pryor and told him he must be very still or they wouldn't come. So we waited and waited, but he didn't seem at all tired. At last I heard one. I touched Mr. Pryor's sleeve to warn him to keep his eyes on the trail. Pretty soon the lion came in sight. Really it was only a little gray rabbit hopping along, but when it was opposite us, I pinged it in the side, it jumped up and turned a somersault with surprise, and squealed a funny little squeal,—well, I wondered if Mr. Pryor's people didn't hear him, and think he had gone crazy as Paddy Ryan. I never did hear any one laugh so. I thought if he enjoyed it like that, I'd let him shoot one. I do May sometimes; so we went to another place I knew where there was a tiger's den, and I loaded with tiger lily bullets, gave him the gun and showed him where to aim. After we had waited a long time out came a muskrat, and started for the river. I looked to see why Mr. Pryor didn't shoot, and there he was gazing at it as if a snake had charmed him; his hands shaking a little, his cheeks almost red, his eyes very bright.

"Shoot!" I whispered. "It won't stay all day!"

He went and forgot how to push the ramrod like I showed him, so he reached out and tried to hit it with the gun, just as it got to the water and began to swim.

"Don't do that!" I said.

"But it's getting away! It's getting away!" he cried.

"Well, what if it is?" I asked, half provoked. "Do you suppose I really would hurt a poor little muskrat? Maybe it has six hungry babies in its home."

"Oh *that* way," he said, but he kept looking at it, so he made me think if I hadn't been there, he would have thrown a stone or hit it with a stick. It is perfectly wonderful about how some men can't get along without killing things, such little bits of helpless creatures too. I thought he'd better be got from the jungle, so I invited him to see the place at the foot of the hill below our orchard where some men thought they had discovered gold before the war. They had been to California in '49, and although they didn't come home with millions, or anything else except sick and tired, they thought they had learned enough about gold to know it when they saw it, and the fever was in their blood yet.

I told him about it and he was interested and anxious to see the place. If there had been a shovel, I am quite sure he would have gone to digging. He kept poking around with his boot toe, and he said maybe the yokels didn't look good. I told him they didn't plow with a yoke of oxen—men dug with mattocks and shovels. My father was one of them, but they didn't find the gold.

He said our meadow was a beautiful place, and when he praised the creek I told him about the wild ducks, and he laughed again. Like as not he had more fun that morning than any time in years. He didn't seem to be the same man when we went back to the road. I pulled some sweet marsh grass and gave his horse bites, so Mr. Pryor asked if I liked animals. I said I loved horses, Laddie's best of all. He asked about it and I told him.

"Hasn't your father but one thoroughbred?" he inquired.

"Father hasn't any," I said. "Flos really belongs to Laddie, and we are mighty glad he has her."

"You should have one soon, yourself," he said.

"Well, if the rest of them will hurry up and marry off, so the expenses won't be so heavy, maybe I can."

"How many of you are there?" he asked.

"Only twelve," I said.

He looked down the road at our house.

"Do you mean to tell me you have twelve children there?" he inquired.

"Oh no!" I answered. "Some of the big boys have gone into business in the cities around, and some of the girls are married. Mother says she has only to show her girls in the cities to have them snapped up like hot cakes."

"I fancy that is the truth," he said. "I've passed the one who rides the little black pony and she is a picture. A fine, healthy, sensible-appearing young woman!"

"I don't think she's as pretty as your girl," I said.

"Perhaps I don't either," he replied, smiling at me.

Then he mounted his horse.

"I don't remember that I ever have passed that house," he said, "without hearing some one singing. Does it go on all the time?"

"Yes, unless mother is sick."

"And what is it all about?"

"Oh just joy! Gladness that we are alive, that we have things to do that we like, and praising the Lord."

"Umph!" said Mr. Pryor.

"It's just letting out what our hearts are full of," I told him. "Don't you know that song:

'Tis the old time religion
And you cannot keep it still?"

He shook his head.

"It's an awful nice song," I explained. "After it sings about all the other things religion is good for, there is one line that says: *'It's good for those in trouble.'"*

I looked at him straight and hard, but he only turned white and seemed sick.

"So?" said Mr. Pryor. "Well, thank you for the most interesting morning I've had this side England. I should be delighted if you would come and hunt lions in my woods with me some time."

"Oh, do you open the door to children?" I cried in surprise.

"Certainly we open the door to children," he said, and as I live, he looked so sad I couldn't help thinking he was sorry to close it against any one. A mystery is the dreadfulest thing. If you think about it much, I'm sure you'd soon get so you couldn't sleep for thinking.

"Then if children don't matter, maybe I can come lion-hunting some time with the Princess, after she has made the visit at our house she said she would."

He seemed very much surprised.

"Indeed! I hadn't been informed that my daughter contemplated visiting your house," he said. "When was it arranged?"

"My mother invited her at Sabbath-school last Sunday."

I didn't like the way he said: "O-o-o-h!" Some way it seemed insulting to my mother.

"She did it to please me," I said. "There was a Fairy Princess told me the other day that your girl felt like a stranger, and that to be a stranger was the hardest thing in all the world. She sat a little way from the others, and she looked so lonely. I pulled my mother's sleeve and led her to your girl and made them shake hands, and then mother *had* to ask her to come to dinner with us. She always invites every one she meets coming down the aisle; she couldn't help asking your girl, too. She said she was expected at home, but she'd come some day and get acquainted. She needn't if you object. My mother only asked her because she thought she was lonely, and maybe she wanted to come."

He sat there staring straight ahead and he seemed to grow whiter, and older, and colder every minute. I began to think I'd better not have explained how it happened.

"Possibly she is lonely," he said at last. "This isn't much like the life she left. Perhaps she does feel herself a stranger. It was very kind of your mother to invite her. If she wants to come, I shall make no objections."

"No, but my father will," I said.

He straightened up as if something had hit him. Maybe there did.

"Why will he object?"

"On account of what you said about God at our house," I told him. "And then, too, father's people were from England, and he says real Englishmen have their doors wide open, and welcome people who offer friendliness."

Mr. Pryor hit his horse an awful blow. It reared and went racing up the road until I thought it was running away. I could see I had made him angry enough to burst. All my fault, too! Mother always tells me not to repeat things; but I'm not smart enough to know what to say, so I don't see what is left but to tell what mother, or father, or Laddie says when grown people ask me questions.

I went home, but every one was too busy even to look at me, so I took Bobby under my arm, hunted father, and told him all about the morning. I wondered what he would think. I never found out. He wouldn't say anything, so Bobby and I went across the lane, and climbed the gate into the orchard to see if Hezekiah were there and wanted to fight. He hadn't time to fight Bobby because he was busy chasing every wild jay from our orchard. By the time he got that done, he was tired, so he came hopping along on branches above us as Bobby and I went down the west fence beside the lane.

If I had been compelled to choose the side of our orchard I liked best, I don't know which I would have selected. The west side—that is, the one behind the dooryard—was running over with interesting things. Two gates opened into it, one from near each corner of the yard. Between these there was quite a wide level space, where mother fed the big chickens and kept the hens in coops with little ones. She had to have them close enough that the big hawks were afraid to come to earth, or they would take more chickens than they could pay for, by cleaning rabbits, snakes, and mice from the fields. Then came a double row of prize peach trees, rare fruit that mother canned to take to county fairs. One bore big, white freestones, and around the seed they were pink as a rose. One was a white cling, and one was yellow. There was a yellow freestone as big as a young sun, and as golden, and the queerest of all was a cling purple as a beet.

Sometimes father read about the hairs of the head being numbered, because we were so precious in the sight of the Almighty. Mother was just as particular with her purple tree; every peach on it was counted, and if we found one on the ground, we had to carry it to her, because it *might* be sound enough to can or spice for a fair, or she had promised the seed to some one halfway across the state. At each end of the peach row was an enormous big pear tree; not far from one the chicken house stood on the path to the barn, and beside the other the smoke house with the dog kennel a yard away. Father said there was a distinct relationship between a smoke house and a dog kennel, and bulldogs were best. Just at present we were out of bulldogs, but Jones, Jenkins and Co. could make as much noise as any dog you ever heard. On the left grew the plum trees all the way to the south fence, and I think there was one of every kind in the fruit catalogues. Father spent hours pruning, grafting, fertilizing, and spraying them. He said they required twice as much work as peaches.

Around the other sides of the orchard were two rows of peach trees, hundreds of them in all, and of every variety; but one cling on the north was just a little the best of any, and we might eat all we wanted from any tree we liked, after father tested them and said: "Peaches are ripe!" In the middle were the apple; selected trees, planted, trimmed, and cultivated like human beings. The apples were so big and fine they were picked by hand, wrapped in paper, packed in barrels, and all we could not use at home went to J. B. White in Fort Wayne for the biggest fruit house in the state. My! but father was proud! He always packed especially fine ones for Mr. White's family. He said he liked him, because he was a real sandy Scotchman, who knew when an apple was right, and wasn't afraid to say so.

On the south side of the orchard there was the earliest June apple tree. The apples were small, bright red with yellow stripes, crisp, juicy and sweet enough to be just right. The tree was very large, and so heavy it leaned far to the northeast. This sounds like make-believe, but it's gospel truth. Almost two feet from the ground there was a big round growth, the size of a hash bowl. The tree must have been hurt when very small and the place enlarged with the trunk. Now it made a grand step. If you understood that no one could keep from running the last few rods from that tree, then figured on the help to be had from this step, you could see how we went up it like squirrels. All the bark on the south side was worn away and the trunk was smooth and shiny. The birds loved to nest among the branches, and under the peach tree in the fence corner opposite was a big bed of my mother's favourite wild flowers, blue-eyed Marys. They had dainty stems from six to eight inches high and delicate heads of bloom made up of little flowers, two petals up, blue, two turning down, white. Perhaps you don't know about anything prettier than that. There were maidenhair ferns among them too! and the biggest lichens you ever saw on the fence, while in the hollow of a rotten rail a little chippy bird always built a hair nest. She got the hairs at our barn, for most of them were gray from our carriage horses, Ned and Jo. All down that side of the orchard the fence corners were filled with long grass and wild flowers, a few alder bushes left to furnish berries for the birds, and wild roses for us, to keep their beauty impressed on us, father said.

The east end ran along the brow of a hill so steep we coasted down it on the big meat board all winter. The board was six inches thick, two and a half feet wide, and six long. Father said slipping over ice and snow gave it the good scouring it needed, and it was thick enough to last all our lives, so we might play with it as we pleased. At least seven of us could go skimming down that hill and halfway across the meadow on it. In the very place we slid across, in summer lay the cowslip bed. The world is full of beautiful spots, but I doubt if any of them ever were prettier than that. Father called it swale. We didn't sink deep, but all summer there was water standing there. The grass was long and very sweet, there were ferns and a few calamus flowers, and there must have been an acre of cowslips—cowslips with big-veined, heart-shaped, green leaves, and large pale gold flowers. I used to sit on the top rail of that orchard fence and look down at them, and try to figure out what God was thinking when He created them, and I wished that I might have been where I could watch His face as He worked.

Halfway across the east side was a gulley where Leon and I found the Underground Station, and from any place along the north you looked, you saw the Little Creek and the marsh. At the same time the cowslips were most golden, the marsh was blue with flags, pink with smart weed, white and yellow with dodder, yellow with marsh buttercups having ragged frosty leaves, while the yellow and the red birds flashed above it, the red crying, "Chip," "Chip," in short, sharp notes, the yellow spilling music all over the marsh while on wing.

It would take a whole book to describe the butterflies; once in a while you scared up a big, wonderful moth, large as a sparrow; and the orchard was alive with doves, thrushes, catbirds, bluebirds, vireos, and orioles. When you climbed the fence, or a tree, and kept quiet, and heard the music and studied the pictures, it made you feel as if you had to put it into words. I often had meeting all by myself, unless Bobby and Hezekiah were along, and I tried to tell God what I thought about things. Probably He was so busy making more birds and flowers for other worlds, He never heard me; but I didn't say anything disrespectful at all, so it made no difference if He did listen. It just seemed as if I must tell what I thought, and I felt better, not so full and restless after I had finished.

All of us were alike about that. At that minute I knew mother was humming, as she did a dozen times a day:

I think when I read that sweet story of old,
  When Jesus was here among men
How He called little children as lambs to His fold,
  I should like to have been with Him then.

Lucy would be rocking her baby and singing, "Hush, my dear, lie still and slumber." Candace's favourite she made up about her man who had been killed in the war, when they had been married only six weeks, which hadn't given her time to grow tired of him if he hadn't been "all her fancy painted." She arranged the words like "Ben Battle was a soldier bold," and she sang them to suit herself, and cried every single minute:

They wrapped him in his uniform,
  They laid him in the tomb,
My aching heart I thought 'twould break,
  But such was my sad doom.

Candace just loved that song. She sang it all the time. Leon said our pie always tasted salty from her tears, and he'd take a bite and smile at her sweetly and say: "How *uniform* you get your pie, Candace!" Father never could see why she always got angry about it. Every time Leon came near when she was singing, he would begin to recite about a man who wanted Candace to quite crying, and keep company with him.

Ebeneezer stood on the burning deck,
  His arm around Can-dicie's neck.

His father called, he would not go,
 Because he loved Can-dicie so.

He always had to do the last two lines on the run, for if she got close enough she hit him just as hard as she could with the broomstick, or anything she could lay her fingers on, or threw water on him, even when it was hot.

May's favourite was "Joy Bells." Father would be whispering over to himself the speech he was preparing to make at the next prayer-meeting. We never could learn his speeches, because he read and studied so much it kept his head so full, he made a new one every time. You could hear Laddie's deep bass booming the "Bedouin Love Song" for a mile; this minute it came rolling across the corn:

"Open the door of thy heart,
 And open thy chamber door,
And my kisses shall teach thy lips
 The love that shall fade no more
  Till the sun grows cold,
  And the stars are old,
  And the leaves of the Judgment Book unfold!"

I don't know how the Princess stood it. If he had been singing that song where I could hear it and I had known it was about me, as she must have known he meant her, I couldn't have kept my arms from around his neck. Over in the barn Leon was singing:

"A life on the ocean wave,
A home on the rolling deep,
Where codfish waggle their tails
'Mid tadpoles two feet deep."

The minute he finished, he would begin reciting "Marco Bozzaris," and you could be perfectly sure that he would reach the last line, only to commence on the speech of "Logan, Chief of the Mingoes," or any one of fifty others. He could make your hair stand a little straighter than any one else; the best teachers we ever had, or even Laddie, couldn't make you shivery, shaky, and creepy as he could. Because all of us kept going like that every day, people couldn't pass without hearing, so *that* was what Mr. Pryor meant.

I had a pulpit in the southeast corner of the orchard. I liked that place best of all because from it you could see two sides at once. The very first little, old log cabin that had been on our land, the one my father and mother moved into, had stood in that corner. It was all gone now; but a flower-bed of tiny, purple iris, not so tall as the grass, spread there, and some striped grass in the shadiest places, and among the flowers a lark brooded every spring. In the fence corner mother's big white turkey hen always nested. To protect her from rain and too hot sun, father had slipped some boards between the rails about three feet from the ground. After the turkey left, that was my pulpit. I stood there and used the top of the fence for my railing.

The little flags and all the orchard and birds were behind me; on one hand was the broad, grassy, meadow with the creek running so swiftly I could hear it, and the breath of the cowslips came up the hill. Straight in front was the lane running down from the barn, crossing the creek and spreading into the woods pasture, where the water ran wider and yet swifter, big forest trees grew, and bushes of berries, pawpaws, willow, everything ever found in an Indiana thicket; grass under foot, and many wild flowers and ferns wherever the cattle and horses didn't trample them, and bigger, wilder birds, many having names I didn't know. On the left, across the lane, was a large cornfield, with trees here and there, and down the valley I could see the Big Creek coming from the west, the Big Hill with the church on top, and always the white gravestones around it. Always too there was the sky overhead, often with clouds banked until you felt if you only could reach them, you could climb straight to the gates that father was so fond of singing about sweeping through. Mostly there was a big hawk or a turkey buzzard hanging among them, just to show us that we were not so much, and that we couldn't shoot them, unless they chose to come down and give us a chance.

I set Bobby and Hezekiah on the fence and stood between

them. "We will open service this morning by singing the thirty-fifth hymn," I said. "Sister Dover, will you pitch the tune?"

Then I made my voice high and squeally like hers and sang:

"Come ye that love the Lord,
And let your joys be known,
Join in a song of sweet accord,
And thus surround the throne."

I sang all of it and then said: "Brother Hastings, will you lead us in prayer?"

Then I knelt down, and prayed Brother Hastings' prayer. I could have repeated any one of a dozen of the prayers the men of our church prayed, but I liked Brother Hastings' best, because it had the biggest words in it. I loved words that filled your mouth, and sounded as if you were used to books. It began sort of sing-songy and measured in stops, like a poetry piece:

Our Heavenly Father: We come before Thee this morning,
Humble worms of the dust, imploring thy blessing.
We beseech Thee to forgive our transgressions,
Heal our backslidings, and love us freely.

Sometimes from there on it changed a little, but it always began and ended exactly the same way. Father said Brother Hastings was powerful in prayer, but he did wish he'd leave out the "worms of the dust." He said we were not "worms of the dust;" we were reasoning, progressive, inventive men and women. He said a worm would never be anything except a worm, but we could study and improve ourselves, help others, make great machines, paint pictures, write books, and go to an extent that must almost amaze the Almighty Himself. He said that if Brother Hastings had done more plowing in his time, and had a little closer acquaintance with worms, he wouldn't be so ready to call himself and every one else a worm. Now if you are talking about cutworms or fishworms, father is right. But there is that place where—"Charles his heel had raised, upon the humble worm to tread," and the worm lifted up its voice and spake thus to Charles:

I know I'm now among the things
  Uncomely to your sight,
But, by and by, on splendid wings,
  You'll see me high and bright.

And there is another poetry piece where it comes in:

Daughter, do you remember, dear,
  The cold, dark thing you brought,
And laid upon the casement here?
  A withered worm, you thought.

I told you, that Almighty power
  Could break that withered shell;
And show you, in a future hour,
  Something would please you well.

O yes, mamma! how very gay
  Its wings of starry gold!
And see! it lightly flies away
  Beyond my gentle hold.

Now I'll bet a cent *that* is the kind of worm Brother Hastings said we were. I must speak to father about it. I don't want him to be mistaken; and I really think he is about worms. Of course he knows the kind that have wings and fly. Brother Hastings mixed him up by saying "worms of the dust" when he should have said worms of the leaves. Those that go into little round cases in earth or spin cocoons on trees always live on leaves, and many of them rear the head, having large horns, and wave it in a manner far from humble. So father and Brother Hastings are both partly right, and partly wrong.

When the prayer came to a close, where every one always said "Amen," I punched Bobby and whispered, "Crow, Bobby, crow!" and he stood up and brought it out strong, like he always did when I told him. I had to stop the service to feed him a little wheat, to pay him for crowing; but as no one was there except us, that didn't matter. Then Hezekiah crowded over for some, so I had to pretend I was Mrs. Daniels feeding her children caraway cake, like she always did in meeting. If I had been the mother of children who couldn't have gone without things to eat in church I'd have kept them at home. Mrs. Daniels always had the carpet greasy with cake crumbs wherever she sat, and mother didn't think the Lord liked a dirty church any more than we would have wanted a mussy house. When I had Bobby and Hezekiah settled I took my text from my head, because I didn't know the meeting feeling was coming on me when I started, and I had brought no Bible along; so I made up a text as well as I could.

"Blessed are all men, but most blessed are they who hold their tempers." I had to stroke Bobby a little and pat Hezekiah once in a while, to keep them from flying down and fighting, but mostly I could give my attention to my sermon.

"We have only to look around us this morning to see that all men are blessed," I said. "The sky is big enough to cover every one. If the sun gets too hot, there are trees for shade or the clouds come up for a while. If the earth becomes too dry, it always rains before it is everlastingly too late. There are birds enough to sing for every one, butterflies enough to go around, and so many flowers we can't always keep the cattle and horses from tramping down and even devouring beautiful ones, like Daniel thought the lions would devour him—but they didn't. Wouldn't it be a good idea, O Lord, for You to shut the cows' mouths and save the cowslips also; they may not be worth as much as a man, but they are lots better looking, and they make fine greens. It doesn't seem right for cows to eat flowers; but maybe it is as right for them as it is for us. The best way would be for our cattle to do like that piece about the cow in the meadow exactly the same as ours:

And through it ran a little brook,
  Where oft the cows would drink,
And then lie down among the flowers,
  That grew upon the brink.

"You notice, O Lord, the cows did not eat the flowers in this instance; they merely rested among them, and goodness knows, that's enough for any cow. They had better done like the next verse, where it says:

"They like to lie beneath the trees,
  All shaded by the boughs,
Whene'er the noontide heat came on:
  Sure, they were happy cows!"

"Now, O Lord, this plainly teaches that if cows are happy, men should be much more so, for like the cows, they have all Thou canst do for them, and all they can do for themselves, besides. So every man is blessed, because Thy bounty has provided all these things for him, without money and without price. If some men are not so blessed as others, it is their own fault, and not Yours. You made the earth, and all that is therein, and You made the men. Of course You had to make men different, so each woman can tell which one belongs to her; but I believe it would have been a good idea while You were at it, if You would have made all of them enough alike that they would all work. Perhaps it isn't polite of me to ask more of You than You saw fit to do; and then, again, it may be that there are some things impossible, even to You. If there is anything at all, seems as if making Isaac Thomas work would be it. Father says that man would rather starve and see his wife and children hungry than to take off his coat, roll up his sleeves, and plow corn; so it was good enough for him when Leon said, 'Go to the ant, thou sluggard,' right at him. So, of course, Isaac is not so blessed as some men, because he won't work, and thus he never knows whether he's going to have a big dinner on Sunday, until after some one asks him, because he looks so empty. Mother thinks it isn't fair to feed Isaac and send him home with his stomach full, while Mandy and the babies are sick and hungry. But Isaac is some blessed, because he has religion and gets real happy, and sings, and shouts, and he's going to Heaven when he dies. He must wish he'd go soon, especially in winter.

"There are men who do not have even this blessing, and to

make things worse, O Lord, they get mad as fire and hit their horses, and look like all possessed. The words of my text this morning apply especially to a man who has all the blessings Thou hast showered and flowered upon men who work, or whose people worked and left them so much money they don't need to, and yet a sadder face I never saw, or a crosser one. He looks like he was going to hit people, and he does hit his horse an awful crack. It's no way to hit a horse, not even if it balks, because it can't hit back, and it's a cowardly thing to do. If you rub their ears and talk to them, they come quicker, O our Heavenly Father, and if you hit them just because you are angry, it's a bigger sin yet.

"No man is nearly so blessed as he might be who goes around looking killed with grief when he should cheer up, no matter what ails him; and who shuts up his door and says his wife is sick when she isn't, and who scowls at every one, when he can be real pleasant if he likes, as some in Divine Presence can testify. So we are going to beseech Thee, O Lord, to lay Thy mighty hand upon the man who grew angry this beautiful morning and make him feel Thy might, until he will know for himself and not another, that You are not a myth. Teach him to have a pleasant countenance, an open door, and to hold his temper. Help him to come over to our house and be friendly with all his neighbours, and get all the blessings You have provided for every one; but please don't make him have any more trouble than he has now, for if You do, You'll surely kill him. Have patience with him, and have mercy on him, O Lord! Let us pray."

That time I prayed myself. I looked into the sky just as straight and as far as I could see, and if I had any influence at all, I used it then. Right out loud, I just begged the Lord to get after Mr. Pryor and make him behave like other people, and let the Princess come to our house, and for him to come too; because I liked him heaps when he was lion hunting, and I wanted to go with him again the worst way. I had seen him sail right over the fences on his big black horse, and when he did it in England, wearing a red coat, and the dogs flew over thick around him, it must have looked grand, but it was mighty hard on the fox. I do hope it got away. Anyway, I prayed as hard as I could, and every time I said the strongest thing I knew, I punched Bobby to crow, and he never came out stronger. Then I was Sister Dover and started: "Oh come let us gather at the fountain, the fountain that never goes dry."

Just as I was going to pronounce the benediction like father, I heard something, so I looked around, and there went he and Dr. Fenner. They were going toward the house, and yet, they hadn't passed me. I was not scared, because I knew no one was sick. Dr. Fenner always stopped when he passed, if he had a minute, and if he hadn't, mother sent some one to the gate with buttermilk and slices of bread and butter, and jelly an inch thick. When a meal was almost cooked she heaped some on a plate and he ate as he drove and left the plate next time he passed. Often he was so dead tired, he was asleep in his buggy, and his old gray horse always stopped at our gate.

I ended with "Amen," because I wanted to know if they had been listening; so I climbed the fence, ran down the lane behind the bushes, and hid a minute. Sure enough they had! I suppose I had been so in earnest I hadn't heard a sound, but it's a wonder Hezekiah hadn't told me. He was always seeing something to make danger signals about. He never let me run on a snake, or a hawk get one of the chickens, or Paddy Ryan come too close. I only wanted to know if they had gone and listened, and then I intended to run straight back to Bobby and Hezekiah; but they stopped under the greening apple tree, and what they said was so interesting I waited longer than I should, because it's about the worst thing you can do to listen when older people don't know. They were talking about me.

"I can't account for her," said father

"I can!" said Dr. Fenner. "She is the only child I ever have had in my practice who managed to reach earth as all children should. During the impressionable stage, no one expected her, so there was no time spent in worrying, fretting, and discontent. I don't mean that these things were customary with Ruth. No woman ever accepted motherhood in a more beautiful spirit; but if she would have protested at any time, it would have been then. Instead, she lived happily, naturally, and enjoyed herself as she never had before. She was in the fields, the woods, and the garden constantly, which account for this child's outdoor tendencies. Then you must remember that both of you were at top notch intellectually, and physically, fully matured. She had the benefit of ripened minds, and at a time when every faculty recently had been stirred by the excitement and suffering of the war. Oh, you can account for her easily enough, but I don't know what on earth you are going to do with her. You'll have to go careful, Paul. I warn you she will not be like the others."

"We realize that. Mother says she doubts if she can ever teach her to sew and become a housewife."

"She isn't cut out for a seamstress or a housewife, Paul. Tell Ruth not to try to force those things on her. Turn her loose out of doors; give her good books, and leave her alone. You won't be disappointed in the woman who evolves."

Right there I realized what I was doing, and I turned and ran for the pulpit with all my might. I could always repeat things, but I couldn't see much sense to the first part of that; the last was as plain as the nose on your face. Dr. Fenner said they mustn't force me to sew, and do housework; and mother didn't mind the Almighty any better than she did the doctor. There was nothing in this world I disliked so much as being kept in doors, and made to hem cap and apron strings so particularly that I had to count the number of threads between every stitch, and in each stitch, so that I got all of them just exactly even. I liked carpet rags a little better, because I didn't have to be so particular about stitches, and I always picked out all the bright, pretty colours. Mother said she could follow my work all over the floor by the bright spots. Perhaps if I were not to be kept in the house I wouldn't have to sew any more. That made me so happy I wondered if I couldn't stretch out my arms and wave them and fly. I sat on the pulpit wishing I had feathers. It made me pretty blue to have to stay on the ground all the time, when I wanted to be sailing up among the clouds with the turkey buzzards. It called to my mind that place in McGuffey's Fifth where it says:

Sweet bird, thy bower is ever green,
Thy sky is ever clear;
Thou hast no sorrow in thy song,
No winter in thy year.

Of course, I never heard a turkey buzzard sing. Laddie said they couldn't; but that didn't prove it. He said half the members of our church couldn't sing, but they *did;* and when all of them were going at the tops of their voices, it was just grand. So maybe the turkey buzzard could sing if it wanted to; seemed as if it should, if Isaac Thomas could; and anyway, it was the next verse I was thinking most about:

Oh, could I fly, I'd fly with thee!
We'd make with joyful wing,
Our annual visit o'er the globe,
Companions of the spring.

That was so exciting I thought I'd just try it, so I stood on the top rail, spread my arms, waved them, and started. I was bumped in fifty places when I rolled into the cowslip bed at the foot of the steep hill, for stones stuck out all over the side of it, and I felt pretty mean as I climbed back to the pulpit.

The only consolation I had was what Dr. Fenner had said. That would be the greatest possible help in managing father or mother. I was undecided about whether I would go to school, or not. Must be perfectly dreadful to dress like for church, and sit still in a stuffy little room, and do your "abs," and "bes," and "bis," and "bos," all day long. I could spell quite well without looking at a schoolhouse, and read too. I was wondering if I ever would go at all, when I thought of something else. Dr. Fenner had said to give me plenty of good books. I was wild for some that were already promised me. Well, what would they amount to if I couldn't understand them when I got them? *That* seemed to make it sure I would be compelled to go to school until I learned enough to understand what the books contained about birds, flowers, and moths, anyway; and perhaps there would be some having Fairies in them. Of course those would be interesting.

I never hated doing anything so badly, in all my life, but I could see, with no one to tell me, that I had put it off as long as I dared. I would just have to start to school when Leon and May went in September. Tilly Baher, who lived across the swamp near Sarah Hood, had gone two winters already, and she was only a year older, and not half my size. I stood on the pulpit and looked a long time in every direction, into the sky the longest of all. It was settled. I must go; I might as well start and have it over. I couldn't look anywhere, right there at home, and not see more things I didn't know about than I did. When mother showed me in the city, I wouldn't be snapped up like hot cakes; I'd be a blockhead no one would have. It made me so vexed to think I had to go, I set Hezekiah on my shoulder, took Bobby under my arm, and went to the house. On the way, I made up my mind that I would ask again, very politely, to hold the little baby, and if the rest of them went and pigged it up straight along, I'd pinch it, if I got a chance.

4

The Last Day in Eden

'Tis the sunset of life gives me mystical lore,
And coming events cast their shadows before.

Of course the baby was asleep and couldn't be touched; but there was some excitement, anyway. Father had come from town with a letter from the new school teacher, that said she would expect him to meet her at the station next Saturday. Mother thought she might as well get the room ready and let her stay at our house, because we were most convenient, and it would be the best place for her. She said that every time, and the teacher always stayed with us. Really, it was because father and mother wanted the teacher where they could know as much as possible about what was going on. Sally didn't like having her at all; she said with the wedding coming, the teacher would be a nuisance. Shelley had finished our school, and the Groveville high school, and instead of attending college she was going to Chicago to study music. She was so anxious over her dresses and getting started, she didn't seem to think much about what was going to happen to us at home; so she didn't care if Miss Amelia stayed at our house. May said it would be best to have the teacher with us, because she could help us with our lessons at home, and we could get ahead of the others. May already had decided that she would be at the head of her class when she finished our school, and the high school, and every time you wanted her and couldn't find her, if you would look across the foot of mother's bed, May would be there with a spelling book. Once she had spelled down our school, when Laddie was not there.

Father had met Peter Dover in town, and he had said that he was coming to see Sally, because he had something of especial importance to tell her.

"Did he say what it was?" asked Sally.

"Only what I have told you." replied father.

Sally wanted to take the broom and sweep the parlour.

"It's clean as a ribbon. You can't improve it," said mother.

"If you go in there, you'll wake the baby," said Lucy.

"Will it kill it if I do?" asked Sally.

"No, but it will make it cross as fire, so it will cry all the time Peter is here," said Lucy.

"I'll be surprised to death if it doesn't scream every minute anyway," said Sally.

"I hope it will," said Lucy. "That will make Peter think a while before he comes so often."

That made Sally so angry she couldn't speak, so she went out and began killing chickens. I helped her catch them. They were so used to me they would come right to my feet when I shelled corn, and I could pick up all I wanted.

"I'm going to kill three," said Sally. "I'm going to be sure we have enough, but don't you tell until their heads are off."

While she was working on them mother came out and asked how many she had, so Sally said three. Mother counted us and said that wasn't enough; there would have to be four at least.

After she was gone Sally looked at me and said: "Well for land's sake!"

It was so funny she had to laugh, and by the time I caught the fourth one, and began helping pick them, she was over being provoked and we had lots of fun.

The minute I saw Peter Dover he made me think of something. I rode his horse to the barn with Leon leading it. There we saw Laddie.

"Guess what!" I cried.

"Never could!" said Laddie.

"Down in the blue-eyed Mary bed, I heard the Fairy Queen tell the Lord High Chamberlain to tell the King that the Princess had lost her letters from the Knight she loved best, and the Jester had found them. The King has her locked in a moth mullein bloom and she is crying her eyes out and won't stop until he sends for the Knight."

"No doubt you heard the King send the Jester to tell the Knight to hurry up and come?" said Laddie.

"No I didn't, but I think he's going to."

"You think something that will never happen!"

"Most anything will happen if the Princess cries hard enough. Moth mulleins shut awful tight."

"I haven't much of an opinion of the Knight who can't go to his Princess without her crying to make a way for him. Her eyes would be all dim and red."

"That's so too!" I said. "Guess what else!"

"Never could!" laughed Laddie, giving Peter Dover's horse a slap as it passed him on the way to a stall.

"Four chickens, ham, biscuit, and cake!" I announced.

"Is it a barbecue?" asked Laddie.

"No, the extra one is for the baby," said Leon. "Squally little runt, I call it."

"It's a nice baby!" said Laddie.

"What do you know about it?" demanded Leon.

"Well, considering that I started with you, and have brought up two others since, I am schooled in all there is to know," said Laddie.

"Guess what else!" I cried.

"More?" said Laddie.

I nodded delightedly. It was such fun to tell surprising things and see people look astonished, and hear what they said.

"Out with it!" said Laddie. "Don't kill me with suspense."

"Father is going to town Saturday to meet the new teacher, and she will stay at our house as usual."

Leon yelled and fell back in a manger, while Laddie held the harness oil to his nose.

"More!" cried Leon, grabbing the bottle with both hands.

"Are you sure?" asked Laddie of me earnestly.

"It's decided. Mother said so," I told him.

"Name of a black cat, why?" demanded Laddie.

"Mother said we were most convenient for the teacher."

"Aren't there enough of us?" asked Leon, straightening up and sniffing harness oil as if his life depended on it.

"Any unprejudiced person would probably say so to look in," said Laddie.

"I'll bet she'll be sixty and a cat," said Leon. "Won't I have fun with her?"

And his eyes began to dance.

"Maybe so, maybe not!" said Laddie. "You can't always tell, for sure. Remember your Alamo! You were going to have fun with the teacher last year, but she had it with you."

Leon threw the oil bottle at him. Laddie caught it and set it on the shelf.

"I don't understand," said Leon.

"I do," said Laddie dryly. "*This* is one reason." He hit Peter Dover's horse another slap.

"Maybe yes," said Leon.

"Shelley to music school, two."

"Yes," said Leon. "Peter Dovers are the greatest expense, and Peter won't happen but once. Shelley will have at least two years in school before it is her turn, and you come next, anyway."

"Shut up!" cried Laddie.

"Thanky!" said Leon. "Your orders shall be obeyed gladly."

He laid down the pitchfork, went outside, closed the door and latched it. Laddie called to him, but he ran to the house. When Laddie and I finished our work and his, and wanted to go, we had to climb the stairs and leave through the front door on the embankment.

"The monkey!" said Laddie, but he didn't get angry; he just laughed.

The minute I stepped into the house and saw the parlour door closed, I thought of that "something" again. I walked past it, but couldn't hear anything. Of course mother wanted to know; and she would be very thankful to me if I could tell her. I went out the front door, and thought deeply on the situation. The windows were wide open, but I was far below them and I could only hear a sort of murmur. Why can't people speak up loud and plain, anyway? Of course they would sit on the big haircloth sofa. Didn't Leon call it the "sparking bench?" The hemlock tree would be best. I climbed quieter than a cat, for they break bark and make an awful scratching with their claws sometimes; my bare feet were soundless. Up and up I went, slowly, for it was dreadfully rough. They were not on the sofa. I could see through the needles plainly. Then I saw the spruce would have been better, for they were standing in front of the parlour door and Peter had one hand on the knob. His other arm was around my sister Sally. Breathlessly I leaned as far as I could, and watched.

"Father said he'd give me the money to buy a half interest, and furnish a house nicely, if you said 'yes,' Sally," said Peter.

Sally leaned back all pinksome and blushful, and while she laughed at him she

Carelessly tossed off a curl
That played on her delicate brow,

exactly like Mary Dow in McGuffey's Third.

"Well, what *did* I say?" she asked.

"Come to think of it, you didn't say anything," said Peter.

Sally's face was all afire with dancing lights, and her eyes were shining, and she laughed the gayest little laugh.

"Are you so very sure of that, Peter?" she said.

"I'm not sure of anything," said Peter, "except that I am so happy I could fly."

"Try it, fool!" said I to myself, deep in my throat.

Sally laughed again, and Peter took his other hand from the door and put that arm around Sally too, and he drew her to him, and he kissed her, the longest, hardest kiss I ever saw. I let go and rolled, tumbled, slid, and scratched down the hemlock tree, dropped from the last branch to the ground, and scampered around the house. I reached the dining-room door when every one was gathering for supper.

"Mother!" I cried. "Mother! Yes! They're engaged! He's kissing her, mother! Yes, Lucy, they're engaged!"

I rushed in to tell all of them what they would be glad to know, and if there didn't stand Peter and Sally! How they ever got through that door, and across the sitting-room before me, I don't understand. Sally made a dive at me, and I was so astonished I forgot to run, so she caught me. She started for the wood house with me, and mother followed. Sally turned at the door and she was the whitest of anything you ever saw.

"This is my affair," she said. "I'll attend to this young lady."

"Very well," said mother, and as I live she turned and left me to my sad fate, as it says in a story book we have. I wish when people are going to punish me, they'd take a switch and strike respectably, like mother does. This thing of having some one get all over me, and not having an idea where I'm going to be hit, is the worst punishment that I ever had. I'd been down the hill and up the hemlock that day, anyway. I'd always been told Sally didn't want me. She *proved* it right then. Finally she quit, because she was too tired to strike again, so I crept among the shavings on the work bench and went to sleep. I *thought* they wanted to know, and that I was going to please them.

Anyway, they found out, for by the time Sally got back Peter had told them about the store, and the furnished house, and asked father for Sally right before all of them, which father said was pretty brave; but Peter knew it was all right or he couldn't have come like he'd been doing.

After that, you couldn't hear anything at our house but wedding. Sally's share of linen and bedding was all finished long ago. Father took her to Fort Wayne on the cars to buy her wedding, travelling, and working dresses, and her hat, cloak, and linen, like you have when you marry.

It was strange that Sally didn't want mother to go, but she said the trip would tire her too much. Mother said it was because Sally could coax more dresses from father. Anyway, mother told him to set a limit and stick to it. She said she knew he hadn't done it as she got the first glimpse of Sally's face when they came back, but the child looked so beautiful and happy she hadn't the heart to spoil her pleasure.

The very next day a sewing woman came; then she, and Sally, and mother, and Lucy were shut up all day in the sitting-room, and the sewing machine just whizzed on the working dresses. Sally said the wedding dress had to be made by hand. She kept the room locked, and every new thing that they made was laid away on the bed in the parlour bedroom, and none of us had a peep until everything was finished. It was awfully exciting, but I wouldn't pretend I cared, because I was huffy at her. I told her I wouldn't kiss her good-bye, and I'd be *glad* when she was gone.

Sally said the school-ma'am simply had to go to Winters', or some place else, but mother said possibly a stranger would have some ideas, and know some new styles, so Sally then thought maybe they had better try it a few days, and she could have her place and be company when she and Shelley left. Shelley was rather silent and blue, and before long I found her crying, because mother had told her she couldn't start to Chicago until after the wedding, and that would make her miss six weeks at the start.

Next day word was sent around that school was to begin the coming Monday; so Saturday afternoon the people who had children large enough to go sent the biggest of them to clean the schoolhouse. May, Leon, and I went to do our share. We took a bucket, a broom, and cloths to wash windows. We forgot the soap. So did every one else. In fact, most of them failed to go, and those who went never took a thing to work with. We used the water bucket, and Mary Hood borrowed a pan and some soap from the nearest family, and after we had played tag until we were tired, and it was getting late, the big ones went to work. Leon tied the broom to a long pole and told Billy Wilson to sweep the ceiling and side walls. Silas Shaw cleaned the blackboard and polished the stove. Jimmy Hood carried water and scrubbed the floor. The girls cleaned out all the desks and dusted them, filled the ink bottles, and washed the windows. I was too little to do much except hand the soap and wait on people, so I carried water and filled the pitcher on the teacher's desk and gathered purple asters from our land just across the road from the schoolhouse. I brought enough goldenrod for the bucket too, when they were through scrubbing. Just when there were about a bushel of nut shells, and withered apple cores, and inky paper on the floor, the blackboard half cleaned, and ashes trailed deep between the stove and the window Billy Wilson was throwing them from, some one shouted: "There comes Mr. Stanton with Her."

All of us dropped everything and ran to the south windows. I tell you I was proud of our big white team as it came prancing down the hill, and the gleaming patent leather trimmings, and the brass side lamps shining in the sun. Father sat very straight, driving rather fast, as if he would as lief get it over with, and instead of riding on the back seat, where mother always sat, the teacher was in front beside him, and she seemed to be talking constantly. We looked at each other and groaned when father stopped at the hitching post and got out. If we had tried to see what a dreadful muss we could make, things could have looked no worse. I think father told her to wait in the carriage, but we heard her cry: "Oh Mr. Stanton, let me see the dear children I'm to teach, and where I'm to work."

Hopped is the word. She hopped from the carriage and came hopping after father. She was as tall as a clothes prop and scarcely as fat. There were gray hairs coming on her temples. Her face was sallow and wrinkled, and she had faded, pale-blue eyes. Her dress was like my mother had worn several years before, in style, and of stiff gray stuff. She made me feel that no one wanted her at home, and probably that was the reason she had come so far away. When father reached the door he looked as if he had so much to say he had no idea where to begin; so he stepped back and let the new teacher see for herself. Evidently she had seen places like that before, maybe so many of them it accounted for her first despairful glance. But she soon cheered up and no gay young thing of sixteen ever gushed worse. Leon called her explosive. She hopped on the steps, beamed on us the best she could when she couldn't have felt so very beamy, and bubbled: "Oh you dear young things! How lovely of you to be cleaning the schoolhouse for me!"

Every one stood dumb. Mother always went to meet people and May was old enough to know it. She went, but she looked exactly as she does when the wafer bursts and the quinine gets in her mouth, and she doesn't dare spit it out, because it costs five dollars a bottle, and it's going to do her good. Father introduced May and some of the older children, and May helped him with the others, and then he told us to "dig in and work like troopers," and he would take Miss Pollard on home.

"Oh do let me remain and help the dear children!" she cried.

"We can finish!" we answered in full chorus.

"How lovely of you!" she chirped.

Chirp makes you think of a bird; and in speech and manner Miss Amelia Pollard was the most birdlike of any human being I ever have seen. She hopped from the step to the walk, turned to us, her head on one side, playfulness in the air around her, and shook her finger at us.

"Be extremely particular that you leave things immaculate at the consummation of your labour," she said. "'Remember that cleanliness is next to Godliness!'"

"Two terms of that!" gasped Leon, sinking on the stove hearth. "Behold Job mourning as close the ashes as he can."

Billy Wilson had the top lid off, so he reached down and got a big handful of ashes and sifted them over Leon. But it's no fun to do anything like that to him; he only sank in a more dejected heap, and moaned: "Send for Bildad and Zophar to comfort me, and more ashes, please."

"Why does the little feathered dear touch earth at all? Why doesn't she fly?" demanded Silas Shaw.

"I'm going to get a hundred wads ready for Monday," said Jimmy Hood. "We can shoot them when we please."

"Bet ten cents you can't hit her," said Billy Wilson. "There ain't enough of her for a decent mark."

"Let's quit and go home," proposed Leon. "This will look worse than it does now by Monday night."

Then every one began talking at once. Suddenly May seized the poker and began pounding on the top of the stove for order.

"We must clean this up," she said. "We might as well go at it and finish. Maybe you'll shoot wads and do what you please, and maybe you won't. Her eyes went around like a cat that smells mice. If she can spell the language she uses, she is the best we've ever had."

That made us blink, and I never forgot it. Many times afterward while listening to people talk, I wondered if they could spell the words they used.

"Well, come on, then!" said Leon. He seized the broom and handed it to Billy Wilson, quoting as he did so, "Work, work, my boy, be not afraid;" and he told Silas Shaw as he gave him the mop, to "Look labour boldly in the face!" but he never did a thing himself, except to keep every one laughing.

So we cleaned up as well as we could, and Leon strutted like Bobby, because he locked the door and carried the key. When we reached home I was sorry I hadn't gone with father, so I could have seen mother, Sally, Candace, and Laddie when first they met the new teacher. The shock showed yet! Miss Amelia had taken off her smothery woollen dress and put on a black calico, but it wasn't any more cheerful. She didn't know what to do, and you could see plainly that no one knew what to do with her, so they united in sending me to show her the place. I asked her what she would like most to see, and she said everything was so charming she couldn't decide. I thought if she had no more choice than that, one place would do as well as another, so I started for the orchard. Quick as we got there, I knew what to do. I led her straight to our best cling peach tree, told her to climb on the fence so she could reach easily, and eat all she chose. We didn't dare shake the tree, because the pigs ran on the other side of the fence, and they chanked up every peach that fell there. Those peaches were too good to feed even father's finest Berkshires. They were delicious enough to make you forget yourself.

By the time Miss Amelia had eaten nine or ten, she was so happy to think she was there, she quit tilting her head and using big words. Of course she couldn't know how I loved to hear them, and maybe she thought I wouldn't know what they meant, and that they would be wasted on me. If she had understood how much spelling and defining I'd heard in my life, I guess she might have talked up as big as she could, and still I'd have got most of it. When she reached the place where she ate more slowly, she began to talk. She must have asked me most a hundred questions. What all our names were, how old we were, if our girls had lots of beaus, and if there were many men in the neighbourhood, and dozens of things my mother never asked any one. She always inquired if people were well, if their crops were growing, how much fruit they had, how near their quilts were finished, and who in the neighbourhood was sick.

I told her all about Sally and the wedding, because no one cared who knew it, after I had been pounded to mince-meat for telling. She asked if Shelley had any beaus, and I said there wasn't any one who came like Peter, but every man in the neighbourhood wanted to be her beau. Then she asked about Laddie, and I was taking no risks, so I said: "I only see him at home. I don't know where he goes when he's away. You'll have to ask him, if you want to know whether he visits the girls or not."

"Oh, I never would dare," she said. "But he must. He is so handsome! They would just compel him to go to see them."

"Not if he didn't want to go," I said.

I knew a few things about Laddie, myself.

"You must never, never tell him I said so, not for anything, but I do think he is the handsomest man I ever saw."

"So do I," I said, "and it wouldn't make any difference if I told him. No one could see him and not think he's good looking; but he can't help that. His job is to be as good as he looks, father says, and he is, every bit, and better too."

"Then do you mean you're going to tell him my foolish remark?" she giggled.

"No use," I said. "He knows it now. Every time he parts his hair he sees how good looking he is. He doesn't care. He says the only thing that counts with a man is to be big, strong, manly, and well educated."

"Is he well educated?"

She had so many peaches by this time that she picked the skin from them with her fingers, and nibbled the red part that stuck to the seed.

"Yes, I think so, as far as he's gone," I answered. "Of course he will go on being educated every day of his life, same as father. He says it is all rot about 'finishing' your education. You never do. You learn more important things each day as you grow older, and by the time you are old enough to die, you have just about enough sense to know how to live comfortably. Pity, isn't it?"

"Yes," said Miss Amelia, "it's an awful pity but it's the truth. Is your mother being educated too?"

"Whole family," I said. "We learn things all the time, mother most of any, because father always looks out for her. You see, it takes so much of her time to manage the house, and sew, and knit, and darn, that she can't study so much as the others; so father reads all the worth while books to her, and tells her about every single thing he finds out anywhere, and so do all of us. Just ask her if you think she doesn't know most everything."

"I wouldn't know what to ask," said Miss Amelia.

"Ask how long it took to make this world, who was the wisest man, who invented printing, where English was first spoken, who was the father of this country, why Greeley changed his politics, how to pickle pigs' feet, make hair oil, bluebell perfumery, cut out a dress, crochet a collar, or cure a baby of worms. Just ask her!"

Miss Amelia threw a peach stone through a fence crack and hit a pig. It was a pretty neat shot.

"I don't need ask any of that," she said scornfully. "I know all of it now."

"All right! What is best for worms?" I asked.

"Jayne's vermifuge," said Miss Amelia.

"Wrong!" I cried. "That's a patent medicine. Tea made from male fern root is best, because there's no morphine in it!"

The supper bell rang and I was glad of it. Peaches are not very filling after all, for I couldn't see but that Miss Amelia ate as much as any of us. For a few minutes every one was slow in speaking, then mother asked about cleaning the schoolhouse, Laddie had something to explain to father about corn mould, Sally and the dressmaker talked about pipings—not a bird—a new way to fold goods to make trimmings, and soon everything was going on the same as if the new teacher were not there. I noticed that she kept her head straight, and was not nearly so glib-tongued and birdlike before mother and Sally as she had been at the schoolhouse. Maybe that was why father told mother that night that the new teacher would bear acquaintance.

Sally asked Miss Amelia if she knew any of the latest New York styles to make dresses, and she said hoop skirts were not worn any more. Sally said they hadn't been for an age, and then Miss Amelia told of a beautiful way to colour your old hoops green, slip out the side and front straps, bend the wire into a figure eight, sew cloth to hold it, and paste gilt paper over the cloth. Then you joined the eights at each curve in the same way, sewed in a pasteboard bottom, and had a new kind of paper holder. I could see mother speculating on how the one she intended to make Monday would appear on the wall; she even glanced around to locate the place she could hang it.

Sunday was like every other Sabbath, except that I felt so sad all day I could have cried, but I was not going to do it. Seemed as if I never could put on shoes and so many clothes Monday morning, quite like church, and be shut in a room for hours, to try to learn what was in books, when the world was running over with things to find out where you could have your feet in water, leaves in your hair, and little living creatures in your hands. In the afternoon Miss Amelia asked Laddie to take her for a walk to see the creek, and the barn, and he couldn't escape.

I suppose our barn was exactly like hundreds of others. It was built against an embankment so that on one side you could drive right on the threshing floor with big loads of grain, and it broke the winds. On the sunny side in the lower part were the sheep pens, cattle stalls, and horse mangers. It was always half bursting with overflowing grain bins and haylofts in the fall; the swallows twittered under the roof until time to go south for winter, as they sailed from the ventilators to their nests plastered against the rafters or eaves. The big swinging doors front and back could be opened to let the wind blow through in a strong draft. From the east doors you could see for miles across the country. Father always tied the rope that belonged to the hayfork to a beam as soon as harvest was over, and it made a swing that would carry you almost to the roof, and when you went high enough to touch the beams with the tips of your toes your heart grew all big and swelly.

I said our barn was like hundreds of others, but it was not. There was not another like it in the whole world. Father, the boys, and the hired men always kept it cleaned and in proper shape every day. The upper floor was as neat as some women's houses. It was swept, the sun shone in, the winds drifted through, the odours of drying hay and grain were heavy, and from the top of the natural little hill against which it stood you could see for miles in all directions.

The barn was our great playhouse on Sundays. It was clean there, we were where we could be called when wanted, and we liked to climb the ladders to the top of the haymows, walk the beams to the granaries, and jump to the hay. One day May came down on a snake that had been brought in with a load. I can hear her yell now, and it made her so frantic she's been killing them ever since. It was only a harmless little garter snake, but she was so surprised. We loved that swing, so we took turns and kept count. Each one was pushed so many times, run under so often, and then had so long for the old cat to die.

Miss Amelia held her head very much on one side all the time she walked with Laddie, and she was so birdlike Leon slipped him a brick and told him to have her hold it to keep her down. Seemed as if she might fly any minute. She thought our barn was the nicest she ever had seen and the cleanest. When Laddie opened the doors on the east side, and she could see the big, red, yellow, and green apples thick as leaves on the trees in the orchard, the lane, the woods pasture, and the meadow with scattering trees, two running springs, and the meeting of the creeks, she said it was the loveliest sight she ever saw—I mean beheld. Laddie liked that, so he told her about the beautiful town, and the lake, and the Wabash River, that our creek emptied into, and how people came from other states and big cities and stayed all summer to fish, row, swim, and have good times. He told her that often they came in carriages or walked and followed up the creeks, crossing our land; and she said she was going to see if she couldn't arrange with father to teach a summer school, and then Laddie seemed as if he wished he hadn't told her.

She asked him to take her to the meadow, but he excused himself, because he had an engagement. So she stood in the door, and watched him saddle Flos and start to the house to dress in his riding clothes. After that she didn't care a thing about the meadow, so we went back.

Our house looked as if we had a party. We were all dressed in our best, and every one was out in the yard, garden, or orchard. Peter and Sally were under the big pearmain apple tree at the foot of the orchard, Shelley and a half dozen beaus were everywhere, May had her spelling book in one hand and was in my big catalpa talking to Billy Stevens, who was going to be her beau as soon as mother said she was old enough. Father was reading a wonderful new book to mother and some of the neighbours. Leon was perfectly happy because no one wanted him, so he could tease all of them by saying things they didn't like to hear. When Laddie came out and mounted, Leon asked him where he was going, and Laddie said he hadn't fully decided: he might ride to Elizabeth's, and not come back until Monday morning.

"You think you're pretty slick," said Leon. "But if we could see north to the cross road we could watch you turn west, and go past Pryors to show yourself off, or try to find the Princess on the road walking or riding. I know something I'm saving to tell next time you get smart, Mr. Laddie."

Laddie seemed annoyed and no one was quicker to see it than Leon. Instantly he jumped on the horse block, pulled down his face long as he could, stretched his hands toward Laddie, and making his voice all wavery and tremulous, he began reciting from "Lochiel's Warning," in tones of agonizing pleading:

"Laddie, Laddie, beware of the day!
For, dark and despairing, my sight, I may seal,
But man cannot cover what God would reveal;
'Tis the sunset of life gives me mystical lore,
And coming events cast their shadows before."

That scared me. I begged Leon to tell, but he wouldn't say a word more. He went and talked to Miss Amelia as friendly as you please, and asked her to take a walk in the orchard and get some peaches, and she went flying. He got her all she could carry and guided her to Peter and Sally, introduced her to Peter, and then slipped away and left her. Then he and Sally couldn't talk about their wedding, and Peter couldn't squeeze her hand, and she couldn't fix his tie, and it was awful. Shelley and her boys almost laughed themselves sick over it, and then she cried, "To the rescue!" and started, so they followed. They captured Miss Amelia and brought her back, and left her with father and the wonderful book, but I'm sure she liked the orchard better.

I took Grace Greenwood under my arm, Hezekiah on my shoulder, and with Bobby at my heels went away. I didn't want my hair pulled, or to be teased that day. There was such a hardness around my heart, and such a lump in my throat, that I didn't care what happened to me one minute, and the next I knew I'd slap any one who teased me, if I were sent to bed for it. As I went down the lane Peter called to me to come and see him, but I knew exactly how he looked, and didn't propose to make up. There was not any sense in Sally clawing me all over, when I only tried to help mother and Lucy find out what they wanted to know so badly. I went down the hill, crossed the creek on the stepping-stones, and followed the cowpath into the woods pasture. It ran beside the creek bank through the spice thicket and blackberry patches, under pawpaw groves, and beneath giant oaks and elms. Just where the creek turned at the open pasture, below the church and cemetery, right at the deep bend, stood the biggest white oak father owned. It was about a tree exactly like this that an Englishman wrote a beautiful poem in McGuffey's Sixth, that begins:

A song to the oak, the brave old oak,
    Who hath ruled in the greenwood long;
Here's health and renown to his broad green crown,
    And his fifty arms so strong.

I knew it was the same, because I counted the arms time and again, and there were exactly fifty. I thought I'd go to the Big Woods and count some there to see if all oaks had that many. There was a pawpaw and spice hedge around three sides of this one, and water on the other. Wild grapes climbed from the bushes to the lower branches and trailed back to earth again. Here, I had two secrets I didn't propose to tell. One was that in the crotch of some tiptop branches the biggest chicken hawks you ever saw had their nest, and if they took too many chickens father said they'd have to be frightened a little with a gun. I can't begin to tell how I loved those hawks. They did the one thing I wanted to most, and never could. When I saw them serenely soar above the lowest of the soft fleecy September clouds, I was wild with envy. I would have gone without chicken myself rather than have seen one of those splendid big brown birds dropped from the skies. I was so careful to shield them, that I selected this for my especial retreat when I wanted most to be alone, and I carefully gathered up any offal from the nest that might point out their location, and threw it into the water where it ran the swiftest.

I never got so nearly in touch with the Fairies as I did here. All my life I had been free to travel as far as my curiosity led or my heels would carry me; this was my chosen place. When starting, I thought company would be nice, but on coming closer I couldn't bear it, so I hid Grace Greenwood in the grass, set Bobby on the fence, and sent Hezekiah back to the orchard. Then I parted the vines and crept where the roots of the big oak stretched like bony fingers over the water, that was slowly eating under it and baring its roots. I sat on them above the water and thought. I decided it was all a mistake about children *not* thinking; that they thought much more than grown people. They have time, and there is so much they do not understand. Big folks have to work, plan, and worry, but we can spend days looking nature in the face, and are not afraid to ask questions, because people would be more surprised if we know than if we don't.

I had decided the day before about going to school, and the day before that, and many, many times before that, and here I was having to settle it all over again. Doubled on the oak roots, a troubled little soul, I settled it once more. No books or teachers were needed to tell me about flowing water and fish, how hawks raised their broods and kept house, about the softly cooing doves of the spice thickets, the cuckoos slipping snakelike in and out of the wild crab-apple bushes, or the brown thrush's weird call from the thorn bush. I knew what they said and did, but their names, where they came from, where they went when the wind blew and the snow fell—how was I going to find out that? Worse yet were the flowers, butterflies, and moths; they were mysteries past learning alone, and while the names I made up for them were pretty and suitable, I knew in all reason they wouldn't be the same in the books. I had to go, but no one will ever know what it cost. When the supper bell rang, I sat still. I'd have to wait until at least two tables had been served, anyway, so I sat there and nursed my misery, looked and listened, and by and by I felt better. I couldn't see or hear a thing that was standing still. Father said even the rocks grew larger year by year. The trees were getting bigger, the birds were busy, and the creek was in a dreadful hurry to reach the river. It was like that poetry piece that says:

When a playful brook, you gambolled,

(Mostly that gambolled word is said about lambs)

  And the sunshine o'er you smiled,
On your banks did children loiter,
  Looking for the spring flowers wild?

The creek was more in earnest and working harder at pushing steadily ahead without ever stopping than anything else; and like the poetry piece again, it really did "seem to smile upon us as it quickly passed us by." I had to quit playing, and go to work some time; it made me sorry to think how behind I was, because I had not started two years before, when I should. But that couldn't be helped now. All there was left was to go this time, for sure. I got up heavily and slowly as an old person, and then slipped out and ran down the path to the meadow, because I could hear Leon whistle as he came to bring the cows.

By fast running I could start them home for him: Rose, Brindle, Bess, and Pidy, Sukey and Muley; they had eaten all day, but they still snatched bites as they went toward the gate. I wanted to surprise Leon and I did.

"Getting good, ain't you?" he asked. "What do you want?"

"Nothing!" I said. "I just heard you coming and I thought I'd help you."

"Where were you?"

"Playing."

"You don't look as if you'd been having much fun."

"I don't expect ever to have any, after I begin school," I said.

"Oh!" said Leon. "It is kind of tough the first day or two, but you'll soon get over it. You should have behaved yourself. and gone when they started you two years ago."

"Think I don't know it?"

Leon stopped and looked at me sharply.

"I'll help you nights, if you want me to," he offered.

"Can I ever learn?" I asked, almost ready to cry.

"Of course you can," said Leon. "You're smart as the others, I suppose. The sevens and nines of the multiplication table are the stickers, but you ought to do them if other girls can. You needn't feel bad because you are behind a little to start on; you are just that much better prepared to work, and you can soon overtake them. You know a lot none of the rest of us do, and some day it will come your turn to show off. Cheer up, you'll be all right."

Men are such a comfort. I pressed closer for more.

"Do you suppose I will?" I asked.

"Of course," said Leon. "Any minute the woods, or birds, or flowers are mentioned your time will come; and all of us will hear you read and help nights. I'd just as soon as not."

That was the most surprising thing. He never offered to help me before. He never acted as if he cared what became of me. Maybe it was because Laddie always had taken such good care of me, Leon had no chance. He seemed willing enough now. I looked at him closely.

"You'll find out I'll learn things if I try," I boasted. "And you'll find out I don't tell secrets either."

"I've been waiting for you to pipe up about—"

"Well, I haven't piped, have I?"

"Not yet."

"I am not going to either."

"I almost believe you. A girl you could trust would be a funny thing to see."

"Tell me what you know about Laddie, and see if I'm funny."

"You'd telltale sure as life!"

"Well, if you know it, he knows it anyway."

"He doesn't know *what* I know."

"Well, be careful and don't worry mother. You know how she is since the fever, and father says all of us must think of her. If it's anything that would bother her, don't tell before her."

"Say, looky here," said Leon, turning on me sharply, "is all this sudden consideration for mother or are you legging for Laddie?"

"For both," I answered stoutly.

"Mostly for Laddie, just the same. You can't fool me, missy. I won't tell you one word."

"You needn't!" I answered, "I don't care!"

I don't know why I said that, for I did care dreadfully, and Leon knew it.

"Yes you do," he said. "You'd give anything to find out what I know, and then run to Laddie with it, but you can't fool me. I'm too smart for you."

"All right," I said. "You go and tell anything on Laddie, and I'll watch you, and first trick I catch you at, I'll do some telling myself, Smarty."

"That's a game more than one can play at," said Leon. "Go ahead!"

I stopped to get Grace Greenwood.

"What did you put your doll there for?" asked Leon.

"Because I wanted to be alone."

"Oh cracky! A girl! How does a piece of painted china, a few rags, and a quart of sawdust prevent you from being alone?"

"It doesn't. But if you pretend long enough and hard enough a thing is really that way."

"You mean it is to a girl," said Leon. "It never could be to a boy."

5

The First Day of School

Birds in their little nests agree,
   And why can't we?

"B-i-r-d-s, birds, i-n, in, t-h-e-i-r, their, l-i-t-t-l-e, little, n-e-s-t-s, nests, a-g-r-e-e, agree."

My feet burned in my new shoes, but most of my body was chilling as I stood beside Miss Amelia on the platform, before the whole school, and followed the point of her pencil, as, a letter at a time, I spelled aloud my first sentence. Nothing ever had happened to me as bad as that. I was not used to so much clothing. It was like taking a colt from the woods pasture and putting it into harness for the first time. That lovely September morning I followed Leon and May down the dusty road, my heart sick with dread.

May was so much smaller that I could have picked her up and carried her. She was a gentle, loving little thing, until some one went too far, and then they got what they deserved, all at once and right away.

Many of the pupils were waiting before the church. Leon climbed the steps, made a deep bow, waved toward the school building across the way, and what he intended to say was, "Still sits the schoolhouse by the road," but he was a little excited and the s's doubled his tongue so that we heard: "Shill stits the school-house by the road." We just yelled and I forgot a little about my-self.

When Miss Amelia came to the door and rang the bell, May must have remembered something of how her first day felt, for as we reached the steps she waited for me, took me in with her, and found me a seat. If she had not, I'm quite sure I'd have run away and fought until they left me in freedom, as I had two years be-fore. All forenoon I had shivered in my seat, while classes were arranged, and the elder pupils were started on their work; then Miss Amelia called me to her on the platform and tried to find out how much schooling I had. I was ashamed that I knew so little, but there was no sense in her making me spell after a pencil, like a baby. I'd never seen the book she picked up. I could read the line she pointed to, and I told her so, but she said to spell the words; so I thought she had to be obeyed, for one poetry piece I know says:

Quickly speed your steps to school
And there mind your teacher's rule.

I can see Miss Amelia to-day. Her pale face was lined deeper than ever, her drab hair was dragged back tighter. She wore a black calico dress with white huckleberries, and a white calico apron figured in large black apples, each having a stem and two leaves. In dress she was a fruitful person. She had been a surprise to all of us. Chipper as a sparrow, she had hopped, and chattered, and darted here and there, until the hour of opening. Then in the stress of arranging classes and getting started, all her birdlike ways slipped from her. Stern and bony she stood before us, and with a cold light in her pale eyes, she began business in a manner that made Johnny Hood forget all about his paper wads, and Leon commenced studying like a good boy, and never even tried to have fun with her. Every one was so surprised you could no-tice it, except May, and she looked, "I told you so!" even in the back. She had a way of doing that very thing as I never saw any one else. From the set of her head, how she carried her shoulders, the stiffness of her spine, and her manner of walking, if you knew her well, you could tell what she thought, the same as if you saw her face.

I followed that pencil point and in a husky voice repeated the letters. I could see Tillie Baher laughing at me from behind her geography, and every one else had stopped what they were doing to watch and listen, so I forgot to be thankful that I even knew my a b c's. I spelled through the sentence, pronounced the words and repeated them without much thought as to the meaning; at that moment it didn't occur to me that she had chosen the lesson because father had told her how I made friends with the birds. The night before he had been putting me through memory tests, and I had recited poem after poem, even long ones in the Sixth Reader, and never made one mistake when the piece was about birds. At our house, we heard next day's lessons for all ages gone over every night so often, that we couldn't help knowing them by heart, if we had any brains at all, and I just loved to get the big folks' readers and learn the bird pieces. Father had been telling her about it, so for that reason she thought she would start me on the birds, but I'm sure she made me spell after a pencil point, like a baby, on purpose to shame me, because I was two years behind the others who were near my age. As I repeated the line Miss Amelia thought she saw her chance. She sprang to her feet, tripped a few steps toward the centre of the platform, and cried: "Classes, attention! Our Youngest Pupil has just completed her first sentence. This sentence contains a Thought. It is a wonderfully beautiful Thought. A Thought that suggests a great moral lesson for each of us. 'Birrrds—in their little nests—agreeee.'"

Never have I heard cooing sweetness to equal the melting tones in which Miss Amelia drawled those words. Then she continued, after a good long pause in order to give us time to allow the "Thought" to sink in: "There is a lesson in this for all of us. We are here in our schoolroom, like little birds in their nest. Now how charming it would be if all of us would follow the example of the birds, and at our work, and in our play, agreeee—be kind, loving, and considerate of each other. Let us all remember always this wonderful truth: 'Birrrds—in their little nests—agreeeee!'"

In three steps I laid hold of her apron. Only last night Leon had said it would come, yet whoever would have thought that I'd get a chance like this, so soon.

"Ho, but they don't!" I cried. "They fight like anything! Every day they make the feathers fly!"

In a backward stroke Miss Amelia's fingers, big and bony, struck my cheek a blow that nearly upset me. A red wave crossed her face, and her eyes snapped. I never had been so surprised in all my life. I was only going to tell her the truth. What she had said was altogether false. Ever since I could remember I had watched courting male birds fight all over the farm. After a couple had paired, and were nest building, the father always drove every other bird from his location. In building I had seen him pecked for trying to place a twig. I had seen that happen again for merely offering food to the mother, if she didn't happen to be hungry, or for trying to make love to her when she was brooding. If a young bird failed to get the bite it wanted, it sometimes grabbed one of its nestmates by the bill, or the eye even, and tried to swallow it whole. Always the oldest and strongest climbed on top of the youngest and fooled his mammy into feeding him most by having his head highest, his mouth widest, and begging loudest. There could be no mistake. I had seen! I knew! I was so amazed I forgot the blow, as I stared at the fool woman.

"I don't see why you slap me!" I cried. "It's the truth! Lots of times old birds pull out bunches of feathers fighting, and young ones in the nests bite each other until they squeal."

Miss Amelia caught my shoulders and shook me as hard as she could; and she proved to be stronger than you ever would have thought to look at her.

"Take your seat!" she cried. "You are a rude, untrained child!"

"They do fight!" I insisted, as I held my head high and walked to my desk.

Leon laughed out loud, and that made every one else. Miss Amelia had so much to do for a few minutes that she forgot me, and I know now why Leon started it, at least partly. He said afterward it was the funniest sight he ever saw. My cheek smarted and burned. I could scarcely keep from feeling to learn whether it were swelling, but I wouldn't have shed a tear or raised my hand for anything you could offer.

Recess was coming and I didn't know what to do. If I went to the playground, all of them would tease me; and if I sat at my desk Miss Amelia would have another chance at me. That was too much to risk, so I followed the others outdoors, and oh joy! there came Laddie down the road. He set me on one of the posts of the hitching rack before the church, and with my arms around his neck, I sobbed out the whole story.

"She didn't understand," said Laddie quietly. "You stay here until I come back. I'll go and explain to her about the birds. Perhaps she hasn't watched them as closely as you have."

Recess was over before he returned. He had wet his handkerchief at the water bucket, and now he bathed my face and eyes, straightened my hair with his little pocket comb, and then he began unlacing my shoes.

"What are you going to do?" I asked. "I must wear them. All the girls do. Only the boys are barefoot."

"You are excused," answered Laddie. "Three-fourths of the day is enough to begin on. Miss Amelia says you may come with me."

"Where are you going?"

Laddie was stripping off my stockings as he looked into my eyes, and smiled a peculiar little smile.

"Oh Laddie!" I cried. "Will you take me? Honest!"

He laughed again and then he rubbed my feet.

"Poor abused feet," he said. "Sometimes I wish shoes had never been invented."

"They feel pretty good when there's ice," I reminded him.

"So they do!" said Laddie.

He swung me to the ground, and we crossed the road, climbed the fence, and in a minute our redbird swamp shut the schoolhouse and cross old Miss Amelia from sight. Then we turned and started straight toward our Big Woods. I could scarcely keep on the ground.

"How are the others getting along?" asked Laddie.

"She's cross as two sticks," I told him. "Johnny Hood hasn't shot one paper wad, and Leon hadn't done a thing until he laughed about the birds, and I guess he did that to make her forget me."

"Good!" cried Laddie. "I didn't suppose the boy thought that far."

"Oh you never can tell by looking at him, how far Leon is thinking," I said.

"That's so, too," said Laddie. "Are your feet comfortable now?"

"Yes, but Laddie, isn't my face marked?"

"I am afraid it is a little," said Laddie. "We'll bathe it again at the creek. We must get it fixed so mother won't notice."

"What will the Princess think?"

"That you fell, perhaps," said Laddie.

"Do the tears show?"

"Not at all. We washed them all away."

"Did I do wrong, Laddie?"

"Yes, I think you did."

"But it wasn't true, what she said."

"That's not the point."

We had reached the fence of the Big Woods. He lifted me to the top rail and explained, while I combed his waving hair with my fingers.

"She didn't strike you because what you said was not so, for it was. She knew instantly you were right, if she knows anything at all about outdoors. This is what made her angry: It is her first day. She wanted to make a good impression on her pupils, to arouse their interest, and awaken their respect. When you spoke, all of them knew you were right, and she was wrong; that made her ridiculous, for she had just called you her 'youngest pupil.' Can't you see how it made her look and feel?"

"I didn't notice how she looked, but from the way she hit me, you could tell she felt bad enough."

"She surely did," said Laddie, kissing my cheek softly. "Poor little woman! What a world of things you have to learn!"

"Shouldn't I have told her how mistaken she was, at all?"

"If you had gone to her alone, at recess or noon, or to-night, probably she would have thanked you. Then she could have corrected herself at some convenient time and kept her dignity."

"Must I ask her pardon?"

"What you should do, is to put yourself in Miss Amelia's place and try to understand how she felt. Then if you think you wouldn't have liked any one to do to you what you did to her, you'll know."

I hugged Laddie tight and thought fast—there was no need to think long to see how it was.

"I got to tell her I was wrong," I said. "Now let's go to the Enchanted Wood and see if we can find the Queen's daughter."

"All right!" said Laddie.

He leaped the fence, swung me over, and started toward the pawpaw thicket. He didn't do much going around. He crashed through and over; and soon he began whistling the loveliest little dancy tune. It made your head whirl, and your toes tingle, and you knew it was singing that way in his heart, and he was just letting out the music. That was why it made you want to dance and whirl; it was so alive. But that wasn't the way in an Enchanted Wood. I pulled his hand.

"Laddie!" I cautioned, "keep in the path! You'll step on the Fairies and crush a whole band with one foot. No wonder the Queen makes her daughter grow big when she sends her to you. If you make so much noise, some one will hear you, then this won't be a secret any more."

Laddie laughed, but he stepped carefully in the path after that, and he said: "There are times, Little Sister, when I don't care whether this secret is secret another minute or not. Secrets don't agree with me. I'm too big, and broad, and too much of a man, to go creeping through the woods with a secret. I prefer to print it on a banner and ride up the road waving it."

"Like,—'A youth who bore mid snow and ice, A banner with a strange device,'" I said.

"That would be 'a banner with a strange device,'" laughed Laddie. "But, yes—something like!"

"Have you told the Princess?"

"I have!" Laddie fairly shouted it.

"Does *she* like secrets?"

"No more than I do!"

"Then why—?"

"There you go!" said Laddie. "Zeus, but the woman is beginning to measle out all over you! You know as well as any one that there's something wrong at her house. I don't know what it is; I can't even make a sensible guess as yet, but it's worse than the neighbours think. It's a thing that has driven a family from their home country, under a name that I have doubts about being theirs, and sent them across an ocean, 'strangers in a strange land,' as it says in the Bible. It's something that keeps a cultured gentleman and scholar raging up and down the roads and over the country like a madman. It shuts a white-faced, lovely, little woman from her neighbours, but I have passed her walking the road at night with both hands pressed against her heart. Sometimes it tries the Princess past endurance and control; and it has her so worn and tired struggling with it that she is willing to carry another secret, rather than try to find strength to do anything that would make more trouble for her father and mother."

"Would it trouble them for her to know you, Laddie?"

"So long as they don't and won't become acquainted with me, or any one, of course it would."

"Can't you force them to know you?"

"That I can!" said Laddie. "But you see, I only met the Princess a short time ago, and there would be no use in raising trouble, unless she will make me her Knight!"

"But hasn't she, Laddie?"

"Not in the very littlest least," said Laddie. "For all I know, she is merely using me to help pass a lonely hour. You see, people reared in England have ideas of class, that two or three generations spent here wash out. The Princess and her family are of the unwashed British. Father's people have been here long enough to judge a man on his own merits."

"You mean the Princess' family would think you're not good enough to be her Knight?"

"Exactly!"

"And we know that our family thinks they are infidels, and wicked people; and that if she would have you, mother would be sick in bed over it. Oh Laddie!"

"Precisely!"

"What are you going to do?"

"That I must find out."

"When it will make so much trouble, why not forget her, and go on like you did before she came? Then, all of us were happy. Now, it makes me shiver to think what will happen."

"Me too," said Laddie. "But look here, Little Sister, right in my face. Will you ever forget the Princess?"

"Never!"

"Then how can you ask me to?"

"I didn't mean forget her, exactly. I meant not come here and do things that will make every one unhappy."

"One minute, Chick-a-Biddy," said Laddie. Sometimes he called me that, when he loved me the very most of all. I don't believe any one except me ever heard him do it. "Let me ask you this: Does our father love our mother?"

"Love her?" I cried. "Why he just loves her to death! He turns so white, and he suffers so, when her pain is the worst. Love her? And she him? Why, don't you remember the other day when he tipped her head against him and kissed her throat as he left the table; that he asked her if she 'loved him yet,' and she said right before all of us, 'Why Paul, I love you, until I scarcely can keep my fingers off you!' Laddie, is it like that with you and the Princess?"

"It is with me," said Laddie. "Not with the Princess! Now, can I forget her? Can I keep away from even the chance to pass her on the road?"

"No," I said. "No, you can't, Laddie. But can you ever make her love you?"

"It takes time to find that out," said Laddie. "I have got to try; so you be a woman and keep my secret a little while longer, until I find a way out, but don't bother your head about it!"

"I can't help bothering my head, Laddie. Can't you make her understand that God is not a myth?"

"I'm none too sure what I believe myself," said Laddie. "Not that there is no God—I don't mean that—but I surely don't believe all father's teachings."

"If you believe God, do other little things matter, Laddie?"

"I think not," said Laddie, "else Heaven would be all Methodists. As for the Princess, all she has heard in her life has been against there being a God. Now, she is learning something on the other side. After a while she can judge for herself. It is for us, who profess to be a Christian family, to prove to her why we believe in God, and what He does for us."

"Well, she would think He could do a good deal, if she knew how mother hated asking her to come to our house; and yet she did it, beautifully too, just to give her a chance to see that very thing. But I almost made her do it. I don't believe she ever would alone, Laddie, or at least not for a long time yet."

"I saw that, and understood it perfectly," said Laddie. "Thank you, Little Sister." He picked me up and hugged me tight. "If I could only make you see!"

"But Laddie, I do! I'm not a baby! I know how people love and make homes for themselves, like Sally and Peter are going to. If it is with you about the Princess as it is with father and mother, why I do know."

"All right! Here we are!" said Laddie.

He parted the willows and we stepped on the Magic Carpet, and that minute the Magic worked. I forgot every awful, solemn, troublous thing we had been talking about, and looked around while Laddie knelt and hunted for a letter, and there was none. That meant the Princess was coming, so we sat on the throne to wait. We hadn't remembered to bathe my cheek, we had been so busy when we passed the water, and I doubt if we were thinking much then. We just waited. The willow walls waved gently, the moss carpet was spotted with little gold patches of sunlight, in the shade a few of the red flowers still bloomed, and big, lazy bumble-bees hummed around them, or a hummingbird stood on air before them. A sort of golden throbbing filled the woods, and my heart began to leap, why, I don't know; but I'm sure Laddie's did too, for I looked at him and his eyes were shining as I never had seen them before, while his cheeks were a little red, and he was breathing like when you've been running; then suddenly his body grew tense against mine, and that meant she was coming.

Like that first day, she came slowly through the woods, stopping here and there to touch the trunk of a tree, put back a branch, or bend over a flower face. Brown as the wood floor was her dress, and cardinal flowers blazed on her breast, and the same colour showed on her cheeks and lips. Her eyes were like Laddie's for brightness, and she was breathing the same way. I thought sure there was going to be something to remember a lifetime—I was so excited I couldn't stand still. Before it could happen Laddie went and said it was a "beautiful day," and she said "it didn't show in the woods, but the pastures needed rain." Then she kissed me. Well if I ever! I sank on the throne and sat there. They went on talking like that, until it was too dull to bear, so I slipped out and wandered away to see what I could find. When I grew tired and went back, Laddie was sitting on the Magic Carpet with his back against the beech, and the Princess was on the throne reading from a little book, reading such interesting things that I decided to listen. After a while she came to this:

Thou art mated with a clown,
And the grossness of his nature, will have weight to bear thee
down.

Laddie threw back his head, and how he laughed! The Princess put down the book and looked at him so surprised.

"Are you reading that to me because you think it is appropriate?" asked Laddie.

"I am reading it because it is conceded to be one of the most beautiful poems ever written," said the Princess.

"You knew when you began that you would come to those lines."

"I never even thought of such a thing."

"But you knew that is how your father would regard any relationship, friendly or deeper, with me!"

"I cannot possibly be held responsible for what my father thinks."

"It is natural that you should think alike."

"Not necessarily! You told me recently that you didn't agree with your father on many subjects."

"Kindly answer me this," said Laddie: "Do you feel that I'm a 'clown' because I'm not schooled to the point on all questions of good manners? Do you find me gross because I plow and sow?"

"You surprise me," said the Princess. "My consenting to know and to spend a friendly hour with you here is sufficient answer. I have not found the slightest fault with your manners. I have seen no suspicion of 'grossness' about you."

"Will you tell me, frankly, exactly what you do think of me?"

"Surely! I think you are a clean, decent man, who occasionally kindly consents to put a touch of human interest into an hour, for a very lonely girl. What has happened, Laddie? This is not like you."

Laddie sat straight and studied the beech branches. Father said beech trees didn't amount to much; but I first learned all about them from that one, and what it taught me made me almost worship them always. There were the big trunk with great rough spreading roots, the bark in little ridges in places, smooth purple gray between, big lichens for ornament, the low flat branches, the waxy, wavy-edged leaves, with clear veins, and the delicious nuts in their little brown burrs. The Princess and I both stared at the branches and waited while a little breath of air stirred the leaves, the sunshine flickered, and a cricket sang a sort of lonesome song. Laddie leaned against the tree again, and he was thinking so hard, to look at him made me begin to repeat to myself the beech part of that beautiful churchyard poem our big folks recite:

There, at the foot of yonder nodding beech,
That wreathes its old fantastic roots so high,
His listless length at noontide he would stretch,
And pore upon the brook that babbles by.

Only he was studying so deeply you could almost feel what was in his mind, and it was not about the brook at all, even if one ran close. Soon he began talking to himself.

"Not so bad!" he said. "You might think worse. I admit the cleanliness, I strive for decency, I delight in being humanely interesting, even for an hour; you might think worse, much worse! You might consider me a 'clown.' 'A country clod.' Rather a lowdown, common thing, a 'clod,' don't you think? And a 'clown!' And 'gross' on top of that!"

"What can you mean?" asked the Princess, her face troubled.

"Since you don't seem to share the estimate of me, I believe I'll tell you," said Laddie. "The other day I was driving from the gravel pit with a very heavy load. The road was wide and level on either side. A man came toward me on horseback. Now the law of the road is to give half to a vehicle similar to the one you are driving, but to keep all of it when you are heavily loaded, if you are passing people afoot or horseback. The man took half the road, and kept it until the nose of his horse touched one of the team I was driving. I stopped and said: 'Good morning, sir! Do you wish to speak with me?' He called angrily: 'Get out of my way, you clod!' 'Sorry sir, but I can't,' I said. 'The law gives me this road when I am heavily loaded, and you are on foot or horseback!'"

"What did he do?" asked the Princess.

And from the way she looked I just knew she guessed the man was the same one I thought of.

"He raised his whip to strike my horse," said Laddie.

"Ah, surely!" said the Princess. "Always an arm raised to strike. And you, Man? What did you do?" she cried eagerly.

"I stood on my load, suddenly," said Laddie, "and I called: 'Hold one minute!'"

"And he?" breathed the Princess.

"Something made him pause with his arm still raised. I said to him: 'You must not strike my horse. It never has been struck, and it can't defend itself. If you want to come a few steps farther and tackle me, come ahead! I can take it or return it, as I choose!'"

"Go on!" said the Princess.

"That's all," said Laddie, "or at least almost all."

"Did he strike?"

"He did not. He stared at me a second, and then he rode around me; but he was making forceful remarks as he passed about 'country clods,' and there was an interesting one about a 'gross clown.' What you read made me think of it, that is all."

The Princess stared into the beech branches for a time and then she said: "I will ask your pardon for him. He always had a domineering temper, and trouble he had lately has almost driven him mad; he is scarcely responsible at times. I would hesitate about making him too angry."

"I think perhaps," said Laddie, "I would have done myself credit if I had recognized that, and given him the road, when he made a point of claiming it."

"Indeed no!" cried the Princess. "To be beaten at the game he started was exactly what he needed. If you had turned from his way, he would have considered you a clod all his life. Since you made him go around, it may possibly dawn on him that you are a man. You did the very best thing."

Then she began to laugh, and how she did laugh.

"I would give my allowance for a quarter to have seen it," she cried. "I must hurry home and tell mother."

Laddie turned to her and stared almost impolitely.

"Does your mother know about me?" he demanded. "Does she know that you come here?"

The Princess arose and stood very tall and straight.

"You may beg my pardon or cease to know me," she said. "Whatever led you to suppose that I would know or meet you without my mother's knowledge?"

Then she started toward the entrance.

"One minute!" cried Laddie.

A leap carried him to her side. He caught her hands and held them tight, and looked straight into her eyes. Then he kissed her hands over and over. I thought from the look on her face he could have kissed her cheek if he had dared risk it; but he didn't seem to notice. Then she stooped and kissed me, and turned toward home, while Laddie and I crossed the woods to the west road, and went back past the schoolhouse. I was so tired Laddie tied the strings together and hung my shoes across his shoulders and took me by the arm the last mile.

All of them were at home when we got there, and Miss Amelia came to the gate to meet us. She was mealy-mouthed and good as pie, not at all as I had supposed she would be. I wonder what Laddie said to her. But then he always could manage things for every one. That set me to wondering if by any possible means he could fix them for himself. I climbed to the catalpa to think, and the more I thought, the more I feared he couldn't; but still mother always says one never can tell until they try, and I knew he would try with every ounce of brain and muscle in him. I sat there until the supper bell rang, and then I washed and reached the table last. The very first thing, mother asked how I bruised my face, and before I could think what to tell her, Leon said just as careless like: "Oh she must have run against something hard, playing tag at recess." Laddie began talking about Peter coming that night, and every one forgot me, but pretty soon I slipped a glance at Miss Amelia, and saw that her face was redder than mine.

6

The Wedding Gown

The gay belles of fashion may boast of excelling
  In waltz or cotillon, at whist or quadrille;
And seek admiration by vauntingly telling
  Of drawing and painting, and musical skill;
But give me the fair one, in country or city,
  Whose home and its duties are dear to her heart,
Who cheerfully warbles some rustical ditty,
  While plying the needle with exquisite art.
The bright little needle, the swift-flying needle,
  The needle directed by beauty and art.

The next morning Miss Amelia finished the chapter—that made
two for our family. Father always read one before breakfast—no
wonder I knew the Bible quite well—then we sang a song, and
she made a stiff, little prayer. I had my doubts about her prayers; she was on no such terms with the Lord as my father. He
got right at Him and talked like a doctor, and you felt he had
some influence, and there was at least a possibility that he might
get what he asked for; but Miss Amelia prayed as if the Lord
were ten million miles away, and she would be surprised to
pieces if she got anything she wanted. When she asked the Almighty to make us good, obedient children, there was not a

word she said that showed she trusted either the Lord or us, or thought there was anything between us and heaven that might make us good because we wanted to be. You couldn't keep your eyes from the big gad and ruler on her desk; she often fingered them as she prayed, and you knew from her stiff, little, sawed-out petition that her faith was in her implements, and she'd hit you a crack the minute she was the least angry, same as she had me the day before. I didn't feel any too good toward her, but when the blood of the Crusaders was in the veins, right must be done even if it took a struggle. I had to live up to those little gold shells on the trinket. Father said they knew I was coming down the line, so they put on a bird for me; but I told him I would be worthy of the shells too. This took about as hard a fight for a little girl as any Crusade would for a big, trained soldier; but it had to be done. I had been wrong, Laddie had made me see that. So I held up my hand, and Miss Amelia saw me as she picked up Ray's arithmetic.

"What is it?"

I held to the desk to brace myself, and tried twice before I could raise my voice so that she heard.

"Please, Miss Amelia," I said, "I was wrong about the birds yesterday. Not that they don't fight—they do! But I was wrong to contradict you before every one, and on your first day, and if you'll only excuse me, the next time you make a mistake, I'll tell you after school or at recess."

The room was so still you could hear the others breathing. Miss Amelia picked up the ruler and started toward me. Possibly I raised my hands. That would be no Crusader way, but you might do it before you had time to think, when the ruler was big and your head was the only place that would be hit. The last glimpse I had of her in the midst of all my trouble made me think of Sabethany Perkins.

Sabethany died, and they buried her at the foot of the hill in our graveyard before I could remember. But her people thought heaps of her, and spent much money on the biggest tombstone in the cemetery, and planted pinies and purple phlox on her, and went every Sunday to visit her. When they moved away, they missed her so, they decided to come back and take her along. The men were at work, and Leon and I went to see what was going on.

They told us, and said we had better go away, because possibly things might happen that children would sleep better not to see. Strange how a thing like that makes you bound you will see. We went and sat on the fence and waited. Soon they reached Sabethany, but they could not seem to get her out. They tried, and tried, and at last they sent for more men. It took nine of them to bring her to the surface. What little wood was left, they laid back to see what made her so fearfully heavy, and there she was turned to solid stone. They couldn't chip a piece off her with the shovel. Mother always said, "For goodness sake, don't let your mouth hang open," and as a rule we kept ours shut; but you should have seen Leon's when he saw Sabethany wouldn't chip off, and no doubt mine was as bad.

"When Gabriel blows his trumpet, and the dead arise and come forth, what on earth will they do with Sabethany?" I gasped. "Why, she couldn't fly to Heaven with wings a mile wide, and what use could they make of her if she got there?"

"I can't see a thing she'd be good for except a hitching post," said Leon, "and I guess they don't let horses in. Let's go home."

He acted sick and I felt that way; so we went, but the last glimpse of Sabethany remained with me.

As my head went down that day, I saw that Miss Amelia looked exactly like her. You would have needed a pick-ax or a crowbar to flake off even a tiny speck of her. When I had waited for my head to be cracked, until I had time to remember that a Crusader didn't dodge and hide, I looked up, and there she stood with the ruler lifted; but now she had turned just the shade of the wattles on our fightingest turkey gobbler.

"Won't you please forgive me?"

I never knew I had said it until I heard it, and then the only way to be sure was because no one else would have been likely to speak at that time.

Miss Amelia's arm dropped and she glared at me. I wondered whether I ever would understand grown people; I doubted if they understood themselves, for after turning to stone in a second—father said it had taken Sabethany seven years—and changing to gobbler red, Miss Amelia suddenly began to laugh. To laugh, of all things! And then, of course, every one else just yelled. I was so mortified I dropped my head again and began to cry as I never would if she'd hit me.

"Don't feel badly!" said Miss Amelia. "Certainly, I'll forgive you. I see you had no intention of giving offense, so none is taken. Get out your book and study hard on another lesson."

That was surprising. I supposed I'd have to do the same one over, but I might take a new one. I was either getting along fast, or Miss Amelia had her fill of birds. I wiped my eyes as straight in front of me as I could slip up my handkerchief, and began studying the first lesson in my reader: "Pretty bee, pray tell me why, thus from flower to flower you fly, culling sweets the livelong day, never leaving off to play?" That was a poetry piece, and it was quite cheery, although it was all strung together like prose, but you couldn't fool me on poetry; I knew it every time. As I studied I felt better, and when Miss Amelia came to hear me she was good as gold. She asked if I liked honey, and I started to tell her about the queen bee, but she had no time to listen, so she said I should wait until after school. Then we both forgot it, for when we reached home, the Princess' horse was hitched to our rack, and I fairly ran in, I was so anxious to know what was happening.

I was just perfectly amazed at grown people! After all the things our folks had said! You'd have supposed that Laddie would have been locked in the barn; father reading the thirty-second Psalm to the Princess, and mother on her knees asking God to open her eyes like Saul's when he tried to kick against the pricks, and make her to see, as he did, that God was not a myth. Well, there was no one in the sitting-room or the parlour, but there were voices farther on; so I slipped in. I really had to slip, for there was no other place they could be except the parlour bedroom, and Sally's wedding things were locked up there, and we were not to see until everything was finished, like I told you.

That was sort of a game Sally enjoyed playing, and as it was her wedding, she had a right to do as she pleased. Shelley said if she were ever going to do it, that was her time, for goodness knew, she'd never have a chance after she was tied to a man. I couldn't see why. Mother was tied to father just as Sally would be to Peter; every one was talking about who was to tie the knot, those days; but mother did exactly as she liked, and when father did anything he asked her what she thought, and they talked it over and decided. Maybe she asked him about what she did, after I was asleep, and I didn't hear it. I knew I missed a lot from sleeping so soundly, because my bed shoved under theirs in the daytime, and stood right beside it at night; so if I only could have kept awake I would have known much more than I did.

Well, this was what I saw: Our bedroom had been a porch once, and when we had been crowded on account of all of us coming, father enclosed it and made a room. But he never had taken out the window in the wall. So all I had to do when I wanted to know how fast the dresses were being made, was to shove up the window above my bed, push back the blind, and look in. I didn't care what she had. I just wanted to get ahead of her and see before she was ready, to pay her for beating me. I started her wedding for her, right from that minute, and one would have thought that she'd have been thankful to me. But thanks nothing! She stuck up her head and sailed around as if she had done it every bit herself. Peter always acted kind of grateful, as if I had helped him out, and he was glad of it. But then men were not so beating as women, anyway, at least young ones. I knew what she had, and I meant to tell her, and walk away with my nose in the air when she offered to show me; but this was different. I was wild to see what was going on because the Princess was there. The room was small, and the big cherry four-poster was very large, and all of them were talking, so no one paid the slightest attention to me.

Mother sat in the big rocking chair, with Sally on one of its arms, leaning against her shoulder. Shelley and May and the sewing woman were crowded between the wall and the footboard, and the others lined against the wall. The bed was heaped in a tumble of everything a woman ever wore. Seemed to me there was more stuff there than all the rest of us had, put together. The working dresses and aprons had been made on the machine, but there were heaps and stacks of handmade underclothes. I could see the lovely chemise mother embroidered lying on top of a pile of bedding, and over and over Sally had said that every stitch in the wedding gown must be taken by hand. The Princess stood beside the bed. A funny little tight hat like a man's and a riding whip lay on a chair close by. I couldn't see what she wore—her usual riding clothes probably—for she had a nip in each shoulder of a dress she was holding to her chin and looking down at. After all, I hadn't seen everything! Never before or since have I seen a lovelier dress than that. It was what always had been wrapped in the sheet on the foot of the bed and I hadn't got a peep at it. The pale green silk with tiny pink moss roses in it, that I had been thinking was the wedding dress, looked about right to wash the dishes in, compared with this.

This was a wedding dress. You didn't need any one to tell you. The Princess had as much red as I ever had seen in her cheeks, her eyes were as bright, and she was half-laughing and half-crying.

"Oh you lucky, lucky girl!" she was saying. "What a perfectly beautiful bride you will be! Never have I seen a more wonderful dress! Where did you get the material?"

Now we had been trained always to wait for mother to answer a visitor as she thought suitable, or at least to speak one at a time and not interrupt; but about six of those grown people told the Princess all at the same time how our oldest sister Elizabeth was married to a merchant who had a store at Westchester and how he got the dress in New York, and gave it to Sally for her wedding present, or she never could have had it.

The Princess lifted it and set it down softly. "Oh look!" she cried. "Look! It will stand alone!"

There it stood! Silk stiff enough to stand by itself, made into a little round waist, cut with a round neck and sleeves elbow length and flowing almost to where Sally's knees would come. It was a pale pearl-gray silk crossed in bars four inches square, made up of a dim yellow line almost as wide as a wheat straw, with a thread of black on each side of it, and all over, very wide apart, were little faint splashes of black as if they had been lightly painted on. The skirt was so wide it almost filled the room. Every inch of that dress was lined with soft, white silk. There was exquisite lace made into a flat collar around the neck, and ruffled from sight up the inside of the wide sleeves. That was the beginning. The finish was something you never saw anything like before. It was a trimming made of white and yellow beads. There was a little heading of white beads sewed into a pattern, then a lacy fringe that was pale yellow beads, white inside, each an inch long, that dangled, and every bead ended with three tiny white ones. That went around the neck, the outside of the sleeves, and in a pattern like a big letter V all the way around the skirt. And there it stood—alone!

The Princess, graceful as a bird and glowing like fire, danced around it, and touched it, and lifted the sleeves, and made the bead fringe swing, and laughed, and talked every second. Sally, and mother, and all of them had smiled such wide smiles, for so long, their faces looked almost as set as Sabethany's, but of course far different. Being dead was one thing, getting ready for a wedding another. Any one could have seen that our folks were as crazy as Pete Billings, about that wedding. It wouldn't have surprised me a mite if Sally had shinned up a bedpost and yowled just like Pete did, until father cut his yowling tree. She was hugging one as if she would start up it any minute.

And it looked too as if God might be a myth, for all they cared, so long as the Princess could make the wedding dress stand alone, and talk a blue streak of things that pleased them. It was not put on either, for there stood the dress, shimmering like the inside of a pearl-lined shell, white as a lily, and the tinkly gold fringe. No one *could* have said enough about it, so no matter what the Princess said, it had to be all right. She kept straight on showing all of them how lovely it was, exactly as if they hadn't seen it before, and she had to make them understand about it, as if she felt afraid they might have missed some elegant touch she had seen.

"Do look how the lace falls when I raise this sleeve! Oh how will you wear this and think of a man enough to say the right words in the right place?"

Mother laughed, and so did all of them.

"Do please show me the rest," begged the Princess. "I know there are slippers and a bonnet!"

Sally just oozed pride. She untied the strings and pushed the prettiest striped bag from a lovely pink bandbox and took out a dear little gray bonnet with white ribbons, and the yellow bead fringe, and a bunch of white roses with a few green leaves. These she touched softly. "I'm not quite sure about the leaves," she said.

The Princess had the bonnet, turning and tilting it.

"Perfect!" she cried. "Quite perfect! You need that touch of colour, and it blends with everything. How I envy you! Oh why doesn't some one ask me, so I can have things like these? I think your brother is a genius. I'm going to ride to Westchester to-morrow and give him an order to fill for me the next time he goes to the city. No one shows me such fabrics when I go, and Aunt Beatrice sends nothing from London I like nearly so well. Oh! Oh!"

She was on her knees now, lifting the skirt to set under little white satin slippers with gold buckles, and white bead buttons. When she had them arranged to suit her, she sat on the floor and kept straight on saying the things my mother and sisters seemed crazy to hear. When Sally showed her the long white silk mitts that went with the bonnet, the Princess cried: "Oh do ride home with me and let me give you a handkerchief Aunt Beatrice sent me, to carry in your hand!"

Then her face flushed and she added without giving Sally time to say what she would do: "Or I can bring it the next time I come past? It belongs with these things and I have no use for it. May I?"

"Please do! I'll use it for the thing I borrow."

"But I mean it to be a gift," said the Princess. "It was made to go with these lace mitts and satin slippers. You must take it!"

"Thank you very much," said Sally. "If you really want me to have it, of course I'd love to."

"I'll bring it to-morrow," promised the Princess. "And I wish you'd let me try a way I know to dress hair for a wedding. Yours is so beautiful."

"You're kind, I'm sure," said Sally. "I had intended to wear it as I always do, so I would appear perfectly natural to the folks; but if you know a more becoming way, I could begin it now, and they would be familiar with it by that time."

"I shan't touch it," said the Princess, studying Sally's face. "Your idea is right. You don't want to commence any new, unfamiliar style that would make you seem different, just at a time when every one should see how lovely you are, as you always have been. But don't forget to wear something blue, and something borrowed for luck, and oh do please put on one of my garters!"

"Well for mercy sake!" cried my mother. "Why?"

"So some one will propose to me before the year is out," laughed the Princess. "I think it must be the most fun of all, to make beautiful things for your very own home, and lovely dresses, and be surrounded by friends all eager to help you, and to arrange a house and live with a man you love well enough to marry, and fix for little people who might come—"

"You know perfectly there isn't a single man in the county who wouldn't propose to you, if you'd let him come within a mile of you," said Shelley.

"When the right man comes I'll go half the mile to meet him, you may be sure of that; won't I, Mrs. Stanton?" the Princess turned to mother.

"I have known girls who went even farther," said my mother rather dryly.

"I draw the line at half," laughed the Princess. "Now I must go; I have been so long my people will be wondering what I'm doing."

Standing in the middle of the room she put on her hat, picked up her whip and gloves, and led the way to the hitching rack, while all of us followed. At the gate stood Laddie as he had come from the field. His old hat was on the back of his head, his face flushed, his collar loosened so that his strong white neck showed, and his sleeves were rolled to the elbow, as they had been all summer, and his arms were burned almost to blisters. When he heard us coming he opened the gate, went to the rack, untied the Princess' horse and led it beside the mounting block. As she came toward him, he took off his hat and pitched it over the fence on the grass.

"Miss Pryor, allow me to make you acquainted with my son," said mother.

I felt as if I would blow up. I couldn't keep my eyes from turning toward the Princess. Gee! I could have saved my feelings. She made mother the prettiest little courtesy I ever set eyes on, and then turned and made a deeper one to Laddie.

"I met your son in one of the village stores some time ago," she said. "Back her one step farther, please!"

Laddie backed the horse, and quicker than you could see how it was done, she flashed up the steps and sat in the saddle; but as she leaned over the horse's neck to take the rein from Laddie, he got one level look straight in the eyes that I was sure none of the others saw, because they were not watching for it, and I was.

Laddie bowed from the waist, and put the reins in her fingers all in one movement. He caught the glance she gave him too; I could almost feel it like a band passing between them. Then she called a laughing good-bye to all of us at once, and showed us how to ride right, as she flashed toward the Little Hill. She and the horse and the saddle worked together like they were all one piece, and the same muscle moved them. That was riding, you may believe, and mother sighed as she watched her.

"If I were a girl again," she said, "I would ride as well as that, or I'd never mount a horse."

"She's been trained from her cradle, and her father deals in horses. Half the battle in riding is a thoroughbred," said Laddie. "No such horse as that ever stepped these roads before."

"And no such girl ever travelled them," said my mother, folding her hands one over the other on top of a post of the hitching rack. "I must say I don't know how this is coming out, and it troubles me."

"Why, what's up?" asked Laddie, covering her hands with his and looking her straight in the eyes.

"Just this," said my mother. "She's more beautiful of face and form than God ought to allow any woman to be, in mercy to the men who will be forced to meet her. Her speech is highly cultured. Her manners are perfect, and that is a big and unusual thing in a girl of her age. She is older than she looks, or whatever their trouble is, it has made her think beyond her years. Every word she said, every move she made to-day, was exactly as I would have been proud to hear, and to see a daughter of mine speak and move. If I had only myself to consider, I would take her into my heart, and make her my friend, because I'm seasoned in the ways of the world, and she could influence me only as I chose to allow her. With you youngsters it is different. You'll find her captivating, and you may let her sway you without even knowing it. All these outward things are not essential; they are pleasing, I grant, but they have nothing to do with the one big, elemental fact that a Godless life is not even half a life. I never yet have known any man or woman who attempted it who did not waste life's grandest opportunities, and then come crawling and defeated to the foot of the cross in the end, asking God's mercy where none was deserved or earned. It seems to me a craven way. I know all about the forgiveness on the cross! I know God is big enough and merciful enough to accept even deathbed repentance, but what is that to compare with laying out your course and running it a lifetime without swerving? I detest and distrust this infidel business. I want no child of mine under its influence, or in contact with it."

"But when your time comes, if you said just those things to her, and won her, what a triumph, little mother!" cried Laddie.

" 'If!' " answered mother. "That's always the trouble! One can't be sure! 'If' I knew I could accomplish that, I would get on my knees and wrestle with the Lord for the salvation of the soul of a girl like that, not to mention her poor, housebound mother, and that man with the unhappiest face I ever have seen, her father. It's worth trying, but suppose I try and fail, and at the same time find that in bringing her among us she has influenced some of mine to the loss of their immortal souls—*then,* what will I have done?"

"Mother," said Laddie; "mother, have you such a poor opinion of things you and father have taught us, and the lives you've lived before us, that you're really afraid of a slip of a girl, almost a stranger?"

"The most attractive girl I ever have seen, and mighty willing to be no longer a stranger, Lad."

"Well, I can't promise for the others," said Laddie, "but for myself I will give you my word of honour that I won't be influenced the breadth of one hair by her, in a doctrinal way."

"Humph!" said my mother. "And it is for you I fear. The girls will resent her just enough to keep them on the safe side, but if a young man is given the slighest encouragement by a girl like that, even his God can't always hold him; and you never have made a confession of faith, Laddie. It is you she will be most likely to captivate."

"If you think I have any chance, I'll go straight over and ask her father for her this very evening," said Laddie, and even mother laughed; then all of us started to the house, for it was almost supper time. I got ready and thought I'd take one more peep at the dress before Sally pinned it in the sheet again, and when I went back, there all huddled in a bunch before it stood Miss Amelia, the tears running down her cheeks.

"Did Sally say you might come here?" I asked.

"No," said Miss Amelia, "but I've been so crazy to see I just slipped in to take a peep when I noticed the open door. I'll go this minute. Please don't tell her."

I didn't say what I would do, but I didn't intend to, unless so everlastingly many things were piled on me to keep that I forgot myself.

"What are you crying about?" I inquired.

"Ah, I too have known love," sobbed Miss Amelia. "Once I made a wedding dress, and expected to be a happy bride."

I hope it didn't look anything like her best dress now.

"Well, wasn't you?" I asked, and knew at once it was a silly question, for of course she would not be a miss, if she had not missed marrying.

"He died!" sobbed Miss Amelia.

If he could have seen her then, I believe he'd have been glad of it; but maybe he looked as bony and dejected as she did before he went; and he may have turned to stone afterward, as sometimes happens. Right then I heard Sally coming, so I grabbed Miss Amelia and dragged her under the fourposter, where I always hid when caught doing something I shouldn't. But Sally had so much stuff she couldn't keep all of it on the bed, and when she stooped and lifted the ruffle to shove a box under, she pushed it right against us, and knelt to look, and there we were.

"Well upon my soul!" she cried, and sat flat on the floor, holding the ruffle, peering in. "Miss Amelia! And in tears! Whatever is the trouble?"

Miss Amelia's face was redder than any crying ever made it, and I saw she wanted to kill me for getting her into such a fix, and if she became too angry probably she'd take it out on me in school the next day, so I thought I'd better keep her at work shedding tears.

"*He died!*" I told Sally as pathetically as ever I could.

Sally dropped the ruffle instantly, but I saw her knees shake against the floor. After a while she lifted the curtain and offered Miss Amelia her hand.

"I was leaving my dress to show you before putting it away," she said.

I didn't believe it; but that was what she said. Maybe it was an impulse. Mother always said Sally was a creature of impulse. When she took off her flannel petticoat and gave it to poor little half-frozen Annie Hasty, that was a good impulse, but it sent Sally to bed for a week. And when she threw a shovel of coals on Bill Ramsdell's dog, because Bill was a shiftless lout, and the dog was so starved it all the time came over and sucked our eggs, that was a bad impulse, because it didn't do Bill a particle of good, and it hurt the dog, which would have been glad to suck eggs at home, no doubt, if Bill hadn't been too worthless to keep hens.

That was a good impulse she had then, for she asked Miss Amelia to help her straighten the room and of course that meant to fold and put away wedding things. Any woman would have been wild to do that. Then she told Miss Amelia that she was going to ask father to dismiss school for half a day, and allow her to see the wedding, and she asked her if she would help serve the breakfast. Miss Amelia wiped her eyes, and soon laughed and was just beaming. I would have been willing to bet my three cents for lead pencils the next time the huckster came, that Sally never thought of wanting her until that minute; and then she arranged for her to wait on table to keep her from trying to eat with the wedding party, because Miss Amelia had no pretty clothes for one thing, and for another, you shouldn't act as if you were hungry out in company, and she ate every meal as if she were breaking a forty days' fast. I wondered what her folks cooked at home.

After supper Peter came, and the instant I saw him I thought of something, and it was such a teasing thought I followed him and stared harder at him every minute. At last he noticed me, and put his arms around me.

"Well, what is it, Little Sister?" he asked.

I did wish he would quit that. No one really had a right to call me that, except Laddie. Maybe I had to put up with Peter doing it when I was his sister in a married way, but before, the old name the preacher baptized on me was good enough for Peter. I was thinking about that so hard, I didn't answer, and he asked again.

"I have seen Sally's wedding dress," I told him.

"But that's no reason why you should stare at me so," he said.

"That's just exactly the reason," I answered. "I was trying to see what in the world there is about you to be worth a dress like that."

Peter laughed and laughed. At last he said that he was not really worth even a calico dress; and he was so little worthy of Sally that he would button her shoes, if she would let him. He got that mixed. The buttons were on her slippers: her shoes laced. But it showed a humble spirit in Peter. Not that I care for humble spirits. I am sure the Crusaders didn't have them. I don't believe Laddie would lace even the Princess' shoes, at least not to make a steady business of it. But maybe Peter and Sally had an agreement to help each other. She was always fixing his tie, and straightening his hair. Maybe that was an impulse, though, and mother said Sally would get over being so impulsive when she cut her eye teeth.

CHAPTER 7

When Sally Married Peter

Mid pleasures and palaces though we may roam,
Be it ever so humble there's no place like home!
A charm from the skies seems to hallow us there,
Which, seek through the world, is ne'er met with elsewhere.

When they began arranging the house for the wedding, it could be seen that they had been expecting it, and getting ready for a long time. From all the closets, shelves and chests poured heaps of new things. First, the walls were cleaned and some of them freshly papered, then the windows were all washed long before regular housecleaning time, the floors were scrubbed and new carpets put down. Mother had some window blinds that Winfield had brought her from New York in the spring, and she had laid them away; no one knew why, then. We all knew now. When mother was ready to put them up, father had a busy day and couldn't help her, and she was really provoked. She almost cried about it, when Leon rode in bringing the mail, and said Hannah Dover had some exactly like ours at her windows, that her son had sent from Illinois. Father felt badly enough then, for he always did everything he could to help mother to be first with everything; but so she wouldn't blame him, he said crosslike that if she had let him put them up when they came, as he wanted to, she'd have been six months ahead.

When they finally got ready to hang the blinds no one knew how they went. They were a beautiful shiny green, plain on one side, and on the other there was a silver border across the bottom and one pink rose as big as a pie plate. Mother had neglected to ask Winfield on which side the rose belonged. Father said from the way the roll ran, it went inside. Mother said they were rolled that way to protect the roses, and that didn't prove anything. Laddie said he would jump on a horse and ride around the section, and see how Hannah Dover had hers, and exactly opposite would be right. Every one laughed, but no one thought he meant it. Mother had father hold one against the window, and she stepped outside to see if she could tell from there. When she came in she said the flower looked mighty pretty, and she guessed that was the way, so father started hanging them. He had only two up when Laddie came racing down the Big Hill bareback calling for him to stop.

"I tell you that's not right, mother!" he said as he hurried in.

"But I went outside and father held one, and it looked real pretty," said mother.

"One! Yes!" said Laddie. "But have you stopped to consider how two rows across the house are going to look? Nine big pink roses with the sun shining on them! Anything funnier than Dovers' front I never saw. And look here."

Laddie picked up a blind. "See this plain back? It's double coated like a glaze. That is so the sun shining through glass won't fade it. The flowers would be gone in a week. They belong inside, mother, sure as you live."

"Then when the blinds are rolled to the middle sash in the daytime no one can see them," wailed mother, who was wild about pink roses.

"But at night, when they are down, you can put the curtains back enough to let the roses show, and think how pretty they will look then."

"Laddie is right!" said father, climbing on the barrel to take down the ones he had fixed.

"What do you think, girls?" asked Mother.

"I think the Princess is coming down the Little Hill," said

Shelley. "Hurry, father! Take them down before she sees! I'm sure they're wrong."

Father got one all right, but tore the corner of the other. Mother scolded him dreadfully cross, and he was so flustered he forgot about being on the barrel, so he stepped back the same as on the floor, and fell crashing. He might have broken some of his bones, if Laddie hadn't seen and caught him.

"If you are *sure* the flowers go inside, fix one before she comes!" cried mother.

Father stepped too close to the edge of the chair, and by that time he didn't know how to hang anything, so Laddie climbed up and had one nailed before the Princess stopped. She came to bring Sally the handkerchief, and it was the loveliest one any of us ever had seen. There was a little patch in the middle about four inches square, and around it a wide ruffle of dainty lace. It was made to carry in a hand covered with white lace mitts, when you were wearing a wedding gown of silver silk, lined with white. Of course it wouldn't have been the slightest use for a funeral or with a cold in your head. And it had come from across the sea! From the minute she took it by a pinch in the middle, Sally carried her head so much higher than she ever had before, that you could notice the difference.

Laddie went straight on nailing up the blinds, and every one he fixed he let down full length so the Princess could see the roses were inside; he was so sure he was right. After she had talked a few minutes she noticed the blinds going up. Laddie, in a front window, waved to her from the barrel. She laughed and answered with her whip, and then she laughed some more, just laughed and laughed.

"Do you know," she said, "there is the funniest thing at Dovers'. I rode past on the way to Groveville this morning and they have some blinds like those you are putting up."

"Indeed?" inquired my mother. "Winfield sent us these from New York in the spring, but I thought the hot summer sun would fade them, so I saved them until fall cleaning. The wedding coming on makes us a little early, but—"

"Well, they may not be exactly the same," said the Princess. "I only saw from the highway." She meant road; there were many things she said differently. "Have yours big pink roses and silver scrolls inside?"

"Yes," said mother.

The Princess bubbled until it made you think one of those yellow oriole birds had perched on her saddle. "That poor woman has gone and put hers up wrong side out. The effect of all those big pink roses on her white house front is most amusing. It looks as if the house were covered with a particularly gaudy piece of comfort calico. Only fancy!"

She laughed again and rode away. Mother came in just gasping.

"Well, for all His mercies, large and small, the Lord be praised!" she cried piously, as she dropped into the big rocking chair. "*That* is what I consider escaping by the skin of your teeth!"

Then father and Laddie laughed, and said they thought so too. When the blinds were up, the outside looked well, and you should have seen the inside! The woodwork was enamelled white, and the wall paper was striped in white and silver. Every so far on the silver there was a little pink moss rose having green leaves. The carpet was plum red and green in wide stripes, and the lace curtains were freshly washed, snowy, and touched the floor. The big rocker, the straight-backed chairs, and the sofa were beautiful red mahogany wood, and the seats shining haircloth. If no one happened to be looking, you could sit on a sofa arm, stick your feet out and shoot off like riding down a haystack; the landing was much better. On the sofa you bounced two feet high the first time; one, the second, and a little way the third. On the haystack, maybe you hit a soft spot, and maybe you struck a rock. Sometimes if you got smart, and tried a new place, and your feet caught in a tangle of weeds and stuck, you came up straight, pitched over, and landed on your head. *Then* if you struck a rock, you were still, quite a while. I was once. But you never dared let mother see you—on the sofa, I mean; she didn't care about the haystack.

There were pictures in oval black frames having fancy edges, and a whatnot where all our Christmas and birthday gifts, almost too dainty to handle, were kept. You fairly held your breath when you looked at the nest of spun green glass, with the white dove in it, that George Washington Mitchell gave to Shelley. Of course a dove's nest was never deep, and round, and green, and the bird didn't have red eyes and a black bill. I thought whoever could blow glass as beautifully as that, might just as easy have made it right while he was at it; but anyway, it was pretty. There were pitchers, mugs, and vases, almost too delicate to touch, and the cloth-covered box with braids of hair coiled in wreathes from the heads of the little fever and whooping cough sisters.

Laddie asked Sally if she and Peter were going to have the ceremony performed while they sat on the sofa. Seemed the right place. They had done all their courting there, even on hot summer days; but I supposed that was because Sally didn't want to be seen fixing Peter's tie until she was ready. She made no bones about it then. She fixed it whenever she pleased; likewise he held her hand. Shelley said that was disgusting, and you wouldn't catch her. Leon said he bet a dollar he would; and I said if he knew he'd get beaten as I did, I bet two dollars he wouldn't tell what he saw. The mantel was white, with vases of the lovely grasses that grew beside the stream at the foot of the Big Hill. Mother gathered the fanciest every fall, dried them, and dipped them in melted alum coloured with copperas, aniline, and indigo. Then she took bunches of the colours that went together best and made bouquets for the big vases. They were pretty in the daytime, but at night you could watch them sparkle and shimmer forever.

I always thought the sitting-room was nicer than the parlour. The woodwork was white enamel there too, but the bureau and chairs were just cherry and not too precious to use. They were every bit as pretty. The mantel was much larger. I could stand up in the fireplace, and it took two men to put on an everyday log, four the Christmas one. On each side were the book shelves above, and the linen closets below. The mantel set between these, and mother always used the biggest, most gorgeous bouquets there, because she had so much room. The hearth was a slab of stone that came far into the room. We could sit on it and crack nuts, roast apples, chestnuts, and warm our cider, then sweep all the muss we made into the fire. The wall paper was white and pale pink in stripes, and on the pink were little handled baskets filled with tiny flowers of different colours. We sewed the rags for the carpet ourselves, and it was the prettiest thing. One stripe was wide, all gray, brown, and dull colours, and the other was pink.

There were green blinds and lace curtains here also, and nice braided rugs that all of us worked on of winter evenings. Everything got spicker and spanner each day.

Mother said there was no use in putting down a carpet in a dining-room where you constantly fed a host, and the boys didn't clean their feet as carefully as they should in winter; but there were useful rugs where they belonged, and in our bedroom opening from it also. The dining-room wall paper had a broad stripe of rich cream with pink cabbage roses scattered over it and a narrow pink stripe, while the woodwork was something perfectly marvellous. I didn't know what kind of wood it was, but a man who could turn his hand to anything, painted it. First, he put on a pale yellow coat and let it dry. Then he added wood brown, and while it was wet, with a coarse toothed comb, a rag, and his fingers, he imitated the grain, the even wood, and knotholes of dressed lumber, until many a time I found myself staring steadily at a knot to see if a worm wouldn't really come working out. You have to see a thing like that to understand how wonderful it is. You couldn't see why they washed the bedding, and even took the feathers from the pillows and steamed them in mosquito netting bags and dried them in the shade, when Sally's was to be a morning wedding, but they did. I even had to take a bucket and gather from around the walls all the little heaps of rocks and shells that Uncle Abraham had sent mother from California, take them out and wash and wipe them, and stack them back, with the fanciest ones on top. He sent her a ring made of gold he dug himself and lots of things. She always kept the ring in a bottle in her bureau, and she meant to wear it at the wedding, with her new silk dress. I had a new dress too. I don't know how they got everything done. All of them worked, until the last few days they were perfect cross patches.

When they couldn't find another thing indoors to scour, they began on the yard, orchard, barn and road. Mother even had Leon stack the wood pile straighter. She said when corded wood leaned at an angle, it made people seem shiftless; and she never passed a place where it looked that way that her fingers didn't just itch to get at it. He had to pull every ragweed on each side of the road as far as our land reached, and lay every rail straight in the fences. Father had to take spikes and our biggest maul and go to the bridges at the foot of the Big and Little Hill, and see that every plank was fast, so none of them would rattle when important guests drove across. She said she just simply wouldn't have them in such a condition that Judge Pettis couldn't hear himself think when he crossed; for you could tell from his looks that it was very important that none of the things he thought should be lost. There wasn't a single spot about the place inside or out that wasn't gone over; and to lots of it you never would have known anything had been done if you hadn't seen, because the place was always in proper shape anyway; but father said mother acted just like that, even when her sons were married at other people's houses; and if she kept on getting worse, every girl she married off, by the time she reached me, we'd all be scoured threadbare and she'd be on the verge of the grave. May and I weeded the flowerbeds, picked all the ripe seed, and pulled up and burned all the stalks that were done blooming. Father and Laddie went over the garden carefully; they scraped the walks and even shook the palings to see if one were going to come loose right at the last minute, when every one would be so flustrated there would be no time to fix it.

Then they began to talk about arrangements for the ceremony, whether we should have our regular minister, or Presiding Elder Lemon, and what people they were going to invite. Just when we had planned to ask every one, have the wedding in the church, and the breakfast at the house, and all drive in a joyous procession to Groveville to give them a good send-off, in walked Sally. She had been visiting Peter's people, and we planned a lot while she was away.

"What's going on here?" she asked, standing in the doorway, dangling her bonnet by the ties.

She never looked prettier. Her hair had blown out in little curls around her face from riding, her cheeks were so pink, and her eyes so bright.

"We were talking about having the ceremony in the church, so every one can be comfortably seated, and see and hear well," answered mother.

Sally straightened up and began jerking the roses on her bonnet far too roughly for artificial flowers. Perhaps I surprised you with that artificial word, but I can spell and define it; it's easy divided into syllables. Goodness knows, I have seen enough flowers made from the hair of the dead, and wax, and paper, where you get the shape, but the colour never is right. These of Sally's were much too bright, but they were better than the ones made at our house. Hers were of cloth and bought at a store. You couldn't tell why, but Sally jerked her roses; I wished she wouldn't, because I very well knew they would be used to trim my hat the next summer, and she said: "Well, people don't have to be comfortable during a wedding ceremony; they can stand up if I can, and as for seeing and hearing, I'm asking a good many that I don't intend to have to see or hear either one!"

"My soul!" cried mother, and she dropped her hands and her mouth fell open, like she always told us we never should let ours, while she stared at Sally.

"I don't care!" said Sally, straightening taller yet; her eyes began to shine and her lips to quiver, as if she would cry in a minute; "I don't care—!"

"Which means, my child, that you *do* care, very much," said father. "Suppose you cease such reckless talk, and explain to us exactly what it is that you do want."

Sally gave her bonnet an awful jerk. Those roses would look like sin before my turn to wear them came, and she said: "Well then, I do care! I care with all my might! The church is all right, of course; but I want to be married in my very own home! Every one can think whatever they please about their home, and so can I, and what I think is, that this is the nicest and the prettiest place in all the world, and I belong here—"

Father lifted his head, his face began to shine, and his eyes to grow teary; while mother started toward Sally. She put out her hand and held mother from her at arm's length, and she turned and looked behind her through the sitting-room and parlour, and then at us, and she talked so fast you never could have understood what she said if you hadn't known all of it anyway, and thought exactly the same thing yourself.

"I have just loved this house ever since it was built," she said, "and I've had as good times here as any girl ever had. If any one thinks I'm so very anxious to leave it, and you, and mother, and all the others, why it's a big mistake. Seems as if a girl is expected to marry and go to a home of her own; it's drummed into her and things fixed for her from the day of her birth; and of course I do like Peter, but no home in the world, not even the one he provides for me, will ever be any dearer to me than my own home; and as I've always lived in it, I want to be married in it, and I want to stay here until the very last second—"

"You shall, my child, you shall!" sobbed mother.

"And as for having a crowd of men that father is planning to ask, staring at me, because he changes harvest help and wood chopping with them, or being criticised and clawed over by some women simply because they'll be angry if they don't get the chance, I just won't—so there! Not if I have to stand the minister against the wall, and turn our backs to every one. I think—"

"That will do!" said father, wiping his eyes. "That will do, Sally! Your mother and I have got a pretty clear understanding of how you feel, now. Don't excite yourself! Your wedding shan't be used to pay off our scores. You may ask exactly whom you please, want, and feel quite comfortable to have around you—"

Then Sally fell on mother's neck and every one cried a while; then we wiped up, Leon gave Sally his slate, and she came and sat beside the table and began to make out a list of those she really wanted to invite. First she put down all of our family, even many away in Ohio, and all of Peter's, and then his friends, and hers. Once in the list of girls she stopped and said: "If I take that beautiful imported handkerchief from Pamela Pryor, I have just got to invite her—"

"And she will outdress and outshine you at your own wedding," put in Shelley.

"Let her, if she can!" said Sally calmly. "She'll have to hump herself if she beats that dress of mine; and as for looks, I know lots of people who think gray eyes, pink cheeks, and brown curls far daintier and prettier than red cheeks and black eyes and curls. If she really is better looking than I am, it isn't her fault; God made her that way, and He wouldn't like us to punish her for it; and it would, because any one can see she wants to be friends; don't you think, mother?"—mother nodded—"and besides, I think she's better looking than I am, myself!"

Sally said that, and wrote down the Princess' name in big letters, and no one cheeped.

Then she began on our neighbourhood, thinking out loud and writing what she thought. Every one was quiet, like you held your breath and waited while father decided if you had been bad enough to be taken to the barn. Father wouldn't punish one of us, or even say what had to be said, only all alone with us. He said a child lost its self-respect if you punished it and talked over its shortcomings before others. But if he heard what you had done, and decided to take you to the barn, why you perfectly well knew what was coming, and it was so awful that for a few seconds while he thought over whether you must go, it was worse than when you were really there and at it. At least it most always was. Once in a while it came out different, usually with Leon. There was the time he fought Absalom Saunders something awful. Abby was bruised all over, and had to go to bed. He was older and bigger than Leon too, but when Leon really fought, it was good-bye to the boy he was angry with, no matter how big or how old he was. Leon was so tough, and wiry, he dodged and turned so quickly, and he practised fighting a bag of wheat hung from a beam in the barn, if no one would wrestle with him. I'll bet Leon would have made a splendid Crusader. He'd have reached the Holy City if any one did. So he thrashed Absalom so badly his father came over and told our father about it, and Mr. Saunders said he was going to whip Leon.

Father said, no, that wouldn't do, but *he'd* punish him as he deserved. He told Leon to go into the orchard and cut a good, big stick, take it to the barn and wait until he came. I heard father tell mother about it that night while he pulled his boots. He said when he reached the barn there stood Leon in the middle of the threshing floor—that was a thrashing floor for more than wheat—and he looked bigger around than Laddie. For a minute father was puzzled, and then he saw a little tag of wool sticking through where Leon's shirt buttoned in the back and he knew the boy had taken the sheepskin from the wagon seat and wrapped it around him, and put on his shirt over it. He had three immense big whips laid in a row across the wheelbarrow; father said a man would have been ashamed to strike a balky mule with sticks the size of those, but every one of them was a last year's alder shoot, and light and rotten as wood could be. Father said he picked up one, tried it across Leon's back, and the wood broke in three pieces, while the feel of the stroke on the wool was so funny, he was laughing before he knew it, and then he couldn't go farther. He helped Leon take off the wool so he wouldn't become overheated, threw the sticks from the barn door, and asked Leon to tell him how it happened. Leon said it was because Absalom used ugly words before the children coming home from school, and father said: "Umph! I expected as much. I hope you gave him a good one!"

When father told mother, he forgot to tell her he said that; he only told her he was mighty thankful he worded that promise to neighbour Saunders as he did, for when he had heard the other side of the story, he didn't think Leon "deserved" any punishment at all. The funny thing about it was that Leon hadn't been to the barn again. He watched father respectful-like, and did exactly as he said; and if he got in any trouble anywhere, he went straight and told father himself just how it had been, before any one else had a chance.

So all of us were as still, and held our breath in softly and waited, and Sally said slow and musing like, "Of course we couldn't have anything at *this* house without Sarah Hood. She dressed most of us when we were born, nursed us when we were sick, helped with threshing, company, and parties, and she's just splendid anyway; we better ask all the Hoods;" so she wrote them down. "And it will be lonely for Widow Willis and the girls to see every one else here—we must have them; and of course Deams—Amanda is always such splendid help; and the Widow Fall is so perfectly lovely, we want her for decorative purposes; and we could scarcely leave out Shaws; they always have all of us everything they do; and Dr. Fenner's of course; and we'll want Flo and Agnes Kuntz to wait on table, so their folks might as well come too—"

So she went on taking up each family we knew, and telling what they had done for us, or what we had done for them; and she found some good reason for inviting them, and pretty soon father settled back in his chair and never took his eyes from Sally's shining head as she bent over the slate, and then he began pulling his lower lip, like when it won't behave, and his eyes danced exactly as I've seen Leon's. I never had noticed that before.

Sally went straight on and at last she came to Freshetts. "I am going to have all of them, too," she said. "The children are good children, and it will help them along to see how things are done when they are done right; and I don't care what any one says, I *like* Mrs. Freshett. I'll ask her to help work, and that will keep her from talking, and give the other women a chance to see that she's clean, and human, and would be a good neighbour if they'd be friendly. If we ask her, then the others will."

When she finished—as you live—there wasn't a soul she had left out except Bill Ramsdell, who starved his dog until it sucked our eggs, and Isaac Thomas, who was so lazy he wouldn't work enough to keep his wife and children dressed so they ever could go anywhere, but he always went, even with rags flying, and got his stomach full just by talking about how he loved the Lord. To save me I couldn't see Isaac Thomas without beginning to myself:

'Tis the voice of the sluggard; I hear him complain,
You have waked me too soon, I must slumber again.
I passed by his garden, I saw the wild brier,
The thorn, and the thistle, grow broader and higher;
The clothes that hang on him are turning to rags;
And his money he wastes, till he starves or he begs.

That described Isaac to the last tatter, only he couldn't waste money; he never had any. Once I asked father what he thought Isaac would do with it, if by some unforeseen working of Divine Providence, he got ten dollars. Father said he could tell me exactly, because Isaac once sold some timber and had a hundred all at once. He went straight to town and bought Mandy a red silk dress and a brass breastpin, when she had no shoes. He got the children an organ, when they were hungry; and himself a plug hat. Mandy and the children cried because he forgot candy and oranges until the last cent was gone. Father said the only time Isaac ever worked since he knew him was when he saw how the hat looked with his rags. He actually helped the men fell the trees until he got enough to buy a suit, the remains of which he still wore on Sunday. I asked father why he didn't wear the hat too, and father said the loss of that hat was a blow, from which Isaac never had recovered. Once at campmeeting he laid it aside to pray his longest, most impressive prayer, and an affectionate cow strayed up and licked the nap all off before Isaac finished, so he never could wear it again.

Sally said: "I'll be switched if I'll have that disgusting creature around stuffing himself on my wedding day; but if you're not in bed, when it's all over, mother, I do wish you'd send Mandy and the children a basket."

Mother promised, and father sat and looked on and pulled his lower lip until his ears almost wiggled. Then Sally said she wanted Laddie and Shelley to stand at the parlour door and keep it tight shut, and seat every one in the dining- and sitting-rooms except a special list she had made out to send in there. She wanted all our family and Peter's, and only a few very close friends, but it was enough to fill the room. She said when she and Peter came downstairs every one could see how they looked when they crossed the sitting-room, and for all the difference the door would make, it could be left open then; she would be walled in by people she wanted around her, and the others could have the fun of being there, seeing what they could, and getting all they wanted to eat. Father and mother said that was all right, only to say nothing about the plan to shut the door; but when the time came just to close it and everything would be satisfactory.

Then Sally took the slate upstairs to copy the list with ink, so every one went about something, while mother crossed to father and he took her on his lap, and they looked at each other the longest and the hardest, and neither of them said a word. After a while they cried and laughed, and cried some more, and it was about as sensible as what a flock of geese say when they are let out of the barn and start for the meadow in the morning. Then father, all laughy and criey, said: "Thank God! Oh, thank God, the girl loves the home we have made for her!"

Just said it over and over, and mother kept putting in: "It pays, Paul! It pays!"

I never knew there was a thing to be paid. If there were, why didn't they use some of all that money in the Underground Station!

Maybe they didn't mean money; you can't always understand clearly, but anyway, it was exactly like the geese passing around the good word that they had escaped the foxes and were on the way to a day of tender grass and water feeding.

Next day Sally put on her riding habit and fixed herself as pretty as ever she could, and went around to have a last little visit with every one, and invited them herself, and then she wrote letters to people away. Elizabeth and Lucy came home, and every one began to work. Father and mother went to the village in the carriage and brought home the bed full of things to eat, and all we had was added, and mother began to pack butter and save eggs for cakes, and the day before, I thought there wouldn't be a chicken left on the place. They killed and killed, and Sarah Hood, Amanda Deam, and Mrs. Freshett picked and picked.

"I'll bet a dollar we get something this time besides ribs and neck" said Leon. "How do you suppose thigh and breast would taste?"

"I was always crazy to try the tail," I said.

"Much chance you got," sniggered Leon. "'Member the time that father asked the Presiding Elder, 'Brother Lemon, what piece of the fowl do you prefer?' and he up and said: 'I'm partial to the rump, Brother Stanton.' There sat father bound he wouldn't give him mother's piece, so he pretended he couldn't find it, and forked all over the platter and then gave him the ribs and the thigh. Gee, how mother scolded him after the preacher had gone! You notice father hasn't asked that since. Now, he always says: 'Do you prefer light or dark meat?' Much chance you have of ever tasting a tail, if father won't even give one to the Presiding Elder!"

"But as many as they are killing—"

"Oh *this* time," said Leon with a flourish, "this time we are going to have livers, and breast, and thighs, *and* tails, if you are beholden to tail."

"I'd like to know how we are?"

"Well, since you have proved that you can keep your mouth shut, for a little while, anyway, I'm going to take you in on this," said Leon. "You keep your eyes on me. When the wedding gets going good, you watch me, and slip out. That's all! I'll be fixed to do the rest. But mind this, get out when I do."

"All right," I promised.

They must have wakened about four o'clock on the wedding day; it wasn't really light when I got up. I had some breakfast in my night dress, and then I was all fixed up in my new clothes, and made to sit on a chair, and never move for fear I would soil my dress, for no one had time to do me over, and there was only one dress anyway. There was so much to see you could keep interested just watching, and I was as anxious to look nice before the boys and girls, and the big people, as any one.

Every mantel and table and bureau was covered with flowers, and you could have smelled the kitchen a mile away, I know. The dining table was set for the wedding party, our father and mother, and Peter's, and the others had to wait. You couldn't have laid the flat of your hand on that table anywhere, it was so covered with things to eat. Miss Amelia, in a dress none of us ever had seen before, a real nice white dress, pranced around it and smirked at every one, and waved the peacock feather brush to keep the flies from the jelly, preserves, jam, butter, and things that were not cooked.

For hours Mrs. Freshett had stood in the kitchen on one side of the stove frying chicken and heaping it in baking pans in the oven, and Amanda Deam on the other, frying ham, while Sarah Hood cooked other things, and made a wash boiler of coffee. Everything was ready by the time it should have been. I had watched them until I was tired, when Sally came through the room where I was, and she said I might come along upstairs and see her dressed. When we reached the door I wondered where she would put me, but she pushed clothing together on a bed, and helped me up, and that was great fun.

She had been bathed and had on her beautiful new linen underclothing that mother punched full of holes and embroidered in flowers and vines, and Shelley was brushing her hair, when some one called out: "The Princess is coming!"

I jumped for the window, and all of them, even Sally, crowded behind. Well, talk about carriages! No one had ever seen *that* one before. It *was* a carriage. And such horses! The funny "'orse, 'ouse" man who made the Pryor garden was driving. He stopped at the gate, got out and opened a door, and the Princess' father stepped down, tall and straight, all in shiny black. He turned around and held out his hand, bowing double, and the Princess laid her hand in his and stepped out too. He walked with her to the gate, made another bow, kissed her hand, and stepped back, and she came down the walk alone. He got in the carriage, the man closed the door, and they drove away.

Sally must have arranged before that the Princess was to come early, for she came straight upstairs. She wore a soft white silk dress with big faded pink roses in it, and her hair was fastened at each ear with a bunch of little pink roses. She was lovely, but she didn't "outdress or outshine" Sally one bit, and she never even glanced at the mirror to see how she looked; she began helping with Sally's hair, and to dress her. When Bess Kuntz prinked so long she made every one disgusted, the Princess said: "Oh save your trouble. No one will look at you when there's a bride in the house."

There was a roll almost as thick as your arm of garters that all the other girls wanted Sally to wear for them so they would get a chance to marry that year, and Agnes Kuntz's was so large it went twice around, and they just laughed about it. They put a blue ribbon on Sally's stays for luck, and she borrowed Peter's sister Mary's comb to hold her back hair. They had the most fun, and when she was all ready except her dress they went away, and Sally stood in the middle of the room trembling a little. Outside you could hear carriage wheels rolling, the beat of horses' hoofs, and voices crying greetings. "There was a sound of revelry," by day. Mother came in hurriedly. She wore her new brown silk, with a lace collar pinned at the throat with the pin that had a brown goldstone setting in it, and her precious ring was on her finger. She was dainty and pretty enough to have been a bride herself. She turned Sally around slowly, touching her hair a little and her skirts; then she went to the closet, took out the wedding dress, put the skirt over Sally's head, and she came up through the whiteness, pink and glowing. She slipped her arms into the sleeves, and mother fastened it, shook out the skirt, saw that the bead fringe hung right, and the lace collar lay flat, then she took Sally in her arms, held her tight and said: "God bless you, dear, and keep you always. Amen."

Then she stepped to the door, and Peter, all shining and new, came in. He hugged Sally and kissed her like it didn't make the least difference whether she had on calico or a wedding dress, and he just stared, and stared at her, and never said a word, so at last she asked: "Well Peter, do you like my dress?"

And the idiot said: "Why Sally, I hadn't even seen it!"

Then both of them laughed, and the Presiding Elder came.

I never liked to look at him very well because something had happened, and he had only one eye. I always wondered if he had "plucked it out" because it had "offended" him; but if you could forget his eye, and just listen to his voice, it was like the sweetest music. He married those two people right there in the bedroom, all but about three words at the end. I heard and saw every bit of it. Then Sally said it was time for me to go to mother, but she followed me into the boys' room and shut the door. Then she knelt in her beautiful silver dress, and put her arms around me and said: "Honest, Little Sister, aren't you going to kiss me good-bye?"

"Oh I can if you want me to," I said, but I didn't look at her; I looked out of the window.

She laughed a breathless little catchy sort of laugh and said: "That's exactly what I do want."

"You didn't even want me, to begin with," I reminded her.

"There isn't a doubt but whoever told you that, could have been in better business," said Sally, angry-like. "I was much younger then, and there were many things I didn't understand, and it wasn't *you* I didn't want; it was just no baby at all. I wouldn't have wanted a boy, or any other girl a bit more. I foolishly thought we had children enough in this house. I see now very plainly that we didn't, for this family never could get along without you, and I'm sorry I ever thought so, and I'd give anything if I hadn't struck you and—"

"Oh be still, and go on and get married!" I said. I could just feel a regular beller coming in my throat. "I was only fooling to pay you up. I meant all the time to kiss you good-bye when the others did. I'll nearly die being lonesome when you're gone—"

Then I ran for downstairs, and when I reached the door, where the steps went into the sitting-room, I stopped, scared at all the people. It was like camp-meeting. You could see the yard full through the windows. Just as I was thinking I'd go back to the boys' room, and from there into the garret, and down the back stairway, Laddie went and saw me. He came over, led me to the parlour door, put me inside, and there mother took my hand and held me tight, and I couldn't see Leon anywhere.

I was caught, but they didn't have him. Mother never hung on as she did that day. I tried and tried to pull away, and she held tight. It was only a minute until the door opened, people crowded back, and the Presiding Elder, followed by Sally and Peter, came into the room, and they began being married all over again.

If it hadn't grown so solemn my mother sprung a tear, I never would have made it. She just had to let me go to sop her face, because tears are salty, and they would turn her new brown silk front yellow. The minute my hand was free, I slipped between the people and looked at the parlour door. It was wedged full and more standing on chairs behind them. No one could get out there. I thought I would fail Leon sure, and then I remembered the parlour bedroom. I got through that door easy as anything, and it was no trick at all to slip behind the blind, raise the window, and drop into mother's room from the sill. From there I reached the back dining-room door easy enough, went around to the kitchen, and called Leon softly. He opened the door at once and I slipped in. He had just got there. We looked all around and couldn't see where to begin at first. There was enough cooked food there to load two wagons.

An old pillow-case that had dried sage in it was lying across a chair and Leon picked it up and poured the sage into the woodbox, and handed the case to me. He went over and knelt before the oven, while I followed and held open the case. Leon rolled his eyes to the ceiling and said so exactly like father when he is serving company that not one of us could have told the difference: "Which part of the fowl do you prefer, Brother Lemon?"

It was so funny it made me snigger, but I straightened up and answered as well as I could: "I'm especially fond of the rump, Brother Stanton."

Leon stirred the heap and piled four or five tails in the case. I thought that was all I could manage before they would spoil, so I said: "Do you prefer light or dark meat, Sister Abigail?"

"I wish to choose breast," said Leon, simpering just like that silly Abigail Webster. He put in six breasts. Then we found them hidden away back in the oven in a pie pan, for the bride's table, I bet, and we took two livers apiece; we didn't dare take more for fear they had been counted. Then he threw in whatever he came to that was a first choice big piece, until I was really scared, and begged him to stop; but he repeated what the fox said in the story of the "Quarrelsome Cocks"—"Poco was very good, but I have not had enough yet," so he piled in pieces until I ran away with the pillow-case; then he slid in a whole plateful of bread, another of cake, and put the plates in a tub of dishes under the table. Then we took some of everything that wasn't too runny. Just then the silence broke in the front part of the house, and we scooted from the back door, closing it behind us, ran to the wood house and climbed the ladder to the loft over the front part. There we were safe as could be, we could see to the road, hear almost everything said in the kitchen, and "eat our bites in peace," like Peter Justice told the Presiding Elder at the church trial that he wanted his wife to, the time he slapped her. Before very long, they began calling us, and called, and called. We hadn't an idea what they wanted, so we ate away. We heard them first while I was holding over a back to let Leon taste kidney, and it made him blink when he got it good.

"Well my soul!" he said. "No wonder father didn't want to feed that to another man when mother isn't very well, and likes it! No wonder!"

Then he gave me a big bite of breast. It was sort of dry and tasteless; I didn't like it.

"Why, I think neck or back beats that all to pieces!" I said in surprise.

"Fact is, they do!" said Leon. "I guess the people who 'wish to choose breast,' do it to get the biggest piece."

I never had thought of it before, but of course that would be the reason.

"Allow me, Sister Stanton," said Leon, holding out a piece of thigh.

That was really chicken! Then we went over the backs and picked out all the kidneys and ate the little crusty places, and all the cake we could swallow; then Leon fixed up the bag the best he could, and set it inside an old cracked churn and put on the lid. He said that would do almost as well as the cellar, and the food would keep until to-morrow. I wanted to slip down and put it in the Underground Station; but Leon said father must be spending a lot of money right now, and he might go there to get some, so that wouldn't be safe. Then he cleaned my face, and I told him when he got his right, and we slipped from the back door, crossed the Lawton blackberry patch, and went to the house from the orchard. Leon took an apple and broke it in two, and we went in eating as if we were starving. When father asked us where in this world we had been, Leon told him we thought it would be so awful long before the fourth or fifth table, and we hadn't had much breakfast, and we were so hungry we went and hunted something to eat.

"If you'd only held your horses a minute," said father; "they were calling you to take places at the first table."

Well for land's sake! Our mouths dropped open until it's a wonder the cake and chicken didn't show, and we never said a word. There didn't seem to be anything to say, for Leon loved to be with grown folks, and to have eaten at the bride's table would have been the biggest thing that ever happened to me. At last, when I could speak, I asked who had taken our places, and bless your heart if it wasn't that mealy-faced little sister of Peter's, and one of the aunts from Ohio. The bride's table had finished, and Sally was upstairs putting on her travelling dress, while the guests were eating, when I heard Laddie ask the Princess to ride with him and Sally's other friends, who were going to escort her to the depot.

"You'll want all your horses," she said. "What could I ride?"

"If I find you a good horse and saddle will you go?" he asked.

"I will," said the Princess. "I think it would be fine sport."

Laddie turned and went from sight that minute. The Princess laughed and kept on making friends with every one, helping wait on people, thinking of nice things to do, and just as the carriage was at the gate for father and mother, and Sally and Peter, and every one else was untying their horses to ride in the procession to the village, from where I was standing on the mounting block I saw something coming down the Little Hill. I took one good look, ran for the Princess, and almost dragged her.

Up raced Laddie, his face bright, his eyes snapping with fun. He rode Flos, was leading the Princess' horse Maud, and carrying a big bundle under his arm. He leaped from the saddle and fastened both horses.

"Gracious Heaven! What have you done?" gasped the Princess.

"Brought your mount," said Laddie, quite as if he were used to going to Pryors' after the sausage grinder or the grain sacks. But the Princess was pale and trembling. She stepped so close she touched him, and he immediately got a little closer. You couldn't get ahead of Laddie, and he didn't seem to care who saw, and neither did she.

"Tell me exactly what occurred," she said, just as father does when he means to whale us completely.

"I rapped at the front door," said Laddie.

"And who opened it?" cried the Princess.

"Your father!"

"My father?"

"Yes, your father!" said Laddie. "And because I was in such a hurry, I didn't wait for him to speak. I said: 'Good morning, Mr. Pryor. I'm one of the Stanton boys, and I came for Miss Pryor's mount and habit. All the young people who are on horseback are going to ride an escort to the village, around my sister's bridal carriage, and Miss Pryor thinks she would enjoy going. Please excuse such haste, but we only this minute made the plan, and the train won't wait."

"And he?"

"He said: 'Surely! Hold one minute.' I stood on the step and waited, and I could hear him give the order to some one to get your riding habit quickly, and then he blew a shrill whistle, and your horse was at the gate the fastest of anything I ever saw."

"Did he do or say—"

"Nothing about 'clods, and clowns, and grossness!' Every other word he spoke was when I said, 'Thank you, and good morning,' and was turning away. He asked: 'Did Miss Pryor say whether she preferred to ride home, or shall I escort her in the carriage?'

" 'She did not!' I answered. 'The plan was so sudden she had no time to think that far. But since she will have her horse and habit, why not allow my father to escort her?' So you see, I'm going to take you home," exulted Laddie.

"But you told him your *father*," said the Princess.

"And thereby created the urgent necessity," said Laddie with a flourish, "for speaking to him again, and telling him that my father had visitors from Ohio, and couldn't leave them. We will get all the fun from the day that we can; but before dusk, too early for them to have any cause for cavil, 'the gross country clod' is going to take you home!"

One at a time, Laddie pounded those last words into the hitching post, with his doubled fist.

"Suppose he sets the dogs on you! You know he keeps two dreadful ones."

Laddie just roared. He leaned closer.

"Beaucheous Lady," he said, "I have fed those same dogs and rubbed their ears so many nights lately, he'll get the surprise of his life if he tries that."

The Princess drew away and stared at Laddie the funniest.

"On my life!" she said at last. "Well for a country clod—!"

Then she turned with the habit bundle, and ran into the house. Father and mother came from the front door arm in arm and walked to the carriage, and Sally and Peter followed. My! but they looked fine! The Princess had gone to the garden and gathered flowers and lined all the children in rows down each side of the walk. They were loaded with blooms to throw at Sally; but when she came out, in her beautiful gray poplin travelling dress, trimmed in brown ribbon, the same shade as her curls, her face all pink, her eyes shining, and the ties of her little brown bonnet waving to her waist, she was so perfectly beautiful, every single child watched her open mouthed, gripped its flowers, and forgot to throw them at all.

And this you scarcely will believe after what she had said the day she made her list, and when all of us knew her heart was all torn up, Sally just swept along smiling at every one and calling "good-bye" to those who had no way to ride to the village, as if leaving didn't amount to much. At the carriage a little white, but still smiling, she turned and took one long look at everything, and then she got in and called for me, right out loud before every one, so I got to hold up my head as high as it would go, and step in too, and ride all the way to Groveville between her and Peter, and instead of holding his hand, she held mine, just gripped it tight. She gripped so hard she squeezed all the soreness at her from my heart, and when she kissed me good-bye the very last of all, I whispered in her ear that I wouldn't ever be angry any more, and I wasn't, because after she had explained I saw how it had been. It wasn't *me* she didn't want; it was just no baby at all.

After our carriage came Peter's people, then one father borrowed for the Ohio relatives, then the other children, and all the neighbours followed, and when we reached the high hill where you turn beside the woods, I saw father gather up the lines and brace himself, for Ned and Jo were what he called "mettlesome." "Then came a burst of thunder sound," as it says in "Casabianca," and the horseback riders came sweeping around us, Laddie and the Princess leading. These two rode ahead of us, and the others lined three deep on either side, and the next carriage dropped back and let them close in behind, so Sally and Peter were "in the midst thereof." Instead of throwing old shoes, as always had been done, the Princess coaxed them to throw rice and roses, and every other flower pulled from the bouquets at home, and from the gardens we had passed. Every one was out watching us go by, and when William Justus rode beside the fences crying, "Flowers for the bride! Give us flowers for the bride!" some of the women were so excited they pulled things up by the roots and gave him armloads, and he rode ahead and supplied Laddie and the Princess, and they kept scattering them in the road until every foot of the way to Groveville was covered with flowers, "the fair young flowers that lately sprang and stood." He even made side-cuts into swampy places and gathered armloads of those perfectly lovely, fringy blue gentians, caught up, and filled the carriage and scattered them in a wicked way, because you should only take a few of those rare, late flowers.

Sally looked just as if she had come into her own and was made for it; I never did see her look so pretty, but Peter sweated and acted awful silly. Father had a time with the team. Ned and Jo became excited and just ranted. They simply danced. Laddie had braided their manes and tails, and they waved like silken floss in the sunshine, and the carriage was freshly washed and the patent leather and brass shone, and we rode flower-covered. Ahead, Laddie and the Princess fairly tried themselves. She hadn't put on her hat or habit after all. When Laddie told her they were going to lead, she said: "Very well! Then I shall go as I am. The dress makes no difference. It's the first time I've had a chance to spoil one since I left home."

When the other girls saw what she was going to do, nearly every one of them left off their hats and riding skirts. Every family had saddle horses those days, and when the riders came racing up they looked like flying flowers, they were all laughing, bloom ladened, singing and calling jokes. Ahead, Laddie and the Princess just plain showed off. Her horse came from England with them, and Laddie said it had Arab blood in it, like the one in the Fourth Reader poem, "Fret not to roam the desert now, With all thy winged speed," and the Princess loved her horse more than that man did his. She said she'd starve before she'd sell it, and if her family were starving, she'd go to work and earn food for them, and keep her horse. Laddie's was a Kentucky thoroughbred he'd saved money for years to buy; and he took a young one and trained it himself, almost like a circus horse. Both of them *could* ride; so that day they did. They ran those horses neck and neck, right up the hill approaching Groveville, until they were almost from sight, then they whirled and came sweeping back fast as the wind. The Princess' eyes were like dead coals, and her black curls streamed, the thin silk dress wrapped tight around her and waved back like a gossamer web such as spiders spin in October. Laddie's hair was blowing, his cheeks and eyes were bright, and with one eye on the Princess— she didn't need it—and one on the road, he cut curves, turned, wheeled, and raced, and as he rode, so did she.

"Will they break their foolish necks?" wailed mother.

"They are the handsomest couple I ever have seen in my life!" said father.

"Yes, and you two watch out, or you'll strike trouble right there," said Sally, leaning forward.

I gave her an awful nudge. It made me so happy I could have screamed to see them flying away together like that.

"Well, if that girl represents trouble," said father, "God knows it never before came in such charming guise."

"You can trust a man to forget his God and his immortal soul if a sufficiently beautiful woman comes along," said my mother dryly, and father, Sally, and Peter laughed.

She didn't mean that to be funny, though. You could always tell by the set of her lips and the light in her eyes if she did.

Just this side Groveville we passed a man on horseback. He took off his hat and drew his horse to one side when Laddie and the Princess rode toward him. He had a big roll of papers under his arm, to show that he had been for his mail. But I knew, so did Laddie and the Princess, that he had been compelled to saddle and ride like mad, to reach town and come that far back in time to watch us pass; for it was the Princess' father, and *watch* was exactly what he was doing; he wanted to see for himself. Laddie and the Princess rode straight at him, neck and neck, and then both of them made their horses drop on their knees and they waved a salute, and then they were up and away. Of course father and mother saw, so mother bowed, and father waved his whip as we passed. He sat there like he'd turned the same on horseback as Sabethany had in her coffin; but he had to see almost a mile of us driving our best horses and carriages, wearing our wedding garments and fine raiment, and all that "cavalcade," father called it, of young, reckless riders. You'd have thought if there were a hint of a smile in his whole being it would have shown when Sally leaned from the carriage to let him see that her face and clothes were as good as need be and smiled a lovely smile on him, and threw him a rose. He did leave his hat off and bow low, and then Shelley, always the very dickens for daring, rode right up to him and laughed in his face, and she leaned and thrust a flower into his bony hands; you would have thought he would have been simply forced to smile then, but he looked far more as if he would tumble over and roll from the saddle. My heart ached for a man in trouble like that. I asked the Lord to preserve us from secrets we couldn't tell the neighbours!

At the station there wasn't a thing those young people didn't do. They tied flowers and ribbons all over Sally's satchel and trunk. They sowed rice as if it were seeding time in a wheatfield. They formed a circle around Sally and Peter and as mushy as ever they could they sang, "As sure as the grass grows around the stump, You are my darling sugar lump," while they danced.

When the train came, they put Sally on, and held Peter until Sally got off, and then they put Peter on, and held her until the train really started, and mother was almost scared to death. She said a railroad train was not a safe thing to fool with. But at last it pulled out, and Sally and Peter stood laughing and waving. They just smiled all the time no matter what was done to them. Some of it made me angry, but I suppose to be pleasant was the right way. Sally was strong on always doing the right thing, so she just laughed, and so did all of us. Going home it was wilder yet, for all of them raced and showed how they could ride.

At the house people were hungry again, so the table was set and they ate up every scrap in sight, and Leon and I ate with them that time and saved ours. Then one by one the carriages, spring wagons, and horseback riders went away, all the people saying Sally was the loveliest bride, and hers had been the prettiest wedding they'd ever seen, and the most good things to eat, and Laddie and the Princess went with them. When the last one was gone, and only the relatives from Ohio were left, mother pitched on the bed, gripped her hands and cried as if she'd go to pieces, and father cried too, and all of us, even Mrs. Freshett, who stayed to wash up the dishes. She was so tickled to be there, and see, and help, that mother had hard work to keep her from washing the linen that same night. She did finish the last dish, scrub the kitchen floor, black the stove, and pack all the borrowed china in tubs, ready to be taken home, and things like that. Mother said it was a burning shame for any neighbourhood to let a woman get so starved out and lonesome she'd act that way. She said enough was enough, and when Mrs. Freshett had cooked all day, and washed dishes until the last skillet was in place, she had done as much as any neighbour ought to do, and the other things she went on and did were a rebuke to us.

I felt sore, weepy, and tired out. It made me sick to think of the sage bag in the cracked churn, so I climbed my very own catalpa tree in the corner, watched up the road for Laddie, and thought things over. If I ever get married I want a dress, and a wedding exactly like that, but I would like a man quite different from Peter; like Laddie would suit me better. When he rode under the tree, I dropped from a limb into his arms, and went with him to the barn.

He asked me what was going on at the house, and I told him about Mrs. Freshett being a rebuke to us; and Laddie said she was, and he didn't believe one word against her. When I told him mother was in bed crying like anything, he said: "I knew that had to come when she kept up so bravely at the station. Thank the Lord, she showed her breeding by holding in until she got where she had a right to cry if she pleased."

Then I whispered for fear Leon might be around: "Did he set the dogs on you?"

"He did not," said Laddie, laughing softly.

"Did he call you names again?"

"He did!" said Laddie, "but I started it. You see, when we got there, Thomas was raking the grass and he came to take the Princess' horse. Her father was reading on a bench under a tree. I helped her down, and walked with her to the door and said good-bye, and thanked her for the pleasure she had added to the day for us, loudly enough that he could hear; then I went over to him and said: 'Good evening, Mr. Pryor. If my father knew anything about it, he would very much regret that company from Ohio detained him and compelled me to escort your daughter home. He would greatly have enjoyed the privilege, but I honestly believe that I appreciated it far more than he could.'"

"Oh Laddie, what did he say?"

"He arose and glared at me, and choked on it, and he tried several times, until I thought the clods were going to fly again, but at last he just spluttered: 'You blathering rascal, you!' That was such a compliment compared with what I thought he was going to say that I had to laugh. He tried, but he couldn't keep from smiling himself, and then I said: 'Please think it over, Mr. Pryor, and if you find that Miss Pryor has had an agreeable, entertaining day, won't you give your consent for her to come among us again? Won't you allow me to come here, if it can be arranged in such a way that I intrude on no one?'"

"Oh Laddie!"

"He exploded in a kind of a snarl that meant, I'll see you in the Bad Place first. So I said to him: 'Thank you very much for to-day, anyway. I'm sure Miss Pryor has enjoyed this day, and it has been the happiest of my life—one to be remembered always. Of course

I won't come here if I am unwelcome, but I am in honour bound to tell you that I intend to meet your daughter elsewhere, whenever I possibly can. I thought it would be a better way for you to know and have us where you could see what was going on, if you chose, than for us to meet without your knowledge.'"

"Oh, Laddie," I wailed, "now you've gone and ruined everything!"

"Not so bad as that, Little Sister," laughed Laddie. "Not half so bad! He exploded in another growl, and he shook his walking stick at me, and he said—guess what he said."

"That he would kill you," I panted, clinging to him.

"Right!" said Laddie. "You have it exactly. He said: 'Young man, I'll brain you with my walking stick if ever I meet you anywhere with my daughter, when you have not come to her home and taken her with my permission.'"

"What!" I stammered. "What! Oh Laddie, say it over! Does it mean—?"

"It means," said Laddie, squeezing me until I was near losing my breath, "it means, Little Sister, that I shall march to his door and ask him squarely, and if it is anywhere the Princess wants to go, I shall take her."

"Like, 'See the conquering hero comes?'"

"Exactly!" laughed Laddie.

"What will mother say?"

"She hasn't made up her mind yet," answered Laddie.

"Do you mean—?" I gasped again.

"Of course!" said Laddie. "I wasn't going to let a girl get far ahead of me. The minute I knew she had told her mother, I told mine the very first chance."

"Mother knows that you feel about the Princess as father does about her?"

"Mother knows," answered Laddie, "and so does father. I told both of them."

Both of them knew! And it hadn't made enough difference that any one living right with them every day could have told it. Time and work will be needed to understand grown people.

8

The Shropshire and the Crusader

For, among the rich and gay,
  Fine, and grand, and decked in laces,
None appear more glad than they,
  With happier hearts, or happier faces.

Every one told mother for a week before the wedding that she would be sick when it was over, and sure enough she was. She had been on her feet too much, and had so many things to think about, and there had been such a dreadful amount of work for her and Candace, even after all the neighbours helped, that she was sick in bed and we couldn't find a thing she could eat, until she was almost wild with hunger and father seemed as if he couldn't possibly bear it a day longer.

After Candace had tried everything she could think of, I went up and talked it over with Sarah Hood, and she came down, pretending she happened in, and she tried thickened milk, toast and mulled buttermilk; she kept trying for two days before she gave up. Candace thought of new things, and Mrs. Freshett came and made all the sick dishes she knew, but mother couldn't even taste them; so we were pretty blue, and we nearly starved ourselves, for how could we sit and eat everything you could mention, and mother lying there, almost crying with hunger?

Saturday morning I was hanging around her room hoping maybe she could think of some least little thing I could do for her, even if no more than to bring a glass of water, or a late rose to lay on her pillow; it would be better than not being able to do anything at all. After a while she opened her eyes and looked at me, and I scarcely knew her. She smiled the bravest she could and said: "Sorry for mother, dear?"

I nodded. I couldn't say much, and she tried harder than ever to be cheerful and asked: "What are you planning to do to-day?"

"If you can't think of one thing I can do for you, guess I'll go fishing," I said.

Her eyes grew brighter and she seemed half interested.

"Why, Little Sister," she said, "if you can catch some of those fish like you do sometimes, I believe I could eat one of them."

I never had such a be-hanged time getting started. I slipped from the room, and never told a soul even where I was going. I fell over the shovel and couldn't find anything quick enough but my pocket to put the worms in, and I forgot my stringer. At last, when I raced down the hill to the creek and climbed over the water of the deep place, on the roots of the Pete Billings yowling tree, I had only six worms, my apple sucker pole, my cotton cord line, and bent pin hook. I put the first worm on carefully, and if ever I prayed! Sometimes it was hard to understand about this praying business. My mother was the best and most beautiful woman who ever lived. She was clean, and good, and always helped "the poor and needy who cluster round your door," like it says in the poetry piece, and there never could have been a reason why God would want a woman to suffer herself, when she went flying on horseback even dark nights through rain or snow, to doctor other people's pain, and when she gave away things like she did—why, I've seen her take a big piece of meat from the barrel, and a sack of meal, and heaps of apples and potatoes to carry to Mandy Thomas—when she gave away food by the wagonload at a time, God couldn't have *wanted* her to be hungry, and yet she *was* that very minute almost crying for food; and I prayed, oh how I did pray! and a sneaking old back-ended crayfish took my very first worm. I just looked far into the sky and said: "Well, when it's for a sick woman, can't You do any better than that?"

I suppose I shouldn't have said it, but if it had been your mother, how would you have felt? I pinched the next worm in two, so if a crayfish took that, it wouldn't get but half. I lay down across the roots and pulled my bonnet far over my face and tried to see to the bottom. I read in school the other day:

And by those little rings on the water I know
The fishes are merrily swimming below.

There were no rings on the water, but after a while I saw some fish darting around, only they didn't seem to be hungry; for they would come right up and nibble a tiny bit at my worm, but they wouldn't swallow it. Then one did, so I jerked with all my might, jerked so hard the fish and worm both flew off, and I had only the hook left. I put on the other half and tried again. I prayed straight along, but the tears would come that time, and the prayer was no powerful effort like Brother Hastings would have made; it was little torn up pieces mostly: "O Lord, please do make only one fish bite!" At last one did bite good, so I swung carefully that time, and landed it on the grass, but it was so little and it hit a stone and was killed. I had no stringer to put it back in the water to keep cool, and the sun was hot that day, like times in the fall. Stretched on the roots, with it shining on my back, and striking the water and coming up from below, I dripped with heat and excitement.

I threw that one away, put on another worm, and a big turtle took it, the hook, and broke my line, and almost pulled me in. I wouldn't have let go if it had, for I just had to have a fish. There was no help from the Lord in that, so I quit praying, only what I said when I didn't know it. Father said man was born a praying animal, and no matter how wicked he was, if he had an accident, or saw he had just got to die, he cried aloud to the Lord for help and mercy before he knew what he was doing. That was the truth, because several times that day when the sun almost scorched, and the turtles took the bait, and I had made up my mind the Lord was far away making a new world, where He couldn't possibly know what trouble I was in, why still I knew my voice was begging Him to help me get only one fish.

I could hear the roosters in the barnyard, the turkey gobbler, and the old ganders screamed once in a while, and sometimes a bird sang a skimpy little fall song; nothing like spring, except the killdeers and larks; they were always good to hear—and then the dinner bell rang. I wished I had been where I couldn't have heard that, because I didn't intend going home until I had a fish that would do for mother if I stayed until night. If the best one in the family had to starve, we might as well all go together; but I wouldn't have known how hungry I was, if the bell hadn't rung and told me the others were eating. So I bent another pin and tried again. I lost the next worm without knowing how, and then I turned baby and cried right out loud. I was so thirsty, the salty tears running down my cheeks tasted good, and doing something besides fishing sort of rested me; so I looked around and up at the sky, wiped my face on the skirt of my sunbonnet, and put on another worm. I had only one more left, and I began to wonder if I could wade in and catch a fish by hand; I did teeny ones sometimes, but I knew the water there was far above my head, for I had measured it often with the pole; it wouldn't do to try that; instead of helping mother any, a funeral would kill her, too, so I fell back on the Crusaders, and tried again.

Strange how thinking about them helped. I pretended I was fighting my way to the Holy City, and this was the Jordan just where it met the sea, and I had to catch enough fish to last me during the pilgrimage west or I'd never reach Jerusalem to bring home a shell for the Stanton crest. I pretended so hard, that I got braver and stronger, and asked the Lord more like there was some chance of being heard. All at once there was a jerk that almost pulled me in, so I jerked too, and a big fish flew over my head and hit the bank behind me with a thump. Of course by a big fish I don't mean a red horse so long as my arm, like the boys bring from the river; I mean the biggest fish I ever caught with a pin in our creek. It looked like the whale that swallowed Jonah, as it went over my head. I laid the pole across the roots, jumped up and turned, and I had to grab the stump to keep from falling in the water and dying. There lay the fish, the biggest one I ever had seen, but it was flopping wildly, and it wasn't a foot from a hole in the grass where a muskrat had burrowed through. If it gave one flop that way, it would slide down the hole straight back into the water;

and between me and the fish stood our cross old Shropshire ram. I always looked to see if the sheep were in the meadow before I went to the creek, but that morning I had been so crazy to get something for mother to eat, I never once thought of them—and there it stood!

That ram hadn't been cross at first, and father said it never would be if treated right, and not teased, and if it were, there would be trouble for all of us. I was having more than my share that minute, and it bothered me a lot almost every day. I never dared enter a field any more if it were there, and now it was stamping up and down the bank, shaking its head, and trying to get me; while one flop the fish went *almost* in the hole, and the next a little away from it. Everything put together, I thought I couldn't stand it. I never wanted anything as I wanted that fish, and I never hated anything as I hated that sheep. It wasn't the sheep's fault either; Leon teased it on purpose, just to see it chase Polly Martin; but that was more her doings than his.

She was a widow and she crossed our front meadow going to her sister's. She had two boys big as Laddie, and three girls, and father said they lived like 'the lilies of the field; they toiled not, neither did they spin.' They never looked really hungry or freezing, but they never plowed, or planted, they had no cattle or pigs or chickens, only a little corn for meal, and some cabbage, and wild things they shot for meat, and coons to trade the skins for more powder and lead—bet they ate the coons—never any new clothes, never clean, they or their house. Once when father and mother were driving past, they saw Polly at the well and they stopped for politeness sake to ask how she was, like they always did with every one. Polly had a tin cup of water and was sopping at her neck with a carpet rag, and when mother asked, "How are you, Mrs. Martin?" she answered: "Oh I ain't very well this spring; I gest I got the go-backs!"

Mother said Polly looked as if she'd been born with the "go-backs," and had given them to all her children, her home, garden, fields, and even the *fences*. We hadn't a particle of patience with such people. When you are lazy like that it is very probable that you'll live to see the day when your children will peep through the fence cracks and cry for bread. I have seen those Martin children come mighty near doing it when the rest of us opened our dinner baskets at school; and if mother hadn't always put in enough so that we could divide, I bet they would. If Polly Martin had walked up as if she were alive, and had been washed and neat, and going somewhere to do some one good, Leon never would have dreamed of such a thing as training the Shropshire to bunt her. She was so long and skinny, always wore a ragged shawl over her head, a floppy old dress that the wind whipped out behind, and when she came to the creek, she sat astride the foot log, and hunched along with her hands; that tickled the boys so, Leon began teasing the sheep on purpose to make it get her. But inasmuch as she saw fit to go abroad looking so funny, that any one could see she'd be a perfect circus if she were chased, I didn't feel that it was Leon's fault. If, like the little busy bee, she had "improved each shining hour," he never would have done it. Seems to me, she brought the trouble on her own head.

First, Leon ran at the Shropshire and then jumped aside; but soon it grew so strong and quick he couldn't manage that, so he put his hat on a stick and poked it back and forth through a fence crack, and that made the ram raving mad. At last it would butt the fence until it would knock itself down, and if he dangled the hat again, get right up and do it over. Father never caught Leon, so he couldn't understand what made the sheep so dreadfully cross, because he had thought it was quite peaceable when he bought it. The first time it got after Polly, she threw her shawl over its head, pulled up her skirts, and Leon said she hit just eleven high places crossing an eighty-acre field; she came to the house crying, and father had to go after her shawl, and mother gave her a roll of butter and a cherry pie to comfort her. The Shropshire never really got Polly, but any one could easily see what it would do to me if I dared step around that stump, and it was dancing and panting to begin. If whoever wrote that "Gentle Sheep, pray tell me why," piece ever had seen a sheep acting like that, it wouldn't have been in the books; at least I think it wouldn't, but one can't be sure. He proved that he didn't know much about anything outdoors or he wouldn't have said that sheep were "eating grass and daisies white, from the morning till the night," when daisies are bitter as gall.

Flop! went the fish, and its tail touched the edge of the hole. Then I turned around and picked up the pole. I put my sunbonnet over the big end of it, and poked it at the ram, and drew it back as Leon did his hat. One more jump and mother's fish would be gone. I stood on the roots and waved my bonnet. The sheep lowered its head and came at it with a rush. I drew back the pole, and the sheep's forefeet slid over the edge, and it braced and began to work to keep from going in. The fish gave a big flop and went down the hole. Then I turned Crusader and began to fight, and I didn't care if I were whipped black and blue, I meant to finish that old black-faced Shropshire. I set the pole on the back of its neck and pushed with all my might, and I got it in, too. My! but it made a splash! It wasn't much good at swimming either, and it had no chance, for I stood on the roots and pushed it down with the pole, and hit it over the nose with all my might, and I didn't care how far it came on the cars, or how much money it cost, it never would chase me and make me lose my fish again.

I didn't hear him until he splashed under the roots and then I was so blind angry I didn't really see that it was Laddie; I only knew that it was some one who was going to help out that miserable ram, so I struck and beat with all my might, the sheep when I could hit it, if not, the man.

"You little demon, stop!" cried Laddie.

I got in one good one right on the ram's nose. Then Laddie dropped the sheep and twisted the fish pole from my fingers, and I pushed him as hard as I could, but he was too strong. He lifted the sheep, pulled it to the bank, and rolled it, worked its jaws, and squeezed water from it, and worked and worked.

"Well, I guess you've killed it!" he said at last.

"Goody!" I shouted. "Goody! Oh but I am glad it's dead!"

"What on earth has turned you to a fiend?" asked Laddie, beginning work on the sheep again.

"That ram!" I said. "Ever since Leon made it cross so that it would chase Polly Martin, it's got me oftener than her. I can't go anywhere for it any more, and to-day it made me lose a big fish, and mother is waiting. She thought maybe she could eat some."

Then I just roared. I bet I sounded like Bashan's bull.

"Dear Lord!" said Laddie dropping the sheep and taking me in his wet arms. "Tell me, Biddy! Tell me how it is."

Then I forgot I was a Crusader, and told him all about it as well as I could for choking, and when I finished he bathed my hot face, and helped me from the roots. Then he went and looked down the hole I showed him and he cried out quicklike, and threw himself on the grass, and in a second up came the fish. Some one had rolled a big stone in the hole, so the fish was all right, not even dead yet, and Laddie said it was the biggest one he ever had seen taken from the creek. Then he said if I'd forgive him and all our family, for spoiling the kind of a life I had the perfect right to lead, and if I'd run to the house and get a big bottle from the medicine case quick, he would see to it that some place was fixed for that sheep where it would never bother me again. So I took the fish and ran as fast as I could, but I sent May back with the bottle, and did the scaling myself. No one at our house could do it better, for Laddie taught me the right way long ago, when I was small, and I'd done it hundreds of times.

Then I went to Candace and she put a little bit of butter and a speck of lard in a skillet, and cooked the fish brown. She made a slice of toast and boiled a cup of water and carried it to the door; then she went in and set the table beside the bed, and I took in the tray, and didn't spill a drop. Mother never said a word; she just reached out and broke off a tiny speck and nibbled it, and it stayed; she tried a little bigger piece, and another, and she said: "Take out the bones, Candace!" She ate every scrap of that fish like the hungriest traveller who ever came to our door, and the toast, and drank the hot water. Then she went into a long sleep and all of us walked tiptoe, and when she waked up she was better, and in a few days she could sit in her chair again, and she began getting Shelley ready to go to music school.

I have to tell you the rest, too. Laddie made the ram come alive, and father sold it the next day for more than he paid for it. He said he hoped I'd forgive him for not having seen how it had been bothering me, and that he never would have had it on the place a day if he'd known. The next time he went to town he bought me a truly little cane rod, a real fishing line, several hooks, and a red bobber too lovely to put into the water. I thought I was a great person from the fuss all of them made over me, until I noticed Laddie shrug his

shoulders, and reach back and rub one, and then I remembered.
I went flying, and thank goodness! he held out his arms.

"Oh Laddie! I never did it!" I cried. "I never, never did! I
couldn't! Laddie, I love you best of any one; you know I do!"

"Of course you didn't!" said Laddie! "My Little Sister wasn't anywhere around when that happened. That was a poor little girl I
never saw before, and she was in such trouble she didn't know
what she was doing. And I hope I'll never see her again," he ended,
twisting his shoulder. But he kissed me and made it all right, and
really I didn't do that; I just simply couldn't have struck Laddie.

Marrying off Sally was little worse than getting Shelley ready for
school. She had to have three suits of everything, and a new dress
of each kind, and three hats; her trunk wouldn't hold all there was
to put in it; and father said he never could pay the bills. He had
promised her to go, and he didn't know what in this world to do; because he never had borrowed money in his life, and he couldn't begin; for if he died suddenly, that would leave mother in debt, and
they might take the land from her. That meant he'd spent what he
had in the bank on Sally's wedding, and all that was in the Underground Station, or maybe the station money wasn't his.

Just when he was awfully bothered, mother said to never mind,
she believed she could fix it. She sent all of us into the orchard to
pick the fine apples that didn't keep well, and father made three
trips to town to sell them. She had big jars of lard she wouldn't
need before butchering time came again, and she sold dried apples, peaches, and raspberries from last year. She got lots of
money for barrels of feathers she'd saved to improve her feather
beds and pillows; she said she would see to that later. Father was
so tickled to get the money to help him out that he said he'd get
her a pair of those wonderful new blue geese like Pryors had, that
every one stopped to look at. When there was not quite enough
yet, from somewhere mother brought out money that she'd saved
for a long time, from butter and eggs, and chickens, and turkeys,
and fruit and lard, and things that belonged to her. Father hated to
use it the worst way, but she said she'd saved it for an emergency,
and now seemed to be the time.

She said if the child really had talent, she should be about
developing it, and while there would be many who would have far

finer things than Shelley, still she meant her to have enough that she wouldn't be the worst looking one, and so ashamed she couldn't keep her mind on her work. Father said, with her face it didn't make any difference what she wore, and mother said that was just like a man; it made all the difference in the world what a girl wore. Father said maybe it did to the girl, and other women; what he meant was that it made none to a man. Mother said the chief aim and end of a girl's life was not wrapped up in a man; and father said maybe not with some girls, but it would be with Shelley: she was too pretty to escape. I do wonder if I'm going to be too pretty to escape, when I put on long dresses. Sometimes I look in the glass to see if it's coming, but I don't suppose it's any use. Mother says you can't tell a thing at the growing age about how a girl is going to look at eighteen.

When everything was almost ready, Leon came in one day and said: "Shelley, what about improving your hair? Have you tried your wild grape sap yet?"

Shelley said: "Why, goodness me! We've been so busy getting Sally married, and my clothes made, I forgot all about that. Have you noticed the crock in passing? Is there anything in it?"

"It was about half full, once when I went by," said Leon. "I haven't seen it lately."

"Do please be a dear and look, when you go after the cows this evening," said Shelley. "If there's anything in it, bring it up."

"Do it yourself for want of me,
The boy replied quite manfully,"

quoted Leon from "The Little Lord and the Farmer." He was always teasing.

"I think you're mean as dirt if you don't bring it," said Shelley.

Leon grinned, and you should have heard the nasty, teasing way he said more of that same piece:

"Anger and pride are both unwise,
Vinegar never catches flies—"

I wondered she didn't slap him. You could see she wanted to.

"I can get it myself," she said angrily.

"What will you give me to bring it?" asked Leon, who never missed a chance to make a bargain.

"My grateful thanks. Are they not a proper reward?" asked Shelley.

"Thanks your foot!" said Leon. "Will you bring something pretty from Chicago for Susie Fall's Christmas present?"

Every one laughed, but Leon never cared. He liked Susie best of any of the girls, and he wanted every one to know it. He went straight to her whenever he had a chance, and he'd already told her mother to keep all the other boys away, because he meant to marry her when he grew up, and Widow Fall said that was fair enough, and she'd save her for him. Leon said that was the way to manage the marrying business; pick out a sweet little girl you knew, and make all your plans, and help her grow up like you wanted her, and then you'd have a decent wife, with no going crazy fuss about it. Nevertheless he was crazy enough right then to beat the life almost out of any boy who looked at Susie, for some excuse he'd think up. So Shelley said she would get him something for Susie, and Leon brought the crock. Shelley looked at it sort of dubious-like, tipped it, and stared at the dirt settled in the bottom, and then stuck in her finger and tasted it. She looked at Leon with a queer grin and said: "Smarty, smarty, think you're smart!" She threw the creek water into the swill bucket. No one said a word, but Leon looked much sillier than she did. After he was gone I asked her if she would bring him a Christmas present for Susie *now,* and she said she ought to bring him a pretty glass bottle labelled perfume, with hartshorn in it, and she would, if she thought he'd smell it first.

Shelley felt badly about leaving mother when she wasn't very well; but mother said it was all right, she had Candace to keep house, and May and me, and father, and all of us to take care of her, and it would be best for Shelley to go now and work hard as she could, while she had the chance. So one afternoon father took her trunk to the depot and bought the tickets and got the checks, and the next day Laddie drove to Groveville with father and Shelley, and she was gone. Right at the last, she didn't seem to want to leave so badly, but all of them said she must. Peter's cousin, who had gone last year, was to meet her, and have a room ready where she boarded if she could, and if she couldn't right away, then the first one who left, Shelley was to have the place, so they'd be together.

There were eight of us left, counting Candace and Miss Amelia, and you wouldn't think a house with eight people living in it could be empty, but ours was. Everything seemed to wilt. The roses on the window blinds didn't look so bright as they had; mother said the only way she could get along was to keep right on working. She helped Candace all she could, but she couldn't be on her feet very much, so she sat all day long and peeled peaches to dry, showed Candace how to jelly, preserve, and spice them, and peeled apples for butter and to dry, quantities more than we could use, but she said she always could sell such things, and with the bunch of us to educate yet, we'd need the money.

When it grew cold enough to shut the doors, and have fire at night, first thing after supper all of us helped clear the table, then we took our slates and books and learned our lessons for the next day, and then father lined us against the wall, all in a row from Laddie down, and he pronounced words—easy ones that divided into syllables nicely, for me, harder for May, and so up until I might sit down. For Laddie, May and Leon he used the geography, the Bible, Roland's history, the *Christian Advocate,* and the *Agriculturist.* My! but he had them so they could spell! After that, as memory tests, all of us recited our reading lesson for the next day, especially the poetry pieces. I knew most of them, from hearing the big folks repeat them so often and practise the proper way to read them. I could do "Rienzi's Address to the Romans," "Casabianca," "Gray's Elegy," or "Mark Antony's Speech," but best of all, I liked "Lines to a Water-fowl." When he was tired, if it were not bedtime yet, all of us, boys too, sewed rags for carpet and rugs. Laddie braided corn husks for the kitchen and outside door mats, and they were pretty, and "very useful too," like the dog that got his head patted in McGuffey's Second.

Then they picked the apples. These had to be picked by hand, wrapped in soft paper, packed in barrels, and shipped to Fort Wayne. Where they couldn't reach by hand, they stood on barrels or ladders, and used a long handled picker, so as not to bruise the fruit. Laddie helped with everything through the day, worked at his books at night, and whenever he stepped outside he looked in the direction of Pryors'. He climbed to the topmost limbs of the trees with a big basket, picked it full and let it down with a long piece of clothesline. I loved to be in the orchard when they were working; there were plenty of summer apples to eat yet; it was fun to watch the men, and sometimes I could be useful by handing baskets or heaping up apples to be buried for us. When I was not needed I could play with Bobby and Hezekiah. Mother said I had to turn the jay out before winter, because he was too big and mussy to keep in the house, but if I would, I might let Bobby sleep in the kitchen on cold nights, and I liked Bobby best, anyway. I didn't know if I ever could get another chicken like Bobby, but every summer brought an orchard full of jays and there was no harm in playing with one, if you fed it lots of the right kind of food, and let it go in time to learn to fly well before winter. All I raised flew wherever they pleased.

One night father read about a man who had been hanged for killing another man, and they cut him down too soon, so he came alive, and they had to hang him over; and father got all worked up about it. He said the man who suffered death the first time to "all intents and purposes," so that fulfilled the requirements of the law, and they were wrong when they hanged him again. Laddie said it was a piece of bungling sure enough, but the law said a man must be "hanged by his neck until he was dead," and if he weren't dead, why, it was plain he hadn't fulfilled the requirements of the law, so they were forced to hang him again. Father said that law was wrong; the man never should have been hanged in the first place. They talked and argued until we were all excited about it, and the next evening after school Leon and I were helping pick apples, and when father and Laddie went to the barn with a load we sat down to rest and we thought about what they said.

"Gee, that was tough on the man!" said Leon, "but I guess the law is all right. Of course he wouldn't want to die, and twice over at that, but I don't suppose the man he killed liked to die either. I think if you take a life, it's all right to give your own to pay for it."

"Leon," I said, "some time when you are fighting Absalom

Saunders or Lou Wicks, just awful, if you hit them too hard on some tender spot and kill them, would you want to die to pay for it?"

"I wouldn't want to, but I guess I'd have to," said Leon. "That's the law, and it's as good a way to make it as any. But I'm not going to kill any one. I've studied my physiology hard to find all the spots that will kill. I never hit them behind the ear, or in the pit of the stomach; I just black their eyes, and bloody their snoots, and knock them down on their chins to finish off with."

"Well, suppose they don't study their physiologies like you do, and hit *you* in the wrong place, and kill you, would you want *them* hanged by the neck until they were dead, to pay for it?"

Leon grinned.

"I don't think I'd want anything if I were dead," he said. "I wonder how it feels to die. Now *that* man knew. I'd like to be hanged enough to find out how it goes, and then come back, and brag about it. I don't think it hurts much; I believe I'll try it."

So Leon took the rope Laddie lowered the baskets with, and threw it over a big limb. Then he rolled up a barrel and stood on it and put my sunbonnet on with the crown over his face, for a black cap, and made the rope into a slip noose over his head, and told me to stand back by the apple tree and hold the rope tight, until he said he was hanged enough. Then he stepped from the barrel. It jerked me toward him about a yard, as he came down smash! on his feet. I held with all my might, but he was too heavy—and falling that way. So he went to trying to fix some other plan, and I told him the sensible thing to do would be for him to hang me, because he'd be strong enough to hold me and I could tell him how it felt just as well. So we fixed me up like we had him, and when Leon got the rope stretched, he wrapped it twice around the apple tree so it wouldn't jerk him as it had me, and when he said "Ready," I stepped from the barrel. The last thing I heard was Leon telling me to say when I was hanged enough. I was so heavy, the rope stretched, and I went down until it almost tore off my head, and I couldn't get a single breath, so of course I didn't tell him, and I couldn't get on the barrel, and my tongue went out, and my chest swelled up, and my ears roared, and I kicked and struggled, and all the time I could hear Leon laughing, and shouting to keep it up, that I was dying fine; only he didn't know that I really was, and at last I didn't feel or know anything more.

When I came to, I was lying on the grass, while father was pumping my arms, and Laddie was pouring creek water on my face from his hat, and Leon was running around in circles, clear crazy. I heard father tell him he'd give him a scutching he'd remember to the day of his death; but inasmuch as I had told Leon to do it, I had to grab father and hold to him tight as I could, until I got breath enough to explain how it happened. Even then I wasn't sure what he was going to do.

After all that, when I tried to tell Leon how it felt, he just cried like a baby, and he wouldn't listen to a word, even when he'd wanted to know so badly. He said if I hadn't come back, he'd have gone to the barn and used the swing rope on himself, so it was a good thing I did, for one funeral would have cost enough, when we needed money so badly, not to mention how mother would have felt to have two of us go at once, like she had before. And anyway, it didn't amount to so awful much. It was pretty bad at first, but it didn't last long, and the next day my neck was only a little blue and stiff, and in three days it was all over, only a rough place where the rope grained the skin as I went down; but I never got to tell Leon how it felt; I just couldn't talk him into hearing, and it was quite interesting too; but still I easily saw why the man in the paper would object to dying twice, to pay for killing another man once.

When the apples were picked and the cabbage, beets, turnips, and potatoes were buried, some corn dried in the garret for new meal, pumpkins put in the cellar, the field corn all husked, and the butchering done, father said the work was in such fine shape, with Laddie to help, and there was so much more corn than he needed, for us, and the price was so high, and the turkeys did so well, and everything, that he could pay back what mother helped him, and have quite a sum over.

It was Thanksgiving by that time, and all of Winfield's, Lucy's, Sally and Peter, and our boys came home. We had a big time, all but Shelley; it was too expensive for her to come so far for one day, but mother sent her a box with a whole turkey for herself and her friends; and cake, popcorn, nuts, and just everything that wasn't too drippy. Shelley wrote such lovely letters that mother saved them and after we had eaten as much dinner as we could, she read them before we left the table.

I had heard most of them, but I liked to listen again, because they sounded so happy. You could hear Shelley laugh on every page. She told about how Peter's cousin was waiting when the train stopped. They couldn't room together right away, but they were going to the first chance they had. Shelley felt badly because they were so far apart, but she was in a nice place, where she could go with other girls of the school until she learned the way. She told about her room and the woman she boarded with and what she had to eat; she wrote mother not to worry about clothes, because most of the others were from the country, or small towns, and getting ready to teach, and lots of them didn't have *nearly* as many or as pretty dresses as she did. She told about the big building, the classes, the professors, and of going to public recitals where some of the pupils who knew enough played; and she was working her fingers almost to the bone, so she could next year. She told of people she met, and how one of the teachers took a number of girls in his class to see a great picture gallery. She wrote pages about a young Chicago lawyer she met there, and only a few lines about the pictures, so father said as that was the best collection of art work in Chicago, it was easy enough to see that Shelley had been far more impressed with the man than she had been with the pictures. Mother said she didn't see how he could say a thing like that about the child. Of course she couldn't tell in a letter about hundreds of pictures, but it was easy enough to tell all about a man.

Father got sort of spunky at that, and he said it was mighty little that mattered most, that could be told about a Chicago lawyer; and mother had better caution Shelley to think more about her work, and write less of the man. Mother said that would stop the child's confidences completely and she'd think all the time about the man, and never mention him again, so she wouldn't know what *was* going on. She said she was glad Shelley had found pleasing, refined friends, and she'd encourage her all she could in cultivating them; but of course she'd caution her to be careful, and she'd tell her what the danger was, and after that Shelley wrote and wrote. Mother didn't always read the letters to us, but she answered every one she got that same night. Sometimes she pushed the pen so she jabbed the paper, and often she smiled or laughed softly.

I liked Thanksgiving. We always had a house full of company, and they didn't stay until we were tired of them, as they did at Christmas, and there was as much to eat; the only difference was that there were no presents. It wasn't nearly so much work to fix for one day as it was for a week; so it wasn't so hard on mother and Candace, and father didn't have to spend much money. We were wearing all our clothes from last fall that we could, and our coats from last winter to help out, but we didn't care. We had a lot of fun, and we wanted Sally and Shelley to have fine dresses, because they were in big cities where they needed them, and in due season, no doubt, we would have much more than they, because, as May figured it, there would be only a few of us by that time, so we could have more to spend. That looked sensible, and I thought it would be that way, too. We were talking it over from school one evening, and when we had settled it, we began to play "Dip and Fade." That was a game we made up from being at church, and fall and spring were the only times we could play it, because then the rains filled all the ditches beside the road where the dirt was plowed up to make the bed higher, and we had to have the water to dip in and fade over.

We played it like that, because it was as near as we could come to working out a song Isaac Thomas sang every time he got happy. He had a lot of children at home, and more who had died, from being half-fed and frozen, mother thought; and he was always talking about meeting the "pore innocents" in Heaven, and singing that one song. Every time he made exactly the same speech in meeting. It began like reciting poetry, only it didn't rhyme, but it sort of cut off in lines, and Isaac waved back and forth on his feet, and half sung it, and the rags waved too, but you just couldn't feel any thrills of earnestness about what he said, because he needed washing, and to go to work and get him some clothes and food to fill out his frame. He only looked funny, and made you want to laugh. It took Emanuel Ripley to raise your hair. I don't know why men like my father, and the minister, and John Dover stood it; they talked over asking Isaac to keep quiet numbers of times, but the minister said there were people like that in every church, they always came among the Lord's anointed, and it was better to pluck out your right eye than to offend one of them, and he was doubtful about doing it. So we children all knew that the grown people scarcely could stand Isaac's speech, and prayer, and song, and that they were afraid to tell him plain out that he did more harm than good. Every meeting about the third man up was Isaac, and we had to watch him wave, and rant, and go sing-songy:

"Oh brethering and sistering—ah,
It delights my heart—ah to gather with you,
In this holy house of worship—ah.
In his sacred word—ah,
The Lord—ah tells us,
That we are all his childring—ah.
And now, lemme exhort you to-night—ah.
As one that loves you—ah,
To choose that good part, that Mary chose—ah,
That the worrrr-uld kin neither give ner take away—ah."

That went on until he was hoarse, then he prayed, and arose and sang his song. Other men spoke where they stood. Isaac always walked to the altar, faced the people, and he was tired out when he finished, but so proud of himself, so happy, and he felt so sure that his efforts were worth a warm bed, sausage, pancakes, maple syrup, and coffee for breakfast, that it was mighty seldom he failed to fool some one else into thinking so too, and if he could, he wouldn't have to walk four miles home on cold nights, with no overcoat. In summer, mostly, they let him go. Isaac always was fattest in winter, especially during revivals, but at any time mother said he looked like a sheep's carcass after the buzzards had picked it. It could be seen that he was perfectly strong, and could have fed and clothed himself, and Mandy and the children, quite as well as our father did us, if he had wanted to work, for we had the biggest family of the neighbourhood. So we children made fun of him and we had to hold our mouths shut when he got up all tired and teary-like, and began to quaver:

"Many dear childurn we know dew stan',
Un toon ther harps in the better lan',
Their little hans frum each soundin' string,
Bring music sweet, wile the Anguls sing,
Bring music sweet, wile the Anguls sing,—
  We shell meet them agin on that shore,
  We shell meet them agin on that shore,
  With fairer face, un angel grace,
  Each loved un ull welcome us ther.

"They uster mourn when the childurn died,
Un said goo-bye at the river side,
They dipped ther feet in the glidin' stream
Un faded away, like a loveli dream,
Un faded away like a loveli dream."

Then the chorus again, and then Isaac dropped on the front seat exhausted, and stayed there until some good-hearted woman, mostly my mother, felt so sorry about his shiftlessness she asked him to go home with us and warmed and fed him, and put him in the traveller's bed to sleep. The way we played it was this: we stood together at the edge of a roadside puddle and sang the first verse and the chorus exactly as Isaac did. Then I sang the second verse, and May was one of the "many dear childurn," and as I came to the lines she dipped her feet in the "glidin' stream," and for "fading away," she jumped across.

Now May was a careful little soul, and always watched what she was doing, so she walked up a short way, chose a good place, and when I sang the line, she was almost birdlike, she dipped and faded so gracefully. Then we laughed like dunces, and then May began to sway and swing, and drone through her nose for me, and I was so excited I never looked. I just dipped and faded on the spot. I faded all right too, for I couldn't jump nearly across, and when I landed in pure clay that had been covered with water for three weeks, I went down to my knees in mud, to my waist in water, and lost my balance and fell backward.

A man passing on horseback pried me out with a rail and helped me home. Of course he didn't know how I happened to fall in, and I was too chilled to talk. I noticed May only said I fell, so I went to bed scorched inside with red pepper tea, and never told a word about dipping and fading. Leon whispered and said he bet it was the last time I would play that, so as soon as my coat and dress were washed and dried, and I could go back to school, I did it again, just to show him I was no cowardy-calf; but I had learned from May to choose a puddle I could manage before I faded.

CHAPTER
9

"Even So"

All things whatsoever ye would
That men should do to you,
Do ye even so to them.

Our big girls and boys always made a dreadful fuss and said we would catch every disease you could mention, but mother and father were set about it, just like the big rocks in the hills. They said they, themselves, once had been at the mercy of the people, and they knew how it felt. Mother said when they were coming here in a wagon, and she had ridden until she had to walk to rest her feet, and held a big baby until her arms became so tired she drove while father took it, and when at last they saw a house and stopped, she said if the woman hadn't invited her in, and let her cook on the stove, given her milk and eggs, and furnished her a bed to sleep in once in a while, she couldn't have reached here at all; and she never had been refused once. Then she always quoted: "All things whatsoever ye would that men should do to you, do ye *even so* to them."

Father said there were men who made a business of splitting hairs, and of finding different meanings in almost everything in the Bible. I would like to have seen any one split hairs about that, or it made to mean something else. Of all the things in the Bible that you had to do because it said to, whether you liked it or not, that was the one you struck oftenest in life and it took the hardest pull to obey. It was just the hatefulest text of any, and made you squirm most. There was no possible way to get around it. It meant, that if you liked a splinter new slate, and a sharp pencil all covered with gold paper, to make pictures and write your lessons, when Clarissa Polk sat next you and sang so low the teacher couldn't hear until she put herself to sleep on it, "I *wisht* I had a slate! I wisht I *had* a slate! I wisht I had a *slate!* Oh, I *wisht I had a slate!"*— it meant that you just had to wash up yours and stop making pictures yourself, and pass it over; you even had to smile when you offered it, if you did it right. I seldom got through it as the Lord would, for any one who loaned Clarissa a slate knew that it would come back with greasy, sweaty finger marks on it you almost had to dig a hole to wash off, and your pencil would be wet. How on earth do people get clammy fingers, like all the Polks have? And if there were the least flaw of crystal in the pencil, she found it, and bore down so hard that what she wrote never would come off.

The Lord always seemed bigger and more majestic to me, than at any other time, when I remembered that He could have known all that, and yet smiled as He loaned Clarissa His slate. And that old Bible thing meant, too, that if you would like it if you were travelling a long way, say to California to hunt gold, or even just to Indiana, to find a farm fit to live on—it meant that if you were tired, hungry, and sore, and would want to be taken in and fed and rested, you had to let in other people when they reached your house. Father and mother had been through it themselves, and they must have been tired as could be, before they reached Sarah Hood's and she took them in, and rested and fed them, even when they were only a short way from the top of the Little Hill, where next morning they looked down and stopped the wagon, until they chose the place to build their house. Sarah Hood came along, and helped mother all day, so by night she was settled in the old cabin that was on the land, and ready to go to work making money to build a new one, and then a big house, and fix the farm all beautiful like it was then. They knew so well how it felt, that they kept one bed in the boys' room, and any man who came at dusk got his supper, to sleep there, and his breakfast, and there never was anything to pay. The girls always scolded dreadfully about the extra washing, but mother said she slept on sheets when she came out, and some one washed them.

One time Sally said: "Mother, have you ever figured out how many hundred sheets you've washed since, to pay for that?"

Mother said: "No, but I just hope it will make a stack high enough for me to climb from into Heaven."

Sally said: "The talk at the church always led me to think that you flew to Heaven."

Mother answered: "So I get there, I don't mind if I creep."

Then Sally knew it was time to stop. We always knew. And we stopped, too!

We had heard that "All things" quotation, until the first two words were as much as mother ever needed repeat of it any more, and we had cooked, washed for, and waited on people travelling, until Leon got so when he saw any one coming—of course we knew all the neighbours, and their horses and wagons and carriages—he always said: "Here comes another 'Even So!'" He said we had done "even so" to people until it was about our share, but mother said our share was going to last until the Lord said, "Well done, good and faithful servant," and took us home. She had much more about the stranger at the gate and entertaining angels unawares; why, she knew every single thing in the Bible that meant it was her duty to feed and give a bed to any one, no matter how dirty or miserable looking he was! So when Leon came in one evening at dusk and said, "There's another 'Even So' coming down the Little Hill!" all of us knew that we'd have company for the night, and we had.

I didn't like that man, but some of the others seemed to find him amusing. Maybe it was because I had nothing to do but sit and watch him, and so I saw more of him than the ones who came and went all the time. As long as there was any one in the room, he complained dreadfully about his sore foot, and then cheered up and talked, and he could tell interesting things. He was young, but he must have been most everywhere and seen everything. He was very brave and could stand off three men who were going to take from him the money he was carrying to buy a piece of land in

Illinois. It was exactly like father had walked here from Ohio to buy our land, but only two men followed him, and he saw them, so he slipped from a side door and went a different way for a few miles, and they didn't find him again. Father never hunted trouble, but he faced it, if it came to him. That seemed a familiar story, but from the way the man boasted, you would have thought he had a bank in his pocket, and could have shown Adam Poe how to whip Big Foot much easier than he did. The minute the grown folks left the room to milk, do the night feeding, and begin supper, he twisted in his chair and looked at every door, and went and stood at the back dining-room window, where he could see the barn and what was out there, and coming back he took a peep into father's and mother's room, and although he limped dreadfully when he came, he walked like any one when he went over and picked up father's gun and looked to see if it were loaded, and seemed mighty glad when he found it wasn't. Father said he could load in a flash when it was necessary, but he was dubious about a loaded gun in a houseful of children. Not one of us ever touched it, until the boys were big enough to have permission, like Laddie and Leon had. He said a gun was such a great "moral persuader," that the sight of one was mostly all that was needed, and no one could tell by looking at it whether it was loaded or not. This man could, for he examined the lock and smiled in a pleased way over it, and he never limped a step going back to his chair. He kept right on complaining, until father told him before bedtime that he had better stay and rest a day or two, and mother said that would be a good idea.

He talked so much we couldn't do our lessons or spell very well, but it was Friday and we'd have another chance Saturday, so it didn't make so much difference. Father said the traveller must be tired and sleepy and Leon should take a light and show him to bed. He stayed so long father went to the foot of the stairway, and asked him why he didn't come down and he said he was in bed too. The next morning he was sleepy at breakfast and Laddie said it was no wonder, because Leon and the traveller were talking when he went upstairs. The man turned to father and said: "That's a mighty smart boy you have, Mr. Stanton." Father frowned and said: "Praise to the face is open disgrace. I hope he will be smart enough not to disgrace us, anyway."

The traveller said he was sure he would be, and we could see that he had taken a liking to Leon, for he went with him to the barn to help do the morning feeding. They stayed so long mother sent me to call them, and when I got there, the man was telling Leon how foolish it was for boys to live on a farm; how they never would amount to anything unless they went to cities, and about all the fun there was there, and how nice it was to travel, even along the roads, because every one fed you, and gave you a good bed. He forgot that walking had made his foot lame, and I couldn't see, to save me, why he was going to spend his money to buy a farm, if he thought a town the only place where it was fit to live.

He stayed all Saturday, and father said Sunday was no suitable time to start on a journey again, and the man's foot was bad by spells, mostly when father was around, so it would be better to wait until Monday. The traveller tagged Leon and told him what a fine fellow he was, how smart he was, and to prove it, Leon boasted about everything he knew, and showed the man all over the farm.

I even saw them pass the Station in the orchard, and heard Leon brag how father had been an agent for the Governor; but of course he didn't really show him the place, and probably it would have made no difference if he had, for all the money must have been spent on Sally's wedding. Of course father might have put some there he had got since, or that money might never have been his at all, but it seemed as if it would be, because it was on his land.

Sunday evening all of us attended church, but the traveller was too tired, so when Leon said he'd stay with him, father thought it was all right. I could see no one wanted to leave the man alone in the house. He said they'd go to bed early, and we came in quite late. The lamp was turned low, the door unlocked, and everything in place. Laddie went to bed without a candle, and said he'd undress and slip in easy so as not to waken them.

In the morning when he got up the traveller's bed hadn't been slept in, and neither had Leon's. The gun was gone, and father stared at mother, and mother stared at Laddie, and he turned and ran straight toward the Station, and in a minute he was back, whiter than a plate. He just said: "All gone!" Father and mother both sat down suddenly and hard. Then Laddie ran to the barn and came back and said none of the horses had been taken. Soon they went into the parlour and shut the door, and when they came out father staggered and mother looked exactly like Sabethany. Laddie ran to the barn, saddled Flos and rode away. Father wanted to ring an alarm on the dinner bell, like he had a call arranged to get all the neighbours there quickly if we had sickness or trouble, and mother said: "Paul, you shall not! He's so young! We've got to keep this as long as we can, and maybe the Lord will help us find him, and we can give him another chance."

Father started to say something, and mother held up her hand and just said, "Paul!" and he sank back in the chair and kept still. Mother always had spoken of him as "the Head of the Family," and here he wasn't at all! He minded her quickly as I would.

When Miss Amelia came downstairs they let her start to school and never told her a word, but mother said May and I were not to go. So I slipped out and ran through the orchard to look at the Station, and sure enough! the stone was rolled back, the door open and the can lying on the floor. I slid down and picked it up, and there was one sheet of paper money left in it stuck to the sides. It was all plain as a pikestaff. Leon must have thought the money had been spent, and showed the traveller the Station, just to brag, and he guessed there might be something there, and gone while we were at church and taken it. He had all night the start of us, and he might have a horse waiting somewhere, and be almost to Illinois by this time, and if the money belonged to father, there would be no Christmas; and if happened to be the money the county gave him to pay the men who worked the roads every fall, and Miss Amelia, or collections from the church, he'd have to pay it back, even if it put him in debt; and if he died, they might take the land, like he said; and where on earth was Leon? Knew what he'd done and hiding, I bet! He needed the thrashing he would get that time, and I started out to hunt him and have it over with, so mother wouldn't be uneasy about him yet; and then I remembered Laddie had said Leon hadn't been in bed all night. He was gone too!

Maybe he wanted to try life in a city, where the traveller had said everything was so grand; but he must have known that he'd kill his mother if he went, and while he didn't kiss her so often, and talk so much as some of us, I never could see that he didn't run quite as fast to get her a chair or save her a step. He was so slim and light he could race for the doctor faster than Laddie or father, either one. Of course he loved his mother, just as all of us did; he never, never could go away and not let her know about it. If he had gone, that watchful-eyed man, who was lame only part of the time, had taken the gun and made him go. I thought I might as well save the money he'd overlooked so I gripped it tight in my hand, and put it in my apron pocket, the same as I had Laddie's note to the Princess, and started to the barn, on the chance that Leon might be hiding. I knew precious well I would, if I were in his place. So I hunted the granaries, the haymow, the stalls, then I stood on the threshing floor and cried: "Leon! If you're hiding come quick! Mother will be sick with worrying and father will be so glad to see you, he won't do anything much. Do please hurry!"

Then I listened, and all I could hear was a rat gnawing at a corner of the granary under the hay. Might as well have saved its teeth, it would strike a strip of tin when it got through, but of course it couldn't know that. Then I went to every hole around the haystack, where the cattle had eaten; none were deep yet, like they would be later in the season, and all the way I begged of Leon to come out. Once a rooster screamed, flew in my face, and scared me good, but no Leon; so I tried the corn crib, the implement shed, and the wood house. I climbed the ladder with the money still gripped in one hand, and then slipped in the front door, up the stairs, and searched the garret, even away back where I didn't like to very well. At last I went to the dining-room, and I don't think either father or mother had moved, while Sabethany turned to stone looked good compared with them. Seemed as if it would have been better if they'd cried, or scolded, or anything but just sit there as they did, when you could see by their moving once in a while that they were alive. In the kitchen Candace and May finished the morning work, and both of them cried steadily. I slipped to May, "Whose money was it?" I whispered. "Father's, or the county's, or the church's?"

"All three," said May.

"The traveller took it."

"How would he find it? None of us knew there was such a place before."

"Laddie seemed to know!"

"Oh Laddie! Father trusts him about everything."

"They don't think *he* told?"

"Of course not, silly. It's Leon who is gone!"

"Leon may have told about the Station!" I cried. "He didn't touch the money. He never touched it!"

Then I looked at father, and went straight to him. Keeping a secret was one thing; seeing the only father you had look like that, was another. I held out the money.

"There's one piece old Even So didn't get, anyway," I said. "Found it on the floor of the Station, where it was stuck to the can. And I thought Leon must be hiding for fear he'd be whipped for telling, but I've hunted where we usually hide, and promised him everything under the sun if he'd come out; but he didn't, so I guess that traveller man must have used the gun to make him go along."

Father sat and stared at me. He never offered to touch the money, not even when I held it against his hand. So I saw that money wasn't the trouble, else he'd have looked quick enough to see how much I had. They were thinking about Leon being gone, at least father was. Mother called me to her and asked: "You knew about the Station?"

I nodded.

"When?"

"On the way back from taking Amanda Deam her ducks this summer."

"Leon was with you?"

"He found it."

"What were you doing?"

"Sitting on the fence eating apples. We were wondering why that ravine place wasn't cleaned up, when everywhere else was, and then Leon said there might be a reason. He told about having seen a black man, and that he was hidden some place, and we hunted there and found it. We rolled back the stone, and opened the door, and Leon went in, and both of us saw a can full of money."

"Go on!"

"We didn't touch it, mother! Truly we didn't! Leon said we'd found something not intended for children, and we'd be whipped sick if we ever went near or told, and we never did, not even once, unless Leon wanted to boast to the traveller man, but if he showed him the place, he thought sure the money had all been spent on the wedding and sending Shelley away."

Father's arms shot out, and his head pitched on the table. Mother got up and began to walk the floor, and never went near or even touched him. I couldn't bear it. I went and pulled his arm and put the bill under his hand.

"Leon didn't take your money! He didn't! He didn't! I just know he didn't! He does tricks because they are so funny, or he thinks they'll be, but he doesn't steal! He doesn't touch a single thing that is not his, only melons, or chicken out of the skillet, or bread from the cellar; but not money and things. I take gizzards and bread myself, but I don't steal, and Leon or none of us do! Oh father, we don't! Not one of us do! Don't you remember about 'Thou shalt not,' and the Crusaders? Leon's the best fighter of any of us. I'm not sure that he couldn't even whip Laddie, if he got mad enough! Maybe he can't whip the traveller if he has the gun, but, father, Leon simply couldn't take the money. Laddie will stay home and work, and all of us. We can help get it back. We can sell a lot of things. Laddie will sell Flos before he'll see you suffer so; and all of us will give up Christmas, and we'll work! We'll work as hard as ever we can, and maybe you could spare the little piece Joe Risdell wants to build his cabin on. We can manage about the money, father, indeed we can. But you don't dare think Leon took it! He never did! Why, he's yours! Yours and mother's!"

Father lifted his head and reached out his arms.

"You blessing!" he said. "You blessing from the Lord!"

Then he gave me a cold, stiff kiss on the forehead, went to mother, took her arm, and said: "Come, mommy, let's go and tell the Lord about it, and then we'll try to make some plan. Perhaps Laddie will be back with word soon."

But he had to almost carry her. Then we could hear him praying, and he was so anxious, and he made it so earnest it sounded exactly like the Lord was in our room and father was talking right to

His face. I tried to think, and this is what I thought: As father left the room, he looked exactly as I had seen Mr. Pryor more than once, and my mother had both hands gripped over her heart, and she said we must not let any one know. Now if something could happen to us to make my father look like the Princess' and my mother hold her heart with both hands, and if no one were to know about it like they had said, how were we any different from Pryors? We might be of the Lord's anointed, but we could get into the same kind of trouble the infidels could, and have secrets ourselves, or at least it seemed as if it might be very nearly the same, when it made father and mother look and act the way they did. I wondered if we'd have to leave our lovely, lovely home, cross a sea and be strangers in a strange land, as Laddie said; and if people would talk about us, and make us feel that being a stranger was the loneliest, hardest thing in all the world. Well, if mysteries are like this, and we have to live with one days and years, the Lord have mercy on us! Then I saw the money lying on the table, so I took it and put it in the Bible. Then I went out and climbed the catalpa tree to watch for Laddie.

Soon I saw a funny thing, such as I never before had seen. Coming across the fields straight toward our house, sailing over the fences like a bird, came the Princess on one of her horses. Its legs stretched out so far its body almost touched the ground, and it lifted up and swept over the rails. She took our meadow fence lengthwise-like, and at the hitching rack she threw the bridle over the post, dismounted, and then I saw she had been riding astride, like a man. I ran before her and opened the sitting-room door, but no one was there, so I went on to the dining-room. Father had come in, and mother was sitting in her chair. Both of them looked at the Princess coming through the house that way, and never said a word.

She stopped inside the dining-room door and spoke breathlessly, as if she as well as the horse had raced.

"I hope I'm not intruding," she said, "but a man north of us told our Thomas in the village that robbers had taken quite a large sum of hidden money you held for the county, and church, and of your own, and your gun, and got away while you were at church last night. Is it true?"

"Practically," said my father.

"When my mother heard it," said the Princess, "the only way I could keep her from coming to you was to come myself. She isn't strong. She has—she has—heart trouble, very badly; and I feared she'd become excited, so I came for her. What she wanted you told was this: I don't know that it will help you any, or do the least good, but she couldn't rest until I came, so I am here."

Then my mother motioned toward a chair.

"You are kind to come," she said. "Won't you be seated?"

The Princess stepped to the chair, but she gripped the back in both hands and stood straight, breathing fast, her eyes shining with excitement, her lips and cheeks red, so lovely you just had to look, and look.

"No," she said. "I'll tell you why I came, and then if there is nothing I can do here, and no errand I can ride for you, I'll go. Mother has heart trouble, the worst in all the world, the kind no doctor can ever hope to cure, and sometimes, mostly at night, she is driven to have outside air. She seems to suffocate if she isn't in the open. Last night she was unusually ill, and I heard her leave the house, after I'd gone to my room. I watched from my window and saw her take a seat on a bench under the nearest tree. I was moving around and often I looked to see if she were still there. Then the dogs began to rave, and I hurried down. They used to run free, but lately, on account of her going out, father has been forced to tie them at night. They were straining at their chains, and barking dreadfully. I met her at the door, but she would only say some one passed and gave her a fright. When Thomas came in and told what he had heard, she said instantly that she had seen the man.

"She said he was about the size of Thomas, that he came from your direction, that he ran when our dogs barked, but he kept beside the fences, and climbed over where there were trees. He crossed our barnyard and went toward the northwest. Mother saw him distinctly as he reached the road, and she said he was not a large man, he stooped when he ran, and she thought he moved like a slinking, city thief. She is sure he's the man who took your money; she says he acted exactly as if he were trying to escape pursuit; but I was to be *sure* to tell you that he didn't carry a gun. If your gun is gone, there must have been two, and the other man took that and went a different way. Did two men stop here?"

"No," said father. "Only one."

The Princess looked at him thoughtfully.

"Do you think, Mr. Stanton," she said, "that the man who took the money would burden himself with a gun? Isn't a rifle heavy for one in flight to carry?"

"It is," said father. "Your mother saw nothing of two men?"

"Only one, and she knows he didn't carry a gun. Except the man you took in, no stranger has been noticed around here lately?"

"No one. We are quite careful. Even the gun was not loaded as it stood; whoever took it carried the ammunition also, but he couldn't fire until he loaded."

Father turned to the corner where the gun always stood and then he stooped and picked up two little white squares from the floor. They were bits of unbleached muslin in which he wrapped the bullets he made for the gun.

"The rifle was loaded before starting, and in a hurry," he said, as he held up the squares of muslin. Then he scratched a match, bent, and ran it back and forth over the floor, and at one place there was a flash, and the flame went around in funny little fizzes as it caught a grain of powder here and there. "You see the measure was overrun."

"Wouldn't the man naturally think the gun was loaded, and take it as it stood?"

"That would be a reasonable conclusion," said father.

"But he looked!" I cried. "That first night when you and the boys went to the barn, and the girls were getting supper, he looked at the gun, and he *liked* it when he saw it wasn't loaded. He smiled. And he didn't limp a mite when I was the only one in the room. He and Leon knew it wasn't loaded, and I guess he didn't load it, for he liked having it empty so well."

"Ummmm!" said father. "What it would save in this world if a child only knew when to talk and when to keep still. Little Sister, the next time you see a stranger examine my gun when I'm not in the room, suppose you take father out alone and whisper to him about it."

"Yes, sir," I said.

The way I wished I had told that at the right time made me dizzy, but then there were several good switchings I'd had for telling things, besides what Sally did to me about her and Peter. I would have enjoyed knowing how one could be sure. Hereafter, it will be all right about the gun, anyway.

"Could I take my horse and carry a message anywhere for you? Are both your sons riding to tell the neighbours?"

Father hesitated, but it seemed as if he stopped to think, so I just told her: "Laddie is riding. Leon didn't take a horse."

Father said there was nothing she could do, so she took my hand and we started for the gate.

"I do hope they will find him, and get the money, and give him what he deserves!" she cried.

"Yes, father and mother are praying that they'll find him," I said. "It doesn't seem to make the least difference to them about the money. Father didn't even look at a big paper piece I found where it was hidden. But they are anxious about the man. Mother says he is so young, we just must find him, and keep this a secret, and give him another chance. You won't tell, will you?"

The Princess stood still on our walk, and then of all things! if she didn't begin to go Sabethany like. The colour left her cheeks and lips and she shivered and shook and never said one word. I caught her arm. "Say, what ails you?" I cried. "You haven't gone and got heart trouble too, have you?"

She stood there trembling, and then, wheeling suddenly, ran back into the house, and went to my mother. On her knees, the Princess buried her face in mother's breast and said: "Oh Mrs. Stanton! Oh, if I only could help you!"

She began to cry as if something inside her had broken, and she'd shake to pieces.

Mother stared above her head at father, with her eyebrows raised high, and he waved his hand toward me. Mother turned to me, but already she had put her arms around the Princess, and was trying to hold her together.

"What did you tell her that made her come back?" she asked sternlike.

"You forgot to explain that the man was so young, and you

wanted to keep it a secret and give him another chance," I said. "I just asked her not to tell."

Mother looked at father and all the colour went from her face, and she began to shake. He stared at her, then he opened her door and lifted the Princess with one arm, and mother with the other, and helped them into mother's room, stepped back and closed the door. After a while it opened and they came out together, with both mother's arms around the Princess, and she had cried until she staggered. Mother lifted her face and kissed her, when they reached the door and said: "Tell your mother I understand enough to sympathize. Carry her my love. I do wish she would give herself the comfort of asking God to help her."

"She does! Oh, I'm sure she does!" said the Princess. "It's father who has lost all judgment and reason."

Father went with her to the gate, and this time she needed help to mount her horse, and she left it to choose its way and go where it pleased on the road. When father came in he looked at mother, and she said: "I haven't the details, but she understands too well. The Pryor mystery isn't much of a mystery any more. God help their poor souls, and save us from suffering like that!"

She said so little and meant so much, I couldn't figure out exactly what she did mean, but father seemed to understand.

"I've often wondered," he said, but he didn't say what he wondered, and he hurried to the barn and saddled our best horse and came in and began getting ready to ride, and we knew he would go northwest. I went back to the catalpa tree and wondered myself; but it was too much for me to straighten out: just why my mother wanting to give the traveller man another chance would make the Princess feel like that. If she had known my mother as I did, she'd have known that she *always* wanted to give every man a second chance, no matter whether he was young or old.

Then I saw Laddie coming down the Big Hill beside the church, but he was riding so fast I thought he wouldn't want to bother with me, so I slid from the tree, and ran to tell mother. She went to the door and watched as he rode up, but you could see by his face he had not heard of them.

"Nothing, but I have some men out. I am going east now," he said. "I wish, father, you would rub Flos down, blanket her, and if you can, walk her slowly an hour while she cools off. I am afraid I've ruined her. How much had you there?"

"I haven't stopped to figure," said father. "I think I'd better take the horse I have ready and go on one of the northwest roads. The Pryor girl was here a few moments ago, and her mother saw a man cross their place about the right time last evening. He ran and acted suspiciously when the dogs barked. But he was alone and he didn't have a gun."

"Was she sure?"

"Positive."

"Then it couldn't have been our man, but I'll ride in that direction and start a search. They would keep to the woods, I think! You'd better stay with mother. I'll ask Jacob Hood to take your place."

So Laddie rode away again without even going into the house, and mother said to father: "What can he be saying to people, that the neighbours don't come?"

Father answered: "I don't know, but if any one can save the situation, Laddie will."

Mother went to bed, while father sat beside her reading aloud little scraps from the Bible, and they took turns praying. From the way they talked to the Lord, you could plainly see that they were reminding Him of all the promises He had made to take care of people, comfort those in trouble, and heal the broken-hearted. One thing was so curious, I asked May if she noticed, and she had. When they had made such a fuss about money only a short while before, and worked so hard to get our share together, and when they would have to pay back all that belonged to the county and church, neither of them ever even mentioned money then. Every minute I expected father to ask where I'd put the piece I found, and when he opened right at it, in the Bible, he turned on past, exactly as if it were an obituary, or a piece of Sally's wedding dress, or baby hair from some of our heads. He went on hunting places where the Lord said sure and strong that He'd help people who loved Him. When either of them prayed, they asked the Lord to help those near them who were in trouble, as often and earnestly as they begged Him to help them. There were no people near us who were in trouble that we knew of, excepting Pryors. Hard as father and mother worked, you'd have thought the Lord wouldn't have minded if they asked only once to get the money back, or if they forgot the neighbours, but they did neither one. May said because they were big like that was why all of us loved them so.

I would almost freeze in the catalpa, but as I could see far in all directions there, I went back, and watched the roads, and when I remembered what Laddie had said, I kept an eye on the fields too. At almost dusk, and frozen so stiff I could scarcely hang to the limb, I heard the bulldogs at Pryors' begin to rave. They kept on steadily, and I thought Gypsies must be passing. Then from the woods came a queer party that started across the cornfield toward the Big Meadow in front of the house, and I thought they were hunters. I stood in the tree and watched until they climbed the meadow fence, and by that time I could see plainly.

The traveller man got over first, then Leon and the dogs, and then Mr. Pryor handed Leon the gun, leaped over, and took it. I looked again, and then fell from the tree and almost bursted. As soon as I could get up, and breathe, I ran to the front door, screaming: "Father! Father! Come open the Big Gate. Leon's got him, but he's so tired Mr. Pryor is carrying the gun, and helping him walk!"

Just like one, all of us ran; father crossed the road and opened the gate. The traveller man wouldn't look up, he just slouched along. But Leon's chin was up and his head high. He was scratched, torn, and dirty. He was wheezing every breath most from his knees, and Mr. Pryor half carried him and the gun. When they met us, Leon reached in his trousers pocket and drew out a big roll of money that he held toward father. "My fault!" he gasped. "But I got it back for you."

Then he fell over and father caught him in his arms and carried him into the house, and laid him on the couch in the dining-room. Mr. Pryor got down and gathered up the money from the road. He followed into the house and set the gun in the corner.

"Don't be frightened," he said to mother. "The boy has walked all night, and all day, with no sleep or food, and the gun was a heavy load for him. I gathered from what he said, when the dogs let us know they were coming, that this hound took your money. Your dog barked and awakened the boy and he loaded the gun and followed. The fellow had a good start and he didn't get him until near daybreak. It's been a stiff pull for the youngster and he seems to feel it was his fault that this cowardly cur you sheltered learned where you kept your money. If that is true, I hope you won't be hard on him!"

Father was unfastening Leon's neckband, mother was rubbing his hands, Candace was taking off his shoes, and May was spilling water father had called for, all over the carpet, she shook so. When Leon drew a deep breath and his head rolled on the pillow, father looked at Mr. Pryor. I don't think he heard all of it, but he caught the last words.

"'Hard on him! Hard on him!'" he said, the tears rolling down his cheeks. "'This my son, who was lost, is found!'"

"Oh!" shouted Mr. Pryor, slamming the money on the table. "Poor drivel to fit the circumstances. If I stood in your boots, sir, I would rise up in the mighty strength of my pride and pull out foundation stones until I shook the nation! I never envied mortal man as I envy you to-day!"

Candace cried out: "Oh look, his poor feet! They are blistered and bleeding!"

Mother moved down a little, gathered them in her arms, and began kissing them. Father wet Leon's lips and arose. He held out his hand, and Mr. Pryor took it.

"I will pray God," he said, "that it may happen 'even so' to you."

Leon opened his eyes and caught only the last words.

"You had better look out for the 'Even So's,' father," he said.

And father had to laugh, but Mr. Pryor went out, and slammed the door, until I looked to see if it had cracked from top to bottom; but we didn't care if it had, we were so happy over having Leon back.

I went and picked up the money and carried it to father to put away, and that time he took it. But even then he didn't stop to see if he had all of it.

"You see!" I said, "I told you —"

"You did indeed!" said father. "And you almost saved our reason. There are times when things we have come to feel we can't live without, so press us, that money seems of the greatest importance. This is our lesson. Hereafter, I and all my family, who have been through this, will know that money is not even worth thinking about when the life and honour of one you love hangs in the balance. When he can understand, your brother shall know of the wondrous faith his Little Sister had in him."

"Maybe he won't like what you and mother thought. Maybe we better not tell him. I can keep secrets real well. I have several big ones I've never told, and I didn't say a word about the Station when Leon said I shouldn't."

"After this there will be no money kept on the place," said father. "It's saving time at too great cost. All we have goes into the bank, and some of us will cheerfully ride for what we want, when we need it. As for not telling Leon, that is as your mother decides. For myself, I believe I'd feel better to make a clean breast of it."

Mother heard, for she sobbed as she bathed Leon's feet, and when his eyes came open so they'd stay a little while, he kept looking at her so funny, between sips of hot milk.

"Don't *cry,* mammy!" he said. "*I'm* all right. Sorry such a rumpus! Let him fool me. Be smart as the next fellow, after this! Know how glad you are to get the money!"

Mother sat back on her heels and roared as I do when I step in a bumblebee's nest, and they get me. Leon was growing better every minute, and he stared at her, and then his dealish, funny old grin began to twist his lips and he cried: "Oh golly! You thought *I* helped take it and went with him, didn't you?"

"Oh my son, my son!" wailed mother until she made me think of Absalom under the oak.

"Well, I be ding-busted!" said Leon, sort of slow and wondering-like, and father never opened his head to tell him that was no way to talk.

Mother cried more than ever, and between sobs she tried to explain that I heard what the traveller man had said about how bad it was to live in the country; and how Leon was now at an age where she'd known boys to get wrong ideas, and how things looked, and in the middle of it he raised on his elbow and took her in his arms and said: "Well of all the geese! And I 'spose father was in it too! But since it's the first time, and since it is you — Go to bed now, and let me sleep — But see that you don't ever let this happen again."

Then he kissed her over and over and clung to her tight and at last dropped back and groaned:

*"My reputation, O my reputation!
I've lost my reputation!"*

She had to laugh while the tears were still running, and father and Laddie looked at each other and shouted. I guess they thought Leon was about right after that. Laddie went and bent over him and took his hand.

"Don't be in quite such a hurry, old man," he said. "Before you wink out I have got to tell you how proud I am of having a brother who is a real Crusader. The Lord knows this took nerve! You're great, boy, simply great!"

Leon grabbed Laddie's hand with both of his and held tight and laughed. You could see the big tears squeeze out, although he fought to wink them back. He held to Laddie and said lowlike, only for him to hear: "It's all right if you stay by a while, old man."

He began to talk slowly.

"It was a long time before I caught up, and then I had to hide, and follow until day, and he wasn't so very easy to handle. Once I thought he had me sure! It was an awful load, but if it hadn't been for the good old gun, I'd never have got him. When we mixed up, I had fine luck getting that chin punch on him; good thing I worked it out so slick on Absalom Saunders, and while old Even So was groggy I got the money away from him, took the gun, and stood back some distance, before he came out of it. Once we had it settled who walked ahead, and who carried the money and gun, we got along better, but I had to keep an eye on him every minute. To come through the woods was the shortest, but I'm tired out, and so is he. Getting close I most felt sorry for him, he was so forlorn, and so scared about what would be done to him. He stopped and pulled out another roll, and offered me all of it, if I'd let him go. I didn't know whether it was really his, or part of father's, so I told him he could just drop it until I found out. Made him sweat blood, but I had the gun, and he had to mind. I was master then. So there may be more in the roll I gave father than Even So took. Father can figure up and keep what belongs to him. Even So had gone away past Flannigans' before I tackled him, and I was sleepy, cold, and hungry; you'd have thought there'd have been a man out hunting, or passing on the road, but not a soul did we see 'til

Pryors'! Say, the old man was bully! He helped me so, I almost thought I belonged to him! My! he's fine when you know him! After he came on the job, you bet old Even So walked up. Say, where is he? Have you fed him?"

Laddie looked at father, who was listening, and we all rushed to the door, but it must have been an hour, and Even So hadn't waited. Father said it was a great pity, because a man like that shouldn't be left to prey on the community; but mother said she didn't want to be mixed up with a trial, or to be responsible for taking the liberty of a fellow creature, and father said that was exactly like a woman. Leon went to sleep, but none of us thought of going to bed; we just stood around and looked at him, and smiled over him, and cried about him, until you would have thought he had been shipped to us in a glass case, and cost, maybe, a hundred dollars.

Father got out his books and figured up his own and the road money, and Miss Amelia's, and the church's. Laddie didn't want her around, so he stopped at the schoolhouse and told her to stay at Justices' that night, we'd need all our rooms; bet she didn't like being sent away when there was such excitement, but every one minded Laddie when he said so for sure.

When father had everything counted there was more than his, quite a lot of it, stolen from other people who sheltered the traveller no doubt, father said. We thought he wouldn't be likely to come back for it, and father said he was at loss what to do with it, but Laddie said he wasn't—it was Leon's—he had earned it; so father said he would try to find out if anything else had been stolen, and he'd keep it a year, and then if no one claimed it, he would put it on interest until Leon decided what he wanted to do with it.

When you watched Leon sleep you could tell a lot more about what had happened to him than he could. He moaned, and muttered constantly, and panted, and felt around for the gun, and breathed like he was running again, and fought until Laddie had to hold him on the couch, and finally awakened him. But it did no good; he went right off to sleep again, and it happened all over. Then father began getting his Crusader blood up, although he always said he was a man of peace. But it was a lucky thing Even So got away; for after father had watched Leon a while, he said if that man had been on the premises, his fingers itched so to get at him, he was positive he'd have vented a little righteous indignation on him that would have cost him within an inch of his life. And he'd have done it too! He was like that. It took a lot, and it was slow coming, but when he became angry enough, and felt justified in it, why you'd be much safer to be some one else than the man who provoked him.

After ten o'clock the dog barked, some one tapped, and father went; he always would open the door; you couldn't make him pretend he was asleep, or not at home when he was, and there stood Mr. Pryor. He said they could see the lights and they were afraid the boy was ill, and could any of them help. Father said there was nothing they could do; Leon was asleep. Then Mr. Pryor said: "If he is off sound, so it won't disturb him, I would like to see him again."

Father told him Leon was restless, but so exhausted a railroad train wouldn't waken him, so Mr. Pryor came in and went to the couch. He took off his hat, like you do beside a grave, while his face slowly grew whiter than his hair, and that would be snow-white; then he turned at last and stumbled toward the door. Laddie held it for him, but he didn't seem to remember he was there. He muttered over and over: "Why? Why? In the name of God, why?" Laddie followed to the gate to help him on his horse, because he thought he was almost out of his head, but he had walked across the fields, so Laddie kept far behind and watched until he saw him go safely inside his own door.

I think father and Laddie sat beside Leon all night. The others went to sleep. A little after daybreak, just as Laddie was starting to feed, there was an awful clamour, and here came a lot of neighbours with Even So. Mr. Freshett had found him asleep in a cattle hole in the straw stack, and searched him, and he had more money, and that made Mr. Freshett sure; and as he was very strong, and had been for years a soldier, and really loved to fight, he marched poor Even So back to our house. Every few rods they met more men out searching who came with them, until there were so many, our front yard and the road were crowded. Of all the sights you ever saw, Even So looked the worst. You could see that he'd drop over at much more. Those men kept crying they were going to hang him; but mother went out and talked to them, and said they mustn't kill a man for taking only money. She told them how little it was worth compared with other things; she had Candace bring Even So a cup of hot coffee, lots of bread, and sausage from the skillet, and she said it was our money, and our lad, and we wanted nothing done about it. The men didn't like it, but the traveller did. He grabbed and gobbled like a beast at the hot food and cried, and mother said she forgave him, and to let him go.

Then Mr. Freshett looked awful disappointed, and he came up to father, with his back toward mother, and asked: "That's your say too, Mr. Stanton?" Father grinned sort of rueful-like, but he said to give Even So his money and let him go. He told all about getting ours back, and having had him at the house once before. He brought the money Leon took from him, but the men said no doubt he had stolen that, and Leon had earned it bringing him back, so the traveller shouldn't have it. They took him away on a horse and said they'd let him go, but that they'd escort him from the county. Father told Mr. Freshett that he was a little suspicious of them, and he would hold him responsible for the man's life. Mr. Freshett said that he'd give his word that the man would be safe; they only wanted to make sure he wouldn't come back, and that he'd be careful in the future how he abused hospitality, so they went, and all of us were glad of it.

I don't know what Mr. Freshett calls safe, for they took Even So to Groveville and locked him up until night. Then they led him to the railroad, and made him crawl back and forth through an old engine beside the track, until he was blacker than any negro ever born; and then they had him swallow a big dose of croton oil for his health. That was the only *kind* thing they did, for afterward they started him down the track and told him to run, and all of them shot at his feet as he went. Hannah Freshett told me at school the next day. Her father said Even So just howled, and flew up in the air, and ducked, and dodged and ran like he'd never walked a step, or was a bit tired. We made a game of it, and after that one of the boys was Even So, and the others were the mob, and the one who could howl nicest, jump highest, and go fastest, could be "It" oftenest. We used a big hollow sycamore log in Sill's woods, for the engine, kept an oil bottle beside it, and our guns were sticks. I can see one of the boys come crawling out; the worse scared he could look and the shakier he was, the better. Then another would step up with the bottle and roar as much like Doc DePaw had at Even So as possible, "Here begad, you got to take this yet!" and then came the running part. We just screamed when we played it, but yet, even pretending we could see enough about how it had gone with Even So, when all those big men, with guns, had really wanted to hang him—only for promising mother to not—we could clearly understand that there wasn't the slightest danger of him ever coming back. It made the most exciting game we played, and we never became tired of it.

Leon grew all right faster than you would think. He went to school day after next, and the boys were sick with envy. They asked and asked, but Leon wouldn't tell much. He didn't seem to like to talk about it, and he wouldn't play the game or even watch us. He talked a blue streak about the money. Father was going to write to every sheriff of the counties along the way the man said he had come, and if he could find no one before spring who had been robbed, he said Leon might do what he liked with the money. I used to pretend it was coming to me, and each day I thought of a new way to spend it. Leon was so sure he'd get it he marched right over and asked Mr. Pryor about a nice young thoroughbred horse, from his stables, and when he came back he could get a coltlike one so very cheap that father and Laddie looked at each other and gasped, and never said a word. They figured up, and if Leon got the money, he could have the horse, and save some for college, and from the start he never changed a mite about those two things he wanted to do with it. He had the horse picked out and went to the field to feed and pet it and make it gentle, so he could ride bareback, and mother said he would be almost sick if the owner of the money turned up.

Pulling his boots one night, father said so too, and that the thoughts of it worried him. He said Mr. Pryor had shaded his price so that if the money had to go, he would be tempted to see if we couldn't manage it ourselves. I don't know how shading the price of a horse would make her feel better, but it did, and maybe Leon is going to get it.

CHAPTER

10

Laddie Takes the Plunge

This is the state of man: to-day he puts forth
The tender leaves of hopes; to-morrow blossoms,
And bears his blushing honors thick upon him;
The third day comes a frost, a killing frost,
And, when he thinks, good, easy man, full surely
His greatness is a-ripening, nips his root,
And then he falls, as I do.

"Watch me take the plunge!" said Laddie.

"Mad frenzy fires him now," quoted Leon.

It was Sunday after dinner. We had been to church and Sunday-school in the forenoon, and we had a houseful of company for dinner. All of them remained to spend the afternoon, because in our home it was perfectly lovely. We had a big dinner with everything good to start on, and then we talked and visited and told all the news. The women exchanged new recipes for cooking, advised each other about how to get more work done with less worry, to doctor their sick folks, and to make their dresses. At last, when everything was talked over, and there began to be a quiet time, father would reach across the table, pick up a paper and read all the interesting things that had happened in the country during the past week; the jokes too, and they made people think of funny stories to tell, and we just laughed. In the *Agriculturist* there were new ways to farm easier, to make land bear more crops; so he divided that with the neighbours, also how to make gardens, and prune trees. Before he finished, he always managed to work in a lot about being honest, kind, and loving God.

He and mother felt so good over Leon, and by this time they were beginning to see that they were mighty glad about the money too. It wouldn't have been so easy to work, and earn, and pay back all that for our school, roads, and the church; and every day you could see plainer how happy they felt that they didn't have to do it. Because they were so glad about these things, they invited every one they met that day; but we knew Saturday mother felt that probably she would ask a crowd, from the chickens, pie, and cake she got ready. When the reading part was over, and the women were beginning to look at the clock, and you knew they felt they should go home, and didn't want to, Laddie arose and said that, and Leon piped up like he always does and made every one laugh. Of course they looked at Laddie, and no one knew what he meant, so all the women and a few of the men asked him.

"Watch me, I said," laughed Laddie as he left the room.

Soon Mrs. Dover, sitting beside the front window, cried: "Here he is at the gate!"

He was on his horse, but he hitched it and went around the house and up the back way. Before long the stair door of the sitting-room opened, and there he stood. We stared at him. Of course he was bathed, and in clean clothing to start with, but he had washed and brushed some more, until he shone. His cheeks were as smooth and as clear pink as any girl's, his eyes blue-gray and big, with long lashes and heavy brows. His hair was bright brown and wavy, and he was so big and broad. He never had been sick a day in his life, and he didn't look as if he ever would be.

And clothes *do* make a difference. He would have had exactly the same hair, face, and body, wearing a hickory shirt and denim trousers; but he wouldn't have looked as he did in the clothes he wore at college, when it was Sunday there, or he was invited to a party at the President's. I don't see how any man could possibly be handsomer or look finer. His shirt, collar, and cuffs were snow-white, like everything had to be before mother got through with it;

his big loose tie almost reached his shoulders; and our men could do a thing no other man in the neighbourhood did: They could appear easier in the finest suit they could put on than in their working clothes.

Mother used to say one thing she dreaded about Sunday was the evident tortures of the poor men squirming in boots she knew pinched them, coats too tight, and collars too high. She said they acted like half-broken colts fretting over restriction. Always she said to father and the boys when they went to buy their new clothes: "Now, *don't* join the harness fighters! Get your clothing big enough to set your bodies with comfort and ease."

I suppose those other men would have looked like ours if their mothers had told them. You can always see that a man needs a woman to help him out awful bad.

Of course Laddie knew he was handsome; he had to know all of them were looking at him curiously, but he stood there buttoning his glove and laughing to himself until Sarah Hood asked: "Now what are you up to?"

He took a step toward her, ran one hand under her lantern-jaw chin, pulled her head against his side and turned up her face.

"Sarah," he said, "'member the day we spoiled the washing?"

Every one laughed. They had made jokes about it until our friends knew what they meant.

"What are you going to spoil now?" asked Sarah.

"The Egyptians! The 'furriners.' I'm going right after them!"

"Well, you could be in better business," said Sarah Hood sharply.

Laddie laughed and squeezed her chin, and hugged her head against him.

"Listen to that, now!" he cried. "My best friend going back on me. Sarah, I thought you, of all people, would wish me luck."

"I do!" she said instantly. "And that's the very reason I don't want you mixed up with that mysterious, offish, stuck-up mess."

"Bless your dear heart!" said Laddie, giving her a harder squeeze than ever. "You got that all wrong, Sarah. You'll live to see the day, very shortly, when you'll change every word of it."

"I haven't done anything but get surer about it every day for two years, anyway," said Sarah Hood.

"Exactly!" said Laddie, "but wait until I have taken the plunge! Let me tell you how the Pryor family strikes me. I think he is a high-tempered, domineering man, proud as Lucifer! For some cause, just or not, he is ruining his life and that of his family because he so firmly believes it just; he is hiding here from his home country, his relatives, and friends. I think she is, barring you and mother, the handsomest woman of her age I ever saw —"

All of them laughed, because Sarah Hood was nearly as homely as a woman could grow, and maybe other people didn't find our mother so lovely as we thought her. I once heard one of her best friends say she was "distinctly plain." I didn't see how she could; but she said that.

"— and the most pitiful," Laddie went on. "Sarah, what do you suppose sends a frail little woman pacing the yard, and up and down the road, sometimes in storm and rain, gripping both hands over her heart?"

"I suppose it's some shameful thing I don't want you mixed up with!" said Sarah Hood promptly, and people just shouted.

"Sarah," said Laddie, "I've seen her closely, watched her move, and studied her expression. There's not one grain of possibility that you, or mother, or Mrs. Fall, or any woman here, could be any closer connected with *shame*. Shame there is," said Laddie, "and what a word! How it stings, burns, withers, and causes heart trouble and hiding; but shame in connection with that woman, more than shame thrust upon her, which might come to any of us, at any time, shame that is her error, in the life of a woman having a face like hers, Sarah, I am ashamed of you! Your only excuse is that you haven't persisted as I have until you got to see for yourself."

"I am not much on persistence in the face of a locked door, a cast-iron man with a big cane, and two raving bulldogs," said Mrs. Hood. "Wait, young man! Just wait until he sets them on you."

Laddie's head went back and how he laughed.

"Hist! A word with you, Sarah!" he said. "'Member I have a sort of knack with animals. I never yet have failed with one I undertook to win. Now those bulldogs of Pryors' are as mild as kittens with a man who knows the right word. Reason I know, Sarah, I've said the word to them, separately and collectively, and it worked.

There is a contrast, Sarah, between what I say and do to those dogs, and the kicks and curses they get from their owner. I'll wager you two to one that if you can get Mr. Pryor to go into a 'sic-ing' contest with me, I can have his own dogs at his throat, when he can't make them do more than to lick my hands."

They laughed as if that were funny.

"Well, I didn't know about this," said Sarah. "How long have you lived at Pryors'?"

You couldn't have heard what Laddie said if he'd spoken; so he waited until he could be heard, and it never worried him a speck. He only stood and laughed too; then, "Long enough," he said, "to know that all of us are making a big and cruel mistake in taking them at their word, and leaving them penned up there weltering in misery. What we should do, is to go over there, one at a time, or in a body, and batter at the door of their hearts, until we break down the wall of pride they have built around them, ease their pain, and bring them with us socially, if they are going to live among us. You people who talk loudly and often about loving God, and 'doing unto others,' should have gone long ago, for Jesus' sake; I'm going for the sake of a girl, with a face as sweet, and a heart as pure, as any accepted angel at the foot of the throne. Mother, I want a cup of peach jelly, and some of that exceptionally fine cake you served at dinner, to take to our sick neighbour."

Mother left the room.

"Father, I want permission to cut and carry a generous chestnut branch, burred, and full fruited, to the young woman. There is none save ours in this part of the country, and she may never have seen any, and be interested. And I want that article about foot disease in horses, for Mr. Pryor. I'll bring it back when he finishes."

Father folded the paper and handed it to Laddie, who slipped it in his pocket.

"Take the finest branch you can select," father said, and I almost fell over.

He had carried those trees from Ohio, before I had been born, and mother said for years he wrapped them in her shawl in winter and held an umbrella over them in summer, and father always went red and grinned when she told it. He was wild about trees, and bushes, so he made up his mind he'd have chestnuts. He planted them one place, and if they didn't like it, he dug them up and set them another where he thought they could have what they needed and hadn't got the last place. Finally, he put them, on the fourth move, on a little sandy ridge across the road from the wood yard, and that was the spot. They shot up, branched, spread, and one was a male and two were females, so the pollen flew, the burrs filled right, and we had a bag of chestnuts to send each child away from home, every Christmas. The brown leaves and burrs were so lovely, mother cut one of the finest branches she could select and hung it above the steel engraving of "Lincoln Freeing the Slaves," in the boys' room, and nothing in the house was looked at oftener, or thought prettier. That must have been what was in the back of Laddie's head when he wanted a branch for the Princess.

Mother came in with the cake and jelly in a little fancy basket, and Laddie said: "Thank you! Now every one wish me luck! I'm going to ride to Pryors', knock at the door, and present these offerings with my compliments. If I'm invited in, I'm going to make the effort of my life at driving the entering wedge toward social intercourse between Pryors and their neighbours. If I'm not, I'll be back in thirty minutes and tell you what happened to me. If they refuse my gifts, you shall have the jelly, Sarah; I'll give Mrs. Fall the olive branch, bring back the paper, and eat the cake to console my wounded spirits."

Of course every one laughed; they couldn't help it. I watched father and he laughed hardest of the men, but mother was more stiff-lipped about it; she couldn't help a little, though. And I noticed some of those women acted as if they had lost something. Maybe it was a chance to gossip about Laddie, for he hadn't left them a thing to guess at, and mother says the reason gossip is so dreadful is because it is always *guesswork*. Well, that was all fair and plain. He had told those people, our very best friends, what he thought about everything, the way they acted included. He was carrying something to each member of the Pryor family, and he'd left a way to return joking and unashamed, if they wouldn't let him in. He had fixed things so no one had anything to guess at, and it would look much worse for the Pryors than it would for him, if he did come back.

I wondered if he had been born that smart, or if he learned it in college. If he did, no wonder Leon was bound to go. Come to think of it, though, mother said Laddie was always like that. She said he never bit her when he nursed; he never mauled her as if she couldn't be hurt when he was little, he never tore his clothes and made extra work as he grew, and never in his life gave her an hour's uneasiness. But I guess she couldn't have said that about uneasiness lately, for she couldn't keep from looking troubled as all of us followed to the gate to see him start.

How they joked, and tried to tease him! But they couldn't get a breath ahead. He shot back answers as fast as they could ask questions, while he cut the branch and untied the horse. He gave the limb and basket to mother to hold, kissed her good-bye, and me too, before he mounted. With my arms around his neck—I never missed a chance to try to squeeze into him how I loved him—I whispered: "Laddie, is it a secret any more?"

He threw back his head and laughed the happiest.

"Not the ghost of a secret!" he said. "But you let me do the talking, until I tell you." Then he went on right out loud: "I'm riding up the road waving the banner of peace. If I suffer repulse, the same thing has happened to better men before, so I'll get a different banner and try again. Fare-ye-well, Brother Crawford-ah!"

Maybe you don't understand what he meant about Brother Crawford, but all of us knew. It was a funny story father read about a Methodist minister who was preaching his farewell sermon to his congregation. He had to move and he didn't want to very bad. He was uncertain as to what would happen next; so he arose before the people and told how as he drove to church that morning, everything seemed to say: "Fare-ye-well, Brother Crawford-ah!" When he had made the land, the trees, the horses, dogs and cats he passed all say it like that to him, it got to be mighty funny, at least it was the way father read it. So when any of us started away and were not sure about what would happen to us, that was the way we said good-bye.

As he drawled that out, he swept a circle in the road, dropped Flos on her knees in a bow, and waved the branch. Leon began to sing at the top of his voice, "Nothing but leaves, nothing but leaves," while Laddie went flashing up the road.

The women went back to the house; the men stood around the

gate, watched him from sight, talked about his horse, how he rode, and made wagers that he'd get shut out, like every one did, but they said if that happened he wouldn't come back. Father was annoyed.

"You heard Laddie say he'd return immediately if they wouldn't let him in," he said. "He's a man of his word. He will either enter or come home at once."

It was pitch dark and we had supper before some of them left; they never stayed so late. After we came from church, father read the chapter and we were ready for bed; still Laddie hadn't come back. And father liked it! He just plain liked it! He chuckled behind the *Advocate* until you could see it shake; but mother had very little to say, and her lips closed tight.

At bedtime he said to mother: "Well, they don't seem in a hurry about sending the boy back."

"Did you really think he *would* be sent back?" asked mother.

"Not ordinarily," said father, "no! If he had no brain, no wit, and no culture, on an animal basis, a woman would look twice before she'd send him away; but with such fanatics as Pryors, one can't always tell what will happen."

"In a case like this, one can be reasonably certain," said mother.

"You don't know what social position they occupied at home. Their earmarks are all good. We've no such notions here as they have."

"Thank God for so much, at any rate," said mother. "How old England would rise up and exult if she had a man in line with Laddie's body, blood and brain, to set on her throne. This talk about class and social position makes me sick. Men are men, and Laddie is as much above the customary timber found in kings and princes, physically and mentally, as the sky is above earth. Talk me no talk about class! If I catch it coming from any of mine, save you, I will beat it out of them. He has admitted he's in love with the girl; the real question is, whether she's fit to be his wife."

"I should say she appears so," said father.

"Drat appearances!" cried mother. "When it's a question of lifetime misery, and the soul's salvation of my son, if things go wrong, I've no time for appearances. I want to know!"

He might have known he would make her angry when he laughed. She punched the pillow, and wouldn't say another word; so I went to sleep, and didn't miss anything that time.

Next morning at breakfast Laddie was beaming, and father hardly waited to ask the blessing before he inquired: "Well, how did you make it, son?"

Laddie laughed and answered: "Altogether, it might have been much worse."

That was all he would say until Miss Amelia started to school, then he took me on his lap and talked as he buttoned my coat.

"Thomas met me at the gate," he said, "and held my horse while I went to the door. One of their women opened it, and I inquired for Mr. Pryor. She said he was in the field looking at the horses, so I asked for Miss Pryor. She came in a minute, so I gave her the branch, told her about it, and offered the jelly and cake for her mother. The Princess invited me to enter. I told her I couldn't without her father's permission, so I went to the field to see him. The dogs were with him and he had the surprise of his life when his man-eaters rolled at my feet, and licked my hands."

"What did he say?" chuckled father.

"Told Thomas they'd been overfed and didn't amount to a brass farthing; to take them to the woods and shoot them. Thomas said he'd see to it the very first thing in the morning, and then Mr. Pryor told him he would shoot him if he did."

"Charming man to work for," said mother.

Laddie laughed.

"Then I told him I'd been at the house to carry a little gift to his wife and daughter, and to inquire if I might visit an hour, and as he was not there, I had come to the field to ask him. Then I looked him in the eye and said: 'May I?'

"'I'll warrant the women asked you to come in,' he said.

"'Miss Pryor was so kind,' I answered, 'but I enter no man's house without his permission. May I talk with your daughter an hour, and your wife, if she cares to see me?'

"'It makes no earthly difference to me' he said, which was not gracious, but might have been worse, so I thanked him, and went back to the house. When I knocked the second time, the Princess came, and I told her the word was that it made 'no difference to her father' if I came in, so she opened the door widely, took my hat and offered me a seat. Then she went to the next room and said: 'Mother, father has given Mr. Stanton permission to pay us a call. Do you feel able to meet him?' She came at once, offering her hand and saying: 'I have already met Mr. Stanton so often, really, we should have the privilege of speaking.'"

"What did she mean by that?" asked mother.

"She meant that I have haunted the road passing their place for two years, and she'd seen me so frequently that she came to recognize me."

"Umph!" said mother.

"Laddie tell on!" I begged.

"Well, I sharpened all the wits I had and went to work. I never tried so hard in my life to be entertaining. Of course I had to feel my way. I'd no idea what would interest a delicate, highbred lady" — mother sniffed again — "so I had to search and probe, and go by guess until I saw a shade of interest, then I worked in more of the same. It was easy enough to talk to the Princess—all young folks have a lot in common, we could get along on fifty topics; it was different with the housebound mother. I did my best, and after a while Mr. Pryor came in. I asked him if any of his horses had been attacked with the trouble some of the neighbours were having, and told him what it was. He had the grace to thank me. He said he would tell Thomas not to tie his horse at the public hitching rack when he went to town, and once he got started, he was wild to talk with a man, and I'd no chance to say a word to the women. He was interested in our colleges, state, and national laws, in land development, and everything that all live men are. When a maid announced dinner I apologized for having stayed so long, and excused myself, because I had been so interested, but Mrs. Pryor merely said: 'I'm waiting to be offered your arm.'

"Well, you should have seen me drop my hat and step up. I did my best, and while I talked to him a little, I made it most to the women. Any one could see they were starved to death for company, so I took the job of entertaining them. I told some college jokes, funny things that had happened in the neighbourhood, and everything of interest I could think up. I know we were at the table for two hours with things coming and going on silver platters."

Mother sat straight suddenly.

"Just what did they have to eat, and how did they serve it?" she asked.

"Couldn't tell if I were to be shot for it, mummy," said Laddie. "Forgive me! Next time I'll take notes for you. This first plunge, I had to use all my brains, not to be a bore to them; and to handle food and cutlery as the women did. It's quite a process, but as they were served first, I could do right by waiting. I never was where things were done quite so elaborately before."

"And they didn't know they would have company until you went to the table?"

"Well, they must have thought likely, there was a place for me."

"Umph!" said mother. "Fine idea! Then any one who drops in can be served, and see that they are not a mite of trouble. Candace, always an extra place after this!"

Father just shouted.

"I thought you'd get something out of it!" he said.

"Happy to have justified your faith!" replied mother calmly. "Go on, son!"

"That's all!" said Laddie. "We left the table and talked an hour more. The women asked me to come again; he didn't say anything on that subject; but when he ordered my horse, he asked the Princess if she would enjoy a little exercise, and she said she would, so he told Thomas to bring their horses, and we rode around the section, the Princess and I ahead, Mr. Pryor following. Where the road was good and the light fine enough that there was no danger of laming a horse, we dropped back, one on either side of him, so we could talk. Mrs. Pryor ate the cake and said it was fine; and the 'conserve,' she called it, delicious as she ever had tasted. She said all our fruits here had much more flavour than at home; she thought it was the dryer climate and more sunshine. She sent her grateful thanks, and she wants your recipe before next preserving time."

Mother just beamed. My! but she did love to have the things she cooked, bragged on.

"Possibly she'd like my strawberries?" she said.

"There isn't a doubt about it," said Laddie. "I've yet to see the first person who doesn't."

"Is that all?" asked mother.

"I can think of nothing more at this minute," answered Laddie. "If anything comes to my mind later, I won't forget to tell you. Oh yes, there was one thing: You couldn't keep Mr. Pryor from talking about Leon. He must have taken a great fancy to him. He talked until he worried the Princess, and she tried to keep him away from the subject, but his mind seemed to run on it constantly. When we were riding she talked quite as much as he, and it will hustle us to think what the little scamp did, any bigger than they do. Of course, father, you understood the price Mr. Pryor made on one of his very finest colts was a joke. There's a strain of Arab in the father—he showed me the record—and the mother is bluegrass. There you get gentleness and endurance combined with speed and nerve. I'd trade Flos for that colt as it stands to-day. There's nothing better on earth in the way of horse. His offer is practically giving it away. I know, with the records to prove its pedigree, what that colt would bring him in any city market."

"I don't like it," said mother. "I want Leon to have a horse, but a boy in a first experience, and reckless as he is, doesn't need a horse like that, for one thing, and what is more important, I refuse to be put under any obligations to Pryors."

"That's the reason Mr. Pryor asked anything at all for the horse. It is my opinion that he would be greatly pleased to give it to Leon, if he could do what he liked."

"Well, that's precisely the thing he can't do in this family," said mother sternly.

"What do you think, father?" asked Laddie.

"I think Amen! to that proposition," said father; "but I would have to take time to thresh it out completely. It appeals to me that Leon is old enough to recognize the value of the animal; and that the care of it would develop and strengthen his character. It would be a responsibility that would steady him. You could teach him to tend and break it."

"Break it!" cried Laddie. "Break it! Why, father, he's riding it bareback all over the Pryor meadow now, and jumping it over logs. Whenever he leaves, it follows him to the fence, and the Princess says almost any hour of the day you look out you can see it pacing up and down watching this way and whinnying for him to come."

"And your best judgment is —?"

Laddie laughed as he tied my hood strings. "Well, I don't feel about the Pryors as the rest of you do," he said. "If the money isn't claimed inside the time you specified, I would let Leon and Mr. Pryor make their own bargain. The boy won't know for years that it is practically a gift, and it would please Mr. Pryor immensely. Now run, or you'll be late!"

I had to go, so I didn't know how they settled it, but if they wouldn't let Leon have that horse, it was downright mean. What if we were under obligations to Mr. Pryor? We were to Sarah Hood, and half the people we knew, and what was more, we *liked* to be.

When I came from school that night father had been to town. He had an ax and was opening a big crate, containing two of the largest, bluest geese you ever saw. Laddie said being boxed that way and seeing them so close made them look so big; really, they were no finer than Pryors', where he had got the address of the place that sold them. Mother was so pleased. She said she had needed a new strain, for a long time, to improve her feathers; now she would have pillows worth while, in a few years. They put them in the barn where our geese stayed over night, and how they did scream. That is, one of them did; the other acted queerly and father said to Laddie that he was afraid the trip was hard on it. Laddie said it might have been hurt, and mother was worried too. Before she had them an hour, she had sold all our ganders; spring had come, she had saved the blue goose eggs, set them under a hen, raised the goslings with the little chickens, never lost one, picked them and made a new pair of pillows too fine for any one less important than a bishop, or a judge, or Dr. Fenner to sleep on. Then she began saving for a featherbed. And still the goose didn't act as spry or feel as good as the gander. He stuck up his head, screamed, spread his wings and waved them, and the butts looked so big and hard, I was not right certain whether it would be safe to tease him or not.

The first person who came to see them was Sarah Hood, and she left with the promise of a pair as soon as mother could raise them. Father said the only reason mother didn't divide her hair with Sarah Hood was because it was fast, and she couldn't. Mother said gracious goodness! she'd be glad to get rid of some of it if she could, and of course Sarah should have first chance at it. Hadn't she kept her over night so she could see her new home when she was rested, and didn't she come with her, and help her get settled, and had she ever failed when we had a baby, or sickness, or trouble, or thrashers, or a party? Of course she'd gladly divide, even the hair of her head, with Sarah Hood. And father said, "Yes, he guessed she would, and come to think of it, he'd just as soon spare Sarah part of his," and then they both laughed, when it was nothing so very funny that I could see.

The next caller the geese had was Mrs. Freshett. My! she thought they were big and fine. Mother promised her a couple of eggs to set under a hen. Father said she was gradually coming down the scale of her feelings, and before two weeks she'd give Isaac Thomas, at least, a quill for a pen. Almost no one wrote with them any more, but often father made a few, and showed us how to use them. He said they were gone with candles, sand boxes, and snuff. Mother said she had no use for snuff, but candles were not gone, she'd make and use them to the day of her death, as they were the nicest light ever invented to carry from room to room, or when you only wanted to sit and think. Father said there was really no good pen except the quill you sharpened yourself; and while he often used steel ones like we children had at school, to write to the brothers and sisters away, and his family, he always kept a few choice quills in the till of his chest, and when he wrote a deed, or any valuable paper, where there was a deal with money, he used them. He said it lent the dignity of a past day to an important occasion.

After mother and Mrs. Freshett had talked over every single thing about the geese, and that they were like Pryors' had been settled, Mrs. Freshett said: "Since he told about it before all of us, and started out the way he did, would it be amiss to ask how Laddie got on at Pryors'?"

Mother smiled.

"Just the way I thought he would," she said. "He stayed until all of us were in bed, and I'd never have known when he came in, if it were not a habit of his always to come to my door to see if I'm sleeping. Sometimes I'm wakeful, and if he pommels my pillow good, brings me a drink, and rubs my head a few strokes with his strong, cool hands, I can settle down and have a good night's rest. I was awake when he came, or I'd never have known. It was almost midnight; but they sat two hours at the table, and then all of them rode."

"Not the Missus?"

"Oh no! She's not strong enough. She really has incurable heart trouble, the worst kind there is; her daughter told me so."

"Then they better look out," said Mrs. Freshett. "She is likely to keel over at a breath."

"They must know it. That's why she keeps so quiet."

"And they had him to supper?"

"It was a dinner served at night. Yes. He took Mrs. Pryor in on his arm, and it was like a grand party, just as they fixed for themselves, alone. Waiters, and silver trays, and things carried in and out in courses."

"My land! Well, I 'spose he had enough schoolin' to get him through it all right!"

My mother's face grew red. She never left any one in doubt as to what she meant. Father said that "was the Dutch of it." And mother always answered that if any one living could put things plainer than the English, she would like to hear them do it.

"He certainly had," said mother, "or they wouldn't have invited him to come again. And all mine, Mrs. Freshett, knew how to sit properly at the table, and manage a knife, fork and napkin, before they ever took a meal away from home."

"No 'fence," laughed Mrs. Freshett. "I meant that maybe his years of college schoolin' had give him ways more like theirs than most of us have. For all the money it takes to send a boy to college, he ought to get somethin' out of it more than jest fillin' his head with figgers, an' stars, an' oratin'; an' most always you can see that he does."

"It is contact with cultivated people," said mother. "You are always influenced by it, without knowing it often."

"Maybe you are, bein' so fine yourself," said Mrs. Freshett. "An' me too, I never get among my betters that I don't carry home a lot I put right into daily use, an' nobody knows it plainer. I come here expectin' to learn things that help me, an' when I go home I know I have."

"Why, thank you," said mother. "I'm sure that is a very nice compliment, and I wish I really could feel that it is well deserved."

"Oh I guess you do!" said Mrs. Freshett laughing. "I often noticed you makin' a special effort to teach puddin' heads like me somethin', an' I always thank you for it. There's a world in right teachin'. I never had any. So all I can pick up an' hammer into mine is a gain for me an' them. If my Henry had lived, an' come out anything like that boy o' yourn an' the show he made last Sunday, I'd do well if I didn't swell up an' bust with pride. An' the little towhaired strip, takin' the gun an' startin' out alone after a robber, even if he wa'n't much of a man, that was downright spunky. If my boys will come out anywhere near like yourn, I'll be glad."

"I don't know how my boys will come out," said mother. "But I work, pray, hope, and hang to them; that's all I know to do."

"Well, if they don't come out right, they ought to be bumped!" said Mrs. Freshett. "After all the chances they've had! I don' know jest how Freshett was brung up, but I'd no chance at all. My folks—well, I guess the less said—little pitchers, you know! I can't see as I was to blame. I was the youngest, an' I knew things was wrong. I fought to go to school, an' pap let me enough that I saw how other people lived. Come night I'd go to the garret, an' bar the trapdoor; but there would be times when I couldn't help seein' what was goin' on. How'd you like chances such as that for a girl of yourn?"

"Dreadful!" said mother. "Mrs. Freshett, please do be careful!"

"Sure!" laughed Mrs. Freshett. "I was jest goin' to tell you about me an' Josiah. He come to our house one night, a stranger off the road. He said he was sick, an' tired, an' could he have a bed. Mother said, 'No, for him to move on.' He tried an' he couldn't. They was somethin' about him—well, you know how them things go! I wa'n't only sixteen, but I felt so sorry for him, all fever burned and mumblin', I helped pap put him to bed, an' doctored him all I could. Come mornin' he was a sick man. Pap went for the county doctor, an' he took jest one look an' says: 'Small pox! All of ye git!'

"I was bound I wouldn't go, but pap made me, an' the doctor said he'd send a man who'd had it; so I started, but I felt so bad, come a chanct when they got to Groveville, I slipped out an' went back. The man hadn't come, so I set to work the best I knowed.

'Fore long Josiah was a little better an' he asked who I was, an' where my folks went, an' I told him, an' he asked *why* I came back, an' I didn't know what to say, so I jest hung my head an' couldn't face him. After a while he says, 'All right! I guess I got this sized up. If you'll stay an' nuss me through, I'll be well enough to pull you out, by the time you get it, an' soon as you're able we'll splice, if you say so.'

"'Marry me, you mean?' says I. They wa'n't ever any talk about marryin' at our house. 'Sure!' says he. 'You're a might likely lookin' girl! I'll do fair by ye.' An' he always has, too! But I didn't feel right to let him go it blind, so I jest up and says, 'You wouldn't if you knowed my folks!' 'You look as decent as I do,' says he; 'I'll chance it!' Then I tole him I was as good as I was born, an' he believed me, an' he always has, an' I was too! So I nussed him, but I didn't make the job of it he did. You 'member he is pitted considerable. He was so strong I jest couldn't keep him from disfigerin' himself, but he tied me. I begged to be loose, an' he wouldn't listen, so I got a clean face, only three little scars, an' they ain't deep to speak of. He says he looks like a piece of side meat, but say! they ain't nothin' the matter with his looks to me!

"The nuss man never did come, but the county doctor passed things in the winder, till I was over the worst, an' Josiah sent for a preacher an' he married us through the winder—I got the writin's to show, all framed an' proper. Josiah said he'd see I got all they was in it long that line, anyway. When I was well, hanged if he didn't perdooce a wad from his clothes before they burnt 'em, an' he got us new things to wear, an' a horse, an' wagon, an' we driv away here where we thought we could start right, an' after we had the land, an' built the cabin, an' jest as happy as heart could wish, long came a man I'd made mad once, an' he tole everythin' up and down. Josiah was good about it. He offered to sell the land, an' pull up an' go furder. 'What's the use?' says I. 'Hundreds know it. We can't go so far it won't be like to follow us; le's stay here an' fight it.' 'All right,' says Josiah, but time an' ag'in he has offered to go, if I couldn't make it. 'Hang on a little longer,' says I, every time he knew I was snubbed an' slighted. I never tole what he didn't notice. I tried church, when my children began to git a size I wanted 'em to have right teachin', an' you come an' welcomed me an' you been my friend, an' now the others is comin' over at last, an' visitin' me, an' they ain't a thing more I want in life."

"I am so glad!" said mother. "Oh my dear, I am so glad!"

"Goin' right home an' tell that to Josiah," said Mrs. Freshett, jumping up laughing and crying like, "an' mebby I'll jest spread wings and fly! I never was so happy in all my life as I was Sunday, when you ast me before all of them, so cordial like, an' says I to Josiah, 'We'll go an' try it once,' an' we come an' nobody turned a cold shoulder on us, an' I wa'n't wearin' specks to see if they did, for I never knowed him so happy in all his days. Orter heard him whistle goin' home, an' he's tryin' all them things he learned, on our place, an' you can see it looks a heap better a'ready, an' now he's talkin' about buildin' in the spring. I knowed he had money, but he never mentioned buildin' before, an' I always thought it was bekase he 'sposed likely we'd have to move on, sometime. 'Pears now as if we can settle, an' live like other folks, after all these years. I knowed ye didn't want me to talk, but I had to tell you! When you ast us to the weddin',' and others began comin' round, says I to Josiah, 'Won't she be glad to know thet my skirts is clear, an' I did as well as I could?' An' he says, 'That she will! An' more am I,' says he. 'I mighty proud of you,' says he. Proud! Think of that! Miss Stanton, I'd jest wade fire and blood for you!"

"Oh my dear!" said mother. "What a dreadful thing to say!"

"Gimme the chanct, an' watch if I don't," said Mrs. Freshett. "Now, Josiah is proud I stuck it out! Now, I can have a house! Now, my children can have all the show we can raise to give 'em! I'm done cringin' and dodgin'! I've always done my best; henceforth I mean to hold up my head an' say so. I sure can't be held for what was done 'fore I was on earth, or since neither. You've given me my show, I'm goin' to take it, but if you want to know what's in my heart about you, gimme any kind of a chanct to prove, an' see if I don't pony right up to it!"

Mother laughed until the tears rolled, she couldn't help it. She took Mrs. Freshett in her arms and hugged her tight, and kissed her might near like she does Sarah Hood. Mrs. Freshett threw her arms around mother, and looked over her shoulder, and said to me, "Sis, when you grow up, always take a chanct on welcomin' the stranger, like your maw does, an' heaven's bound to be your home! My! but your maw is a woman to be proud of!" she said, hugging mother and patting her on the back.

"All of us are proud of her!" I boasted.

"I doubt if you are proud enough!" cried Mrs. Freshett. "I have my doubts! I don't see how people livin' with her, an' seein' her every day, are in a shape to know jest what she can do for a person in the place I was in. I have my doubts!"

First time I saw father I told him Mrs. Freshett had doubts if we were proud enough of mother, and as you live! if he didn't go and say that he had too!

That night when I went home from school mother was worrying over the blue goose. When we went to feed, she told Leon that she was afraid it was weak, and not getting enough to eat when it fed with the others. She said after the work was finished, to take it out alone, and give it all it would eat; so when the horses were tended, the cows milked, everything watered, and the barn ready to close for the night, Laddie took the milk to the house, while Leon and I caught the blue goose, carried her to the well, and began to shell corn. She was starved to death, almost. She ate a whole ear in no time and looked for more, so Leon sent me after another. By the time that was most gone she began to eat slower, and stick her bill in the air to help the grains slip down, so I told Leon I thought she had enough.

"No such thing!" said Leon. "You distinctly heard mother tell me to give her 'all she would eat.' She's eating, isn't she? Go bring another ear!"

So she was, but I was doubtful about more.

Leon said I better mind or he would tell mother, so I got it. She didn't begin on it with any enthusiasm. She stuck her bill higher, and stretched her neck longer to make the corn go down, and she looked so funny when she did it, that we just shrieked. Then Leon reached over, took her by the bill, and stripped her neck to help her swallow, and as soon as he let go, she began to eat again.

"You see!" said Leon, "she's been starved. She can't get enough. I must help her!"

So he did help her every little bit. By that time we were interested in seeing how much she could hold; and she looked so funny that Leon sent me for more corn; but I told him I thought what she needed now was water, so we held her to the trough, and she tried to drink, but she couldn't swallow much. We set her down beside the corn, and she went to eating again.

"Go it, old mill-hopper!" cried Leon.

Right then there was an awful commotion in the barn, and from the squealing we knew one of the horses was loose, and fighting the others. We ran to fix them, and had a time to get Jo back into his stall, and tied. Before we had everything safe, the supper bell rang, and I bet Leon a penny I could reach the house while he shut the door and got there. She was not in sight, there was no corn, and we forgot every single thing about the goose.

At supper mother asked Leon if he fed the goose all she would eat, and I looked at him guilty-like, for I remembered we hadn't put her back. He frowned at me cross as a bear, and I knew that meant he had remembered, and would slip back and put her inside when he finished his supper, so I didn't say anything.

"I didn't feed her *all* she would eat!" said Leon. "If I had, she'd be at it yet. She was starved sure enough! You never saw anything like the corn she downed."

"Well I declare!" said mother. "Now after this, take her out alone, for a few days, and give her as much as she wants."

"All right!" chuckled Leon, because it was a lot of fun to see her run her bill around, and gobble up the corn, and stick up her head.

The next day was Saturday, so after breakfast I went with Leon to drive the sheep and geese to the creek to water; the trough was so high it was only for the horses and cattle, and when we let out the geese, the blue one wasn't there.

"Oh Leon, did you forget to come back and put her in?"

Leon was almost crying.

"Yes I did!" he said. "I meant to when I looked at you to keep still, and I started to do it, but Sammy Deam whistled, so I went down in the orchard to see what he wanted, and we got to planning how to get up a fox chase, and I stayed until father called for night, and then I ran and forgot all about the blame old goose."

"Oh, Leon! Where is she? What will mother say? 'Spose a fox got her!"

"It wouldn't help me any if it had, after I was to blame for leaving her outside. Blast a girl! If you ever amounted to anything, you could have put her in while I fixed the horses. At least you could have told me to."

I stood there dumblike and stared at him. He has got the awfulest way of telling the truth when he is scared or provoked. Of course I should have thought of the goose when he was having such a hard fight with the horses. If I'd been like he was, I'd have told him that he was older, mother told *him* to do it, and it wasn't my fault; but in my heart I knew he did have his hands full, and if you're your brother's keeper, you ought to *help* your brother remember. So I stood gawking, while Leon slowly turned whiter and whiter.

"We might as well see if we can find her," he said at last, so slow and hopeless like it made my heart ache. So he started around the straw stack one way, and I the other, looking into all the holes, and before I had gone far I had a glimpse of her, and it scared me so I screamed, for her head was down, and she didn't look right. Leon came running and pulled her out. The swelled corn rolled in a little trail after her, and the pigs ran up and began to eat it. Pigs are named righter than anything else I know.

"Busted!" cried Leon in tones of awe; about the worst awe you ever heard, and the worst bust you ever saw.

From bill to breast she was wide open, and the hominy spilling. We just stood staring at her, and then Leon began to kick the pigs; because it would be no use to kick the goose; she would never know. Then he took her up, carried her into the barn, and put her on the floor where the other geese had stayed all night. We stood and looked at her some more, as if looking and hoping would make her get up and be alive again. But there's nothing in this world so useless as wishing dead things would come alive; we had to do something.

"What are you going to tell mother?"

"Shut up!" said Leon. "I'm trying to think."

"I'll say it was as much my fault as yours. I'll go with you. I'll take half whatever they do to you."

"Little fool!" said Leon. "What good would that do me?"

"Do you know what they cost? Could you get another with some of your horse money?"

I saw it coming and dodged again, before I remembered the Crusaders.

"All right!" I said. "If that's the way you are going to act, Smarty, I'll lay all the blame on you; I won't help you a bit, and I don't care if you are whipped until the blood runs."

Then I went out of the barn and slammed the door. For a minute I felt better; but it was a short time. I *said* that to be mean, but I did care. I cared dreadfully; I was partly to blame, and I knew it. Coming around the barn, I met Laddie, and he saw in a flash I was in trouble, so he stopped and asked: "What now, Chicken?"

"Come into the barn where no one will hear us," I said.

So we went around the outside, entered at the door on the embankment, and he sat in the wheelbarrow on the threshing floor while I told him. I thought I felt badly enough, but after I saw Laddie, it grew worse, for I remembered we were short of money that fall, that the goose was a fine, expensive one, and how proud mother was of her, and how she'd be grieved, and that was trouble for sure.

"Run along and play!" said Laddie, "and don't tell any one else if you can help it. I'll hide the goose, and see if I can get another in time to take the place of this one, so mother won't be worried."

I walked to the house slowly, but I was afraid to enter. When you are all choked up, people are sure to see it, and ask fool questions. So I went around to the gate and stood there looking up and down the road, and over the meadow toward the Big Woods; and all at once, in one of those high, regular bugle calls, like they mostly scream in spring, one of Pryors' ganders split the echoes for a mile; maybe farther.

I was across the road and slinking down inside the meadow fence before I knew it. There was no thought or plan. I started for Pryors' and went straight ahead, only I kept out of line with our kitchen windows. I tramped through the slush, ice, and crossed fields where I was afraid of horses; but when I got to the top of the Pryor backyard fence, I stuck there, for the bulldogs were loose, and came raving at me. I was going to be eaten alive, for I didn't know the word Laddie did; and those dogs climbed a fence like a person; I saw them the time Leon brought back Even So. I was thinking what a pity it was, after every one had grown accustomed to me, and had begun loving me, that I should be wasted for dog feed, when Mr. Pryor came to the door, and called them; they didn't mind, so he came to the fence, and crossest you ever heard, every bit as bad as the dogs, he cried: "Whose brat are you, and what are you doing here?"

I meant to tell him; but you must have a minute after a thing like that.

"God of my life!" he fairly frothed. "What did anybody send a dumb child here for?"

"Dumb child!" I didn't care if Mr. Pryor did wear a Crown of Glory. It wasn't going to do him one particle of good, unless he was found in the way of the Lord. "Dumb child!" I was no more dumb than he was, until his bulldogs scared me so my heart got all tangled up with my stomach, my lungs, and my liver. That made me mad, and there was nothing that would help me to loosen up and talk fast, like losing my temper. I wondered what kind of a father he had. If he'd been stood against the wall and made to recite, "Speak Gently," as often as all of us, perhaps he'd have remembered the verse that says:

Speak gently to the little child;
  Its love be sure to gain;
Teach it in accents soft and mild;
  It may not long remain.

I should think not, if it had any chance at all to get away! I was so angry by that time I meant to tell him what I thought. Polite or not polite, I'd take a switching if I had to, but I wasn't going to stand that.

"You haven't got any God in your life," I reminded him, "and no one sent me here. I came to see the Princess, because I'm in awful trouble and I hoped maybe she could fix up a way to help me."

"Ye Gods!" he cried. He would stick to calling on God, whether he believed in Him or not. "If it isn't Nimrod! I didn't recognize you in all that bundling."

Probably he didn't know it, but Nimrod was from the Bible too! By bundling, he meant my hood and coat. He helped me from the fence, sent the bulldogs rolling—sure enough he *did* kick them, and they didn't like it either—took my hand and led me straight into the house, and the Princess was there, and a woman who was her mother no doubt, and he said: "Pamela, here is our little neighbour, and she says she's in trouble, and she thinks you might be of some assistance to her. Of course you will be glad if you can."

"Surely!" said the Princess, and she introduced me to her mother, so I bowed the best I knew, and took off my wet mitten, dirty with climbing fences, to shake hands with her. She was so gracious and lovely I forgot what I went after. The Princess brought a cloth and wiped the wet from my shoes and stockings, and asked me if I wouldn't like a cup of hot tea to keep me from taking a chill.

"I've been much wetter than this," I told her, "and I never have taken a chill, and anyway my throat's too full of trouble to drink."

"Why, you poor child!" said the Princess. "Tell me quickly! Is your mother ill again?"

"Not now, but she's going to be as soon as she finds out," I said, and then I told them.

They all listened without a sound until I got where Leon helped the goose eat, and from that on Mr. Pryor laughed until you could easily see that he had very little feeling for suffering humanity. It was funny enough when we fed her, but now that she was bursted wide open there was nothing amusing about it; and to roar when a visitor plainly told you she was in awful trouble, didn't seem very good manners to me. The Princess and her mother never even smiled; and before I had told nearly all of it, Thomas was called to hitch the Princess' driving cart, and she took me to their barnyard to choose the goose that looked most like mother's, and all of them seemed like hers, so we took the first one Thomas could catch, put it into a bag in the back of the cart, and then we got in and started for our barn. As we reached the road, I said to her: "You'd better go past Dovers', for if we come down our Little Hill they will see us sure; it's baking day."

"All right!" said the Princess, so we went the long way round the section, but goodness me! when she drove no way was far.

When we were opposite our barn she stopped, hitched her horse to the fence, and we climbed over, and slipping behind the barn, carried the goose around to the pen and put it in with ours.

She said she wanted the broken one, because her father would enjoy seeing it. I didn't see how he could! We were ready to slip out, when our geese began to run at the new one, hiss and scream, and make such a racket that Laddie and Leon both caught us. They looked at the goose, at me, the Princess, and each other, and neither said a word. She looked back a little bit, and then she laughed as hard as she could. Leon grew red, and he grinned ashamed-like, so she laughed worse than ever. Laddie spoke to me: "You went to Mr. Pryor's and asked for that goose?"

"She did not!" said the Princess before I could answer. "She never asked for anything. She was making a friendly morning call and in the course of her visit she told about the pathetic end of the goose that was expected to lay the golden egg—I mean stuff the Bishop's pillow—and as we have a large flock of blue geese, father gave her one, and he had the best time he's had in years doing it. I wouldn't have had him miss the fun he got from it for any money. He laughed like home again. Now I must slip away before any one sees me, and spoils our secret. Leon, lad, you can go to the house and tell your little mother that the feeding stopped every pain her goose had, and hereafter it looks to you as if she'd be all right."

"Miss Pryor," said Leon, "did you care about what I said at you in church that day?"

"'Thou art all fair, my love. There is no spot in thee.' Well, it *was* a little pointed, but since you ask a plain question, I have survived it."

"I'm awfully sorry," said Leon. "Of course I never would, if I'd known you could be this nice."

The Princess looked at Laddie and almost gasped, and then both of them laughed. Leon saw that he had told her he was sorry he said she was "fair, and no spot in her."

"Oh I don't mean that!" he said. "What I do mean is that I thank you awful much for the goose, and helping me out like such a brick of a good fellow, and what I wish is, that I was old as Laddie, and he'd hump himself if he got to be your beau."

The Princess almost ran. Laddie and I followed to the road, where he unhitched the horse and helped her in. Then he stood stroking its neck, as he held the bridle.

"I don't know what to say!" said Laddie.

"In such case, I would counsel silence," advised the Princess.

"I hope you understand how I thank you."

"I fail to see what for. Father gave the goose to Little Sister. Her thanks and Leon's are more than enough for him. We had great sport."

"I insist on adding mine. Deep and fervent!"

"You take everything so serious. Can't you see the fun of this?"

"No," said Laddie. "But if you can, I am glad, and I'm thankful for anything that gives me a glimpse of you."

"Bye, Little Sister," said the Princess, and when she loosened the lines the mud flew a rod high.

CHAPTER
11

Keeping Christmas Our Way

I remember, I remember
  How my childhood fleeted by,—
The mirth of its December,
  And the warmth of its July.

When dusk closed in it would be Christmas eve. All day I had three points—a chair beside the kitchen table, a lookout melted through the frost on the front window, and the big sitting-room fireplace.

All the perfumes of Araby floated from our kitchen that day. There was that delicious smell of baking flour from big snowy loaves of bread, light biscuit, golden coffee cake, and cinnamon rolls dripping a waxy mixture of sugar, butter, and spice, much better than the finest butterscotch ever brought from the city. There was the tempting odour of boiling ham and baking pies. The air was filled with the smell of more herbs and spices than I knew the names of, that went into mincemeat, fruit cake, plum pudding, and pies. There was a teasing fragrance in the spiced vinegar heating for pickles, a reminder of winesap and rambo in the boiling cider, while the newly opened bottles of grape juice filled the house with the tang of Concord and muscadine. It seemed to me I never got nicely fixed where I could take a sly dip in the cake dough or snipe a fat raisin from the mincemeat but Candace would say: "Don't you suppose the backlog is halfway down the lane?"

Then I hurried to the front window, where I could see through my melted outlook on the frosted pane, across the west eighty to the woods, where father and Laddie were getting out the Christmas backlog. It was too bitterly cold to keep me there while they worked, but Laddie said that if I would watch, and come to meet them, he would take me up, and I might ride home among the Christmas greens on the log.

So I flattened my nose against the pane and danced and fidgeted until those odours teased me back to the kitchen; and no more did I get nicely located beside a jar of pudding sauce than Candace would object to the place I had hung her stocking. It was my task, my delightful all-day task, to hang the stockings. Father had made me a peg for each one, and I had ten feet of mantel front along which to arrange them. But it was no small job to do this to every one's satisfaction. No matter what happened to any one else, Candace had to be pleased: for did not she so manage that most fowls served on mother's table went gizzardless to the carving? She knew and acknowledged the great importance of trying cookies, pies, and cake while they were hot. She was forever overworked and tired, yet she always found time to make gingerbread women with currant buttons on their frocks, and pudgy doughnut men with clove eyes and cigars of cinnamon. If my own stocking lay on the hearth, Candace's had to go in a place that satisfied her—that was one sure thing. Besides, I had to make up to her for what Leon did, because she was crying into the corner of her apron about that.

He slipped in and stole her stocking, hung it over the broomstick, and marched around the breakfast table singing to the tune of—

Ha, ha, ha, who wouldn't go—
  Up on the housetop click, click, click?
Down through the chimney,
  With good Saint Nick—

words he made up himself. He walked just fast enough that she couldn't catch him, and sang as he went:

"Ha, ha, ha, good Saint Nick,
  Come and look at this stocking, quick!
If you undertake its length to fill,
  You'll have to bust a ten-dollar bill.
Who does it belong to? Candace Swartz.
  Bring extra candy,—seven quarts—"

She got so angry she just roared, so father made Leon stop it, but I couldn't help laughing myself. Then we had to pet her all day, so she'd cheer up, and not salt the Christmas dinner with her tears. I never saw such a monkey as Leon! I trotted out to comfort her, and snipped bites, until I wore a triangle on the carpet between the kitchen and the mantel, the mantel and the window, and the window and the kitchen, while every hour things grew more exciting.

There never had been such a flurry at our house since I could remember; for to-morrow would be Christmas and bring home all the children, and a houseful of guests. My big brother, Jerry, who was a lawyer in the city, was coming with his family, and so were Frank, Elizabeth, and Lucy with theirs, and of course Sally and Peter—I wondered if she would still be fixing his tie—and Shelley came yesterday, blushing like a rose, and she laughed if you pointed your finger at her.

Something had happened to her in Chicago. I wasn't so sure as I had been about a city being such a dreadful place of noise, bad air, and wicked people. Nothing had hurt Shelley. She had grown so much that you could see she was larger. Her hair and face—all of Shelley just shone. Her eyes danced, she talked and laughed all the time, and she hugged every one who passed her. She never loved us so before. Leon said she must have been homesick and coming back had given her a spell. I did hope it would be a bad one, and last forever. I would have liked for all our family to have had a spell if it would have made them act and look like Shelley. The Princess was not a speck lovelier, and she didn't act any nicer.

If I could have painted, I'd have made a picture of Shelley with a circle of light above her head like the one of the boy Jesus where He talked with the wise men in the temple. I asked father if he noticed how much prettier and nicer she was, and he said he did.

Then I asked him if he thought now, that a city was such a bad place to live in, and he said where she was had nothing to do with it, the same thing would happen here, or anywhere, when life's greatest experience came to a girl. That was all he would say, but figuring it out was easy. The greatest experience that happened to our girls was when they married, like Sally, so it meant that Shelley had gone and fallen in love with that lawyer man, and she liked sitting on the sofa with him, and no doubt she fixed his ties. But if any one thought I would tell anything I saw when he came they were badly mistaken.

All of us rushed around like we were crazy. If father and mother hadn't held steady and kept us down, we might have raised the roof. We were all so glad about getting Leon and the money back; mother hadn't been sick since the fish cured her; the new blue goose was so like the one that had burst, even father never noticed any difference; all the children were either home or coming, and after we had our gifts and the biggest dinner we ever had, Christmas night all of us would go to the schoolhouse to see our school try to spell down three others to whom they had sent saucy invitations to come and be beaten.

Mother sat in the dining-room beside the kitchen door, so that she could watch the baking, brewing, pickling, and spicing. It took four men to handle the backlog, which I noticed father pronounced every year "just a little the finest we ever had," and Laddie strung the house with bittersweet, evergreens, and the most beautiful sprays of myrtle that he raked from under the snow. Father drove to town in the sleigh, and the list of things to be purchased mother gave him as a reminder was almost a yard long.

The minute they finished the outdoor work Laddie and Leon began bringing in baskets of apples, golden bellflowers, green pippins, white winter pearmains, Rhode Island greenings, and striped rambos all covered with hoarfrost, yet not frozen, and so full of juice you had to bite into them carefully or they dripped and offended mother. These they washed and carried to the cellar ready for use.

Then they cracked big dishes of nuts, and popped corn that popped with the most resounding pops in all my experience—

popped a tubful, and Laddie melted maple sugar and poured over it and made big balls of fluff and sweetness. He took a pan and filled it with grains, selected one at a time, the very largest and whitest, and made an especial ball, in the middle of which he put a lovely pink candy heart on which was printed in red letters: "How can this heart be mine, yet yours, unless our hearts are one?" He wouldn't let any of them see it except me, and he only let me because he knew I'd be delighted.

It was almost dusk when father came through the kitchen loaded with bundles and found Candace and the girls still cooking.

We were so excited we could scarcely be gathered around the supper table, and mother said we chattered until she couldn't hear herself think. After a while Laddie laid down his fork and looked at our father.

"Have you any objection to my using the sleigh tomorrow night?" he asked.

Father looked at mother.

"Had you planned to use it, mother?"

Mother said: "No. If I go, I'll ride in the big sled with all of us. It is such a little way, and the roads are like glass."

So father said politely, as he always spoke to us: "Then it will give me great pleasure for you to take it, my son."

That made Leon bang his fork loudly as he dared and squirm in his chair, for well he knew that if he had asked, the answer would have been different. If Laddie took the sleigh he would harness carefully, drive fast, but reasonably, blanket his horse, come home at the right time, and put everything exactly where he found it. But Leon would pitch the harness on some way, race every step, never think of his steaming horse, come home when there was no one so wild as he left to play pranks with, and scatter the harness everywhere. He knew our father would love to trust him the same as he did Laddie. He wouldn't always prove himself trustworthy, but he envied Laddie.

"You think you'll take the Princess to the spelling bee, don't you?" he sneered.

"I mean to ask her," replied Laddie.

"Maybe you think she'll ride in our old homemade, hickory

cheesebox, when she can sail all over the country like a bird in a velvet-lined cutter with a real buffalo robe."

There was a quick catch in mother's breath and I felt her hand on my chair tremble. Father's lips tightened and a frown settled on his face, while Laddie fairly jumped. He went white to the lips, and one hand dropped on the table, palm up, the fingers closing and unclosing, while his eyes turned first to mother, and then to father, in dumb appeal. We all knew that he was suffering. No one spoke, and Leon having shot his arrow straight home, saw as people so often do in this world that the damage of unkind words could not easily be repaired; so he grew red in the face and squirmed uncomfortably.

At last Laddie drew a deep, quivering breath. "I never thought of that," he said. "She has seemed happy to go with me several times when I asked her, but of course she might not care to ride in ours, when she has such a fine sleigh of her own."

Father's voice fairly boomed down the length of the table.

"Your mother always has found our sleigh suitable," he said.

The fact was, father was rarely proud of it. He had selected the hickory in our woods, cut and hauled it to the mill, cured the lumber, and used all his spare time for two winters making it. With the exception of having the runners turned at a factory and iron-bound at a smithy, he had completed it alone with great care, even to staining it a beautiful cherry colour, and fitting white sheep-skins into the bed. We had all watched him and been so proud of it, and now Leon was sneering at it. He might just as well have undertaken to laugh at father's wedding suit or to make fun of "Clark's Commentaries."

Laddie appealed to mother: "Do you think I'd better not ask her?"

He spoke with an effort.

"Laddie, that is the first time I ever heard you propose to do any one an injustice," she said.

"I don't see how," said Laddie.

"It isn't giving the Princess any chance at all," replied mother. "You've just said that she has seemed pleased to accompany you before, now you are proposing to cut her out of what promises to be the most delightful evening of the winter, without even giving her the chance to say whether she'd go with you or not. Has she ever made you feel that anything you offered her or wanted to do for her was not good enough?"

"Never!" exclaimed Laddie fervently.

"Until she does, then, do you think it would be quite manly and honourable to make decisions for her? You say you never thought of anything except a pleasant time with her; possibly she feels the same. Unless she changes, I would scarcely let a boy's foolish tongue disturb her pleasure. Moreover, as to the matter of wealth, your father may be as rich as hers; but they have one, we have many. If what we spend on all our brood could be confined to one child, we could easily duplicate all her luxuries, and I think she has the good sense to realize the fact as quickly as any one. I've no doubt she would gladly exchange half she has for the companionship of a sister or a brother in her lonely life."

Laddie turned to father, and father's smile was happy again. Mother was little but she was mighty. With only a few words she had made Leon feel how unkind and foolish he had been, quieted Laddie's alarm, and soothed the hurt father's pride had felt in that he had not been able to furnish her with so fine a turnout as Pryors had.

Next morning when the excitement of gifts and greetings was over, and Laddie's morning work was all finished, he took a beautiful volume of poems and his popcorn ball and started across the fields due west; all of us knew that he was going to call on and offer them to the Princess, and ask to take her to the spelling bee. I suppose Laddie thought he was taking that trip alone, but really he was surrounded. I watched him from the window, and my heart went with him. Presently father went and sat beside mother's chair, and stroking her hand, whispered softly: "Please don't worry, little mother. It will be all right. Your boy will come home happy."

"I hope so," she answered, "but I can't help feeling dreadfully nervous. If things go wrong with Laddie, it will spoil the day."

"I have much faith in the Princess' good common sense," replied father, "and considering what it means to Laddie, it would hurt me sore to lose it."

Mother sat still, but her lips moved so that I knew she was

making soft little whispered prayers for her best loved son. But Laddie, plowing through the drift, never dreamed that all of us were with him. He was always better looking than any other man I ever had seen, but when, two hours later, he stamped into the kitchen he was so much handsomer than usual, that I knew from the flush on his cheek and the light in his eye, that the Princess had been kind, and by the package in his hand, that she had made him a present. He really had two, a beautiful book and a necktie. I wondered to my soul if she gave him that, so she could fix it! I didn't believe she had begun on his ties at that time; but of course when he loved her as he did, he wished she would.

It was the very jolliest Christmas we ever had, but the day seemed long. When night came we were in a precious bustle. The wagon bed on bobs, filled with hay and covers, drawn by Ned and Jo, was brought up for the family, and the sleigh made spick-and-span and drawn by Laddie's thoroughbred, stood beside it. Laddie had filled the kitchen oven with bricks and hung up a comfort at four o'clock to keep the Princess warm.

Because he had to drive out of the way to bring her, Laddie wanted to start early; and when he came down dressed in his college clothes, and looking the manliest of men, some of the folks thought it funny to see him carefully rake his hot bricks from the oven, and pin them in an old red breakfast shawl. I thought it was fine, and I whispered to mother: "Do you suppose that if Laddie ever marries the Princess he will be good to her as he is to you?"

Mother nodded with tear-dimmed eyes, but Shelley said: "I'll wager a strong young girl like the Princess will laugh at you for babying over her."

"Why?" inquired Laddie. "It is a long drive and a bitter night, and if you fancy the Princess will laugh at anything I do, when I am doing the best I know for her comfort, you are mistaken. At least, that is the impression she gave me this morning."

I saw the swift glance mother shot at father, and father laid down his paper and said, while he pretended his glasses needed polishing: "Now there is the right sort of a girl for you. No foolishness about her, when she has every chance. Hurrah for the Princess!"

It was easy to see that she wasn't going to have nearly so hard a time changing father's opinion as she would mother's. It was not nearly a year yet, and here he was changed already. Laddie said good-bye to mother—he never forgot—gathered up his comfort and bricks, and started for Pryors' downright happy. We went to the schoolhouse a little later, all of us scoured, curled, starched, and wearing our very best clothes. My! but it was fine. There were many lights in the room and it was hung with greens. There was a crowd even though it was early. On Miss Amelia's table was a volume of history that was the prize, and every one was looking and acting the very best he knew how, although there were cases where they didn't know so very much.

Our Shelley was the handsomest girl there, until the Princess came, and then they both were. Shelley wore one of her city frocks and a quilted red silk hood that was one of her Christmas gifts, and she looked just like a handsome doll. She made every male creature in that room feel that she was pining for him alone. May had a gay plaid frock and curls nearly a yard long, and so had I, but both our frocks and curls were homemade; mother would have them once in a while; father and I couldn't stop her.

Mary Ann Ramsey wore her first store dress of green flannel and was almost bursting with pride, and her best friend, Sarah Marietta Dover, was green with envy as Ann's dress. The girls who had new store dresses took off their wraps and shivered with the cold, and those who had to wear their old ones kept on their coats or shawls and suffered with heat.

All the boys had their hair newly cut just as nicely as their mothers could shear it off, and grease it for them, and wore the very best clothes they owned or could borrow. Little Benny Polk had to wear his father's old army overcoat, so long it trailed, and the sleeves had to be rolled up; and Joseph Thomas wore his sister Alabama's breakfast shawl around his throat—because it was so cold, he said, but I suspect he had no tie and collar. George Washington Justice came with his pantaloons in his boot tops. When he saw that none of the other boys was so dressed, he went behind a back desk and tried to pull up the pantaloons, and put them outside. As the boots were wider than the trousers, he tugged until he was purple in the face and then didn't get them within hailing distance of his feet.

But there was not a soul there who didn't have some sort of gift to rejoice over, and laughter and shouts of "Merry Christmas!" filled the room. It was growing late and there was some talk of choosers, when the door opened and in a rush of frosty air the Princess and Laddie entered. Every one stopped short and stared. There was good reason. The Princess looked as if she had accidentally stepped from a frame. She was always lovely and beautifully dressed, but to-night she was prettier and finer than ever before. You could fairly hear their teeth click as some of the most envious of those girls caught sight of her, for she was wearing a new hat!—a black velvet store hat, fitting closely over her crown, with a rim of twisted velvet, a scarlet bird's wing, and a big silver buckle. Her dress was of scarlet cloth cut in forms, and it fitted as if she had been melted and poured into it. It was edged around the throat, wrists, and skirt with narrow bands of fur, and she wore a loose, long, silk-lined coat of the same material, and worst of all, furs—furs such as we had heard wealthy and stylish city ladies were wearing. A golden brown cape that reached to her elbows, with ends falling to the knees, finished in the tails of some animal, and for her hands a muff as big as a nail keg.

Now, there was not a girl in that room, except the Princess, and she had those clothes, who wouldn't have flirted like a peacock, almost bursting with pride; but because the Princess had them, and they didn't, they sat stolid and sullen, and cast glances at each other as if they were saying: "The stuck-up thing!" "Thinks she's smart, don't she?"

Many of them should have gone to meet her and made her welcome, for she was not of our district and really their guest. Shelley did go, but I noticed she didn't hurry.

The choosers began at once, and Laddie was the first person called for our side, and the Princess for the visitors'. Every one in the room was chosen on one side or the other; even my name was called, but I only sat still and shook my head, for I very well knew that no one except father would remember to pronounce easy ones for me, and besides I was so bitterly disappointed I could scarcely have stood up. They had put me in a seat near the fire; the spellers lined either wall, and a goodly number that refused to spell occupied the middle seats. I couldn't get a glimpse of Laddie or the home folks, or worst of all, of my idolized Princess.

I never could bear to find a fault with Laddie, but I sadly reflected that he might as well have left me at home, if I were to be buried where I could neither hear nor see a thing. I was just wishing it was summer so I could steal out, and go across the road to the cemetery, and have a good visit with the butterflies that always swarmed around Georgiana Jane Titcomb's grave at the corner of the church. I never knew Georgiana Jane, but her people must have been very fond of her, for her grave was scarlet with geraniums, and pink with roses from earliest spring until frost, and the bright colours attracted swarms of butterflies. I had learned that if I stuck a few blossoms in my hair, rubbed some sweet smelling ones over my hands, and knelt and kept so quiet that I fitted into the landscape, the butterflies would think me a flower too, and alight on my hair, dress, and my hands, even. God never made anything more beautiful than those butterflies, with their wings of brightly painted velvet down, their bright eyes, their curious antennae, and their queer, tickly feet. Laddie had promised me a book telling all about every kind there was, the first time he went to a city, so I was wishing I had it, and was among my pet beauties with it, when I discovered him bending over me.

He took my arm, and marching back to his place, helped me to the deep window seat beside him, where with my head on a level, and within a foot of his, I could see everything in the whole room. I don't know why I ever spent any time pining for the beauties of Georgiana Jane Titcomb's grave, even with its handsome headstone on which was carved a lamb standing on three feet and holding a banner over its shoulder with the fourth, and the geraniums, roses, and the weeping willow that grew over it, thrown in. I might have trusted Laddie. He never had forgotten me; until he did, I should have kept unwavering faith.

Now, I had the best place of any one in the room, and I smoothed my new plaid frock and shook my handmade curls just as near like Shelley as ever I could. But it seems that most of the ointment in this world has a fly in it, like in the Bible, for fine as my location was, I soon knew that I should ask Laddie to put me down, because the window behind me didn't fit its frame, and the night was bitter. Before a half hour I was stiff with cold, but I doubt if I would have given up that location if I had known I would freeze, because this was the most fun I had ever seen.

Miss Amelia began with McGuffey's spelling book, and whenever some poor unfortunate made a bad break the crowd roared with laughter. Peter Justice stood up to spell and before three rounds he was nodding on his feet, so she pronounced sleepy to him. Some one nudged Pete and he waked up and spelled it, s-l-e, sle, p-e, pe, and because he really was so sleepy it made every one laugh. James Whittaker spelled compromise with a k, and Isaac Thomas spelled soap, s-o-a-p-e, and it was all the funnier that he couldn't spell it, for from his looks you could tell that he had no acquaintance with it in any shape. Then Miss Amelia gave out "marriage" to the spooniest young man in the district, and "stepfather" to a man who was courting a widow with nine children; and "coquette" to our Shelley, who had been making sheep's eyes at Johnny Myers, so it took her by surprise and she joined the majority, which by that time occupied seats.

There was much laughing and clapping of hands for a time, but when Miss Amelia had let them have their fun and thinned the lines to a half dozen on each side who could really spell, she began business, and pronounced the hardest words she could find in the book, and the spellers caught them up and rattled them off like machines.

"Incompatibility," she gave out, and before the sound of her voice died away the Princess was spelling: "I-n, in, c-o-m, com, incom, p-a-t, pat, incompat, i, incompati, b-i-l, bil, incompatibil, i, incompatibili, t-y, ty, incompatibility."

Then Laddie spelled "incomprehensibility," and they finished up the "bilities" and the "alities" with a rush and changed McGuffey's for Webster, with five on Laddie's side and three on the Princess', and when they quit with it, the Princess was alone, and Laddie and our little May facing her.

From that on you could call it real spelling. They spelled from the grammars, hyperbole, synecdoche, and epizeuxis. They spelled from the physiology, chlorophyll, coccyx, arytenoid, and the names of the bones and nerves, and all the hard words inside you. They tried the diseases and spelled jaundice, neurasthenia, and tongue-tied. They tried all the occupations and professions, and went through the stores and spelled all sorts of hardware, china and dry goods. Each side kept cheering its own and urging them to do their best, and every few minutes some man in the back of the house said something that was too funny. When Miss Amelia pronounced "bombazine" to Laddie our side cried, "Careful, Laddie, careful! you're out of your element!"

And when she gave "swivel-tree" to the Princess, her side whispered, "Go easy! Do you know what it is? Make her define it."

They branched over the country. May met her Jonah on the mountains. Katahdin was too much for her, and Laddie and the Princess were left to fight it out alone. I didn't think Laddie liked it. I'm sure he never expected it to turn out that way. He must have been certain he could beat her, for after he finished English there were two or three other languages he knew, and every one in the district felt that he could win, and expected him to do it. It was an awful place to put him in, I could see that. He stood a little more erect than usual, with his eyes toward the Princess, and when his side kept crying, "Keep the prize, Laddie! Hold up the glory of the district!" he ground out the words as if he had a spite at them for not being so hard that he would have an excuse for going down.

The Princess was poised lightly on her feet, her thick curls, just touching her shoulders, shining in the light; her eyes like stars, her perfect, dark oval face flushed a rich red, and her deep bosom rising and falling with excitement. Many times in later years I have tried to remember when the Princess was loveliest of all, and that night always stands first.

I was thinking fast. Laddie was a big man. Men were strong on purpose so they could bear things. He loved the Princess so, and he didn't know whether she loved him or not; and every marriageable man in three counties was just aching for the chance to court her, and I didn't feel that he dared risk hurting her feelings.

Laddie said, to be the man who conquered the Princess and to whom she lifted her lips for a first kiss was worth life itself. I made up my mind that night that he knew just exactly what he was talking about. I thought so too. And I seemed to understand why Laddie—Laddie in his youth, strength, and manly beauty, Laddie, who boasted that there was not a nerve in his body—trembled before the Princess.

It looked as if she had set herself against him and was working for the honours, and if she wanted them, I didn't feel that he should chance beating her, and then, too, it was beginning to be plain that it was none too sure he could. Laddie didn't seem to be the only one who had been well drilled in spelling.

I held my jaws set a minute, so that I could speak without Laddie knowing how I was shivering, and then I whispered: "Except her eyes are softer, she looks just like a cardinal."

Laddie nodded emphatically and moving a step nearer laid his elbow across my knees. Heavens, how they spelled! They finished all the words I ever heard and spelled like lightning through a lot of others the meaning of which I couldn't imagine. Father never gave them out at home. They spelled epiphany, gaberdine, ichthyology, gewgaw, kaleidoscope, and troubadour. Then Laddie spelled one word two different ways; and the Princess went him one better, for she spelled another three.

They spelled from the Bible, Nebuchadnezzar, Potiphar, Peleg, Belshazzar, Abimelech, and a host of others I never heard the minister preach about. Then they did the most dreadful thing of all. "Broom," pronounced the teacher, and I began mentally, b-r-o-o-m, but Laddie spelled "b-r-o-u-g-h-a-m," and I stared at him in a daze. A second later Miss Amelia gave out "Beecham" to the Princess, and again I tried it, b-e-e-c-h, but the Princess was spelling "B-e-a-u-c-h-a-m-p," and I almost fell from the window.

They kept that up until I was nearly crazy with nervousness; I forgot I was half frozen. I pulled Laddie's sleeve and whispered in his ear: "Do you think she'll cry if you beat her?"

I was half crying myself, the strain had been awful. I was torn between these dearest loves of mine.

"Seen me have any chance to beat her?" retorted Laddie.

Miss Amelia seemed to have used most of her books, and at last picked up an old geography and began giving out points around the coast, while Laddie and the Princess took turns snatching the words from her mouth and spelling them. Father often did that, so Laddie was safe there. They were just going it when Miss Amelia pronounced, "Terra del Fuego," to the Princess. "T-e-r-r-a, Terra, d-e-l, del, F-i-e-u-g-o," spelled the Princess, and sat down suddenly in the midst of a mighty groan from her side, swelled by a wail from one little home district deserter.

"Next!" called Miss Amelia.

"T-e-r-r-a, Terra, d-e-l, del, F-e-u-g-o," spelled Laddie.

"Wrong!" wailed Miss Amelia, and our side breathed one big groan in concert, and I lifted up my voice in that also. Then every one laughed and pretended they didn't care, and the Princess came over and shook hands with Laddie, and Laddie said to Miss Amelia: "Just let me take that book a minute until I see how the thing really does go." It was well done and satisfied the crowd, which clapped and cheered; but as I had heard him spell it many, many times for father, he didn't fool me.

Laddie and the Princess drew slips for the book and it fell to her. He was so pleased he kissed me as he lifted me down and never noticed I was so stiff I could scarcely stand—and I did fall twice going to the sleigh. My bed was warm and my room was warm, but I chilled the night through and until the next afternoon, when I grew so faint and sleepy I crept to Miss Amelia's desk, half dead with fright—it was my first trip to ask an excuse—and begged: "Oh teacher, I'm so sick. Please let me go home."

I think one glance must have satisfied her that it was true, for she said very kindly that I might, and she would send Leon along to take care of me. But my troubles were only half over when I had her consent. It was very probable I would be called a baby and sent back when I reached home, so I refused company and started alone. It seemed a mile past the cemetery. I was so tired I stopped, and leaning against the fence, peeped through at the white stones and the whiter mounds they covered, and wondered how my mother would feel if she were compelled to lay me beside the two little whooping-cough and fever sisters already sleeping there. I decided that it would be so very dreadful, that the tears began to roll down my cheeks and freeze before they fell.

Then I noticed the beautiful angel blowing a horn on Henrietta Angelina Rittenhouse's tombstone. It wore a flowing robe and its breast and arms were bare. I wondered why the Rittenhouses didn't wrap a blanket around it in winter, it looked so cold and blue, and I cried again in sympathy; and then it struck me that it was very probable that Henrietta Angelina died because she was so cold she couldn't live any longer, and so I cried some more.

Down the Big Hill slowly I went. How bare it looked then! Only leafless trees and dried seed pods rattling on the bushes, the sand frozen, and not a rush to be seen for the thick blanket of snow. A few rods above the bridge was a footpath, smooth and well worn, that led down to the creek, beaten by the feet of children who raced it every day and took a running slide across the ice. I struck into the path as always; but I was too stiff to run, for I tried. I walked on the ice, and being almost worn out, sat on the bridge and fell to watching the water bubbling under the glassy crust. I was so dull a horse's feet struck the bridge before I heard the bells—for I had bells in my ears that day—and when I looked up it was the Princess—the Princess in her red dress and furs, with a silk hood instead of her hat, her sleigh like a picture, with a buffalo robe, that it was whispered about the country, cost over a hundred dollars, and her thoroughbred mare Maud dancing and prancing. "Bless me! Is it you, Little Sister?" she asked. "Shall I give you a ride home?"

Before I could scarcely realize she was there, I was beside her and she was tucking the fine warm robe over me. I lifted a pair of dull eyes to her face.

"Oh Princess, I am so glad you came," I said. "I don't think I could have gone another step if I had frozen on the bridge."

The Princess bent to look in my face. "Why, you poor child!" she exclaimed, "you're white as death! Where are you ill?"

I leaned on her shoulder, though ordinarily I would not have offered to touch her first, and murmured: "I am not ill, outdoors, only dull, sleepy, and freezing with the cold."

"It was that window!" she exclaimed. "I thought of it, but I trusted Laddie."

That roused me a little.

"Oh Princess," I cried, "you mustn't blame Laddie! I knew it was too cold, but I wouldn't tell him, because if he put me down I couldn't see you, and we thought, but for your eyes being softer, you looked just like a cardinal."

The Princess hugged me close and laughed merrily. "You darling!" she cried.

Then she shook me up sharply: "Don't you dare go to sleep!" she said. "I must take you home first."

Once there she quieted my mother's alarm, put me to bed, drove three miles for Dr. Fenner and had me started nicely on the road to a month of lung fever, before she left. In my delirium I spelled volumes; and the miracle of it was I never missed a word until I came to "Terra del Fuego," and there I covered my lips and stoutly insisted that it was the Princess' secret.

To keep me from that danger sleep on the road, she shook me up and asked about the spelling bee. I thought it was the grandest thing I had ever seen in my life, and I told her so. She gathered me close and whispered: "Tell me something, Little Sister, please."

The minx! She knew I thought that a far finer title than hers.

"Would Laddie care?" I questioned.

"Not in the least!"

"Well then, I will."

"Can Laddie spell 'Terra del Fuego?'" she whispered.

I nodded.

"Are you sure?"

"I have heard him do it over and over for father."

The Princess forgot I was so sick, forgot her horse, forgot everything. She threw her head back and her hands up, until her horse stopped in answer to the loosened line, and she laughed and laughed. She laughed until peal on peal re-echoed from our Big Woods clear across the west eighty. She laughed until her ringing notes set my slow pulses on fire, and started my numbed brain in one last effort. I stood up and took her lovely face between my palms, turning it until I could see whether the thought that had come to me showed in her eyes, and it did.

"Oh you darling, splendid Princess!" I cried. "You missed it on purpose to let Laddie beat! You can spell it too!"

12

The Horn of the Hunter

The dusky night rides down the sky,
And ushers in the morn:
The hounds all join in glorious cry,
The huntsman winds his horn.

Leon said our house reminded him of the mourners' bench before any one had "come through." He said it was deadly with Sally and Shelley away, that he had a big notion to marry Susie Fall and bring her over to liven things up a little. Mother said she thought that would be a good idea, and Leon started in the direction of Falls', but he only went as far as Deams'. When he came back he had a great story to tell about dogs chasing their sheep, and foxes taking their geese. Father said sheep were only safe behind securely closed doors, especially in winter, and geese also. Leon said every one hadn't as big a barn as ours, and father said there was nothing to prevent any man from building the sized barn he needed to shelter his creatures in safety and comfort, if he wanted to dig in and earn the money to put it up. There was no answer to that, and Mr. Leon didn't try to make any. Mostly, he said something to keep on talking, but sometimes he saw when he had better quit.

I was having a good time, myself. Of course when the fever was the worst, and when I never had been sick before, it was pretty bad, but as soon as I could breathe all right, there was no pain to speak of, and every one was so good to me. I could have Bobby on the footboard of my bed as long as I wanted him, and he would crow whenever I told him to. I kept Grace Greenwood beside me, and spoiled her dress making her take some of each dose of medicine I did, but Shelley wrote that she was saving goods and she would make her another as soon as she came home. I made mother put red flannel on Grace's chest and around her neck, until I could hardly find her mouth when she had to take her medicine, but she swallowed it down all right, or she got her nose held, until she did. She was not nearly so sick as I was, though. We both grew better together, and when Dr. Fenner brought me candy, she had her share.

When I began to get well it was lovely. Such toast, chicken broth, and squirrels, as mother always had. I even got the chicken liver, oranges, and all of them gave me everything they had that I wanted—I must almost have died to make them act like that!

Laddie and father would take me up wrapped in blankets and hold me to rest my back. Father would rock me and sing about "Young Johnny," just as he had when I was little. We always laughed at it, we knew it was a fool song, but we liked it. The tune was smooth and sleepy-like and the words went:

One day young Johnny, he did go,
Way down in the meadow for to mow.

(Chorus)
Li-tu-di-nan-incty, tu-di-nan-incty, noddy O!

He scarce had mowed twice round the field,
When a pesky sarpent bit him on the heel, (Chorus)

He threw the scythe upon the ground,
An' shut his eyes, and looked all round, (Chorus)

He took the sarpent in his hand,
And then ran home to Molly Bland, (Chorus)

O Molly dear, and don't you see,
This pesky sarpent that bit me? (Chorus)

O Johnny dear, why did you go?
Way down in the meadow for to mow? (Chorus)

O Molly dear, 'tis well you knowed,
'Twas Daddy's grass and it must be mowed. (Chorus)

So Johnny dear gave up the ghost,
And to Abraham's bosom he did post. (Chorus)

Now all young men a warning take,
And don't get bit by a rattlesnake. (Chorus)

All of them told me stories, read to me, and Frank, one of my big gone-away brothers, sent me the prettiest little book. It had a green cover with gold on the back, and it was full of stories and poems, not so very hard, because I could read every one of them, with help on a few words. The piece I liked best was poetry. If it hadn't been for that, I'm afraid, I was having such a good time, I'd have lain there until I forgot how to walk, with all of them trying to see who could be nicest to me. The ones who really could, were Laddie and the Princess, except mother. Laddie lifted me most carefully, the Princess told the best stories, but after all, if the burning and choking grew so bad I could scarcely stand it, mother could lay her hand on my head and say, "Poor child," in a way that made me work to keep on breathing. Maybe I only *thought* I loved Laddie best. I guess if I had been forced to take my choice when I had the fever, I'd have stuck pretty tight to mother. Even Dr. Fenner said if I pulled through she'd have to make me, because he couldn't be there enough, so many other people were sick.

One day I asked father if he supposed Dr. Fenner took candy to all the children he went to see, and he said of course he did, and put it in the bill afterward, and mother said: "Why, Paul! I'm ashamed of you!" First time I saw him alone I asked him if he was really giving me that candy. I had a big, flat, round cake of mint that morning that was all waxy and delicious, and cut the cobwebs from my throat fine, and he said mother didn't think so, but he did, so I could take my choice. I studied about it a great deal, and the next time Dr. Fenner came, I asked him, because really, he was the only one who knew, and he laughed and laughed, until he shook the bed, and he said he guessed father was right. Mother's face was so red I thought sure she would scold me good when he was gone, but I must have been sicker than I knew, for she never mentioned it. That was how kind all of them were. I might have been lying there yet, if it hadn't been for the book Frank sent me, with the poetry piece in it. It began:

Somewhere on a sunny bank, buttercups are bright,
Somewhere 'mid the frozen grass, peeps the daisy white.

I read that so often I could repeat it quite as well with the book shut as open, and every time I read it, I wanted outdoors worse. In one place it ran:

Welcome, yellow buttercups, welcome daisies white,
Ye are in my spirit visioned a delight.
Coming in the springtime of sunny hours to tell,
Speaking to our hearts of Him who doeth all things well.

That piece helped me out of bed, and the blue gander screaming opened the door. It was funny about it too. I don't know *why* it worked on me that way; it just kept singing in my heart all day, and I could shut my eyes and go to sleep seeing buttercups in a gold sheet all over our Big Hill, although there never was a single one there; and meadows full of daisies, which were things father said were a pest he couldn't tolerate, because they spread so, and he grubbed up every one he found. Yet that piece filled our meadow until I imagined I could roll on daisies. They might be a pest to farmers, but sheets of them were pretty good if you were burning with fever. Between the buttercups and the daisies I left the bed with a light head and wobbly legs.

Of course I wasn't an idiot. I knew when I looked from our south window exactly what was to be seen. The person who wrote that piece was the idiot. It sang and sounded pretty, and it pulled you up and pushed you out, but really it was a fool thing, as I very well knew. I couldn't imagine daisies peeping through frozen grass. Any baby should have known they bloomed in July. Skunk cabbage always came first, and hepatica. If I had looked from any of our windows and seen daisies and buttercups in March, I'd have fallen over with the shock. I knew there would be frozen brown earth, last year's dead leaves, caved-in apple and potato holes, the cabbage row almost gone, puddles of water and mud everywhere, and I would hear geese scream and hens sing. And yet that poem kept pulling and pulling, and I was happy as a queen—I wondered if they were for sure; mother had doubts—the day I was wrapped in shawls and might sit an hour in the sun on the top board of the back fence, where I could see the barn, orchard, the creek and the meadow, as you never could in summer because of the leaves. I wasn't looking for buttercups and daisies either. I mighty well knew there wouldn't be any.

But the sun was there. A little taste of willow, oak and maple was in the air. You could see the buds growing fat too, and you could smell them. If you opened your eyes and looked in any direction you could see blue sky, big, ragged white clouds, bare trees, muddy earth with grassy patches, and white spots on the shady sides where unmelted snow made the icy feel in the air, even when the sun shone. You couldn't hear yourself think for the clatter of the turkeys, ganders, roosters, hens, and everything that had a voice. I was so crazy with it I could scarcely hang to the fence; I wanted to get down and scrape my wings like the gobbler, and scream louder than the gander, and crow oftener than the rooster. There was everything all ice and mud. They would have frozen, if they hadn't been put in a house at night, and starved, if they hadn't been fed; they were not at the place where they could hunt and scratch, and not pay any attention to feeding time, because of being so bursting full. They had no nests and babies to rejoice over. But there they were! And so was I! Buttercups and daisies be-hanged! Ice and mud really! But if you breathed that air, and shut your eyes, north, you could see blue flags, scarlet lilies, buttercups, cattails and redbirds sailing above them; east, there would be apple bloom and soft grass, cowslips, and bubbling water, robins, thrushes, and bluebirds;

and south, waving corn with wild rose and alder borders, and sparrows, and larks on every fence rider.

Right there I got that daisy thing figured out. It wasn't that there were or ever would be daisies and buttercups among the frozen grass; but it was forever and always that when this *feel* came into the air, you knew they were *coming. That* was what ailed the gander and the gobbler. They hadn't a thing to be thankful for yet, but something inside them was swelling and pushing because of what was coming. I felt exactly as they did, because I wanted to act the same way, but I'd been sick enough to know that I'd better be thankful for the chance to sit on the fence, and think about buttercups and daisies. Really, one old brown and purple skunk cabbage with a half-frozen bee buzzing over it, or a few forlorn little spring beauties, would have set me wild, and when a lark really did go over, away up high, and a dove began to coo in the orchard, if Laddie hadn't come for me, I would have fallen from the fence.

I simply had to get well and quickly too, for the wonderful time was beginning. It was all very well to lie in bed when there was nothing else to do, and every one would pet me and give me things; but here was maple syrup time right at the door, and the sugar camp most fun alive; here was all the neighbourhood crazy mad at the foxes, and planning a great chase covering a circuit of miles before the ground thawed; here was Easter and all the children coming, except Shelley—again, it would cost too much for only one day—and with everything beginning to hum, I found out there would be more amusement outdoors than inside. That was how I came to study out the daisy piece. There was nothing in the silly, untrue lines: the pull and tug was in what they made you think of.

I was still so weak I had to take a nap every day, so I wasn't sleepy as early at night, and I heard father and mother talk over a lot of things before they went to bed. After they mentioned it, I remembered that we hadn't received nearly so many letters from Shelley lately, and mother seldom found time to read them aloud during the day and forgot, or her eyes were tired, at night.

"Are you worrying about Shelley?" asked father one night.

"Yes, I am," answered mother.

"What do you think is the trouble?"

"I'm afraid things are not coming out with Mr. Paget as she hoped."

"If they don't ,she is going to be unhappy?"

"That's putting it mildly."

"Well, I was doubtful in the beginning."

"Now hold on," said mother. "So was I; but what are you going to do? I can't go through the world with my girls, and meet men for them. I trained them just as carefully as possible before I started them out; that was all I could do. Shelley knows when a man appears clean, decent and likable. She knows when his calling is respectable. She knows when his speech is proper, his manners correct, and his ways attractive. She found this man all of these things, and she liked him accordingly. At Christmas she told me freely how much she thought of him."

"Have you any idea how far the thing has gone?"

"She said then that she had seen him about twice a week for two months. He seemed very fond of her. He had told her he cared more for her than any girl he ever had met, and he had asked her to come here this summer and pay us a visit, so she wanted to know if he might.

"Of course you told her yes."

"Certainly I told her yes. I wish now we'd saved money and you'd gone to visit her and met him when she first wrote of him. You could have found out who and what he was, and with your experience you might have pointed out signs that would have helped her to see, before it was too late."

"What do you think is the trouble?"

"I wish I knew! She simply is failing to mention him in her letters; all the joy of living has dropped from them, she merely writes about her work; and now she is beginning to complain of homesickness and to say that she doesn't know how to endure the city any longer. There's something wrong."

"Had I better go now?"

"Too late!" said mother, and I could hear her throat go wrong and the choke come into her voice. "She is deeply in love with him; he hasn't found in her what he desires; probably he is not coming any more; what could you do?"

"I could go and see if there is anything I could do?"

"She may not want you. I'll write her to-morrow and suggest that you or Laddie pay her a visit and learn what she thinks."

"All right," said father.

He kissed her and went to sleep, but mother was awake yet, and she got up and stood looking down at the church and the two little white gravestones she could see from her window, until I thought she would freeze, and she did nearly, for her hands were cold and the tears falling when she examined my covers, and felt my face and hands before she went to bed. My! but the mother of a family like ours is never short of a lot of things to think of! I had a new one myself. Now what do you suppose there was about that man?

Of course after having lived all her life with father and Laddie, Shelley would know how a man should look, and act to be *right;* and this one must have been right to make her bloom out in winter the way other things do in spring; and now what could be wrong? Maybe city girls were prettier than Shelley. But all women were made alike on the outside, and that was as far as you could see. You couldn't find out whether they had pure blood, true hearts, or clean souls. No girl could be so very much prettier than Shelley; they simply were not made that way. She knew how to behave; she had it beaten into her, like all of us. And she knew her books, what our schools could teach her, and Groveville, and Lucy, who had city chances for years, and there never was a day at our house when books and papers were not read and discussed, and your spelling was hammered into you standing in rows against the wall, and memory tests—what on earth could be the matter with Shelley that a man who could make her look and act as she did at Christmas, would now make her unhappy? Sometimes I wanted to be grown up dreadfully, and again, times like that, I wished my bed could stay in mother's room, and I could creep behind father's paper and go to sleep between his coat and vest, and have him warm my feet in his hands forever.

This world was too much for me. I never worked and worried in all my life as I had over Laddie and the Princess, and Laddie said I, myself, never would know how I had helped him. Of course nothing was settled; he had to try to make her love him by teaching her how lovable he was. We knew, because we always had known him, but she was a stranger and had to learn. It was mighty fine for him that he could force his way past the dogs, Thomas, the other men, her half-crazy father, and through the locked door, and go there to try to make her see, on Sunday nights, and week days, every single chance he could invent, and he could think up more reasons for going to Pryors' than mother could for putting out an extra wash. Now just as I got settled a little about him, and we could see they really wanted him there, at least the Princess and her mother did, and Mr. Pryor must have been fairly decent or Laddie never would have gone; and the Princess came to our house to bring me things to eat, and ask how mother was, and once to learn how she embroidered Sally's wedding chemise, and social things like that; and when father acted as if he liked her so much he hadn't a word to say, and mother seemed to begin to feel as if Laddie and the Princess could be trusted to fix it up about God; and the old mystery didn't matter after all; why, here Shelley popped up with another mystery, and it belonged to us. But whatever ailed that man I couldn't possibly think. It had got to be him, for Shelley was so all right at Christmas, it made her look that pretty we hardly knew her.

I was thinking about her until I scarcely could study my lessons, so I could recite to Laddie at night, and not fall so far behind at school. Miss Amelia offered to hear me, but I just begged Laddie, and father could see that he taught me fifty things in a lesson that you could tell to look at Miss Amelia, she never knew. Why, he couldn't hear me read:

We charged upon a flock of geese,
  And put them all to flight,
Except one sturdy gander
  That thought to show us fight,

without teaching me that the oldest picture in all the world was made of a row of geese, some of which were kinds we then had— the earth didn't seem so old when you thought of that—and how a flock of geese once wakened an army and saved a city, and how far wild geese could fly without alighting in migration, and everything you could think of about geese, only he didn't know why eating the same grass made feathers on geese and wool on sheep. Anyway, Miss Amelia never told you a word, but what was in the book, and how to read and spell it. May said that father was very much disappointed in her, and he was never going to hire another teacher until he met and talked with her, no matter what kind of letters she could send. He was not going to help her get a summer school, and O my soul! I hope no one does, for if they do, I have to go, and I'd rather die than go to school in the summer.

Leon came in about that time with more fox stories. Been in Jacob Hood's chicken house and taken his best Dorking rooster, and father said it was time to do something. He never said a word so long as they took Deams', except they should have barn room for their geese, but when anything was the matter at Hoods' father and mother started doing something the instant they heard of it. So father and Laddie rode around the neighbourhood and talked it over, and the next night they had a meeting at our schoolhouse; men for miles came, and they planned a regular old-fashioned foxchase, and every one was wild about it.

Laddie told it at Pryors' and the Princess wanted to go; she asked to go with him, and if you please, Mr. Pryor wanted to go too, and their Thomas. They attended the meeting to tell how people chase foxes in England, where they seem to hunt them most of the time. Father said: "Thank God for even a foxchase, if it will bring Mr. Pryor among his neighbours and help him to act sensibly." They are going away fifteen miles or farther, and form a big circle of men from all directions, some walking in a line, and others riding to bring back any foxes that escape, and with dogs, and guns, they are going to rout out every one they can find, and kill them so they won't take the geese, little pigs, lambs, and Hoods' Dorking rooster. Laddie had a horn that Mr. Pryor gave him, when he told him this country was showing signs of becoming civilized at last; but Leon grinned and said he'd beat that.

Then when you wanted him, he was in the wood house loft at work, but father said he couldn't get into mischief there. He should have seen that churn when it was full of wedding breakfast! We ate for a week afterward, until things were all moulded, and we didn't dare any more. One night I begged so hard and promised so faithfully he trusted me; he did often, after I didn't tell about the Station; and I went to the loft with him, and watched him work an hour. He had a hollow limb about six inches through and fourteen long. He had cut and burned it to a mere shell, and then he had scraped it with glass inside and out, until it shone like polished horn. He had shaved the wool from a piece of sheepskin, soaked, stretched, and dried it, and then fitted it over one end of the drumlike thing he had made, and tacked and bound it in a little groove at the edge. He put the skin on damp so he could stretch it tight. Then he punched a tiny hole in the middle, and pulled through it, down inside the drum, a sheepskin thong rolled in resin, with a knot big enough to hold it, and not tear the head. Then he took it under his arm and we slipped across the orchard below the Station, and went into the hollow and tried it.

It worked! I almost fell dead with the first frightful sound. It just bellowed and roared. In only a little while he found different ways to make it sound by his manner of working the tongue. A long, steady, even pull got that kind of a roar. A short, quick one made it bark. A pull half the length of the thong, a pause, and another pull, made it sound like a bark and a yelp. To pull hard and quick, made it go louder, and soft and easy made it whine. Before he had tried it ten minutes he could do fifty things with it that would almost scare the livers out of those nasty old foxes that were taking every one's geese, Dorking roosters, and even baby lambs and pigs. Of course people couldn't stand that; something had to be done!

Even in the Bible it says, "Beware of the little foxes that spoil the vines," and geese, especially blue ones, Dorking roosters, lambs, and pigs were much more valuable than mere vines; so Leon made that awful thing to scare the foxes from their holes—that's in the Bible too, about the holes I mean, not the scaring. I wanted Leon to slip to the back door and make the dumb-bell—that's what he called it; if I had been naming it I would have called it the thunder-bell—go; but he wouldn't. He said he didn't propose to work as he had, and then have some one find out, and fix one like it. He said he wouldn't let it make a sound until the night before the chase, and then he'd raise the dead. I don't know about the dead; but it was true of the living. Father went a foot above his chair and cried: "Whoo-pee!" All of us, even I, when I was waiting for it, screamed as if Paddy Ryan raved at the door. Then Leon came in and showed us, and every one wanted to work the dumb-bell, even mother. Leon marched around and showed off; he looked "See the conquering hero comes," all over. I never felt worse about being made into a girl than I did that night.

I couldn't sleep for excitement, and mother said I might as well, for it would be at least one o'clock before they would round-up in our meadow below the barn. All the neighbours were to shut up their stock, tie their dogs, or lead them with chains, if they took them, so when the foxes were surrounded, they could catch them alive, and save their skins. I wondered how some of those chasing people, even Laddie, Leon, and father—think of that! father was going too—I wondered how they would have liked to have had something as much bigger than they were, as they were bigger than the foxes, chase them with awful noises, guns and dogs, and catch them alive—to save their skins. No wonder I couldn't sleep! I guess the foxes wouldn't either, if they had known what was coming. Maybe hereafter the mean old things would eat rabbits and weasels, and leave the Dorking roosters alone.

May, Candace, and Miss Amelia were going to Deams' to wait, and when the round-up formed a solid line, they planned to stand outside, and see the sport. If they had been the foxes, maybe they wouldn't have thought it was so funny; but of course, people just couldn't have even their pigs and lambs taken. We had to have wool to spin yarn for our stockings, weave our blankets and coverlids, and our Sunday winter dresses of white flannel with narrow black crossbars were from the backs of our own sheep, and we had to have ham to fry with eggs, and boil for Sunday night suppers, and bacon to cook the greens with—of course it was all right.

Before it was near daylight I heard Laddie making the kitchen fire, so father got right up, Leon came down, and all of them went to the barn to do the feeding. I wanted to get up too, but mother said I should stay in bed until the house was warm, because if I took more cold I'd be sick again. At breakfast May asked father about when they should start for Deams' to be ahead of the chase, and he said by ten o'clock at least; because a fox driven mad by pursuit, dogs, and noise, was a very dangerous thing, and a bite might make hy—the same thing as a mad dog. He said our back barn door opening from the threshing floor would afford a fine view of the meet, but Candace, May, and Miss Amelia wanted to be closer. I might go with them, if they would take good care of me, and they promised to; but when the time came to start, there was such a queer feeling inside me, I thought maybe it was more fever, and with mother would be the best place for me, so I said I wanted to watch from the barn. Father thought that was a capital idea, because I would be on the east side, where there would be no sun and wind, and it would be perfectly safe; also, I really could see what was going on better from that height than on the ground.

The sun was going to shine, but it hadn't peeped above Deams' strawstack when father on his best saddle horse, and Laddie on Flos, rode away, their eyes shining, their faces red, their blood pounding so it made their voices sound excited and different. Leon was to go on foot. Father said he would ride a horse to death. He just grinned and never made a word of complaint. Seemed funny for him.

"I was over having a little confidential chat with my horse, last night," he said, "and next year we'll be in the chase, and we'll show you how to take fences, and cut curves; just you wait!"

"Leon, *don't* build so on that horse," wailed mother. "I'm sure that money was stolen like ours, and the owner will claim it! I feel it in my bones!"

"Aw, shucks!" said Leon. "That money is mine. He won't either!"

When they started, father took Leon behind him to ride as far as the county line. He said he would go slowly, and it wouldn't hurt the horse, but Leon slipped off at Hoods', and said he'd go with their boys, so father let him, because light as Leon was, both of them were quite a load for one horse. Laddie went to ride with the Princess. We could see people moving around in Pryors' barnyard when our men started. Candace washed, Miss Amelia wiped the dishes, May swept, and all of them made the beds, and then they went to Deams', while I stayed with mother. When she thought it was time, she bundled me up warmly, and I went to the barn. Father had the east doors standing open for me, so I could sit in the sun, hang my feet against the warm boards and see every inch of our meadow where the meet was to be. I was really too warm there, and had to take off the scarf, untie my hood, and unbutton my coat.

It was a trifle muddy, but the frost had not left the ground yet, the sparrows were singing fit to burst, so were the hens. I didn't care much for the music of the hen, but I could see she meant well. She liked her nest quite as much as the red velvet bird with black wings, or the bubbly yellow one, and as for baby chickens, from the first peep they beat a little naked, blind, wobbly tree bird, so any hen had a right to sing for joy because she was going to be the mother of a large family of them. A hen had something to sing about all right, and so had we, when we thought of poached eggs and fried chicken. When I remembered them, I saw that it was no wonder the useful hen warbled so proudlike; but that was all nonsense, for I don't suppose a hen ever tasted poached eggs, and surely she wouldn't be happy over the prospect of being fried. Maybe one reason she sang was because she didn't know what was coming; I hardly think she'd be so tuneful if she did.

Sometimes the geese, shut in the barn, raised an awful clatter, and the horses and cattle complained about being kept from the sunshine and fresh air. You couldn't blame them. It was a lovely day, and the big upper door the pleasantest place. I didn't care if the fox hunters never came, there was so much to see, hear, and smell. Everything was busy making signs of spring, and one could become tired of ice and snow after a while, and so hungry for summer that those first days which were just hints of what was coming were almost better than the real thing when it arrived. Bud perfume was stronger than last week, many doves and bluebirds were calling, and three days more of such sunshine would make cross-country riding too muddy to be pleasant. I sat there thinking; grown people never know how much children do think, they have so much time, and so many bothersome things to study out. I heard it behind me, a long, wailing, bellowing roar, and my hood raised right up with my hair. I was in the middle of the threshing floor in a second, in another at the little west door, cut into the big one, opening it a tiny crack to take a peep, and see how close they were.

I could see nothing, but I heard a roar of dreadful sound

steadily closing in a circle around me. No doubt the mean old foxes wished then they had let the Dorking roosters alone. Closer it came and more dreadful. Never again did I want to hear such sounds coming at me; even when I knew what was making them. And then away off, beyond Pryors', and Hoods', and Dovers', I could see a line of tiny specks coming toward me, and racing flying things that must have been people on horses riding back and forth to give the foxes no chance to find a hiding place. No chance! Laddie and the Princess, Mr. Pryor and father, and all of them were after the bad old foxes; and they were going to get them; because they'd have no chance — Not with a solid line of men with raving dogs surrounding them, and people on horseback racing after them, no! the foxes would wish now that they had left the pigs and lambs alone. In that awful roaring din, they would wish, Oh how they would wish, they were birds and could fly! Fly back to their holes like the Bible said they had, where maybe they *liked* to live, and no doubt they had little foxes there, that would starve when their mammies were caught alive, to save their skins.

To save their skins! I could hear myself breathe, and feel my teeth click, and my knees knock together. And then! Oh dear! There they came across our cornfield. Two of them! And they could fly, almost. At least you could scarcely see that they touched the ground. The mean old things were paying up for the pigs and lambs now. Through the fence, across the road, straight toward me they came. Almost red backs, nearly white beneath, long flying tails, beautiful pointed ears, and long tongues, fire red, hanging from their open mouths; their sleek sides pulsing, and that awful din coming through the woods behind them. One second, the first paused to glance toward either side, and threw back its head to listen. What it saw, and heard, showed it. I guess then it was sorry it ever took people's ham, and their greens, and their blankets; and it could see and hear that it had no chance—to save its skin.

"Oh Lord! Dear Lord! Help me!" I prayed.

It had to be me, there was no one else. I never had opened the big doors; I thought it took a man, but when I pushed with all my might—and maybe if the hairs of our heads were numbered, and the sparrows counted, there would be a little mercy for the foxes—I asked for help; maybe I got it. The doors went back, and I climbed up the ladder to the haymow a few steps and clung there, praying with all my might: "Make them come in! Dear Lord, make them come in! Give them a chance! Help them to save their skins, O Lord!"

With a whizz and a flash one went past me, skimmed the cider press, and rushed across the hay; then the other. I fell to the floor and the next thing I knew the doors were shut, and I was back at my place. I just went down in a heap and leaned against the wall and shook, and then I laughed and said: "Thank you, Lord! Thank you for helping with the door! And the foxes! The beautiful little red and white foxes! They've got their chance! They'll save their skins! They'll get back to their holes and their babies! Praise the Lord!"

I knew when I heard that come out, that it was exactly like my father said it when Amos Hurd was redeemed. I never knew father to say it so impressively before, because Amos had been so bad, people really were afraid of him, and father said if once he got started right, he would go at it just as hard as he had gone at wrongdoing. I suppose I shouldn't have said it about a fox, when there were the Dorkings, and ham, and white wool dresses, and all that, but honestly, I couldn't remember that I cared particularly whether Amos Hurd was redeemed or not; he was always lovely to children; while I never in all my life had wanted anything worse than I wanted those foxes to save their skins. I could hear them pant like run out dogs; and I could hear myself, and I hadn't been driven from my home and babies, maybe—and chased miles and miles, either.

Then I just shook. They came pounding, roaring and braying right around the barn, and down the lane. The little door flew open and a strange man stuck in his head.

"Shut that door!" I screamed. "You'll let them in on me, and they bite! They're poison! They'll kill me!"

I hadn't even thought of it before.

"See any foxes?" cried the man.

"Two crossed our barnyard headed that way!" I cried back, pointing east. "Shut the door!"

The man closed it and ran calling as he went: "It's all right! They crossed the barnyard. We've got them!"

I began to dance and beat my hands, and then I stopped and held my breath. They were passing, and the noise was dreadful. They struck the sides of the barn, poked around the strawstack, and something made me look up, and at the edge of the hay stood a fox ready to spring. If it did, it would go from the door, right into the midst thereof. Nothing but my red hood sailing straight at it, and a yell I gave, drove it back. No one hit the barn again, the line closed up, and went on at a run now, they were so anxious to meet and see what they had. Then came the beat of hoofs and I saw that all the riders had dropped back, and were behind the line of people on foot. I watched Laddie as he flew past waving to me, and I grabbed my scarf to wave at him. The Princess flashed by so swiftly I couldn't see how she looked, and then I heard a voice I knew cry: "Ep! Ep! Over Lad!" And I almost fell dead where I stood. Mr. Pryor sailed right over the barnyard fence into the cornfield, ripping that dumb-bell as he went, and neck and neck, even with him, on one of his finest horses, was our Leon. His feet were in the stirrups, he had the reins tight, he almost stood as he arose, his face was crimson, his head bare, his white hair flying, the grandest sight you ever saw. At the top of my voice I screamed after them, "Ep! Ep! Over lad!" and then remembered and looked to see if I had to chase back the foxes, but they didn't mind only me, after what they had been through. Then I sat down suddenly again.

Well! What would father think of that! Leon kill a horse of ours, indeed! There he was on one of Mr. Pryor's, worth as much as six of father's no doubt, flying over fences, and the creek was coming, and the bank was steep behind the barn. I was up again straining to see.

"Ep! Ep! Over!" rang the cry.

There they went! Laddie and the Princess too. I'll never spend another cent on paper dolls, candy, raisins, or oranges. I'll give all I have to help Leon buy his horse; then I'm going to begin saving for mine.

The line closed up, a solid wall of men with sticks, clubs and guns; the dogs raged outside, and those on horseback stopped where they could see best; and inside, raced back and forth, and round and round, living creatures. I couldn't count they moved so, but even at that distance I could see that some were poor little cotton tails. The scared things! A whack over the head, a backward toss, and the dogs were mouthing them. The long tailed, sleek, gracefully moving ones, they were the foxes, the foxes driven from their holes, and nothing on earth could save their skins for them now; those men meant to have them.

I pulled the doors shut suddenly. I was so sick I could scarcely stand. I had to work, but at last I pushed the west doors open again. I don't think the Lord helped me any that time, for I knew what it took—before, they just went. Or maybe He did help me quite as much, but I had harder work to do my share, because I felt so dizzy and ill. Anyway, they opened. Then I climbed the upright ladder to the top beam, walked it to the granary, and there I danced, pounded and yelled so that the foxes jumped from the hay, leaped lightly to the threshing floor, and stood looking and listening. I gave them time to hear where the dreadful racket was, and then I jumped to the hay and threw the pitchfork at them. It came down smash! and both of them sprang from the door. When I got down the ladder and where I could see, they were so rested they were hiking across the cornfield like they never had raced a step before; and as the clamour went up behind me, that probably meant the first fox had lost its beautiful red and white skin, they reached our woods in safety. The doors went shut easier, and I started to the house crying like any blubbering baby; but when mother turned from the east window, and I noticed her face, I forgot the foxes.

"You saw Leon!" I cried.

"That I did!" she exulted, rocking on her toes the same as she does at the Meeting House when she is going to cry, "Glory!" any minute. "That I did! Ah! the brave little chap! Ah! the fine fellow!"

Her cheeks were the loveliest pink, and her eyes blazed. I scarcely knew her.

"What will father say?"

"If his father isn't every particle as proud of him as I am this day, I've a big disappointment coming," she answered. "If Mr. Pryor chose to let him take that fine horse, and taught him how to ride it, father should be glad."

"If he'd gone into the creek, you wouldn't feel so fine."

"Ah! but he didn't! He didn't! He stuck to the saddle and sailed over in one grand, long sweep! It was fine! I hope—to my soul, I hope his father saw it!"

"He did!" I said. "He did! He was about halfway down the lane. He was where he could see fine."

"You didn't notice —?"

"I was watching if Leon went under. What if he had, mother?"

"They'd have taken him out, and brought him to me, and I'd have worked with all the strength and skill God has given me, and if it were possible to us, he would be saved, and if it were not, it would be a proud moment for a woman to offer a boy like that to the God who gave him. One would have nothing to be ashamed of!"

"Could you do it, like you are now, and not cry, mother?" I asked wonderingly.

"Patience no!" said she. "Before long you will find out, child, that the fountain head of tears and laughter lies in the same spot, deep in a woman's heart. Men were made for big things! They must brave the wild animals, the Indians, fight the battles, ride the races, till the fields, build the homes. In the making of a new country men must have the thing in their souls that carried Leon across the creek. If he had checked that horse and gone to the ford, I would have fallen where I stood!"

"Father crossed the ford!"

"True! But that's different. He never had a chance at a horse like that! He never had time for fancy practice, and his nose would have been between the pages of a book if he had. But remember this! Your father's hand has never faltered, and his aim has never failed. All of us are here, safe and comfortable, through him. It was your father who led us across the wilderness, and fended from us the wildcat, wolf, and Indian. He built this house, cleared this land, and gave to all of us the things we love. Get this in your head straight. Your father rode a plow horse; he never tried flourishes in riding; but no man can stick in the saddle longer, ride harder, and face any danger with calmer front. If you think this is anything, you should have seen his face the day he stood between me and a band of Indians, we had every reason to think, I had angered to the fighting point."

"Tell me! Please tell me!" I begged.

All of us had been brought up on that story, but we were crazy to hear it, and mother loved to tell it, so she dropped on a chair and began:

"We were alone in a cabin in the backwoods of Ohio. Elizabeth was only nine months old, and father always said a mite the prettiest of any baby we ever had. Many of the others have looked quite as well to me, but she was the first, and he was so proud of her he always wanted me to wait in the wagon until he hitched the horses, so he would get to take and to carry her himself. Well, she was in the cradle, cooing and laughing, and I had my work all done, and the cabin shining. I was heating a big poker red-hot, and burning holes into the four corners of a board so father could put legs in it to make me a bench. A greasy old squaw came to the door with her papoose on her back. She wanted to trade berries for bread. There were berries everywhere for the picking; I had more dried than I could use in two years. We planted only a little patch of wheat and father had to ride three days to carry to mill what he could take on a horse. I baked in an outoven and when it was done, a loaf of white bread was by far the most precious thing we had to eat. Sometimes I was caught, and forced to let it go. Often I baked during the night and hid the bread in the wheat at the barn. There was none in the cabin that day and I said so. She didn't believe me. She set her papoose on the floor beside the fireplace, and went to the cupboard. There wasn't a crumb there except cornbread, and she didn't want that. She said: 'Brod! Brod!'

"She learned that from the Germans in the settlement. I shook my head. Then she pulled out a big steel hunting knife, such as the whites traded to the Indians so they would have no trouble in scalping us neatly, and walked to the cradle. She took that knife loosely between her thumb and second finger and holding it directly above my baby's face, she swung it lightly back and forth and demanded: 'Brod! Brod!'

"If the knife fell, it would go straight through my baby's head, and Elizabeth was reaching her little hands and laughing. There was only one thing to do, and I did it. I caught that red-hot poker from the fire, and stuck it so close to her baby's face, that the papoose drew back and whimpered. I scarcely saw how she snatched it up and left. When your father came, I told him, and we didn't know what to do. We knew she would come back and bring her band. If we were not there, they would burn the cabin, ruin our crops, kill our stock, take everything we had, and we couldn't travel so far, or so fast, that on their ponies they couldn't overtake us. We endangered any one with whom we sought refuge, so we gripped hands, knelt down and told the Lord all about it, and we felt the answer was to stay. Father cleaned the gun, and hours and hours we waited.

"About ten o'clock the next day they came, forty braves in war paint and feathers. I counted until I was too sick to see, then I took the baby in my arms and climbed to the loft, with our big steel knife in one hand. If your father fell, I was to use it, first on Elizabeth, then on myself. The Indians stopped at the woodyard, and the chief of the band came to the door, alone. Your father met him with his gun in reach, and for a whole eternity they stood searching each other's eyes. I was at the trapdoor where I could see both of them.

"To the depths of my soul I enjoyed seeing Leon take the fence and creek: but what was that, child, to compare with the timber that stood your father like a stone wall, between me and forty half-naked, paint besmeared, maddened Indians? Don't let any showing the men of to-day can make set you to thinking that father isn't a king among men. Not once, but again and again in earlier days, he fended danger from me like that. I can shut my eyes and see his waving hair, his white brow, his steel blue eyes, his unfaltering hand. I don't remember that I had time or even thought to pray. I gripped the baby, and the knife, and waited for the thing I must do if an arrow or a shot sailed past the chief and felled father. They stood second after second, like two wooden men, and then slowly and deliberately the chief lighted his big pipe, drew a few puffs and handed it to father. He set down his gun, took the pipe and quite as slowly and deliberately he looked at the waiting band, at the chief, and then raised it to his lips.

"'White squaw brave! Heap much brave!' said the chief.

"'In the strength of the Lord. Amen!' said father.

"Then he reached his hand and the chief took it, so I came

down the ladder and stood beside father, as the Indians began to file in the front door and out the back. As they passed, every man of them made the peace sign and piled in a heap, venison, fish, and game, while each squaw played with the baby and gave me a gift of beads, a metal trinket, or a blanket she had woven. After that they came often, and brought gifts, and if prowling Gypsies were pilfering, I could look to see a big Indian loom up and seat himself at my fireside until any danger was past. I really got so I liked and depended on them, and father left me in their care when he went to mill, and I was safe as with him. You have heard the story over and over, but to-day is the time to impress on you that an exhibition like *this* is the veriest child's play compared with what I have seen your father do repeatedly!"

"But it was you, the chief said was brave!"

Mother laughed.

"I had to be, baby," she said. "Mother had no choice. There's only one way to deal with an Indian. I had lived among them all my life, and I knew what must be done."

"I think both of you were brave," I said, "you, the bravest!"

"Quite the contrary," laughed mother. "I shall have to confess that what I did happened so quickly I'd no time to think. I only realized the coal red iron was menacing the papoose when it drew back and whimpered. Father had all night to face what was coming to him, and it was not one to one, but one to forty, with as many more squaws, as good fighters as the braves, to back them. It was a terror, but I never have been sorry we went through it together. I have rested so securely in your father ever since."

"And he is as safe in you," I insisted.

"As you will," said mother. "This world must have her women quite as much as her men. It is shoulder to shoulder, heart to heart, business."

The clamour in the meadow arose above our voices and brought us back to the foxes.

"There goes another!" I said, the tears beginning to roll again.

"It *is* heathenish business," said mother. "I don't blame you! If people were not too shiftless to care for their stuff, the foxes wouldn't take their chickens and geese. They never get ours!"

"Hoods aren't shiftless!" I sobbed.

"There are always exceptions," said mother, "and they are the exception in this case."

The door flew open and Leon ran in. He was white with excitement, and trembling.

"Mother, come and see me take a fence on Pryor's Rocket!" he cried.

Mother had him in her arms.

"You little whiffet!" she said. "You little tow-haired whiffet!"

Both of them were laughing and crying at the same time, and so was I.

"I saw you take one fence and the creek, Weiscope!" she said, holding him tight, and stroking his hair. "That will do for to-day. Ride the horse home slowly, rub it down if they will allow you, and be sure to remember your manners when you leave. To trust such a child as you with so valuable a horse, and for Mr. Pryor to personally ride with you and help you, I think that was a big thing for a man like him to do."

"But, mother, he's been showing me for weeks, or I couldn't have done it to-day. It was our secret to surprise you. When I get *my* horse, I'll be able to ride a little, as well as Mr. Laddie."

"Leon, don't," said mother, gripping him tighter. "You must bear in mind, word about that money may come any day."

"Aw, it won't either," said Leon, pulling away. "And say, mother, that dumb-bell was like country boys make in England. He helped me hunt the wood and showed me, and I couldn't ride and manage it, so he had it all day, and you should have heard him make it rip. Say, mother, take my word, he was some pumpkins in England. I bet he ordered the Queen around, when he was there!"

"No doubt!" laughed mother, kissing him and pushing him from the door.

Some people are never satisfied. After that splendid riding and the perfect day, father, Leon, and Laddie came home blaming every one, and finding fault, and trying to explain how it happened, that the people from the east side claimed two foxes, and there was only one left for the west side, when they had seen and knew they had driven three for miles. They said they lost them in our Big Woods.

I didn't care one speck. I would as lief wear a calico dress, and let the little foxes have their mammies to feed them; and I was willing to bet all my money that we would have as much ham, and as many greens next summer as we ever had. And if the foxes took Hoods' Dorkings again, let them build a coop with safe foundations. The way was to use stone and heap up dirt around it in the fall, to be perfectly sure, and make it warmer.

We took care of our chickens because we had to have them. All the year we needed them, but most especially for Easter. Mother said that was ordained chicken time. Turkeys for Thanksgiving, sucking pigs for Christmas, chickens for Easter, goose, she couldn't abide. She thought it was too strong. She said the egg was a symbol of life; of awakening, of birth, and the chickens came from the eggs, first ones about Easter, so that proved it was chicken time.

I am going to quit praying about little things I can manage myself. Father said no prayer would bring an answer unless you took hold and pulled with all your being for what you wanted. I had been intending for days to ask the Lord to help me find where Leon hid his Easter eggs. It had been the law at our house from the very first, that for the last month before Easter, aside from what mother had to have for the house, all of us might gather every egg we could find and keep them until Easter. If we could locate the hiding place of any one else, we might take all theirs. The day before Easter they were brought in, mother put aside what she required, and the one who had the most got to sell all of them and take the money. Sometimes there were two washtubs full, and what they brought was worth having, for sure. So we watched all year for safe places, and when the time came we almost ran after the hens with a basket. Because Laddie and Leon were bigger they could outrun us, and lots of hens laid in the barn, so there the boys always had first chance. Often during the month we would find and take each other's eggs a dozen times. We divided them, and hid part in different places, so that if either were found there would still be some left.

Laddie had his in the hopper of the cider press right on the threshing floor, and as he was sure to get more than I had anyway, I usually put mine with his. May had hers some place, and where Leon had his, none of us could find or imagine. I almost lay awake of nights trying to think, and every time I thought of a new place, the next day I would look, and they wouldn't be there. Three days before Easter, mother began to cook and get the big dinner ready, and she ran short of eggs. She told me to go to the barn and tell the boys that each of them must send her a dozen as quickly as they could. Of course that was fair, if she made both give up the same number. So I went to the barn.

The lane was muddy, and as I had been sick, I wore my rubbers that spring. I thought to keep out of the deep mud, where horses and cattle trampled, I'd go up the front embankment, and enter the little door. My feet made no sound, and it so happened that the door didn't either, and as I started to open it, I saw Leon disappearing down the stairway, with a big sack on his back. I thought it was corn for the horses, and followed him, but he went to the cow stable door and started toward the lane, and then I thought it was for the pigs, so I called Laddie and told him about the eggs. He said he'd give me two dozen of his, and Leon could pay him back. We went together to get them, and there was only one there.

Wasn't that exactly like Leon? Leave *one* for a nest egg! If he were dying and saw a joke or a trick, he'd stop to play it before he finished, if he possibly could. If he had no time at all, then he'd go with his eyes twinkling over the thoughts of the fun it would have been if he possibly could have managed it. Of course when we saw that one lonely egg in the cider hopper, just exactly like the "Last Rose of Summer, left to pine on the stem," I thought of the sack Leon carried, and knew what had been in it. We hurried out and tried to find him, but he was swallowed up. You couldn't see him or hear a sound of him anywhere.

Mother was as cross as she ever gets. Right there she made a new rule, and it was that two dozen eggs must be brought to the house each day, whether any were hidden or not. She had to stop baking until she got eggs. She said a few times she had used a goose egg in custard. I could fix that. I knew where one of our gray geese had a nest, and if she'd cook any goose egg, it would be a gray one. Of course I had sense enough not to take a blue one. So I slipped from the east door, crossed the yard and orchard corner, climbed the fence and went down the lane. There was the creek up and tearing. It was half over the meadow, and the floodgate between the pasture and the lane rocked with the rush of water; still, I believed I could make it. So I got on the fence and with my feet on the third rail, and holding by the top one, I walked sidewise, and so going reached the floodgate. It was pretty wobbly, but I thought I could cross on the run. I knew I could if I dared jump at the other end; but there the water was over the third rail, and that meant above my head.

It was right at that time of spring when you felt so good you thought you could do most anything, except fly—I tried that once—so I went on. The air was cold for all the sun shone, the smell of catkin pollen, bursting buds, and the odour of earth steaming in the sun, was in every breath; the blackbirds were calling, and the doves; the ganders looked longingly at the sky and screamed a call to every passing wild flock, and Deams' rooster wanted to fight all creation, if you judged by the boasting he was doing from their barnyard gate. He made me think of eggs, so I set my jaws, looked straight ahead, and scooted across the floodgate to the post that held it and the rails of the meadow fence. I made it too, and then the fence was easy, only I had to double quite short, because the water was over the third rail there, but at last it was all gone, and I went to the fence corner and there was the goose on the nest, laying an egg. She had built on a little high place, among puddles, wild rose bushes, and thorns, and the old thing wouldn't get off. She just sat there and stuck out her head and hissed and hissed. I never noticed before that geese were so big and so aggravating. I wasn't going to give up, after that floodgate, so I hunted a big stick, set it against her wing, pushed her off and grabbed three eggs and ran. When I got to the fence, I was in a pickle for sure. I didn't know what in the world to do with the eggs.

At last I unbuttoned my coat, put them in my apron front, gathered it up, and holding it between my teeth, started back. I had to double more than ever on account of the eggs, and when I reached the floodgate it rocked like a branch in the wind; but I had to get back, so I rested and listened to the larks a while. That was a good plan. They were calling for mates, and what they said was so perfectly lovely, you couldn't think of anything else; and the less you thought about how that gate rocked, and how deep and swift the water ran, the better for you. At last one lark went almost from sight, and he rang, twisted and trilled his call, until my heart swelled so big it hurt. I crossed on the jump with no time to think at all. That was a fine plan, for I made it, but I hit the post so hard I broke the middle egg. I was going to throw it away, but there was so much starch in my apron it held like a dish, and it had been clean that morning, now the egg soiled it anyway, so I ran and got home all right.

Mother was so pleased about the eggs she changed the apron and never said a word, except to brag on me. She said she couldn't keep house without me, and I guess that was a fact. I came in handy a lot of times. But at dinner when she scolded the boys about the eggs, and told them I brought the goose eggs for her custard, else there would have been no pie, father broke loose, and I thought he was going to whip me sure. He told mother all about the water and the gate, and how I had to cross, and he said, 'it was a dispensation of Providence that we didn't have a funeral instead of celebrating Easter,' so I said: "Well, if you think I came so near drowning myself, when you rejoice because Christ is risen from the dead, you can be glad I am too, and that will make it all the better."

The boys laughed, but father said it was no laughing matter. I think that speech saved me from going on the threshing floor, for he took me on his lap when I thought I'd have to go, and told me never, never to do anything like that again, and then he hugged me until I almost broke. Gracious! He should have seen us going to school some days. Why, we even walked the top rail when it was the only one above water, and we could cross the bridge if we wanted to. At least when Laddie or Miss Amelia was not around, we did.

Leon was so bursting full he scarcely could eat, and Laddie looked pretty glum when he had to admit he had no eggs; so Leon had to hand over the whole two dozen. Leon didn't mind that, but he said if he must, then all of us should stay in the dining-room until he brought them, because of course he couldn't walk straight and get them in broad daylight with us watching, and not show where they were. Father said that was fair, so Leon went out and before so very long he came back with the eggs.

I thought until my skull almost cracked, about where he *could* have gone, and I was almost to the place where the thing seemed serious enough that I'd ask the Lord to help me find Laddie's eggs, when mother sent me to the garret for red onion skins. She had an hour to rest, and she was going to spend it fixing decorations for our eggs. Of course there were always red and black aniline ones, and yellow and blue, but none of us ever liked them half so well as those mother coloured, herself.

She took the dark red skins and cut boys, girls, dogs, cats, stars, flowers, butterflies, fish, and everything imaginable, and wet the skins a little and laid them on very white eggs that had been soaked in alum water to cut the grease, and then wrapped light yellow skins over, and then darker ones, and at last layer after layer of cloth, and wet that, and roasted them an hour in hot ashes and then let them cool and dry, before unwrapping. When she took them out, rubbed on a little grease and polished them— there they were! They would have our names, flowers, birds, animals, all in pale yellow, deep rich brown, almost red, and perfectly beautiful colours, while you could hunt and hunt before you found everything on one egg. And sometimes the onion skins slipped, and made things of themselves that she never put on.

I was coming from the bin with an apron full of skins and I almost fell over. I couldn't breathe for a long time. I danced on my toes, and held my mouth to keep from screaming. On the garret floor before me lay a little piece of wet mud, and the faintest outline of a boot, a boot about Leon's size. That was all I needed to know. As soon as I could hold steady, I took the skins to mother, and slipped back and hunted good; and of course I had to find them—grain sacks half full of them—carried in the front door in the evening, and up the front stairs, where no one went until bedtime, unless there were company. Away back under the eaves, across the joists, behind the old clothing waiting to be ripped, coloured and torn for carpet rags and rugs, Mr. Leon had almost every egg that had been laid on the place for a month. *Now* he'd see what he'd get for taking Laddie's!

Then I stopped short. What I thought most made me sick, but

I didn't propose to lie in bed again for a year at least, for it had its bad parts as well as its good; so I went straight and whispered to Laddie. He never looked pleased at all, so I knew I had been right. He kissed me, and thanked me, and then said slowly: "It's mighty good of you, Little Sister, but you see it wouldn't be *fair*. He found mine himself, so he had a right to take them. But I don't dare touch his, when you tell me where they are. I never in a month of Sundays would have looked for them in the house. I was going to search the wood house and smoke house this afternoon. I can't take them. But thank you just as much."

Then I went to father and he laughed. How he did laugh!

"Laddie is right!" he said at last. "He didn't find them, and he mustn't take them. But you may! They're yours! That front door scheme of Leon's was fairly well, but it wasn't quite good enough. If he'd cleaned his feet as he should, before he crossed mother's carpet and climbed the stairs, he'd have made it all right. 'His tracks betrayed him,' as tracks do all of us, if we are careless enough to leave any. The eggs are yours, and to-night is the time to produce them. Where do you want to hide them?"

Well of all things! and after I had stumbled on them without pestering the Lord, either! Just as slick as anything! Mine! I never even thought of it. But when I did think, I liked it. The more I thought, the funnier it grew.

"Under mother's bed," I whispered. "But I never can get them. They're in wheat sacks, and full so high, and they'll have to be handled like eggs."

"I'll do the carrying," laughed father. "Come show me!"

So we took all those eggs, and put them under mother's bed.

Of course she and Candace saw us, but they didn't hunt eggs and they'd never tell. If ever I thought I'd burst wide open! About dusk I saw Leon coming from the barn carrying his hat at his side—more eggs—so I ran like a streak and locked the front door, and then slipped back in the dining-room and almost screamed, when I could hear him trying it, and he couldn't get in. After a while he came in, fussed around, and finally went into the sitting-room, and the key turned and he went upstairs. I knew I wouldn't dare look at him when he came down, so I got a reader and began on a piece I just love:

A nightingale made a mistake;
  She sang a few notes out of tune:
Her heart was ready to break,
  And she hid away from the moon.

When I did get a peep, gracious but he was black! Maybe it wasn't going to be so much fun after all. But he had the money last year, and the year before, and if he'd cleaned his feet well—I was not hunting his eggs, when I found them. "His tracks betrayed him," as father said. I was thankful supper was ready just then, and while it was going on mother said: "As soon as you finish, all bring in your eggs. I want to wrap the ones to colour to-night, and bury them in the fireplace so they will colour, dry, and be ready to open in the morning."

No one said a word, but neither Laddie nor Leon looked very happy, and I took awful bites to keep my face straight. When all of us finished May brought a lot from the bran barrel in the smoke house, but Laddie and Leon only sat there and looked silly; it really was funny.

"I must have more eggs than this?" said mother. "Where are they to come from?"

Father nodded to me and I said: "From under your bed!"

"Oh, it was you! And I never once caught you snooping!" cried Leon.

"Easy son!" said father. "That will do. You lost through your own carelessness. You left wet mud on the garret floor, and she saw it when mother sent her for the onion skins. You robbed Laddie of his last egg this morning; be a good loser yourself!"

"Well, anyway, you didn't get 'em," said Leon to Laddie. "And she only found them by accident!"

Then we had a big time counting all those eggs, and such another heap as there was to sell, after mother filled baskets to cook with and colour. When the table was cleared, Laddie and Leon made tallow pencils from a candle and wrote all sorts of things over eggs that had been prepared to colour. Then mother boiled them in copperas water, and aniline, and all the dyes she had, and the boys polished them, and they stood in shining black, red, blue, and yellow heaps. The onion ones would be done in the morning. Leon had a goose egg and mother let him keep it, so he wrote and wrote on it, until Laddie said it would be all writing, and no colour, and he boiled it in red, after mother finished, and polished it himself. It came out real pretty with roses on it and lots of words he wouldn't let any of us read; but of course it was for Susie Fall.

Next morning he slipped it to her at church. When we got home, all of us were there except Shelley, and we had a big dinner and a fine time and Laddie stayed until after supper, before he went to Pryors'.

"How is he making it?" asked Sally.

You could see she was making it all right; she never looked lovelier, and mother said Peter was letting her spend away too much money on her clothes. She told him so, but Peter just laughed and said business was good, and he could afford it, and she was a fine advertisement for his store when she was dressed well."

"All I know is," said mother, "that he goes there every whip-stitch, and the women, at least, seem glad to have him. He says Mr. Pryor treats him decently, and that is more than he does his own family and servants. He and the girl and her mother are divided about something. She treats her father respectfully, but she's in sympathy with her mother."

"Laddie can't find out what the trouble is?"

"I don't think that he tries."

"Maybe he'd feel better not to know," said Peter.

"Possibly!" said mother.

"Nonsense!" said father.

"You seem to be reconciled," said Elizabeth.

"That girl would reconcile a man to anything," said father.

"Not to the loss of his soul, I hope," said mother stiffly.

"Souls are not so easy to lose," said father. "Besides, I am counting on Laddie saving hers."

13

The Garden of the Lord

With what content and merriment,
Their days are spent, whose minds are bent
To follow the useful plow.

That spring I decided if school didn't stop pretty soon, I'd run away again, and I didn't in the least care what they did to me. A country road was all right and it was good enough, if it had been heaped up, leveled and plenty of gravel put on; and of course our road would be fine, because father was one of the commissioners, and as long as he filled that office, every road in the county would be just as fine as the law would allow him to make it. I have even heard him tell mother that he "stretched it a leetle mite," when he was forced to by people who couldn't seem to be made to understand what was required to upbuild a nation. He said our language was founded on the alphabet, and to master it you had to begin with "a". And he said the nation was like that; it was based on townships, and when a township was clean, had good roads, bridges, schoolhouses, and churches, a county was in fine shape, and when each county was in order, the state was right, and when the state was prosperous, the nation could rejoice in its strength.

He said Atlas in the geography book, carrying the world on his back, was only a symbol, but it was a good one. He said when the county elected him to fill an important office, it used his shoulder as a prop for the nation, so it became his business to stand firmly, and use every ounce of strength and brains he had, first of all to make his own possessions a model, then his township, his county, and his state, and if every one worked together doing that, no nation on earth had our amount of territory and such fine weather, so none of them could beat us.

Our road was like the barn floor, where you drove: on each side was a wide grassy strip, and not a weed the length of our land. All the rails in the fences were laid straight, the gates were solid, sound, and swung firmly on their beams, our fence corners were full of alders, wild roses, sumac, blackberry vines, masses of wild flowers beneath them, and a bird for every bush. Some of the neighbours thought that to drive two rails every so often, lay up the fences straight, and grub out the shrubs was the way, but father said they were vastly mistaken. He said that was such a shortsighted proceeding, he would be ashamed to indulge in it. You did get more land, but if you left no place for the birds, the worms and insects devoured your crops, and you didn't raise half so much as if you furnished the birds shelter and food. So he left mulberries in the fields and fence corners and wild cherries, raspberries, grapes, and every little scrub apple tree from seeds sown by Johnny Appleseed when he crossed our land.

Mother said those apples were so hard a crane couldn't dent them, but she never watched the birds in winter when snow was beginning to come and other things were covered up. They swarmed over those trees until spring, for the tiny sour apples stuck just like oak leaves waiting for next year's crop to push them off. She never noticed us, either. After a few frosts, we could almost get tipsy on those apples; there was not a tree in our orchard that had the spicy, teasing tang of Johnny Appleseed's apples. Then too, the limbs could be sawed off and rambo and maiden's-blush grafted on, if you wanted to; father did on some of them, so there would be good apples lying beside the road for passers-by, and they needn't steal to get them. You could graft red haws on them too, and grow great big, little haw-apples, that were the prettiest things you ever saw, and the best to eat. Father said if it didn't spoil the looks of the road, he wouldn't care how many of his neighbours straightened their fences. If they did, the birds would come to him, and the more he had, the fewer bugs and worms he would be troubled with, so he would be sure of big crops, and sound fruit. He said he would much rather have a few good apples picked by robins or jays, than untouched trees, loaded with wormy falling ones he could neither use nor sell. He always patted my head and liked every line of it when I recited, sort of tearful-like and pathetic:

Don't kill the birds! the happy birds,
  That bless the field and grove;
So innocent to look upon,
  They claim our warmest love.

The roads crossing our land were all right, and most of the others near us; and a road is wonderful, if it is taking you to the woods or a creek or meadow; but when it is walking you straight to a stuffy little schoolhouse where you must stand up to see from a window, where a teacher is cross as fire, like Miss Amelia, and where you eternally *hear* things you can't see, there comes a time about the middle of April when you had quite as soon die as to go to school any longer; and what you learn there doesn't amount to a hill of beans compared with what you can find out for yourself outdoors.

Schoolhouses are made wrong. If they must be, they should be built in a woods pasture beside a stream, where you could wade, swim, and be comfortable in summer, and slide and skate in winter. The windows should be cut to the floor, and stand wide open, so the birds and butterflies could pass through. You ought to learn your geography by climbing a hill, walking through a valley, wading creeks, making islands in them, and promontories, capes, and peninsulas along the bank. You should do your arithmetic sitting under trees adding hickorynuts, subtracting walnuts, multiplying butternuts, and dividing hazelnuts. You could use apples for fractions, and tin cups for liquid measure. You could spell everything in sight and this would teach you the words that are really used in the world. Every single one of us could spell incompatibility, but I never heard father, or the judge, or even the Bishop, put it in a speech.

If you simply can't have school *that* way, then you should be shut in black cells, deep under the ground, where you couldn't see, or hear a sound, and then if they'd give you a book and candle and Miss Amelia, and her right-hand man, Mister Ruler, why you might learn something. This way, if you sat and watched the windows you could see a bird cross our woods pasture to the redbird swamp every few minutes; once in a while one of my big hawks took your breath as he swept, soared, sailed, and circled, watching the ground below for rabbits, snakes, or chickens. The skinny old blue herons crossing from the Wabash to hunt frogs in the cowslip swale in our meadow, sailed so slow and so low, that you could see their sharp bills stuck out in front, their uneven, ragged looking feathers, and their long legs trailing out behind. I bet if Polly Martin wore a blue calico dress so short her spindle-shanks showed, and flew across our farm, you couldn't tell her from a heron.

There were so many songs you couldn't decide which was which to save you; it was just a pouring jumble of robins, larks, doves, blackbirds, sparrows, everything that came that early; the red and the yellow birds had not come yet, or the catbirds or thrushes. You could hear the thumping wings of the roosters in Sills' barnyard nearest the schoolhouse, and couldn't tell which was whipping, so you had to sit there and wonder; and worst of all you must stand Miss Amelia calmly telling you to pay attention to your books or you would be kept in, and all the time you were forced to bear torments, while you watched her walk from window to window to see every speck of the fight. One day they had thumped and fought for half an hour; she had looked from every window in the room, and at last there was an awful whacking, and then a silence. It grew so exciting I raised my hand, and almost before she nodded permission, "Which whipped?" I asked.

Miss Amelia turned red as a beet. Gee, but she was mad!

"I did!" she said. "Or at least I will. You may remain for it after school is dismissed."

Now if you are going to be switched, they never do it until they are just so angry anyway, and then they always make it as hard as they dare not to stripe you, so it isn't much difference *how* provoked they are, it will be the same old thrashing, and it's sure to sting for an hour at least, so you might as well be beaten for a little more as hardly anything at all. At that instant from the fence not far from my window came a triumphant crow that fairly ripped across the room.

"Oh, it was the Dorking!" I said. "No wonder you followed clear around the room to see him thrash a Shanghai three times his size! I bet a dollar it was great!"

Usually, I wouldn't have put up more than five cents, but at that time I had over six dollars from my Easter eggs, and no girl of my age at our school ever had half that much. Miss Amelia started toward me, and I braced my feet so she'd get a good jolt herself, when she went to shake me; she never struck us over the head since Laddie talked to her that first day; but John Hood's foot was in the aisle. I thought maybe I'd have him for my beau when we grew up, because I bet he knew she was coming, and stuck out his foot on purpose; anyway, she pitched, and had to catch a desk to keep off the floor, and that made her so mad at him, that she forgot me, while he got his scolding; so when my turn came at last, she had cooled down enough that she only marched past to her desk, saying I was to remain after school. I had to be careful after that to be mighty good to May and Leon.

When school was out they sat on the steps before the door and waited. Miss Amelia fussed around and there they sat. Then her face grew more gobblerish than usual, and she went out and told them to go home. Plain as anything I heard May say it: "She's been awful sick, you know, and mother wouldn't allow it." And then Leon piped up: "You *did* watch the roosters, all the time they fought, and of course all of us wanted to see just as badly as you did."

She told them if they didn't go right home she'd bring them back and whip them too; so they had to start, and leave me to my sad fate. I was afraid they had made it sadder, instead of helping me; she was so provoked when she came in she was crying, and over nothing but the plain truth too; if we had storied on her, she'd have had some cause to beller. She arranged her table, cleaned the board, emptied the water bucket, and closed the windows.

Then she told me I was a rude, untrained child. I was rude, I suppose, but goodness knows, I wasn't untrained; that was hard on father and mother; I had a big notion to tell them; and then, she never whipped me at all. She said if I wanted her to love me, I mustn't be a saucy, impudent girl, and I should go straight home and think it over.

I went, but I was so dazed at her thinking I wanted her to love me, that I hardly heard May and Leon calling; when I did I went to the cemetery fence and there they lay in the long grass waiting.

"If you cried, we were coming back and pitch into her," said Leon.

There was a pointer. Next time, first cut she gave me, I decided to scream bloody murder. But that would be no Crusader way. There was one thing though. No Crusader ever sat and heard a perfectly lovely fight going on, and never even wondered which whipped.

May and Leon stepped one on each side, took a hand, and we ran like Indians, and slid down the hill between the bushes, climbed the fence, crossed the pasture back of the church, and went to the creek. There we sat on a log, I told them, and we just laughed. I didn't know what I could do to pay them, for they saved me sure as fate that time.

I wished we lived in the woods the way it was when father and mother were married and moved to Ohio. The nearest neighbours were nine miles, and there wasn't a dollar for school funds, so of course the children didn't have to go, and what their fathers and mothers taught them was all they knew. That would not have helped me much though, for we never had one single teacher who knew anything to compare with what father and mother did, and we never had one who was forever reading books, papers, and learning more things that help, to teach other people. I wished father had time to take our school. It would have been some fun to go to him, because I just knew he would use the woods for the room, and teach us things it would do some good to know about.

I began debating whether it was a big enough thing to bother the Lord with: this being penned up in the schoolhouse droning over spelling and numbers, when you could smell tree bloom, flower bloom, dozens of birds were nesting, and everything was beginning to hum with life. I couldn't think for that piece about "Spring" going over in my head:

I am coming, I am coming:
Hark! the little bee is humming:
See! the lark is soaring high,
In the bright and sunny sky;
All the birds are on the wing:
Little maiden, now is spring.

I made up my mind that it was of enough importance to call for the biggest prayer I could think of and that I would go up in the barn to the top window, stand on a beam, and turn my face to the east, where Jesus used to be, and I'd wrestle with the Lord for freedom, as Jacob wrestled with the Angel on the banks of the Jabbok in the land of Ammon. I was just getting up steam to pray as hard as ever I could; for days I'd been thinking of it, and I was nearly to the point where one more killdeer crying across the sky would have sent me headlong from the schoolhouse anywhere that my feet were on earth, and the air didn't smell of fried potatoes, kraut, sweat, and dogs, like it did whenever you sat beside Clarissa Polk. When I went to supper one night, father had been to Groveville, and he was busy over his papers. After he finished the blessing, he seemed worried, at last he said the funds were all out, and the county would make no appropriation, so school would have to close next week.

Well that beats me! I had faith in that prayer I was going to make, and here the very thing I intended to ask for happened before I prayed. I decided I would save the prayer until the next time I couldn't stand anything another minute, and then I would try it with all my might and see if it really did any good. After supper I went out the back door, spread my arms wide, and ran down the orchard to the fence in great bounds, the fastest I ever went in my life. I climbed my pulpit in the corner and tried to see how much air my lungs would hold without bursting, while I waved my arms and shouted at the top of my voice: "Praise ye the Lord! Praised be His holy name!"

"Ker-awk!" cried an old blue heron among the cowslips below

me. I had almost scared it to death, and it arose on flapping wings and paid me back by frightening me so I screamed as I dodged its shadow.

"What is all this?" asked father behind me.

"Come up and take a seat, and I'll try to tell you," I said.

So he stepped on my pulpit and sat on the top rail, while I stood between his knees, put my arms around his neck, took off his hat and loosened his hair so the wind could wave it, and make his head feel cool and good. His hair curled a little and it was black and fine. His cheeks were pink and his eyes the brightest blue, with long lashes, and heavier brows than any other man I ever have seen. He was the best looking—always so clean and fresh, and you never had to be afraid of him, unless you had been a bad, sinful child. If you were all right, you could walk into his arms, play with his hair, kiss him all you pleased, and there wasn't a thing on earth you couldn't tell him, excepting a secret you had promised to keep.

So I explained all this, and more too. About how I wanted to hunt for the flowers, to see which bloomed first, and watch in what order the birds came, and now it was a splendid time to locate nests, because there were no leaves, so I could see easily, and how glad mother would be to know where the blue goose nested, and her white turkey hen; because she wanted her geese all blue, and the turkeys all white, as fast as she could manage. Every little thing that troubled me or that I wanted, I told him. He sat there and he couldn't have listened with more interest or been quieter if I had been a bishop, which is the biggest thing that ever happened at our house: his name was Ninde and he came from Chicago to dedicate our church when it was new. So father listened and thought and held his arms around me, and kept asking questions until I had not a thing more to tell, then he inquired: "And what were you praising the Lord for, child?"

"Because school is so near out! Because I got what I was going to pray for before I asked."

"And you think the Lord was at the bottom of the thing that makes you happy?"

"Well, you always go to Him about what concerns you, and you say, 'Praise the Lord,' when things go to please you."

"I do indeed!" said father. "But I had thought of this running short of school funds as a calamity. If I had been praying about it, I would have asked Him to show me a way to raise money to continue until middle May at least."

"Oh father!"

I just crumpled up in his arms and began to cry; to save me I couldn't help it. He held me tight. At last he said: "I think you are a little overstrained this spring. Maybe you were sicker than we knew, or are growing too fast. Don't worry any more about school. Possibly father can fix it."

Next morning when I wakened, my everyday clothes lay across the foot of the bed, so I called mother and asked if I should put them on; she took me in her arms, and said father thought I had better be in the open, and I needn't go to school any more that spring. I told her I thought I could bear it a few more days, now it was going to be over so soon; but she said I might stay at home, father and Laddie would hear me at night, and I could take my books anywhere I pleased and study when I chose, if I had my spelling and reading learned at evening. *Now,* say the Lord doesn't help those who call on Him in faith believing!

Think of being allowed to learn your lessons on the top of the granary, where you could look out of a window above the treetops, lie in the cool wind, and watch swallows and martins. Think of studying in the pulpit when the creek ran high, and the wild birds sang so sweetly you seemed to hear them for the first time in all your life, and hens, guineas, and turkeys made prime music in the orchard. You could see the buds swell, and the little blue flags push through the grass, where Mrs. Mayer had her flower bed, and the cowslips greening under the water of the swale at the foot of the hill, while there might be a Fairy under any leaf. I was so full, so swelled up and excited, that when I got ready to pick up a book, I could learn a lesson in a few minutes, tell all about it, spell every word, and read it back, front, and sideways. I never learned lessons so quick and so easy in all my life; father, Laddie, and every one of them had to say so. One night, father said to Laddie: "This child is furnishing evidence that our school system is wrong, and our methods of teaching far from right."

"Or is it merely proof that she is different," said Laddie, "and you can't run her through the same groove you could the rest of us?"

"A little of both," said father, "but most that the system is wrong. We are not going at children in a way to gain and hold their interest, and make them love their work. There must be a better way of teaching, and we should find different teachers. You'll have to try the school next year yourself, Laddie."

"I have a little plan about a piece of land I am hoping to take before then," answered Laddie. "It's time for me to try my wings at making a living, and land is my choice. I have fully decided. I stick to the soil!"

"Amen!" cried father. "You please me mightily. I hate to see sons of mine thriving on law, literally making their living out of the fruit of other men's discord. I dislike seeing them sharpen their wits in trade, buying at the lowest limit, extorting the highest. I don't want their horizons limited by city blocks, their feet on pavements, everything under the sun in their heads that concerns a scheme to make money; not room for an hour's thought or study in a whole day, about the really vital things of life. After all, land and its products are the basis of everything; the city couldn't exist a day unless we feed and clothe it. In the things that I consider important, you are a king among men, with your feet on soil you own."

"So I figure it," said Laddie.

"And you are the best educated man I have reared," said father. "Take this other thought with you: On land, the failure of the bank does not break you. The fire another man's carelessness starts, does not wipe out your business or home. You are not in easy reach of contagion. Any time you want to branch out, your mother and I will stand back of you."

"Thank you!" said Laddie. "You backed none of the others. They would resent it. I'll make the best start I can myself, and as they did, stand alone."

Father looked at him and smiled slowly.

"You are right, as always," he said. "I hadn't thought so far. It would make trouble. At any rate, let me inspect and help you select your land."

"That of course!" said Laddie.

I suspect it's not a very nice thing for me to tell, but all of us were tickled silly the day Miss Amelia packed her trunk and left for sure. She begged father to promise her our school next winter; she even asked mother to urge him, but mother said she could scarcely interfere. Father said he'd think about it, and let her know; which didn't mean a thing but that he was too tender-hearted to tell her right out that he didn't like her teaching. None of us cared for *her,* either. Mother said she never tried harder in all her days, but Miss Amelia was the most distinctly unlovable person she ever had met. She sympathized with us so, she never said a word when Leon sang:

"Believe me, if all those endearing young charms,
  Which I gaze on so fondly to-day,
Were to change by to-morrow, and fleet in my arms,
  Like fairy-gifts fading away,
Thou wouldst still be adored, as this moment thou art,
  Let thy loveliness fade as it will,
And around the dear ruin each wish of my heart
  Would entwine itself verdantly still—"

while Miss Amelia drove from sight up the Groveville road.

As he sang Leon stretched out his arms after her vanishing form. "I hope," he said, "that you caught that touching reference to 'the dear ruin,' and could anything be expressed more beautifully and poetically than that 'verdantly still?'"

I feel sorry for a snake. I like hoptoads, owls, and shitepokes. I envy a buzzard the way it can fly, and polecats are beautiful; but I never could get up any sort of feeling at all for Miss Amelia, whether she was birdlike or her true self. So no one was any gladder than I when she was gone.

After that, spring came pushing until you felt shoved. Our family needed me then. If they never had known it before, they found out there was none too many of us. Every day I had to watch the blue goose, and bring in her egg before it was chilled, carrying it carefully so it would not be jarred. I had to hunt the turkey nests and gather their eggs so they would be right for setting. There had to be straw carried from the stack for new nests, eggs marked, and hens set by the dozen. Garden time came, so leaves had to be raked from the beds and from the dooryard. No one was busier than I; but every little while I ran away, and spent some time all by myself in the pulpit, under the hawk oak, or on the roof.

I loved it up there. You could see farther than from any place else, the air was so fresh and fine, it cleared your brain until it made you think such big things, you shook and trembled sometimes, so that you almost fell from the eaves. Father made those eaves himself, they were very wide and hollowed only enough to catch the rain, and run it to the pipes that led to the cistern. I often lay in them, and watched the sky. I could climb from the back window of the girls' room, but my hand against the wall to steady me, and walk up the roof of the back part of the house to the ridge, and sit or lie in the big wide white eave trough of the front part. It was finest on cloudy days so the sun didn't make it too warm, and in a storm it was wonderful. My! but the world does look slashed around and helpless in a stiff wind, under black clouds, and when the sky cracks to let the lightning through, and the thunder rolls. One cloudy day, I went to sleep staring straight up, and a big storm came. I never knew it until the rain pelted on my face, and at the same time the thunder rolled. I jumped so I fell from the eaves, but I lit on my stomach across the ridge of the back part of the house, so it didn't hurt much or break me, like it would if I had fallen on either side, rolled down the roof, and bounced on the ground. I got down pretty quick though, and after that, if I felt sleepy, I lay on a bed beside a window.

Coming from church that Sunday, when we reached the top of the Big Hill, mother touched father's arm. "Stop a minute," she said, and he checked the horses, while we sat there and wondered why, as she looked and looked all over the farm, then, "Now drive to the top of the Little Hill and turn, and stop exactly on the place from which we first viewed this land together," she said. "You know the spot, don't you?"

"You may well believe I know it," said father. "I can hit it to the inch. You see, children," he went on, "your mother and I arranged before the words were said over us"—he always put it that way—I never in my life heard him say, "when we were married;" he read so many books he talked exactly like a book—"that we would be partners in everything, as long as we lived. When we decided the Ohio land was not quite what we wanted, she sent me farther west to prospect, while she stayed at home and kept the baby. When I reached this land, found it for sale, and within my means, I bought it, and started home happy. Before I'd gone a mile, I turned to look back, and saw that it was hilly, mostly woods, and there was no computing the amount of work it would require to make it what I could see in it; so I began to think maybe she wouldn't like it, and to wish I had brought her, before I closed the deal. By the time I returned home, packed up, and travelled this far on the way back with her, there was considerable tension in my feelings—considerable tension," repeated father as he turned the horses and began driving carefully, measuring the distance from Hoods' and the bridge. At last he stopped, backed a step, and said: "There, mommy, did I hit the spot?"

"You did!" said mother, stepping from the carriage and walking up beside him. She raised one hand and laid it on the lamp near him. He shifted the lines, picked up her hand, and held it tight. Mother stood there looking, just silently looking. May jabbed me in the side, leaned over and whispered:

"Could we but stand where Moses stood,
*   And view the landscape o'er,*
Not our Little Creek, nor dinner getting cold,
*   Could fright us from that shore."*

I couldn't help giggling, but I knew that was no proper time, so I hid my head in her lap and smothered the sound the best I could; but they were so busy soft-soddering each other they didn't pay a bit of attention to us.

It was May now, all the leaves were fresh and dustless, everything that flowered at that time was weighted with bloom, bees hummed past, butterflies sailed through the carriage, while birds at the tops of their voices, all of them, every kind there was, sang fit to split; friendly, unafraid bluebirds darted around us, and talked a blue streak from every fence rider. Made you almost crazy to know what they said. The Little Creek flowed at our feet across the road, through the blue-flag swamp, where the red and the yellow birds lived. You could see the sun flash on the water where it emptied into the stream that crossed Deams', and flowed through our pasture; and away beyond the Big Hill arose, with the new church on top, the graveyard around it, the Big Creek flashing at its base. In the valley between lay our fields, meadows, the big red barn, the white house with the yard filled with trees and flowering shrubs, beyond it the garden, all made up, neat and growing; and back of it the orchard in full bloom.

Mother stood and looked, and looked. Suddenly she raised her face to father. "Paul," she said, "that first day, did you ever dream it could be made to look like this?"

"No!" said father. "I never did! I saw houses, barns, and cleared fields; I hoped for comfort and prosperity, but I didn't know any place could grow to be so beautiful, and there is something about it, even on a rainy November day, there is something that catches me in the breast, on the top of either of these hills, until it almost stifles me. What is it, Ruth?"

"The Home Feeling!" said mother. "It is in my heart so big this morning I am filled with worship. Just filled with the spirit of worship."

She was rocking on her toes like she does when she becomes too happy at the Meeting House to be quiet any longer, and cries, "Glory!" right out loud. She pointed to the orchard, an immense orchard of big apple trees in full bloom, with two rows of peach trees around the sides. It looked like a great, soft, pinkish white blanket, with a deep pink border, spread lightly on the green earth.

"We planted that way because we thought it was best; how could we know how it would look in bloom time? It seems as if you came to these hilltops and figured on the picture you would make before you cleared, or fenced a field."

"That's exactly what I did," said father. "Many's the hour, all told, that I have stopped my horse on one of these hilltops and studied how to make the place beautiful, as well as productive. That was a task you set me, my girl. You always considered *beauty* as well as *use* about the house and garden, and wherever you worked. I had to hold my part in line."

"You have made it all a garden," said mother. "You have made it a garden growing under the smile of the Master; a very garden of the Lord, father."

Father drew up her hand and held it tight against his heart.

"Your praise is sweet, my girl, sweet!" he said. "I have tried, God knows I have tried, to make it first comfortable, then beautiful, for all of us. To the depths of my soul I thank Him for this hour. I am glad, Oh I am so glad you like your home, Ruth! I couldn't endure it if you complained, found fault and wished you lived elsewhere."

"Why, father!" said my mother in the most surprised voice. "Why, father, it would kill me to leave here. This is ours. We have made it by and through the strength of the Lord and our love for each other. All my days I want to live here, and when I die, I want to lie beside my blessed babies and you, Paul, down by the church we gave the land for, and worked so hard to build. I love it, Oh I love it! See how clean and white the dark evergreens make the house look! See how the big chestnuts fit in and point out the yellow road. I wish we had a row the length of it!"

"They wouldn't grow," said father. "You mind the time I had finding the place those wanted to set their feet?"

"I do indeed!" said mother, drawing her hand and his with it where she could rub her cheek against it. "Now we'll go home and have our dinner and a good rest. I'm a happy woman this day, father, a happy, happy woman. If only one thing didn't worry me—"

"Must there always be a 'fly in the ointment,' mother?"

She looked at him with a smile that was like a hug and kiss, and she said: "I have found it so, father, and I have been happy in spite of it. Where one has such wide interests, at some point there is always a pull, but in His own day, in His own way, the Lord is going to make everything right."

"'Thy faith hath made thee whole,'" quoted father.

Then she stepped into the carriage, and he waited a second, quite long enough to let her see that he was perfectly willing to sit there all day if she wanted him to, and then he slowly and carefully drove home, as he always did when she was in the carriage. Times when he had us children out alone, he went until you couldn't see the spokes in the wheels. He just loved to "speed up" once in a while on a piece of fine road to let us know how going fast felt.

Mother sat there trembling a little, smiling, misty-eyed. I was thinking, for I knew what the "fly in the ointment" was. She had a letter from Shelley yesterday, and she said there wasn't a reason on earth why father or Laddie should spend money to come to Chicago, she would soon be home, she was counting the hours, and she never wanted to leave again. In the start she didn't want to go at all, unless she could stay three years, at the very least. Of course it was that dreadful man, who had made her so beautiful and happy, and then taken away all the joy; how *could* a man do it? It was the hardest thing to understand.

Next morning mother was feeling fine, the world was lovely, Miss Amelia was gone, May was home to help, so she began housecleaning by washing all the curtains. She had been in the kitchen to show Candace how. I had all my work done, and was making friends with a robin brooding in my very own catalpa tree, when Mr. Pryor rode up, tied his horse, and started toward the gate. I knew he and father had quarreled; that is, father had told him he couldn't say "God was a myth" in his house, and he'd gone home mad as hops; so I knew it would be something mighty important that was bringing him back. I slid from the tree, ran and opened the gate, and led the way up the walk. I opened the front door and asked him in, and then I did the wrong thing. I should have taken his hat, told him to be seated, and said I would see if I could find father; I knew what to do, and how to do it, but because of that about God, I was so excited I made a mistake. I never took his hat, or offered him a chair; I just bolted into the dining-room, looking for father or mother, and left the door wide open, so he thought that wasn't the place to sit, because I didn't give him a chair, and he followed me. The instant I saw mother's face, I knew what I had done. The dining-room was no place for particular company like him, and bringing him in that way didn't give her time to smooth her hair, pull shut her dress band at the neck, put on her collar, and shiny goldstone pin, her white apron, and rub her little flannel rag, with rice flour on it, on her nose to take away the shine. I had made a mess of it.

There she came right in the door, just as she was from the tub. Her hair was damp and crinkled around her face, her neckband had been close in stooping, so she had unfastened it, and tucked it back in a little V-shaped place to give her room and air. Her cheeks were pink, her eyes bright, her lips red as a girl's, and her neck was soft and white. The V-shaped place showed a little spot like baby skin, right where her neck went into her chest. Sure as father kissed her lips, he always tipped back her head, bent lower and kissed that spot too. I had seen hundreds of them go there, and I had tried it myself, lots of times, and it *was* the sweetest place. Seeing what I had done, I stopped breathless. You have to beat most everything you teach a child right into it properly to keep it from making such a botch of things as that. I hardly dared peep at mother, but when I did, she took my breath worse than the mistake I had made.

Caught, she stood her ground. She never paused a second. Straight to him she went, holding out her hand, and I could see that it was red and warm from pressing the lace in the hot suds. A something flashed over her, that made her more beautiful than she was in her silk dress going to town to help Lucy give a party, and her voice was sweet as the bubbling warbler on the garden fence when he was trying to coax a mate into the privet bush to nest.

"So glad to see you!" she cried. "How are you, and all your family this fine morning?"

"I think we are feeling spring a little too," he said formally.

Mother asked him to be seated, so he took one of the chairs nearest him, and sat holding his hat in one hand, his whip in the other. Mother drew a chair beside the dining table, dropped her hands on each other, and looking in his eyes, she smiled at him. I tell the same thing over about people's looks, but I haven't told of this smile of mother's; because I never saw exactly how it was, or what it would do to people, until that morning. Then as I watched her—for how she felt decided what would happen to me, after Mr. Pryor was gone—I saw something I never had noticed until that minute. She could laugh all over her face, before her lips parted until her teeth showed. She was doing it now. With a wide smile running from cheek to cheek, pushing up a big dimple at each end, her lips barely touching, her eyes dancing, she sat looking at him.

"This *is* the most blessed season for warming up the heart," she said. "If you want the half of my kingdom, ask quickly. I'm in the mood to bestow it."

How she laughed! He just had to loosen up a little, and smile back, even though it looked pretty stiff.

"Well, I'll not tax you so far," he said. "I only want Mr. Stanton."

"But he is the whole of the kingdom, and the King to boot!" she laughed, dimpled, and flamed redder.

Mr. Pryor stared at her wonderingly. You could even see the wonder, like it was something you could take hold of. I suppose he wondered what could make a woman so happy, like that.

"Lucky man!" he said. "All of us are not so fortunate."

"Then it must be you don't covet the place or the title," said mother more soberly. "Any woman will crown the man she marries, if he will allow her. Paul went farther. He compelled it."

"I wonder how!" said Mr. Pryor, his eyes steadily watching mother's face.

"By never failing in a million little things, that taken as a whole, make up one mighty big thing, on which he stands like the Rock of Ages."

"Yet they tell me that you are the mother of twelve children," he said, as if he marvelled at something.

"Yes!" cried mother, and the word broke right through a bubbling laugh. "Am I not fortunate above most women? We had the grief to lose two little daughters at the ages of eight and nine, through a complication of scarlet fever and whooping cough; but they were beautiful children whom it was joy to have been permitted to love, and to hold for that long; all the others I have, and I rejoice in them."

She reached out, laid a hand on me, drew me to her, and lightly touched my arm, sending my spirits sky-high. She wasn't going to do a thing to me, not even scold! Mr. Pryor stared at her like Jacob Hood does at Laddie when he begins rolling Greek before him, so I guess what mother said must have been Greek to Mr. Pryor.

"I came to see Mr. Stanton," he said suddenly, and crosslike as if he didn't believe a word she said, and had decided she was too foolish to bother with any longer; but he kept on staring. He couldn't quit that, no matter how cross he was. The funniest thing came into my mind. I wondered what on earth he'd have done if she'd gone over, sat on his lap, put her arms around his neck, took his face between her hands and kissed his forehead, eyes, lips, and tousled his hair, like she does father and our boys. I'll bet all I got, he'd have turned to stonier stone than Sabethany. You could see that no one ever served *him* like that in all his old, cold, hard, cross, mysterious, shut-in life. I was crazy to ask, "Say, did anybody ever kiss you?" but I had such a close escape bringing him in wrong, I thought it would be wise not to take any risks so soon after. It was enough to stand beside mother, and hear every word they said. What was more, she wanted me, because she kept her hand on mine, or touched my apron every little while.

"I'm so sorry!" she said. "He was called to town on business. The County Commissioners are sitting to-day."

"They are deciding about the Groveville bridge, and pike?"

"Yes. He is working so hard for them."

"The devil you say! I beg pardon! But it was about that I came. I'm three miles from there, and I'm taxed over sixty pounds for it."

"But you cross the bridge every time you go to town, and travel the road. Groveville is quite a resort on account of the water and lovely country. Paul is very anxious to have the work completed before the summer boarders come from surrounding cities. We are even farther from it than you; but it will cost us as much."

"Are you insane?" cried Mr. Pryor, not at all politely; but you could see that mother was bound she wouldn't become provoked about anything, for she never stopped a steady beam on him. "Spend all that money for strangers to lazy around on a few weeks and then go!"

"But a good bridge and fine road will add to their pleasure, and when they leave, the improvements remain. They will benefit us and our children through all the years to come."

"Talk about 'the land of the free!'" cried Mr. Pryor. "This is a tax-ridden nation. It's a beastly outrage! Ever since I came, it's been nothing but notice of one assessment after another. I won't pay it! I won't endure it. I'll move!"

Mother let go of me, gripped her hands pretty tight together on the table, and she began to talk.

"As for freedom—no man ever was, or is, or will be free," she said, quite as forcibly as he could speak. "The wildest savage in darkest Africa is not a free man. He is subject to the law of nature, the power of savage, or beast stronger than he. The higher men advance in civilization, the more cords they furnish to bind themselves with, the tighter they are held by national and state law; and above all, by the law of God. You probably knew when you came here that you would find a land tax-ridden from a great civil war of years' duration, and from newness of vast territory to be opened up and improved. You certainly studied the situation. Most of our taxes are levied by each state. You'll have to leave the country to avoid them."

"'Studied the situation!'" His whip beat across his knee. "'Studied the situation!' My leaving England was—er—the result of intolerable conditions there—in the nature of flight from things not to be endured. I had only a vague idea of the States."

"If England is intolerable, and the United States an outrage, I don't know where in this world you'll go," said mother softly.

Mr. Pryor stared at her sharply.

"Madame is pleased to be facetious," he said sneeringly.

Mother's hands parted, and one of them stretched across the table toward him.

"Forgive me!" she cried. "That was unkind. I know you are in dreadful trouble. I'd give—I'd almost give this right hand to comfort you. I'd do nearly anything to make you feel that you need bear no burden alone; that we'd love to help support you."

"I believe you would," he said slowly, his eyes watching her again. "I believe you would. I wonder why!"

"All men are brothers, in the broader sense," said mother, "and if you'll forgive me, your face bears marks of suffering almost amounting to torture."

She stretched out the other hand.

"You couldn't possibly let us help you?"

Slowly he shook his head.

"Think again!" urged mother. "A trouble shared is half over to start with. You lay a part of it on your neighbours, and your neighbours in this case would be glad, glad indeed, to see you care-free and happy as all men should be."

"We'll not discuss it," he said. "You can't possibly imagine the root of my trouble."

"I shan't try!" said mother. "But let me tell you this: I don't care if you have betrayed your country, blasphemed your God, or killed your own child! So long as you're a living man, daily a picture of suffering before me, you're a burden on my heart. You're a load on my shoulders, without your consent. I have implored God, I shall never cease to implore Him, until your brow clears, your head is lifted, and your heart is at rest. You can't prevent me! This hour I shall go to my closet and beg Him to have mercy on your poor soul, and when His time comes, He will. You can't help yourself, or you would have done so, long ago. You must accept aid! This must end, or there will be tragedy in your house."

"Madame, there has been!" said Mr. Pryor, shaking as he sat.

"I recognize that," said mother. "The question is whether what has passed is not enough."

"You simply cannot understand!" he said.

"I understand only too well!" said mother.

He kept his eyes on her, but for a wonder he didn't become angry.

"You don't know when Mr. Stanton will be home?" he asked at last.

"Before night, I think."

"But the matter will have been decided when he comes?"

"I don't know. It is probable."

"He is working for the road?"

"With all his heart!"

"Yet he can't afford it; and the taxes will be an added burden on you."

Mother laughed aloud.

"Mr. Pryor," she said, "you're in the position of a man doubly bereft. You are without a country, and without a God. Your face tells every passer-by how you are enjoying that kind of life. Forgive me, if I speak plainly. I admire some things about you so much, I am venturing positive unkindness to try to make you see that in shutting out your neighbours you will surely make them think more, and worse things, than are true. I haven't a doubt in my mind but that your trouble is not one half so dreadful as you imagine while brooding over it. We will pass that. Let me tell you how we feel about this road matter. You see we did our courting in Pennsylvania, married and tried Ohio, and then came on here. We took this land when it was mostly woods. I could point you to the exact spot where we stopped; we visited it yesterday, looked down the hill and selected the place where we would set this house, when we could afford to build it. We moved into the cabin that was on the land first, later built a larger one, and finally this home as we had planned it. Every fruit tree, bush, vine, and flower we planted. Here our children have been born, lived, loved, and left us; some for the graveyard down yonder, some for homes of their own. Always we have planned and striven to transform this into the dearest, the most beautiful spot on earth. In making our home the best we can, in improving our township, county, and state, we are doing our share toward upbuilding this nation."

She began at the a b c's, and gave it to him straight: the whole thing, just as we saw it; and he listened, as if he were a prisoner, and she a judge telling him what he must do to gain his freedom. She put in the birds to keep away the worms, the trees to break the wind, the creeks to save the moisture. She whanged him, and she banged him, up one side, and down the other. She didn't stop to be mincy. She shot things at him like a man talking to another man who had plenty of sense but not a particle of reason. She gave him the reason. She told him exactly why, and how, and where, and also just *what* he must do to feel *right* toward his neighbours, his family, and his God. She never stopped until there wasn't a single thing left to tell him; and he sat and stared at her, and she stared straight back at him, while she hammered away as I never heard or knew she could possibly speak. I don't see why on earth they don't put *her* in the pulpit to tell every one things like that. No preacher ever talked half so well. Yea verily, she was as interesting as the Bishop himself, and far pleasanter to look at. When she ran short of breath, and out of words, she reached both hands toward him again.

"Oh do please think of these things!" she begged. "Do try to believe that I am a sensible person, and know what I am talking about."

"Madame," said Mr. Pryor, "there's no doubt in my mind but you are the most wonderful woman I ever have met. Surely I believe you! Surely I know your plan of life is the true, the only right way. It is one degree added to my humiliation that the ban I am under keeps me from friendly intercourse with so great a lady."

"'Lady?'" said my mother, her eyes widening. "'Lady?' Now it is you who are amused."

"I don't understand!" he said. "Certainly you are a lady, a very great lady."

"Goodness, gracious me!" cried my mother, laughing until her dimples would have held water. "That's the first time in all my life I was ever accused of such a thing."

"Again, I do not comprehend," said Mr. Pryor, as if vexed about all he would endure.

Mother laughed on, and as she did so she drew back her hands and studied them. Then she looked at him again, one pink dimple flashing here and there, all over her face.

"Well, to begin at the root of the matter," she said, "that is an enormous big word that you are using lightly. Any one in petticoats is not a lady,—by no means! A lady must be born of unsullied blood for at least three generations, on each side of her house. Think for a minute about where you are going to fulfil that condition. Then she must be gentle by nature, and rearing. She must know all there is to learn from books, have wide experience to cover all emergencies, she must be steeped in social graces, and diplomatic by nature. She must rise unruffled to any emergency, never wound, never offend, always help and heal, she must be perfect in deportment, virtue, wifehood and motherhood. She must be graceful, pleasing and beautiful. She must have much leisure to perfect herself in learning, graces and arts —"

"Madame, you draw an impossible picture!" cried Mr. Pryor.

"I draw the picture of the only woman on earth truly entitled to be called a lady. You use a good word lightly. I have told you what it takes to make a lady—now look at me!"

How she laughed! Mr. Pryor looked, but he didn't laugh.

"More than ever you convince me that you are a lady, indeed," he said.

Mother wiped her eyes.

"My dear man!" she cried. "I'm the daughter of a Dutch miller, who lived on a Pennsylvania mountain stream. There never was a school anywhere near us, and father and mother only taught us to work. Paul Stanton took a grist there, and saw me. He married me, and brought me here. He taught me to read and write. I learned my lessons with my elder children. He has always kept school in our house, every night of his life. Our children supposed it was for them; I knew it was quite as much for me. While I sat at knitting or sewing, I spelled over the words he gave out. I know nothing of my ancestors, save that they came from the lowlands of Holland, down where there were cities, schools, and business. They were well educated, but they would not take the trouble to teach their children. As I have spoken to you, my husband taught me. All I know I learn from him, from what he reads aloud, and places he takes me. I exist in a twenty-mile radius, but through him, I know all lands, principalities and kingdoms, peoples and customs. I need never be ashamed to go, or afraid to speak, anywhere."

"Indeed not!" cried Mr. Pryor.

"But when you think on the essentials of a real lady—and then picture me patching, with a First Reader propped before me; facing Indians, Gypsies, wild animals—and they used to be bad enough—why, I mind one time in Ohio when our first baby was only able to stand beside a chair, and through the rough puncheon floor a copperhead stuck up its gleam of bronzy gold, and shot its darting tongue within a foot of her bare leg. By all accounts, a lady would have reached for her smelling salts and gracefully fainted away; in fact, a lady never would have been in such a place at all. It was my job to throw the first thing I could lay my hands on so straight and true that I would break that snake's neck, and send its deadly fangs away from my baby. I did it with Paul's plane, and neatly too! Then I had to put the baby on the bed and tear up every piece of the floor to see that the snake had not a mate in hiding there, for copperheads at that season were going pairs. Once I was driven to face a big squaw, and threatened the life of her baby with a red-hot poker while she menaced mine with a hunting knife. There is not one cold, rough, hard experience of pioneer life that I have not endured. Shoulder to shoulder, and heart to heart, I've stood beside my man, and done what had to be done, to build this home, rear our children, save our property. Many's the night I have shivered in a barn doctoring sick cattle and horses we could ill afford to lose. Time and again I have hung on and brought things out alive, after the men gave up and quit. A lady? How funny!"

"The amusement is all on your part, Madame."

"So it seems!" said mother. "But you see, I know so well how ridiculous it is. When I think of the life a woman must lead in order to be truly a lady, when I review the life I have been forced to live to do my share in making this home, and rearing these children, the contrast is too great. I thank God for any part I have been able to take. Had I life to live over, I see now where I could do more; but neighbour, believe me, my highest aspiration is to be a clean, thrifty housekeeper, a bountiful cook, a faithful wife, a sympathetic mother. That is life work for any woman, and to be a good woman is the greatest thing on earth. Never mind about the ladies; if you can honestly say of me, she is a good woman, you have paid me the highest possible tribute."

"I have nothing to change, in the face of your argument," said Mr. Pryor. "Our loved Queen on her throne is no finer lady."

That time mother didn't laugh. She looked straight at him a minute and then she said: "Well, for an Englishman, as I know them, you have said the last word. Higher praise there is none. But believe me, I make no such claim. To be a good wife and mother is the end toward which I aspire. To hold the respect and love of my husband is the greatest object of my life."

"Then you have succeeded," said Mr. Pryor. "The other day I stood in a shop in Groveville, talking with the owner, and while we chatted, you and Mr. Stanton passed each other going in different directions. He removed his hat, and bowed with formal ceremony. 'What do you think of that?' asked Mr. Andrews of me. 'I think that is exactly as it should be,' I answered. 'He has been in love with his wife for over thirty years,' he said. No doubt he has; I can see exactly why, and from my soul I envy him."

Mother's face flushed, and she looked as if she didn't know what to say, so I thought I'd help her out.

"That time when the lightning struck our house and knocked

her over, and she didn't move or say a word for such a long time, why he just kissed her feet," I told him.

I guess I knew how much our father thought of mother.

"No doubt!" said Mr. Pryor. "No doubt! Any man understanding the life of such a woman would. That was his high privilege!"

"You shame me!" cried mother. "I never in my life have done anything above the average. To keep clean, to strive to learn as much as my husband and children know, to be as good a wife and mother as I can, that is nothing! All women do that! I deserve no credit whatever; I am humbled by your words."

"You stand a monument to wifehood; your children prove your idea of motherhood," said Mr. Pryor. "How in this world have you managed it? The members of your family whom I have seen are fine, interesting men and women, educated above the average. It is not idle curiosity. I am deeply interested in knowing how such an end came to be accomplished here on this farm. I wish you would tell me just how you have gone about schooling your children."

"By educating ourselves before their coming, and with them afterward. Self-control, study, work, joy of life, satisfaction with what we have had, never-ending strife to go higher, and to do better—Dr. Fenner laughs when I talk of these things. He says he can take a little naked Hottentot from the jungle, and educate it to the same degree that I can one of mine. I don't know; but if these things do not help before birth, at least they do not hinder; and afterward, you are in the groove in which you want your children to run. With all our twelve there never has been one who at nine months of age did not stop crying if its father lifted his finger, or tapped his foot and told it to. From the start we have rigorously guarded our speech and actions before them. From the first tiny baby my husband has taught all of them to read, write and cipher some, before they went to school at all. He is always watching, observing, studying: the earth, the stars, growing things; he never comes to a meal but he has seen something that he has or will study out for all of us. There never has been one day in our home on which he did not read a new interesting article from book or paper; work out a big problem, or discuss some phase of politics, religion, or war. Sometimes there has been a little of all of it in one day, always reading, spelling, and memory exercises at night. He has a sister who twice in her life has repeated the Bible as a test before a committee. He, himself, can go through the New Testament and all of the Old save the books of the generations. He always says he considers it a waste of gray matter to learn them. He has been a schoolmaster, his home his schoolroom, his children, wife and helpers his pupils; the common things of life as he meets them every day, the books from which we learn.

"I was ignorant at first of bookish subjects, but in his atmosphere, if one were no student, and didn't even try to keep up, or forge ahead, they would absorb much through association. Almost always he has been on the school board and selected the teachers; we have made a point of keeping them here, at great inconvenience to ourselves, in order to know as much of them as possible, and to help and guide them in their work. When the children could learn no more here, for most of them we have managed the high school of Groveville, especially after our daughter moved there, and for each of them we have added at least two years of college, music school, or whatever the peculiar bent of the child seemed to demand.

"Before any daughter has left our home for one of her own, she has been taught all I know of cleanliness about a house, cookery, sewing, tending the sick, bathing and dressing the new born. She has to bake bread, pie, cake, and cook any meat or vegetable we have. She has had her bolt of muslin to make as she chose for her bedding, and linen for her underclothing. The quilts she pieced and the blankets she wove have been hers. All of them have been as well provided for as we could afford. They can knit, darn, patch, tuck, hem, and embroider, set a hen and plant a garden. I go on a vacation and leave each of them to keep house for her father a month, before she enters a home of her own. They are strong, healthy girls; I hope all of them are making a good showing at being useful women, and I know they are happy, so far at least."

"Wonderful!" said Mr. Pryor.

"Father takes the boys in hand and they must graduate in a straight furrow, an even fence, planting and tending crops, trimming and grafting trees, caring for stock, and handling plane, augur and chisel. Each one must select his wood, cure, fashion, and fit his own ax with a handle, grind and swing it properly, as well as cradle, scythe and sickle. They must be able to select good seed grain, boil sap, and cure meat. They must know animals, their diseases and treatment, and when they have mastered all he can teach them, and done each thing properly, they may go for their term at college, and make their choice of a profession. As yet I'm sorry to say but one of them has come back to the land."

"You mean Laddie?"

"Yes."

"He has decided to be a farmer?"

"He has determined to make the soil yield his living."

"I am sorry—sorry indeed to hear it," said Mr. Pryor. "He has brain and education to make a brilliant figure at law or statesmanship; he would do well in trade."

"What makes you think he would *not* do well on land?"

"Wasted!" cried Mr. Pryor. "He would be wasted!"

"Hold a bit!" said mother, her face flushing as it did when she was very provoked. "My husband is, and always has been, on land. He is far from being wasted. He is a power in this community. He has sons in cities in law and in trade. Not one of them has the friends, and the influence on his time, that his father has. Any day he says the word, he can stand in legislative halls, and take any part he chooses in politics. He prefers his home and family, and the work he does here, but let me tell you, no son of his ever had his influence or opportunity, or ever will have."

"All this is news to me," said Mr. Pryor.

"You didn't expect us to come over, force our way in and tell you?"

It was his turn to blush and he did.

"Laddie has been at our house often," he said. "He might have mentioned —"

Mother laughed. She was the gayest that morning.

"He 'might,' but he never would. Neither would I if you hadn't seemed to think that the men who do the things Mr. Stanton *refuses* to do are the ones worth while."

"He could accomplish much in legislative halls."

"He figures in the large. He thinks that to be a commissioner, travel his county and make all of it the best possible, to stand in primaries and choose only worthy men for all offices, is doing a much bigger work than to take one place for himself, and strive only for that. Besides, he really loves his land, his house, and family. He says no man has a right to bring twelve children into the world and not see personally to rearing and educating them. He thinks the farm and the children too much for me, and he's sure he is doing the biggest thing for the community at large, to go on as he does."

"Perhaps so," said Mr. Pryor slowly. "He should know best. Perhaps he is."

"I make no doubt!" said mother, lifting her head proudly. "And as Laddie feels and has fitted himself, I look to see him go head and shoulders above any other son I have. Trade is not the only way to accumulate. Law is not the only path to the legislature. Comfort, independence, and freedom, such as we know here, is not found in any city I ever have visited. We think we have the best of life, and we are content on land. We have not accumulated much money; we have spent thousands; we have had a big family for which to provide, and on account of the newness of the country, taxes always have been heavy. But we make no complaint. We are satisfied. We could have branched off into fifty different things after we had a fair start here. We didn't, because we preferred life as we worked it out for ourselves. Paul says when he leaves the city, and his horses' hoofs strike the road between our fields, he always lifts his head higher, squares his shoulders, and feels a man among men. To own land, and to love it, is a wonderful thing, Mr. Pryor."

She made me think of something. Ever since I had added to my quill and arrow money, the great big lot at Easter, father had shared his chest till with me. The chest stood in our room, and in it lay his wedding suit, his every Sunday clothes, his best hat with a red silk handkerchief in the crown, a bundle of precious newspapers he was saving on account of rare things in them he wanted for reference, and in the till was the wallet of ready money he kept in the house for unexpected expense, his deeds, insurance papers, all his particular private papers, the bunches of lead pencils, slate pencils, and the box of pens from which he supplied us for school. Since I had grown so rich, he had gone partners with me, and I might lift the lid, open the till and take out my little purse that May bought from the huckster for my last birthday. I wasn't to touch a thing, save my own, and I never did; but I knew precious well what was there. If Mr. Pryor thought my father didn't amount to much because he lived on land; if it made him think more of him, to know that he could be in the legislature if he chose, maybe he'd think still more —

I lifted the papers, picked it up carefully, and slipping back quietly, I laid it on Mr. Pryor's knee. He picked it up and held it a minute, until he finished what he was saying to mother, and then he looked at it. Then he looked long and hard. Then he straightened up and looked again.

"God bless my soul!" he cried.

You see when he was so astonished he didn't know what he was saying, he called on God, just as father says every one does. I took a side look at mother. Her face was a little extra flushed, but she was still smiling; so I knew she wasn't angry with me, though of course she wouldn't have shown the thing herself. She and father never did, except as each of us grew big enough to be taught about the Crusaders. Father said he didn't care the snap of his finger about it, except as it stood for hardihood and bravery. But Mr. Pryor cared! He cared more than he could say. He stared, and stared, and over and over he wonderingly repeated: "God bless my soul!"

"Where did you get the crest of the Earl of Eastbrooke, the master of Stanton house?" he demanded. "Stanton house!" he repeated. "Why—why, the name! It's scarcely possible, but —"

"But there it is!" laughed mother. "A mere bauble for show and amounting to nothing on earth save as it stands a mark for brave men who have striven to conquer."

"Surgere tento!" read Mr. Pryor, from the little shield. "Four shells! Madame, I know men who would give their lives to own this, and to have been born with the right to wear it. It came to your husband in straight line?"

"Yes," said mother, "but generations back. He never wore it. He never would. He only saves it for the children."

"It goes to your eldest son?"

"By rights, I suppose it should," said mother. "But father mentioned it the other night. He said none of his boys had gone as he tried to influence them, unless Laddie does now in choosing land for his future, and if he does, his father is inclined to leave it to him, and I agree. At our death it goes to Laddie I am quite sure."

"Well, I hope—I hope," said Mr. Pryor, "that the young man has the wit to understand what this would mean to him in England."

"His wit is just about level with his father's," said mother. "He never has been in England, and most probably he never will be. I don't think it means a rap more to Laddie than it does to my husband. Laddie is so busy developing the manhood born in him, he has no time to chase the rainbow of reflected glory, and no belief in its stability if he walked in its light. The child of my family to whom that trinket really means something is Little Sister, here. When Leon came in with the thief, I thought he should have it; but after all, she is the staunchest little Crusader I have."

Mr. Pryor looked me over with much interest.

"Yes, yes! No doubt!" he said. "But the male line! This priceless treasure should descend to one of the male line! To one whose name will remain Stanton! To Laddie would be best, no doubt! No doubt at all!"

"We will think about it," said mother serenely as Mr. Pryor arose to go.

He apologized for staying so long, and mother said it hadn't been long, and asked him the nicest ever to come again. She walked in the sunlight with him, and pointed out the chestnuts. She asked what he thought of a line of trees to shade the road, and they discussed whether the pleasure they would give in summer would pay for the dampness they would hold in winter. They wandered around the yard and into the garden. She sent me to bring a knife, trowel, and paper, so when he started home, he was carrying a load of cuttings, and roots to plant.

When father came from town that evening, at the first sight of him, she went straight into his arms, her face beaming; she had been like a sun all that day. Some of it must have been joy carried over from yesterday.

"Praise God, the wedge is in!" she cried.

Father held her tight, stroked her hair, and began smiling without having the least idea why, but he very well knew that whatever pleased her like that was going to be good news for him also.

"What has happened, mother?" he asked.

"Mr. Pryor came over about the road and bridge tax, and Oh Paul! I've said every word to him I've been bursting to say from the very start. Every single word, Paul!"

"How did he take it?"

"Time will tell. Anyway, he heard it, all of it, and he went back carrying a load of things to plant. Only think of that! Once he begins planting, and watching things grow, the home feeling is bound to come. I tell you, Paul, the wedge is in! Oh I'm so happy!"

The Crest of Eastbrooke

Sow;—and look onward, upward,
  Where the starry light appears,—
Where, in spite of coward's doubting,
  Or your own heart's trembling fears,
You shall reap in joy the harvest
  You have sown to-day in tears.

"Any objections to my beginning to break ground on the west eighty to-day?" asked Laddie of father at breakfast Monday morning.

"I had thought we would commence on the east forty, when planning the work."

"So had I," said Laddie. "But since I thought that, a very particular reason has developed for my beginning to plow the west eighty at once, and there is a charming little ditty I feel strongly impelled to whistle every step of the way."

Father looked at him sharply, and so, I think, did all of us. And because we loved him deeply, we saw that his face was a trifle pale for him; his clear eyes troubled, in spite of his laughing way. He knew we were studying him too, but he wouldn't have said anything that would make us look and question if he had minded our doing it. That was exactly like Laddie. He meant it when he said he hated a secret. He said there was no place on earth for a man to look for sympathy and love if he couldn't find it in his own family; and he never had been so happy since I had been big enough to notice his moods as he had been since all of us knew about the Princess. He didn't wait for father to ask why he'd changed his mind about the place to begin.

"You see," he said, "a very charming friend of mine expressed herself strongly last night about the degrading influence of farming, especially that branch of agriculture which evolves itself in a furrow; hence it is my none too happy work to plow the west eighty where she can't look our way without seeing me; and I have got to whistle my favourite toon where she must stop her ears if she doesn't hear; and then it will be my painful task, I fear, to endeavour to convince her that I am still clean, decent, and not degraded."

"Oh Laddie!" cried mother.

"Abominable foolishness!" roared father like he does roar once in about two years.

"Isn't it now?" asked Laddie sweetly. "I don't know what has got into her head. She has seen me plowing fifty times since their land has joined ours, and she never objected before."

"I can tell you blessed well!" said mother. "She didn't care two hoots how much my son plowed, but it makes a difference when it comes to her lover."

"Maw, you speak amazing reckless," said Laddie, "if I thought there was anything in *that* feature of the case, I'd attempt a Highland fling on the ridgepole of our barn."

"Be serious!" said father sternly. "This is no laughing matter."

"That's precisely why I am laughing," said Laddie. "Would it help me any to sit down and weep? I trow not! I have thought most of the silent watches—by the way they are far from silent in May—and as I read my title clear, it's my job to plow the west eighty immejit."

Father tried to look stern, but he just had to laugh.

"All right then, plow it!" he said.

"What did she say?" asked mother.

"Phew!" Laddie threw up both hands. "She must have been bottled some time on the subject. The ferment was a spill of considerable magnitude. The flood rather overwhelmed me, because it was so unexpected. I had been taking for granted that she accepted my circumstances and surroundings as she did me. But no, kind friends, far otherwise! She said last night, in the clearest English I ever heard spoken impromptu, that I was a man suitable for her friend, but I would have to change my occupation before I could be received on more than a friendly footing."

"'On more than a friendly footing?'" repeated mother.

"You have her exact words," said Laddie. "Kindly pass the ham."

"What did you say!"

"Nothing! I am going to plow the answer. Please don't object to my beginning this morning."

"You try yourself all winter to get as far as you have, and then upset the bowl like this?" cried mother.

"Softly, mummy, softly!" said Laddie. "What am I to do? I've definitely decided on my work. I see land and life, as you and father taught me, in range and in perspective far more than you've got from it. You had a first hand wrestle. The land I covet has been greatly improved already. I can do what I choose with it, making no more strenuous effort than plowing; and I am proud to say that I *love* to plow. I like my feet in the soil. I want my head in the spring air. I can become almost tipsy on the odours that fill my nostrils. Music evolved by the Almighty is plenty good enough for me. I'm proud of a spanking big team, under the control of a touch or a word. I enjoy farming, and I am going to be a farmer. Plowing is one of the most pleasing parts of the job. Sowing the seed beats it a little, from an artistic standpoint, either is preferable to haying, threshing, or corn cutting: all are parts of my work, so I'm going to begin. Mother, I hope you don't mind if I take your grays. I'll be very careful; but the picture I present to my girl to-day is going to go hard with her at best, so I'd like to make it level best."

He arose, went around and knelt beside mother. He took her, chair and all, in his arms:

"Best of mothers! on my breast
Lean thy head, and sink to rest."

he quoted. Mother laughed.

"Mammy," he asked bending toward her, "am I clean?"

"You goose!" she said, putting her arms around him and holding him tight.

"Gander love," said Laddie, turning up his face for a kiss. "Honest mother, you have been through nigh unto forty years of it, tell me, can a man be a farmer and keep neat enough not to be repulsive to a refined woman?"

"Your father is the answer," said mother. "All of you know how perfectly repulsive he is and always has been to me."

"'Repulsive,'" said father. "That's an ugly word!"

"There are a whole lot of unpleasant things that peep around corners occasionally," said Laddie. "But whoever of you dear people it was that showed Mr. Pryor the Crest of Eastbrooke, brought out this particular dragon for me to slay."

"Tut, tut! Now what does that mean?" said father. "Have we had a little exhibition of that especial brand of pride that goes before a fall?"

"We have! and I take the tumble," said Laddie. "Watch me start! 'Jack fell down and broke his crown.' Question—will 'Jill come tumbling after?'"

My heart stopped and I was shaking in my bare feet, because I wore no shoes to shake in. Oh my soul! No matter how Laddie jested I knew he was almost killed; the harder he made fun, the worse he was hurt. I opened my mouth to say I did it, I had to, but Leon began to talk.

"Well, I think she's smart!" he cried. "If she was going to give you the mitten, why didn't she do it long ago?"

"She had to find out first whether there were a possibility of her wanting to keep it," said Laddie.

"You're sure you are all signed, sealed, and delivered on this plowing business, are you?" asked Leon.

"Dead sure!" said Laddie.

"All right, if you like it!" said Leon. "None for me after college! But say, you can be a farmer and not plow, you know. You go trim the trees, and work at cleaner, more gentlemanly jobs. I'll plow that field. I'd just as soon as not. I plowed last year and you said I did well, didn't you, father?"

"Yes, on the potato patch," said father. "A cornfield is a different thing. I fear you are too light."

"Oh but that was a year ago!" cried Leon.

He pushed back his chair and went to father.

"Just feel my biceps now! Most like steel!" he boasted. "A fellow can grow a lot in a year, and all the riding I've been doing, and all the exercise I've had. Cert' I can plow that meadow."

"You're all right, shaver," said Laddie. "I'll not forget your offer; but in this case it wouldn't help. Either the Princess takes her medicine or I take mine. I'm going to live on land: I'm going to plow in plain sight of the Pryor house this week, if I have to hire to Jacob Hood to get the chance. May I plow, and may I take the grays, father?"

"Yes!" said father roundly.

"Then here goes!" said Laddie. "You needn't fret, mother. I'll not overheat them. I must give a concert simultaneous with this plowing performance, and I'm particular about the music, so I can't go too fast. Also, I'll wrap the harness."

"Goodness knows I'm not thinking about the horses," said mother.

"No, but if they turned up next Sunday, wind-broken, and with nice large patches of hair rubbed from their sides, you would be! If you were me, would you whistle, or vocalize to start on?"

Mother burst right out crying and laid her face all tear-wet against him. Laddie kissed her, and wiped away the tears, teased her, and soon as he could he bolted from the east door; but I was closest, so I saw plainly that his eyes were wet too. My soul and body! *And I had done it!* I might as well get it over.

"I showed Mr. Pryor the trinket," I said.

"How did you come to do that?" asked father sternly.

"When he was talking with mother. He told her Laddie would be 'wasted' farming —"

"'Wasted?'"

"That's what he said. Mother told him you had always farmed and you were a 'power in this community.' She told him about what you did, because you wanted to, and what you *could* do if you chose, about holding office, you know, and that seemed to make him think heaps more of you, so I thought it would be a good thing for him to know about the Crusaders too, and I ran and got the crest. I *thought* it would help —"

"And so it will," said mother. "They constantly make the best showing they can, we might as well, too. The trouble is they got more than they expected. They thought they could look down on us, and patronize us, if they came near at all; when they found we were quite as well educated as they, had as much land, could hold prominent offices if we chose, and had the right to that bauble, they veered to the other extreme. Now they seem to demand that we quit work —"

"Move to the city, 'sit on a cushion and sew a fine seam,'" suggested father.

"Exactly!" said mother. "They'll have to find out we are running our own business; but I'm sorry it fell to Laddie to show them. You could have done it better. It will come out all right. The Princess is not going to lose a man like Laddie on account of how he makes his money."

"Don't be too confident," said father. "With people of their stripe, how much money a man can earn, and at what occupation, constitute the whole of life."

She wasn't too confident. Yesterday she had been so happy she almost flew. To-day she kept things going, and sang a lot, but nearly every time you looked at her you could see her lips draw tight, a frown cross her forehead, and her head shake. Pretty soon we heard a racket on the road, so we went out. There was Laddie with the matched team of carriage horses and a plow. Now, in dreadfully busy times, father let Ned and Jo work a little, but not very much. They were not plow horses; they were roadsters. They liked to prance, and bow their necks and dance to the carriage. It shamed them to be hitched to a plow. They drooped their heads and slunk along like dogs caught sucking eggs. But they were a sight on the landscape. They were lean and slender and yet round too, matched dapple gray on flank and side, with long snow-white manes and tails. No wonder mother didn't want them to work. Laddie had reached through the garden fence and hooked a bunch of red tulips and yellow daffodils. The red was at Jo's ear, and the yellow at Ned's, and they did look fine. So did he! Big, strong, clean, a red flower in his floppy straw hat band; and after he drove through the gate, he began a shrill, fifelike whistle you could have heard a half mile:

See the merry farmer boy, tramp the meadows through,
Swing his hoe in careless joy, while dashing off the dew.
Bobolink in maple high, trills a note of glee,
Farmer boy a gay reply now whistles cheerily.

The chorus was all whistle, and it was written for folks who could. It went up until it almost split the echoes, and Laddie could easily sail a measure above the notes. He did it too. As for me, I kept from sight. For a week Laddie whistled and plowed. He wore that tune threadbare, and got an almost continuous pucker on his lips. Leon said if he didn't stop whistling, and sing more, the girls would think he was doing a prunes and prisms stunt. So after that he sang the words, and whistled the chorus. But he made no excuse to go, and he didn't go, to Pryors'. When Sunday came, he went to Westchester to see Elizabeth, and stayed until Monday morning. Not once that week did the Princess ride past our house, or her father either. By noon Monday Laddie was back in the field, and I had all I could bear. He was neither whistling nor singing so much now, because he was away at the south end, where he couldn't be seen or heard at Pryors'. He almost scoured the skin from him, and he wore his gloves more carefully than usual. If he soiled his clothing in the least, and it looked as if he would make more than his share of work, he washed the extra pieces at night.

Tuesday morning I hurried with all my might, and then I ran to the field where he was. I climbed on the fence, sat there until he came up, and then I gave him some cookies. He stopped the horses, climbed beside me and ate them. Then he put his arms around me and hugged me tight.

"Laddie, do you know I did it?" I wailed.

"Did you now?" said Laddie. "No, I didn't know for sure, but I had suspicions. You always have had such a fondness for that particular piece of tinware."

"But Laddie, it means so much!"

"Doesn't it?" said Laddie. "A few days ago no one could have convinced me that it meant anything at all to me, or ever could. Just look at me now!"

"Don't joke, Laddie! Something must be done."

"Well, ain't I doing it?" asked Laddie. "Look at all these acres and acres of Jim-dandy plowing!"

"Don't!" I begged. "Why don't you go over there?"

"No use, Chicken," said Laddie. "You see her exact stipulation was that I must *change my occupation* before I came again."

"What does she want you to do?"

"Law, I think. Unfortunately, I showed her a letter from Jerry asking me to enter his office this fall."

"Hadn't you better do it, Laddie?"

"How would you like to be shut in little stuffy rooms, and set to droning over books and papers every hour of the day, all your life, and to spend the best of your brain and bodily strength straightening out other men's quarrels?"

"Oh Laddie, you just couldn't!" I cried.

"Precisely!" said Laddie. "I just couldn't, and I just won't!"

"What can you do?"

"I might compromise on stock," he said. "I could follow the same occupation as her father, and with better success. Neither he nor his men get the best results from horses. They don't understand them; especially the breeds they are attempting to handle. Most Arab horsemen are tent dwellers. They travel from one oasis to another with their stock. At night their herds are gathered around them as children. As children they love them, pet them, feed them. Each is named for a divinity, a planet or a famous ruler, and the understanding between master and beast is perfect. Honestly, Little Sister, I think you have got to believe in the God of Israel, in order to say the right word to an Arabian horse; and I know you must believe in the God of love. A beast of that breed, jerked, kicked, and scolded is a fine horse ruined. If I owned half the stock Mr. Pryor has over there, I could put it in such shape for market that I could get twice from it what his men will."

"Are Thomas and James rough with the horses?"

"'Like master, like man,'" quoted Laddie. "They are! They are foolish with the Kentucky strain, and fools with the Arab; and yet, that combination beats the world. But I must get on with the P.C. job."

He slid from the fence, took a drink from his water jug, and pulled a handful of grass for each horse. As he stood feeding them, I almost fell from the top rail.

"Laddie!" I whispered. "Look! Mr. Pryor is half-way across the field on Ranger."

"So?" said Laddie. "Now I wonder —"

"Shall I go?"

"No indeed!" said Laddie. "Stay right where you are. It can't be anything of much importance."

At first it didn't seem to be. They talked about the weather, the soil, the team. Laddie scooped a handful of black earth, and holding it out, told Mr. Pryor all about how good it was, and why, and he seemed interested. Then they talked about everything; until if he had been Jacob Hood, he would have gone away. But just at the time when I expected him to start, he looked at Laddie straight and hard.

"I missed you Sabbath evening," he said.

Then I looked at him. He had changed, some way. He seemed more human, more like our folks, less cold and stern.

"I sincerely hope it was unanimous," said Laddie.

Mr. Pryor had to laugh.

"It was a majority, at any rate."

Laddie stared dazed. You see that was kind of a joke. An easy one, because I caught it; but we were not accustomed to expecting a jest from Mr. Pryor. Not one of us dreamed there was a joke between his hat crown and his boot soles. Then Laddie laughed; but he sobered quickly.

"I'm mighty sorry if Mrs. Pryor missed me," he said. "I thought of her. I have grown to be her devoted slave, and I hoped she liked me."

"You put it mildly," said Mr. Pryor. "Since you didn't come when she expected you, we've had the worst time with her that we have had since we reached this da—ah—er—um—this country."

"Could you make any suggestion?" asked Laddie.

"I could! I would suggest that you act like the sensible fellow I know you to be, and come as usual, at your accustomed times."

"But I'm forbidden, man!" cried Laddie.

Ugh! Such awful things as Mr. Pryor said.

"Forbidden!" he cried. "Is a man's roof his own, or is it not? While I live, I propose to be the head of my family. I invite you! I ask you! Mrs. Pryor and I want you! What more is necessary?"

"*Two* things," said Laddie, just as serenely. "That Miss Pryor wants me, and that I want to come."

"D'ye mean to tell me that you *don't* want to come, eh? After the fight you put up to force your way in!"

Laddie studied the sky, a whimsy smile on his lips.

"Now wasn't that a good fight?" he inquired. "I'm mighty proud of it! But not now, or ever, do I wish to enter your house again, if Miss Pryor doesn't want, and welcome me."

Then he went over, took Mr. Pryor's horse by the head, and began working with its bridle. It didn't set right some way, and Mr. Pryor had jerked, spurred, and mauled, until there was a big space tramped to mortar. Laddie slid his fingers beneath the leather, eased it a little, and ran his hands over the fretful creature's head. It just stopped, stood still, pushed its nose under his arm, and pressed against his side. Mr. Pryor arose in one stirrup, swung around and alighted. He looped an arm through the bridle rein, and with both hands gripped his whipstock.

"How the devil do you do it?" he asked, as if he were provoked.

"First, the bridle was uncomfortable; next, you surely know, Mr. Pryor, that a man can transfer his mental state to his mount."

Laddie pointed to the churned up earth.

"*That* represents your mental state; *this*"—he slid his hand down the neck of the horse—"portrays mine."

Mr. Pryor's face reddened, but Laddie was laughing so heartily he joined in sort of sickly-like.

"Oh I doubt if you are so damnably calm!" he cried.

"I'm *calm* enough, so far as that goes," said Laddie. "I'm not denying that I've got about all the heartache I can conveniently carry."

"Do you mind telling me how far this affair has gone?"

"Wouldn't a right-minded man give the woman in the case the first chance to answer that question? I greatly prefer that you ask Miss Pryor."

If ever I felt sorry for any one, I did then for Mr. Pryor. He stood there gripping the whip with both hands, and he looked exactly as if the May wind might break him into a thousand tiny pieces, and every one of them would be glass.

"Um—er—" he said at last. "You're right, of course, but unfortunately, Pamela and her mother did not agree with my motives, or my course in coming to this country; and while there is no outward demonstration—er—um—other than Mrs. Pryor's seclusion; yet, er—um!—I am forced to the belief that I'm *not* in their confidence."

"I see!" said Laddie. "And of course you love your daughter as any man would love so beautiful a child, and when she is all he has —" I thought the break was coming right there, but Mr. Pryor clenched his whip and put it off; still, any one watching with half an eye could see that it was only put off, and not for long at that,— "It has been my idea, Mr. Pryor, that the proper course for me was to see if I could earn any standing with your daughter. If I could, and she gave me permission, then I intended coming to you the instant I knew how she felt. But in such a case as this, I don't think I shall find the slightest hesitation in telling you anything you want to know, that I am able."

"You don't know how you stand with her?"

Laddie took off his hat and ran his fingers through his hair. His feet were planted widely apart, and his face was sober enough for any funeral now. At last he spoke.

"I've been trying to figure that out," he said slowly. "I believe the situation is as open to you as it is to me. She was a desperately lonely, homesick girl, when she caught my eye and heart; and I placed myself on her horizon. In her case the women were slow in offering friendship, because, on account of Mrs. Pryor's seclusion, none was felt to be wanted; then Miss Pryor was different in dress and manner. I found a way to let her see that I wanted to be friends, and she accepted my friendship, and at the same time allowed it go only so far. On a few rare occasions, I've met her alone, and we've talked out various phases of life together; but most of our intercourse has taken place in your home, and in your presence. You probably have seen her meet and entertain her friends frequently. I should think you would be more nearly able to gauge my standing with her than I am."

"You haven't told her that you love her?"

"Haven't I though?" cried Laddie. "Man alive! What do you think I'm made of? Putty? Told her? I've told her a thousand times. I've said it, and sung it, and whistled it, and looked it, and lived it. I've written it, and ridden it, and this week I've plowed it! Your daughter knows as she knows nothing else, in all this world, that she has only to give me one glance, one word, one gesture of invitation, to find me before her, six feet of the worst demoralized beefsteak a woman ever undertook to handle. Told her? Ye Gods! I should say I've told her!"

If any of the Pryors had been outdoors they certainly could have heard Mr. Pryor. How he laughed! He shook until he tottered. Laddie took his arm and led him to the fence. He lifted a broad top rail, pushed it between two others across a corner and made a nice comfortable seat for him. After a while Mr. Pryor wiped his eyes. Laddie stood watching him with a slow grin on his face.

"And she hasn't given the signal you are waiting for?" he asked at last.

Laddie slowly shook his head.

"Nary the ghost of a signal!" he said. "Now we come to Sunday before last. I only intimated, vaguely, that a hint of where I stood would be a comfort—and played Jonah. The whale swallowed me at a gulp, and for all my inches, never batted an eye. You see, a few days before I showed her a letter from my brother Jerry, because I thought it might interest her. There was something in it to which I had paid little or no attention, about my going to the city and beginning work in his law office; to cap that, evidently you had mentioned before her, our prize piece of family tinware. There was a culmination like a thunder clap in a January sky. She said everything that was on her mind about a man of my size and ability doing the work I am, and then she said I must change my occupation before I came again."

"And for answer you've split the echoes with some shrill, abominable air, and plowed, before her very eyes, for a week!"

Then Laddie laughed.

"Do you know?" he said; "that's a good one on me! It never occurred to me that she would not be familiar with that air, and understand its application. Do you mean to crush me further by telling me that all my perfectly lovely vocalizing and whistling was lost?"

"It was a dem irritating, challenging sort of thing," said Mr. Pryor. "I listened to it by the hour, myself, trying to make out exactly what it did mean. It seemed to combine defiance with pleading, and through and over all ran a note of glee that was really quite charming."

"You have quoted a part of it, literally," said Laddie. "'A note of glee'—the cry of a glad heart, at peace with all the world, busy with congenial work."

"I shouldn't have thought you'd have been so particularly joyful."

"Oh, the joy was in the music," said Laddie. "That was a whistle to keep up my courage. The joy was in the song, not in me! Last week was black enough for me to satisfy the most exacting pessimist."

"I wish you might have seen the figure you cut! That fine team, flower bedecked, and the continuous concert!"

"But I did!" cried Laddie. "We have mirrors. That song can't be beaten. I know this team is all right, and I'm not dwarfed or disfigured. That was the pageant of summer passing in review. It represented the tilling of the soil; the sowing of seed, garnering to come later. You buy corn and wheat, don't you? They are vastly necessary. Much more so than the settling of quarrels that never should have taken place. Do you think your daughter found the spectacle at all moving?"

"Damn you, Sir, what I should do, is to lay this whip across your shoulders!" cried Mr. Pryor.

But if you will believe it, he was laughing again.

"I prefer that you don't," said Laddie, "or on Ranger either. See how he likes being gentled."

Then he straightened and drew a deep breath.

"Mr. Pryor," he said, "as man to man, I have got this to say to you—and you may use your own discretion about repeating it to your daughter: I can offer her six feet of as sound manhood as you can find on God's footstool. I never in my whole life have had enough impure blood in my body to make even one tiny eruption on my skin. I never have been ill a day in my life. I never have touched a woman save as I lifted and cared for my mother, and hers, or my sisters. As to my family and education she can judge for herself. I can offer her the first and only love of my heart. She objects to farming, because she says it is dirty, offensive work. There are parts of it that are dirty. Thank God, it only soils the body, and that can be washed. To delve and to dive into, and to study and to brood over the bigger half of the law business of any city is to steep your brain in, and smirch your soul with, such dirt as I would die before I'd make an occupation of touching. Will you kindly tell her that word for word, and that I asked you to?"

Mr. Pryor was standing before I saw him rise. He said those awful words again, but between them he cried: "You're right! It's the truth! It's the eternal truth!"

"It *is* the truth," said Laddie. "I've only to visit the offices, and examine the business of those of my family living by law, to *know* that it's the truth. Of course there's another side! There are times when there are great opportunities to do good; I recognize that. To some these may seem to overbalance that to which I object. If they do, all right. I am merely deciding for myself. Once and for all, for me it is land. It is born in me to love it, to handle it easily, to get the best results from stock. I am going to take the Merriweather place adjoining ours on the west, and yours on the south. I intend to lease it for ten years, with purchase privilege at the end, so that if I make of it what I plan, my work will not be lost to me. I had thought to fix up the place and begin farming. If Miss Pryor has any use whatever for me, and prefers stock, that is all .ight with me. I'll go into the same business she finds suitable for you. I can start in a small way and develop. I can afford a maid for her from the beginning, but I couldn't clothe her as she has been accustomed to being dressed, for some time. I would do my best, however. I know what store my mother sets by being well gowned. And as a husband, I can offer your daughter as loving consideration as woman ever received at the hands of man. Provided by some miracle I could win her consent, would you even consider me, and such an arrangement?"

"Frankly sir," said Mr. Pryor, "I have reached the place where I would be ———" (whenever you come to a long black line like that, it means that he just roared a lot of words father never said, and never will) "glad to! To tell the truth, the thing you choose to jestingly refer to as 'tinware'—I hope later to convince of the indelicacy of such allusion—would place you in England on a social level above any we ever occupied, or could hope to. Your education equals ours. You are a physical specimen to be reckoned with, and I believe what you say of yourself. There's something so clean and manly about you, it amounts to confirmation. A woman should set her own valuation on that; and the height of it should correspond with her knowledge of the world."

"Thank you!" said Laddie. "You are more than kind! more than generous!"

"As to the arrangements you could make for Pamela," said Mr. Pryor, "she's all we have. Everything goes to her, ultimately. She has her stipulated allowance now; whether in my house or yours, it would go with her. Surely you wouldn't be so callous as to object to our giving her anything that would please us!"

"Why should I?" asked Laddie. "That's only natural on your part. Your child is your child; no matter where or what it is, you expect to exercise a certain amount of loving care over it. My father and mother constantly send things to their children absent from home, and they take much pleasure in doing it. That is between you and your daughter, of course. I shouldn't think of interfering. But in the meantime, unless Miss Pryor has been converted to the beauties of plowing through my continuous performance of over a week, I stand now exactly where I did before, so far as she is concerned. If you and Mrs. Pryor have no objection to me, if you feel that you could think of me, or find for me any least part of a son's place in your hearts, I believe I should know how to appreciate it, and how to go to work to make myself worthy of it."

Mr. Pryor sat down so suddenly, the rail almost broke. I thought the truth was, that he had heart trouble, himself. He stopped up, choked on things, flopped around, and turned so white. I suppose he thought it was womanish, and a sign of weakness, and so he didn't tell, but I bet anything that he had it—bad!

"I'll try to make the little fool see!" he said.

"Gently, gently! You won't help me any in that mood," said

Laddie. "The chances are that Miss Pryor repeated what she heard from you long ago, and what she knows you think and feel; unless you've changed recently."

"That's the amount of it!" cried Mr. Pryor. "All my life I've had a lot of beastly notions in my head about rank, and class, and here they don't amount to a damn! There's no place for them. Things are different. Your mother, a grand, good woman, opened my eyes to many things recently, and I get her viewpoint—clearly, and I agree with her, and with you, sir!—I agree with you!"

"I am more than glad," said Laddie. "You certainly make a friend at court. Thank you very much!"

"And you will come —?"

"The instant Miss Pryor gives me the slightest sign that I am wanted, and will be welcomed by her, I'll come like a Dakota blizzard! Flos can hump herself on time for once."

"But you won't come until she does?"

"Man alive! I can't!" cried Laddie. "Your daughter said positively exactly what she meant. It was unexpected and it hit me so hard I didn't try to argue. I simply took her at her word, her very explicit word."

"Fool!" cried Mr. Pryor. "The last thing on earth any woman ever wants or expects is for a man to take her at her word."

"What?" cried Laddie.

"She had what she said in her mind of course, but what she wanted was to be argued out of it! She wanted to be convinced!"

"I think not! She was entirely too convincing herself," said Laddie. "It's my guess that she has thought matters over, and that her mind is made up; but I would take it as a mighty big favour if you would put that little piece of special pleading squarely up to her. Will you?"

"Yes," said Mr. Pryor, "I will. I'll keep cool and do my best, but I am so unfortunate in my temper. I could manage slaves better than women. This time I'll be calm, and reason things out with her, or I'll blow out my brains."

"Don't you dare!" laughed Laddie. "You and I are going to get much pleasure, comfort and profit from this world, now that we have come to an understanding."

Mr. Pryor arose and held out his hand. Laddie grasped it tight, and they stood there looking straight at each other, while a lark on the fence post close by cried, "Spring o' ye-ar!" at them, over and over, but they never paid the least attention.

"You see," said Mr. Pryor, "I've been thinking things over deeply, deeply! ever since talking with your mother. I've cut myself off from going back to England, by sacrificing much of my property in hasty departure, if by any possibility I should ever want to return, and there is none, not the slightest! There's no danger of any one crossing the sea, and penetrating to this particular spot so far inland; we won't be molested! And lately—lately, despite the rawness, and the newness, there is something about the land that takes hold, after all. I should dislike leaving now! I found in watching some roots your mother gave me, that I wanted them to grow, that I very much hoped they would develop, and beautify our place with flowers, as yours is. I find myself watching them, watching them daily, and oftener, and there seems to be a sort of home feeling creeping around my heart. I wish Pamela would listen to reason! I wish she would marry you soon! I wish there would be little children. Nothing else on earth would come so close to comforting my wife, and me also. Nothing! Go ahead, lad, plow away! I'll put your special pleading up to the girl."

He clasped Laddie's hand, mounted and rode back to the gate he had entered when he came. Laddie sat on the rail, so I climbed down beside him. He put his arm around me.

"Do I feel any better?" he asked dubiously.

"Of course you do!" I said stoutly. "You feel whole heaps, and stacks, and piles better. You haven't got *him* to fight any more, or Mrs. Pryor. It's now only to convince the Princess about how it's all right to plow."

"Small matter, that!" said Laddie. "And easy! Just as simple and easy!"

"Have you asked the Fairies to help you?"

"Aye, aye, sir," said Laddie. "Also the winds, the flowers, the birds and the bees! I have asked everything on earth to help me except you, Little Sister. I wonder if I have been making a mistake there?"

"Are you mad at me, Laddie?"

"'Cause for why?"

"About the old crest thing!"

"Forget it!" laughed Laddie. "I have. And anyway, in the long run, I must be honest enough to admit that it may have helped. It seems to have had its influence with Mr. Pryor, no doubt it worked the same on Mrs. Pryor, and it may be that it was because she had so much more to bank on than she ever expected, that the Princess felt emboldened to make her demand. It may be, you can't tell! Anyway, it's very evident that it did no real harm. And forget my jesting, Chicken. A man can't always cry because there are tears in his heart. I think quite as much of that crest as you do. In the sum of human events, it is a big thing. No one admires a Crusader more than I. No one likes a good fight better. No Crusader ever put up a stiffer battle than I have in the past week while working in these fields. Every inch of them is battlefield, every furrow a separate conflict. Gaze upon the scene of my Waterloo! When June covers it with green, it will wave over the resting place of my slain heart!"

"Oh Laddie!" I sobbed. "There you go again! How can you?"

"Whoo-pee!" cried Laddie. "That's the question! How can I? Got to, Little Sister! There's no other way. Up you go! We'll strike down the south line, up the east, and stop at the schoolhouse pump, for a real drink. That jug water makes thirst faster than it quenches it."

When we were opposite the schoolhouse, Nancy Dover rode past on the way to her sister's, so she saw what we were doing.

"Come on and pump, Che-oild!" she cried. "I'll carry the water."

She rode to the fence and took the jug. Nancy was Peter's sister, so she was almost related to us. I hurried over and ran to the pump. She rode her horse right up the schoolhouse stile three steps, and back down, twice over. It was a pretty piece of work, and she put on all the flourishes. Maybe she wanted Laddie to see that some folks could ride as well as others. If she did, she showed him. She was beside the fence holding the jug, and Laddie with laughing, upturned face was drinking his fill, when up the Groveville road, around the corner and smash past them went the Princess! Of course she must have seen that ride over the stile; she also saw Nancy, one dimpled laugh, bending down, holding the jug for Laddie to drink from, then she was gone. She *must* have bowed, but if she did it was such a feeble little one, it needed wrapping in a blanket and warming to make it strong enough to stand alone. Laddie sat on the plow when they were both gone, looked at me and groaned. There wasn't any make-believe about it either.

"Did she speak at all, Chicken?" he asked.

"Of course she did!" I said. "There was no reason why she shouldn't! It was going so fast that made it show so little."

"It certainly wasn't anything pronounced," said Laddie.

"No," I was forced to admit, "it wasn't. What are we going to do now?"

"Life-saver, we'll now go to dinner," said Laddie. "That 'we' saves me. Father Pryor had me bolstered up a little. The proud and haughty Princess snatched the bolster in headlong flight; nothing except the partnership implied in 'we' sustains me now. *You'll find a way to help me out, won't you, Little Sister?*"

"Of course I will!" I promised, without ever stopping a minute to think what kind of a job that was going to be.

Did you ever wish with all your might that something would happen, and wait for it, expect it, and long for it, and nothing did, until it grew so bad, it seemed as if you had to go on another minute you couldn't bear it? Now I thought when Mr. Pryor talked to her, maybe she'd send for Laddie that very same night; but send nothing! She didn't even ride on our road any more. Of course her father had made a botch of it! Bet I could have told her Laddie's message straighter than he did. I could think it over, and see exactly how he'd do. He'd talk nicely about one minute, and the first word she said, that he didn't like, he'd be ranting, and using unsuitable words. Just as like as not he told her that he'd lay his whip across her shoulders, like he had Laddie. Any one could see that as long as she was his daughter, she might be slightly handy with whips herself; at least she wouldn't be likely to stand still and tell him to go ahead and beat her.

Sunday Laddie went to Lucy's. He said he was having a family reunion on the installment plan. Of course we laughed, but none of us missed the long look he sent toward Pryors' as he mounted to start in the opposite direction.

"'But Enoch yearned to see her face again'"—Leon started in on that dreadful poem, and Laddie raised his whip and rode at him, so he jumped the fence and climbed a tree. When Laddie was gone mother said to Leon: "That was in poor taste. How could you?"

"Why, Laddie didn't really care," said Leon. "He knows I'd do anything to get his girl back for him, or any of us would."

"That's so too!" said mother.

Everything went on. I didn't see how it could, but it did. It even got worse, for another letter came from Shelley that made matters concerning her no brighter, and while none of us talked about Laddie, all of us knew mighty well how we felt; and what was much worse, how he felt. Father and mother had quit worrying about God; especially father. He seemed to think that God and Laddie could be trusted to take care of the Princess, and I don't know exactly what mother thought. No doubt she saw she couldn't help herself, and so she decided it was useless to struggle.

The plowing on the west side was almost finished, and some of the seed was in. Laddie went straight ahead flower-trimmed and whistling until his face must have ached as badly as his heart. In spite of how hard he tried to laugh, and keep going, all of us could see that he fairly had to stick up his head and stretch his neck like the blue goose, to make the bites go down. And you couldn't help seeing the roundness and the colour go from his face, a little more every day. My! but being in love when you couldn't have the one you loved, was the worst of all. I wore myself almost as thin as Laddie, hunting a Fairy to ask if she'd help me to make the Princess let Laddie go on and plow, when he was so crazy about it. I prayed beside my bed every night, until the Lord must have grown so tired He quit listening to me, for I talked right up as impressively as I knew how, and it didn't do the least bit of good. I hadn't tried the one big prayer toward the east yet; but I was just about to the place where I intended to do it soon.

Laddie, the Princess, and the Pie

O whistle, and I'll come to you, my lad.

Candace was baking the very first batch of rhubarb pies for the season and the odour was so tempting I couldn't keep away from the kitchen door. Now Candace was a splendid cook about chicken gizzards—the liver was always mother's—doughnuts and tarts, but I never really did believe she would cut into a fresh rhubarb pie, even for me. As I reached for the generous big piece I thought of Laddie—poor Laddie, plowing away at his Crusader fight, and not a hint of victory. No one in the family liked rhubarb pie better than he did. I knew there was no use to ask for a plate.

"Wait—oh wait!" I cried.

I ran to the woodshed, pulled a shining new shingle from a bale stacked there, and held it for Candace. Then I slipped around the house softly. I didn't want to run any one's errands that morning. I laid the pie on the horseblock and climbed the catalpa carefully, so as not to frighten my robins. They were part father's too, because robins were his favourite birds; he said their song through and after rain was the sweetest music on earth, and mostly he was right; so they were not all my robins, but they were most mine after him; and I owned the tree. I hunted the biggest leaf I could see, and wiped it clean on my apron, although it was early for much dust. It covered the pie nicely, because it was the proper shape, and I held the stem with one hand to keep it in place.

There was no use in carrying food to Laddie unless it looked neat and clean. Once I had taken him cookies and he just couldn't swallow them, and when I was almost crying he admitted that it was because they had been in my pocket. Poor Laddie! Of course he could not eat anything from my apron pocket. I couldn't myself, when I stopped to think of it, and as much as I thought over other things, it was a wonder that hadn't occurred to me before. You see, I probably came as near being a bird as anything alive, without wings and feathers. I had sixty nests located right then, and I could easily raise that to a hundred by the middle of June. The minute my work for mother was done, I gathered seed, dug worms and bugged bushes for the fun of feeding the babies. It was the greatest sport alive to tap the edge of a nest, see the little wobbly heads fly up, and drop food in the wide-open yellow mouths. Of course I had sense enough to watch first and see exactly what their mammies fed them; I didn't go and give a hummingbird wheat, or a warbler fish worms; but the baby robins just loved them and they could down one six inches long. I always divided the big worms when the birds were very young, so I was sure not to choke them. Having so many to feed, I got all loaded up at times, and before I knew it my pocket was full of everything, cabbage and fish worms especially; so of course Laddie couldn't very well eat from it.

If I had made that morning myself I couldn't have done better. It was sunny, spring air, but it was that cool, spicy kind that keeps you stopping every few minutes to see just how full you can suck your lungs without bursting. It seemed to wash right through and through and make you all over. The longer you breathed it the clearer your head became, and the better you felt, until you would be possessed to try again, and see if you really couldn't fly. I tried that last summer, and knocked myself into jelly. You'd think once would have been enough, but there I was going down the road with Laddie's pie, and wanting with all my heart to try again.

Sometimes I raced, but I was a little afraid the pie would shoot from the shingle and it was like pulling eye teeth to go fast that morning. I loved the soft warm dust, that was working up on the road. Spat! Spat! I brought down my bare feet, already scratched and turning brown, and laughed to myself at the velvety feel of it. There were little puddles yet, where May and I had "dipped and faded" last fall, and it was fun to wade them. The roadsides were covered with meadow grass and clover that had slipped through the fence. On slender green blades, in spot after spot, twinkled the delicate bloom of blue-eyed grass. Never in all this world was our Big Creek lovelier. It went slipping, and whispering, and lipping, and lapping over the stones, tugging at the rushes and grasses as it washed their feet; everything beside it was in masses of bloom, a blackbird was gleaming and preening on every stone, as it plumed after its bath. Oh there's no use to try—it was just *Spring* when it couldn't possibly be any better.

But even spring couldn't hold me very long that morning, for you see my heart was almost sick about Laddie; and if he couldn't have the girl he wanted, at least I could do my best to comfort him with the pie. I was going along being very careful the more I thought about how he would like it, so I was not watching the road so far ahead as I usually did. I always kept a lookout for Paddy Ryan, Gypsies, or Whitmore's bull. When I came to an unusually level place, and took a long glance ahead, my heart turned right over and stopped still, and I looked long enough to be sure, and then right out loud some one said, "I'll *do* something!" and as usual, I was the only one there.

For days I'd been in a ferment, like the vinegar barrel when the cider boils, or the yeast jar when it sets too close to the stove. To have Laddie and the Princess separated was dreadful, and knowing him as I did, I knew he never really would get over it. I had tried to help once, and what I had done started things going wrong; no wonder I was slow about deciding what to try next. That I was going to do something, I made up my mind the instant Laddie said he was not mad at me; that I was his partner, and asked me to help; but exactly *what* would do any good, took careful thought. Once, I considered going hunting in their woods, and trying to reach the house with Mr. Pryor. He had asked me to come. I had thought of slipping over, hiding along the fence, and trying to see Mrs. Pryor. Mr. Pryor had said he was not in their confidence, so if she and the Princess had their confidences together, and she wanted Laddie to come, maybe she could tell me what would help him. I thought she would; but after all, it seemed as if the best way, and the most Crusaderish, would be to walk spang up to the Princess and talk it over with her, straight from the reel.

Here was my chance coming right at me. She was far up the road, riding Maud like racing. I began to breathe after a while, like you always do, no matter how you are worked up, and with my brain whirling, I went slowly toward her. How would I manage to stop her? Oh what could I say that would help Laddie? I was shaking, and that's the truth; but through and over it all, I was watching her too. I only wish you might have seen her that morning. Of course the morning was part of it. A morning like that would make a fence post better looking. Half a mile away you could see she was tipsy with spring as I was, or the song sparrows, or the crazy babbling old bobolinks on the stakes and riders. She made such a bright splash against the pink fence row, with her dark hair, flushed cheeks, and red lips, she took my breath. Father said she was the loveliest girl in three counties, and Laddie stretched that to the whole world. As she came closer, smash! through me went the thought that she looked precisely as Shelly had at Christmas time; and Shelley had been that way because she was in love with the Paget man. Now if the Princess was gleaming and flashing like that, for the same reason, there wasn't any one for her to love so far as I knew, except Laddie.

Then smash! came another thought. She *had* to love him! She couldn't help herself. She had all winter, all last summer, and no one but themselves knew how long before that, and where was there any other man like Laddie? Of course she loved him! Who so deserving of love? Who else had his dancing eyes of deep tender blue, cheeks so pink, teeth so white, such waving chestnut hair, and his height and breadth? There was no other man who could ride, swim, leap, and wrestle as he could. None who could sing the notes, do the queer sums with letters having little figures at the corners in the college books, read Latin as fast as English, and even the Greek Bible. Of course she loved him! Every one did! Others might plod and meander, Laddie walked the tired, old road that went out of sight over the hill, with as prideful a step as any king; his laugh was as merry as the song of the gladdest thrush, while his touch was so gentle that when mother was in dreadful pain I sometimes thought she would a little rather have him hold her than father, even.

Now, he was in this fearful trouble, the colour was going from his face, his laugh was a little strained, and the heartache almost more than he could endure—and there she came! I stepped squarely in the middle of the road so she would have to stop or ride over me, and when she was close, I stood quite still. I was watching with my eyes, heart, and brain, and I couldn't see that she was provoked, as she drew rein and cried: "Good morning, Little Queer Person!"

I had supposed she would say Little Sister, she had for ages, just like Laddie, but she must have thought it was queer for me to stop her that way, so she changed. I was in for it. I had her now, so I smiled the very sweetest smile that I could think up in such a hurry, and said, "Good morning," the very politest I ever did in all my life. Then I didn't know what to do next, but she helped me out.

"What have you there?" she asked.

"It's a piece of the very first rhubarb pie for this spring, and I'm carrying it to Laddie," I said, as I lifted the catalpa leaf and let her peep, just to show her how pie looked when it was right. I bet she never saw a nicer piece.

The Princess slid her hand down Maud's neck to quiet her prancing, and leaned in the saddle, her face full of interest. I couldn't see a trace of anything to discourage me; her being on our road again looked favourable. She seemed to think quite as much of that pie as I did. She was the finest little thoroughbred. She understood so well, I was sorry I couldn't give it to her. It made her mouth water all right, for she drew a deep breath that sort of quivered; but it was no use, she didn't get that pie. It was on the way to Laddie.

"I think it looks delicious," she said. "Are you carrying it for Candace?"

"No! She gave it to me. It's my very own."

"And you're doing without it yourself to carry it to Laddie, I'll be bound!" cried the Princess.

"I'd much rather," I said.

"Do you love Laddie so dearly?" she asked.

My heart was full of him right then; I forgot all about when I had the fever, and as I never had been taught to lie, I told her what I thought was the truth, and I guess it *was:* "Best of any one in all this world!"

The Princess looked across the field, where she must have seen him finishing the plowing, and thought that over, and I waited, sure in my mind, for some reason, that she would not go for a little while longer.

"I have been wanting to see you," she said at last. "In fact I think I came this way hoping I'd meet you. Do you know the words to a tune that goes like this?"

Then she began to whistle "The Merry Farmer Boy." I wish you might have heard the flourishes she put to it.

"Of course I do," I answered. "All of us were brought up on it."

"Well, I have some slight curiosity to learn what they are," she said. "Would you kindly repeat them for me?"

"Yes," I said. "This is the first verse:

"See the merry farmer boy tramp the meadows through,
Swing his hoe in careless joy while dashing off the dew.
Bobolink in maple high —

"Of course you can see for yourself that they're not. There isn't a single one of them higher than a fence post. The person who wrote the piece had to put it that way so high would rhyme with reply, which is coming in the next line."

"I see!" said the Princess.

"Bobolink in maple high, trills a note of glee.
Farmer boy a gay reply now whistles cheerily.

"Then you whistle the chorus like you did it."

"You do indeed!" said the Princess. "Proceed!"

"Then the farmer boy at noon, rests beneath the shade,
Listening to the ceaseless tune that's thrilling through the glade.

Long and loud the harvest fly winds his bugle round,
Long, and loud, and shrill, and high, he whistles back the sound."

"He does! He does indeed! I haven't a doubt about that!" cried the Princess. "'Long, and loud, and shrill, and high,' he whistles over and over the sound, until it becomes maddening. Is that all of that melodious, entrancing production?"

"No, evening comes yet. The last verse goes this way:

"When the busy day's employ, ends at dewy eve,
Then the happy farmer boy, doth haste his work to leave,
Trudging down the quiet lane, climbing o'er the hill,
Whistling back the changeless wail, of plaintive whip-
  poor-will,—

and then you do the chorus again, and if you know how well enough you whistle in, 'whip-poor-will,' 'til the birds will answer you. Laddie often makes them."

"My life!" cried the Princess. "Was that he doing those bird cries? Why, I hunted, and hunted, and so did father. We'd never seen a whip-poor-will. Just fancy us!"

"If you'd only looked at Laddie," I said.

"My patience!" cried the Princess. "Looked at him! There was no place to look without seeing him. And that ear-splitting thing will ring in my head forever, I know."

"Did he whistle it too high to suit you, Princess?"

"He was perfectly welcome to whistle as he chose," she said, "and also to plow with the carriage horses, and to bedeck them and himself with the modest, shrinking red tulip and yellow daffodil."

Now any one knows that tulips and daffodils are *not* modest and shrinking. If any flowers just blaze and scream colour clear across a garden, they do. She was provoked, you could see that.

"Well, he only did it to please you," I said. "He didn't care anything about it. He never plowed that way before. But you said he mustn't plow at all, and he just had to plow, there was no escaping that, so he made it as fine and happy as possible to show you how nicely it could be done."

"Greatly obliged, I'm sure!" cried the Princess. "He showed me! He certainly did! And so he feels that there's 'no escaping' plowing, does he?"

Then I knew where I was. I'd have given every cent of mine in father's chest till, if mother had been in my place. Once, for a second, I thought I'd ask the Princess to go with me to the house, and let mother tell her how it was; but if she wouldn't go, and rode away, I felt I couldn't endure it, and anyway, she had said she was looking for me; so I gripped the shingle, dug in my toes and went at her just as nearly like mother talked to her father as I could remember, and I'd been put through memory tests, and descriptive tests, nearly every night of my life, so I had most of it as straight as a string.

"Well, you see, he *can't* escape it," I said. "He'd do anything in all this world for you that he possibly could; but there are some things no man *can* do."

"I didn't suppose there was anything you thought Laddie couldn't do," she said.

"A little time back, I didn't," I answered. "But since he took the carriage horses, trimmed up in flowers, and sang and whistled so bravely, day after day, when his heart was full of tears, why I learned that there was something he just *couldn't do; not to save his life, or his love, or even to save you.*"

"And of course you don't mind telling me what that is?" coaxed the Princess in her most wheedling tones.

"Not at all! He told our family, and I heard him tell your father. The thing he can't do, not even to win you, is to be shut up in a little office, in a city, where things roar, and smell, and nothing is like this —"

I pointed out the orchard, hill, and meadow, so she looked where I showed her—looked a long time.

"No, a city wouldn't be like this," she said slowly.

"And that isn't even the beginning," I said. "Maybe he could bear that, men have been put in prison and lived through years and years of it, perhaps Laddie could too; I doubt it! but anyway the worst of it is that he just couldn't, not even to save you, spend all the rest of his life trying to settle other people's old fusses. He despises a fuss. Not one of us ever in our lives have been able to make him quarrel, even one word. He simply won't. And if he possibly could be made to by any one on earth, Leon would have done it long ago, for he can start a fuss with the side of a barn. I don't like to quarrel myself, but he can make me so mad, I want to kill him and die too. But he can't make Laddie fuss, and nobody can. He *never* would at school, or anywhere. Once in a while if a man gets so overbearing that Laddie simply can't stand it, he says: 'Now, you'll take your medicine!' Then he pulls off his coat, and carefully, choosing the right spots, he just pounds the breath out of that man, but he never stops smiling, and when he helps him up he always says: 'Sorry! hope you'll excuse me, but you *would* have it.' That's what he said about you, that you had to take your medicine —"

I made a mistake there. That made her too angry for any use.

"Oh," she cried, "I do? I'll jolly well show the gentleman!"

"Oh, you needn't take the trouble," I cried. "He's showing you!"

She just blazed like she'd break into flame. Any one could fuss with her all right; but that was the last thing on earth I wanted to do.

"You see he already knows about you," I explained as fast as I could talk, for I was getting into an awful mess. "You see he knows that you want him to be a lawyer, and that he must quit plowing before he can be more than friends with you. That's what he's plowing for! If it wasn't for that, probably he wouldn't be plowing at all. He asked father to let him, and he borrowed mother's horses, and he hooked the flowers through the fence. Every night when he comes home, he kneels beside mother and asks her if he is 'repulsive,' and she takes him in her arms and the tears roll down her cheeks and she says: 'Father has farmed all his life, and you know how repulsive he is.'"

I ventured an upward peep. I was doing better. Her temper seemed to be cooling, but her face was a jumble. I couldn't find any one thing on it that would help me, so I just stumbled ahead guessing at what to say.

"He didn't *want* to do it. He perfectly *hated* it. Those fields were his Waterloo. Every furrow was a *fight,* but he was *forced* to show you."

"Exactly *what* was he trying to show me?"

"I can think of three things he told me," I answered. "That plowing could be so managed as not to disfigure the landscape —"

"The dunce!" she said.

"That he could plow or do dirtier work, and not be repulsive —"

"The idiot!" she said.

"That if he came over there, and plowed right under your nose, when you'd told him he mustn't, or he couldn't be more than friends; and when you knew that he'd much rather die and be laid beside the little sisters up there in the cemetery than to *not* be more than friends, why, you'd see, if he did *that,* he couldn't help it, that he just *must.* That it was not his fault. That he was *forced* —"

"The soldier!" she said.

"Oh Princess, he didn't want to!" I cried. "He tells me secrets he doesn't any one else, unless you. He told me how it hurt, how he hated it; but he just had to do it."

"Do you know *why?*"

"Of course! It's the way he's *made!* Father is like that! He has chances to live in cities, make big business deals, and go to the legislature at Indianapolis; I've seen his letters from his friend Oliver P. Morton, our Governor, you know; they're in his chest till now; but father can't do it, because he is made so he stays at home and works for us, and this farm, and township, and county where he belongs. He says if all men will do that the millennium will come to-morrow. I 'spose you know what the millennium is?"

"I do!" said the Princess. "But I don't know what your father and his friend Oliver P. Morton have to do with Laddie."

"Why, everything on earth! Laddie is father's son, you see, and he is made like father. None of our other boys is. Not one of them loves land. Leon is going away as quick as ever he finishes college; but the more you educate Laddie, the better he likes to make things grow, the more he loves to make the world beautiful, to be kind to every one, to gentle animals—why, the biggest fight he ever had, the man he whipped 'til he most couldn't bring him back again, was one who kicked his horse in the stomach. Gee, I thought he'd killed him! Laddie did too for a while, but he only said the man deserved it."

"And so he did!" cried the Princess angrily. "How beastly!"

"That's one reason Laddie sticks so close to land. He says he doesn't meet nearly so many two-legged beasts in the country. Almost every time he goes to town, he either gets into a fight or he sees something that makes him fighting mad. Princess, you think this beautiful, don't you?"

I just pointed anywhere. All the world was in it that morning. You couldn't look right or left and not see lovely places, hear music, and smell flowers.

"Yes! It is altogether wonderful!" she said.

"Would you like to live among this all your life, and have your plans made to fix you a place even nicer, and then be forced to leave it and go to a little room in the city, and make all the money you earned off of how much other men fight over business, and land and such perfectly awful things, that they always have to be whispered when Jerry tells about them? Would you?"

"You little dunce!" she cried.

"I know I'm a fool. I know I'm not telling you a single thing I should! Maybe I'm hurting Laddie far more than I'm helping him, and if I am, I wish I would die before I see him; but oh! Princess, I'm trying with all my might to make you understand how he feels. He *wants* to do every least thing you'd like him to. He will, almost anything else in the world, he would this—he would in a minute, but he just *can't*. All of us know he can't! If you'd lived with him since he was little and always had known him, you wouldn't ask him to; you wouldn't want him to! You don't know what you're doing! Mother says you don't! You'll kill him if you send him to the city to live, you just will! You are doing it now! He's getting thinner and whiter every day. Don't! Oh please don't do it!"

The Princess was looking at the world. She was gazing at it so dazed-like she seemed to be surprised at what she saw. She acted as if she'd never really seen it before. She reminded me of Saul after the scales had fallen from his eyes, that time when he tried to kick against the pricks, and found it such hard work. She looked and she looked. She even turned her horse a full circle to see all of it, and she went around slowly. I stepped from one foot to the other and sweat; but I kept quiet and let her look. At last when she came around, she glanced down at me, and she was all melted, and lovely as any one you ever saw, exactly like Shelly at

Christmas, and she said: "I don't think I ever saw the world before. I don't know that I'm so crazy about a city myself, and I perfectly hate lawyers. Come to think of it, a lawyer helped work ruin in our family, and I never have believed, I never will believe —"

She stopped talking and began looking again. I gave her all the time she needed. I was just straining to be wise, for mother says it takes the very wisest person there is to know when to talk, and when to keep still. As I figured it, now was the time not to say another word until she made up her mind about what I had told her already. If Pryors didn't know what we thought of them by that time, it wasn't mother's fault or mine. As she studied things over she kept on looking. What she saw seemed to be doing her a world of good. Her face showed it every second plainer and plainer. Pretty soon it began to look like she was going to come through as Amos Hurd did when he was redeemed. Then, before my very eyes, it happened! I don't know how I ever held on to the pie or kept from shouting, "Praise the Lord!" as father does at the Meeting House when he is happiest. Then she leaned toward me all wavery, and shining eyed, and bloomful, and said: "Did you ever hurt Laddie's feelings, and make him angry and sad?"

"I'm sure I never did," I answered.

"But suppose you had! What would you do?"

"Do? Why, I'd go to him on the run, and I'd tell him I never intended to hurt his feelings, and how sorry I was, and I'd give him the very best kiss I could."

The Princess stroked Maud's neck a long time and thought while she studied our farm, theirs beyond it, and at the last, the far field where Laddie was plowing. She thought and thought, and afraid to cheep, I stood gripping the shingle and waited. Finally she said: "The last time Laddie was at our house, I said to him those things he repeated to you. He went away at once, hurt and disappointed. Now, if you like, along with your precious pie, you may carry him this message from me. You may tell him that I said I am sorry!"

I could have cried "Glory!" and danced and shouted in the road, but I didn't. It was no time to lose my head. That was all so fine and splendid, as far as it went, but it didn't quite cover the case. I never could have done it for myself; but for Laddie I would venture anything, so I looked her in the eyes, straight as a dart, and said: "He'd want the kiss too, Princess!"

You could see her stiffen in the saddle and her fingers grip the reins, but I kept on staring right into her eyes.

"I could come up, you know," I offered.

A dull red flamed in her cheeks and her lips closed tight. One second she sat very still, then a dancing light leaped sparkling into her eyes; a flock of dimples chased each other around her lips like swallows circling their homing place at twilight.

"What about that wonderful pie?" she asked me.

I ran to the nearest fence corner, and laid the shingle on the gnarled roots of a Johnny Appleseed apple tree. Then I set one foot on the arch of the Princess' instep and held up my hands. One second I thought she would not lift me, the next I was on her level and her lips met mine in a touch like velvet woven from threads of flame. Then with a turn of her stout little wrist, she dropped me, and a streak went up our road. Nothing so amazing and so important ever had happened to me. It was an occasion that demanded something unusual. To cry, "Praise the Lord!" was only to repeat an hourly phrase at our house; this demanded something out of the ordinary, so I said just exactly as father did the day the brown mare balked with the last load of seed clover, when a big storm was breaking—"Jupiter Ammon!"

When I had calmed down so I could, I climbed the fence, and reached through a crack for the pie. As I followed the cool, damp furrow, and Laddie's whistle, clear as the lark's above the wheat, thrilled me, I was almost insane with joy. Just joy! Pure joy! Oh what a good world it was!—most of the time! Most of the time! Of course, there *were* Paget men in it. But anyway, *this* couldn't be beaten. I had a message for Laddie from the Princess that would send him to the seventh heaven, wherever that was; no one at our house spent any time thinking farther than the first one. I had her kiss, that I didn't know what would do to him, and I also had a big piece of juicy rhubarb pie not yet entirely cold. If that didn't wipe out the trouble I had made showing the old crest thing, nothing ever could. I knew even then, that men were pretty hard to satisfy, but I was quite certain that Laddie would be satisfied that morning. As I hurried along I wondered whether it would be better to give him my gift first, or the Princess'. I decided that joy would keep, while the pie was cold enough, with all the time I had stopped; and if I told him about her first, maybe he wouldn't touch it at all, and it wasn't so easy as it looked to carry it to him and never even once stick in my finger for the tiniest lick—joy would keep; but I was going to feed him; so with shining face, I offered the pie and stood back to see just how happy I could get.

"Mother send it?" asked Laddie.

People were curious that morning, as if I had a habit of stealing pie. I only took pieces of cut ones from the cellar when mother didn't care. So I explained again that Candace gave it to me, and I was free to bring it.

"Oh I see!" said Laddie.

After nearly two weeks of work, the grays had sobered down enough to stand without tying; so he wound the lines around the plow handle, sat on the beam, and laid aside his hat, having a fresh flower in the band. Once he started a thing, he just simply wouldn't give up. He unbuttoned his neckband until I could see his throat where it was white like a woman's, took out his knife and ate that pie. Of course we knew better than to use a knife at the table, but there was no other way in the field. He ate that pie, slowly and deliberately, and between bites he talked. I watched him with a wide grin, wondering what in this world he *would* say, in a minute. I don't think I ever had quite such a good time in all my life before, and I never expect to again. He was saying: "Talk about nectar and ambrosia! Talk about the feasts of Lucullus! Talk about food for the Gods!"

I put on his hat, sat on the ground in front of him, and was the happiest girl in the world, of that I am quite sure. When the last morsel was finished, Laddie looked at me steadily.

"I wonder," he said, "I wonder if there's another man in the world who is blest with quite such a loving, unselfish little sister as mine?" Then he answered himself: "No! By all the Gods, and half-Gods, I swear it—No!"

It was grand as a Fourth of July oration or the most exciting part when the Bishop dedicated our church. I couldn't hold in another second, I could hear my heart beat.

"Oh, Laddie!" I shouted, jumping up, "that pie is only the

beginning of the good things I have brought you. I have a message, and a gift besides, Laddie!"

"A message and a gift?" Laddie repeated. "What! More?"

His eyes were on my apron pocket. I could feel my face burn.

"Oh Laddie," I cried. "I wouldn't do that again. I didn't think! Indeed I didn't! Truly, I have a message and a gift for you, and Laddie—they are from the Princess!"

His eyes raised to mine now, and slowly he turned Sabethany-like.

"From the Princess!" he exclaimed. "A message and a gift for me, Little Sister? You never would let Leon put you up to serve me a trick?"

That hurt. He should have *known* I wouldn't, and besides, "Leon feels just as badly about this as any of us," I said. "Have you forgotten he offered to plow, and let you do the clean, easy work?"

"Forgive me! I'm overanxious," said Laddie, his arms reaching for me. "Go on and tell carefully, and if you truly love me, don't make a mistake!"

Crowding close, my arms around his neck, his crisp curls against my lips, I whispered my story softly, for this was such a fine and splendid secret, that not even the shining blackbirds, and the pert robins in the furrows were going to get to hear a word of it. Before I had finished Laddie was breathing as Flos does when he races her the limit. He sat motionless for a long time, while over his face slowly crept a beauty that surpassed that of Apollo in his Greek book.

"And her gift?"

It was only a breath.

"She helped me up, and she sent you this," I answered.

Then I set my lips on his, and held them there a second, trying my level best to give him her very kiss, but of course I could only try.

"Oh Laddie," I cried. "Her eyes were like when stars shine down in our well! Her cheeks were like mother's damask roses! She smelled like flowers, and when her lips touched mine little stickers went all over me!"

Then Laddie's arms closed around me and I thought sure every bone in my body was going to be broken; when he finished there wasn't a trace of that kiss left for me. Remembering it would be all I'd ever have. It made me see what would have happened to the Princess if she had been there; and it was an awful pity for her to miss it, because he'd sober down a lot before he reached her, but I was sure as shooting that he wouldn't be so crazy as to kiss her hands again. Peter wasn't a patching to him!

That night Laddie rode to Pryors'. When he brought Flos to the gate you could see the shadow of your face on her shining flank; her mane and tail were like ravelled silk, her hoofs bright as polished horn, and her muzzle was clean as a ribbon. I broke one of those rank green sprouts from the snowball bush and brushed away the flies, so she wouldn't fret, stamp, and throw dust on herself. Then Laddie came, fresh from a tubbing, starched linen, dressed in his new riding suit, and wearing top hat and gauntlets. He looked the very handsomest I ever had seen him; and at the same time, he seemed trembling with tenderness, and bursting with power. Goodness sake! I bet the Princess took one good look and "came down" like Davy Crockett's coon. Mother was on his arm and she walked clear to the gate with him.

"Laddie, are you sure enough to go?" I heard her ask him whisper-like.

"Sure as death!" Laddie answered.

Mother looked, and she had to see how it was with him; no doubt she saw more than I did from having been through it herself, so she smiled kind of a half-sad, half-glad smile. Then she turned to her damask rose bush, the one Lucy brought her from the city, and that she was so precious about, that none of us dared touch it, and she searched all over it and carefully selected the most perfect rose. When she borrowed Laddie's knife and cut the stem as long as my arm, I knew exactly how great and solemn the occasion was; for always before about six inches had been her limit. She held it toward him, smiling bravely and beautifully, but the tears were running straight down her cheeks.

"Take it to her," she said. "I think, my son, it is very like."

Laddie took her in his arms and wiped away the tears; he told her everything would come out all right about God, and the mystery, even. Then he picked me clear off the ground, and he tried to see how near he could come to cracking every bone in my body without really doing it, and he kissed me over and over. It hadn't been so easy, but I guess you'll admit that paid. Then he rode away with the damask rose waving over his heart. Mother and I stood beside the hitching rack and looked after him, with our arms tight around each other while we tried to see which one could bawl the hardest.

16

The Homing Pigeon

A millstone and the human heart,
Are ever driven round,
And if they've nothing else to grind,
They must themselves be ground.

It seemed to me that my mother was the person who really could
have been excused for having heart trouble. The more I watched
her, the more I wondered that she didn't. There was her own life,
the one she and father led, where everything went exactly as she
wanted it to; and if there had been only themselves to think of, no
people on earth could have lived happier, unless the pain she
sometimes suffered made them trouble, and I don't think it would,
for neither of them were to blame for that. They couldn't help it.
They just had it to stand, and fight the stiffest they could to cure
it, and mother always said she was better; every single time any
one asked, she was better. I hoped soon it would all be gone. Then
they could have been happy for sure, if some of us hadn't popped
up and kept them in hot water all the time.

I can't tell you about Laddie when he came back from Pryors'.
He tore down the house, then tore it up, and then threw around
the pieces, and none of us cared. Every one was just laughing,
shouting, and every bit as pleased as he was, while I was the

Queen Bee. Laddie said so, himself, and if he didn't know, no one did. Pryors had been lovely to him. When mother asked him how he made it, he answered: "I rode over, picked up the Princess and helped myself. After I finished, I remembered the little unnecessary formality of asking her to marry me; and she said right out loud that she *would*. When I had time for them, I reached Father and Mother Pryor, and maybe it doesn't show, but somewhere on my person I carry their blessing, genially and heartily given, I am proud to state. Now, I'm only needing yours, to make me a king among men."

They gave it quite as willingly, I am sure, although you could see mother scringe when Laddie said "Father and Mother Pryor." I knew why. She adored Laddie, like the Bible says you must adore the Almighty. From a tiny baby Laddie had taken care of her. He used to go back, take her hand, and try to help her over rough places while he still wore dresses. Straight on, he had been like that; always seeing when there was too much work and trying to shield her; always knowing when a pain was coming and fighting to head it off; always remembering the things the others forgot, going to her last at night, and his face against hers on her pillow the first in the morning, to learn how she was before he left the house. If you were the mother of a man like that, how would you like to hear him call some one else mother, and have the word slip from his tongue so slick you could see he didn't even realize that he had used it? The answer would be, if you were honest, that you wouldn't have liked it any more than she did. She knew he had to go. She wanted him to be happy. She was as sure of the man he was going to be as she was sure of the mercy of God. That is the strongest way I know to tell it. She was unshakably sure of the mercy of God, but I wasn't. There were times when it seemed as if He couldn't hear the most powerful prayer you could pray, and when instead of mercy, you seemed to get the last torment that could be piled on. Take right now. Laddie was happy, and all of us were, in a way; and in another we were almost stiff with misery.

I dreaded his leaving us so, I would slip to the hawk oak and cry myself sick, more than once; whether any of the others were that big babies I don't know; but anyway, *they* were not his Little Sister. I was. I always had been. I always would be, for that matter;

but there was going to be a mighty big difference. I had the poor comfort that I'd done the thing myself. Maybe if it hadn't been for stopping the Princess when I took him that pie, they never would have made up, and she might have gone across the sea and stayed there. Maybe she'd go yet, as mysteriously as she had come, and take him along. Sometimes I almost wished I hadn't tried to help him; but of course I didn't really. Then, too, I had sense enough to know that loving each other as they did, they wouldn't live on that close together for years and years, and not find a way to make up for themselves, like they had at the start. I liked Laddie saying I had made his happiness for him; but I wasn't such a fool that I didn't know he could have made it for himself just as well, and no doubt better. So everything was all right with Laddie; and what happened to us, the day he rode away for the last time, when he went to stay—what happened to us, then, was our affair. We had to take it, but every one of us dreaded it, while mother didn't know how to bear it, and neither did I. Once I said to her: "Mother, when Laddie goes we'll just have to make it up to each other the best we can, won't we?"

"Oh my soul, child!" she cried, staring at me so surprised-like. "Why, how unspeakably selfish I have been! No little lost sheep ever ran this farm so desolate as you will be without your brother. Forgive me baby, and come here!"

Gee, but we did cry it out together! The God she believed in has wiped away her tears long ago; this minute I can scarcely see the paper for mine. If you could call anything happiness, that was mixed with feeling like that, why, then, we were happy about Laddie. But from things I heard father and mother say, I knew they could have borne his going away, and felt a trifle better than they did. I was quite sure they had stopped thinking that he was going to lose his soul, but they couldn't help feeling so long as that old mystery hung over Pryors that he *might* get into trouble through it. Father said if it hadn't been for Mr. Pryor's stubborn and perverted notions about God, he would like the man immensely, and love to be friends; and if Laddie married into the family we would have to be as friendly as we could anyway. He said he had such a high opinion of Mr. Pryor's integrity that he didn't believe he'd encourage Laddie to enter his family if it would involve the boy in serious trouble. Mother didn't know. Anyway, the thing was done, and by fall, no doubt, Laddie would leave us.

Just when we were trying to keep a stiff upper lip before him, and whistling as hard as ever he had, to brace our courage, a letter came for mother from the head of the music school Shelley attended, saying she was no longer fit for work, so she was being sent home at once, and they would advise us to consult a specialist immediately. Mother sat and stared at father, and father went to hitch the horses to drive to Groveville.

There's only one other day of my life that stands out as clearly as that. The house was clean as we could make it. I finished feeding early, and had most of the time to myself. I went down to the Big Hill, and followed the top of it to our woods. Then I turned around, and started toward the road, just idling. If I saw a lovely spot I sat down and watched all around me to see if a Fairy really would go slipping past, or lie asleep under a leaf. I peeked and peered softly, going from spot to spot, watching everything. Sometimes I hung over the water, and studied tiny little fish with red, yellow, and blue on them, bright as flowers. The dragonflies would alight right on me, and some wore bright blue markings and some blood red. There was a blue beetle, a beautiful green fly, and how the blue wasps did flip, flirt and glint in the light. So did the blackbirds and the redwings. That embankment was left especially to shade the water, and to feed the birds. Every foot of it was covered with alders, wild cherry, hazelbush, mulberries, everything having a berry or nut. There were several scrub apple trees, many red haws, the wild strawberries spread in big beds in places, and some of them were colouring.

Wild flowers grew everywhere, great beds were blue with calamus, and the birds flocked in companies to drive away the water blacksnakes that often found nests, and liked eggs and bird babies. When I came to the road at last, the sun was around so the big oak on the top of the hill threw its shadow across the bridge, and I lay along one edge and watched the creek bottom, or else I sat up so the water flowed over my feet, and looked at the embankment and the sky. In a way, it was the most peculiar day of my life. I had plenty to think of, but I never thought at all. I only lived. I sat watching the world go past through a sort of golden haze the sun made. When a pair of kingbirds and three crows chased one of my hawks pell-mell across the sky, I looked on and didn't give a cent what happened. When a big blacksnake darted its head through sweet grass and cattails, and caught a frog that had climbed on a mossy stone in the shade to dine on flies, I let it go. Any other time I would have hunted a stick and made the snake let loose. To-day I just sat there and let things happen as they did.

At last I wandered up the road, climbed the back garden fence, and sat on the board at the edge of a flower bed, and to-day, I could tell to the last butterfly about that garden: what was in bloom, how far things had grown, and what happened. Bobby flew under the Bartlett pear tree and crowed for me, but I never called him. I sat there and lived on, and mostly watched the bees tumble over the bluebells. They were almost ready to be cut to put in the buttered tumblers for perfume, like mother made for us. Then I went into the house and looked at Grace Greenwood, but I didn't take her along. Mother came past and gave me a piece of stiff yellow brocaded silk as lovely as I ever had seen, enough for a dress skirt; and a hand-embroidered chemise sleeve that only needed a band and a button to make a petticoat for a Queen doll, but I laid them away and wandered into the orchard.

I dragged my bare feet through the warm grass, and finally sat under the beet red peach tree. If ever I seemed sort of lost and sorry for myself, that was a good place to go; it was so easy to feel abused there because you didn't dare touch those peaches. Fluffy baby chickens were running around, but I didn't care; there was more than a bird for every tree, bluebirds especially; they just loved us and came early and stayed late, and grew so friendly they nested all over the wood house, smoke house, and any place we fixed for them, and in every hollow apple limb. Bobby came again, but I didn't pay any attention to him.

Then I heard the carriage cross the bridge. I knew when it was father, every single time his team touched the first plank. So I ran like an Indian, and shinned up a cedar tree, scratching myself until I bled. Away up I stood on a limb, held to the tree and waited. Father drove to the gate, and mother came out, with May, Candace, and Leon following. When Shelley touched the ground and straightened, any other tree except a spruce having limbs to hold me up, I would have fallen from it. She looked exactly as if she had turned to tombstone with eyes and hair alive. She stopped a second to brush a little kiss across mother's lips, to the others she said without even glancing at them: "Oh do let me lie down a minute! The motion of that train made me sick."

Well, I should say it did! I quit living, and began thinking in a hooray, and so did every one else at our house. Once I had been sick and queened it over them for a while, now all of us strained ourselves trying to wait on Shelley; but she wouldn't have it. She only said she was tired to death, to let her rest, and she turned her face to the wall and lay there. Once she said she never wanted to see a city again so long as she lived. When mother told her about Laddie and the Princess to try to interest her, she never said a word; I doubted if she even listened. Father and mother looked at each other, when they thought no one would see, and their eyes sent big, anxious questions flashing back and forth. I made up my mind I'd keep awake that night and hear what they said, if I had to take pins to bed with me and stick myself.

Once mother said to Shelley that she was going to send for Dr. Fenner, and she answered: "All right, if *you* need him. Don't you dare for me! I'll not see him. All I want is a little peace and rest."

The idea! Not one of us ever had spoken to mother like that before in all our born days. I held my breath to see what she would do, but she didn't seem to have heard it, or to notice how rude it had been. Well, *that* told about as plain as anything what we had on our hands. I wandered around and *now* there was no trouble about thinking things. They came in such a jumble I could get no sense from them; but one big black thought came over, and over, and over, and wouldn't be put away. It just stood, stayed, forced you, and made you look it in the face. If Shelley weren't stopped quickly she was going up on the hill with the little fever and whooping cough sisters. There it was! You could try to think other things, to play, to work, to talk it down in the pulpit, to sing it out in a tree, to slide down the haystack away from it—there it stayed! And every glimpse you had of Shelley made it surer.

There was no trouble about keeping awake that night; I couldn't sleep. I stood at the window and looked down the Big Hill through the soft white moonlight, and thought about it, and then

I thought of mother. I guess *now* you see what kind of things
mothers have to face. All day she had gone around doing her
work, every few minutes suggesting some new thing for one of us
to try, or trying it herself; all day she had talked and laughed, and
when Sarah Hood came she told her she thought Shelley must be
bilious, that she had travelled all night and was sleeping; but she
would be up the first place she went, and then they talked all over
creation and Mrs. Hood went home and never remembered that
she hadn't seen Shelley. She worked Mrs. Freshett off the same
way, but you could see she was almost too tired to do it, so by
night she was nearly as white as Shelley, yet keeping things
going. When the house was still, she came into the room, and
stood at the window as I had, until father entered, then she turned,
and I could see they were staring at each other in the moonlight,
as they had all day.

"She's sick?" asked father, at last.

"Heartsick!" said mother bitterly.

"We'd better have Doc come?"

"She says she isn't sick, and she won't see him."

"She will if I put my foot down."

"Best not, Paul! She'll feel better soon. She's so young! She
must get over it."

They were silent for a long time and then father asked in a
harsh whisper: "Ruth, can she possibly have brought us to
shame?"

"God forbid!" cried mother. "Let us pray."

Then those two people knelt on each side of that bed, and I
could hear half the words they muttered, until I was wild enough
to scream. I wished with all my heart that I hadn't listened. I had
always known that it was no nice way. I must have gone to sleep
after a while, but when I woke up I was still thinking about it, and
to save me, I couldn't quit. All day, wherever I went that question
of father's kept going over in my head. I thought about it until I
was almost crazy, and I just couldn't see where anything about
shame came in.

She was only mistaken. She *thought* he loved her, and he
didn't. She never could have been so bloomy, so filled with song,
laughter, and lovely like she was, if she hadn't truly believed with

all her heart that he loved her. Of course it would almost finish her to give him up, when she felt like that; and maybe she did wrong to let herself care so much, before she was sure about him; but that would only be foolish, there wouldn't be even a shadow of shame about it. Besides, Laddie had done exactly the same thing. He loved the Princess until it nearly killed him when he thought he had to give her up, and he loved her as hard as ever he could, when he hadn't an idea whether she would love him back, even a tiny speck; and the person who wasn't foolish, and never would be, was Laddie.

The more I thought, the worse I got worked up, and I couldn't see how Shelley was to blame for anything at all. Love just came to her, like it came to Laddie. She would hardly have knelt down and beseeched the Lord to make her fall in love with a man she scarcely knew, and when she couldn't be sure what he was going to do about it—not the Lord, the man, I mean. You could see for yourself she wouldn't do that. I finished my work, and then I tried to do things for her, and she wouldn't let me. Mother told me to ask her to make Grace Greenwood the dress she promised when I was sick; so I took the Scotch plaid to her and reminded her, and she pushed me away and said: "Some time!"

I even got Grace, and showed Shelley the spills on her dress, and how badly she needed a new one, but she never looked, she said: "Oh bother! My head aches. Do let me be!"

Mother was listening. I could see her standing outside the door. She motioned to me to come away, so I went to her and she was white as Shelley. She was sick too, she couldn't say a word for a minute, but after a while she kissed me, I could feel the quivers in her lips, and she said stifflike: "Never mind, she'll be better soon, then she will! Run play now!"

Sometimes I wandered around looking at things and living dully. I didn't try to study out anything, but I must have watched closer than I knew, for every single thing I saw then, over that whole farm, I can shut my eyes and see to-day; everything, from the old hawk tilting his tail to steer him in soaring, to a snake catching field mice in the grass, lichens on the fence, flowers, butterflies, every single thing. Mostly I sat to watch something that promised to become interesting, and before I knew it, I was back on the shame question. That's the most dreadful word in the dictionary. There's something about it that makes your face burn, only to have it in your mind.

Laddie said he never had met any man who knew the origin of more words than father. He could even tell every clip what nationality a man was from his name. Hundreds of times I have heard him say to stranger people, "From your name you'd be of Scotch extraction," or Irish, or whatever it was, and every time the person he was talking with would say, "Yes." Some day away out in the field, alone, I thought I would ask him what people first used the word "shame," and just exactly what it did mean, and what the things were that you could do that would make the people who loved you until they would die for you, ashamed of you.

Thinking about that and planning out what it was that I wanted to know, gave me another idea. Why not ask her? She was the only one who knew what she had done away there in the city, alone among strangers; I wasn't sure whether all the music a girl could learn was worth letting her take the chances she would have to in a big city. From the way Laddie and father hated them, they were a poor place for men, and they must have been much worse for girls. Shelley knew, why not ask *her?* Maybe I could coax her to tell me, and it would make my life much easier to know; and only think what was going on in father's and mother's heads and hearts, when I felt that way, and didn't even know what there was to be ashamed about. She wouldn't any more than slap me; and sick as she was, I made up my mind not to get angry at her, or ever to tell, if she did. I'd rather have her hit me when she was so sick than to have Sally beat me until she couldn't strike another lick, just because she was angry. But I forgave her that, and I was never going to think of it again—only I did.

Mother kept sending Leon to the post-office, and she met him at the gate half the time herself and fairly snatched the letters from his hands. Hum! She couldn't pull the wool over my eyes. I knew she hoped somehow, some way, there would be a big fat one with Paget, Legal Adviser, or whatever a Chicago lawyer puts on his envelopes. Jerry's just say: "Attorney at Law." I don't believe it's right, either. "At" means the place you are in, like "The man is at home." "Of" means the thing you are a part of, like "The Board of Commissioners;" anyway, Dr. Fenner is "of," for when I asked him what the M. D. after his name meant, he said: "Doctor of Medicine." Next time Jerry or Frank comes, I'm going to ask if "at" isn't a mistake.

No letter ever came that had Paget in the corner, or anything happened that did Shelley any good. Far otherwise! Just before supper Leon came from Groveville one evening, and all of us could see at a glance that he had been crying like a baby. He had wiped up, and was trying to hold in, but he was killed, next. I nearly said, "Well, for heaven's sake, another!" when I saw him. He slammed down a big, long envelope, having printing on it, before father, and glared at it as if he wanted to tear it to smithereens, and he said: "If you want to know why it looks like that, I buried it under a stone once; but I had to go back, and then I threw it as far as I could send it, into Ditton's gully, but after a while I hunted it up again!"

Then he keeled over on the couch mother keeps for her in the dining-room, and sobbed until he looked like he'd come apart. Mother drew a deep breath that sounded as if it hurt her throat, and looked at father; and he stared at the letter corner, peered over his glasses at Leon, then examined the flap carefully, and when he was satisfied that it hadn't been opened, he slowly drew out his knife. Mother just couldn't stand it. She caught up a knife from the table, ran it under and across the flap, pulled the sheet out, gave it a shake, and held it before father's eyes, all in one moment. Then she dropped on a chair, gripped her hands and waited. *Now,* I guess you see what a woman fixes up for herself when she marries and brings a houseful of children into the world. She and father alone could have beaten any pair of doves in our orchard, at having a loving time. But because of us, she had to face Laddie leaving, and how she felt over it; that shame word in her mind, and worry about Shelley's health; and now on top of that, she had to be grieved sick for Leon.

Of course all of us knew exactly what that letter was from the way he acted. Mother had told him, time and again, not to set his heart so; father had, too, and Laddie, and every one of us, but that little half-Arab, half-Kentucky mare was the worst temptation a man who loved horses could possibly have; and while father and mother stopped at good work horses, and matched roadsters for the carriage, they managed to prize and tend them so that every one of us had been born horse crazy, and we had been allowed to ride, care for, and taught to love horses all our lives. Treat a horse ugly and we'd have gone on the thrashing floor ourselves.

Father laid the letter face down, his hand on it, and shook his head. Mother shook hers too, like you've seen folks in a funeral procession. Of course this wasn't nearly so bad as a funeral; but it was enough to make you think of one, and Leon couldn't have cried harder if some of us really had been on the way to the graveyard. I guess it was a funeral for him.

"This is too bad!" said father. "It's a burning shame, but the money, the exact amount, was taken from a farmer in Medina County, Ohio, by a traveller he sheltered a few days, because he complained of a bad foot. The description of the man who robbed us is perfect. The money was from the sale of some prize cattle. It will have to be returned."

"Just let me see the letter a minute," said Laddie.

He read it over thoughtfully. He was long enough about it to have gone over it three times; then he looked at Leon, and his forehead creased in a deep frown. I looked at Leon too. I could see that fox hunt all over again; how bravely he sat, his tow hair waving in the wind as he sailed across the fence and took the creek. "Ep! Ep! Over, lad!" before I knew what I was doing I shouted it. Then I cried right out loud and ran to mother. The tears slid down her cheeks, but she didn't know it, or else she'd have wiped them away. She was never mussy about the least little thing.

"Father!" she said. "Father —!"

That was as far as she could go.

"The man must have his money," said father, "but we'll look into this —"

He pushed back the plates and tablecloth, and cleared his end of the table. Mother never budged to stack the plates, or straighten the cloth so it wouldn't be wrinkled. Then father brought his big account book from the black walnut chest in our room, some little books, and papers, sharpened a pencil and began going up and down the columns and picking out figures here and there that he set on a piece of paper. I never had seen him look either old or tired before; but he did then. Mother noticed it too, for her lips tightened, she lifted her head, wiped her eyes, and pretended that she felt better. Laddie said something about doing the feeding, and slipped out. Just then Shelley came into the room, stopped, and looked questioningly at us. Her eyes opened wide, and she stared hard at Leon.

"Why what ails him?" she asked mother.

"You remember what I wrote you about a man who robbed us, and the money Leon was to have, provided no owner was found in a reasonable time; and the horse the boy had planned to buy, and how he had been going to Pryors'—Oh, I think he's slipped over there once a day, and often three times, all this spring! Mr. Pryor encouraged him, let him take his older horses to practise on, even went out and taught him cross country riding himself —"

"I remember!" said Shelley.

Leon sobbed out loud. Shelley crossed the room swiftly, dropped beside him and whispered something in his ear. Quick as a shot his arm reached out and went around her. She hid her head deep in the pillow beside him, and they went to pieces together. Clear to pieces! Pretty soon father had to take off his glasses and wipe them so he could see the figures. Mother took one long look at him, a short one at Leon and Shelley, then she arose, her voice as even and smooth, and she said: "While you figure, father, I'll see about supper. I have tried to plan an extra good one this evening."

She left the room. *Now,* I guess you know about all I can tell you of mother! I can't see that there's a thing left. That was the kind of a soldier she was. Talk about Crusaders, and a good fight! All the blood of battle in our family wasn't on father's side, not by any means! The Dutch could fight too!

Father's pencil scraped a little, a bee that had slipped in buzzed over the apple butter, while the clock ticked as if it used a hammer. It was so loud one wanted to pitch it from the window. May and I sat still as mice when the cat is near. Candace couldn't keep away from the kitchen door to save her, and where mother went I hadn't an idea, but she wasn't getting an extra good supper. Shelley and Leon were quieter now. May nudged me, and I saw that his arm around her was gripping her tight, while her hand on his head was patting him and fingering his hair.

Ca-lumph! Ca-lumph! came the funniest sound right on the stone walk leading to the east door, then a shrill whicker that made father drop his pencil. Leon was on his feet, Shelley beside him, while at the door stood Laddie grinning as if his face would split, and with her forefeet on the step and her nose in the room, stood the prettiest, the very prettiest horse I ever saw. She was sticking her nose toward Leon, whinnying softly, as she lifted one foot, and if Laddie hadn't backed her, she would have walked right into the dining-room.

"Come on, Weiscope, she's yours!" said Laddie. "Take her to the barn, and put her in one of the cow stalls, until we fix a place for her."

Leon crossed the room, but he never touched the horse. He threw his arms around Laddie's neck.

"Son! Son! Haven't you let your feelings run away with you? What does this mean?" asked father sternly.

"There's nothing remarkable in a big six-footer like me buying a horse," said Laddie. "I expect to purchase a number soon, and without a cent to pay, in the bargain. I contracted to give five hundred dollars for this mare. She is worth more; but that should be satisfactory all around. I am going to earn it by putting five of Mr. Pryor's fancy, pedigreed horses in shape for market, taking them personally, and selling them to men fit to own, and handle, real horses. I get one hundred each, and my expenses for the job. I'll have as much fun doing it as I ever had at anything. It suits me far better than plowing, even."

Mother entered the room at a sweep, and pushed Leon aside.

"Oh you man of my heart!" she cried. "You man after my own heart!"

Laddie bent and kissed her, holding her tight as he looked over her head at father.

"It's all right, of course?" he said.

"I never have known of anything quite so altogether right," said father. "Thank you, lad, and God bless you!"

He took Laddie's hand and almost lifted him from the floor, then he wiped his glasses, gathered up his books with a big, deep breath of relief, and went into his room. If the others had looked to see why he was gone so long, they would have seen him on his knees beside his bed thanking God, as usual. Leon couldn't have come closer than when he said, "The same yesterday, to-day, and forever," about father.

Leon had his arms around the neck of his horse now, and he was kissing her, patting her, and explaining to Shelley just why no other horse was like her. He was pouring out a jumble all about the oasis of the desert, the tent dwellers, quoting lines from "The Arab to His Horse," bluegrass, and gentleness combined with spirit, while Shelley had its head between her hands, stroking it and saying, "Yes," to every word Leon told her. Then he said: "Just hop on her back from that top step and ride her to the barn, if you want to see the motion she has."

Shelley said: "Has a woman ever been on her back? Won't she shy at my skirts?"

"No," explained Leon. "I've been training her with a horse blanket pinned around me, so Susie could ride her! She'll be all right."

So Shelley mounted, and the horse turned her head, and tried to rub against her, as she walked away, tame as a sheep. I wondered if she could be too gentle. If she went "like the wind," as Leon said, it didn't show then. I was almost crazy to go along, and maybe Leon would let me ride a little while; but I had a question that it would help me to know the answer and I wanted to ask father before I forgot; so I waited until he came out. When he sat down, smiled at me and said, "Well, is the girl happy for brother?" I knew it was a good time, and I could ask anything I chose, so I sat on his knee and said: "Father, when you pray for anything that it's all perfectly right for you to have, does God come down from heaven and do it Himself, or does He send a man like Laddie to do it for him?"

Father hugged me tight, smiling the happiest.

"Why, you have the whole thing right there in a nutshell, Little Sister," he said. "You see it's like this: the Book tells us most distinctly that 'God is love.' Now it was love that sent Laddie to bind himself for a long, tedious job, to give Leon his horse, wasn't it?"

"Of course!" I said. "He wouldn't have been likely to do it if he hated him. It was love, of course!"

"Then it was God," said father, "because 'God is love.' They are one and the same thing."

Then he kissed me, and *that* was settled. So I wondered when you longed for anything so hard you really felt it was worth bothering God about, whether the quickest way to get it was to ask Him for it, or to try to put a lot of love into the heart of some person who could do what you wanted. I decided it all went back to God though, for most of the time probably we wouldn't know who the right one was to try to awaken love in. I was mighty sure none of us ever dreamed Laddie could walk over to Pryors', and come back with that horse, in a way perfectly satisfactory to every one, slick as an eel.

You should have seen Leon following around after Laddie, trying to do things for him, taking on his work to give him more time with the horses, getting up early to finish his own stunts, so he could go over to Pryors' and help. Mother said it had done more to make a man of him than anything that ever happened. It helped Shelley, too. Something seemed to break in her, when she cried so with Leon, because he was in trouble. Then he was so crazy to show off his horse he had Shelley ride up and down the lane, while he ran along and led, so she got a lot of exercise, and it made her good and hungry. If you don't think by this time that my mother was the beatenest woman alive, I'll prove it to you. When the supper bell rang there were strawberry preserves instead of the apple butter, biscuit, fried chicken, and mashed potatoes. She must have slapped those chickens into the skillet before they knew their heads were off. When Shelley came to the table, for the first time since she'd been home, had pink in her cheeks, and talked some, and ate too, mother forgot her own supper. She fumbled over her plate, but scarcely touched even the livers, and those delicious little kidneys in the tailpiece like Leon and I had at Sally's wedding. When we finished, and it was time for her to give the signal to arise, no one had asked to be excused, she said: "Let us have a word with the Most High." Then she bowed her head, so all of us did too. "O Lord, we praise Thee for all Thy tender mercies, and all Thy loving kindness. Amen!"

Of course father always asked the blessing to begin with, and mostly it was the same one, and that was all at meal time, but this was a little extra that mother couldn't even wait until night to tell the Almighty, she was so pleased with Him. Maybe I haven't told everything about her, after all. Father must have thought that was lovely of her; he surely felt as happy as she did, to see Shelley better, for he hugged and kissed her over and over, finishing at her neck like he always did, and then I be-hanged, if he didn't hug and kiss every last one of us—tight, even the boys. Shelley he held long and close, and patted her a little when he let her go. It made me wonder if the rest of us didn't get ours, so he'd have a chance at her without her noticing it. One thing was perfectly clear. If shame came to us, they were going to love her, and stick tight to her right straight through it.

Now that everything was cleared up so, Shelley seemed a little more like herself every day, although it was bad enough yet; I thought I might as well hurry up the end a little, and stop the trouble completely, so I began watching for a chance to ask her. But I wanted to get her away off alone, so no one would see if she slapped me. I didn't know how long I'd have to wait. I tried coaxing her to the orchard to see a bluebird's nest, but she asked if bluebirds were building any different that year, and I had to admit they were not. Then I tried the blue-eyed Mary bed, but she said she supposed it was still under the cling peach tree, and the flower, two white petals up, two blue down, and so it was. Just as I was beginning to think I'd have to take that to the Lord in prayer, I got my chance by accident.

May and Candace were forever going snake hunting. You would think any one with common sense would leave them alone and be glad of the chance, but no indeed! They went nearly every day as soon as the noon work was finished, and stayed until time to get supper. They did have heaps of fun and wild excitement. May was gentle, and tender with everything else on earth; so I 'spose she had a right to bruise the serpent with her heel—really she used sticks and stones—if she wanted to. I asked her how she *could,* and she said there was a place in the Bible that told how a snake coaxed Eve to eat an apple, that the Lord had told her she mustn't touch; and so she got us into most of the trouble there was in the world. May said it was all the fault of the *snake* to begin with, and she meant to pay up every one she could find, because she had none of the apple, and lots of the trouble. Candace cried so much because Frederick Swartz had been laid in the tomb, that mother was pleased to have her cheer up, even enough to go snake hunting.

That afternoon Mehitabel Heasty had come to visit May, so she went along, and I followed. They poked around the driftwood at the floodgate behind the barn, and were giving up the place. Candace had crossed the creek and was coming back, and May had started, when she saw a tiny little one and chased it. We didn't know then that it was a good thing to have snakes to eat moles, field mice, and other pests that bother your crops; the Bible had no mercy on them at all, so we were not saving our snakes; and anyway we had more than we needed, while some of them were too big to be safe to keep, and a few poison as could be. May began to bruise the serpent, when out of the driftwood where they hadn't found anything came its mammy, a great big blacksnake, maddest you ever saw, with its pappy right after her, mad as ever too. Candace screamed at May to look behind her, but May was busy with the snake and didn't look quick enough, so the old mammy struck right in her back. She just caught in the hem of May's skirt, and her teeth stuck in the goods—you know how a snake's teeth turn back—so she couldn't let go. May took one look and raced down the bank to the crossing, through the water, and toward us, with the snake dragging and twisting, and trying her best to get away. May was screaming at every jump for Candace, and Mehitabel was flying up and down crying: "Oh there's snakes in my shoes! There's snakes in my shoes!"

That was a fair sample of how much sense a Heasty ever had. It took all Mehitabel's shoes could do to hold her feet, for after one went barefoot all week, and never put on shoes except on Sunday or for a visit, the feet became so spread out, shoes had all they could do to manage them, and then mostly they pinched until they made one squirm. But she jumped and said that, while May ran and screamed, and Candace gripped her big hickory stick and told May to stand still. Then she bruised that serpent with her whole foot, for she stood on it, and swatted it until she broke its neck. Then she turned ready for the other one, but when it saw what happened to its mate, it decided to go back. Even snakes, it doesn't seem right to break up families like that; so by the time Candace got the Mammy killed, loose from May's hem, and stretched out with the back up, so she wouldn't make it rain, when Candace wasn't sure that father wanted rain, I had enough. I went down the creek until I was below the orchard, then I crossed, passed the cowslip bed, climbed the hill and fence, and stopped to think what I would do first; and there only a few feet away was Shelley. She was sitting in the shade, her knees drawn up, her hands clasped around them, staring straight before her across the meadow at nothing in particular, that I could see. She jumped as if I had been a snake when she saw me, then she said, "Oh, is it you?" like she was half glad of it. My chance had come.

I went to her, sat close beside her and tried snuggling up a little. It worked. She put her arm around me, drew me tight, rubbed her cheek against my head and we sat there. I was wondering how in the world I could ask her, and not get slapped. I was growing most too big for that slapping business, anyway. We sat there; I was looking across the meadow as she did, only I was watching everything that went on, so when I saw a grosbeak fly from the wild grape where Shelley had put the crock for sap, it made me think of her hair. She used to like to have me play with it so well, she'd give me pennies if I did. I got up, and began pulling out her pins carefully. I knew I was getting a start because right away she put up her hand to help me.

"I can get them," I said just as flannel-mouthed as ever I could, like all of us talked to her now, so I got every one and never pulled a mite. When I reached over her shoulder to drop them in her lap, being so close I kissed her cheek. Then I shook down her hair, spread it out, lifted it, parted it, and held up strands to let the air on her scalp. She shivered and said: "Mercy child, how good that does feel! My head has ached lately until it's a wonder there's a hair left on it."

So I was pleasing her. I never did handle hair so carefully. I tried every single thing it feels good to you to have done with your hair, rubbed her head gently, and to cheer her up I told her about May and the snake, and what fool Mehitabel had said, and she couldn't help laughing; so I had her feeling about as good as she could, for the way she actually felt, but still I didn't really get ahead. Come right to the place to do it, that was no very easy question to ask a person, when you wouldn't hurt their feelings for anything; I was beginning to wonder if I would lose my chance, when all at once a way I could manage popped into my mind.

"Shelley," I said, "they told you about Laddie and the Princess, didn't they?"

I knew they had, but I had to make a beginning some way.

"Yes," she said. "I'm glad of it! I think she's pretty as a picture, and nice as she looks. Laddie may have to hump himself to support her, but if he can't get her as fine clothes as she has, her folks can help him. They seem to have plenty, and she's their only child."

"They're going to. I heard Mr. Pryor ask Laddie if he'd be so unkind as to object to them having the pleasure of giving her things."

"Well, the greenhorn didn't say he would!"

"No. He didn't want to put his nose to the grindstone quite that close. He said it was between them."

"I should think so!"

"Shelley, there's a question I've been wanting to ask some one for quite a while."

"What?"

"Why, this! You know, Laddie was in love with the Princess, like you are when you want to marry folks, for a long, long time, before he could be sure whether she loved him back."

"Yes."

"Well, now, 'spose she never had loved him, would he have had anything to be ashamed of?"

"I can't see that he would. Some one must start a courtship, or there would be no marrying, and it's conceded to be the place of the man. No. He might be disappointed, or dreadfully hurt, but there would be no shame about it."

"Well, then, suppose she loved him, and wanted to marry him, and he hadn't loved her, or wanted her, would *she* have had anything to be ashamed of?"

"I don't think so! If she was attracted by him, and thought she would like him, she would have a right to go to a certain extent, to find out if he cared for her, and if he didn't, why, she'd just have to give him up. But any sensible girl waits for a man to make the advances, and plenty of them, before she allows herself even to dream of loving him, or at least, I would."

Now I was getting somewhere!

"Of course you would!" I said. "That would be the way mother would do, wouldn't it?"

"Surely!"

"If that Paget man you used to write about had seemed to be just what you liked, you'd have waited to know if he wanted you, before you loved him, wouldn't you?"

"I certainly would!" answered Shelley. "Or at least, I'd have waited until I *thought* sure as death, I knew. It seems that sometimes you can be fooled about those things."

"But if you thought sure you knew, and then found out you had been mistaken, you wouldn't have anything to be *ashamed* of, would you?"

"Not-on-your-life-I-wouldn't!" cried Shelley, hammering each word into her right knee with her doubled fist. "What are you driving at, Blatherskite? What have you got into your head?"

"Oh just studying about things," I said, which was exactly the truth. "Sally getting married last fall, and Laddie going to this, just started me to wondering."

Fooled her, too!

"Oh well, there's no harm done," she said. "The sooner you get these matters straightened out, the better able you will be to take care of yourself. If you ever go to a city, you'll find out that a girl needs considerable care taken of her."

"You could look out for yourself, Shelley?"

"Well, I don't know as I made such a glorious fist of it," she said, "but at least, as you say, I've nothing to be ashamed of!"

I almost hugged her head off.

"Of course you haven't!" I cried. "Of course you wouldn't have!"

I just kissed her over and over for joy; I was so glad my heart hurt for father and mother. Shame had not come to them!

"Now, I guess I'll run to the house and get a comb," I told her.

"Go on," said Shelley. "I know you are tired."

"I'm not in the least," I said. "Don't you remember I always use a comb when I fuss with your hair?"

"It *is* better," said Shelley. "Go get one."

As I got up to start I took a last look at her, and there was something in her face that I couldn't bear. I knelt beside her, and put both arms around her neck.

"Shelley, it's a secret," I said in a breathless half whisper. "It's a great, big secret, but I'm going to tell you. Twice now I've had a powerful prayer all ready to try. It's the kind where you go to the barn, all alone, stand on that top beam below the highest window and look toward the east. You keep perfectly still, and just think with all your might, and you look away over where Jesus used to be, and when the right feeling comes, you pray that prayer as if He stood before you, and it will come true. I *know* it will come true. The reason I know is because twice now I've been almost ready to try it, and what I intended to ask for happened before I had time; so I've saved that prayer; but Shelley, shall I pray it about the Paget man, for you?"

She gripped me, and she shook until she was all twisted up; you could hear her teeth click, she chilled so. The tears just gushed, and she pulled me up close and whispered right in my ear: "Yes!"

It was only pretend about the comb; what I really wanted was to get to father and mother quick. I knew he was at the barn and he was going to be too happy for words in a minute. But as I went up the lane, I wasn't sure whether I'd rather pray about that Paget man or bruise him with my heel like a serpent. The only way I could fix it was to remember if Shelley loved him so, he *must* be mighty nice. Father was in the wagon shoveling corn from it to a platform where it would be handy to feed the pigs; so I ran and called him, and put one foot on a hub and raised my hands. He pulled me up and when he saw how important it was, he sat on the edge of the bed, so I told him: "Father, you haven't got a thing in the world to be ashamed of about Shelley."

"Praise the Lord!" said father like I knew he would, but you should have seen his face. "Tell me about it!"

I told him and he said: "Well, I don't know but this is the gladdest hour of my life. Go straight and repeat to your mother exactly what you've said to me. Take her away all alone, and then forget about it, you little blessing."

"Father, have you got too many children?"

"No!" he said. "I wish I had a dozen more, if they'd be like you."

When I went up the lane I was so puffed up with importance I felt too dignified to run. I strutted like our biggest turkey gobbler. The only reason you couldn't hear my wings scrape, was because through mistake they grew on the turkey. If I'd had them, I would have dragged them sure, and cried "Ge-hobble-hobble!" at every step.

I took mother away alone and told her, and she asked many more questions than father, but she was even gladder than he. She almost hugged the breath out of me. Sometimes I get things *right*, anyway! Then I took the comb and ran back to Shelley.

"I thought you'd forgotten me," she said.

She had wiped up and was looking better. If ever I combed carefully I did then. Just when I had all the tangles out, there came mother. She had not walked that far in a long time. I thought maybe she could comfort Shelley, so I laid the comb in her lap and went to see how the snake hunters were coming on. It must be all right, when the Bible says so, but the African Jungle will do for me, and a popgun is not going to scatter families. I never felt so strongly about breaking home ties in my life as I did then. There was nothing worse. It was not where I wanted to be, so I thought I'd go back to the barn, and hang around father, hoping maybe he'd brag on me some more. Going up the lane I saw a wagon passing with the biggest box I ever had seen, and I ran to the gate to watch where it went. It stopped at our house and Frank came toward me as I hurried up the road.

"Where are the folks?" he asked, without paying the least attention to my asking him over and over what was in the box.

"May and Candace are killing every snake in the driftwood behind the barn, Shelley and mother are down in the orchard, and father and the boys are hauling corn."

"Go tell the boys to come quickly and keep quiet," he said. "But don't let any one else know I'm here."

That was so exciting I almost fell over my feet running, and all three of them came quite as fast. I stood back and watched, and

I just danced a steady hop from one foot to the other while those men got the big box off the wagon and opened it. On the side I spelled Piano, so of course it was for Shelley. It was so heavy it took all six of them, father and the three boys, the driver and another very stylish looking man to carry it. They put it in the parlour, screwed a leg on each corner, and a queer harp in the middle, then they lifted it up and set it on its feet, under the whatnot, and it seemed as if it filled half the room. Then Frank spread a beauteous wine coloured cover all embroidered in pink roses with green leaves over it, and the stylish man opened a lid, sat down and spread out his hands. Frank said: "Soft pedal! Mighty soft!" So he smothered it down, and tried only enough to find that it had not been hurt coming, and then he went away on the wagon. Father and the boys gathered up every scrap, swept the walk, and put all the things they had used back where they got them, like we always did.

Then Frank took a card from his pocket and tied it to the music rack, and it read: "For Shelley, from her brothers in fact, and in law." To a corner of the cover he pinned another card that read: "From Peter."

"What is that?" asked father.

"That's from Peter," said Frank. "Peter is great on finishing touches. He had to outdo the rest of us that much or bust. Fact is, none of us thought of a cover except him."

"How about this?" asked father, staring at it as if it were an animal that would bite.

"Well," said Frank, "it was apparent that practising her fingers to the bone wouldn't do Shelley much good unless she could keep it up in summer, and you and mother always have done so much for the rest of us, and now mother isn't so strong and the expenses go on the same with these youngsters; we knew you were figuring on it, but we beat you. Put yours in the bank, and try the feel of a surplus once more. Haven't had much lately, have you, father!"

"Well, not to speak of," said father. "Sally's wedding cleaned me up slick as a whistle."

"Now let's shut everything up, ring the bell to call them, and get Shelley in here and surprise her."

"She's not very well," said father. "Mother thinks she worked too hard."

"She's all right now, father," I said. "She is getting pink again and rounder, and this will fix her grand."

Wouldn't it though! There wasn't one anywhere, short of the city. Even the Princess had none. Father hunted up a song book, opened it and set it on the rack. Then all of us went out.

"We'll write to the boys, mother and I, and Shelley also," said father. "I can't express myself just now. This is a fine thing for all of you to do."

Frank seemed to think so too, and looked rather puffed up, until Leon began telling about his horse. When Frank found out that Laddie, who had not yet branched out for himself, had given Leon much more than any one of them had Shelley, he looked a little disappointed. He explained how the piano cost eight hundred dollars, but by paying cash all at once, the man took seven hundred and fifty, so it only cost them one hundred and fifty a piece, and none of them felt it at all.

"Sometimes the clouds loom up pretty black, and mother and I scarcely know how to go on, save for the help of the Lord, but we certainly are blest with good children, children we can be proud of. Your mother will like that instrument as well as Shelley, son," said father.

Frank went out and rang the bell, tolled it, and made a big noise like he always did when he came unexpectedly, and then sat on the back fence until he saw them coming, and went to meet them. He walked between mother and Shelley, with an arm around each one. If he thought Shelley looked badly, he didn't mention it. What he did say was that he was starved, and to fly around and get supper. I thought I'd burst. They began to cook, and the boys went to feed and see Leon's horse, and then we had supper. I just sat and stared at Frank and grinned. I couldn't eat.

"Do finish your supper," said mother. "I never saw anything take your appetite like seeing your brother. You'll be wanting a piece before bedtime."

I didn't say a word, because I was afraid to, but I kept looking at Leon and he smiled back, and we had great fun. Secrets are lovely. Mother couldn't have eaten a bite if she'd known about that great shining thing, all full of wonderful sound, standing in our parlour. When the last slow person had finished, father said: "Shelley, won't you step into the front room and bring me that book I borrowed from Frank on 'Taxation.' I want to talk over a few points."

All of us heard her little breathless cry, and mother said, "There!" as if she'd been listening for something, and she beat all of us to the door. Then she cried out too, and such a time as we did have. At last after all of us had grown sensible enough to behave, Shelley sat on the stool, spread her fingers over the keys and played at the place father had selected, and all of us sang as hard as we could: "Be it ever so humble, There's no place like home"; and there *was* no place like ours, of *that* I'm quite sure.

17

In Faith Believing

Nor could the bright green world around
  A joy to her impart,
For still she missed the eyes that made
  The summer of her heart.

Soon as she had the piano, Shelley needed only the Paget man to make her happy as a girl could be; and having faith in that prayer, I decided to try it right away. So I got Laddie to promise surely that he'd wake me when he got up the next morning. I laid my clothes out all ready; he merely touched my foot, and I came to, slipped out with him, and he helped me dress. We went to the barn when the morning was all gray.

"What the dickens have you got in your head now, Chicken?" he asked. "Is it business with the Fairies?"

"No, this is with the Most High," I said solemnly, like father. "Go away and leave me alone."

"Well of all the queer Chickens!" he said, but he kissed me and went.

I climbed the stairs to the threshing floor, then the ladder to the mow, walked a beam to the wall, there followed one to the east end, and another to the little, high-up ventilator window. There I stood looking at the top of the world. A gray mist was rising like steam from the earth, there was a curious colour in the east, stripes of orange and flames of red, where the sun was coming. I folded my hands on the sill, faced the sky, and stood staring. Just stood, and stood, never moving a muscle. By and by I began to think how much we loved Shelley, how happy she had been at Christmas, the way she was now, and how much all of us would give in money, or time, or love, to make her sparkling, bubbling, happy again; so I thought and thought, gazing at the sky, which every second became a grander sight. Little cold chills began going up my back, and soon I was talking to the Lord exactly as if He stood before me on the reddest ray that topped our apple trees.

I don't know all I said. That's funny, for I usually remember to the last word; but this time it was so important, I wanted it so badly, and I was so in earnest that words poured in a stream. I began by reminding Him that He knew everything, and so He'd understand if what I asked was for the best. Then I told Him how it looked to us, who knew only a part; and then I went at Him and implored and beseeched, if it would be best for Shelley, and would make her happy, to send her the Paget man, and to be quick about it. When I had said the last word that came to me, and begged all I thought becoming—I don't think with His face, that Jesus wants us to grovel to Him, at least He looks too dignified to do it Himself—I just stood there, still staring.

I didn't expect to see a burning bush, or a pillar of fire, or a cloud of flame, or even to hear a small, still voice; but I watched, so I wouldn't miss it if there should be anything different in that sunrise from any other I ever had seen, and there was not. Not one thing! It was so beautiful, and I was so in earnest my heart hurt; but that was like any other sunrise on a fine July morning. There wasn't the least sign that Jesus had heard me, and would send the man; yet before I knew it, I was amazed to find the feeling creeping over me that he was coming. If I had held the letter in my hand saying he would arrive on the noon train, I couldn't have grown surer. Why, I even looked down the first time I moved, to see if I had it; but I was certain anyway. So I looked steadily toward the east once more and said, "Thank you, with all my heart, Lord Jesus," then I slowly made my way down and back to the house.

Shelley was at the orchard gate, waiting; so I knew they had missed me, and Laddie had told them where I was and not to call. She had the strangest look on her face, as she asked: "Where have you been?"

I looked straight and hard at her and said, "It's all right, Shelley. He's going to come soon;" but I didn't think it was a thing to mouth over, so I twisted away from her, and ran to the kitchen to see if breakfast had all been eaten. I left Shelley standing there with her eyes wide, also her mouth. She looked about as intelligent as Mehitabel Heasty, and it wouldn't have surprised me if she had begun to jump up and down and say there were snakes in *her* shoes. No doubt you have heard of people having been knocked silly; I knew she was, and so she had a perfect right to look that way, until she could remember what she was doing and come back to herself. Maybe it took her longer, because mother wasn't there, to remind her about her mouth, and I didn't propose to mention it.

At breakfast, mother said father was going to drive Frank home in the carriage, and if I would like, I might go along. I would have to sit on the back seat alone, going; but coming home I could ride beside and visit with father. I loved that, for you could see more from the front seat, and father would stop to explain every single thing. He always gave me the money and let me pay the toll. He would get me a drink at the spring, let me wade a few minutes at Enyard's riffles, where their creek, with the loveliest gravel bed, ran beside the road; and he always raced like wildfire at the narrows, where for a mile the railroad ran along the turnpike. Our team never could seem to get over being afraid of the cars. So father always listened at the place, and if no train could be heard coming, he cut the wind going through. It was a real chariot race. I was always crazy to stand up and cheer, but of course I never dared. I was more than glad to go along.

We took Frank to his office, stopped a little while to visit Lucy, and give her the butter and cream mother sent, went to the store to see Peter, and then to the post-office. From there we could see that the veranda of the hotel across the street was filled with gayly dressed people, and father said that the summer boarders from big cities around must be pouring in fast. When he came out with the mail he said he better ask if the landlord did not want some of mother's corn and milk fed spring chickens, because last year he had paid her more than the grocer. So he drove across the street, stopped at the curb, and left me to hold the team.

Maybe you think I wasn't proud! I've told you about Ned and Jo, with their sharp ears, dappled sides, and silky tails, and the carriage almost new, with leather seats, patent leather trimmings, and side lamps, so shiny you could see yourself in the brass. We never drove into the barn with one speck of mud or dust on it. That was how particular mother was. I sat up very straight and dignified. When Ned reached over and nipped Jo's neck, I pulled him up sharply and said: "Steady boy! Behave yourself!" The horses didn't know it wasn't father speaking to them.

I watched the team carefully; I had to if I didn't want my neck broken; but I also kept an eye on that veranda. You could see at a glance that those were stylish women. Now my mother liked to be in fashion as well as any one could; so I knew she'd be mightily pleased if I could tell her a new place to set her comb, a different way to fasten her collar, or about an unusual pattern for a frock.

I got my drink at the spring, father offered to stop at the riffle, but I was enjoying the ride so much, and I could always wade at home, although our creek was not so beautiful as Enyard's, but for common wading it would do; we went through the narrows, like two shakes of a sheep's tail, then we settled down to a slow trot, and were having the loveliest visit possible, when in the bundle on my lap, I saw the end of something that interested me. Mr. Agnew always made our mail into a roll with the *Advocate* and the *Agriculturist* on the outside, and because every one was so anxious about their letters, and some of them meant so much, I felt grown and important while holding the package.

I was gripping it tight when I noticed the end of one letter much wider and fatter than any I ever had seen, so when father was not looking I began pushing it a little at one end, and pulling it at the other, to work it up, until I could read the address. I got it out so far I thought every minute he'd notice, and tell me not to do that, but I could only see Stanton. All of us were Stanton, so it might be for me, for that matter. Jerry might be sending me pictures, or a book, he did sometimes, but there was an exciting thing about it. Besides being fatter than it looked right at the end, it was plastered with stamps—lots of them, enough to have brought it clear around the world. I pushed that end back, pulled out the other, and took one good look. I almost fell from the carriage. I grabbed father's arm and cried: "Stop! Stop this team quick. Stop them against the fence, and see if I can read."

"Are you crazy, child?" asked father, but he checked the horses.

"No, but you are going to be in a minute," I said. "Look at that!"

I yanked the letter from the bundle, and held it over. I *thought* I could read, but I was too scared to be sure. I thought it said in big, strong, upstanding letters, Miss Shelley Stanton, Groveville, Indiana. And in the upper corner, Blackburn, Yeats and *Paget,* Counsellors of Law, 37 to 39 State St., Chicago. I put my finger on the Paget, and looked into father's face. I was no fool after all. He was not a bit surer that *he* could read than I was, from the dazed way he stared.

"You see!" I said.

"It says Paget!" he said, like he would come nearer believing it if he heard himself pronounce the word.

"I *thought* it said 'Paget,'" I gasped, "but I wanted to know if you thought so too."

"Yes, it's Paget plain enough," said father, but he acted like there was every possibility that it might change to Jones any minute. "It says 'Paget,' plain as print."

"Father!" I cried, clutching his arm, "father, see how fat it is! There must be pages and pages! Father, it wouldn't take all that to tell her he didn't like her, and he never wanted to see her again. Would it, father?"

"It doesn't seem probable," said father.

"Father, don't you think it means there's been some big mistake, and it takes so much to tell how it can be fixed?"

"It seems reasonable."

I gripped him tighter, and maybe shook him a little.

"Father!" I cried. "Father, doesn't it just look *hurry,* all over? Can't you speed up a little? They have all day to cool off. Oh father, won't you speed a little?"

"That I will!" said father. "Get a tight hold, and pray God it is good word we carry."

"But I prayed the one big prayer to get this," I said. "It wouldn't be sent if it wasn't good. The thing to do now is to thank the Lord for 'all his loving kindnesses,' like mother said. Drive father! Make them go!"

At first he only touched them up; I couldn't see that we were getting home so fast; but in a minute a cornfield passed like a streak, a piece of woods flew by a dark blur, a bridge never had time to rattle, and we began to rock from side to side a little. Then I gripped the top supports with one hand, the mail with the other, and hung on for dear life. I took one good look at father.

His feet were on the brace, the lines looked as if he pushed against strips of wood, his face was clear, even white, his eyes steely, and he never moved a muscle. When Jo thought it was funny, that he was loose in the pasture, and kicked up a little behind, father gave him a sharp cut with the whip and said: "Steady boy! Get along there!"

Sometimes he said, "Aye, aye! Easy!" but he never stopped a mite. We whizzed past the church and cemetery, and scarcely touched the Big Hill. People ran to their doors, even to the yards, and I was sure they thought we were having a runaway, but we were not, we were just "Up Joris—I galloped, we galloped," only there were two of us, it was plain running in harness that we were doing, and from our hearts we hoped that it was *"good news"* we were carrying. Father began to stop at the lane gate, he pulled all the way past the garden, and it was as much as he could do to get them slowed down so that I could jump out by the time we reached the hitching rack. He tied them, and followed me into the house instead of going to the barn. I ran ahead calling: "Shelley! Where is Shelley?"

"What in this world has happened, child?" asked mother, catching my arm.

"Her letter has come! Her Paget letter! The one *you* looked for until you gave up. It's come at last! Oh, where is she?"

"Be calmer, child, you'll frighten her," said mother.

May snatched the letter from my fingers and began to read all that was on it aloud. I burst out crying.

"Make her give that back!" I sobbed to father. "It's mine! I found it. Father, make her let me take it!"

"Give it to her!" said father. "I rather feel that it is her right to deliver it."

May passed it back, but she looked so disappointed, that by how she felt I knew how much I wanted to take it myself; so I reached my hand to her and said: "You can come along! We'll both take it! Oh where is she?"

"She went down in the orchard," said mother. "I think probably she's gone back where she was the other day."

Gee, but we ran! And there she was! As we came up, she heard us and turned.

"Shelley!" I cried. "Here's your letter! Everything is all right! He's coming, Shelley! Look quick, and see when! Mother will want to begin baking right away!"

Shelley looked at me, and said coolly: "Paddy Ryan! What's the matter?"

"Your letter!" I cried, shoving it right against her hands. "Your letter from Robert! From the Paget man, you know! I *told* you he was coming! Hurry, and see when!"

She took it, and sat there staring at it, so much like father, that it made me think of him, so I saw that she was going to have to come around to it as we did, and that one couldn't hurry her. She just had to take her time to sense it.

"Shall I open it for you?" I asked, merely to make her see that it was time she was doing it herself.

Blest if she didn't reach it toward me!—sort of woodenlike. I stuck my finger under the flap, gave it a rip across and emptied what was inside into her lap. Bet there were six or seven letters in queer yellow envelopes I never before had seen any like, and on them was the name, Robert Paget, while in one corner it said, "Returned Dead Letter;" also there was a loose folded white sheet. She sat staring at the heap, touching one, another, and repeating "Robert Paget?" as she picked each up in turn.

"What do you suppose it means?" she asked May.

May examined them.

"You must read the loose sheet," she advised. "No doubt that will explain."

But Shelley never touched it. She handled those letters and stared at them. Father and mother came through the orchard and stood together behind us, so father knelt down at last, reached across Shelley's shoulder, picked one up and looked at it.

"Have you good word, dear?" asked mother of Shelley.

"Why, I don't understand at all," said Shelley. "Just look at all these queer letters, addressed to Mr. Paget. Why should they be sent to me? I mustn't open them. They're not mine. There must be some mistake."

"These are *dead letters,*" said father. "They've been written to you, couldn't be delivered, and so were sent to the Dead Letter Office at Washington, which returned them to the writer, and unopened he has forwarded them once more to you. You've heard of dead letters, haven't you?"

"I suppose so," said Shelley. "I don't remember just now; but there couldn't be a better name. They've come mighty near killing me."

"If you'd only read that note!" urged May, putting it right into her fingers.

Shelley still sat there.

"I'm afraid of it," she said exactly like I'd have spoken if there had been a big rattlesnake coming right at me, when I'd nothing at hand to bruise it.

Laddie and Leon came from the barn. They had heard me calling, seen May and me run, and then father and mother coming down, so they walked over.

"What's up?" asked Leon. "Has Uncle Levi's will been discovered, and does mother get his Mexican mines?"

"What have you got, Shelley?" asked Laddie, kneeling beside her, and picking up one of the yellow letters.

"I hardly know," said Shelley.

"I brought her a big letter with all those little ones and a note in it, and they are from the Paget man," I explained to him. "But she won't even read the note, and see what he writes. She says she's afraid."

"Poor child! No wonder!" said Laddie, sitting beside her and putting his arm around her. "Suppose I read it for you. May I?"

"Yes," said Shelley. "You read it. Read it out loud. I don't care."

She leaned against him, while he unfolded the white sheet.

"Umph!" he said. "This *does* look bad for you. It begins: 'My own darling Girl.'"

"Let me see!" cried Shelley, suddenly straightening, and reaching her hand.

Laddie held the page toward her, but she only looked, she didn't offer to touch it.

"'My own darling Girl:'" repeated Laddie tenderly, making it mean just all he possibly could, because he felt so dreadfully sorry for her—"'On my return to Chicago, from the trip to England I have so often told you I intended to make some time soon —'"

"Did he?" asked mother.

"Yes," answered Shelley. "He couldn't talk about much else. It was his first case. It was for a friend of his who had been robbed of everything in the world; honour, relatives, home, and money. If Robert won it, he got all that back for his friend and enough for himself—that he could—a home of his own, you know! Read on, Laddie!"

"'I was horrified to find on my desk every letter I had written you during my absence returned to me from the Dead Letter Office, as you see.'"

"Good gracious!" cried mother, picking up one and clutching it tight as if she meant to see that it didn't get away again.

"Go on!" cried Shelley.

"'I am enclosing some of them as they came back to me, in proof of my statement. I drove at once to your boarding place and found you had not been there for weeks, and your landlady was distinctly crabbed. Then I went to the college, only to find that you had fallen ill and gone to your home. That threw me into torments, and all that keeps me from taking the first train is the thought that perhaps you refused to accept these letters, for some reason. Shelley, you did not, did you? There is some mistake somewhere, is there not —'"

"One would be led to think so," said father sternly. "Seems as if he might have managed some way —"

"Don't you blame him!" cried Shelley. "Can't you see it's all my fault? He'd been coming regularly, and the other girls envied me; then he just disappeared, and there was no word or anything, and they laughed and whispered until I couldn't endure it; so I moved in with Peter's cousin, as I wrote you; but that left Mrs. Fleet with an empty room in the middle of the term, and it made her hopping mad. I bet anything she wouldn't give the postman my new address, to pay me back. I left it, of course. But if I'd been half a woman, and had the confidence I should have had in myself and in him — Oh how I've suffered, and punished all of you —!"

"Never you mind about that," said mother, stroking Shelley's hair. "Likely there isn't much in Chicago to give a girl who never had been away from her family before, 'confidence' in herself or any one else. As for him,—just disappearing like that, without a word or even a line— Go on Laddie!"

"'Surely, you knew that I was only waiting the outcome of this trip to tell you how dearly I love you. Surely, you encouraged me in thinking you cared for me a little, Shelley. Only a little will do to begin with —'"

"You see, I *did* have something to go on!" cried Shelley, wiping her eyes and straightening up.

"'No doubt you misunderstood and resented my going without coming to explain, and bid you good-bye in person, but Shelley, *I simply dared not.* You see, it was this way: I got a cable about the case I was always talking of, and the only man who could give the testimony I *must have* was dying!'"

"For land's sake! The poor boy!" cried mother, patting Shelley's shoulder.

"'An hour's delay might mean the loss of everything in the world to me, even you. For if I lost any time, and the man escaped me, there was no hope of winning my case, and everything, even you, as I said before, depended on him —'"

"Good Lord! I mean land!" cried Leon.

"'If I could catch the train in an hour, I could take a boat at New York, and go straight through with no loss of time. So I wrote you a note that probably said more than I would have ventured in person, and paid a boy to deliver it.'"

"Kept the money and tore up the note, I bet!" said May.

"'I wrote on the train, but found after sailing that I had rushed so I had failed to post it in New York. I kept on writing every day on the boat, and mailed you six at Liverpool. All the time I have written frequently; there are many more here that this envelope will not hold, that I shall save until I hear from you.'"

"Well, well!" said father.

"'Shelley, I beat death, reached my man, got the testimony I had to have, and won my case.'"

"Glory!" cried mother. "Praise the Lord!"

"'Then I scoured England, and part of the continent, hunting some interested parties; and when I was so long finding them, and still no word came from you, I decided to come back and get you, if you would come with me, and go on with the work together.'"

"Listen to that! More weddings!" cried Leon. He dropped on his knees before Shelley. "'Will you marry me, my pretty maid?'" he begged.

"Young man, if you cut any capers right now, I'll cuff your ears!" cried father. "This is no proper time for your foolishness!"

"'Shelley, I beg that you will believe me, and if you care for me in the very least, telegraph if I may come. Quick! I'm half insane to see you. I have many things to tell you, first of all how dear you are to me. Please telegraph. Robert.'"

"Saddle a horse, Leon!" father cried as he unstrapped his wallet. "Laddie, take down her message."

"Can you put it into ten words?" asked Laddie.

"Mother, what would you say?" questioned Shelley.

Leon held up his fingers and curled down one with each word. "Say, 'Dear Robert. Well and happy. Come when you get ready.' "

"But then I won't know when he's coming," objected Shelley.

"You don't need to," said Leon. "You can take it for granted from that epistolary effusion that he won't let the grass grow under his feet while coming here. That's a bully message! It sounds as if you weren't crazy over him, and it's a big compliment to mother. Looks as if she didn't have to know when people are coming—like she's ready all the time."

"Write it out and let me see," said Shelley.

So Laddie wrote it, and she looked at it a long time, it seemed to me, at last she said: "I don't like that 'get.' It doesn't sound right. Wouldn't 'are' be better?"

"Come when you are ready," repeated Laddie. "Yes, that's better. 'Get' sounds rather saucy."

"Why not put it, 'Come when you choose?'" suggested mother. "That will leave you a word to spare, so it won't look as if you had counted them and used exactly ten on purpose, and it doesn't sound as if you expected him to make long preparations, like the other. That will leave it with him to start whenever he likes."

"Yes! yes!" cried Shelley. "That's much better! Say, 'Come when you choose!'"

"Right!" said Laddie as he wrote it. "Now I'll take this!"

"Oh no you won't!" cried Leon. "Father told me to saddle my horse. She's got enough speed in her to beat yours a mile. I take that! Didn't you say for me to saddle, father?"

"Such important business, I think I better," said Laddie, and Leon began to cry.

"I think you should both go," said Shelley. "It is so important, and if one goes to make a mistake, maybe the other will notice it."

"Yes, that's the best way," said mother.

"Yes, both go," said father.

It was like one streak when they went up the Big Hill. Father shook his head. "Poor judgment—that," he said. "Never run a horse up hill!"

"But they're in such a hurry," Shelley reminded him.

"So they are," said father. "In this case I might have broken the rule myself. Now come all of you, and let the child get at her mail."

"But I want you to stay," said Shelley. "I'm so addle-pated this morning. I need my family to help me."

"Of course you do, child," said mother. "Families were made to cling together, and stand by each other in every circumstance of life—joy or sorrow. Of course you need your family."

May began sorting the letters by dates so Shelley could start on the one that had been written first. Father ran his knife across the top of each, and cut all the envelopes, and Shelley took out the first and read it; that was the train one. In it he told her about sending the boy with the note again, and explained more about how it was so very important for him to hurry, because the only man who could help him was so sick. We talked it over, and all of us thought the boy had kept the money and torn up the note. Father said the way would have been to send the note and pay the boy when he came back; but Shelley said Mr. Paget would have been gone before the boy got back, so father saw that wouldn't have been the way, in such a case.

Next she read one written on the boat. He told more about sending the boy; how he loved her, what it would mean to both of them if he got the evidence he wanted and won his first case; and how much it would bring his friend. The next one told it all over again, and more. In that he wrote a little about the ocean, the people on board the ship, and he gave Shelley the name of the place where he was going and begged her to write to him. He told her if the ship he was on passed another, they were going to stop and send back the mail. He begged her to write often, and to say that she forgave him for starting away without seeing her, as he had been forced to.

The next one was the same thing over, only a little more yet. In the last he had reached England, the important man was still living, but he was almost gone, and Mr. Paget took two good witnesses, all the evidence he had, and went to see him; and the man saw it was no use, so he made a statement, and Robert had it all written out, signed and witnessed. For the real straight sense there was in that letter, I could have done as well myself. It was a wild jumble, because Robert was so crazy over having the evidence that would win his case; and he told Shelley that now he was perfectly free to love her all she would allow him. He said he had to stay a while longer to find his friend's people so they would get back their share of the money, but it was not going to be easy to locate them. You wouldn't think the world so big, but maybe it seemed smaller to me because as far as I could see from the top of our house, was all I knew about it. After Shelley had read the letters, and the note again, father heaved a big sigh that seemed to come clear from his boot soles and he said: "Well Shelley, it looks to me as if you had found a *man*. Seems to me that's a mighty important case for a young lawyer to be trusted with, in a first effort."

"Yes, but it was for Robert's best friend, and only think, he has won!"

"I don't see how he could have done better if he'd been old as Methuselah, and wise as Solomon," boasted mother.

"But he hasn't found the people who must have back their money," said May. "He will have to go to England again. And he wants to take you, Shelley. My! You'll get to sail on a big steamer, cross the Atlantic Ocean, and see London. Maybe you'll even get a peep at the Queen!"

Shelley was busy making a little heap of her letters; when the top one slid off I reached over and put it back for her. She looked straight at me, and smiled the most wonderful and the most beautiful smile I ever saw on any one's face, so I said to her: "You see! I *told* you he was coming!"

"I can't understand it!" said Shelley.

"You *know* I told you."

"Of course I do! But what made you think so?"

"That was the answer. Just that he was coming."

"What are you two talking about?" asked mother.

Shelley looked at me, and waited for me to tell mother as much as I wanted to, of what had happened. But I didn't think things like that were to be talked about before every one, so I just said: "Oh nothing! Only, I told Shelley this very morning that the Paget man was coming soon, and that everything was going to be all right."

"You did? Well of all the world! I can't see why."

"Oh something told me! I just *felt* that way."

"More of that Fairy nonsense?" asked father sharply.

"No. I didn't get that from the Fairies."

"Well, never mind!" said Shelley, rising, because she saw that I had told all I wanted to. "Little Sister *did* tell me this morning that he was coming, that everything would be made right, and it's the queerest thing, but instantly I believed her. Didn't I sing all morning, mother? The first note since Robert didn't come when I expected him in Chicago, weeks ago."

"Yes," said mother. "That's a wonderfully strange thing. I can't see what made you think so."

"Anyway, I did!" I said. "Now let's go have dinner. I'm starving."

I caught May's hand, and ran to get away from them. Father and mother walked one on each side of Shelley, while with both hands she held her letters before her. When we reached the house we just talked about them all the time. Pretty soon the boys were back, and then they told about sending the telegram. Leon vowed he gave the operator a dime extra to start that message with a shove, so it would go faster.

"It will go all right," said Laddie, "and how it will go won't be a circumstance to the way he'll come. If there's anything we ought to do, before he gets here, we should hustle. Chicago isn't a thousand miles away. That message can reach him by two o'clock, it's probable he has got ready while he was waiting, so he will start on the first train our way. He could reach Groveville on the ten, to-morrow. We better meet it."

"Yes, we'll meet it," said mother. "Is the carriage perfectly clean?"

Father said: "It must be gone over. Our general manager here ordered me to speed up, and we drove a little coming from town."

Mother went to planning what else should be done.

"Don't do anything!" cried Shelley. "The house is all right. There's no need to work and worry into a sweat. He won't notice or care how things look."

"I miss my guess if he doesn't notice and care very much indeed," said mother emphatically. "Men are not blind. No one need think they don't see when things are not as they should be, just because they're not cattish enough to let you know it, like a woman always does. Shelley, wouldn't you like to ride over and spend the afternoon with the Princess?"

"Nope!" said Shelley. "It's her turn to come to see me. Besides, you don't get me out of the way like that. I know what you'll do here, and I intend to help."

"Do you need one of the boys at the house?" asked father, and if you'll believe it, both of them wanted to stay.

Father said he must have one to help wash the carriage and do a little fixing around the barn; so he took Leon, but he didn't like to go. He said: "I don't see what all this fuss is about, anyway. Probably he'll be another Peter."

Shelley looked at him: "Oh Mr. Paget isn't nearly so large as Peter," she said, "and his hair is whiter than yours, while his eyes are not so blue."

"Saints preserve us!" cried Leon. "Come on, father, let's only dust the carriage! He's not worth washing it for."

"Is he like that?" asked mother anxiously.

"Wait and see!" said Shelley. "Looks don't make a man. He has proved what he can do."

Then all of us went to work. Before night we were hunting over the yard, and beside the road, to see if we could find anything to pick up. Six chickens were in the cellar, father was to bring meat and a long list of groceries from town in the morning. He was to start early, get them before train time, put them under the back seat, and take them out after he drove into the lane, when he came back. That made a little more trouble for father, but there was not the slightest necessity for making Mr. Paget feel that he had ridden in a delivery wagon.

Next morning I wakened laughing softly, because some one was fussing with my hair, patting my face, and kissing me, so I put up my arms and pulled that loving person down on my pillow, and gave back little half-asleep kisses, and slept on; but it was Shelley, and she gently shook me and began repeating that fool old thing I have been waked up with half the mornings of my life:

"Get up, Little Sister, the morning is bright,
The birds are all singing to welcome the light,
Get up; for when all things are merry and glad.,
Good children should never be lazy and sad;
For God gives us daylight, dear sister, that we
May rejoice like the lark and work like the bee."

Usually I'd have gone on sleeping, but Shelley was so sweet and lovely, and she kissed me so hard, that I remembered it was going to be a most exciting day, so I came to quick as snap and jumped right up, for I didn't want to miss a single thing that might happen.

The carriage was shining when it came to the gate, so was father. I thought there was going to be a vacant seat beside him, and I asked if I might go along. He said: "Yes, if mother says so." He always would stick that in. So I ran to ask her, and she didn't care, if Shelley made no objections. I was just starting to find her, when here she came, all shining too, but Laddie was with her. I hadn't known that he was going, and I was so disappointed I couldn't help crying.

"What's the matter?" asked Shelley.

"Father and mother both said I might go, if you didn't care."

"Why, I'm dreadfully sorry," said Shelley, "but I have several things I want Laddie to do for me."

Laddie stooped down to kiss me good-bye and he said: "Don't cry, Little Sister. The way to be happy is to be good."

Then they drove to Groveville, and we had to wait. But there was so much to do, it made us fly to get all of it finished. So mother sent Leon after Mrs. Freshett to help in the kitchen, while Candace wore her white dress, and waited on the table. Mother cut flowers for the dining table, and all through the house. She left the blinds down to keep the rooms cool, chilled buttermilk to drink, and if she didn't think of every single, least little thing, I couldn't see what it was. Then all of us put on our best dresses. Mother looked as glad and sweet as any girl, when she sat to rest a little while. I didn't dare climb the catalpa in my white dress, so I watched from the horse block, and when I saw the grays come over the top of the hill, I ran to tell. As mother went to the gate, she told May and me to walk behind, to stay back until we were spoken to, and then to keep our heads level, and remember our manners. I don't know where Leon went. He said he lost all interest when he found there was to be another weak-eyed towhead in the family, and I guess he was in earnest about it, because he wasn't even curious enough to be at the gate when Mr. Paget came.

Father stopped with a flourish, Laddie hurried around and helped Shelley, and then Mr. Paget stepped down. Goodness, gracious, sakes alive! Little? Towhead? He was taller than Laddie. His hair was most as black as ink, and wavy. His eyes were big and dark; he was broad and strong and there was the cleanest, freshest look about him. He put his arm spang around Shelley, right there in the road, and mother said: "Hold there! Not so fast, young man! I haven't given my consent to that."

He laughed, and he said: "Yes, but you'ah going to!" And he put his other arm around mother, so May and I crowded up, and we had a family reunion right between the day lilies and the snowball bush. We went into the house, and he *liked* us, his room, and everything went exactly right. He was crazy about the cold buttermilk, and while he was drinking it Leon walked into the dining room, because he thought of course Mr. Paget and Shelley would be on the davenport in the parlour. When he saw Robert he said lowlike to Shelley: "Didn't Mr. Paget come? Who's that?"

Shelley looked so funny for a minute, then she remembered what she had told him and she just laughed as she said: "Mr. Paget, this is my brother."

Robert went to shake hands, and Leon said right to his teeth: "Well a divil of a towhead you are!"

"Towhead?" said Robert, bewildered-like.

"Shelley said you were a little bit of a man, with watery blue eyes, and whiter hair than mine."

"Oh I say!" cried Robert. "She must have been stringin' you!"

Leon just whooped; because while Mr. Paget didn't talk like the 'orse, 'ouse people, he made you think of them in the way he said things, and the sound of his voice. Then we had dinner, and I don't remember that we ever had quite such a feast before. Mother had put on every single flourish she knew. She used her very best dishes, and linen, and no cook anywhere could beat Candace alone; now she had Mrs. Freshett to help her, and mother also. If she tried to show Mr. Paget, she did it! No visitor was there except him, but we must have been at the table two hours talking, and eating from one dish after another. Candace *liked* to wear her white dress, and carry things around, and they certainly were good.

And talk! Father, Laddie, and Robert talked over all creation. Every once in a while when mother saw an opening, she put in her paddle, and no one could be quicker, when she watched sharp and was trying to make a good impression. Shelley was very quiet; she scarcely spoke or touched that delicious food. Once the Paget man turned to her, looking at her so fondlike, as she picked up one of her sauce dishes and her spoon and wanted to feed her. And he said: "Heah child, eat your dinnah! You have nawthing to be fussed ovah! I mean to propose to you, and your parents befowr night. That is what I am heah for."

Every one laughed so, Shelley never got the bite; but after that she perked up more and ate a little by herself.

At last father couldn't stand it any longer, so he began asking Robert about his trip to England, and the case he had won. When the table was cleared for dessert, Mr. Paget asked mother to have

Candace to bring his satchel. He opened it and spread papers all over, so that father and Laddie could see the evidence, while he told them how it was.

It seemed there was a law in England, all of us knew about it, because father often had explained it. This law said that a man who had lots of money and land must leave almost all of it to his eldest son; and the younger ones must go into law, the army, be clergymen, or enter trade and earn a living, while the eldest kept up the home place. Then he left it to his eldest son, and his other boys had to work for a living. It kept the big estates together; but my! it was hard on the younger sons, and no one seemed even to think about the daughters. I never heard them mentioned.

Now there was a very rich man; he had only two sons, and each of them married, and had one son. The younger son died, and sent his boy for his elder brother to take care of. He pretended to be good, but for sure, he was bad as ever he could be. He knew that if his cousin were out of the way, all that land and money would be his when his uncle died. So he went to work and he tried for years, and a lawyer man who had no conscience at all, helped him. At last when they had done everything they could think of, they took a lot of money and put it in the pocket of the son they wanted to ruin; then when his father missed the money, and the house was filled with policemen, detectives, and neighbours, the bad man said he'd feel more comfortable to have the family searched too, merely as a formality, so he stepped out and was gone over, and when the son's turn came, there was the money on him! That made him a public disgrace to his family, and a criminal who couldn't inherit the estate, and his father went raving mad and tried to kill him, so he had to run away. At first he didn't care what he did, so he came over here. Robert said that man was his best friend, and as men went, he was a decent fellow, so he cheered him up all he could, and went to work with all his might to prove he was innocent, and to get back his family, and his money for him.

When Robert had enough evidence that he was almost ready to start to England, his man got a cable from an old friend of his father's who always had believed in him, and it said that the bad man was dying—to come quick. So Robert went all of a sudden, like the Dead Letters told about. Now, he described how he reached there, took the old friend of the father of his friend with him, and other witnesses, and all the evidence he had, and went to see the sick man. When Robert showed him what he could prove, the bad man said it was no use, he had to die in a few days, so he might as well go with a clean conscience, and he told about everything he had done. Robert had it all written out, signed and sworn to. He told about all of it, and then he said to father: "Have I made it clear to you?"

Leon was so excited he forgot all the manners he ever had, for he popped up before father could open his head and cried: "Clear as mud! I got that son business so plain in my mind, I'd know the party of the first part, from the party of the second part, if I met him promenading on the Stone Wall of China!"

Father and Laddie knew so much law they asked dozens of questions; but that Robert man wasn't a smidgin behind, for every clip he had the answer ready, and then he could go on and tell much more than he had been asked. He said as a Case, it was a pretty thing to work on; but it was much more than a case to him, because he always had known that his friend was not guilty; that he was separated from his family, suffering terribly under the disgrace, and they must be also. He had worked for life for his friend, because the whole thing meant so much to both of them. He said he must go back soon and finish up a little more that he should have done while he was there, if it hadn't been that he received no word from Shelley.

"When I didn't heah from heh for so long, and wrote so many letters, and had no reply, I thought possibly some gay 'young Lochinvah had come out from the west,' and taken my sweet-'eart," he said, "and while I had my armour on, I made up my mind that I'd give him a fight too. I didn't propose to lose Shelley, if it were in my powah to win heh. I hadn't been able to say to heh exactly what I desiahed, on account of getting a start alone in this country; but if I won this case, I would have ample means. When I secuahed the requiahed evidence, I couldn't wait to finish, so I came straight over, to make sure of heh."

He arose and handed the satchel to father.

"I notice you have a very good looking gun convenient," he

said. "Would you put these papahs where you consider them safe until I'm ready to return. Our home, our living, and the honah of a man are there, and we are mighty particular about that bag, are we not, Shelley?"

"Well I should think we are!" cried Shelley. "For goodness sake, father, hang to it! Is the man still living? Could you get that evidence over again?"

"He was alive when I left, but the doctors said ten days would be his limit, so he may be gone befowr this."

Father picked up the satchel, set it on his knees, and stroked it as if it were alive.

"Well! Well!" he said. "Now would any one think such a little thing could contain so much?"

Shelley leaned toward Robert.

"Your friend!" she cried. "Your friend! What *did* he say to you? What did he *do?*"

"Well, for a time he was wildly happy ovah having the stain removed from his honah, and knowing that he would have his family and faw'tn back; but there is an extremely sad feature to his case that is not yet settled, so he must keep his head level until we work that out. Now about that hoss you wanted to show me—" he turned to Leon.

Mother gave the signal, and we left the table. Father carried the satchel to his chest, made room for it, locked it in and put the key in his pocket. Then our men started to the barn to show the Arab-Kentucky horse. Mr. Paget went to Shelley and took her in his arms exactly like Peter did Sally before the parlour door that time when I got into trouble, and he looked at mother and laughed as he said: "I hope you will excuse me, but I've been having a very nawsty, anxious time, and I cawn't conform to the rules for a few days, until I become accustomed to the fawct that Shelley is not lost to me. It was beastly when I reached Chicago, had back all my letters, and found she had gone home ill. I've much suffering to recompense. I'll atone for a small portion immediately."

He lifted Shelley right off the floor—that's how big and strong he was—he hugged her tight, and kissed her forehead, cheeks, and eyes.

"When I've gone through the fahmality of asking your parents for you, and they have said a gracious 'yes,' I'll put the fust one on your lips," he said, setting her down carefully. "In the meantime, you be fixing your mouth to say, 'yes,' also, when I propose to you, because it's coming befowr you sleep."

Shelley was like a peach blossom. She reached up and touched his cheek, while she looked at mother all smiling, and sparkling, as she said: "You see!"

Mother smiled back.

"I do, indeed!" she answered.

Leon pulled Mr. Paget's sleeve.

"Aw quit lally-gaggin' and come see a real horse," he said.

Robert put his other arm around Leon, drew him to his side and hugged him as if he were a girl. "I'm so glad Shelley has a lawge family," he said. "Big families are jolly. I'm so proud of all the brothers I'm going to have. I was the only boy at home."

"You haven't told us about your family," said mother.

"No," said Robert, "but I intend to. I have a family! One of the finest on uth. We'll talk about them after this hoss is inspected."

He let Shelley go and walked away, his arm still around Leon. Shelley ran to mother and both of them sobbed out loud.

"Now you see how it was!" she said.

"You poor child!" cried mother. "Indeed I *do* see how it was. You've been a brave girl. A good, brave girl! Father and I are mighty proud of you!"

"Oh mother! I thought you were ashamed of me!" sobbed Shelley.

"Oh my child!" said mother quavery-like. "Oh my child! You surely see that none of us could understand, as we do now."

She patted Shelley, and told her to run upstairs and lie down for a while, because she was afraid she would be sick.

"We mustn't have a pale, tired girl right now," said mother.

"Well!" said Shelley, but she just stood there holding mother.

"Well?" said mother gripping her.

"You see!" said Shelley.

"Child," said mother, "I *do* see! I see six feet of as handsome manhood as I ever have seen anywhere. His manner is perfect, and I find his speech most attractive. I am delighted with him. I do see indeed! Your father is quite as proud and pleased as I am. Now go to bed."

Shelley held up her lips, and then went. I ran to the barn, where the men were standing in the shade, while Leon led his horse up and down before them, told about its pedigree, its record, how he came to have it. The Paget man stood there looking and listening gravely, as he studied the horse. At last he went over her, and Gee! but he knew horse! Then Laddie brought out Flos and they talked all about her, and then went into the barn. Father opened the east doors to show how much land he had, which were his lines; and while the world didn't look quite so pretty as it had in May, still it was good enough. Then they went into the orchard, sat under the trees and began talking about business conditions. That was so dry I went back to the house. And maybe I didn't strike something interesting there!

As I came up the orchard path to the back yard gate, I saw a carriage at the hitching rack in front of the house, so I took a peep and almost fell over. It was the one the Princess had come to Sally's wedding in; so I knew she was in the house visiting Shelley. I went to the parlour and there I had another shock; for lo and behold! in our big rocking chair, and looking as well as any one, so far as you could see—of course you can't see heart trouble, though—sat Mrs. Pryor. The Princess and mother were there, all of them talking, laughing and having the best time, while on the davenport enjoying himself as much as any one, was Mr. Pryor. They talked about everything, and it was easy to see that the Pryor door was *open* so far as we were concerned, anyway. Mrs. Pryor was just as nice and friendly as she could be, and so was he. Shelley sat beside him, and he pinched her cheek and said: "Something seems to make you especially brilliant to-day, young woman!"

Shelley flushed redder, laughed, and glanced at mother, so she said: "Shelley is having a plain old-fashioned case of beau. She met a young man in Chicago last fall and he's here now to ask our consent. All of us are quite charmed with him. That's why she's so happy."

Then the Princess sprang up and kissed Shelley, so did Mrs. Pryor, while such a chatter you never heard. No one could repeat what they said, for as many as three talked at the same time.

"Oh do let's have a double wedding!" cried the Princess when the excitement was over a little. "I think it would be great fun; do let's! When are you planning for?"

"Nothing is settled yet," said Shelley. "We've had no time to talk!"

"Mercy!" cried the Princess. "Go make your arrangements quickly! Hurry up, then come over, and we'll plan for the same time. It will be splendid! Don't you think that would be fine, Mrs. Stanton?"

"I can't see any objections to it," said mother.

"Where is your young man? I'm crazy to see him," cried the Princess. "If you have gone and found a better looking one than mine, I'll never speak to you again."

"She hasn't!" said Mrs. Pryor calmly, like that settled it. I like her. "They're not made!"

"I am not so sure of that," said Shelley proudly. "Mother, isn't my man quite as good looking, and as nice in every way, as Laddie?"

"Fully as handsome, and so far as can be seen in such a short time, quite as fine," said mother.

I was perfectly amazed at her; as if any man could be!

"I don't believe it, I won't stand it, and I shan't go home until I have seen for myself!" cried the Princess, laughing, and yet it sounded as if she were half-provoked, and I knew I was. The Paget man was all right, but I wasn't going to lose my head over him. Laddie was the finest, of course!

"Well, he's somewhere on the place with our men, this minute," said Shelley, "but you stay for supper, and meet him."

"When you haven't your arrangements made yet! You surely are unselfish! Of course I won't do that, but I'd love to have one little peep, then you bring him and come over to-morrow, so all of us can become acquainted, and indeed, I'm really in earnest about a double wedding."

"Go see where the men are," said Shelley to me.

I went to the back door, and their heads were bobbing far down in the orchard.

"They're under the greening apple tree," I reported.

"If you will excuse us," said Shelley to Mr. and Mrs. Pryor, "we'll walk down a few minutes and prove that I'm right."

"Don't stay," said Mrs. Pryor. "This trip is so unusual for me that I'm quite tired. For a first venture, in such a long time, I think I've done well. But now I'm beginning to feel I should go home."

"Go straight along," said the Princess. "I'll walk across the fields, or Thomas can come back after me."

So Mr. and Mrs. Pryor went away, while the Princess, Shelley, May, and I walked through the orchard toward the men. They were standing on the top of the hill looking over the meadow, and talking with such interest they didn't hear us or turn until Shelley said: "Mr. Paget, I want to present you to Laddie's betrothed—Miss Pamela Pryor."

He swung around, finishing what he was saying as he turned, the Princess took a swift step toward him, then, at the same time, both of them changed to solid tombstone, and stood staring, and so did all of us, while no one made a sound. At last the Paget man drew a deep, quivery breath and sort of shook himself as he gazed at her.

"Why, Pam!" he cried. "Darling Pam, cawn it possibly be you?"

If you ever heard the scream of a rabbit when the knives of a reaper cut it to death, why that's exactly the way she cried out. She covered her eyes with her hands. He drew back and smiled, the red rushed into his face, and he began to be alive again. Laddie went to the Princess and took her hands.

"What does this mean?" he begged.

She pulled away from him, and went to the Paget man slowly, her big eyes wild and strained.

"Robert!" she cried. "Robert! how did you get here? Were you hunting us?"

"All ovah England, yes," he said. "Not heah! I came heah to see Shelley. But you? How do you happen to be in this country?"

"We've lived on adjoining land for two years!"

"You moved heah! To escape the pity of our friends?"

"Father moved! Mother and I had no means, and no refuge. We were forced. We never believed it! Oh Robert, we never—not for a minute! Oh Robert, say you never did it!"

"Try our chawming cousin Emmet your next guess!"

"That devil! Oh that devil!"

She cried out that hurt way again, so he took her tight in his arms; but sure as ever Laddie was my brother, he was hers, so that was all right. When they were together you wondered why in this world you hadn't thought of it the instant you saw him alone. They were like as two peas. They talked exactly the same, only he sounded much more so, probably from having just been in England for weeks, while in two years she had grown a little as we were. We gazed at them, open-mouthed, like as not, and no one said a word.

At last Mr. Paget looked over the Princess' shoulder at father and said: "I can explain this, Mr. Stanton, in a very few wuds. *I am my friend. The case was my own. The evidence I secuahed was for myself. This is my only sisteh. Heh people are mine —*"

"The relationship is apparent," said father. "There is a striking likeness between you and your sister, and I can discern traces of your parents in your face, speech and manner."

"If you know my father," said Robert, "then you undehstand what happened to me when I was found with his money on my pehson, in the presence of our best friends and the police. He went raving insane on the instant, and he would have killed me if he hadn't been prevented; he tried to; has he changed any since, Pam?"

The Princess was clinging to him with both hands, staring at him, wonder, joy, and fear all on her lovely face.

"Worse!" she cried. "He's much worse! The longer he broods, the more mother grieves, the bitterer he becomes. Mr. Stanton, he is always armed. He'll shoot on sight. Oh what shall we do?"

"Miss Pamela," said Leon, "did your man Thomas know your brother in England?"

"All his life."

"Well, then, we'd better be doing something quick. He tied the horses and was walking up and down the road while he waited, and he saw us plainly when we crossed the wood yard a while ago. He followed us and stared so, I couldn't help noticing him."

"Jove!" cried Robert. "I must have seen him in the village this morning. A man reminded me of him, then I remembered how like people of his type are, and concluded I was mistaken. Mr. Stanton, you have agreed that the evidence I hold is sufficient. Pam cawn tell you that while I don't deny being full of tricks as a

boy they weh not dirty, not low, and while father always taking
Emmet's paht against me drove me to recklessness sometimes, I
nevah did anything underhand or disgraceful. She knows what
provocation I had, and exactly what happened. Let heh tell you!"

"I don't feel that I require any further information," said father.
"You see, I happen to be fairly well acquainted with Mr. Pryor."

"Pryor?"

"He made us use that name here," explained the Princess.

"Well, his name is Paget!" said Robert angrily.

Laddie told me long ago he didn't believe it was Pryor.

"Then, if you are acquainted with my father, what would you
counsel? Unless I'm prepahed to furnish the central figyah of
interest in a funeral, I dare not meet him, until he has seen this
evidence, had time to digest it, and calm himself."

Shelley caught him by the arm. No wonder! She hadn't been
proposed to, or even had a kiss on her lips. She pulled him.

"You come straight to the house," she said. "Thomas may tell
your father he thought he saw you."

That was about as serious as anything could be, but nothing
ever stopped Leon. He sidled away from father, repeating in a low
voice:

"For sore dismayed, through storm and shade
  His child he did discover;
One lovely hand she stretched for aid,
  And one was round her lover—"

Shelley just looked daggers at him, but she was too anxious to
waste any time.

"Would Thomas tell your father?" she asked the Princess.

"The instant he saw him alone, yes. He wouldn't before
mother."

"Hold one minute!" cried father. "We must think of our mother,
just a little. Shelley, you and the girls run up and explain how this
is. Better all of you go to the house, except Mr. Paget. He'll be safe
here as anywhere. Mr. Pryor will stop there, if he comes. So it
would be best for you to keep out of sight, Robert, until I have had
a little talk with him."

"I'll stay here," I offered. "We'll sit and talk until you get Mr. Pryor cooled off. He can be awful ragesome when he's excited, and it doesn't take much to start him."

"You're right about that!" agreed Robert.

So we sat under the greening and were having a fine visit while the others went to break the news gently to mother that the Pryor mystery had gone up higher than Gilderoy's kite. My! but she'd be glad! It would save her many a powerful prayer. I was telling Robert all about the time his father visited us, and what my mother said to him, and he said: "She'd be the one to talk with him now. Possibly he'd listen to her, until he got it through his head that his own son is not a common thief."

"Maybe he'll have to be held, like taking quinine, and made to listen," I said.

"That would be easy, if he were not a walking ahsenal," said Robert. "You have small chance to reason with a half-crazy man while he is handling a pistol."

He meant revolver.

"But he'll shoot!" I cried. "The Princess said he'd shoot!"

"So he will!" said Robert. "Shoot first, then find out how things are, and kill himself and every one else with remorse, afterward. He is made that way."

"Then he doesn't dare see you until he finds out how mistaken he has been," I said, for I was growing to like Robert better every minute longer I knew him. Besides, there was the Princess, looking like him as possible, and loving him of course, like I did Laddie, maybe. And if anything could cure Mrs. Pryor's heart trouble, having her son back would, because that was what made it in the first place, and even before them, there was Shelley to be thought of, and cared for.

18

The Pryor Mystery

And now old Dodson, turning pale,
Yields to his fate—so ends my tale.

It didn't take me long to see why Shelley liked Robert Paget. He was one of the very most likeable persons I ever had seen. We were sitting under the apple tree, growing better friends every minute, when we heard a smash, so we looked up, and it was the sound made by Ranger as Mr. Pryor landed from taking our meadow fence. He had ridden through the pasture and was coming down the creek bank. He was a spectacle to behold. A mile away you could see that Thomas had told him he had seen Robert, and where he was. Father had been mistaken in thinking Mr. Pryor would go to the house. He had lost his hat, his white hair was flying, his horse was in a lather, and he seemed to be talking to himself. Robert took one good look. "Ye Gods!" he cried. "There he comes now, a chattering madman!"

"The Station," I panted. "Up that ravine! Roll back the stone and pull the door shut after you. Quick!"

He never could have been inside, before Mr. Pryor's horse was raving along the embankment beside the fence.

"Where is he?" he cried. "Thomas saw him here!"

I didn't think his horse could take the fence at the top of the hill, but it looked as if he intended trying to make it, and I had to stop him if I could.

"Saw who?" I asked with clicking teeth.

"A tall, slender man, with a handsome face, and the heart of a devil."

"Yes, there was a man here like that in the face. I didn't see his heart," I said.

"Which way?" raved Mr. Pryor. "Which way? Is he at your house?"

Then I saw that he had the reins in his left hand, and a big revolver in his right. So there was no mistake about whether he'd really shoot. But that gun provoked me. People have no business to be careless with those things. They're dangerous!

"He didn't do what you think he did," I cried, "and he can prove he didn't, if you'll stop cavorting, and listen to reason."

Mr. Pryor leaned over the fence, dark purple like a beet now.

"You tell me where he is, or I'll choke it out of you," he said.

I guess he meant it. I took one long look at his lean, clawlike fingers, and put both hands around my neck.

"He knew Thomas saw him. He went that way," I said, waving off toward the north.

"Hah! striking for petticoats, as usual!" he cried, and away he went in the direction of his house. Then I flew for the Station.

"Come from there, quick!" I cried. "I've sent him back to his house, but when he finds you're not there, he will come here again. Hurry, and I'll put you in the woodshed loft. He'd never think of looking there."

He came out and we started toward the house, going pretty fast. Almost to the back gate we met Shelley.

"Does mother know?" I asked.

"I just told her," she said.

"Father," I cried, going in the back dining-room door. "Mr. Pryor was down in the meadow on Ranger. Thomas did see Robert, and his father is hunting him with a gun. We saw him coming, so I hid Robert in the Station and sent Mr. Pryor back home—I guess I told him a lie, father, or at least part of one, I said he went 'that way,' and he did, but not so far as I made his father think; so he started back home, but when he gets there and doesn't find Robert he'll come here again, madder than ever. Oh father, he'll come again, and he's crazy, father! Clear, raving crazy! I know he'll come again!"

"Yes," said father calmly. "I think it very probable that he will come again."

Then he started around shutting and latching windows, closing and locking the doors, and he carefully loaded his gun, and leaned it against the front casing. Then he put on his glasses and began examining the papers they had brought out again. Robert stood beside him, and explained and showed him.

"You see with me out of the way, the English law would give everything to my cousin," he said, and he explained it all over again.

"And to think how he always posed for a perfect saint!" cried the Princess. "Oh I hope the devil knows how to make him pay for what all of us have suffered!"

"Child! Child!" cried mother.

"I can't help it!" said the Princess. "Let me tell you, Mr. Stanton."

Then *she* told everything all over again, but it was even more interesting than the way Robert explained it, because what she said was about how it had been with her and her mother.

"It made father what he is," she said. "He would have killed Robert, if our friends hadn't helped him away. He will now, if he isn't stopped. I tell you he will! He sold everything he could legally control, for what any one chose to give him, and fled here stricken in pride, heartbroken, insane with anger, the creature you know. In a minute he'll be back again. Oh what are we going to do?"

Father was laying out the papers that he wanted to use very carefully.

"These constitute all the proof any court would require," he said to Robert. "If he returns, all of you keep from sight. This is *my* house; I'll manage who comes here, in my own way."

"But you must be allowed to take no risk!" cried Robert. "I cawn't consent to youah facing danger for me."

"There will be no risk," said father. "There is no reason why he should want to injure me. As the master of this house, I am accustomed to being obeyed. If he comes, step into the parlour there, until I call you."

He was busy with the papers when we saw Mr. Pryor coming. I wondered if he would jump the yard fence and ride down mother's flowers, but he left his horse at the hitching rack, and pounded on the front door.

"Did any of you notice whether he was displaying a revolver?" asked father.

"Yes father! Yes!" I cried. "And he's shaking so I'm afraid he'll make it go, when he doesn't really intend to."

Father picked up and levelled his rifle on the front door.

"Leon," he said, "you're pretty agile. Open this door, keep yourself behind it, and step around in the parlour. The rest of you get out, and stay out of range."

Those nearest hurried into the parlour. Candace, May, and I crouched in the front stairway, but things were so exciting we just had to keep the door open a tiny crack so we could see plain as anything. There had been nothing for Mrs. Freshett to do all afternoon, so she had gone over to visit an hour with Amanda Deam. Now Mr. Pryor probably thought father would meet him with the Bible in his hand, and read a passage about loving your neighbour as yourself. I'll bet anything you can mention that he never expected to find himself looking straight down the barrel of a shining big rifle when that door swung open. It surprised him so, he staggered, and his arm wavered. If he had shot and hit anything then, it would have been an accident.

"Got you over the heart," said father, in precisely the same voice he always said, "This is a fine day we are having." "Now why are you coming here in such shape?" This was a little cross. "I'm not the man to cringe before you!" This was quite boastful. "You'll get bullet for bullet, if you attempt to invade my house with a gun." This pinged as if father shot words instead of bullets.

"I want my daughter to come home," said Mr. Pryor. "And if you're sheltering the thief she is trying to hide, yield him up, if you would save yourself."

"Well, I'm not anxious about dying, with the family I have on my hands, neighbour," said father, his rifle holding without a waver, "but unless you put away that weapon, and listen to reason, you cannot enter my house. Calm yourself, man, and hear what there is to be said! Examine the proof, that is here waiting to be offered to you."

"Once and but once, send them out, or I'll enter over you!" cried Mr. Pryor.

"Sorry," said father, "but if only a muscle of your trigger finger moves, you fall before I do. I've the best range, and the most suitable implement for the work."

"Implement for the work!" Well, what do you think of father? Any one who could not see, to have heard him, would have thought he was talking about a hoe. We saw a shadow before we knew what made it; then, a little at a time, wonderingly, her jolly face a bewildered daze, her mouth slowly opening, Mrs. Freshett half-bent and peering, stooped under Mr. Pryor's arm and looked in our door. She had come back to help get supper, and because the kitchen was locked, she had gone around the house to see if she could get in at the front. What she saw closed her mouth, and straightened her back.

"Why, you two old fools!" she cried. *"If ye ain't drawed a bead on each other!"*

None of us saw her do it. We only knew after it was over what must have happened. She had said she'd risk her life for mother. She never stopped an instant when her chance came. She must have turned, and thrown her big body against Mr. Pryor. He was tired, old, and shaking with anger. They went down together, she gripping his right wrist with both hands, and she was strong as most men. Father set the gun beside the door, and bent over them. A minute more and he handed the revolver to Leon, and helped Mrs. Freshett to her feet. Mr. Pryor lay all twisted on the walk, his face was working, and what he said was a stiff jabber no one could understand. He had broken into the pieces we often feared he would.

Robert and Laddie came running to help father carry him in, and lay him on the couch.

"I hope, Miss Stanton," said Mrs. Freshett, "that I wa'n't too rough with him. He was so shaky-like, I was 'feered that thing would go off without his really makin' it, and of course I couldn't see none of yourn threatened with a deadly weapon, 'thout buttin' in and doin' the best I could."

Mother put her arms around her as far as they would reach. She would have had to take her a side at a time to really hug all of her, and she said: "Mrs. Freshett, you are an instrument in the hands of the Lord this day. Undoubtedly you have kept us from a fearful tragedy; possibly you have saved my husband for me. None of us ever can thank you enough."

"Loosen his collar and give him air," said Mrs. Freshett pushing mother away. "I think likely he has bust a blood vessel."

Father sent Leon flying to bring Dr. Fenner. Laddie took the carriage and he and Robert went after Mrs. Pryor, while father, mother, Mrs. Freshett, the Princess, May, and I, every last one, worked over Mr. Pryor. We poured hot stuff down his throat, put warm things around him, and rubbed him until the sweat ran on us, trying to get his knotted muscles straightened out. When Dr. Fenner came he said we were doing all he could; *maybe* Mr. Pryor would come to and be all right, and maybe his left side would be helpless forever; it was a stroke. Seemed to me having Mrs. Freshett come against you like that, could be called a good deal more than a stroke, but I couldn't think of the right word then. And after all, perhaps stroke was enough. He couldn't have been much worse off if the barn had fallen on him. I didn't think there was quite so much of Mrs. Freshett; but then she was scared, and angry; and he was about ready to burst, all by himself, if no one had touched him. He had much better have stayed at home and listened to what was to be said, reasonably, like father would; and then if he really had to shoot, he would have been in some kind of condition to take aim.

After a long hard fight we got him limber, straightened out, and warm, it didn't rip so when he breathed, then they put him in the parlour on the big davenport. Leon said if the sparkin' bench didn't bring him to, nothing would. Laddie sat beside him and mother kept peeping. She wouldn't let Dr. Fenner go, because she said Mr. Pryor just must come out of it right, and have a few years of peace and happiness.

Mrs. Pryor came back with Laddie and Robert. He carried her in, put her in the big rocking chair again, and he sat beside her, stroking and kissing her, while she held him with both hands. I didn't see, myself, where Shelley was going to get much show at him, but she smiled on both of them whenever she passed, and never seemed to mind at all. Perhaps she hadn't seen him for so long, she was not used to him very much, or maybe she never had fixed his tie yet. I suppose that doesn't begin until after you are promised. My! but he was kind, thoughtful, and quick, and he was also good looking; phew! but he *was* good looking. No wonder Shelley felt badly when she thought she'd lost him. Most any one would.

You could see *now* why his mother couldn't sleep, walked the road, and held her hands over her heart. She was a brave woman, and she had done well to keep alive and going in any shape at all. You see we knew. There had been only the few hours when it seemed possible that one of our boys had taken father's money and was gone. I well remembered what happened to our mother then. And if she had been disgraced before every one, dragged from her home away across a big sea to live among strangers, and not known where her boy was for years, I'm not a bit sure that she'd have done better than Mrs. Pryor. Yes, she would too; come to think it out—she'd have kept on believing the Lord had something to do with it, and that He'd fix it some way; and I know she and father would have held hands no matter what happened or where they went. I guess the biggest thing the matter with Pryors was that they didn't know how to go about loving each other right; maybe it was because they didn't love God, so they couldn't know exactly what *proper love* was; because God is love, like father said.

Mrs. Pryor didn't want to see Mr. Pryor—I can't get used to calling them Paget—and she didn't ask anything about him. I guess she was pretty mad at him. She never had liked the Emmet cousin, and she'd had nothing but trouble with him all the time he had been in her family, and then that awful disgrace, that she always *thought* was all him, but she couldn't prove it, and she had no money.

That's a very bad thing. A woman should always have some money. She works as hard as any one, and usually she has more that worries her, so it's only fair for her to have part of what the work and worry bring. No one ever knows how good it feels until they own a roll as big as I have; and after I sell my arrows and quills, it will be bigger. Ever after, I'm going to hunt and hide

Easter eggs, without any giving away, and fooling around. Mother always has money. Why, she has so much, she can help father out when he is pushed with bills, as she did last fall, to start Shelley to music school. It's no way to be forced to live with a man, just to get a home, food, and clothing. I don't believe mother ever would do it in all this world. But then mother has worked all her life, and so if father doesn't do as she wants him to, she'd know exactly how to go about taking care of herself.

After all Mrs. Pryor didn't need to sit back on her dignity and look so abused. He couldn't knock her down, and drag her clear here. Why didn't she say right out, in the beginning, that her son *couldn't* be a thief, that she knew it, and she'd stay at home and wait for him to come back? She could have put a piece in the paper saying she knew her boy was all right, and for him to come back, so they could go to work and *prove* it. I bet if she'd had one tenth of the ginger mother has, she'd have stopped the whole fuss in the start. I looked at her almost steadily, trying to figure out just what mother would have done in her place. Maybe I'm mistaken about exactly how she would have set to work, but this I *know:* she'd have stuck to the Lord; she'd have loved father, so dearly, he just *couldn't* have wanted her to do things that hurt her until it gave her heart trouble; and she never, never would have given up one of us, and sat holding her heart for months, refusing to see or to speak to any one, while she waited for some one else to do something. Mother never waits. She always thinks a minute, if she's in doubt she asks father; if he can't decide, both of them ask God; and then you ought to see things begin to fly. When they come out right, they "praise the Lord for his goodness and mercy which endureth forever;" but if they'd shut their mouths and their doors, while they held their hearts and moped, I guess the Lord would be too busy with more important things to pay any attention to them. I have made up my mind that the times when things happen is when you set your feet, brace your back, and push for what you want, like mother does. As a pusher, she's away ahead of father.

The more I watched Mrs. Pryor, the more I began to think she was a lady; and just about when I was sure that was what ailed her, I heard father say: "Perhaps the lady would like a cup of tea." I had a big notion to tell her to come on, and I would show her where the canister was, but I thought I better not. I wanted to, though. She'd have felt much better if she had got up and worked like the rest of us. With all the excitement, and everything happening at once, you'd have thought mother would be flat on her back, but flat nothing! Everything was picked up and slid back, fast as it was torn down; she found time to flannel her nose and brush her hair, her collar was straight, and the goldstone pin shone in the light, while her starched white apron fluttered as she went through the doors. She said a few words to Candace and Mrs. Freshett, May took out a linen cloth and began to set places for all the grown people, so I knew there'd be strawberry preserves and fried ham, but in all that, would you ever have thought that she'd find a second to make biscuit, and tea cakes herself? Plain as preaching I heard her say to Mrs. Freshett: "I do hope and pray that Mr. Pryor will come out of it right, so we can take him home, and teach him to behave himself; but if he's gone this minute, I intend to have another decent meal for Shelley to offer her young man; and I don't care if I show Mrs. Pryor that we're not hungry over here, if we do lack servants to carry in food on silver platters."

"That I jest would!" said Mrs. Freshett. "Even if he turns up his toes, 'tain't *your* funeral, thank the Lord! an' looky here, I'd jest as soon set things in a bake pan an' pass 'em for you, myself. I'll do it, if you say the word."

Mother bit her lip, and fought her face to keep it straight, as she said confidential-like: "No, I'm not going to toady to her. I only want her to see that a meal really consists of food after all; I don't mind putting my best foot foremost, but I won't ape her."

"Huccome they to fuss like this, peaceable as Mr. Stanton be, an' what's Shelley's beau to them?"

"I should think you could tell by looking at Pryors," said mother. "He's their mystery, and also their only son. Shelley met him in Chicago, he came here to see her, and ran right into them. I'll tell you all about it before you go. Now, I must keep these applications hot, for I've set my head on pulling Mr. Pryor out so that he can speak, and have a few decent years of life yet."

"But why did the old devil—*ex*-cuse me, I mean the old *gentleman,* want to shoot your man?"

"He didn't! I'll tell you all about it after they're gone."

"I bet you don't get shet of them the night," said Mrs. Freshett.

"All right!" said mother. "Whatever Dr. Fenner thinks. I won't have Mr. Pryor moved until it can't hurt him, if he stays a week. I blame her quite as much as I do him; from what I know. If a woman is going to live with a man, there are times when she's got to put her foot down—flat—most unmercifully flat!"

"Ain't she though!" said Mrs. Freshett; then she and mother just laughed.

There! What did I tell you? I feel as good as if father had patted me on the head and bragged on me a lot. I *thought* mother wouldn't think that Mr. Pryor was *all* to blame, and she didn't. I figured that out by myself, too.

Every minute Mr. Pryor grew better. He breathed easier, and mother tilted on her toes and waved her hands, when he moved his feet, threw back his head, lifted his hand to it, and acted like he was almost over it, and still in shape to manage himself. She hurried to tell Mrs. Pryor, and I know mother didn't like it when she never even said she was glad, or went to see for herself.

Laddie and the Princess watched him, while every one else went to supper. Laddie picked up Mrs. Pryor's chair, carried her to the dining-room, and set her in my place beside father. He placed Dr. Fenner next her, and left Robert to sit with Shelley. I don't think Mrs. Pryor quite liked that, but no one asked her. Father must have had Dr. Fenner out beside the beehives explaining things a little, for he didn't seem at all mystified. He talked, laughed and shook his old fat sides until I know mother would have liked it better if he'd been primmer. That's not the right word to describe Dr. Fenner; but you'll know what I mean. Why, he even went and asked Mrs. Pryor if she ever took a hand at breaking horses. She almost fainted. I doubt if she even *likes* a horse. Afterward mother asked him how he could; and he said what she needed was a shaking up, and whenever he was around her, she'd always get it, because it was his work in life to give folks the medicine they needed most, whether they wanted to take it or not.

"You know, sometimes, I even have to hold their noses to make them down it, Ruth," he said, and mother laughed.

I watched and listened until everything seemed to be going right there, and then I slipped into the parlour, where Laddie and the Princess were caring for Mr. Pryor. With one hand Laddie held hers, the other grasped Mr. Pryor's wrist. Laddie never took his eyes from that white, drawn face, except to smile at her, and squeeze her hand every little while. At last Mr. Pryor turned over and sighed, pretty soon he opened his eyes, and looked at Laddie, then at the Princess, and it was nothing new to see them, so he smiled and dozed again. After a while he opened them wider, then he saw the piano—that was an eye-opener for any one—and the strange room, so he asked, most as plain as he ever talked, why he was at our house again, and then he began to remember. He struggled to sit up and the colour came into his face. So Laddie let go the Princess, and held him down while he said: "Mr. Pryor, answer me this. Do you want to spend the remainder of your life in an invalid's chair, or would you like to walk abroad and sit a horse again?"

He glared at Laddie, but he heard how things were plainly enough. Laddie held him, while he explained what a fight we had to unlock his muscles, and start him going again, and how, if we hadn't loved him, and wanted him so, and had left him untouched until the Doctor came, very likely he'd have been paralyzed all the rest of his life, if he hadn't died; and he said he wished he *had,* and he didn't *thank* any one for saving him.

"Oh yes you do!" said Laddie, the same as he'd have talked to Leon. "You can't stuff me on that, and you needn't try. Being dead is a cold, clammy proposition, that all of us put off as long as we can. You know you want to see Pamela in her own home. You know you are interested in how I come out with those horses. You know you want the little people you spoke of, around you. You know the pain and suspense you have borne have almost driven you insane, and it was because you cared so deeply. Now lie still, and keep quiet! All of us are tired and there's no sense in making us go through this again, besides the risk of crippling yourself that you run. Right here in this house are the papers to prove that your nephew took your money, and hid it in your son's clothing, as he already had done a hundred lesser things, before, purposely to estrange you. Hold steady! You must hear this! The sooner you know it, the better you'll feel. You remember, don't you, that before your nephew entered your home, you idolized your son. You thought the things he did were amusing. A boy is a boy, and if he's alive, he's very apt to be lively. Mother could tell you a few pranks that Leon has put us through; but they're only a boy's foolishness, they are not unusual or unforgivable. I've gone over the evidence your son brings, with extreme care, so has father. Both of us are quite familiar with common law. He has every proof you can possibly desire. You can't get around it, even if your heart wasn't worn out with rebellion, and you were not crazy to have the loving sympathy of your family again."

"I don't believe a word of it!"

"You have got to! I tell you it is *proof*, man! The documents are in this house now."

"He forged them, or stole them, as he took the money!"

Laddie just laughed.

"How you do long, and fight, to be convinced!" he said. "I don't blame you! When anything means this much, of course you have got to be sure. But you'll know your nephew's signature; also your lawyer's. You'll know letters from old friends who are above question. Sandy McSheel has written you that he was with Robert through all of it, and he gives you his word that everything is all right. You will believe him, won't you?"

Big tears began to squeeze from under Mr. Pryor's lids, until Laddie and the Princess each tried to see how much of him they could hold to keep him together-like.

"Tell me!" he said at last, so they took turns explaining everything plain as day, and soon he listened without being held. When they had told him everything they could think of, he asked: "Did Robert kill Emmet?"

"I am very happy to be able to tell you that he did not. It would have been painful, and not helped a bad matter a particle. Your nephew had dissipated until he was only a skeleton just breathing his last. It's probable that his fear of death helped your son out, so that he got the evidence he wanted easier than he hoped to in the beginning. I don't mean that he is dead now; but he is passing slowly, and loathsomely. Robert thinks word that he has gone will come any hour. Think how pleasant it will be to have your son!

Think how happy your home will be now! Think how you will love to see Sandy, and all your old friends! Think how glad you'll be to go home, and take charge of your estate!"

"Think!" cried Mr. Pryor, pushing Laddie away and sitting up: "Think how I shall enjoy wringing the last drop of blood from that craven's body with these old hands!"

What a sight he did look to be sure! Sick, half-crazy, on the very verge of the grave himself, and wanting to kill a poor man already dying. Aren't some people too curious?

Laddie carefully laid him down, straightened him out and held him again. Mother always said he was "patient as Job," and that day it proved to be a mighty good thing.

"You're determined to keep yourself well supplied with trouble," laughed Laddie. I don't believe any one else would have dared. "Now to an unbiased observer, it would seem that you'd be ready to let well enough alone. You have your son back, you have him fully exonerated, you have much of your property, you are now ready for freedom, life, and love, with the best of us; you have also two weddings on your hands in the near future. Why in the name of sense are you anxious for more?"

"I should have thought that Sandy McSheel, if he's a real friend of mine —"

"Sandy tells you all about it in the letter he has sent. He went with Robert fully intending to do that very thing for you, but the poor creature was too loathsome. The sight of him made Sandy sick. He writes you that when he saw the horrible spectacle, all he could think of was to secure the evidence needed and get away."

Suddenly the Princess arose and knelt beside the davenport. She put her arms around her father's neck and drew his wrinkled, white old face up against her lovely one.

"Daddy! Dear old Daddy!" she cried. "I've had such a hard spot in my heart against you for so long. Oh do let's forget everything, and begin all over again; begin away back where we were before Emmet ever came. Oh Daddy, do let's forget, and begin all over new, like other people!"

He held her tight a minute, then his lips began whispering against her ear. Finally he said: "Take yourselves off, and send Robert here. I want my son. Oh I want my boy!"

It was a long time before Robert came from the parlour; when he did, it was only to get his mother and take her back with him; then it was a still longer time before the door opened; but when it did, it was perfectly sure that they were all friends again. Then Leon went to tell Thomas, and he came with the big carriage. White and shaking, Mr. Pryor was lifted into it and they went home together, taking Shelley with them to stay that night; so no doubt she was proposed to and got her kiss before she slept.

That fall there were two weddings at our church at the same time. Sally's had been fine; but it wasn't worth mentioning beside Laddie and the Princess, and Robert and Shelley. You should have seen my mother! She rocked like a kingbird on the top twig of the winesap, which was the tallest tree in our orchard, and for once there wasn't a single fly in her ointment, not one, she said so herself, and so did father. As we watched the big ve-hi-acklé, as Leon called it, creep slowly down the Little Hill, it made me think of that pathetic poem, "The Three Warnings," in McGuffey's Sixth. I guess I gave Mr. Pryor the first, that time he got so angry he hit his horse until it almost ran away. Mother delivered the second when she curry-combed him about the taxes, and Mrs. Freshett finished the job. The last two lines read as if they had been especially written about him:

And now old Dodson, turning pale,
Yields to his fate—so ends my tale.

The End

People Making A Difference

Family Bookshelf offers the finest in good wholesome Christian literature, written by best-selling authors. All books are recommended by an Advisory Board of distinguished writers and editors.

We are also a vital part of a compassionate outreach called **Bowery Mission Ministries**. Our evangelical mission is devoted to helping the destitute of the inner city.

Our ministries date back more than a century and began by aiding homeless men lost in alcoholism. Now we also offer hope and Gospel strength to homeless, inner-city women and children. Our goal, in fact, is to end homelessness by teaching these deprived people how to be independent with the Lord by their side.

Downtrodden, homeless men are fed and clothed and may enter a discipleship program of one-on-one professional counseling, nutrition therapy and Bible study. This same Christian care is provided at our women and children's shelter.

We also welcome nearly 1,000 underprivileged children each summer at our Mont Lawn Camp located in Pennsylvania's beautiful Poconos. Here, impoverished youngsters enjoy the serenity of nature and an opportunity to receive the teachings of Jesus Christ. We also provide year-round assistance through teen activities, tutoring in reading and writing, Bible study, family counseling, college scholarships and vocational training.

During the spring, fall and winter months, our children's camp becomes a lovely retreat for religious gatherings of up to 200. Excellent accommodations include heated cabins, chapel, country-style meals and recreational facilities. Write to Paradise Lake Retreat Center, Box 252, Bushkill, PA 18324 or call: (717) 588-6067.

Still another vital part of our ministry is **Christian Herald magazine**. Our dynamic, bimonthly publication focuses on the true personal stories of men and women who, as "doers of the Word," are making a difference in their lives and the lives of others.

Bowery Mission Ministries are supported by voluntary contributions of individuals and bequests. Contributions are tax deductible. Checks should be made payable to Bowery Mission.

 **Fully accredited Member
of the Evangelical Council
for Financial Accountability**

Every Monday morning, our ministries staff joins together in prayer. If you have a prayer request for yourself or a loved one, simply write to us.

 **Administrative Office:
40 Overlook Drive, Chappaqua,
New York 10514 Telephone: (914) 769-9000**